TREGARR BOOKS

Tregarr Books, 46 Forest Rd, Richmond, Surrey TW9 3BZ.

Copywright.© Sally Wheldon 2006
All rights reserved.
The moral rights of the author have been asserted.
ISBN   0-9554331-0-X
13 Digit   ISBN   978-0-9554331-0-8

All the characters in this book are entirely fictional and any similarity to any person is purely coincidental.

Printed and bound by CPI Antony Rowe, Eastbourne

To My Friends.

Sally Wheldon

<u>The Lonely Tide</u>

T

Tregarr Books

Chapter One

'Two of 'em found dead. Stone dead.'
The cabbie sucked on a peppermint sweet and glanced back through the rear view mirror at his passenger, who was staring impassively out of the window.
'Dead of cold; been the coldest night,' the driver paused, momentarily distracted by the necessity of forcing his way into the traffic at Holborn junction, 'Of the year. One of them,' he flicked the chalky, dissolving mint to the underside of his tongue, 'Was over Highbury Fields, the other, can you believe, just outside the Houses of Parliament.'
The cabbie, whose name was Derek, peered into the mirror again. There was no reaction from the passenger. Had he frozen too? No, the heater was full on.
Derek didn't know why he bothered some days.
'It's like a protest, innit, dying outside the Mother of Parliaments?' That was what he wanted to say. Not that Derek was clear what protest this frozen death implied. A protest against what? Winter? Capitalism? Derek thought that people ought to look after themselves. He was against the idea of the nanny state. People ought to work hard and look after themselves and their loved ones; of course, their loved ones.
Cold, miserable bastard. Derek hated miserable bastards in the back of his cab. He shot a further brief hostile glance into the mirror. He might as well not have spoken. Derek pulled up and the passenger disembarked. Derek grunted the fare and slid out his fat, doughy hand to meet the hand coming in through the cab window. In that brief commercial exchange Derek noted the expensive cashmere coat sleeve, the crisp white cotton fold down cuffs secured by onyx links, the quality watch, the gold signet ring on the little finger. The kind of hand that got mugged, Derek hoped. As he drove off back to Essex he looked once more curiously through the rear view mirror. He could see his passenger

standing on the banks of the river of traffic, poised to jump, a figure receding into the distance of his perspective.

The coldest day of the year. On the Strand people walked albino faced against the shock of the ice wind. Tall buildings on either side channelled the cold and compacted it like an invisible glacier grinding down towards St Clement Danes and the iron statue of Bomber Harris. On the base of the statue red graffiti said, 'Murderer,' and below that was scrawled, 'Someone has to do society's dirty work,' and then for good measure, as an after thought, 'You twat.'

Michael Easton stood on the North side of the Strand where the cab had dropped him by the Royal Courts of Justice. The outline of the building's turrets, peaks, spires and rococo crenulations resembled mountain crags, inaccessible and lonely. Up there a bird flapped its feathers in wide blue silence.

Easton stepped out in front of a double decker, onto the stripes of the zebra crossing that formed a pathway from the black orifice of the court door over to the green tiled cave wherein lodged Lloyds Strand cash-point machine. The bus driver had to brake quickly and swore, his face contorted with road rage. The man in the way of his bus didn't even look. There was something contemptuous about the manner in which he had crossed the road; an appearance of certainty that the bus would halt for him. "Arrogant fucker," mouthed the bus driver and wished he could replay the seconds so that the bus was just a fraction too late in stopping.

There was a woman already at the cash point, and Easton was obliged to wait. She dotted the buttons with long red polished nails. She made an error and had to start again, her card being tongued out in disgust. Easton felt his jaw tighten involuntarily. Running through the stream of consciousness in his head were the sort of words that howled expression, fucking come on, come on, suppressed.

The woman balanced on cheap high heels with little black leather bows on the back of them. Her hair was unnaturally dark. Her clothes were black, too, the office clothes of an office junior. When she eventually concluded her transaction she turned, eying Easton in brief assessment, holding on just a little too long. The image of a raven came into Easton's head, blue black feathered, red clawed, red beaked and open winged.

The girl registered the haughty rejection of his body language and tottered off on her ridiculous shoes, feeling somehow humiliated, somehow common.

At her departure he breathed a long sigh of relief through closed teeth. He had his card ready in his hand, slid it in, and with rapid movements pressed the digits and anticipated mentally the screen's instructions. As the machine hummed and thought its mechanical thoughts he held his hand in poised readiness over the slit so that as his card emerged he pulled it out without the waste of a single second in time. He swiped the proffered notes and inserted them into his wallet.

As he turned, his body collided with another body, a repellent, unexpected, unwanted physical contact. A man had been waiting right behind.

'Sorry mate, got any spare change?'

The beggar was smaller than Easton, (who was a well built man,) as shrunken and wizened as a goblin, with dull watchful eyes. His clothes were too large, cast offs doled out by the Army of Salvation. He held out his palm, hand up. Easton inhaled a draught of foul, alcohol stained breath. He dropped his gaze down to the man's outstretched hand, saw the dirt in the creases of the palm, lines grained into the hollow cup. The stench was unbearable. The man smiled with teeth missing, knocked out or fallen out through neglect. The smile faltered first from the eyes, then from the lips, as Easton raised his eyes and looked at the beggar. The beggar recoiled. Days and weeks of faces passing and passing, faces that looked right through him, faces arrested, averted, cold, glassy, disgusted, superior. More than money,

3

more than food, the derelict wanted a face to smile at him. This look he had from the expensive, walleted man was more than he could endure, a look that went right in to him and searched the bottom of the person he was. It was an outrage, a vile intrusion.

'Got any change?' the beggar asked again, mortified by his own wretchedness, seeing his degradation anew in the eyes of the man in front of him.

The wallet opened and the clean nailed hand took out a twenty pound note. The beggar took it.

'You should clean yourself up,' said the rich man to the beggar, softly.

As Easton walked away he turned and glanced behind him. The beggar was watching. He shouted 'Fuck off,' at Easton, and spat, before pushing in to Starbuck's warm interior to spend his money on a coffee, cake and keeping the cold at bay.

Chapter Two

Dr. Alice Christie entered the High Court's Great Hall, a cavernous space, a pew-less cathedral, architraves soaring high above the heads of the ants below. Marble judges, not saints, lined the walls, staring from sightless eyes at the folly of human weakness.

Through the strutting robed barristers and milling uncertain claimants Alice spied her patient, Lorette, a tiny black woman with mangy hair in tight scraggy knots, half sitting hunched on one of the cold slab seats built into the walls. Standing by her was a woman with blonde, cropped hair, in a pinstripe suit, cradling an overflowing lever arch file in her arms.

'Good morning, Lorette,' greeted Alice.

Lorette was the kind of person to whom no one else was polite.

'Awright?' Lorette's voice was a surprise, incongruously deep and rasping from her child like throat.

It was the first day of Lorette's hearing, a hearing in court that would determine whether or not she would be allowed a chance to retain the care of her six month boy. The Local Authority wanted him adopted. Lorette was seventeen and this was her first baby. Lorette had been abused by one of her mother's men. She had been put in care too late, fostered, rejected, fostered again, rejected again, placed in a children's home where they openly dealt drugs on the doorstep. By fifteen she was on the street, a sex worker, funding her heroin habit. She didn't know who was the father of her baby. It could have been any of the twenty men a day she admitted rutting into her skinny body in order to get the money to buy the heroin. She went to no antenatal appointments and it was with disbelief that she gave birth, two months early, on the concrete landing of a high rise in Shoreditch. A man from the flats had come out swearing foully at the noise. "Stop that fucking screaming," he snarled, then he saw Lorette and said 'Jesus," in an Irish accent and went back in and in a second a woman came out and said to Lorette, 'Breath, breath, like this, love,' and Lorette breathed and panted like a cow lowing and a little brown otter slivered out between her legs and the cutting pain made her wail. The ambulance men took them off the concrete and in the ambulance Lorette looked into the puzzled violet eyes of her son for the first time. Lorette, who had never been loved, now screamed in love.

The child was born heroin addicted. His first experience was coughing and trembling and sweating and shivering with the pain of withdrawal, cramp and diarrhoea and the sure curse of descent from the high place his baby self had visited. Baby smack head, flailing his fists in justifiable rage.

After his medical recovery he was released from hospital, where Lorette had stayed with him and had fed him, into care.

'Don't want no foster carer looking after him,' Lorette wept. 'Look what happened to me.' She beat her breastbone. It sounded porous, the bone of a bird.

Lorette knew she'd never kick junk in the street. Heroin ran through the street like blood through a syringe. She went into rehab, a dingy house they euphemistically called Beginnings, situated off the Mile End Road. It was exactly like the children's home. At least she stopped having to fuck sweat stained stinking men and got clean.

Temporarily.

And each week day she went to see him. She called him Rosco and held his little hair slicked head in her arms and marvelled at his finger nails, bathed him, fed him, changed him and made wide eye contact. She was there for his first smile, and she sparked back laughter in delight. Her first, her only happy time.

Lorette relapsed, having unluckily (it's all down to luck,) bumped into an old dealer at King's Cross. Beginnings became endings, they 'terminated her contract', using formalities of language to obscure the human tragedy and make it easier for the staff to do this terrible job.

Lorette had no choice but to go back to her flat, which had become a crack house in her absence. She wanted a second chance. For herself, for the baby. She wanted an order under S38.6 of the Children Act, obliging the Local Authority to put her and her baby together in a mother and baby unit. That was her application. It was all about second chances.

'Dr Christie?' said the blonde woman and held out her hand to Alice. 'I'm Deborah Morton, Lorette's barrister.'

Deborah Morton had strikingly huge blue eyes. They registered concern. Alice shot a rapid glance of scrutiny at Lorette and understood why.

Alice placed a hand on Lorette's shoulder and bent so that their faces were at the same level.

'Did you miss your methadone this morning?'

'I did, I did. I wanted to be here in time and the chemist don't open til nine thirty.'

Alice read the barrister's unspoken cue. The two professional women moved down the hall so that Lorette couldn't hear them speaking.

'Is she going to have to be in court all day?' asked Alice.

'Yes.'

'She's withdrawing. She won't last.'

'What will she be like?'

'A write off. Trembling, sweating, crapping, puking and in pain, not to mention the emotional slide. If you get her out early I'll take her to the chemist for her methadone. What are her chances of success today?'

'It all depends on the Judge. The problem is,' said Miss Morton, 'it's a borderline case. Some judges will give her a chance, others won't. We'd better go up to the courts. It's nearly time.'

'Right.' Deborah Morton dropped her bundle heavily on the table outside Court 44 in the modern block attached to the old Victorian court building. There were three floors of

7

Family Courts. Big plate glass windows, greasy with finger and breath marks lined the corridor. The windows were fixed so they could never open, so that the light came in but never the day. It heaved with a hot claustrophobic airlessness. Already people were gathering in pools, each pool representing a discrete case. There were too many cases. The courts were bursting at the seams, the waiting list grinding away into impossible distance.

'Let's see who we've got.' Deborah Morton spoke to herself. The moment of truth. Her adrenalin surged. Court is tense. She peered at the list pinned up on the wall. The sight of the name of the judge was like a kick in the teeth. 'Easton,' she pronounced. Alice, behind her, heard the note of despairing finality. She turned and looked at Lorette, whose top lip was beginning to glisten with sweat.

At the front of the court there was a high wooden podium, above which was an heraldic device, and underneath, on a scroll, the words 'Dieu et mon Droit'. Arrayed before the judge's podium were five rows of benches, each with a narrow desk. The second desk from the front bore the weight of the three sets of bundles, and the additional weight of Janice Drake, the barrister for the Local Authority, who was resting her fat gunwales on it, irritably discussing last moment aspects of the case with the social workers for the Local Authority that wanted to take away Lorette's baby. Miss Drake wore bizarre make up. It was as if she were smeared in grease paint, ready for some theatrical performance, bright crimson lips, high rouged cheeks, turquoise eyelids. The court has much in common, superficially, with the theatre, with the difference being that the final act in the theatre usually contains resolution.

Miss Drake was a formidable, bass voiced tank of an advocate, but now she was reduced to a state of nervous fussing and recriminations against her instructing solicitor who had failed to file the judge's bundle within the required time scale. The bundle was late and the judge was Easton.

"Start off on the wrong foot with this judge and you'll know it. He's notorious," said Janice, grimly.

The bundle is the name given to the collection of documents that form the evidence in a court trial. There is a paginated set for each party and for the witnesses and, of course, for the judge. Applications, statements, experts' reports, orders, case summaries, chronologies; mountains of words that go to comprise the flesh and bones of a legal case. A good advocate will know the words in the bundles like the contours of a lover's body.

'Court rise,' called the lugubrious clerk, holding wide the door to the right of the judge's podium.

Mr Justice Easton entered the court. He was not robed, Family judges never are. He wore a dark suit. He nodded curtly in the direction of the lawyers and sat down. So too did everyone else except Miss Drake.

'My Lord,' she began, in the plummy, artificial tones of High Court counsel. They have to do this, because every word counts and has to be heard. There is no scope for mumbling, no scope for hiding ambivalence or disguising uncertainty with inaudibility or fudge. Janice had decided to meet the unpleasantness head on. It was always best, especially with Easton. 'I'm afraid I have to open with an apology.'

The judge stared stonily ahead. Janice persevered. 'I understand your bundle was delivered to you only last evening.'

That was why he was so difficult, his lack of response. It created an atmosphere. It made everything worse. Awkwardness mingled with apprehension. Easton allowed his expressionless eyes to settle for a moment on the mother. Lorette shifted her gaze. The judge frightened her. She was withdrawing and saw the court in a heightened state of paranoia. He was like a wolf from a fairy story. She thought she might see him lick his lips with a long, red tongue between cruel, white canines. Lorette felt a cramp fix in her stomach. She saw the glint in his eyes, saw him part his lips and exhale, saw the rise and fall of his woolly chest under the human shirt. Lorette shifted in her seat to avoid the cramp and the stare of the wolf judge.

'I am assuming therefore, My Lord, that you will require reading time. Again I can only apologise.' Janice waited.

There was a secondary silence. Then the judge said, impassively, 'I've read the bundle.' Five hundred pages. Eight hours reading, overnight. 'Put the Local Authority solicitor in the witness box. She can explain to me why she's unfamiliar with the court process, and after that she can apologise in court to my clerk, who had to wait for the papers.'

After being destroyed and humiliated by the judge, the young woman solicitor left the witness box restraining tears.

By the time of the luncheon adjournment Lorette's itching and cramp and dryness of mouth were raging. 'How's it going?' she asked, with pathetic hopefulness.

'You're doing really well,' encouraged Deborah Morton, and as soon as Lorette had walked away down the corridor to get a drink of water, the barrister flashed her eyes at Alice, who had been sent away for the morning, to return for the afternoon session. 'That judge is a bastard,' Deborah Morton pronounced.

'Has Lorette lost?' asked Alice, in consternation.

Miss Morton bit into her tuna mayo on brown to give herself time to think. She had been pinning her hopes on Alice Christie. There was something in the name Alice Mabel Christie that had suggested gravitas, a grey haired bun and pince-nez spectacles.

But Alice was twenty nine, with shoulder length liquorice black hair, overgrown at the fringe, so that she had to flick it out of her eyes. Those eyes were intelligent, serious and restless. She wore no make up. She ought to have worn make up. It might have made her look older.

'You'll have to tell the judge we can't go ahead this afternoon,' said Alice.

Back in court after lunch Deborah Morton rose to her feet. The judge kept his eyes on Lorette's suffering. The sound of her sniffs and moans punctured the air intermittently. Alice found it almost unbearable, like watching a kitten tortured to death. Who would allow the hearing to proceed with the mother in that state?

'My Lord, I wonder if it might be possible to adjourn until tomorrow morning?' Deborah asked, thinking, please, please give this mother a break.

'Is your expert here?' asked the judge.

'My Lord, Dr Christie behind me.'

'Then I shall continue.'

Alice ascended the witness box. She looked up at the judge in perplexity. Had he not understood? For a fraction of a second their eyes met. With a shock Alice realised he was cold, that he understood and discounted all that suffering.

'Do you have a religion?' asked the robed usher.

How much time do you have, wondered Alice, for the answer to that one?

'Anglican,' she replied, for the want of a better description. Alice swore to tell the truth the whole of it and nothing but.

She turned to face the judge.

'Can I ask that the mother be allowed to go?'

The judge replied, 'State your name.'

'Alice Mabel Christie.'

'And do you hold any professional qualifications?' She realised the judge's question to be personal, designed to denigrate. He did not look at her. She wanted to make him look at her.

'My qualifications are set out in my report, at page C 87 of the bundle, if you have read it.' Yes, see me, she thought. You see me now.

Deborah Morton and Janice Drake sucked in their breath individually and together. Such insolence. The doctor must be mad. She remained impassive in the witness box.

'Sit or stand as you please,' said Easton, with as much concern as if she were a nameless tube traveller.

'Might I ask for the mother's release?' Alice interceded for Lorette.

'On what basis?' The judge looked into the high distance. Lorette had her eyes closed, her head low on her arms. She frowned and grunted and shifted in discomfort, barely listening.

'I think it's crystal clear,' replied Alice.

The judge stared at her.

Alice continued. 'She didn't take her medication this morning, so she's withdrawing. The symptoms of withdrawal are distressing her. And she'll only deteriorate during the course of the afternoon. She needs to go to the chemist and take her script.'

There was a silence.

The judge stopped addressing Alice. He said, 'Miss Morton, I shall release your client at the request of Dr Christie, on the basis that Miss Gurley is unable to sit through the afternoon's proceedings, having failed to take her methadone script. But she will have to wait until the end of Dr Christie's evidence, which I doubt will delay me long.'

Alice recognised the operative word; failed. The judge had given Lorette the worst of both worlds, exposed as incapacitated, but having to stay and suffer, tossing in a post script of contempt for a professional opinion that couldn't detain him long.

Deborah Morton began her examination in chief.

'Dr Christie, in your report you recommend the resumption of Ms Gurley's rehabilitation treatment.'

'Yes, but not at Beginnings. I recommend the Lyall Centre, which is in Ladbroke Grove.'

'Can you say why you believe she would succeed in The Lyall Centre but not in Beginnings?'

'It's a different regime. Just as a medical doctor would try different drugs to treat a medical condition so it is that one would expect to try out alternative regimes of rehabilitation.

12

It's not a matter of one size fits all.' Alice found her nerves settling a little as she got into her swing.

'My problem,' interrupted the judge, 'is that I have the timescale of a young baby to consider.'

'I accept that, My Lord,' said Alice. What she accepted was that she could not allow the afternoon to turn into a sparring match between her and the judge, a match that only the judge could win, with Lorette's baby as the prize. She had antagonised the judge, she had rattled his cage. She now offered the humility of her answer to soothe him.

'How long do you say Ms Gurley will need?'

'The physical recovery can be effected relatively quickly properly managed. The psychological recovery takes longer. The longer the abstinence, the better the prognosis. Part of the consideration is the length of the addiction and the age of the patient. Lorette's addiction is relatively short, two years, and she's young. And she has the motivation, her baby. Her child is very important to her.'

'That didn't stop her relapsing before,' observed the judge, cruelly. Alice sensed the cruelty was a strike at her, a response to the feelings of irritation she had caused him. She looked across to Lorette.

Alice was glad the mother was barely listening, though she doubted that the judge would have been more careful in his remarks if Lorette had been attentive. Truths hurt, and she got the feeling this man was brutal. Treat her like shit, why not, take her kid away and make her feel like nothing as you're doing it.

'Beginnings' regime didn't work for her,' she said, neutrally.

'And what would 'work for her'?' Easton used the expression like a rag of slang.

'She needs an intensely therapeutic structure and intelligent mentoring. She also needs to be in an all female environment, treated by females.'

'Why is that, Dr Christie?'

Alice detected the warning drop in tone.

13

'Because she's been abused, raped and used as a prostitute by men.'

The accusation swung in the air. Easton faced the eyes of the women and knew that they were asking themselves if he ever fucked desperate girls in back alleys, on car seats, in seedy rooms and sat there still, judging. For a moment the roles were reversed and he was the accused.

'What if Miss Gurley were a man?' he said.

'I'm sorry?' Alice was caught off guard.

'If she were a he, a man with an addiction, used by other men as a prostitute? Would he need an all female environment?'

Alice paused. It was an unexpected question, a good question. 'It would depend on the man.'

The judge gazed around the court. 'Uncharted territory,' he said, with contempt at their incapacity to rationalise beyond gender fashion. He quashed the stirrings of anger and nodded brusquely at them to carry on.

Alice rushed to the newsagents across the road from the court and purchased a bar of Turkish Delight. As she walked down the street towards the tube she ripped off its deep pink silky wrapper, the pink of cheap sex, and rammed the confection into her mouth. The sticky goo tasted of bliss, momentarily, until it was all gone, after which the sugary assault nauseated her taste buds. She sat on the subterranean platform at the Temple feeling guilty. She wished she had bought a bottle of water instead. She regretted the momentary but urgent impulse of the chocolate bar. She had such a pain behind her eyes, the effect of dehydration and stress. Although she had given evidence before it was only at mental health tribunals or once at a criminal magistrates' court, and the ordeal she had had today cast them in the shade. This had been of a completely different order. She analysed. Was it the set out of the court itself, with its benches in rows, its high judicial dias? No. The magistrates' was much the same. Was it the stakes, a woman's loss of her

14

child? Was it the infectious tension? The fear of being exposed as a fool or a liar? Was the tension caused by the judge himself? She thought of the judge. There was something about him, a compelling forcefulness. She wondered what his real life was like, mulled him over, but then she slid over to thinking about little fucked up Lorette. Alice had no children, but it didn't take a mind reader to empathise with the idea of the pain of losing a child. She supposed it was worse to have your child taken away than to be hung. Alice knew at the back of her mind that she was being more optimistic in her recommendations for Lorette than she ought to be, seduced by pity. On the other hand it was true to say that with continual support Lorette could probably provide good enough mothering to her kid. The problem was that continual support cost money. There wasn't enough money continually to support all the Lorettes. There was nothing innately wrong with Lorette, she was reasonably intelligent, hitting 107 on the Wechsler test.

Alice had once tested herself; she had a score of 133, categorised as 'Superior'. She had enjoyed the fact that her boyfriend Toby had scored only 126, a mere 'High Average'. At first she had cheated in marking them so that Toby had come out under 62, which is 'mild mental retardation'. She had tittered at the expression of blank puzzlement that adorned his credulous face for a few seconds as he examined the paper. 'Dummy,' she said, that he had been taken in by her deceit. Alice smiled a little at this recollection, then the smile faded and a lump grew in her gut when she remembered that she had to go back to Court 44 tomorrow. She had a feeling she knew what was going to happen. She knew what would happen to Lorette, too, if she lost her baby. The baby was Lorette's only hope. If he went she would relapse big time, restraint drowned in despair, she would go back on the game, inject, inject, carry on injecting until she died in some horrible way and her life would have been a short, wholly unnoticed existence of indignity, pain and rejection. What's your religion, the usher asked her.

15

Something to do with God but I couldn't tell you what. I can only see it out of the corner of my eye, but it's gone when I turn. Oddly, Alice had felt that sense of God in the court; not actual God, but that same sense of omnipotence, the sense of scales being balanced by a higher authority, of chaff being burned. The court was a ruthless God, the God of the Old Testament, an eye for an eye sort of God. Alice didn't believe in a God that would burn Lorette. Wasn't Lorette one of the little ones he loved? But Lorette was going to be fucked by men over and over again like a thing, like a nothing, unloved and inhuman forever and then she would die.

Alice thought of the face of the judge. It could be an image of God, an Old Testament image, righteous wrath, sweeping his enemies into a boiling sea.

The tube rolled in. She had to stand. The men were hogging all the seats. There was an elderly lady hanging on to one of the straps. Alice said loudly, 'Could you do with a seat?' and still none of the men stood up. A plump lady in her forties gathered her bags and came and stood up and said to the old dear, 'Please sit down.' The old woman tottered unsteadily to the vacant seat. The men looked shifty. What is it that makes people unkind? Alice answered her own internalised question; in this case lack of social disapprobation. While all the men were ignoring the old lady it was acceptable. Once the woman with the bags had stood up the standard of acceptable behaviour had shifted and the men found themselves uncomfortably below standard. Possibly if one person went to help Lorette others would follow. She would like to think so, but the world was not that simple.

She thought, what if there were a train crash? What happens to all the hopes and fears of the people in this carriage? She glanced around and wondered how the individuals would respond to carnage. The middle aged suited man with a copy of the Times, for example, would he crawl back into burning wreckage to save the injured inside, or would he stand on peoples faces to get out? Did it depend on whether you had

16

hero DNA or just on what sort of mood you were in at the time, or again, on the behaviour of the others around you, or again on the entire fabric of your belief system and upbringing? She decided that her sister Helen would definitely die rescuing the injured without thinking twice because she was would want to be in control of the situation. Toby would be in there next to her because it was the right thing. Her sister Marion would rescue them because she had to be in the thick of any drama. She, Alice, would also be a rescuer, though recalcitrant, because she would want to live to analyse the event afterwards. Human behaviour was so endlessly complex.

It was only twenty past five, but she felt as if she'd done a thirty-six hour shift on the secure wing, completely knackered.

When she reached the flat where she lived with Toby she found it all neat and tidy. There were no dishes or mugs in the sink, the bag in the bin had been removed and taken outside to the back garbage deposit, the bed was made, the shoes were in the shoe rack in the bedroom wardrobe. This was Toby. The flat, on the top floor of a formerly grand Victorian house, was too small to be untidy, though Alice knew it would be a mess if she lived there alone. The presence of Toby, not the confined dimensions of her physical surroundings, made her a tidy person. There, it came back to conformity to the standards and expectation of others.

Alice pulled off her court suit, her one good item of clothing, and hung it up. It occurred to her that she could throw it over the back of the chair as she would be wearing it tomorrow, but she knew Toby would only hang it up when he got back.

She put on tracksuit bottoms and a sweatshirt that Marion had given her from the States with a picture of the Statue of Liberty on the back and rumbled in the shoe rack for her running shoes.

As she left the flat she flicked the flashing answering machine. As usual there were messages from Toby.

'How was court? Tried you on your mobile but it was off, you should leave it on. Can I play rugby on Saturday? Grudge match, London Welsh. Oh there's a meat pie in the freezer, can you defrost it so we can...' He ran out of message space.

Alice turned North and ran up Haverstock Hill, past rows of big old houses joined together almost all of which had been converted to flats. It was dark and it was rush hour, that euphemism for what happens to traffic in London after five thirty. She ran past a static jam of cars, the headlamps adding to the yellow light of the night city. She detoured down a side road and more Victorian terraces. On the smaller roads the houses were more likely to have been retained as single dwellings, family homes.

Her breath made a transitory vapour trail behind her in the frosty air. She moved fast. The year before she had run the London Marathon. She was addicted to running. She hadn't always been a runner. She had taken it up when she started on the psychiatric wards. Running wasn't a hobby. It was essential.

At the end of the road she could turn left and get on to Hampstead Heath. Toby had made her promise not to run on the Heath after dark. It worried him. Lots of things worried him.

She turned ran past the cinema and the shops at the bottom of East Heath Road, past the patisserie and the bakers and the art gallery and crossed the road to the beginning of the Heath. It was easier to run on grass, and she liked the dark and the emptiness. In London the yellow dome of the city obscured the burning of the stars, but there on the Heath she could sometimes pretend she was out on a boat, lifted by the rolls of the sea surface so close she could dangle her hand in its stone cold depths.

She ran up to Highgate and back, more than five miles.

On her return there was a follow up message from Toby on the machine.

'Aren't you back? Its six fifty seven. Don't run on the Heath. Don't forget to defrost the pie.'

Alice took the pie out to defrost, dithered, wondered if Toby would notice if she cooked it from frozen, then put it back in the freezer and looked in the fridge to see if there was anything else. She decided they could have pasta. Again.

She went into the bathroom and ran a hot bath. Her clothes were covered in mud, a tell tale sign of Heath running. She threw them directly in the washing machine, economically adding the washing already in the basket as a mental sop to Toby, and returned to her bath.

Her body was bright red with cold and exercise. Her skin tingled with a billion pinpricks as she sank into the hot water. She lay in great physical pleasure.

'Didn't you get my messages?' His tone was mildly irate.

'I went for a run, only just got back.' Her tone was placatory. She was watching the news. Toby dropped his rucksack. He was beginning to lose the angelic look he had possessed as a youth, with his blonde wavy hair, cornflower eyes and clear skin. At the age of thirty three his face was filling out, lines were forming in fans from his nose to the outer edges of his lips and from the corners of his eyes and a frown furrow was developing between the brows. Despite the blondeness and blue eyes Toby was not actually good looking. There was something about the narrowness of his face, a pointiness of the features that detracted from handsomeness. When Alice first met him he reminded her of the foxy whiskered gentleman who was the undoing of Jemima Puddleduck, apart from the fact that Toby would never have taken advantage of an unsophisticated lady duck. He would have given her sound practical advice on the protection of her eggs.

He put his arm around Alice's neck and kissed her briefly. He was about to chide her about not returning his call, but as he bent he smelled the scent of her hair and the call faded into unimportance.

'We're having pasta,' she said, without turning round. He realised she'd forgotten the pie too. He gave a resigned smile that she didn't see.

He began to talk about the patients he had seen, working through them in order. Alice wasn't really listening. It wasn't necessary to listen. It was the talking that was therapeutic. She heard his voice, raised, ploughing on from the bedroom as he hung up his jacket. The words were muffled by the telly commentary.

Alice got up at six to meet Lorette at the clinic. Alice was attached two days a week to the substance misuse team in Camden, a combined clinic and therapy centre. She had arranged to give Lorette her methadone script there early so she could get to court in time and in shape. Lorette didn't come. Alice decided to go to Lorette's last known address and see if she was there. As she approached the entrance of the run down block she thought to herself that this was exactly the sort of thing Toby would worry about. He would be furious if he could see her now, on her own going up the echoey concrete stairwell. Polystyrene burger cartons, lager cans and used nappies littered the walkway. The door to the flat she was aiming for stood ajar, the lock splintered off. Alice knocked. A giant Jamaican man answered and glowered aggressively at her.

'Is Lorette in, please?'

He disappeared and didn't return.

Alice stood outside. No one came out.

She pushed the door open and walked in. The Jamaican guy and a friend of his were lolling in the kitchen cutting foil. As she passed the first man came up behind her. He raised his voice, very threatening.

'Who you want?'

'Lorette. Is she here?'

'No,' he said aggressively. Just then Lorette emerged from one of the bedrooms, looking poorly.

'I've got your script.'

'Oh fuch is zat duh time?' Lorette licked back the methadone. 'Yeah, right man.'

'We'd better go,' Alice wanted to be out of the flat. It stank of piss, and the two men in the kitchen were still hanging around with dark suspicious stares.

It was Janice Drake's turn to cross examine Alice. Alice tried to conceal her nerves. She was the only witness with a good word to say for Lorette. She had to get it right. As she ascended the witness box she caught the judge observing her. Up there, on the stand, she was completely exposed.

'Dr Christie.' Even the intonation of her name on Janice Drake's lips carried formal hostility. 'Dr Christie, have you read the report of Dr Mirrish?'

'Yes.' Alice addressed her responses to the judge.

'Dr Mirrish concludes that Miss Gurley's prognosis for recovery is poor. You disagree with his conclusion?'

Alice knew what was coming.

'Yes, I do.'

'For how long have you been practising as a psychiatrist?'

'I'm not fully qualified yet.'

'But you are employed as a senior registrar.'

'Yes.'

Janice Drake pushed her bully form forward. 'Dr Mirrish is a Consultant Psychiatrist of some thirty eight years experience, is he not?'

'He is.'

Thirty eight years of dealing with substance abusers. Alice reckoned it was a miracle he wasn't in a straight jacket himself. Everyone knew Mirrish was jaded. Everyone knew he was sick of the sight of addicts and alcoholics and wanted only to do his research and churn out tired, lucrative experts reports for court cases. He barely looked at the patients as they sat in his consulting room, answering the same faded set of questions.

'Why should the court prefer your evidence to his?' Janice Drake asked her question with an incredulous lift of the eyebrows.

'Dr Mirrish met Miss Gurley on only one occasion for an hour, very shortly after her relapse. At that time she would have presented badly, really at her worst. I have been her treating doctor and I have seen her over a longer period and I know what she is like drug free. She's a completely different person. She is warm, intelligent and she has insight.'

'But when she is using?'

'She'd be lethargic, chaotic, unmotivated, irritable, disorientated, aggressive, even violent.' Oh, yes. Alice knew exactly what Lorette would be like when she was using.

'Dr Christie, how could such a person possibly have the care of a baby?'

'Her drug use would have to be regulated to a minimum.'

'Are you saying that heroin use can be compatible with the care of an infant?' Again the theatrical tinge of incredulity in the voice. Janice Drake pinned her eyes on Alice.

'Yes, as long as the use is carefully monitored and the user is well supported and housed. Over time the use can be reduced to nil and abstinence achieved. It is dependent on the user's motivation and the accuracy of the support provided. The mother loves her baby. That is her motivation.'

'Quite apart from the drug issues, this lady has a chaotic and disturbing background, has she not?' Janice's voice dropped back to the brusque note of business.

'She was deprived of love, which always leads to difficulties later on.'

'So she has no model of loving parenting?' Janice had practiced this phrase. She rather liked it.

'Her model is absent or abusive parenting. The parenting we receive has a major affect on the way in which we function as adults, but adverse consequences can be minimised. Miss Gurley has an all too clear awareness of the way in which her early experiences have impacted on her, which in itself is a good indicator. Many people cannot acknowledge the damage their parenting caused to them because they are stuck replaying the same model.'

'Dr Mirrish made no reference to any of these factors,' dismissed Janice.

'I'm suggesting that creativity and independent thought be applied to this case.'

Alice knew Dr Mirrish's creativity had been buried in concrete somewhere in the late eighties. Mirrish hadn't given a fuck for twenty years. Alice glanced over at Lorette. What chance had she had to break the evil spell?

She said, 'If Miss Gurley had been given the right therapeutic setting from the start and the parenting classes she requested, and the help with housing she was continually promised we may not be here now.' Alice was aware her voice was upping in tempo. She took a drink of water to cool her self down. She noticed the judge observing her brief disarray. The feeling of being exposed returned.

Janice Drake was used to hurrying past Local Authority incompetence. She said, 'But here we are. Rosco is six months old and needs a safe home now. You will be aware of the significance of his age.'

'Yes.' Alice replaced her plastic cup on the ledge in front of her.

Six months is the crucial time for bonding. Mess them around with multiple carers at six months they have lifelong problems with forming attachments.

'No further questions.' Janice sat down.

'Thank you, Dr Christie,' said the judge. 'You are released.'

'My Lord, would it be acceptable for me to be here for the judgement?'

The judge pursed his lips shrewdly. He understood the reason for her suggestion. He looked at the young doctor carefully. She had anticipated him.

'No objection?' he asked the parties. None made, very well.

Easton had already written his judgement, even before hearing the mother's voice, before hearing the cross examination, before the barrister's final submissions.

23

Obviously he added bits in here and there but the structure was completed on the documentary evidence. The case had been scheduled to last four days. It lasted two. Easton was efficient. He worked fast. He cut through mothers and children, wives and husbands and their money like a red hot knife on butter. God knows, if the judges were all like him, they said in the list office, waiting time would be halved. He was sharp as a guillotine. He went straight to the point.

'I have before me a case concerning a six month boy, Rosco Gurley. The mother is Lorette Gurley. The father is unknown.'

Four-thirty on the second day. Alice sat in court next to Lorette. The effect of the morning methadone was wearing thin. She kept wiping the shiny palm of her hand on her jeans.

'Is he going to go with me?' Lorette asked. 'It was all good what you said. It was all true. I can do it with the right help.'

Lorette nodded. 'I could see he was listening to you, he was looking at you really hard. I think he might be going to give me a chance. Thas all we can ask, innit, a chance. I wouldn't fail again, no I wouldn't, nuh nuh.'

Lorette raised her eyes to the judge, over bright.

The solicitors sitting behind counsel scribbled furiously in their notebooks to take a note of every word that fell from the mouth of the judge.

Alice had the opportunity to examine him. He was late forties, still had brown hair, a few streaks of grey in the sides, parted down the left side, rather longer into the collar and around the ears than you might expect. He had never been beautiful even, Alice guessed, as a child. In fact he might have been an ugly child. His nose was too pronounced, rather curved, like an eagle's beak. His mouth was small and too square, his cheeks were heavy and he had exhausted bags around black mesmerising eyes. He had lines of severity and concentration between the brows and running down from the lips; she thought he had a scar at the left side of his lower jaw. But more than anything else, Alice believed she was looking at a sad man.

He had his eyes directed at a fixed point above the heads of everyone in the court and he spoke to that. He gave his speech without reading, without reference to notes. He listed dates and events in chronological order, he told the mother's story calmly, without passion or, initially, comment. This is the pattern of a judgement. First recount the facts as agreed or as found, then recount the salient parts of the evidence, then balance the evidence, then expound the law, then extract the conclusion.

Alice realised, as the judgement progressed that she was witnessing a carving in words, chip chip chip, no wasted stroke, inexorably producing an inevitable form, the apparently effortless work of a master, the product of mental organisation of fact and reason. But not emotion.

'Dr Mirrish, the expert instructed by the Local Authority, is a very experienced psychiatrist who has been providing this court with the benefit of his opinion for many years...'

Double edged, reflected Alice.

'In his view the mother's prognosis was poor. He based his opinion on the fact of her relapse, on the level of her usage, and on her psychological vulnerability and apparent inability to demonstrate a capacity for self protection in the real world. I believe Dr Mirrish is right. This mother will never be a functioning member of society.'

Alice's chest constricted. The awfulness of these words went beyond anything she had been expecting. She might not have been expecting Lorette to be awarded her child there and then, but she had not expected this. Her nerves tingled for what now lay ahead. She risked a glance at Lorette. Her face had turned ashen under its colour.

'Dr Christie, a qualified doctor and senior registrar, but with no qualification yet in psychiatry, sought to persuade me that the mother did stand a chance of rehabilitation if the right placement and treatment were made available to her.'

Pause.

25

'The doctor gave her view sincerely. I hope that in due course, no matter the outcome of this application, the mother will be given the opportunity to take advantage of such treatment.'

Alice deconstructed his sentence. It was preparing the ground for the final conclusion. She could see his judgement had pattern, symmetry and that it would loop back and pick up threads and themes and that nothing would be left random or hanging out.

'Dr Christie also sought to persuade me that the mother's love for her child was a decisive factor in her prospects of success.'

Pause.

'I have no doubt that Lorette Gurley loves her baby.'

Lorette had stopped breathing. For the first time the judge looked her full in the face.

'But I and the other professionals in this court know that love is not enough. I am not going to order the return of her child to her.'

He carried on. He was talking about timescales of the child, about risk of relapse, but behind the talk there grew a sound, startlingly low at first, like a baby's cry, then increasing in power and pitch until it was one long high ululation, a scream of loss, despair and disbelief.

The judge persevered briefly, then stopped. Deborah Morton had turned and was trying to shut Lorette up. The elderly women ushers were looking on in fascination and the judge's male clerk, sitting below the judge, was watching with an expression of distressed pity. Lorette picked up a cup of water and threw it at the judge. The clerk jumped up and raised his hands, as if to intervene between the stream of water and the judge.

'You,' shouted Lorette and pointed an accusing spidery finger at the judge. 'What do you know about me? What do you know about love? You fuck me, yes, you fuck me and you don't know about love. Its men like you- men like you.'

Deborah Morton rested back inertly against the bench, incapable of reaction. Janice Drake was sitting bolt upright, impassive but vindicated. The social workers looked guilty and uncomfortable. Lorette was raving on. Any minute now she was going to be out of her seat and up to the judge's podium.

The judge looked with a silent message to Alice. It was for this moment, anticipated by them both, that Alice had asked and he had granted permission for her to be in court for the judgement.

'No. Lorette.' It snapped out of Alice spontaneously. She stood up as she said it. 'No point, my darling.' She shook her head and gathered Lorette up in her arms and half carried her weeping and wailing and literally gnashing her teeth out of the court, away from the judge who had become her executioner.

Chapter Three.

As soon as Easton stepped through the door and heard the babble of conversation and the clink of glasses, he knew he had made a mistake. The faces and name badges repelled him. The thought of small talk repelled him. As he entered a blonde had tried to make him wear a badge with his name on; Mr Justice Easton. He had given the girl a look that sent her hand and the badge in it shooting back to her chest. She was a first year trainee, terrified that she had made some unforgivable social and professional blunder. But, she tried to comfort herself, if there was a badge for him, surely it was deemed appropriate that he should wear it. She agitated over the quandary and it spoiled her night, a night she had been looking forward to.

At the entrance to the reception room a waitress in a black and white outfit proffered a tray of drinks. He reached over the champagne to the glasses of carbonated water, with a nod of acknowledgement and no smile. He raised it to his lips and took a sip. The dry fizz stung his mouth. He had an ulcer on the inside of his cheek. He had first developed mouth ulcers when he was sent to boarding school at the age of six, and, at the age of forty nine, he still got them, especially if he was tired, which was all the time.

A solicitor called Adam Dearing appeared out of the forest of suits.

'Sir Michael.' Dearing grasped Easton's hand and shook it vigorously. He was a large, freckled man who smiled with his mouth but not with his eyes. In those circles it was an unspoken code that outer shells were not disturbed. About the inner life they did not wish to know. When someone ended up with a breakdown no one went to visit. There were drinks dos and professional camaraderie but underneath it all was ambition. The exterior was therefore vital.

For some privileged few, success was ready grown, as for Dearing. His maternal great-uncle was Sir Richard Carter, lately senior partner in the firm and knighted for services to families at the highest levels of society. In Carter's day it wasn't barely literate football players or crass furniture magnates who held the money. It was this Duke and that peer, and the storage vaults were piled with embossed black metal boxes containing deeds and wills from landed families. Sir Richard had retired in 1985, depressed with the way things were going.

There was another way to prosper, and that was through sheer force of ability; Easton's method. He was the best, the barrister of choice for any complex or valuable piece of work. It wasn't only the fact that he was cleverer than most, he had accurate judgement, a total command of the law and an unmatchable capacity for work. Also he had a major psychological advantage; he had no inclination to be liked. It didn't matter who you were, if you were on the other side you felt it, even if he knew that the next day you were using him for your client, paying him the fat fee his clerk required, you knew that Easton was always prepared to put the boot in. Not maliciously, not unnecessarily; he didn't even notice you were there. On the other hand he wouldn't go out of his way to run you over. The Bar was very surprised when he took an appointment as a judge. It must have cut his income by four fifths. His private life was an enigma. He did not mix in the gossipy, incestuous, highly social world of the Family Bar and its instructing solicitors.

That he should attend a drinks party was a major coup. Adam Dearing was a man who spotted opportunities. He meant to extract maximum value from the presence of the judge at his firm's reception.

Easton was propelled across the room, under the brilliant light of a magnificent chandelier. Easton would have liked time to study the shape and form and refracting glass drops of the chandelier, but there was no time. Easton noticed Gerald Routledge, another judge, an urbane, slick haired man who enjoyed parties. He was wearing a mauve silk handkerchief flamboyantly in his breast pocket. Routledge liked the attention of pretty young ladies. Easton watched with distaste as Routledge entertained a breathless circle with an anecdote starring him self, drawing them in with languid hand movements and stepping lightly from side to side like a ballroom dancer of exquisite grace.

Then there was the usual sprinkling of District Judges, less elite, more normal. Easton, because of his rarity and his reputation, caused a stir. He was aware that people were surreptitiously taking him in. Grudgingly, he allowed Dearing to present him as an offering at the altar of David Harding, the current senior of the Family Team at Carter Bell. Harding and Easton knew each other. Harding was older than Easton by some ten years. He had used Easton since he was junior barrister, and was one of the first to realise his value. He had respect for Easton's ability, but had never found him a man of easy social graces. Best to talk about work.

'Michael, good to see you. How's the Bench?'

Easton had been sitting as a judge for two years.

'Busy,' he replied, with a grimace.

'Money?'

'Money and children. Lots of children.'

Harding did not imagine that children appealed to Michael Easton. Something stirred far back in his memory about Easton, something he had heard. No, it had gone. The misty recollection stopped him from asking any polite questions about personal life.

'Must be a shock to the system, having to deal with all that. I suppose we're protected from it, at our end of things.'

By this he meant the money.

David Harding's long fingers swooped on a glistening canapé from a passing tray and popped it into his mouth, masticating.

'Have one.' He gestured to the tray, not at the man holding it out. Easton shook his head and tried to think of something to say. Surely that was what he had come for, to recall the art of conversation, to say things to other people and have other people say things to him. You talk, I talk. Social intercourse.

It was part of Easton's duty as a High Court judge to make himself available at least occasionally to the members of the profession who were an integral part of the judicial machine. However, he was incapable of working the room alone. He recognised that his social skills were silting up, and he relied upon Dearing and Harding's remorseless commitment to protect him at their own party from impudent intrusion.

Harding settled him in his new group. There was the Senior District Judge from the Registry, a plump, sensible no-nonsense matronly figure. There was an up and coming old Etonian junior barrister whose decorum could be relied on; there was Mark Thurloe, a fat, tired, bald, rather debauched looking partner from a rival firm. Mark had brought his assistant solicitor with him, a young blonde female. This latter was a part of what seemed to Harding to be a sort of stable, a recent phenomenon he had observed over the last five or six years. Whereas young lady solicitors in the top firms used to be serious and respectable, occasionally attractive in a modest, latent sort of way, there now appeared girls, clever girls, with long blonde hair like porn models, bronzed exposed shoulders in tight Max Mara shift dresses, welcoming pink lips and a forwardness of attitude Harding associated with a certain type of girl, the type that wears a red bra. One could not deny, however that they were decorative.

Mark Thurloe shook hands with Easton. They began a conversation about the development of case law, carefully avoiding specific reference, discoursing by means of analogy, the lawyer's skill.

The girl, as Harding thought of her, though she was a woman of twenty-three with a First in Law from Exeter University, was called Sally French, and the range of her ambition dwarfed that of men like Thurloe and Dearing. Whereas they merely wanted to excel in their profession, Sally French had multiple targets. She wanted to be a partner at her prestigious law firm. She wanted to be attractive and sexually alluring. She wanted to be thin, and this was quite hard because she was naturally curvaceous, so she had to starve herself. She wanted to marry a seriously prestigious man and she wanted that husband to adore her. She wanted to have children and for them to go to top private schools. She wanted to have a beautiful home.

Sally stood up a little bit straighter and pulled back her shoulders so that her breasts pointed out (she was not wearing a red bra) when Easton joined the conversing circle. She may not be the most professionally prominent person there, but she was sure she was the one he would be most interested in. Sally was very interested in the judge. She was a High Court Judge groupie. She had sat behind counsel and watched with real admiration the way in which Easton ran his court.

She swung her blonde hair and mirrored the way he was standing, turning full on towards him. She had had sex with Mark Thurloe but he was married so it had been a brief thing, cementing a certain intimacy between them that might one day come in useful. Sally actually found Thurloe repulsive when she saw his fat white flesh and felt it soft and doughy and sweaty between her thighs. As it happened Mark felt emotionally disgusted by Sally and blamed her for his inability to resist another one night stand. She didn't know it but he was looking for an opportunity to sack her.

Sally listened with an expression of deep concentration to what the judge was saying, nodding vigorously. When anyone else made a comment she used it as a springboard to her own safe interjection. Safe, because she wasn't about to make a prat of herself intellectually and had to be circumspect.

The Etonian, who might have been the focus of her attentions in other circumstances, gave his polished excuses about having a matter to prepare and bowed out.

It was a pity. Easton would have chosen to continue talking to him. He struck Easton as straight, hardworking, sensible, discreet and decent.

Sally French manoeuvred herself in next to the judge. Her pink lips were frosted, like the edge of a cocktail glass dipped in sugar. She kept smiling at him, catching his eye in a gesture of exclusivity, imperceptibly moving nearer and even once risking a light rest of her fingers on his arm as he bent to listen to what she was saying. She smelled overwhelmingly of some heavy scent.

Was this what he had come for? He made a couple of dry comments that served for humour, tentatively touching in his mind the possibility of this young woman and her tanned body. Maybe it was time he slept with a woman again. He was mildly embarrassed at being so blatantly chatted up in front of Harding, Dearing and the lady DJ. The latter was plainly amused, and kindly initiated a slight separation of the group so that Sally and the judge formed a sub group. Sally was facing him now and using a lot of hand language. Harding marvelled. The liberties these girls took.

Sally took another glass of champagne from the tray. Easton declined with a frown and a shake of the head. Sally's signals became gradually more overt.

Eason began to feel wretched. The girl was inching towards the personal, breaching the point of no return. Thus far she had followed conversational gambits about the law. Now she was asking him where he lived, a question concealed in her rapidly delivered verbal cogitations as to the awfulness of public transport from her part of London.

'Excuse me,' Easton said, cutting her off in her flow.

He gave her a small, reproaching, twist of the lips that left Sally confused.

Dearing, seeing the tide turn, took immediate repossession and steered Easton to join him up with Routledge. Easton stayed for a little while longer. He spoke to the judges from the Registry. It was always useful to know how matters were in the lower, interlocking courts. He spoke to the Clerk of the Rules, who said she mustn't grumble then complained bitterly about the state of the waiting list. He spoke to a couple of very senior solicitors about the implications of recent decisions in Family Law. He did what was expected and departed at a quarter to nine, having spent a respectable hour circulating with his professional peers.

In the cab on the way home he avoided thinking about his possible motivation for going to the function. You speak, I speak. Human intercourse? He had fulfilled a professional obligation. That was all.

Easton stopped the cab at the bottom of the hill by the parade of shops. He went in to the late store and bought some bread and milk. He carried the plastic bag in the crook of his arm and walked quickly up the incline past more shops towards the house in which he lived. On the opposite side of the road the pavement turned into a broad tarmac path lined by tall planes, down which there was always a bleak wind sweeping from the open Heath. Easton heard the trees' mottled bent branches groan, and he turned to look at the swaying outlines silhouetted against a streaked purple sky.

His house was opposite the Heath. Its lower floors were invisible from the pavement because of a high brick wall built on its boundary, over the top of which spilled heavy boughs of evergreen. There was a black iron gate set in the wall, beyond which lay the path to the door of the house, but the door itself could not be seen because the house had been built facing away from the world, away from the road and the eyes of the casual passer by, so that the path led to a blank white sided wall and followed the parameter of the house to a garden concealed from all but the occupant. A symmetrical arrangement of sash windows, three to either side of a white door, set out the ground floor. Altogether the house had four bedrooms. The attic bedroom was the only room to have a window to the world. Estate agents would have given much for the commission of this house. The garden was grassed, and tall growing shrubs and trees had been nurtured so that the house could not be overlooked.

Where French windows opened from the kitchen, there was an espalier, a fig outstretched on a wall.

Easton let himself in and turned on the lights. There was a recent smell of furniture polish. The cleaner had been in. Everything in the kitchen was tidy and ordered. There was nothing for him to do. The tiny Sri Lankan woman came in twice a week, for six hours at a time. She vacuumed his carpets, wiped the crumbs from the kitchen and the dust from the shelves, machine washed his shirts and ironed and hung them away, cleaned out his refrigerator, stripped his sheets and laundered them, emptied his bins and put them out for the dust cart. She attended all his domestic needs, but he had no real recollection of what she looked like. He had engaged her seven years before and had given her a key to the door and since the day when she first came he had been out of the house every Monday and Thursday. He left her cash, which he increased by the rate of the RPI each year, on the table in an envelope marked 'Ata', and at Christmas he gave her a hundred pounds. For seven years he had been misspelling her name, which appealed to her tinkling sense of humour so when she wrote her occasional notes to him, (Sir, we need more bleach, or lavatory roll, or cheese lasts longer in the refrigerator if it is wrapped,) she was careful to squiggle her name so as not to disturb her little joke. She planned at the end of twenty five years invisible service to leave him a note with the name 'Jyatah' signed in huge bold letters at the bottom.

Easton took off his overcoat and hung it in the hall. He went into the pristine kitchen, and made a pot of tea. He was a tea addict. He was hungry. He had not eaten at the reception. Putting food into his mouth in front of others was something he did not do. The one domestic chore he performed for himself was to purchase his own food. He seldom bothered to cook. He spent a lot of money at the delicatessen. There was some duck pate in the fridge and a bowl of Lebanese olives. He unwrapped the French loaf he had bought. He took the food out and arranged it on the kitchen table with his tea and began to eat. He listened to the ticking of the clock on the wall, a circular wooden framed timepiece with very clear hands and roman numerals. He thought about reading the newspaper as he ate, or listening to a discussion on the radio, but then sat deliberately in the silence of being alone in his own house.

Going to the function had been a professional obligation, not an attempt to make contact with people, he reminded himself. Out of curiosity he tried to recreate the obscure unpleasantness of the emotion he had experienced while talking to Sally French. He couldn't put a name to it. When he concentrated hard the closest he could come to a description was the word 'exposed'. But it had been much more powerful than that, it was exposure of the most pathetic, derisory, humiliating kind. He didn't understand why, only that it was deep and cold and a place he feared.

He washed up his plate and left it on the side to dry, refilled his tea cup and went into the living room. Because he had gone to the function he had not brought work home. It was his habit to leave chambers around ten at night, often bringing bundles home to look at after he had eaten.

Very unusually therefore he had an empty space of an evening. He went to the study and opened his computer and browsed the Christie's catalogue. There were a couple of interesting paintings, but nothing he must have. He went onto the other mainstream art sites then the less mainstream. At weekends he went to fairs and exhibitions and auctions in London, and occasional weekends he went to Paris or Manhattan, if work allowed, and he had an agent in each of the cities who kept an eye out for pieces he would want to buy. When the time came, and sometimes he kept his pieces of art for many years, he sold. He had had a few extremely good deals, buying the obscure that became celebrated and valuable. Making money from Art was about foresight, ruthlessness, luck and keeping informed. Rather like the Law. But there were also items that he would never sell.

He heard the clock in the hall strike midnight and turned off the screen. He was hungry again so ate dried dates then made a jam sandwich and another cup of tea. He took the tea

36

into the living room and picked a book off the shelf, The Magic Mountain, and sat in an armchair reading. He had bought a paperback copy in the local Oxfam. He'd never been as keen on the Germans as the Russians but now he found he was ready for Mann. Still, as he read his mind slid and intruding into the pages was the thought that instead of reading he could be having sex. For some moments he felt an almost painful desire for the action of moving inside a tight, soft tunnel. He felt a heat pass through his stomach and into his groin. It was an entirely abstract lust. One recollection of the woman at the function and desire faded abruptly. In its place he imagined having to talk to her after the act and he recalled why it was that he hadn't had sex for so long. He didn't want to talk. He had nothing to say, and there was nothing he wanted to hear. It was pointless.

He read six chapters of Thomas Mann and fell asleep.

He awoke. The room was cold. He leaned forward to pick up the book from the carpet. Then he stopped. There were sounds in his house or maybe it wasn't sound but the sense of someone else being present. Easton stiffened and listened intently. He went into the hallway, still holding The Magic Mountain. He heard definite noises coming from the kitchen. It was so shocking he merely stood. There was a telephone in the kitchen and one by his bed, as well as a fax phone in the study. Too late. The kitchen door opened and a swarthy man appeared, unshaven, wearing a long black coat, jeans and a black woolly hat. He had a gold earring in one lobe, and a serrated knife in his hand.

'What are you doing?' Easton asked. The inadequacy of his response struck him as ridiculous.

'I just need some money.'

From the kitchen there was silence. If there was another person he was quiet.

The unshaven one half glanced behind him and said to Easton, 'Go in there,' gesturing with a nod of his head to the drawing room.

Easton backed into the room. There was no point in confrontation unless it became necessary. Fear and rage competed for dominance. Easton considered flinging Thomas Mann, the greatest of all the Germans, at the burglar, at the same time realising that the situation had caused him this ludicrous mental aberration.

The burglar followed him into the drawing room. For a second they stood facing each other. Easton waited for the other to speak.

'Cash,' said the burglar.

Easton put his hand in his pocket and pulled out the contents, some loose change and laid it on the table next to him. He noticed that his hand shook. The man was making him afraid, and this made him unspeakably, almost sickeningly, angry. With a vast effort he brought his anger under control. He looked up and saw a vile scowl of impatience disfigure the man's brow and beetle dark eyes.

'There's more in my wallet upstairs, about eighty pounds. That's all I have in cash.'

The burglar nodded and went to the door, opening it a shifty crack and speaking to another who was standing in the hall.

'He's got cash in his wallet upstairs.'

Easton heard the creak of the stairs as someone ascended.

The first thief risked an examination of the room. Easton kept quiet. He didn't suppose the thief would have any idea of the value of the artefacts. There was a bronze of a girl reclining, which was worth a great deal. There was a long silk antique Persian wall hanging, there was a French textile screen and a number of Turkish rugs. There were several heavy marble sculptures, and a clay bust. On the walls were paintings and sketches by important artists and by not so important. The thief would know no difference. To him it was all the same. Easton was afraid not of the theft of these items, but of their random despoliation, pointless ripping and tearing. His own heart beat so loud he wondered if the thief could hear it. Easton tried to assess the thief's state. He'd seen the look before, sweating and erratic jerky movements. Easton recognised drugs.

There were some obvious pieces of ornate silver dotted around. The thief started putting them, item by item into the pocket of his coat, a small inkwell, a paperknife, a wine stop, a whisky flask.

'You'll get a good price for those, if you sell in the right market,' Easton said. He couldn't stand dumb while he was being robbed. 'Maybe I'll be able to buy them back, if I see them.' He risked a joke. Yes, this was the moment for jokes, not as conversation with young women, but as the response of a civilized man in the face of an uncivilized occurrence. Speech, language, the avoidance of violence, human connection. It struck him as ironic that he was attempting now, in these circumstances to make contact, not with a person to whom he could have made love, but with one who was robbing him and might just as easily attack and kill him. The instinctual capacity for contact reinstated itself in the hour of need, the path was overgrown but not impassable. The thief reached out again.

'Not that.' Easton reached out too, forgetting his danger. 'At least, not the photograph. Take the frame, leave the photograph.' He attempted to negotiate.

With slow and insolent deliberation the thief studied the picture in the frame then put it frame, photograph, all in his pocket.

Easton smiled regretfully and repeated, 'I want my photograph.'

'You can't have it.'

'Why?'

There was a movement outside the door. The thief, watchful, cast a quick look at the other thief, the one Easton couldn't see. No words passed between them, but an obvious understanding.

The first thief made a movement of the door, opened it to leave. Easton stepped forward, he was going to close that

39

door and ask again for his photograph, because there was no reason for it to be taken away from him. No reason.

As his hand closed around the edge of the door the thief, the one with whom he had attempted to joke, slammed it hard, cracking the ends of Easton's fingers. The door was quickly released and Easton felt unspeakable pain. Then the thief jerked the full force of his knee into Easton's groin.

He bent, and fell slowly to his knees. He lost his vision and for a short second there was no pain, no breath, no feeling at all, like the insuck of a child prior to its scream. But only for a second, then there was a searing, excruciating total body agony.

The thief watched, listening to the man on the floor make broken gagging attempts both to breath and to cry out.

The door opened and a second thief spoke.

'Oh! Oh, no! What've you done?'

'He was coming for me. He'll be all right. Let's go.'

It took a long time for the initial violence of the spasm to pass. As soon as it did, Easton vomited. The pain in his stomach and groin prevented him from getting up. Eventually he managed to roll onto all fours, at which point he was sick once more. He spat. He could barely move for the pain. He crawled to the sofa and propped his back against it so that at least he was in an upright position. He had lost control over his body and shivered. He looked at his hand and realised his fingers were broken.

Time passed like a nightmare. He wasn't sure whether it was the shock or the cold that was making him shake.

Raising himself a bit at a time he managed to stand and stagger upstairs, pausing between each step, each movement sending a burning blade through his groin and abdomen. He felt nauseous and his head swam. Upstairs he swallowed four paracetamol and ran a hot bath. He undressed slowly, conscious of his body shaking, and stepped into the hot water, lowering himself with difficulty. The heat of the water on his damaged body forced from him an animal grunt, but he pushed his hand deep into the heat as well. It occurred to him that he might pass out, but he was a big man and didn't think he was likely to drown in the foot of water wallowing around him. He probably did pass out temporarily. The lightness in his head, at any rate, caused a type of absence from reality.

But the heat and drugs helped. The burning changed into an intense throbbing ache. He lifted himself out of the bath. Water dripped onto black and white ceramic tiles. He wrapped a towel around himself and dried his skin.

In the bedroom he noticed from his alarm clock that it was past dawn, four thirty pm.

He lay on the bed. He supposed he ought to have his hand looked at. The pulsing pain made sleep impossible. The night was long.

At eight he telephoned and spoke to Clive, his clerk. For the first time in twenty years Easton called in ill. He said he had had an accident.

His clerk said, 'Oh dear. Oh dear. Are you all right, sir? Ought I to come round? What can I do?'

'Nothing. Don't come. I'll be in tomorrow.'

It wasn't merely the pain. It was that other; the solid, leaden, inescapable awfulness of having been physically assaulted. Easton couldn't stand it. And what was worse, even worse, repeating in his ears, the voice of the second thief.

Chapter Four.

A harassed white coated doctor in an overflowing casualty ward bandaged Easton's fingers.

'How did it happen?' The doctor looked up quizzically to see why there was no reply.

'I trapped my hand in the door. The wind blew it shut.'

'And that?' The doctor nodded knowingly downwards.

Easton hadn't mentioned his lower injury. It showed in his face that he didn't like being asked.

'It's the way you're walking, and sitting,' said the doctor, a tinge of impatience in his tone. Did he look as if he were blind? 'You don't have to tell me, if you don't want to.'

Easton agreed. 'No.'

The doctor wasn't sure he liked this patient very much.

As Easton rolled down his sleeve, the doctor said, 'Do you think you might need other tests?' He met Easton's eye in an inferential manner.

'What kind of tests?'

'To inform your behaviour with others.'

'You think…?'

'I don't think anything. I'm just a doctor.'

'I don't need any tests.'

The doctor despaired. Would they ever learn?

'Have you told the police?'

'Why would I do that?'

'To prevent similar…accidents,' said the doctor, drily.

'I had a man in casualty today. Three broken fingers, balls swollen up like coconuts. Obviously been attacked, and hadn't reported it,' said Toby to Alice over dinner in a small inexpensive bistro in Belsize Park. 'What got me, it must have been a homosexual incident…'

'Why?' asked Alice, immediately.

'Because of the nature of the injuries and because he hadn't reported it. He made up some story about trapping his fingers. I don't think he gave a monkey's whether I believed

42

it or not. If it had been a normal attack, a mugging for example, he'd have told the police.'

'People have their reasons.'

'What reasons?'

'Maybe he's afraid of whoever did it.'

'He didn't look the frightened kind. Just the opposite, actually. '

'It could have been a woman. That would make it humiliating, explaining the reluctance to report.'

'A woman wouldn't do that,' dismissed Toby, screwing pepper onto his lasagne.

'Just because it never happened to you.'

'Anyway, he wouldn't have an HIV test.'

'Why should he?'

'It's the responsible thing to do,' snapped Toby, exasperated with Alice's obtuseness. Sometimes she took her liberal inclinations to a ridiculous extent.

'You can't make people act responsibly,' she observed, indifferently.

'You bloody well ought to be able to. I'm sick of people who don't act responsibly. They'd be the first to start talking about their rights. They don't want to be infected so why should they infect others willy nilly.'

Alice sat back in her chair as she laughed. 'Willy nilly,' she echoed, and shook her head in mirth.

Toby put down his knife and leaned forward in his chair resentfully. 'I *am* sick of people who don't act responsibly. Smokers, the obese, practising gays who won't have the test, people who don't use condoms.'

'Like us,' said Alice, licking her knife.

'Don't lick your knife. We're different. That's not what I meant. We're not a risk to each other.'

'I could be HIV, for all you know.'

'Don't be stupid.'

'You're not my only lover.'

Toby stared at her.

'I mean, you're not the only sexual partner I've ever had.'

43

'What an extraordinary thing to say.'

'It's true though, isn't it? HIV can stay dormant for ten years. You and I have been together four years. Before that...'

'I don't want to know. I've always said, I don't want to know.'

Toby looked around the restaurant. It was a Saturday night and the tables were full. He put down his knife and fork.

'Why have you started this?' he asked, his eyes lowered.

Alice felt ashamed. It was too easy to hurt Toby. His love made him vulnerable.

'I'm teasing. Forget about it.' She teased him too often these days.

'I can't forget about it.' He looked at her. She was extra beautiful tonight, not that she was wearing anything special. She didn't need to bother with all that make up and dresses nonsense. She was special unadorned.

He leaned forward and whispered, 'When you say these things...' he stopped, unable to express what he felt.

'Forget about it.'

'You know I love you,' he said, resentfully.

'I know.' She pressed his hand. He pulled away and they resumed eating.

In bed after the meal, after they had watched the video he had rented, a sci-fi thing, he lay awake and Alice slept. She lay on her left side and he lay on his left, too, behind her, without touching. He traced the dark outline of her naked shoulder. He took a lock of her hair in his fingers and rubbed the silky strands together. He bent forward and smelled her then licked her skin in the deep valley between the shoulder blades. She tasted of salt. She moved unconsciously onto her back.

'Alice, will you marry me?'

He had done this before. She never replied. He only ever dare ask her while she was asleep.

Chapter Five

On the first day of April, Spring burst in unexpectedly. The winter had run through into March, bleak as Russia, grey and dismal, but on April Fool's Day the sky was dramatically cleared of its misery and turned blue, real cerulean blue, with fat, butter yellow clouds. The sun showered gold.

Alice lay on the rumpled white bed and stretched. A bed alone was a luxury. Toby was on an early shift, so she had the bed and the Saturday morning to herself.

Being the sole occupant of the bed meant she could do what she liked. Toby couldn't bear her late shifts when he had to be alone. Alice felt the opposite. She spread herself out in a star shape, legs and arms wide. She couldn't have done that with Toby in the flat. He would have been aroused despite himself and she would have lost the possession of her own body. Besides she would never have exposed herself to him in that way. Toby was sexually conservative. He would have found her open legs somehow distasteful. For a doctor, he really didn't like bodies.

She sat up. It felt like a day for going out and strolling the High Street. She had a night shift later, on the secure psychiatric wing at the hospital.

Alice walked from the bottom of Haverstock Hill to the Village. The shops, cafés and restaurants along the way thrummed and bustled in a feverish excitement over the incoming Spring. Easter was imminent. They were late in the Lenten period. All the confectionary shops, and there were many to satisfy that sweet toothed area of London, were decked out with imitation fluffy chicks, or bob tailed bunnies. In the children's toy store paper cut outs of gaudy egg shapes had been made by the little customers and stuck up in the window with their names and ages written underneath. There were no nods in the direction of Easter being anything other than an opportunity to spend and gorge on pretty chocolates; this was an intellectual, cosmopolitan area. No one wanted to be tastelessly reminded of crosses and suffering, especially on a day so crystalline.

The previous day Alice had spent too long on the secure psychiatric wing, where, through an unfortunate quirk of the architecture there were no windows.

Inside, the dangerous mad, dangerous to themselves and to others, sat in individual tiny cells euphemistically called rooms, surrounded by the moans of other afflicted souls, closed in a world of unpredictable terrors, fantasies played out, screams, rages, muttering and drug induced stupefaction. It is still Bedlam, intrinsically Victorian. The patients go about in baggy old clothes, wild haired and dead eyed. No wonder the sane are so afraid of the mad, the modern bogeymen.

Alice was writing her thesis about the history of society's attitude to the mentally ill, the different, the isolated, the addicted, the reviled and hated. She had a deadline. But this morning she wanted to stroll in the sun.

Here on Hampstead High Street sanity prevailed. The clean, corduroy clad, bright faced children of the well off gambolled gently, or sat sucking at straws at pavement tables, chocolate mouthed. Reasonable brains sat cross-legged at the outdoor cafes reading broadsheets over strong coffee and croissant; surely this morning on Hampstead High Street epitomised the crowning manifestation of rational civilization, concluding what the Greeks had begun.

Alice snatched her careless happiness. She pushed from her thoughts the wards, the thesis deadline, the clients at the substance misuse clinic. As she strolled she recognised this as a good state of mind, one that was necessary, a brief time out from the stresses. It was her belief that human minds to one degree or another create a web of artificial stresses and concerns that go way beyond actual human needs, ie the need for shelter and food. If it were just shelter and food there would be no problem. But the mind is so amazing, so godlike, so devilish and complex that it needs love as well. And just as the need for shelter mutates into the need to build Versailles, the need for food into the objectively preposterous need for Michelin, so the need for love distorts most alarmingly of all.

Alice rolled this over in her mind. She couldn't stop analysing. That was one of her problems. A day like today, she scolded herself, just enjoy.

She went into Whistles and made herself admire a bottle green silk paisley dress with dark green velvet trim. It was expensive. She didn't try it on. She never tried things on. However, to her surprise, she found being in the shop of luxurious women's accoutrements to be erotic. This interested her and she carefully set it aside for later analysis. She supposed that there had been much marketing strategy in terms of producing her feeling, an orchestration of smell and sight and touch and mind altering music. She wondered if other women were feeling it too. Whatever it was, (she stopped herself from analysing again), it felt pleasant.

Alice didn't have many clothes. Those she did were mainly functional and comfortable. Toby encouraged her in this.

Out in the street once more the power of the women's shop broke and she realised she would far rather buy books. She crossed the road. On the way she dipped into Crabtree and Evelyn and sprayed some vanilla scent onto her wrist and hair. She sniffed and it reminded her of melted caramel. In Waterstone's she bought a couple of books, guiltily. Toby said they ought to make more use of the library, and she supposed, humbly, that he was right.

Carrying her stash in a black Waterstone's bag, she swung it back and forth in a jaunty fashion, liberated by the illicit purchase.

She began to walk down the hill again but diverted into Gayton Street and went in to Oxfam. She was a keen charity shop aficionado.

As Alice approached there was a Mercedes slewed across two parking spaces, boot up and a high maintenance female in shades and Manolo Blahnik kitten heels tottering to and fro from the car to the shop with bin liners full of designer cast offs.

Once, in the shop, Alice had got into conversation with a group of women who were on a coach trip from the North East, the theme of which was London charity stores. In one day, they had set off from Sunderland at 5 in the morning, and covered Hampstead, the King's Road, and Belgravia.

But the best thing about the Hampstead store, and this reflected the intellectual character of the area, was the book section. It was enormous, eclectic and cheap.

While she was in there she idly browsed the clothing section at the far end of the shop.

A man came in with a bulging bin liner and passed it over the counter. She knew him instantly and drew back. He came down the steps to the book section, took out a pair of glasses and put them on, and began to look through the titles, tilting his head to read the spines. He was wearing a black cashmere overcoat, the collar pulled up despite the mellowness of the day, a pale blue shirt open at the top button, black corduroy trousers and black brogues. Alice smiled a little to herself. Not a lot of concession to the weekend, nor the weather.

She found herself in a dilemma. Was he like a celebrity, unavailable to the public while not performing? She was interested in the question of what lay behind the professional mask, and she felt very strongly from him the sense of a highly fortified façade. Fortified facades are erected for a reason. They are designed to repel. She was sure that the last thing he would want to do on a Saturday morning was have to accommodate some professional ship in the night in his private space. But in order to leave the store she would have to squeeze past his back. How, anyway, would she address him?

She inched forward, thinking that if he turned she would speak to him, but if not she would go her way.

He had selected a book and had it open in his hand, reading a page. He was bigger than she remembered, quite burly. He seemed absorbed, and had his back turned, but as she passed he glanced around. In the second that it became obvious to her that he had clearly seen her face she pretended to notice him for the first time.

'It's Mr Justice Easton, isn't it?' she said, even though she had no certainty that he would recognise her. It was, after all, six months ago and he must see many faces. She had no reason to feel that she would stand out in any way.

He lowered his head and looked at her from over his glasses, then reached up quickly and took them off. It was the scent in her hair that made him turn.

'I gave some evidence in court in November last year. You won't remember, probably.'

'Dr. Christie from the Royal Free.'

She gave an embarrassed laugh. 'I just noticed you. I hope you don't mind me addressing you,' she added. He gave a tiny dry smile to himself at her earnestness and slotted the book back onto the shelf. She carefully avoided looking at its title. She didn't think he was the kind of man who liked his tastes to be perused by strangers.

'No, I don't mind.'

'Only, I know how I feel about being recognised by patients in the street.'

'But then I suppose, your patients…'

'Oh, I don't mind their illness. It's just when it's out of context, I mean, you need that distance, between the personal and the professional. Interior and exterior, you know.' She shrugged, effacingly. He considered.

'It must be difficult, what you do,' he said.

She wondered if this was functional level chit chat. She had never been interested in that.

'It is,' she replied, with feeling. 'But I'm off until late shift and it's a beautiful day.'

'So you're putting it behind you.' A challenge weighed in behind the words.

'Don't you? It's not exactly a party game, is it?' She resented the subtext of alleged lack of feeling.

They both flashed back to the screams of the mother, put fastidiously to one side to facilitate the politesse of their chance meeting.

Alice's sense of the glorious morning was dissolved by the memory of the reality of the world. She was sorry she had spoken to him. He had upset her and something in her wanted to disconcert him, just a pinprick incision into the personal, she sensed, would be sufficient.

'So, having a spring clear out?' She nodded at the plastic bag he had brought in, which was still slumped dejectedly in the corner behind the counter. He instinctively followed her gesture.

'Something like that,' he said heavily, fixing his gaze too long on the bag.

'I shop for books here,' she said, to distract him, ashamed that she might have hit upon a real wound. 'When I retire I'm going to run a second hand book store.'

'Are you?' he asked, without any real interest.

'Yes, down in Cornwall.'

'You've got it all planned,' he observed, as if plans were a child's game.

She thought he would make a move to leave, but instead he asked, 'Are you still attached to the substance misuse team?'

She nodded. 'Twice a week. It's the area I'm planning to specialise in. I'm writing a thesis about it.'

'Lots of plans.'

She couldn't decide if it was worldly cynicism or just plain mockery.

She smiled in a non-committal way and shrugged, as if to signify that they had come to the end of their conversational road.

'Well,' he said, without saying goodbye, and moved off.

Alice breathed out slowly. She turned to the books. There was a copy of Hecuba, actually three plays by Euripides. Death, power, war, madness, revenge, morality; voices reaching out across the millennia to a society that has in no real psychological sense changed. She realised that in their haste to get away from each other they had confused their roles and forgotten that she was meant to be the one leaving and him the one staying.

'I'm sorry.' He was there at her shoulder again, running his hand through his hair. 'Have you got time for a coffee?'

'Now?' She was taken aback. 'Yes, all right.'

She followed him out of the shop and into the street. She half expected some breathless revelation, in her recipient role as psychiatrist. She had to step out to keep up with him. He turned to her. 'Just up to the café,' he said, and smiled self consciously, as if smiling were alien to him.

He asked her if she wanted to sit inside or out and waited for her to seat herself before sitting down. He had learned the esoteric rites of English social courtesy. She recognised the hallmark of a public school background, which would explain so much.

They took a table on the pavement. The sun's reflection burned a dazzling O on the silver topped surface. The patch of brilliance was hot to the touch. Alice rested her hands open in the heat. It was good to feel the sun.

He ordered an espresso with a separate jug of hot milk for her and tea for himself. While she carefully mixed the coffee and milk he stole the opportunity to examine her. Her hair fell untidily across her eyes, which were large, expressive, truthful and the blue grey of a winter sea. Her skin was peculiarly lucent, pale cream and white and strawberry pink high on the cheeks. Her brows were clear and straight and the way they formed a curve into the contour of the nose reminded him of a strong Picasso woman. Her mouth was too wide for beauty, but added to the impressionistic effect. He absorbed her as a portrait in bold sweeps of intermingled blueberry black, bright grey and deep red. As soon as she looked directly at him he turned away and faced the road.

'Tell me about the work you do at the clinic.'

'Why?' she asked. He hadn't expected that. He was used to having his questions answered.

'I'm interested.' He lifted up his cup of tea and obscured his face by sipping it. Classic avoidance, she thought; ulterior motive. But she told him about her work. He directed her, shepherding like a sheep dog, keeping her working, keeping her where he wanted her to be. The moment she deviated he brought her back. He asked questions with surgical precision.

She had the uncomfortable feeling that she had been dissected for her parts.

After half an hour he said, oddly, showing the fissure where good manners were used as an inappropriate replacement for human sensitivity, 'Thank you, I've finished,' and leaned back with an air of release.

'I bet you say that to all the girls,' she quipped, instantly, without thinking, rather shocking herself, but once said she had to carry it off. He looked at her sharply. The sexual innuendo was clear. He wished to deny that he acted sexually in this way, and this caused him irritation; that he should feel the need to justify himself sexually, in a mere café conversation. For the first time in many years he was at a loss what to say.

'Is that the time?' she asked, employing an ironic cliché. She stood up. He stood too, facing her over the sun spilled table. She seemed to reflect, to make a decision then said, 'I was brought up in Cornwall. I studied at Guy's. I have two sisters and a mother still alive. My father was a country doctor, but he drowned when I was twelve. I live with my boyfriend in a small flat on Haverstock Hill. Last year I ran the London Marathon. My favourite film is Bad Lieutenant. I like asparagus. I have an uncontrollable passion for chocolate. I am politically agnostic, a religious floater, and I have bad dreams about cold places.'

Easton gazed at her wryly.

'Am I telling you things you don't want to know?' She smiled at him lightly to indicate she was teasing him. As she walked away, she turned and called, 'Thanks for the coffee.' She didn't think she'd ever see him again.

Easton paid the bill and left. On the way home he had to pass the charity shop. He passed, halted, turned back and went in. The bell on the door tinkled at his entry. It was still the same lady on the counter. She remembered him. He bought back the bin liner he had donated, paying twenty pounds for it. It hadn't even been unpacked. He carried it home again.

Chapter Six.

The second thief prepared to inject himself. He sat on the concrete floor of the half derelict council flat they inhabited as squatters. They didn't really even qualify technically for the title of squatter. Formalities have no part in the world of the heroin addict.

'Can't get it in,' he observed, gazing bleakly at the network of collapsed veins in his outstretched arm. In his other hand he held a syringe. His arm was bound tight with a belt.

Chas took the syringe from Tommy's loose fingers and, kneeling over Tommy, concentrated intently on the inside of his arm, searching for a possible needle site.

'Come on,' whined Tommy, impatiently.

'Give us your leg,' replied Chas.

Tommy squirmed and pulled down his jeans. His legs were thin white things, barely legs at all. Chas knelt and examined the inside of the knee. Vivid septic spots tracked the trace of Tommy's latest injection sites.

'Ankles,' directed Chas, and he peeled off Tommy's trainer and sock and finally located a satisfactory vein, pressing the hard spine of the silver needle at an expertly oblique angle.

Tommy moaned and slid inexorably into ecstatic oblivion. His body slumped onto the concrete. Chas, rushing now, cooked up for himself, and using the same needle, injected.

Twenty minutes of well being later Tommy and Chas clanged down the echoey metal staircase of the outside of the flats. They passed another user, coming up, a girl called Eva, with no eyebrows left, and black lines as substitutes, applied under and over the eyes, giving her and her chalk white face a deathly mask. She had on no tights, and her high heeled shoes had rubbed blisters on the back of her feet. She was going up to the flat to use. Maybe it was her flat. Who cared? Eva was on the game.

She stopped. Chas and Tommy and Eva were friends, or that was how Eva thought of it. In other words they were part of the heroin network in that neighbourhood.

'There's a bloke looking for you two,' she said, pleased with her nugget of information. It gave them a reason to look at her. No one really looked at Eva anymore. Come to think of it, no one ever really had.

'Oldish bloke, money, asking at the clinic when I was there to get me syringes. Giving your description. Seemed quite keen.'

She waited for their reaction, which is saying something as she was aching for a hit. The boys exchanged glances and moved off. Eva, having shed her information, dragged up the metal stairs on legs that trembled.

'Where now?' asked Tommy.

'Pig,' replied Chas, decisively.

Chapter Seven.

Alice received a letter sent to her at the hospital.

'Dear Dr Christie,'

(He had deliberated over the name. He couldn't bring himself to say Dear Alice. Nor could he say Dear Alice Christie, as he despised the conjunction of first and family name. It sounded cumbersome, like a letter from a minor civil servant in pre revolution Russia. Nor was Dear Doctor right. It implied a patient/physician relationship.)

Would you and your friend like to come for supper? I'm on West Rise, adjoining the Heath. Let me know if you can.

Regards

Michael EASTON.

Your friend? What did that mean? She had told him she had a boyfriend. Was this the person Easton was inviting along with her? Or was it an open choice; bring the lover or anyone else? Or was there just something uncomfortable for him in the word 'boyfriend'.

The writing was unexpected, a large rapid scrawl, difficult to decipher, the few words taking up all of the page. Doctor's writing was traditionally bad. Toby's wasn't. That hand was small, even, neat and careful.

Alice put the letter in her bag. She decided she wouldn't decide. She would give the letter to Toby, explain the circumstances, and leave it to him. Then it was his responsibility if they formed an acquaintance with Michael Easton.

'We can hardly refuse. He's left an open date.' Toby held the note in his hand as he sat at the table eating his dinner. Toby had no desire to refuse. One look at the headed paper, with Sir Michael Easton written in black at the top, and the West Rise address, secured Toby's immediate agreement.

'I've always wanted to see inside one of those houses,' he said. 'Do you know why he's a sir?'

'All the High Court judges are Sir.'

'Typical lawyers,' sniffed Toby. 'According themselves honours. What about senior consultants, I'd like to know?'

'I didn't think you'd want to go.'

'Why ever not?'

'Because he's a stranger, and you don't like strangers.'

'But he's a judge.'

'So? He's still a stranger.'

'Yes, but he's not likely to be an axe murderer.'

Alice didn't argue with this crushing logic.

She wrote back.

'Dear Sir Michael,'

(They were going to supper. They couldn't call him Judge, or My Lord. If there was to be social intimacy it had to be acknowledged.)

'Toby and I would love to come to supper. Would Saturday week be convenient? Neither of us have shifts. You must let us know what we can bring.'

She toyed with using the word Love, as in Love Alice, but it was too much. It would sound to him like insincerity. She felt she was beginning to form a picture of how he worked, how he thought.

She ended; *'Regards, Alice Christie.'*

Then she had the problem of analysing the situation.

She reflected on the way in which she had parted from him, pressing on him facts about herself. Now she saw it at a distance she saw it as he might see it, self centred and childish. There was nothing wrong with what he had done; did he not after all work with substance mis-users? Make decisions about their lives? Was it not grown up and reasonable to wish to learn more about them, their habits and their treatment? She now flushed with mortification to recall the intimacy she had obliged him to suffer, her potted autobiography. Imagining that people were interested in each other at that level was something she had to shake out of herself. Just because she was interested in the minutiae of minds and how individual histories shape behaviour it did not mean that everyone else should be. It had always been her interest and now it was her professional concern. So? Did a garage mechanic have to analyse his customers' childhoods to see what was wrong with their car engines? Indeed they did not. Forcing others to see and do things your way is an immature reaction, she acknowledged. Not everyone stands where you stand. The variety of human perception is infinite as is the distance between one human being and another. She reminded herself of this argument before coming to the counter argument, that all humans need to be connected with other humans and that it is the absence of connection that leads to and is perceived by others as dysfunctionality.

Alice lay on the bed, staring at the ceiling and putting squares of bitter seventy per cent cocoa chocolate into her mouth, sucking it slowly, letting it melt on her tongue. She remembered the experiment of the Emperor Charlemagne. The Emperor Charlemagne, with his restless imperial curiosity, conducted an experiment on two babies. He kept them in a distant wing of his great castle, attended by expert nurses, whose orders were to provide the infants with all they needed to live; food, drink, warmth, physical safety, and cleanliness, but no affection. On no condition were the babies to be accorded love.

History tells us that the babies died.

Had she been trying to prevent Michael Easton from dying? There are deaths and deaths. Emotional death is a long, painful business. Alice did not wish to believe in emotional death, contrary to the evidence of her own observations of herself and others, and chose instead to recognise what she categorised as severe and sometimes irrevocable emotional disease. Her mind wandered off into the duality of the human condition, soul and body. Plato had them separate, but still couldn't help noticing the effect on the body of the agitated soul. It was a bit like transubstantiation, the incredible doctrine that the Catholics believe, that a little round wafer is really the body of Christ. Body and mind and soul, the three in one, the mystery mirror of the Trinity.

Constant human struggle to reconcile the body and the mind. Alzheimer's, schizophrenia, the organic causes of mental aberration, the body cruelly mutilating the mind; paranoia, neurosis, hysteria, the mind destroying the capacity of the body.

'Have you seen my box?' asked Toby, distractedly, riffling through the contents of his Rugby bag.

'What would I want with your box?' she retorted. He was referring to his groin protector. 'Do you think I lie and sniff it in your absence?'

Toby was disgusted and turned from his search to cast a disapproving eye at her.

'That's revolting.' Toby didn't like bodily smells. He always washed himself after having sex. Alice had to wash herself before having sex, in order to present cleanly to him.

'You know when I met Easton on the high street and we went for that coffee, he only wanted to talk about work. He didn't ask anything about me.'

'Why should he? He knows you in a professional context. He might have thought it rude to go prying into your personal arrangements. He was just extending an interest in an area that he has to deal with in his job.'

'So why has he invited us to dinner?' She wanted to see if Toby had any suspicions.

'Because…I don't know. Maybe he likes to keep up with new ideas.'

Alice laughed out loud and lifted herself onto her elbow, regarding Toby mischievously. 'Poor Easton. He longs for radical thinking and he gets you.'

Toby looked peeved. 'I keep up with developments,' he protested. 'What about my thesis.' Toby was working on a paper about the treatment of spine trauma.

Alice was chastened when she remembered the hours of work and dedication he was putting in to this and to the paralysed victims on his wards. The sad thing about spinal wards was that it was full of young men there because of sporting or motorcycle accidents. Alice remembered Toby's hard work and stopped laughing.

'Only kidding. Oh, have you looked on the window ledge? I think I might have put your box out there, to prevent festering.'

Toby tutted and went to the window and recovered his property. He flipped the raindrops off it and tossed it into his bag.

'Is he married?'

Alice genuinely hadn't thought of that. Even the idea of it surprised her.

'I suppose he must be,' she said, now she came to consider it. Rationally she acknowledged the likelihood of Easton having a wife. He was successful, monied, intelligent; such men always had wives. Even vile, ugly, boring men get wives easily if they have money and status. It was inconceivable that such a prize as he would be allowed to remain unclaimed. But thinking of it disconcerted her. It made it necessary completely to revise her picture of him as a man alone; a lonely man.

She tried to imagine what kind of wife Easton would have. Alice envisaged an elegant, cool, dark haired intellectual, in a white French blouse with good breasts and dramatic make up, like a fifties movie star.

'You'd better pick up some flowers, then,' said Toby, with a hint of irony, 'For Lady Easton.'

Alice realised she needed a dress. It occurred to her, now that she had created the Eastons, Sir Michael and Lady Easton, that their casual supper could easily be a sophisticated soiree and that she could not arrive looking like a bag lady. It was nine in the morning on Saturday, the Saturday of the dinner party (it had become a dinner party to her now) and she had a shift from ten to seven. Toby was playing rugby in Hertfordshire somewhere, and this usually took all day. She sighed. She would just have to do flowers and dress at lunch time, if there was no emergency.

As it happened she had time only for the dress. They had a new Section coming in and Alice had to manage the admission. The woman was a short Philippine of the most massive circumference, convinced that she was the Virgin Mary, a common problem with Catholics.

This left a short half hour to run up the hill and buy. She had time only for one shop, the shop she had browsed the day she had met Easton, and she had time for only one dress, the previously admired green silk paisley. She tried it on in a hurry. She looked at herself in the mirror and felt uncomfortable. It showed too much; her shoulders, her cleavage, the curve of her hips, but at least it was of reasonable length, past her knees.

She gagged when she checked the price label. She handed over her card knowing she would never wear this dress but once.

Toby was late back from Rugby. He called as he always did to keep her in touch with his every movement and said sorry, the match had gone on and they were having a 'quick' drink at the clubhouse and he had to wait for Trevor Saunders who was his lift.

On the way back from the hospital Alice went into the florists and bought some flowers. She held the image of the dark sophistication of Lady Easton in her mind and bought deep velvety red roses.

'Nice, those,' commented the aproned vendor as he wrapped them elaborately. 'Nice for a lady.'

She left the flowers on the sofa and threw herself into the shower. She was rather glad that Toby was not there to watch her get ready. She sluiced the ward off her skin and hair, and washed her self all over with rose scented oil Toby had bought for her one Christmas and which had remained unopened for over a year as it was too good to be used.

She dried her hair quickly with the dryer, too quickly, and it curled, but there was nothing she could do about that. Her hair had a power of its own.

Then she put on the dress. She realised she couldn't wear a bra with it, unless grubby grey straps were back in fashion. She stood at the mirror and looked at herself.

It was a different her.

As a response she went to her neglected make up bag and took out an ancient lipstick. She stood close to the glass and ran its tip over her lips. Someone had once told her you could get salmonella from old lipstick, as it was infused with animal fat, or placenta. She hoped she wouldn't be so infected.

She heard the door slam. Toby appeared in the bedroom doorway, carrying his rugby bag. He stopped.

'Well,' he said. She could tell at once he didn't like it.

'I had to get something, Tobe,' she said, excusing her profligacy.

He changed, putting on a pair of chinos, a clean shirt and a jacket.

She stood next to him at the mirror.

'You look nice,' she said, wanting to make him feel better.

Toby nodded shortly. 'Better go. We'll take the car.'

They parked outside the house on West Rise.

'Must be worth two million at least,' said Toby. 'Do they make that much, High Court Judges?'

'Why don't you ask him?'

The black iron gate was open. Alice had an impression that it was usually locked. There was a chain around the bar that had been looped around one of the sections, held by a padlock with an inset number code. The padlock was undone.

They walked along the laurel hedged path around the side of the house and to the front door. Alice thought of fairy stories, beating a way through the thorn forest to the Sleeping Beauty, or more apposite, the forbidding castle of the Beast. The path, the garden and the house were all overgrown with evergreens and dark ivies.

Toby carried a bottle of wine and some gold wrapped chocolates and she carried the roses.

They knocked.

Easton opened the door. Alice was surprised. She had almost expected a liveried minion, a servant of some kind, a loyal retainer, and instead there was the master of the house.

He moved back so they could step in, staring hard at Toby.

'This is Toby,' introduced Alice. Easton and Toby shook hands.

'Michael Easton,' said Easton, as Alice had failed to use his name. He looked straight into Toby's face. Alice felt a shiver of protectiveness toward Toby.

She peered beyond the hall to see if her impression of Easton having a wife could be substantiated. No one came. The house was lit within by lamps, but empty.

'These are for you.' She held out the roses.

Easton realised the flowers could never have been intended for him.

'And...' Toby offered the chocolates he had bought in case Alice had forgotten the flowers.

He led them through into a room that ran the length of the house. Polished dark floorboards were covered by Turkish rugs. Two ornate Ottoman sofas faced each other across the width of the room. In between them was a low table inlaid with intricate mosaic. All around was clutter that, on closer inspection, comprised articles that Alice could have examined with interest for hours. The rug on the floor was potent with colour. It was exquisitely beautiful. A tall ceramic oil jar stood in one corner. By its side was a sculpture of figures reaching up hands of appeal, long and bony, rising from each other in an interlocking matrix. The walls of the room were painted neutral pale cream, and were a little shabby, as if the owner no longer noticed or cared. And what indeed did it matter, since they were almost entirely covered in paintings? Along the walls with no pictures were shelves of books, stack upon stack. As she passed she noticed one title; Colloquial Arabic. A gorgeous hanging was suspended on a wooden frame, and a tapestry panel screen stood by a walnut bureau. On the bureau was a bronze of a man's head that reminded Alice of a death mask. The room made Alice think of a storage room at one of the great galleries, where items not on display had been left for the private delectation of a solitary curator.

Easton offered wine, and as he was pouring it he lifted his head to Toby.

'I saw you at the hospital, didn't I?'

'Oh, yes. I'd forgotten. Of course,' lied Toby. 'How's the hand?'

Suddenly Alice realised Easton was the man who had refused the HIV test.

Easton was studying her face, checking to see if she knew. She tried to hide it to protect Toby's indiscretion. Too late. He knew she knew. She thought he was capable of seeing everything.

He held out a glass of red to Toby, and poured one for her, too. She noticed that his own glass contained water.

They sat on the Ottoman, Toby and Alice, opposite Easton. It was all such a surprise, so unexpected. Alice spectated while Toby engaged Easton in conversation; mainly about himself and his activities, about rugby, about the hospital, thence to matters general of state provision, to politics and all the things Toby liked to talk about.

Suddenly, out of the blue, it struck her like a sliver of lightning that Easton might be interested in Toby. She looked again. Toby was blonde, athletic, blue eyed, well behaved. Easton was middle aged and mysteriously unmarried and irregular in so many ways. Gay men, she chastised herself for a fool, do not in real life wear their sexuality on a limp wrist. None of her assumptions about this man were working.

'Shall we eat?' said Easton, standing.

They followed him across the stone flagged floor of the hallway into a dining room that had the still air of disuse. A curiously carved mahogany table was laid with silver. The lights were dim and candles licked flame in glinting candle sticks.

Alice offered to help, but Easton pointed wordlessly to her chair, so she sat down. Toby sat opposite her, leaving a space for Easton in the middle at the head of the table.

When they were alone Toby whispered, 'What a house. Have you seen the picture in the hallway? I think it's a Picasso sketch, but it can't be. And the Islamic art in the drawing room? I bet it's worth a mint.'

'He's the man with the sexual injury, isn't he?'

'Ssh. It was him, but clearly I'm wrong. Anyway it's a private matter.'

'Now he's got a house worth two million.'

'For Heaven's sake, Alice. He's obviously an intelligent, cultured man, even if he is a homosexual. They're often very like that.'

Easton entered carrying a china tureen.

'Asparagus, Alice's favourite,' Toby exclaimed. 'Serendipity.'

Easton glanced at her and they shared a moment of intimacy from which Toby was excluded, and which Alice felt was stolen from her.

The green thin stalks glistened with butter melting and sliding down the stems and over the heads.

'Eat as much as you can,' said Easton.

'She's showing restraint,' said Toby, naughtily. 'You'd never know it but she's very greedy. She's only so skinny because she runs. Alice ran the London Marathon last year.'

'Did she?'

Again Easton looked at her. She thought she detected a glint of victory. She realised he was testing to see how much she had told Toby. She sensed that everything he did was an aspect of cross examination. Was he saving up the fruits of his explorations for some devastating final attack?

He gave them a tagine of lamb, with apricots and lemons and olives baked in a clay dish.

She asked 'Have you lived in the Middle East?' The house, its carved chairs and tables, the mosaics, the lamps, the rugs and the art suggested it. Now even the food.

Easton hesitated. He had no desire to answer questions himself.

'Yes. When I was a young boy.' He forked down his food rapidly and with no attention to what he was consuming.

There was a silence that forbade further enquiry.

Easton kept leaning over and filling Toby's glass. Toby kept complimenting Easton on the wine, the kind of wine Toby could never have afforded. He had been drinking already at the rugby and Alice knew he could slip quickly from mellow to comatose.

Soon Toby's head began to loll.

Alice watched him and when Easton went out with the plates she kicked at Toby gently with her foot. He smiled at her with bleary contentment.

She slid to her feet and collected the clay pot in her hands and carried it through to the kitchen.

Easton turned as she entered.

'Can you get into the garden from here?' she asked.

From the kitchen window, over the butler's sink, she could see an icy round moon hanging in the tangerine tinted black expanse.

Easton opened the narrow French doors, and bent to raise the security grille behind it. She remembered the story of the accidental injury.

'New?' she asked.

He straightened up without replying but gave her a dry, warning look.

She persevered. 'You don't keep them locked?'

'Not when I'm in the house.'

'Surely that's when it's most dangerous.' Two can play at cross examination, she thought.

'I could say fuck off,' he replied, his voice retaining its politely conversational level.

She stared at him, amazed. He left the door ajar.

'Would you like to go outside?' he asked, in evenly courteous tones.

She stepped into the chill of the night. The dark closed around her under the high damp wall and overhanging foliage.

Right outside the door a fruit tree was nailed with outstretched arms against the facing wall. She moved onto the grass. She felt him come and stand just behind her. She was instinctively afraid of him and sorry they had come.

'Is that a fig?' she asked, turning her face to the wall. 'Espalier trees always make me think of crucifixions.'

'There are some roses,' he said. 'But you can't see them.'

Did bees hum lazily in this garden in the summer? Was there ever a summer here?

'Why are we here?' she turned to him suddenly. 'Why have you invited us?'

'You like to know things about people, don't you?'

'That's what relationships are made of. It's a question of trust.'

She faced him. He looked at her, unsmiling.

A shape darkened the doorway. Toby's voice called out, 'Is that you?'

'Yes, Tobe, coming.'

She cast a look back at Easton and went in. The grass had stained her shoes. She felt the wet absorbed in the material and thought she would never get the stain out.

Easton followed them into the dining room, carrying the gold box of chocolates they had given him.

'Godiva chocolates, Alice's dream dessert,' said Toby, sluggishly.

Easton gave them to Alice to unwrap. The chocolates, miniature works of art, shone like treasures.

The two men watched her. Behind Toby's head, on a dresser made of oak, an ornate ormolu ticked the seconds.

Alice hovered over the box. Just as she had seen Toby accept a false version of the truth with a glass of wine so now she felt she was accepting Easton's version of relationships with a handmade chocolate.

'I don't think I will,' she said, deliberately. 'I've had too much already.'

'Don't be silly,' slurred Toby. 'Choose one for her, Michael.'

Easton considered. He closed his fingers around a gold wrapped chocolate. He unfolded the foil slowly and held the dark confection between his finger and thumb and held it out to her. She hesitated and then took it from his hand.

She cracked the shell with her teeth and a sweet sticky liquid flooded down her throat.

'Shall we go into the other room?' suggested Easton.

Alice supported Toby by the arm and he sank down into the corner of the ottoman next to the fire.

'Do you have some coffee, Easton?' she asked, seeing Toby slipping away. She didn't know why she had used his surname. Perhaps it was an instinctive distance.

'I'll make some.'

He turned to go. She followed him.

'The bathroom?'

'Upstairs. Along the corridor. I'll show you.'

He waited for her to precede him. On the upper landing she stopped, arrested by a painting of a bedroom in a Mediterranean light.

He said, 'Mattise, very early.'

'The cover on the bed.'

'Yes. The cover.' The broad stroked cover in the painting was bright and real.

She noticed more art in the receding shadows of the corridor. A refracted oblong of milky white fell on the wall at the end from a long window.

'Third on the left,' he said.

She felt him still standing there behind her watching as she stepped into the shadow. He had not offered her any light. Then she felt him move, fast as an animal, and take her by the shoulder and turn her. His mouth was on hers, his hands on her face, on her neck, her clavicles, in her hair. The urgency shocked her. It was over in a second.

'Easton.' She murmured this small cry of protest, and at her word, his name, he fell on her again. He moved his lips on hers, forced his tongue into her mouth, tasted chocolate, inhaled attar of rose. His fingertips grazed the outline of her breast, warm and heavy under thin silk. Momentarily she moved against him. He put his hands on her hips, holding her captive, crushing himself onto her.

'No,' she said.

He stared at her in the half dark, his eyes yellow in the reflection of the moon, heavy with bewilderment and suspicion.

He turned and walked rapidly down the stairs.

When she returned to the drawing room Easton was sitting back on the Ottoman watching Toby, who was sipping at a tiny, beautiful china cup of coffee.

Alice went around the back of the Ottoman and stood behind Toby. As Easton watched she moved her fingers down Toby's shoulders and onto his chest, dipped her head and rested her cheek at the side of his.

'He was on casualty last night. He's tired. I must take him back home.'

In the night air of the doorstep their breath made puffy swirls that melted instantly.

Toby reached out for Easton's hand. 'You must come to us next time,' said Toby, expansively.

Alice led him away. Easton watched them then turned inwards and closed the door.

69

Chapter Eight

The crack house had been raided and was now boarded up with planks nailed to the door.

'Where shall we go?' asked Tommy.

'There's always other places,' said Chas roughly and walked with rapid, angry steps down the passage. He half turned to check that Tommy was coming after him.

They walked and came to a stop at a bench in a children's park area.

Kids picked their way through the broken glass.

'There was a park a bit like this near my house,' recollected Tommy.

Chas had no memories of parks.

'Do they think that because we're users we don't need a place to sleep? At night? In this?' he asked.

It had begun to drizzle. The warm spell had collapsed into blustery wind and showers, as the weatherman puts it.

'How much have we got?' asked Tommy.

Chas fumbled wearily in his pocket. He carried the money for both of them.

'Two pounds.' They regarded the coins in Chas' hand.

'Not enough for two tickets,' observed Tommy, sadly.

'Enough for one,' said Chas. 'You go on the tube. I'll see what I can find.'

'What will you do?'

'Oxford Street.'

'I'll come.'

'No. You go on the tube. Look. It's wet.'

The drizzle was hardening into curtains of rain.

Chas tipped the coins into Tommy's hand. Tommy watched Chas' progress from the park, a kind of bitter, jumpy, ready-for-you swagger. He clanged out of the gate and disappeared round the wall.

Tommy waited for a minute and looked at the two kids. The park was in the middle of a council estate. A man slumped on a bench, supervising the kids. He pulled his collar up and shouted at them to come in. He had waited with them until it had become clear that play was no longer possible. Tommy didn't suppose this was the man's ideal way of spending a Thursday morning. The kids, two boys, ran up to their dad and he put his arms around their small shoulders and steered them home, as they shouted shrill kid stuff at him, looking right up into his face for reaction.

Tommy made his way to the Tube stop. He bought a ticket, the cheapest one available. He went down to the platform. He was so tired. They had had the last hit in an alley at the back of the boarded up flat, and now they had no more dough. Tommy got on the train. It was the Jubilee line. He travelled down to where that line intersected with the Circle line, and crossed over. A Circle line train pulled in and Tommy got on in the back carriage. There were a few people. No one took any notice of him. He found a seat and folded his arms around himself and put his head against the window. He could sit in the warm and go around and around on the line, never arriving at any destination. At least it was warm. In a short time he would start to feel an increase in the need for another hit. Maybe he might last another few hours. He hoped Chas would come up with something.

Chas knew they needed a place and he knew they needed to score. It was a full time job, being a junkie. No sooner was the last rush faded than the need began again.

Chas hung around the tube at Oxford Circus, sizing up the people.

He put on a hopeless expression, hung his head abjectly and called in a reedy voice, 'Small change.'

No one gave him anything. He didn't look sufficiently pitiable. Tommy made a much better beggar.

He moved along a bit and sat down cross legged against the wall by Marks and Spencers. He put his hat on the pavement. Eventually a woman in a smart black suit bent down and offered him a cheese and celery sandwich in a plastic box. Chas took it, her successful and directly administered charity making the woman feel elated with herself, and ate half of it, putting the rest back in the triangular plastic shell and keeping it. He picked up about three quid. That might get them a drink in the Pig, nothing else.

Chas was not feeling good. No, not feeling happy at all. He was sliding down, from the lofty fabulous heights of euphoria and well being back down into the shittiness of the world. Chas was more advanced in his addiction than Tommy. Chas started sniffing glue when he was twelve and worked up. Now he was nineteen, taking three times a day. Tommy had started smack at fifteen. Obviously there was other stuff as well. People hardly ever keep to one addiction. For Tommy and Chas though junk was the real deal, the queen of the land. The other stuff was to help the days along. It made all the pain drift away. All they needed was a gaffe and a score.

Chas used the Marks and Spencers money and bought a cheap ticket for the tube. He strolled casually along the platform, in and out of the islands of people, without catching anybody's eye.

Finally he settled on a late middle aged woman, short pepper and salt grey hair, large glasses and flat black shoes. She looked like some horrible social worker to Chas.

Chas fingered the Stanley knife in his pocket, running his thumb across the blade.

He positioned himself inconspicuously behind the woman. A distant susurration announced the approach of the train. Chas felt the onrushing wind, heard the growl of the train as it came blasting into the station. The crowd began to shuffle forward with one solitary aim. The doors opened with a creaking swish and disobedient passengers lunged forward before those on the train could get off. The woman held back, in a civilized manner, an expression of pained toleration on her face. She stepped on, wholly unconscious of the man behind her and the blade. Chas moved in as the panic stricken bleeping announcing the closing of the doors.

He slid the knife out of his pocket and slit the strap of her bag, pulling back just as the doors closed, bag in hand, before the woman had realised what was happening. The train pulled out, chugging and clanking. The woman's shocked face appeared at the window, her hands beating at the Perspex.

Chas was halfway up the escalator.

Outside he jumped on a bus, one of the old fashioned type with the open door at the back, allowing easy egress.

He had a quick glance in the bag. There was a mobile, a little hand held psion thing, a purse with thirty pounds and some coins, a rainbow of credit cards, an organ donor card, an Islington library card and a photo of a balding man on a beach in swim trunks smiling happily into the camera. There were also her house keys and a diary.

Chas met up with Tommy.

'Thirty quid and some stuff we can sell.'

Chas showed Tommy the bag and its contents. He passed him the remnant of the sandwich.

'I'm not hungry,' said Tommy.

'Eat it,' said Chas irritably.

Tommy bit into the bread, and looked around.

'What?' snapped Chas, the need for a score getting intense.

'Bin?' queried Tommy, wrapper in hand.

'God,' shouted Chas, rage at everything buzzing in his brain. He snatched the plastic wrapper and hurled it onto the floor.

Tommy looked at it, an expression of anxiety on his face.

Chas bent down and seized the thing in his hand.

'All right. Come on.' They moved off. Chas dropped the plastic sandwich container in a litter bin as they passed.

Chapter Nine

Alice's client wept.

There's a line in an old Tamla Mowtown song that goes,
'They say a crying man is only half a man.'

Alice saw men crying who had been reduced to much less than half; shells, ghosts, reflections, men whose entire lives had been eaten away by addiction.

Today it was Gary.

Gary had worked in the City and had made a lot of money. He had had a house in the Algarve where he loved his game of golf. He had had a house in Primrose Hill, a nice sports car and a wife and a child.

Now his debt was floating around his ears and every minute of every day Gary felt he was rolling downhill over razor wire.

Gary was addicted to crack cocaine. Actually his marriage hadn't really been very good. He married too young. By the time he reached his twenties it was plain that his blonde stiletto wearing wife didn't fit in with the life he was carving out for himself. He was mixing with a different type of person and little Karen was looking a bit incongruous and she was a lot more stupid than he had thought. Karen knew this and had become resentful, so as insurance she had had a baby, whom Gary adored. Unfortunately Karen got Post Natally Depressed and cried and whined and blamed and sat around the house all day in her dressing gown with the curtains closed. Gary came home to a house that smelled of Hell.

By contrast crack was Heaven. One short line and everything was fine, everything was beautiful. Life was foxy. There was no stress, no worry. Gary was good, Gary was the star of the show, laughing and chatting- all his jokes were hilarious, all his mates loved him, he was a sexual athlete. The problem with being up though is that you have to come down and when Gary came down what did he see?

He saw a fat, unattractive bloke with a wife who called him a wanker and made him sleep in the spare room. Gary lay in that room with his brain turning over like a Formula 1 racer, eyes out on stalks, tortured by insomnia, the whole world a terrifying vortex into which he was falling.

Whereas Gary had once been a likeable bloke, quite popular, one of the lads at least, now he was moody, irritable, impatient, sweaty, paranoid and just generally unpleasant to be around, except of course for the five minutes after he came out of the men's toilets.

It got so bad that his boss told him to kick the habit or leave. The bank even paid for him to have three weeks in rehab, and given him plenty of sick time, but he'd only been out a week when he accidentally overdosed in the loo at work, and had to be rushed to hospital, which was upsetting for the other workers, especially the ones who were managing their coke habit, and Gary got the sack.

Now fat, jolly, matey Gary was an emaciated, depressed, paranoid, impotent, insomniac bankrupt divorcee in a bedsit on his own in Camden Town having one hour's weekly supervised contact with his toddler and sitting in clothes that hung off him like a clown and crying like a baby in front of Alice. Huge fat tears dripped from his nose. At least he hadn't killed himself yet.

'I feel so lonely,' he sobbed.

Gary sat two feet away from her, crying, his head in his hands. The two foot distance said it all. Gary needed someone to hold him, physically. Alice registered this with detached but acute compassion and did not hold him. Only the complete giving of herself to a person like Gary could make a difference, and she did not give herself, her real self, to anybody. She wanted to say, you need to find someone to love you, only it has to be real love. She hoped that Gary would find love, but knew that he would not.

'You're not alone,' she said, and realised with weary guilt that this denied him his feeling of loneliness and beside, it wasn't true. Gary was alone. And therein lay Gary's real problem. As he sat in his chilly bedsit he knew for a fact that he wasn't in anybody's thoughts, that it would be better objectively for everyone if he were dead.

Alice gave Gary addresses and numbers for support groups, another appointment and sent him out into the world. At least he had had an hour when he had been in a room with another human being.

At the Unit, she was working in a team building up a holistic environment for addicts to resolve their issues and kick their old life. That was what it was really about, for Alice, getting them to junk their old lives. Actually, it was her mission. The hardest ones to help were the ones without family, though it was the families that had caused them to be there in the first place. Starting treating a drug addict was like starting with a tight tangled knot. Straightening the knot took limitless hours of intense, patient work, checking all the time to see where the strands were lying, how they connected, where they had come from and where they had to go, then when it was untangled it had to be kept that way. Alice sometimes wondered if the myth of Sisyphus was really an ancient cipher for the treatment of addicts.

Professional wisdom says that the treating room of a psychiatrist ought to be bright, informal, restful, unchallenging, impersonal, welcoming and comfortable. The chairs had to be positioned carefully so that you, the professional, are never sitting higher than the client, so there is no obstacle like a desk between you and the client, and so that there is an escape route, because you might need to leave in a hurry.

But when Alice first moved in to her treatment room at the Unit she found it hard to know where to begin.

It was in the basement, a gloomy dungeon. It had horrible dirty brown carpet, one filthy frosted glass window with five metal bars, mushroom coloured walls all chipped and smeared and it stank of damp, like an open grave. The room intoned to all who sat in it, you are shit and your situation is shit.

Alice was sensitive to surroundings. There was no way she could have sat in that room, let alone worked or treated clients there.

She spent time and money ripping out the carpet and installing a dehumidifier, painting the walls and ceiling, replacing the window and painting the bars clean white, (the bars had to stay because of regulations), fitting new lights and a new plain carpet. She put up shelves with books on them and her photographs of Cornwall and it became a room that a person in distress could sit in and feel respected.

'Alice, there's a man in reception. He's been waiting twenty minutes.'

Maxine the imperturbable, receptionist of the unit, put her head around the door. Alice thought Maxine was a therapeutic tool in herself. She was motherly without being bossy, kind but firm, sympathetic without over indulgence. Hers was a hard task, manning the front line, handling the drop-ins; the desperate, the emergencies, the violent and abusive, the withdrawing, speeding, pleading hopeless human beings that pressed on the buzzer twenty times a day.

'No appointment?' asked Alice.

'He won't go away. Asking specifically for you.'

'I've just had Gary,' protested Alice. Gary is enough, more than enough. The needs of a man like Gary drain the energy levels so that Alice felt completely empty, weak and brittle dry.

'How was Gary?' asked Maxine.

'Depressed.'

'Aw.' Maxine made a deep long sound of pity, then, because it had to be done, 'And what about our gentleman in reception?'

'Oh, I'll have a look at him.'

Alice climbed the stairs as if they were stages of a mountainside.

She recognised the back of the man staring out of the window.

'Hello, Easton.'

She hadn't returned his call. He had made only one in the six weeks since his dinner evening. She had thought it might go away if she ignored it, if she didn't do it again, that what had happened could remain in the realms of the unreal, like a dream or a fantasy or a story she had heard when she was a little girl, or the nightmares of reality that she preferred not to acknowledge.

But he was here, a man whose presence confirmed that in the real world actions have consequences and do not just fade into the ether of convenient oblivion.

'I've not got long,' she said, and hooked her thumbs into her belt.

He nodded as if accepting the offer of a deal, the best he was going to get.

'Would you like some tea?' she asked him, leading him down the stairs.

'No, thank you.' She saw in his eye and heard in his voice that it was not for tea or any other social convention that he had come.

Her heart began to flutter like a bird in a hand. He made her feel.

Now he was standing in the middle of the room he seemed to have nothing to say to her. He looked at her. There was no desk, no island in the room for her to hide behind. He didn't smile, just looked. Then he turned his gaze to the photographs on the walls.

'Cornwall?'

'They call it Gull Rock. It's just off the coast near where I lived.'

She had taken the photos of the rock early one morning, while she was completely alone on the beach, the tide rushing in across black smooth stones and sea sculpted boulders, while a celluloid dawn bleached the sky. Easton examined the formation closely.

'Summer?'

'August. It turned into a beautiful day. Very hot, very blue, virtually no wind, except on the cliff. It was the summer of 2001.'

Summer of 2001. The last summer before Toby, when she had been on her own and her sisters called for her to find a real man, just as they had found men. She couldn't scramble over rocks forever, crouching and puzzling over the enclosed brine aquatic worlds left behind after the retreat of the tide. She had to grow up and think of grown up things.

These pools were still the sea, they had sea in them, they had salt, they had sea creatures living their shallow depths. They were the sea, separated from the main body of the immensity only for an infinitesimal moment in the scheme of time and then, at the turn of the tide they would rejoin the body completely, merging and becoming one, having had their tiny piece of unique existence on the beach.

'You didn't get my message?' He fingered the books on the shelf, speaking casually.

Always questions.

He waited for a reply, turned to watch the curve of her cheek, the still, hesitant line of her lips.

He didn't want to be there. He wished he were somewhere else. He felt intensely humiliated by the coming. He had taken a cab in the hour between cases and time was running out. As the cab traversed the London streets he felt sick of himself. He also felt a sense of fear. Some huge thing had broken off inside him, and was drifting like an iceberg in the cold deep.

Now he was close enough to reach out and touch her. Why didn't she answer his question?

The kiss on the stair had been forced from him. She had forced something out of him as a bully brutally unfolds the reluctant clench of a younger boy's hand. She made him feel powerless.

Silence can be a very effective reply. Easton was used to silence. He gathered the torn strands of his dignity.

'Is this where you see your patients?'

'We call them clients.'

'Word play.'

She lifted her eyebrows inconsequentially. She wasn't going to let him make her unhappy. There was something he wanted to tell her. For her to be told she had to be in neutral gear. She wanted to hear his inner heart. For a moment she felt he might say something that meant something.

'I expect they tell you everything in here.' He could almost hear the whispered confessions, confidences, secrets dripping like sweat.

'You make it sound like an accusation. But, yes. People talk.'

He leant close to her ear. She felt his breath on the side of her face.

'You come and see me,' he said.

No more accusation. Naked demand.

One of the techniques for maintaining abstinence is distraction, keeping busy, staying away from people and places connected with the drug of choice, talking to your friends, using stop signals, like envisaging in your mind a big red stop sign at the edge of a precipice. Alice was using all of these.

She was working on her thesis.

'How's it going?' Toby asked, peering at the screen over her shoulder.

'Fine.'

'When's the deadline?'

'September.'

Toby knew and she knew he knew that the deadline for the draft was September. 'Why?' Irked, she had to pursue it, even though she knew it would cause her more irritation.

'Just wanted to be sure.'

'Sure of what?'

'Sure it's going according to plan. And that you're pacing the work. You don't want to have to rush it.' He left a meaningful silence.

'I'm not going to have to rush it,' she said.

He read what she had written.

'Is that meant to be a semi colon?' He pointed. 'That's not how you spell bourgeois. Are you still going to include Sherlock Holmes? I'm not sure you ought. I mean, he's a figure of the imagination.'

'He's a cipher for the Victorian perception of drug use.'

'Hmm. Well, it's your work.' He frowned and went into the bedroom. He came out carrying her glasses. 'You need to wear your specs,' he said. She put them on.

Toby sat on the sofa.

'Would it bother you...?'

She knew what he was going to say.

'Go ahead.'

Toby switched on the T.V news. For a while he was verbally restrained then he began muttering irate ejaculations and comments at the newsreaders, and following that at the panel members on Any Questions. He slumped on the sofa tutting and shaking his head. 'Do these people live in the real world?' he asked.

Finally he turned off the TV and sighed. Alice was still pretending to work.

'It's late,' said Toby.

Alice's eyes were getting tired.

She closed down her screen and tidied up the mugs around her.

'You drink too much coffee,' Toby told her as she clinked her way through to the kitchen.

She undressed rapidly, strewing her clothes on the chair and leaping into bed.

Toby folded her clothes.

He undressed and hung his trousers in the wardrobe, placed his shirt and smalls in the wash basket, turned out the light and got in bed next to Alice.

Toby let a moment elapse.

He took her hand and placed it on his softly growing erection. She touched it. It hardened.

81

'Actually,' she said, drawing back her hand. 'I'm quite tired.'

This was true.

'I'll just stroke you to sleep, then,' he said.

He began to caress her shoulders. She knew what was coming. His hand dipped to her breast.

'No, Tobe,' she said.

'Sorry.' His hand left her breast and went down to her stomach. He kissed her arm. She heard the increase in the pace of his breathing. His kisses became more passionate. His hand moved between her legs. She turned away from him and drew her knees up.

'Can I go in?' he asked. 'I won't be long. I'm ready.'

'No.' She tried to push away the irritation he had caused her. It wasn't his fault.

He sighed and stopped, turning in disappointment.

She closed her eyes.

'Tomorrow,' she said.

'Will you touch me? Just touch me. That's all.'

He started kissing her again.

Reluctantly she took his erection in her hand. He pushed himself against her.

'You do it so well,' he breathed.

She wanted him to come, to get it over with. She moved her hand over him at just the right speed, just the right tension, not too fast, not too slow. She tightened her fingers around the most sensitive part of the tip. Slowly she pressed out a drop of smooth glaze the texture of thick olive oil and used it to slide her thumb up and down the circumcised head. She felt him begin to pulse.

'Let me in, please, Alice.' He lifted himself onto her as he said it.

'No, Tobe.'

He was not listening. She parted her legs and went to a distant place in her head.

'You see. You want it too,' he said as he pushed.

His thrusts were shallow and erratic, stopping and starting. It prolonged the moment for him. She pressed him in to her, wanting it to finish. He made five or six hard ramming movements then stopped, replete. He drew out.

'Was that O.K?' he asked. He had not made her come. 'You see, you liked it.'

He held her tenderly in his arms and kissed her hair.

'I love you so much,' he said.

'What are you doing?' Toby raised himself from sleep. Alice was at the end of the bed in the semi dark.

'I'm going for a run.'

'What time is it?'

'Only six. Go back to sleep.'

He turned over and closed his eyes. 'Don't leave the path,' he warned.

She ran into the brisk cool air of the early morning, turning up the hill and running past the rows of big brick Victorian houses all divided into flats. Further up the shops started and the closed up cafes. The streets were empty. A few cars shushed by. The light was still grey, as if the day had not decided yet what sort of day it was going to be, jealously guarding the secret of its potential.

As she got going into her pace her heart began to beat faster, reaching a stable level after about ten minutes, as she found her rhythm.

She cut off for the Heath, along the pavements from which, if she chose to look, she could see passing glimpses in occasional basement windows of strangers in yellow light wandering groggily into their mornings. From one basement she heard the sound of a piano being played. She recognised the slow notes of Satie.

Down past the hospital, to the green, along where all three buses were queuing up at the end or the beginning of the line, whichever way you chose to see it. The drivers were having desultory conversations standing outside their vehicles, cradling coffee in their hands.

The Heath lay to her right. If she crossed the road she would come to the avenue of limes.

Instead she ran straight ahead.

The iron gate was closed but not chained. It left a small metallic clang behind her.

She went through, into the overgrown garden. The heavy boughs seemed to hang down to watch her movements, as if she were a thief in the night.

He opened the door to her knock.

For a second he stood and looked at her as if she were a stranger. She had no explanation, no reason. She had come. That was the only reality.

He stood back to let her in.

The hall was warm. She was hot from her exercise and from the trembling nerves of her brain. Her heart beat loud, so loud she could hear it and feel it in her head.

He put his hand on her shoulder as she passed in front of him. She twisted her neck to kiss the hand that lay on her. He twined her hair in his other hand, drew back her face to his and kissed her. This was what she wanted. She moved her tongue over his; his mouth tasted so different to Toby's. Her desire was literally painful.

He turned her away from him, against the wall. He pulled down her loose tracksuit and reached round and touched her between her legs. She arched, not concealing the need in her, not concealing anything. He breathed in the scent of her hair, of her skin.

She pushed herself down hard, taking him in.

They came together. He bit into her clothing at her shoulder to keep himself silent.

Buckling his belt, he cast one glance at her. She leaned against the wall. Her clothing had barely been disturbed. She really didn't want him to speak. Speaking would be wrong. It would introduce definition to what had happened, to what existed between them.

It would be a shag, a zipless fuck. But it was not these. Nor was it love, or commitment, nor a moment of unrestrained lust. It carried no reproach, no obligation, no damaged expectation, no demand, no possession, no trust betrayed, no disgust of self or other.

Only wordlessness could truly encompass what had happened.

Chapter Ten

Whatever suffered since Easton met Alice Christie it was not his work. In the moments he had spare he thought of her and therefore he killed spare time.

It was more of the same.

Easton sat at his desk in the room behind his court, this room being known as Chambers, at ten at night.

At seven his clerk, Clive, had come in.

'Can I get you a cup of tea, sir?'

Clive looked like the progeny of a tortoise and a giant bloodhound; large oval drooping eyes, heavy wrinkled lids, strangely elongated hairy ears with pendulous lobes, and a neck that projected almost perpendicular to hunched and rounded shoulders. Clive had been Easton's clerk for twenty five years, the entirety of Easton's career at the Bar.

Clive noticed certain tell tale signs.

'Or perhaps a bicarb?' he ventured.

'Yes. Thank you, Clive.'

Clive went to the kitchen, ripped open a packet of bicarb and fizzed it into a glass of water. He returned down the corridor to the judge's room, placing the glass at Easton's right hand.

'Light's very dim, sir.'

Clive switched on the main overhead light. Easton had been working by a green glass shaded desk lamp.

'Out of the shadows,' said Clive, with satisfaction.

Easton swilled the unpleasant liquid around in his mouth. He thought of Alice's words in the garden, about knowing things about people. That's what relationships are made of, she said. It's a question of trust.

'How's the family, Clive?'

'Very well, sir. Thank you for asking.' Clive faced the judge with curious surprise.

'Your wife?'

'She's,' Clive paused, considering, 'keeping cheerful. She's like that, Mrs Bird.'

Clive's wife had M.S. She spent her days in a wheelchair. Clive, who was stronger than he looked, pushed her about the shops or wherever she wanted to go. He kept her knees warm with a tartan rug and catheterised her three times a night.

Clive was careful only to answer what he had been asked. He made no reciprocal enquiry.

Clive picked up the cups and glass from Easton's desk.

'Anything else, sir?'

'No, thank you.'

Clive was going out the door when Easton said, 'If there's anything I can do.' He kept his eyes fixed on his papers.

When Clive got home Mrs Bird asked him about his day. They lived in a modern house in a part of Essex that still retained a precarious hold on its semi rural status in the face of London's relentless murder of the countryside. Clive had been born and bred in the East End, but with the affluence that his assiduous clerking and Easton's success brought, he and Mrs Bird and their children had been able to move up to the leafy suburbs. Mrs Bird liked gardens and they had a large garden. Now their oldest, Matthew, came round with his wife and his kids on Saturdays and did the garden and they all had lunch together.

'Judge was in a funny mood today,' said Clive.

Mrs Bird creased her face in enquiry, and made a small high sound. The power of speech was gradually slipping away.

Clive lowered Mrs Bird, who was light as a feather, into an armchair. She kept her gaze fixed interrogatively on his face.

'He asked me how the family was. That's the first time in, well, twenty five years. He's not much of a man for personal chit chat, as you know.'

Mrs Bird thought. Then she rocked a little, her shoulders quivering in mirth. 'About time,' she said.

Easton parked in the road just opposite Alice's flat on Haverstock Hill. He turned off the car engine. Its curved bonnet reflected the streetlamp. From his position outside he

87

stared at the top floor window. Inside she carried on her life. The exterior walls of the villa contained her activity, the minutae of her day-to-day existence. Within she was doing something; she might be looking in the refrigerator, might be in the bath, eating supper, washing up, talking on the phone. The thought that she might be in bed with Toby did not float up in his mind as a possibility. It really had no more, possibly less, significance than the mundane activities that marked the fact that she was inside conducting her life, and he was outside.

It was late. The light was still on in the window, though the curtains were drawn.

He had wanted to see how it would feel, just sitting and looking at her house. It was an indulgence and an experiment that no one could see or know. He speculated whether in this huge city there was anyone else doing what he was doing. Quite probably. There was no limit to human loneliness and exclusion. That was how he saw the world. There was pain, there was disappointment and there was isolation. He did not believe in love; there was only transient sexual infatuation and convenience. These were what brought people together and kept them together, hormonal urges and practical survival structures, the hugely critical and competitive struggle to find a mate, to avoid being alone. Easton had contempt for that struggle. He knew it for what it was; a delusion of happiness.

Toby was watching the TV. He always watched the TV after work. He needed to be able to switch his mind off completely and he did this with the assistance of the remote control.

It didn't matter what was on the screen. Right now there was some woman in scruffy jungle clothing, showing her belly and revealing her tits, her skin covered in a slick of perspiration, balancing on a rope bridge over a cavernous gorge, whining to camera about some man called Blake, who had repeatedly interrupted her night's sleep, and, seemingly, who had compounded her troubles by placing a leech surreptitiously on her buttock while she was sunbathing.

'I hope she drops in,' said Toby morosely, mostly to himself, although he probably wouldn't have spoken if Alice hadn't been somewhere in the flat. Her general presence was sufficient.

The bridge swung in long shot, the woman clinging in artificial terror to the thick twists of rope.

'Fall, fall,' implored Toby. 'Fractured femur, gross bruising, dislocated shoulder, inoperable jaw injury,' he predicted hopefully. 'Months, possibly years of traction.'

'I've got the munchies. I'm going to the store.' Alice slouched in the doorway.

'We need milk. Want me to go?' He offered without looking round or making a move, looking on in fixated disgust as the female in the jungle stepped unharmed off the rope bridge. 'Typical,' he huffed.

As she slammed the communal door behind her she lifted her watch. Ten to eleven. The store closed at eleven. There was still traffic swishing up and down the road. The convenience store, run by Mr and Mrs Patel, was on the other side of the street. The shop had everything. The shelves were so close together it wasn't possible to pass anther shopper in the aisles and one had continually to step back politely. The store had an odd mixed smell, engendered by the myriad of products and its own distinctive flavour. Some might say it was not a good smell, but Alice now found it reassuring. Mr and Mrs Patel manned the till in comradeship from seven in the morning to eleven each night including Sunday. They had a daughter studying medicine at Guy's, Alice's old college hospital, so she and the Patels were big friends.

Alice heard her name called and turned involuntarily.

Easton was standing next to a black BMW. He wore an expression of reluctant perplexity. He hadn't meant to see her. That was in no way what he had come for. It was a shock to see her come out of the front door and for an instant

89

he had frozen. He had wanted to shrink into invisibility. Then, because she didn't see him, (why should she see a man sitting in the dark on his own in a row of parked cars,) he watched her and very suddenly he wanted to attract her attention before she disappeared. He got out of the car and went round to the pavement and called her name. It all happened in the blink of a few seconds.

Her name was a short command. It wasn't the voice she recognised, it was the tone.

She went back towards him.

'Get in the car,' he said.

In her head was the warning about getting into cars with strangers. This was exactly the situation her mother, her father, her teachers, her sisters had taught her to avoid and fear.

She looked at the curtain of the safety of her flat, where Toby sat in front of the flickering television.

She got into Easton's car.

He pulled out using the side view mirror to see the traffic behind. He drove up the hill and swung off to the right into a small lane next to some sports fields. He parked and turned off the engine. Only then did he look at her. She waited for him to speak, to say something so that she could take her bearings.

'What do you want?' she asked.

'I don't know,' he replied and surprised him self with the truth contained in this phrase.

She knew what she wanted. She wanted to breach his defences. She moved closer and put her face in front of his so she could feel his breathing. She put her hand down between his legs. She wanted to see the loss of control at close quarters. She unzipped him and took out his erection, holding it lightly in her hand.

He felt a burning heat flow through him, though his whole body, each nerve alive, and mentally, inside, right inside his brain. She began to move her hand, slowly. He had to close his eyes.

The sports field was deserted on the other side of the chicken wire, and stretched into blackness, but there was a street lamp that glowed quite near.

'Go down,' he said.

She looked at him for one second, her grey eyes holding on to his then lowered her head. He placed his hand to his temple, the thumb and index finger spread over his forehead. She kissed him lightly all over at first then used her tongue and then the warm O of her mouth closed tightly around him, sucking softly. It was over quickly. She swallowed his semen. She tasted the bitter bodily saltiness. Because it was him she was able to do it. She never did it for Toby. But still he didn't tell her anything.

She sensed he wanted nothing more yet, no touch, no intimacy. He put his hands on the wheel and stared out in front of him, before driving her back.

'Where *have* you been?' Toby swivelled his head as she came in.

'You know what Mrs Patel's like. I couldn't get away.'

'Did you get the milk?'

'Oh, damn. I forgot.'

'What did you get?' said Toby in exasperation.

'Chocolate, I ate it on the way back.'

'Not pregnant, I hope.'

Alice took this as a joke. 'You'll be the first to know.'

So what does this all mean, she asked herself in bed that night with the duvet pulled up to her chin and the man who loved her lying peacefully asleep at her side. It is so unexpected. No, not unexpected. There was always this irregularity lurking in her, what her family would call 'oddness'. It was very important not to be odd. What was she, a member of her family, a nice girl, a professional, educated woman, with a sensible, successful relationship with a reasonable man, doing being this odd? Going out in a car with a man she barely knew, and giving him a blow job in a side street? She knew there was a school of thought that would consider this acceptable, that there were enough versions of morality for her behaviour to slot in satisfactorily, no guilt, somewhere. Only that wasn't the version she had been brought up with. What had made her do this? She thought of Easton and her heartbeat accelerated. It felt as if a part of her had just awoken, after a long, long time.

Chapter Eleven.

Boats that looked small in perspective bobbed on the glinting, mercurial surface of the estuary as they crossed the Tamar bridge. At this point Alice experienced a revolution in the stomach. It was always the same. Crossing the Tamar brought her home.

The weather was perfect in every respect. Up until the last moment people had been grumbling that yet another summer was passing without delivery, as if the seasons were capable of conscious betrayal. There had been grey and rain and wind. A bad summer in England leaves everybody bereft. The little island, in its outpost position at the edge of Europe, set in a cold iron sea, needs summer, real summer, once each year, otherwise the inhabitants grow bitter.

But now in August in London the air quality stuttered and died. Tarmac simmered stickily, the dusty pavements smelled of heat and there was nowhere to go to be relieved of the oppression. London grumpily insists on doing heat badly and without style. Everyone complains. That is the essence of the British relationship with weather, complaint. The huge throngs of beer clutching jacketless perspiring men outside the pubs are baking and sweltering and the hot sun makes them feel and act as if they are on holiday but they are complaining at the same time. Nothing gets done in London when it is hot. It is worse than the most recalcitrant African village. The city goes through the motions of business as usual but it is a lie.

The only way to manage a hot English summer is to go away to the country, preferably by the sea. Coinciding ones holiday with the occasional bout of good weather in England is a lottery of the most unpredictable nature. The winners who bask on beaches under light blue sky are frenzied with smugness. The losers, who have returned to the city the very day the weather turned glorious, who have sat miserable covered by windbreaks and golf umbrellas and sheltering in cheap cafes watching the rain drizzle down the window panes, are green with envy and black with resentment.

On the motorway, heat threw up wobbling mirages in the distance. There had been a tailback before Bristol which had held them up, and Toby blamed Alice. His opinion was that they should have waited until Monday to travel, but she insisted on Saturday. He said, clasping the wheel in the bumper to bumper jam by the Gordano service station, 'I don't know why I gave in on this,' and she sat silent, no regrets. It was better to get there late on Saturday after a hideous journey than to delay in London until Monday. There was nothing in any event she could say to make Toby feel better, but lots she could say to make him worse, so she remained quiet. Later she would make it up to him by giving him some really nice sex. Toby always succumbed to this. It was his panacea.

She knew anyway, but didn't say, that it was now officially impossible at any time to drive to Cornwall unimpeded by crawling caravans and sluggish cars packed to overcapacity with vacation luggage and children at the end of their tether. Not even commencing their journey at seven in the morning had solved the problem. The whole of Birmingham, the whole of London, even distant Northerners, abjured their own shores to come down to Cornwall in one gelatinous river of cars.

The reason they came in the school holidays was to do with Alice's sisters and her six nieces and nephews. Helen, twelve years Alice's senior, and her husband Paul were both social workers in Exeter. Marion, ten years older than Alice, lived in Connecticut, USA. She had no need to work. She had married well, to a North London Jewish media executive, who reluctantly took time out to perform the horrible duty of visiting his wife's Cornish relatives in the hated countryside once a year in the summer. Alice was the baby.

Alice and Toby had stopped at a little stone pub on the fringe of Dartmoor and had early lunch sitting at a picnic table in the nasturtium covered garden looking out on glorious moorland, brown patched in the distance. From far away Alice heard ponies' whinnies in the quiet air.

Toby had had a few well earned pints. This was their routine. He drove the first part of the journey and she the latter.

Now he was fast asleep.

The traffic had congealed again at Indian Queens, so Alice cut down the side roads, so winding that it probably took as long as sitting in the traffic, but at least she was doing her own thing and not herding with the others.

From there it took a further hour twisting along the coast road to the village.

Every time she came back she was overwhelmed by nostalgia. They drove down the main street. Unlike many villages in Cornwall this one had not been sent to the Devil by tourism. Of course it had been ringed by the usual incoherent developments, white bungalows, hideous both in conception and execution, but people have to live somewhere, and there weren't enough of the cosy granite cottages in the village to go around. The village had originated as a satellite of the mines that now stood abandoned, grim and magnificent, on the cliff edges. A short, tumbling row of cottages had been built on the slope of a hill leading steeply down to the cove back in the eighteenth century. In the next hundred years there appeared a main street, an early Victorian church with a steeple, a big vicarage and, of course, hostelries. There it had been left until the sixties and the prototype bungalows.

The bungalows were a part of Alice's landscape. She didn't resent them, but what she did resent were the modern houses that had been built since her departure. Familiar ugliness was acceptable on the basis that what you know you hardly notice.

As she drove into the top part of the village she passed cottages, shops and little cafes that held in every brick of their substance reminders of her past self.

The centre of the village had maintained a working life beyond the summer crowds and in this way retained its charm against all odds. It wasn't cutely pretty, like so many Cornish honey spots. It had no art, like St Ives. There was no celebrity chef. The beach was too inaccessible to attract vast crowds. There was nowhere to park because the hill and valley sides to which the village clung were too steep, and narrowed violently to the sea. There was a long descent to the bay and people couldn't do it with kids and buckets and spades and wet suits and deckchairs and tents and flasks and towels and balls and bags and all the clobber they seemed to need to sit on a beach for a couple of hours.

Nevertheless, at two o clock on an August Saturday there was still a snake of cars trying optimistically to make it to the sea.

The pavements thronged with holiday people. At The Ship, opposite the church, she had to pause to clear a path with the car bumper through the crowds spilling onto the road.

Toby woke with a snuffle.

'We're here,' he said.

The house in which she had been raised was along the coast road. It was one of those that had been built in the sixties. It sat at the top of a cul de sac of bungalows, all white and blue with palms swaying their prickly fronds. In the summer brilliance they looked almost right. Anything less than perfect hot sunshine revealed them for what they were, simply inappropriate. Alice winced with the shock of revisiting the old familiarity after a long time, like meeting up with your first boyfriend at a school reunion. But she knew that the hours would anaesthetise any feelings of metropolitan superiority.

The house had been inhabited by the builder who had done the development and where the other dwellings were boring two bed affairs he had carefully positioned his own house at the top of the rise, slightly apart from the others, and made it much bigger with a large acreage of garden and the most stupendous views of the bay and cliffs, stretching on and on, headland after hazy headland.

Alice parked on the kerb. She recognised Helen's sensible Volvo and Marion's hire car, and her mother's sparkling clean red Polo.

Even as they stepped stiff out of the car the front door opened and the children poured out. Both Helen and Marion had three kids and Alice was a popular auntie.

The children, and then the adults encircled Alice and Toby. Helen's smiling steps, Marion's shrieks and there at the back, slightly withheld, the mother, Maria Christie. Alice noticed that her mother looked tired and this made her feel guilty.

Toby stood aside from this sisterly reunion.

'Hello, Toby, how are you?' said Helen, giving him a matronly peck on the cheek and his arm a warm little squeeze. 'Can't leave Toby out of the cuddles.'

'Cuddles,' shouted Marion. 'I want more than cuddles. Come here and give me a fat snog, Toby.' Marion squashed him in a bear hug. 'It's so good to see you.' Marion's voice rose higher and higher with self induced emotion.

Her husband David sauntered out of the house with his hands in his pockets. He was short and weedy with a neat tonsure. He wore Ted Baker shorts and sandals, and his skin was very pale, apart from an angry pink on the top of his bald head. Watery, calculating blue eyes were magnified by thick lenses. He was considerably more intelligent than his wife.

'David,' called Marion, 'Say hello to your sister in law.' She gave him a meaningful look. Only that morning in bed they had argued about David's lethargy in respect of her family. Their method of arguing was that Marion would rave and David would maintain an impassive countenance, and say 'These things are not so simple.' He didn't smile a lot and his sense of humour didn't surface too often. Marion moaned that she had married into the race that had all the best jokes, the race that produced Lenny Bruce, Bette Midler, Woody Allen and she still got Boris Karloff.

They piled into the house. The smell of the hallway, of carpet and cooking and the house furniture and spray polish mingled with the smells from the adjoining garage and hit her with a scud of familiarity. Home. And all that goes with it.

'Don't hang on to Toby like that, Sunny, you duh,' cried Marion to her oldest daughter. 'Give him room to breath.'

Helen's gentle tempered, rather fat, soft-spoken Paul came wandering in through the door, hugged Alice and shook Toby's hand.

Alice went into the living room and pulled out a bag.

'Same for everyone,' she laughed and handed out six pairs of reflective black wraparound sunspecs that she'd bought on Camden lock. 'It was either these or shrunken heads.' She had been tempted by the shrunken heads but had realised with sorrow that Helen and her mother would not have approved.

Toby and Alice were dispatched upstairs to deposit their luggage. As usual they had been allocated separate rooms, at supreme inconvenience to the rest of the family. Marion had mentioned to Helen that she thought this was stupid, but Helen said, 'It's for mother. Not for us,' which shut Marion up. She didn't want to upset Helen and she didn't want to upset Mother. Well, she would have liked to but it would have been at too great a cost, even for Marion, whose favourite hobby was emotional conflict.

Alice remembered she owed Toby some physicals. She didn't really feel like it now that they were here. She had never been comfortable with boyfriends at home and nothing had changed. It felt, if anything, worse. But the obligation hung there. She sat on the bed in her tiny room and put her arms around his waist. Toby, she knew, had the same inhibition as her. He kissed the top of her head.

Feet came stamping down the corridor. Sunny burst in, a girl with a mass of wild black hair and strong shining white teeth meshed in braces, wide eyed and breathless. She was followed more sedately by her cousin Gabby, Helen's oldest. Gabby was eleven, the same as Sunny, and secretly she was Alice's favourite of the girls. Sunny was a real starlet, with her funked up hair, skinny hips, rainbow skirt, endless bangles and red monkey boots. Gabby, who hated her name, was in jeans and a little girly blouse and cardy. Her straight mousy brown hair was held back at the fringe with a plain pink plastic clip. Alice felt a surge of exasperation with Helen.

'Why don't you and Toby share a room?' trilled Sunny, who had inherited her mother's love of confrontation.

Gabby sent a gaze of apology to her aunt.

'He snores very badly, don't you, Tobe?' explained Alice.

'Yes, I do,' confirmed Toby. 'If you listen late at night you'll hear it. You'll think it's the sea, but really it's me.'

'That's a poem,' giggled Sunny.

'Mum says there's tea downstairs, Victoria sponge,' Gabby informed them, dutifully discharging her responsibility.

Sunny took Toby by the hand and stood between his legs.

'Carry me,' she breathed.

Toby smiled, concealing his panic.

'I think you'll have to carry me,' he said. 'I've pulled a back muscle carrying your aunt.'

Sunny shot a quick jealous dart at Alice and pulled Toby away by the hand.

Gabby rolled her eyes.

The family had congregated on the sun lawn at the side of the house. They were sitting about in candy striped deckchairs, books open face down at interrupted pages by the side of each chair.

A cake, light perfect buttery yellow sponge, sandwiching whipped cream and strawberry jam stood on a round wooden table under a giant fringed orange parasol. Next to it was a frosty jug of ice clinking Lemon Barley water, and beside that a steaming pot of tea and six Cornish blue and white mugs. Jake and Saul, Marion's boys, aged four and six, carried out a tray of scones with solemn dignity. Jenny and Emily, Helen's twins of eight, identical to each other and their mother, fussed officiously behind with plastic cups and Rodda's clotted cream in a tub.

Helen stood at the table with a knife in her hand, organizing everyone. 'Who's for what? Marion, pour the Lemonade. Paul, do the tea.'

'I want to cut the cake,' screamed Sunny.

There was a momentary frisson in which Helen's smiling disapproval was noted by Marion, and Alice saw the way in which her sister bit back the boiling resentment her older sister's unspoken slight on her daughter had caused. Helen didn't break her stride.

'*I'll* cut the cake, Sunny, in case it crumbles all over the place. Could you give everyone a scone for me, please?'

Gabby stood patient and unallocated by the table.

'Gabby,' said Alice, 'Why don't you come round after me with the cream?'

The stars hung their constellations over a midnight sea. Alice rested her arms on the windowsill in the darkness of her room and looked out. It was the same room she had occupied as a child. It was the same dark and the same stars and the same sea and the same string of orange lights from the village. A sliver of lemony moon curved in the sky.

Many nights they had sailed out, she and her father, nights like this when the dead calm of the wind left them rising and falling and drifting with the tide, fishing lines over the side, the lamp on the prow the centre of a ghostly circle fading in pitch black indigo.

Her father helped her listen to the sounds of the sea, a continual whispering from a half seen world; the slap of waves on the keel, the hollow suck of fish jumping, breakers pounding distant rocks, bells and horns of other craft, the rumble of the moving ocean, the creak in the boat's timber, the sea birds' mournful cries, gulls and cormorants, and the mysterious feathery flap of invisible unfurling wings.

100

For hours he was able to sit without talking, on the sea. Sometimes he showed her knots, sometimes the stars, (he knew all the constellations) and he taught her to read a compass and to read a chart of the deep unending. He showed her the direction of France and of Spain and how to sail to America in emergencies.

Her father smelled of brine, and his moustache was grained with salt. His hands were calloused where he ran the line through them. His face was creased with lines from exposure to the sea. Alice liked to imagine that he was really a fisherman, not a local country GP.

At sea he wore yellow rubber trousers and a big matching coat with a hood and Wellingtons. She had the same outfit. They were two yellow shiny sea creatures, unexpectedly on a boat. There was a tiny cabin where she sheltered if it was wet, though she preferred being out on board, tasting the mixture of sea splash and rain on her face.

They caught crab and lobster, mackerel and other fish. Her father handled the shimmering rainbow bodies with respect, displaying them in the flat of his big hand so she could see the flashes of colour. Many were thrown back in, but some were kept, especially the shell fish. Alice thought the lobster were waving to her, imploring her with their slow red pincers not to eat them. They were pulled up in creels, with the crabs. Sometimes the crabs crawled eccentrically around the deck, their horny backs encrusted with tiny molluscs. Alice thought of her father as encrusted in molluscs. His skin was hardened from the weather. His eyes were buried from squinting into the light. The two of them went fishing day and night. He took her across the sea to Brittany and even to the coast of Spain. She used to dream of being a pirate.

She never wanted him to go without her. Her mother did not like them going to sea. She did not say it in front of Alice, but she was not happy as they left together, packing the creels into the messy interior of the car. Alice remembered her mother's still face peering at them silent and unsmiling from the kitchen window as they drove away.

101

Now every time she came home she was confronted with the loss.

Toby's shape appeared in the doorway.

'Come in my room,' he whispered.

'Tomorrow let's walk to Chapel Porth,' she replied.

She gazed back at the dark expanse that covered everything and everybody. She thought, this is the same moon that is shining over London, over the flat and the Heath. She balanced the fact that there was infinite space, and herself, and that the two co-existed and did not cancel each other out. The human mind had just such capacity; the great philosopher worries about his laundry list. When you have just been told that the person you love most in all the world is dead, you cannot sleep because you have not finished your geography homework. The sky, the moon, space, the sea, the eye, the face, the heart; all part of a whole. For what reason?

'I must get some toenail clippers tomorrow,' mused Toby, 'If I'm going to be wearing sandals.'

Alice grinned in the dark. 'Yes,' she agreed. 'That is important.'

In the morning Alice got up early. She could hear the kids smashing about and shushing each other. Tired bundles in pyjamas squished up on the sofa like hairless puppies, watching cartoons on the TV.

She made a cup of tea and drank it standing by the pond in the garden. The grass was already pale with sun and hot under her bare feet. From that spot she could see down to the bay. It was so white that she couldn't see where the sky ended and the sea started.

Helen appeared in her dressing gown. 'Another scorching hot day. Plenty of sun cream for everyone.'

Helen had rounded out. She was on a permanent diet; cabbage soup diet, no carb diet, no sugar diet, hi-protein diet. They all failed because Helen had a dangerous relationship with food. Food and family. Food and family and activity were comfort. Helen was permanently on her feet, gardening, cleaning, cooking, washing, painting the white on her spotless walls, or if she did sit down it was late at night to address the overwhelming weight of social worker bureaucracy.

'I'm going to clean out this pond today,' said Helen.

'I'll give you a hand,' volunteered Alice, thinking it would be good to have something to focus on.

'You and Toby should be out having a nice time together.'

'What about you and Paul? Shouldn't you be having a nice time?' Alice regretted saying it immediately. She didn't want to raise any issues. She wanted to leave it all as it was, not stir it up. She looked at the festering surface of the pond.

'Too much to do for that, ponds and three children.' Helen smiled, determinedly.

'I'll take the kids to the village for fudge, then.'

'Oh, I'll come. I could do with a row of stamps.'

There's no need, thought Alice. I can take the children for fudge on my own. I am thirty next year. Thirty. At least no one had mentioned her getting married yet. They would, though. They would.

The six children and Alice filled the fudge shop. Each of the children had a pound, from Alice, and the choosing of the flavours was the best bit. They smeared their fingers over the glass. The woman behind the till maintained a fixed smile and chopped up mini pieces of gluey sweet in various different colours. The twins had their white paper bags screwed up in their hot little hands. Fat blue flies were already huzzing around the fudge. Alice tried not to look.

Gabby was last in the queue. She hovered and selected the pink and white coconut ice. At that moment Helen bustled in from the post office.

'What are you having, Gabby?'

'Coconut ice.'

Alice knew what was going to happen next. 'Helen, do we need a paper?' Her attempt at distraction failed. Helen was not easily distracted. 'Not coconut ice, Gabby. Why not have a few pieces of the vanilla?'

'They're all the same, Helen,' said Alice.

'It's so sugary, the coconut ice.'

'But fudge is sugar. That's all it is. Pure sugar.'

'Have the vanilla, Gabby,' said Helen.

Gabby shrugged and Helen asked the woman for four slices of vanilla and laughing, said it was all the same on the hips.

'I'm going to get a paper,' said Alice. 'I'll catch you up.' She walked away to be on her own and behind her Helen shepherded the children onto the pavement. 'Let's have a look in the church,' said Helen.

'Oh, no way,' protested Sunny. 'We're Jews.'

'We're just looking, Sunny. It'll be interesting.' Helen held up her hand and stopped a car so that they could cross in front of it.

They disappeared into the church.

Though Alice recognised that the point was the choice and not the confection, she bought a bag of coconut ice to give to Gabby later, having picked up the Sunday newspapers; a Telegraph for Toby, an Observer for Marion and the Mail for her mother.

She got back to the house before Helen and the children. Toby was up sitting at the kitchen table with Paul and David. David was stoically drinking the cheap instant coffee Maria had made. He wondered wistfully if there were a Starbucks in the village.

Alice delivered the newspapers, which David and Toby sank into immediately.

'I'm going to clean out the pond,' said Alice. No one looked up.

The pond was at the lowest part of the garden enclosed by a hazel hedge. It was thick with rush and pea green weed. Alice parted the rush and saw soupy water. She realised she would have to get in to the pond properly to clean it out.

She went into the garage. For some reason her mother hardly ever kept the car in the garage. It was used for storage. There was a big freezer cabinet stuffed with joints and bags of cooked fruit, labelled with description and date, and bits of left overs, similarly labelled. Her mother never threw any food away. Maria was appalled at the waste when Marion brought the children over. Maria was forced to eat far more than she needed, because she just couldn't put pizza crust in the bin, couldn't stand seeing ketchup covered peas tossed out, or half consumed biscuits. If the worst came to the worst she put anything possible out for the birds, even chicken nuggets. Sunny was shocked. 'It's making cannibals of them,' she said.

'That's why you should eat your food,' reproved Maria.

'No,' retorted Sunny. 'Just because I don't eat it it doesn't mean that the birds have to. It's not my fault.'

Maria looked at Sunny with hard, pursed, meaningful lips, but the child was impervious to this silent disapproval, an imperviousness that Maria found incredibly shocking, a direct personal affront. Maria tightened her face even more, so that Sunny would see. Sunny continued to fail to see. The problem with Sunny, Maria determined, was that she had too much self confidence. Too much self. Marion would have trouble with her.

Alice began to sort through the waterproofs and coats hanging up on the wall pegs. She couldn't find what she wanted. There was an old wardrobe in between the shelves of WD40, paint cans, creosote, car wax and such like. Alice opened it. Her mother's golf clubs stood diagonally across the base. At the far end of the rack of coats, hidden right at the back, were her father's yellow slickers. Seeing them sent a shock to her brain. She took them out and shook them down. Dust rose and tickled her nose. They were hard and stiff to the touch. She decided she would wear them.

Just as she was about to put them on Maria came into the garage from the house door.

Immediately Alice sensed that she had breached one of her mother's invisible conduct barriers. 'Do you mind? I was just going to clean out the pond. It really needs it.'

It was nothing more than that, she meant to say, nothing that had any meaning, just an exercise in clearing up. She stood with the slickers in her hands, nervous of eliciting some sort of emotional scene.

'They haven't been used for a long time. I didn't think anyone would be burrowing in there.' Maria's statements were always capable of translation. Hers was a loaded language.

'I'll put them back.' Years had gone by and Alice had never ventured past that line Maria had drawn. Her mother shot her a stare of reproach.

'They're my mementos. You're young. You have your life ahead of you,' Maria carefully allowed Alice to see her biting back the tears.

Alice didn't have any of her father's personal effects. Her mother had kept them all. Maria had quite quickly taken Edward's clothes to the jumble, retaining in her bedroom only the items she wanted.

'What made you keep these in particular?' Alice asked, curious to see what answer her mother would give.

'After he died,' Maria's face constricted, 'You wouldn't understand what happens with grief. I wasn't thinking normally. I sorted his things and gave them away. I gave away a lot of things I should have kept. His fishing rod, for example.'

Yes, his fishing rod, and all his tackle and everything to do with the boat, the charts, the brass compass, even his lobster creels were given away, and the boat placed in the Yard for sale. Reminders of the sea trips were obliterated, like a secret history.

Maria took the slickers out of Alice's hands and hung them back in the wardrobe and shut its door firmly.

Maria's grief at the funeral had been terrible to see. Maria's grief had not gone away, instead it had calcified, like a rock in her heart. People had comforted her with the promise that the initial stage of bereavement took two years to pass. She hadn't been able to understand how they could say this to her, standing there in the wind as the coffin was lowered down into its mud hole. Perhaps they had not understood how much she loved.

They told her her daughters would be her comfort. Helen and Marion did their best. They were older. Alice was different. Standing at the side of the open grave hole, Maria realised that if Alice had not been born, she would still have had her husband.

Toby emerged from the kitchen and the newspapers into the heat of the sun. He found Alice sludging around in shorts and flip flops in the pond. The reeds and tangle of lily stems had been dredged up and slung slimy wet on the grass. The children frolicked in eccentric circles, shouting and screaming. Alice pulled a rake over and over the surface.

She was good with children, Toby noted with satisfaction. Green brown slime clung to her legs.

'A snake, a snake!' screamed Jake in dreadful excitement, pointing. Toby's smile vanished as he caught a glimpse of silver slide across the grass and into the hedge.

'They're just water snakes,' said Alice. 'It's full of them. They've been eating the frogs.'

Toby grimaced. Alice could put up with all sorts of things he couldn't bear. He really didn't like snakes. He hung back, away from the pond.

'Do you want to go to the cliffs?' he asked.

She threw down the rake.

'I'll finish this later. The worst of it's done.'

It was true. The rectangular York stone outline of the pond was now visible, as was the surface of the water, still green speckled with pond weed.

Gabby held a bin liner open for Alice and she pushed in all the detritus.

'I'd better have a quick shower,' she said, twisting the neck of the bag and taking it off Gabby. Helen came round the hazel hedge.

'Oh, well done,' she said, admiring the pond. Alice knew Helen would 'finish off' the work.

They set off towards the coast path mid morning. Alice had asked if anyone else wanted to come. Helen had cast a meaningful eye around so no one would accept.

The sun was high. A light breeze wafted in from the sea. At first they had to descend a narrow road, down which the occasional misdirected car grunted and groaned then they cut off cross country over a smooth wooden stile with a footpath sign that said 'Porth 4 miles.'

The grass in the field was long and swished their calves as they walked single file on the worn track. At the end of it they had to squeeze past a thorny haw and then they were on the coast path. The sea stretched away, touched with lines of white foam, pools of turquoise merging with translucent emerald according to the depth of the water, dazzling in the brilliant sun.

Toby carried a rucksack in which he had packed two bottles of water, Factor 40 sunscreen, cash, towels, some plasters, his swimming trunks, and his book.

'Might you get bored?' Alice had asked, as she watched him arranging the contents inside.

'No,' he replied. 'But you might.'

The National Trust beach at Chapel Porth was only a ten minute ride in the car from the village, but to walk it, up and down the vertiginous declensions of the craggy shoreline took a good two hours of steady toil. Every so often they halted to look out over the sea filled coves.

They stopped at one of Alice's favourite spots, a high ridge of cliff, from which a semi circle had collapsed, leaving a vast drop and from the base of that drop a massive granite shard had been pushed up by unimaginable forces from the sea bed to form a wave crashed, jutting, lichen covered island, so surrounded that it was permanently in shadow. On

108

the slope, entirely inaccessible to man, perched sea birds in their hundreds, grey and white strutting forms, sitting, flapping, calling their shrill echoes from rock face to rock face. Toby stood carefully back from the precipice, peering cautiously down at the shadow cast rocks below.

'I can't see the attraction. It looks abandoned to me, and unsafe. The ground could give way beneath you at any moment. No one would ever find you. I can't imagine anyone's ever even been down there.'

'That's the attraction.'

'Step back, Alice.'

'When I was a little girl,' she said to Toby, ignoring his instruction, 'I used to stand here and vow that I would never go so far away that I couldn't come back.' She waited to see if he would understand how important this place was to her, not just the place but the notion of having something you never want to leave, something that is representative of oneself, integral and necessary.

'Dangerous,' he commented.

'True. But when you're that age you can't imagine how the future distances you.'

'I meant, letting you come out here on your own to this...' he gestured down, '...desolate place.'

Alice looked at the waves rolling onto the lonely rock. It meant the same to her now as it had then. Her life had changed, but not the meaning of the rock. The part of her that as a child had been real and unchanging was still alive, at the core of her. She said, by way of common explanation, for Toby's sake, 'Not on my own. With my dad. We came here a lot.'

The final ascent rose to an old mine. Despite the excessive heat of the day the interior of the minehouse was cold. They waited there. Toby kissed Alice within the walls, and she kissed him back.

They carried on to the beach. It was dotted with families, their temporary territory marked out by towels and windbreaks, which were needed for shade and privacy today, not for the wind. The tide was on the retreat, and pioneers pitched camp closer and closer to the edge of the still foamy sands.

Toby, used to the city, felt the muscles in his calves twang. It wasn't so much the climb up, it was the descent that did the damage. He wasn't hugely fond of walking. Left to his own devices he wouldn't have walked to the beach, he would have driven in the car. But he followed Alice.

The sky hung low with heat. Only the sea made it bearable. Gulls wheeled high above, throats open, screaming.

They found a spot on unsullied wet sand in an alcove of rocks at the end of the beach and spread out the towels.

Alice stretched out on her back. Toby lay down next to her. She stared upwards, watching a slow white cloud sail across the sky's blue stage and change shape. She closed her eyes and heard the huge rush and suck of the waves, rolling onto the rocks further down the cove.

Imagine this, her father had said, when life is hard. She used the image of the sun behind her eyes and she used the sound in her ears to cleanse herself of anxiety. So many times she had gone there in her head, to where she was now, on the wet sand, her hand extended onto a smooth- washed, half buried rock, feeling and hearing the endless break of the sea.

They lay without speaking. The sun was directly overhead.

Toby scrabbled in his rucksack and brought out his sunscreen. 'Here,' he said and squeezed a snowy white coil of cream into the palm of his hand. She turned onto her front. Toby began to apply the lotion. He slid his oiled fingers in the dip between her shoulders, round and around, covering every little patch of skin, onto her arms, down the felty scoop of her curved back, rubbing each bone of her spine, lower until he reached her bikini. He lifted the edge and moved his hand inside, right down to her coxyx. Toby loved caressing hard bone under soft skin. It was the contrast. She knew Toby hated anything sexual in public. They didn't exactly have an audience, being partially concealed behind the ridge of rocks, but it was open to anyone wandering past to the extreme end of the beach. She glanced at him.

'My turn,' she said, sitting up.

Toby lay on his front, resting his head sideways on his arms and looking at her through squinting eyes. She smiled to herself at his furtiveness.

She massaged the lotion into his skin. Toby, with his golden hair and paleness burned easily. Aware of his vulnerability to the sun's rays Alice forgot she was meant to be involved in sex play and bent intensely to ensure he was covered in great handfuls of protective oil. Only when there were no holes in the milky slick on his body did she remember.

She slipped her hand under his abdomen, feeling the soft sides of his stomach. He inhaled and raised himself slightly, producing a cave for her fingers to explore. She stroked him gently, lower and lower, finally brushing the tip of his penis almost imperceptibly, over and over. He suffered this for several minutes then lifted himself, his body facing hers.

'Not here,' he said.

She laughed and lay down on her stomach, her feet pointing towards the sea, her chin resting on joined hands. Toby propped himself on his elbow and surveyed her. Grains of sand adhered to the stickiness of the sun oil on the swoop of her back. She smelled of melted bounty bars. Toby experienced the most wrenching desire, more than he had ever felt in his life. He didn't know what it was about this moment, but quite suddenly there was no future except with her.

'Alice, will you marry me?'

For a moment, it seemed a very long moment to Toby, she stared at the striated rock in front of her, and listened to the sea. Out there the waters were uncharted, the depths cold. The enormity of it, the loneliness and its cruelty and how much she loved it frightened her. She knew what the sea could do.

Maria was in the kitchen cooking three chickens, far too much effort and far too much food. On the top of the AGA there simmered a gargantuan pan of potatoes and next to it a pan of carrots. In the carrot pan the water had turned orange because the carrots had been boiling for so long. On the gentle stove sat a bubbling bog of wholly unnecessary bread sauce.

'You realise she's mad,' whispered Marion to Alice, as Maria disappeared into the pantry. The temperature in the kitchen had risen beyond the endurable. 'Roast and all the trimmings in this weather? David's bewildered. He keeps asking is it summer or is it winter? He wanted to take us all out for a meal. I suggested it to Mother, but…'

Maria's grudging idea of catering for Jews was to grill endless paper thin pieces of plaice to a rubbery consistency and serve with green veg. Marion was feeding the children secretly at pubs but David was unhappy with this, tolerating it only so his children could eat, but he himself wouldn't touch anything that wasn't kosher and he was hungry, despondently glutting out on cakes and biscuits to make up the difference. Maria didn't disapprove of Jewishness, she disapproved of the rudeness of putting people to trouble, and the Kosher diet fell into her category of 'odd'.

'Tomorrow,' said Alice, 'we will eat out. We will go to the Fish Restaurant.'

'You will never get Mother into the Fish Restaurant.'

'She'll come, to celebrate.'

'Celebrate what?'

'I'm marrying Toby.'

As she said it Alice felt tears unaccountably pricking at her eyes and she had to leave the room and go and stand in the garden. Marion came after her and pulled her by the arm and hugged her and squeaked excitedly, 'Can I go and tell people?'

'Yes,' said Alice, to get rid of her. She went to stand at the pond where it was enclosed. She had not cried for years, but she did now. She thought it was something to do with telling her mother. She couldn't have done it directly. Having Marion do it was just about manageable. She dried her eyes and waited for them to feel normal again before walking casually back into the house. She could hear Marion shouting.

She entered the sitting room and they all looked at her. Toby was there being hugged by Marion. Helen was waiting to embrace him too. Then they embraced Alice, and the men embraced her and shook Toby's hand. Maria still had her apron tied around her waist.

Maria had to say something. Maria and Alice both knew it was unavoidable. Maria forced herself to put her arms around Alice and ignore the shock. She had known this day would come.

'That's lovely,' said Maria, repressing her bitterness. 'I'm so pleased. You'll see how wonderful it is to be married.'

'So when's it going to be?' asked Marion, quickly.

'We haven't really got that far,' said Toby from his side of the room. He was still locked in Marion's arms, Helen the other side of him. Alice thought, he is the brother we never had, the man of the house. He filled the absent space so perfectly. The sisters clutched him to them metaphorically as well as physically. David was always going to be an outsider in this family and he didn't care. Paul was too weak, an all but invisible sideshow to Helen's main performance. Toby was just right. He scooped up the family's entire ration of unused female reverence, and there was a lot of it.

That question, lobbed out by Helen, drove it home to Alice that she had agreed to marry Toby. Alice wondered awkwardly if she should cross the room and close the distance between herself and her future husband, but there didn't seem to be the necessity. He was plainly comfortable in the bosom of the family.

Alice imagined what her father would say if he were here now. She knew instinctively, and the knowledge stabbed at her, that her mother was doing the same thing. The two women tugged in their imaginations for the affections of the dead man.

If he had been alive he would have taken her out on the boat, or to the cliff to the gull covered rock, and she would have told him about Easton. He would have asked what Easton was like. He would have asked her what she felt inside and what it meant and she would have told him. But maybe if he'd been alive she would have had nothing to tell. There would be no Easton.

Maria's chest burned with the effort of suppressing a complete breakdown into tears. It would have been all right to cry if they had been tears of happiness, but the tears she would have cried would betray themselves. She told herself that the feeling she had was because she knew how much Edward ought to be here to share this moment, the announcement of Alice's marriage. But with whom would he have been sharing it? Could any man have come between Edward and Alice? Maria knew what she would have felt if he had been alive and this announcement were taking place in this room with Edward present. She would have felt unutterable relief. She would have been able to feel happiness for her daughter and for herself. She would have laughed gaily.

They would both have been gaining a husband.

'Now then, Mother, happy news.' Helen's voice managed to convey warning, sympathy, rebuke and cheer all at the same time. Maria thought, plain Helen will never understand. Nor will centre stage Marion. Alice is the one able to understand. Alice knows. Even as a little girl she understood things, things a child oughtn't to understand. If she had not had that capacity, those serious, comprehending, watchful, grey eyes, maybe it wouldn't have been possible to blame her. The tears were streaming down Maria's face. Marion came and put her arm around her mother's shoulder.

'Your father should have been here,' said Maria and turned her face away from her youngest daughter.

'He'd have been really happy,' said Marion, misunderstanding. Alice did not misunderstand.

She was pleased she had decided not to cross the room to Toby.

Maria wiped her eyes on a tissue Helen had produced. She said to Alice, 'You're very lucky to have Toby.'

Toby had called in to the off licence and had bought two bottles of cold champagne. The rucksack was on the sofa. He unbuckled the bag and produced one bottle.

'Glasses, Paul, glasses,' ordered Helen. Paul disappeared.

'David also,' said Marion to David. David had been watching with the fixed smile he kept in the closet for occasions marked 'Happy Family.' The smile snapped off and was replaced by the frown that had drawn indelible lines in David's forehead.

Family, thought Alice.

Across the family Toby smiled at her. She smiled back. She did love Toby. She had done the right thing.

After the long meal was over and the plates had been cleared away they sat outside in the still air, drinking wine along the table, like Mediterraneans. The children had been allowed to remain in honour of the occasion, though it was late. They scrambled and played in the night time garden, dim excited figures in the dark. A lozenge of umber light fell onto the scented grass from the kitchen window. Beyond was the black, where the land dropped down to the sea. Way in the distance were the light beads of the next village along the coast, and beyond that the wide Atlantic.

Helen and Marion were locked in argument over the guest list. Helen's argument was controlled and unbreakable, Marion's loud and shrill with younger sister frustration. Alice's childhood had been permeated by that sound.

'Toby, are you going to invite anyone to this wedding?' asked Marion with fake innocence. 'Only I think Helen's just filled the guest list.'

'I'm sure Toby has a long list to give us,' said Helen undaunted, with the bonhomie of the benign control freak.

'Oh, surely not many,' said Marion, 'Just the parents and the brother, maybe the brother's wife. So, that's four on his side and, hmm, let's see, ah, three hundred and twenty on ours. That seems fair.'

Toby, mellow with drink and happiness and family, slouched contentedly lower in his chair. David, a tee-total himself, poured Toby another glass of wine and muttered 'You're going to need it.'

'You're being silly, now,' said Helen to her sister with a steely smile. 'That's the beauty of the Rosemundy. It'll take easily a hundred and fifty with a buffet.'

Alice imagined that her father were there. He would be listening to his two elder daughters arguing and looking with resigned amusement into Alice's eyes. They always shared the joke. He would say, have what you want. He hadn't been able to have what he wanted. He taught her that life was fragile. By his death he had warned her. She had seen and believed. She chose shore and safety.

Chapter Twelve

Easton left his car at the bottom of the dilapidated flats. It occurred to him that it was almost certain in its shiny newness to be vandalised, that he would return to find shards of glass covering the pavement and no CD deck, not that he ever listened to CD's. He didn't like music. He didn't like what music did to him. Once he had gone to a concert at the Festival Hall, one of the violin concertos. He had had to leave in a hurry less than twenty minutes through and he never went back.

A gang of kids in baggy jeans and silver jewellery lolled around the steps to the flats, boys and girls together. Easton had to pass them on his way up.

The place had been built late sixties, long and square and depressing, and was crying out for demolition. Washing hung from windows, flapping in despairing surrender to circumstance.

As he approached the kids watched him from surly faces. They had been drinking and empty cans of laager rolled around metallically on the concrete. A burger, tossed aside in its box, its slimy entrails spilling out on the floor, contributed to the rancid stink of general unpleasantness.

Easton moved past them as if they weren't there. A girl, her hair pulled tightly back, so that her eyes looked elongated, called out an obscenity and they laughed. They didn't attack him, though. He didn't look like a victim.

He climbed the stairs to the third floor. The walkway ran along the row of doors to the flats. The windows of the doors were at best filthy, at worst broken into jagged shapes. The sound of children and a baby's mewling cry reached his ears from the interior of one of the flats. The number he was looking for was at the end of the walkway. When he got there he saw it was derelict. Boards had been nailed across the door windows and a plank affixed with nails across the latch. Graffiti screwed all over the door and walls.

As he stood there a woman came out of the next door flat. She had the appearance of premature age; a bizarrely whitened powder face, the whiteness accentuated by a slash of scarlet lipstick. Heavy mascara clogged bleary eyes. She was fat as dough and wore a black coat and black leggings on fat legs. On her fat fingers rings of bright glass jumped and sparkled.

'Are you the Law?' She pronounced it Lawah.

He nodded.

She sucked her tongue and considered. She wasn't sure she believed him. She didn't like the cold in his eye.

'Too late, if you're after them. Went Thursday. Bad as rats.'

'I'm looking for two of them, one dark, maybe Greek, black short hair, gold ear ring, sunken cheeks. Scowling.'

Something about her interrogator made her think hard.

'Scowling? Yeah, he was. Like a dog, an evil tempered dog. Greek, was he? They was always coming and going all times of the day and night. Like rats they were, only worse than rats, and the noise, doors banging, shouting, arguing, whores too.'

'Do you know where they might have gone?'

'Hell for all I care. Made my life a misery, they did. The old folk are afraid to go out. Scum. I'd hang them. I would.'

She gazed in bitter resentment at his retreating back.

'All right for your kind. You don't have to live with it,' she cawed.

His car had a long, deep scratch gouged into the side, from the front to the end. He glanced back at the group of teenagers. The long eyed girl gave him a stare of vindictive triumph.

Alice's clinic finished late. She had been back from Cornwall for three weeks. London was quiet with the absence of people. Only those who really needed to came into the stifling, airless city. The Heath, with its green space, shady oak glades and cool ponds was rashed with supine, semi naked bodies recklessly exposed to the sun's hypnotic power.

Alice had had all day at the hospital, where windows did not open and radiators were stuck on, blasting out artificial heat to add to the existing blanket. The patients were being driven madder in their tiny closed cells, sweating brows and lank hair, cruel to keep them in, no where for them to go, only the whispering of lips for a breeze. Alice had been infected by lethargy, like a dying sailor in a stranded submarine.

As she emerged from the Hospital into the open, even the oppressive air of heatwave London felt cool and good in her lungs. She cycled home, grotty with sweat, her palms slipping on the handlebars.

She chained her bike at the rear of the house, and banged heavily up the stairs to the flat. Because it was right at the top it absorbed heat from the roof above and the flats below. Opening the windows was futile.

Toby was sitting in the thick air of the living room, cross legged, with a glass of Stella in his hand. Opposite him, on the sofa, sat Easton. He was still wearing his suit. He must have come straight from the court.

'Michael's called by,' said Toby, superfluously. He raised his glass to his lips, his eyes warning her to be polite. He could see she was tired and hot and in a poor mood.

Easton rose.

'Toby's just been telling me your good news.'

She stared at him and he stared back.

What had he come here for? What was it to him if she was engaged to be married? She had made up her mind never to see him again. She felt the same sinking feeling as when a New Year's Resolution is first broken. It means the fragmentation of resolve.

'Excuse me. I need a shower.'

She could hear the hum of their voices as she stripped off her clothes. She switched on the shower and drowned them both out. She stepped under the gush of water before it got hot, gasping with physical shock. She let the cold numb her then

119

turned the dial to warm. Toby liked carbolic soap. He bought this stuff called Wright's Coal Tar, a bright yellow brick that smelled of boys' boarding schools during the War. Getting clean was a luxury. She had read about the European women prisoners of the Japanese in Singapore, and how precious to them was a bar of soap. Yes, she could understand that. It gave you back a clean mind. She washed her hair, squeezing out the water, over and over.

When she came out of the shower she listened. He was still there. He was waiting for her. She rubbed some coconut oil into her skin, and towelled her hair. She made an effort to make no effort, put on some Bermudas of Toby's and an old T shirt.

When she re entered the sitting room she went and stood behind Toby's chair and placed her palm, now fresh, on his shoulder. He raised his hand and covered hers.

If she had expected to see jealousy or pain she was disabused. All she saw in Easton's eyes and in the curl of his mouth was the suggestion of mockery.

He knew she was making a statement. He found her gesture too simplistic to be taken seriously. All he cared about was fucking her, he wanted to fuck her and fuck her over again. He wanted her to suck him and open for him and he wanted to feel how it felt when he pushed in. That was all. He didn't ask if she loved the man he was engaging in conversation. He didn't ask if she came when he fucked her. He didn't care. She could send him coded messages, but he knew she wanted to fuck him too. That was all that counted. There was only that reality. If she wanted to pretend that she was in love, he didn't care. He had no desire to pretend with her and no desire to destroy her pretence. He just wanted to live in a bare world.

'Show him the ring,' said Toby.

Easton felt her mortification. Despite himself, it gave him some pleasure. He saw it in the tiny lowering of her head, the minute pursing of her lips and the indiscernible tightening of her body. He felt as if he could see right through her. He almost felt as if he felt her feelings. It surprised him and he held on to the sensation. It was like being inside her, and her waiting for his next movement, emotionally and physically.

She had no alternative. She stepped forward, close to him, and extended her hand. With a display of profound interest that she found utterly insulting, and he knew she did, he took her fingers in his and examined the small diamond for a long time. She had chosen the ring for its plainness, and because Toby wanted to save for more important things.

Under Easton's scrutiny it became cheap. She knew he would never have bought such a ring.

'Very nice,' he said.

She took her hand away.

As the tip of her fingers left his he regretted his unkindness. It had been deliberate, but also involuntary. He would never have bought such a ring. He would rather she went without. The ring offended him. But he should have hidden his contempt. It was a small, mean response. Had it been anyone else he would have attempted concealment. Had it been anyone else he would have had no interest of any sort. She had elicited his meanness. She had made him small. He felt a shard of disgust at himself.

'Have you eaten?' asked Toby. They both turned to him at once.

'No,' said Easton.

'I'm not hungry,' declined Alice.

'I know it sounds crazy,' said Toby, ignoring her, 'But I could murder a curry.'

'I'm tired,' Alice said, snappily. Toby shot her a glance of reproof at her peevishness. It wasn't like her. He was surprised. He made a joke of it. 'You have to eat. We'll go to Sarits. Do you want to come, Michael?' He hadn't particularly wanted Easton to come, but now felt he had to offer, to make amends. Easton was looking wryly at Alice, presumably also taken aback by her rudeness.

121

Sarits, five minutes down the road was a venerable curry establishment of the old school. Disdainfully it abjured slick innovation, resolutely retaining its swirly patterned shag pile carpet, its furry wallpaper, low brass lamps and white starched tablecloths. The service was silent and deferential.

'Have you been here before?' asked Toby.

'No.' Easton tried to keep his intonation neutral, wary of unintentional condescension.

'Oh, I thought you would, as it's so local.'

'No.'

Toby ordered a chicken korma. He always had chicken korma. Alice had dal and bhindi. Easton barely glanced at the menu before ordering a lamb pasanda and rice.

'Beer?' asked Toby, eyebrows raised in friendly enquiry.

'I'll just have water,' said Alice.

'Yes. Water. No beer,' said Easton.

Toby started a conversation about a senior politician who appeared to have lost all sense of judgement over a woman. It was Toby's opinion that the man would have to resign. He and Alice bickered. She thought he ought to be left alone with his private life. In France, she pointed out, the matter would be accepted with adult discretion. But this was not France, Toby argued. The man clearly hadn't been able to think about the consequences that would assuredly follow and even though Toby accepted that the press were hysterical and hypocritical, the hypocrisy and hysteria of the press were facts of British life and couldn't be ignored.

'And when you get so emotional about something, you can't do your job,' concluded Toby.

'It's not the emotion. It's the scandal. If it weren't for the scandal he could do his job.'

Toby was goaded by her irritation. 'No, no. It's the type of emotion that's the problem. It's the wrong emotion.'

'The wrong emotion?' echoed Alice, surprised despite her long knowledge of Toby's way of thinking. 'Emotions can't be right or wrong. They just are.'

'It's about sex and infatuation. It's not proper love.'

'What's proper love? Emotion isn't just love, not in the way you mean it. What about grief, despair, desire? Aren't those emotions, too?'

'Yes, but not love, obviously. They get in the way of real love.'

'But, if a man's wife or child dies they don't just sack him, do they, on the basis that he's too emotional?'

They turned to Easton to arbitrate their muddled argument. He had put down his knife and fork and was resting his cuffs quietly on the table.

Alice knew, as soon as the words fell, that Toby was thinking the same as she was. Here is a man alone. Improbably alone, maybe left alone through death. They had never asked him and he had never offered any information as to his private life.

In the brittle silence Easton took a long drink from his glass of water.

'No,' he said, at length. 'They don't do that.'

'Anyway,' salvaged Toby. 'Politicians always wriggle out of messes. Whether he ought resign or not, he won't. Life's not like that. Blow.'

He dropped his hand to his belt and unhooked his bleep. 'Oh, I don't believe it. I shouldn't even be wearing this. I'm not on call. I forgot to take it off. Sorry, Michael.'

He took out his mobile and made a call.

'Surely Dr Chaudhi's on call? Tut. What about Caroline Fraser?'

Toby gave a huge sigh and stood up. 'Chaudi's gone home sick and Caroline Fraser's already in casualty and there's a car accident come in, two spinal injuries. I've got to go.' He reached into his jeans pocket.

'No,' said Easton tersely, waving Toby away. 'I'll do it.'

Alice saw Toby hesitate. She saw his parsimony get the better of him.

'Are you sure?' It was crystal clear Toby was going to acquiesce, even though he had issued the invite. The bill should have been his.

123

'Yes,' said Easton.

They still had food in front of them in oval silver dishes.

As soon as Toby left Easton put his knife and fork across his plate and sat back.

'Did your wife die?' asked Alice.

She wasn't sure if she was going to get an answer.

'No. She divorced me.' He said it with casual indifference, glancing around at the restaurant décor as he spoke.

'Why?'

He sighed and looked about again, then pushed his plate away.

'This is dire,' he said, rinsing the remains of Toby's Tiger beer experimentally between his teeth. She couldn't tell if he meant the beer or the situation.

'Do you mind that I'm marrying Toby?'

'No,' he replied.

'Don't drink it if you don't like it.' He was still sipping from Toby's glass. Easton called the waiter over and asked for more water.

'I can't see you anymore. Do you understand?'

'Yes.' He nodded as if she had just asked him to pass the salt.

The waiter placed an iced jug of water on the table.

Easton drank some.

'Could we get the bill, please?' Alice gave the waiter a smile. Easton felt a prick of jealousy. He sneered at himself.

'What?' she asked, observing the curl of his lip.

He shook his head. He would, if he could, have pulled her onto the Heath and fucked her there, in the dark, on the mud. He recognised this as the bitterness of rejection, but it didn't make the desire any less violent.

He took out three twenties and laid them on the table.

'That's way too much.'

'You can take the change to Toby.'

'You see everything, don't you? You're very clever,' she mocked, irked that he saw Toby so clearly.

He said nothing.

'Do you remember that case?' she asked. 'The mother, Lorette Gurley.'

'I can't talk about that. It might come back to me.' Did he mean the case, or the memory?

'It won't. She killed herself. Threw herself from a high balcony.'

She wanted him to know how it had ended. Welcome to the world.

She looked at him, perplexed. He seemed to have frozen. He stood up abruptly and left the restaurant without turning. By the time she had made it to the pavement he had gone.

She stood for a long time staring after him.

Easton wandered about.

He couldn't face going back to his house. He passed a pub on the corner and went in. It was one of those very popular character pubs in good locations. There was sawdust self-consciously sprinkled on the floor and the specials on the board included seared tuna with ginger, coriander and lime leaves. They were just calling last orders. The pub was full. Circles of smoking drinkers squashed up on stools around the tables, chatting and laughing. Easton hated pubs. It was literally years since he had been in one. He hated the proximity to others, the bonhomie, the noise, the drunks, the boring banter. The whole meaning of going to the pub eluded him.

He had to lever open a gap in the row of bodies leaning against the bar. Even the process of catching the barman's eye to get served was singularly distasteful. The barman was a youth with pale spotty skin and gelled hair and a woven string around his wrist. Easton ordered a double whisky. He drank in one it and left.

He went down Well Walk towards the Heath. It was just a black space, clouded with blacker silhouettes in the dark. He crossed the road and passed a big old fashioned Mansion block, before the Heath opened out.

He knew he could walk downhill from where he was now, where in the day there were clear vistas to Highgate, and reach the woods.

As he stepped over uneven ground he stumbled and fell hard, pushing his hands out to save himself. He felt mud on his hands. He carried on walking. They say the Heath at night is infested with sexual bandits, muggers and drunks, but Easton didn't see anyone. He was left quite alone.

Eventually he came to a halt. This is mad, he thought. What I'm doing is mad. He sat on a bench. His watch told him it was quarter past two. He had walked for three hours.

He sat and waited, but he didn't know what for. It was the alternative to going home and going to bed, better than waking from sleep. The colour of night began to drain into day. The old axiom that things seemed better in the morning had never been true. He recalled blankly the dawns in the dormitory when he was a boy. He found the evenings, the endings, more bearable than this, another day opening up before him. Birds stirred and began to chirrup, just one, then all of them. He stood up and began to walk home. He had a professional life. He had avoided sleep, and now he was crucified by tiredness. He never slept well. Sleep slid away from him like shards of shell in raw egg.

He let himself into his own house, listening to the silence, shaved and showered, put on a clean shirt and trousers and went into the kitchen and flicked on the kettle. While he waited for it to boil he opened the lever arch bundle of papers in his study. There was about two hours reading. It was four o clock. The reading would take his mind off all the rest.

At six and six cups of tea later, he brushed his teeth. His mouth tasted like camel's breath. He tried not to think of the curry and the circumstances in which he had eaten it. He tried not to think of the words she had said. He tried not to think of the image of a woman, light as a feather, falling and

126

hitting the floor and the blood forming a pool around lifeless, inscrutable, detached eyeballs, eyeballs connected to the sockets only by strands of ophthalmic nerve, like marbles on the ground. It's because of you, say the eyes.

He stared at himself in the mirror. Why had she fucked him? He was forty-nine and looked it. He did not count himself a handsome man. He was ugly. He knew this because he had been told. But she had fucked him, she had taken him in her mouth, swallowed his semen. She had kissed him. She let him hear sounds of pleasure as he took her. She had trusted him. She had wanted him. She had not asked for anything. And now she did not want him.

He took the tube to Temple and walked up Arundel St to the court. As he did so a weight lifted from his mind. He began to think of the cases he had before him. When he got to his desk he checked the list.

The Clerk of the Rules is the name for the official who masterminds the judges' schedules. Putting together the judges' schedules is a like doing Rubik's cube with the added difficulty that the colours change shade when you are not looking. The Clerk of the Rules, a woman as hard as nuts, with red painted nails, gave thanks each day to some unknown God of the Rules for Mr Justice Easton and his capacity to run through cases. He did all the reading in his own time. He hadn't taken a holiday for...well, as long as the Clerk could remember. She was aware that Easton wasn't liked. They said he was a dysfunctional workaholic, out of step with the touchy feely new ambience of the Family Court. The Clerk didn't care. Mr Justice Easton was the last to leave the Court, the first to arrive.

'Have you been in long, sir?' asked Clive anxiously. His judge was looking really quite awful.

'Not long.'

Clive could see this to be untrue. There were already three cups on Easton's desk. Clive cleared them up.

'Busy list, today, sir.'

127

'What's new? Has anything come in on this Stone case? There should be the protocol documents.'

'Nothing, I'm afraid. No doubt it'll be handed over my head.'

Late documents were handed up to the judge in court, physically, over Clive's head.

'No doubt,' replied Easton. Late filing and generally sloppy representation was a subject that engendered rage in him. Clive balanced him out phlegmatically. How did Clive control the anger?

'Clive.'

Clive stood expectantly on the other side of the desk. Easton fingered the metal staves of the lever arch file mechanically as he wondered what he was doing asking this. The words were coming out from somewhere separate from his rational brain.

'Don't you feel angry?'

Clive frowned. Did the judge mean angry about the late documents? About sloppy preparation? About the things that made the judge angry?

'About...?' He hesitated, to leave way for elucidation.

'About...' and the judge stalled over the sentence, '... your wife.'

'Her condition? No, sir. I did at first. Very angry. Well, you do, don't you. But mainly I felt,' Clive weighed the words carefully. He wanted to be sure he was putting it honestly. 'Mainly I felt terribly sorry that she was going to have to put up with all that, and what I wanted most was to find a way to make things as normal as possible, to go on, to make sure she had a life outside the illness. It's hard to explain. The thing is, we're in it together. I'm sorry. I sound sentimental. But the point is we decided to concentrate on what we had. I think in a way, we've found things out about each other, good things, we might not have discovered otherwise. Not that I'd have asked for it to happen, you understand.'

Easton nodded. He was impelled to ask more, to try to understand this new world of acceptance.

'What about afterwards?'

'When she dies? When Susan dies? I expect I'll be very lonely, sir, if that answers your question.'

'I'm sorry.' Easton was mortified at the impertinence of his question. He couldn't look at the man to whom he was speaking and who was replying to him with such painful honesty.

'I'm lucky to have such a close family, my children and the grandchildren, other people to care for, to care about, really. And, of course, my friends.'

Clive looked at Easton.

The judge didn't reply. He'd had his answer.

Chapter Thirteen

The wedding was booked for the New Year, with all its connotations of new beginnings. Only it wasn't a beginning, but a continuation, a metal rivet seamlessly joining two panels in perpetuity, the before and after barely distinguishable.

Alice stood on the platform at Paddington waiting for Helen's train from Exeter. Alice watched the 10.30 from Penzance pull in to the station, wrenching and clanking. She imagined it rolling back after unloading its human cargo, through the countryside, away from London, finally crossing the Tamar. She identified in her mind the landmarks from Saltash. Paddington was inevitably associated with Cornwall for her.

The fat steaming engine screamed its iron frame into bay. Helen had worked her way through the carriages to the front and Alice could see her waving from the window. Alice smiled and waved back.

This was a compromise. Helen knew a very good seamstress in Exeter. But Alice didn't want to use a seamstress in Exeter for her wedding dress. She lost a couple of nights sleep about it, worrying about saying no to Helen. She had agreed to a wedding in Cornwall with all the trimmings, and to a hundred of her mother's friends, elderly relatives, church acquaintances, distant cousins and long lost godparents. Now she was about to agree to the wedding dress, too.

Alice had handed over every other aspect of the wedding to her family with little more than mild resignation, but she had a blockage where the dress was concerned. She did not want to walk up the aisle as a projection of someone else's idea of who she was.

Toby said, 'She's probably very good, Helen's woman.'

Helen told Alice and Toby that she was going to pay for the wedding dress as a present. She didn't see it as a means of control. She didn't see herself as a controlling person. Toby thought it was a lovely gesture. He rebuked Alice, 'She's loving it. And she's a brilliant organiser. Just let her get on with it. Let's face it, it's not exactly your thing.'

Toby was privately pleased that Helen was doing the wedding. She was a safe pair of hands. He would have been a little uneasy as to what Alice would have produced by way of a wedding. Left to her own devices she could veer towards the unconventional. Then there was the delicate matter of money. Alice wanted to have the wedding in London. Toby couldn't think of the cost of that. Under intractable pressure from Alice they had told their respective parents that they, the happy couple, were paying for the wedding. He was ashamed and hid it, but he had always assumed that the bride's parents... but then of course Maria was a widow and he knew that there wasn't heaps of money. Still, it rankled. At one point he had tried to hint to Alice about the normal arrangement. He hadn't even got that far, she had looked into his eyes, he knew she knew what he was going to say and, wisely, he abandoned the attempt. Alice had very few limits but Toby sensed that crossing them might be terminal. He was pleased, though, that at least Helen was funding the dress.

Alice told Helen she would have trouble going to fittings in Exeter. Only three or four trips, said Helen. Alice said her clinics and her thesis took up all of the time and Helen was forced to concede. To assuage the guilt Alice asked Helen to help her choose, knowing with a sense of despair that this search for a dress for her wedding day would end in her wearing something that was Helen, not her.

Helen bustled off the train. She was wearing a smart brown wool suit, her London clothes.

'Now,' she said. 'I've brought some magazines. I've managed to isolate four shops.' Alice had a vision of her sister in white anti contamination clothing, ruthlessly cordoning off bridal shops.

Helen had a list. She marched ahead, steaming down the escalator in the tube station, stopping and puzzling at the

131

topographical map showing the different lines, in charge of operations in a city she didn't know, with a sister who had lived there for ten years. Alice made no attempt to intervene. In the morning they did a store in Chelsea and one in Knightsbridge. Helen allowed a brief break for a sandwich then they went to Regent Street and New Bond Street.

'You know, there is one place that I want to look,' said Alice. 'It's in Camden. We can get a cab.'

She had tried on frilly, frothy, long gowns and heavy trailing veils, and lace veils, and silk veils, sheath dresses, dresses with bustles (Helen was keen on bustles), Regency dresses and Victorian.

'What's at Camden?' asked Helen, dismissively, who had already identified the dress she wanted her sister to wear. It was cream Regency with delicate embroidery on the bosom. In it, Alice resembled a Jane Austen heroine at the peak of her achievement, that is, marriage.

In the cab, Helen took out her notebook and pencil like a policeman in the thick of an investigation, and put pencil lines through the shops she had discounted.

The shop in Camden was set on a side street. It had a funny little dark shop window, and Helen knew immediately that it was one of Alice's odd ideas.

The shop had bare boards and smelled of incense. A woman, thin as a willow, in a black leotard top, black leggings and black stilettos, smiled as they entered.

'Need any help,' she enquired.

'No thank you. We're just browsing,' Helen replied. In all the other shops Helen had dominated the assistants' time and attention.

Despite herself, however, she began to finger the materials of the dresses. There were rows of garments of all colours. Helen turned. Alice had pulled out one of the dresses from the racks and was standing in front of the mirror holding it against herself.

'It's very pretty,' mouthed Helen, 'but it's not a wedding dress.'

Alice supposed that any dress worn by a bride on her journey to the altar constituted a wedding dress, but didn't advance this argument to her sister. It held too many philosophical implications. When is a wedding dress not a wedding dress? When is a wedding not a wedding?

'I'll try it on, shall I?'

'I'm only thinking there's not a lot of time if we want to get back over to Chelsea.'

Chelsea was where they had seen the dress of Helen's dreams.

Helen herself had worn a dress from Berketex in Truro, utterly traditional. She had been a pretty bride, though she would not have said so herself. If she had shown anyone her wedding photos she would have said, 'Plain as a pikestaff, and the groom not much better.'

Alice emerged from the changing room wearing the pearl coloured fifties style dress.

'I look like Grace Kelly,' said Alice, with a laugh. Self consciousness had smeared her cheeks rose.

'You look fabulous,' admired the shop assistant. 'It's a Dior. Early nineties.'

'You mean its second hand?' Helen was appalled.

The woman laughed. 'Yes,' she said, and bent to adjust the waves of silk on the skirt. The bodice and arms were tightly fitted, showing off Alice's long back and high breasts. The skirt section flowed like a champagne fountain. The pearl carried a soft, almost imperceptible shadow of peach. Alice looked at herself in the mirror.

'Here.' The assistant took a pair of high heeled shoes from the window and placed them at Alice's feet. 'Maybe not your size, but...' The woman shrugged. It was the impression that counted. 'Very beautiful.' She nodded, in silent and expert approval.

Helen bent close to Alice's ear.

'You know, I so liked the Regency dress we saw in Chelsea. It was extremely pretty. And I think on the day itself anything but a proper wedding dress will feel odd. You're

133

not really considering this, are you? It would be terrible to make the wrong decision. Especially at this price.' Helen pressed her finger and thumb meaningfully against the price tag.

Chapter Fourteen

Easton lay in bed. In the oblivion of his tablet induced sleep he heard a distant, distinct voice, the first fruit of returning consciousness as he swam towards waking.

'Easton. Easton.' The voice was harsh and male. 'Get up at once.'

Easton struggled to open his eyes. They were glued shut despite rising panic.

Mr Harwell, the master, stood over him. The seven year olds in the dormitory watched in terrified silence, kneeling or sitting on their beds, clad in striped cotton pyjamas. Easton, prone, the sleeper and the child, crushed his face deeper into the pillow. It smelled of damp, tearstains.

'Easton, are you *crying*?' The word crying was articulated with incomparable disgust. 'I won't tell you again. Get up.'

He did not want to show his crying face. He continued to lie in his bed. He felt the sheets being pulled off him, exposing him. The sleeper saw what the boy could not possibly have seen, Mr Harwell's raised hand and in the hand a thick length of cane. Mr Harwell was dressed in his speckled Norfolk suit and had ginger hair. Anger had turned his lips white as paper. The arm went high, right back over Mr Harwell's head. He was a rugby playing man, very muscular in the shoulders. Mr Harwell used all the strength he had. The sleeper moved in his sleep, a defensive motion. The dream boy felt a sudden unbelievable pain. The dream boy screamed. He screamed hysterically during the second and third strokes and all the way to the tenth stroke, when he suddenly stopped screaming. The boy sensed what the sleeper was telepathically communicating to him. If you stop he stops. Salvation through silence.

'Now get up.'

Mr Harwell slicked back the strands of thin ginger hair that had risen like snakes from his scalp.

The small body, bleeding from ten striped lacerations stood in trembling shock.

Harwell took a deep breath.

'You have been sent to us, Easton, because you have nowhere else to go. Your mother is dead and your father is a busy man. That is the state of matters, and you must get used to it. Crying is for babies. You must not cry. Do you understand? Or I will beat you again and all the other boys will think you are a baby. No body will want to be friends with a boy who cries.'

The vision receded as Easton awoke, breaking through sleep's skin. Reality fell on him like a brick wall. He awoke exhausted.

The bird's dawny orison gathered pace. He closed his eyes again for a few seconds, not to sleep, certainly not that, just to block the day out. But it was worse under the eyelids.

He realised he had curled up. He straightened out, lay flat on his back, extended his arm into the vacancy of the rest of his double bed. He slept naked.

He got up and urinated, put on his dressing gown and went downstairs. It was still early. He made a cup of tea and sat in the kitchen sipping it. The cordless telephone extension lay next to his hand. He sat back in the chair and crossed his arms out of harm's way but continued to look at the thing. He had noticed recently that it barely ever rang. No body called him. The telephone loomed larger and larger until it was virtually the only object in the room, bigger even than Easton himself.

He picked up the phone and dialled, lifting his eyes to the clock. He was safe. It was six in the morning. There wasn't going to be an answer. The line connected. He listened to the tone. The telephone on her desk was ringing. He pretended for a moment that he had status to call, that is, that he was a friend of hers, or a legitimate lover, or even a professional acquaintance. It was only a momentary indulgence he allowed himself. He was appalled when the telephone was answered.

'Hello,' said a deep female tone.

He put the receiver down, feeling ludicrous.

136

Clive was protective of his judge. No body got to Easton except through him.

Easton was sitting in court hearing a trial. In this trial there were many millions of pounds, dollars and euros in bank accounts around the world; there were investments, shares, share options, loans soft and hard, companies, holding companies and directorships all over the place. In essence there was a husband and there were his assets and they did not wish to be divided to fund the increasingly, breathtakingly self indulgent lifestyle of the wife. Easton checked, 'The annual expenditure for clothing, Mr Peters, one hundred and eighty thousand sterling?'

'My Lord, yes. It may at first appear a large sum, but given the extent of the assets in this case it is not disproportionate, indeed in comparison to many such cases it is almost frugal.'

'I understand the significance of proportion, Mr Peters. I also understand the meaning of the word frugal, as I am sure does Mr Chambers, though not perhaps, your respective clients.'

Clive allowed himself a tiny smile. The judge's only islands of relief seemed to lie here, in matters of extreme technical complexity, adjudicating the arguments spun by front rank intellects. In front of Easton were six lever arch files lined up in a row and labelled A-F, one thousand pages of evidence about money. Twelve forensic witnesses, two Q.C's, two junior barristers, Adam Dearing, Mark Thurloe, a four week hearing, million pound legal costs, assimilation of fact and formulation of law.

Clive sat below the Judge, quietly getting on with admin, while the case went on around him. He sometimes wondered how a person could absorb so much information, how arguments could be constructed out of materials invisible to the ordinary human brain, existing only in abstract. Sometimes he had no idea what they were talking about, it was a foreign language. The judge spoke this language with the innate fluency of a native, never the slightest stumble or hesitation. Clive could see why the judge would prefer the money cases. He had noticed they got through a lot more bicarb during the children cases than the money cases. There wasn't much law in children, well, you had to do what you had to do, no matter how sorry you felt for the poor parents. He was glad it wasn't him who had to make the terrible decisions. Susan was always interested in the cases, always eager to hear about the day's incidents and stories. That was the thing about Family work, it was never boring. Clive sometimes felt himself to be the channel between the world and his wife and he was grateful to have such an interesting world to present to her. He related the stories to her over their tea together. It was the details that stood out, the lady who pleaded that she had to have a cook because she had never learned to operate a microwave oven, the wife who wept in the witness box over her poverty, exposed dramatically as the husband's barrister whips out a copy of Hello magazine and finds her in it, grinning, in mink, made up to the nines, stepping out on the arm of an oily rich man, the taxi driver who bought a house with money carried to his solicitors office in wads in a Sainsbury's bag, the child who has never been told that her mother is her grandmother and her sister is her mother, the abuser who sells his daughter, age seven, to men under the railway bridge, the AIDS baby whose African mother consents to his adoption so that he can receive treatment in England. It was the alphabet of the human heart every day in court. Of course, Susan couldn't speak too clearly, but Clive understood what she was saying, by listening hard and watching her face. 'What's that, dear?' he would ask, wrinkling his brow in concentration. He never pretended to understand when he didn't as that would be giving in, and Susan would feel that the lines of communication closing up. They persevered. Nor did Clive believe it would be all right to guess what she was saying on the assumption that he knew what she would be thinking. Her thoughts still had the capacity to surprise him. She had always been an independent thinker, much more so than himself. They had been married for thirty three years.

138

There had been a point a couple of years before when Clive had been depressed, thinking about giving up work. Susan talked him out of it. She knew he needed a matrix of life to cling to when she was gone, she knew the importance of work. Besides, she said, Mr Easton needed to be looked after more than she did. Coincidentally, at this crucial time, Mr Easton became a judge, and asked Clive to come with him as his Clerk. Less money, of course, but better hours. Clive always said he couldn't understand why Mr Easton should give up such a lucrative practice at the bar to go to the Bench at that point in his career. All in all Mr Easton's decision had benefited Clive and Susan very much.

Susan had met Mr Easton once only, years ago, when she had met Clive out of Chambers before going to see a musical show in Town. He had been polite, but he hadn't offered to shake her hand. When he looked at her she could see he was really looking. She thought he had been looking *for* something, but it was only for a second and there was no time to get to the bottom of it. Clive was twenty eight when Mr Easton arrived in Chambers. By that stage Clive was a senior junior. He had come home and said, 'They've given me a new young man to look after.' After six months the senior clerk asked Clive apprehensively if he had any reservations about continuing to clerk for Easton. Clive said no, he had not. Clive couldn't exactly say why he was content to continue. No one else liked Easton. He had a manner about him that one of the other clerks had described as 'fucking rude,' but no one could actually cite an example of this rudeness, only excessive castigation of mistakes or inefficiencies. Clive thought it was more that the man seemed contemptuous. He put people's backs up. Work came before everything. He had no interest in building relationships. His manner said, as plainly as if he had a sign written on his forehead, 'I don't give a toss about you.' What he did care about was the cases. In respect of the cases nothing was too much trouble. Clive supposed this was why the solicitors used Mr Easton as a barrister, and why the

139

clients, especially the ladies, sent him bottles of champagne that he would never drink. He left all his presents on Clive's desk. Clive had had a lot of champagne, whisky and wine in his career looking after Mr Easton. As the briefs became more lucrative and the cases more complex the only person in chambers Easton would let manage him was Clive. Clive never knew why. Mr Easton wasn't difficult in chambers. He never got involved in the bitchy politics. He never fussed about trivialities. He bore any hardship with silent stoicism and never complained.

Clive couldn't exactly say he liked his judge. That would imply a personal relationship. The thing was, Mr Easton trusted Clive and Clive carried the responsibility as a weight on his shoulders. He felt, dimly, for Clive was not one for analysis, that he held in his hands a rare treasure that, once dropped, would shatter and be lost.

At the luncheon adjournment Easton carried the bundle marked A into his chambers. Clive followed him through.

'Shall I order a sandwich, Mr Easton?'

'Thank you, Clive.'

'There was one message, sir, well not really a message. The lady didn't leave a name. She said she'd call you again.'

'When did she call?'

Clive observed an unexpected urgency in his judge.

'Early, just as you went in to court.'

'But not since then?'

'No, sir.'

'If she calls back, hand me a note.'

'In court, sir? You want to speak to the lady even if you're sitting?'

'Yes.'

So Clive did something he had never done before. As he sat in the room adjoining the judge's chambers, transcribing the orders after lunch, the lady called again. The judge was in court, actually hearing evidence. Clive handed up a short note informing him that the lady was holding on the telephone for him.

'Mr Peters,' the judge said to the clever young barrister, in mid flow with his be-suited accountant in the witness box, 'I'm going to have to rise for five minutes, I apologise to the witness.'

Easton stood and nodded. The court rose to its collective feet and bowed, like the subjects of a foreign potentate.

Easton picked up the phone, lying waiting for him on his desk.

He placed the receiver to his ear. She heard his breath and spoke.

'Are you all right?'

He sat down. He didn't know how to answer.

'Why did you call?' she asked.

'I didn't call.'

'The receptionist picked up your number on recall.'

He felt his throat dry up. 'Can I see you?' It was the first time he had asked for something he needed.

'I can see you but, not as we did before. I can come on Saturday at three.'

Not as before. How else? He didn't understand how else. There was no other way.

Chapter Fifteen

Easton knew that people sometimes bought each other presents.

He stood in the queue in the Chocolatier at the top of Hampstead High Street. He listened to the orders of those in the line in front of him. Behind the glass counter was a girl all dressed in white like a respectable masseuse, holding long silver tongs and awaiting with wide blank eyes the customer's lingering instructions. Easton realised that they cared about the composition of the boxes they were creating. Easton tried hard to care as well. He supposed the boxes were being purchased as gifts. He didn't believe that anyone would buy chocolate in this way for themselves. Easton seldom bought chocolate. Chocolate, especially cheap chocolate was something he had disliked since school.

At school, the boys craved chocolate. They craved food of all sorts, since they were kept on small rations of bile inducing rat filth, permanently hungry. Most of the boys were sustained by regular parcels of food from their mothers and aunts. These parcels often contained chocolate, usually bars of Cadbury's Dairy Milk, treasures to be shared only with the most intimate companions in ecstatic huddles. The possession of chocolate signified that a boy was loved. If you had chocolate you had love. If you gave chocolate you loved.

Easton had once been offered three squares of chocolate by a boy. It was in the dormitory late at night. The boy, Dorfield, a dullard, but popular as a consequence of being good at rugby, had that morning received a food parcel. Dorfield's friends, Burnley and Fyldes, Staithely and Quiller sat on his bed. The five boys discussed with animated anticipation the division of the chocolate bar. Easton, the sixth child in the dormitory, lay apart in his bed with his back to them, pretending to sleep. He knew there was no prospect that they would give him any chocolate.

'I should get most,' declared Dorfield, 'because it's my parcel.'

The two others nodded in acceptance. Possession was clearly nine tenths of the law.

'On the other hand though,' negotiated Fyldes, reasonably, 'both I and Staithely divided our bars equally.'

'And I am your best friend,' pointed out Burnley.

'And my mother's taking you to tea at the half holiday,' said Quiller. 'I expect she'll buy us both whole bars each.'

'Give and take,' summarised Fyldes.

Dorfield conceded. 'It's true,' he said. 'We have all shared. Right, so we are five, and there are twenty eight pieces. That means…' He stopped, dismayed. 'It's not even. It's not even halves.'

'If we each have five squares, there will be three left over.' Burnley was good at maths.

'I should have those,' said Dorfield, returning unabashed to his original position, now that the indivisibility of the stock had become clear.

Dorfield sat with the bar of chocolate in his hand, scowling in thought. Suddenly his face cleared. 'I know,' he said. 'Easton,' he called. 'Would you like some chocolate? I say, Easton.'

Easton turned and sat up. Inside he repressed a humiliating swell of gratitude to Dorfield.

No,' exclaimed Burnley, scandalised. 'Don't, Dorfield.'

'No, don't,' echoed Quiller, equally shocked.

'It's all right. It's not because I like him,' Dorfield excused himself. 'If you do my Latin, Easton,' he spoke haughtily, 'you can have three squares of chocolate.' Dorfield was much scared of his Latin homework.

Easton looked at the five faces and the five faces stared back at him.

'I don't like chocolate.'

He turned over and closed his eyes.

'Yes, sir?' He had reached the top of the queue. Easton cast his eyes at the oblong trays of chocolate creations under the glass.

'A selection, please.'

The girl made no move. She was a machine that had to be programmed. He gazed at the trays. Nothing made any sense. What was the link between presents and relationships? Easton had not received a personal present at Christmas for twelve years.

The queue was becoming restive.

'Two each from the top row.'

He left with the chocolates in a bag and walked down the hill. He passed a shop that sold soap and scent in small bottles. As he passed something made him stop. It was what had made him lift his head in the Oxfam store. It was the scent of Alice's hair. He went in to the shop. There were tables spread with gold cloths, upon which stood various boxes and bottles. Easton went to one of the tables. An ivory coloured soap attracted him with its pebble smoothness, and inhaling he was impaled with wholly unexpected intensity. He read the label, Vanilla Dream. He bought two boxes, one for her and one for him to keep. Then he went home to wait.

She did not come at three o clock. There could be no mistake, no unheard knock. Easton had been standing on the top floor of his house, the only floor with a window out to the road, watching the gate. At four he went downstairs, realising that she wasn't going to come. He decided he would do some work. There were bundles in his study. He sat at his desk. Now that the embers of hope were cold he was sickened at the power of what he could only identify as disappointment. It was huge, almost overwhelming. He sat at his desk thinking. He castigated himself mercilessly for allowing this to happen. When would he learn? It wasn't as if he hadn't had lessons. He was pathetic. He despised himself. He hated himself. He had to stop thinking about it. Hurting yourself was hitting your head on the wall, cutting your skin, what mad minds did. He wasn't mad. Why did he feel so like damaging himself? Probably, because he deserved it. Easton sat and forced himself to see everything as it was. People did not love each other. Whatever feelings they had it was not love. It was better, thank God, that Alice Christie had not come. Love and drink and drugs and music were all the same; mind altering, reality denying anaesthetics. Easton wanted to live in the real world. Every day in the real world. He had found that he could survive in it. Mr Harwell had taught him about reality. Mr Harwell's drops of sweat falling on his bare skin, Mr Harwell's grunts of exertion as he did what he did. Every day. Casual cruelties, disappointment, spite, selfishness, betrayals, exclusion, being alone. This was what love and friendship and trust amounted to.

Intellectual rigour had been his salvation, a hiding place to escape from Harwell's squalid hatred, Harwell's personal frustration at a child's obstinate capacity to withhold tears. He had to beat Easton unbelievably hard to get him to cry, so hard it sometimes made his arm ache. But for Harwell it was necessary. And as tears forced inevitably through, Harwell knew pure inexplicable bliss, and taunted, 'It is only babies who weep, Easton. Stop crying at once.' Any pretext would do, though increasingly Harwell sensed the other masters had noticed what was going on, even if no one was sufficiently crass to mention it. It is difficult not to notice when a boy is unable to walk across the classroom.

When the boys discovered Easton's capacity for emotional isolation, a capacity that surprised both him and them, they didn't bother to torment him. He became an accepted part of the scene; Easton, bit of a loner, dead mother, father in the Middle East, scholarship to Cambridge; a cold city, a cold man.

Law was the most rigorous of the disciplines. The Bar was the most rigorous and independent strand of the Law. The professional life he chose was all about competing and winning. As a barrister you worked alone, you had no partners or employers to whom you were accountable. He saw the same bullying ruthless self serving and betrayals there as he had seen at school, powered by adult stakes, greed and status. Family Law confirmed what he had already concluded about love. It was one of the minor emotions, once the hallucinatory power of infatuation had been stripped off.

Only Clive and Mrs Bird tormented Easton's perception.

He must have fallen into a reverie. He became aware of a loud knocking on the door. His fingers held involuntarily onto the arm of his chair. He remained silent, except for the pounding of his heart.

The knock came again and made him stand up. He hesitated a moment, then went to the door.

It was her.

'Sitting in the dark?' Alice glanced behind him quizzically.

He recalled the usual social conventions and dragged them into use. He invited her in and switched on the hall light.

He had forgotten what she looked like, or rather he had imagined her so often that seeing her reminded him of the power of reality.

He took her into the living room, which was also dark until he turned on the lamps.

She was wearing jeans and a zipped, hooded grey sweatshirt. He tried to avoid watching her, though he wanted just to look at her, and thought that was pathetic.

'Drink? There's wine.'

She selected a chair and sat down, open kneed, leaning forward like a man, elbows resting on knees, hands loosely joined. One of the knees of her jeans was ripped.

'I'll have what you're having.'

'Tell me what you want.'

'O.K. I'll have red. You're not drinking? You don't drink, do you? Why's that?'

'You're the analyst.'

'You could say fuck off.' She pursed her lips and shrugged as if that would be perfectly fine. 'I'm sorry I was late.'

'Toby?'

'Yes.'

'Do you love him, I mean, do you think you do?'

'Are you going to get me that wine?'

In the kitchen he picked up the bottle of red wine he had bought and held it to his temple feeling the stone hard of the glass. He wondered how it would feel to have a full bottle smashed in his face. He went back through.

As he pulled the cork out she said 'Yes.'

'Then why are you here?'

'Lots of reasons.' It was too much to explain. There were lots of reasons, and yet all of them together didn't provide the full answer. She wasn't sure, now she thought about it, if what she felt for Toby was love. She fell into contemplation. As if he read her mind he asked, 'What do you feel about Toby? Break it down for me.'

'I know what he's thinking. I know what makes him happy and unhappy. I don't like bad things happening to him. I want him to succeed. I want to help him, to look after him if he needs it.'

'Is that love?'

'It's one version. Now I want to ask you a question?'

He tilted his hand to say go ahead. It was a game, one he had never played before.

'Why did your wife divorce you?'

That was easy. 'Unreasonable behaviour.' The legal terminology rose up to greet him like an old friend.

'Which means?'

'Five paragraphs. Short ones.'

She waited and he sighed in resignation. She made him think about things he didn't want to think about. He was surprised to find he could remember the Petition word for word, like an ancient prayer acquired by heart and which, out of the depths he was obliged to recite.

'One. I was never there.'

Alice recalled a poem she had known as a child.

Late last night upon the stair,
I met a man who wasn't there,

He wasn't there again today,
I wish that man would go away.

'Two. I put my career before my marriage.'

Late nights all nights. A wife alone. Ignored. Meals prepared and in the waste, conversations un-had, lip-stick wiped off before being seen.

'Three. The marriage was characterised by cold and silence.'

Her increasingly hysterical attacks, reaching for reaction, bad better than none at all, her screams, his retreat. Isolation.

Four. I showed no natural love and affection.'

The giving of love and affection has to be learned. This wife needed it in a quantity and form he had never been taught to provide. Instead though, he was able to provide disappointment, rejection, hurt and humiliation not just to one but to both of them, quite an achievement in terms of emotion.

His marriage was a mechanism he couldn't work. It was the patent manifestation of his failure as a human being.

'Five. You said five paragraphs.'

The fifth, endorsed on the legal document in black and white type, and presented to the very courts in which he worked. Although only a few of the judges would have seen the document he couldn't know which ones, and he couldn't know if they were discreet. Discretion was unlikely. When he sat in the court as a barrister, facing the District Judge as he was presenting his client's case he had no idea if they had read what she had said about him, the interior of his life laid bare to the people against whom he had erected his highest walls. Judith really knew how to show her hate. It was her parting shot, sweet retaliation for the razor sharp rejections, for allowing the fertile seam of her sexual love to wither unused, for locking her in an emotional vacuum.

Since fucking Alice, Easton had understood, as in a revelation of flames, that men are almost entirely ignorant of the ferment of women's sexuality. As he felt the soft wetness of her vagina taking him in, the tightening of the contractions as her excitement accumulated, saw the rose pink flush high on her cheeks, the arch of her back and experienced the pressure of her fingers on his shoulders and neck, as she bit her lips and moaned for him he suddenly understood. Men have no conception of what it means for a woman to open her legs and accept penetration into their vulnerability, no idea of the immensity of the deal involved. Self help books (he had read one once, feeling abjectly humiliated to be doing it,) devote preachy pages to the art of foreplay, physical and emotional. Kiss, cuddle, adore, speak to, flatter, appreciate, value, empty the garbage and tenderly prepare for each penile invasion. But of course, like every other human activity it is infinitely more complicated than simplistic explanation. What Easton had learned from Alice was that sex was a means of communication more powerful than words, and what he learned in his marriage was that sex is power, the perfect medium for expressing anger and recrimination, and for getting revenge.

He knew now that sex cannot be underestimated. It works, or doesn't work, on a vast elevator of levels in motion.

When Easton withdrew from sex in his marriage it was the final rejection of his spouse. He hadn't realised at the time that that was what he was doing. At the time he had just stopped being able to do it with her.

Hell hath no fury like an unfucked wife and in the silence between the sheets Judith devised a suitable means of revenge.

One night, after a year of celibacy, Judith came into his room and lay in his bed. She took his penis in her hand and held it. He stirred. He moved his head as if he was having a bad dream. Slowly, softly she caressed the shaft, feeling it grow. Then she slid the head into her mouth. She felt the moment of his awakening, the tensing of his body. But by this time he was hard and stiff in her mouth.

'No, Judith,' she heard him say, and she lashed her tongue over the most sensitive tip. It had to be precisely, intuitively gauged. He reached a level just below no return. Judith moved and sat open legged over him, astride his hips and pushed him inside. She was a beautiful woman. Her blonde waves fell like gold over her forehead. She sank forward. How she hated him in that moment. Her hate was like a drug shot directly into her vein. She made him look at her. His erection faded, as she knew it would. She rocked backwards and forwards as it sank, smiling with malice. She kept him inside her until he fell out of her. She dismounted, victorious, drinking in the humiliation she had inflicted on him.

'I want sex,' Judith had sneered. 'If you can't do anything else, do that.'

Easton had no reason to explain any of this to his listener. Alice regarded him from cloudy grey eyes, sitting forward, her face still, attentive to his words.

'Do you want to tell me?' she asked.

'I couldn't fuck my wife.'

'That was the last paragraph?'

'No.' He shook his head. Sex is never that simple, nor is love, nor hate. Especially not hate. There was no reason to tell Alice the truth. She saw before her a man, one who had fucked her and given her pleasure, one who was a success in the view of the world. Why break it? The only reason for telling her would be to destroy that image and replace it with something ugly. But that was who he was, something ugly, the reverse of the beast under a spell, she had fucked him and broken the spell and now she had to see what ugliness lay beneath. He wanted her to see.

'I needed to learn how to fuck someone when it was about disgust. That's what our marriage was; disgust.'

The girl lounged in the topless bar, bored, blinking aimlessly into the red light of the basement. Easton, sitting at one of the tables, saw her yawn and stretch her arms over her head in an arc of tedium. She was incredibly thin, naked from the waist up. She wore a black PVC mini skirt, black stockings and thigh length boots. Her hair was dyed blonde and had the texture of thin straw. She wasn't ugly, just vacant. Her

150

mouth hung open in an expression of permanent lethargy. As his eyes adjusted another girl, also topless came and handed him an indecipherable menu of drinks. Around the dimly lit drabness of the red tinted cavern a few other men engaged in desultory conversation with bare breasted women, their eyes dropping incessantly to brown round aurioles and purple nipples. The bored girl frowned briefly as if assessing a complex situation, then passed two palms down the front of her skirt to eradicate creases and slouched over to Easton's table. Red light shone upwards from the table lamp and filled the girl's face with strange shadows; her thinness made her seem very young. That was what Easton briefly thought, though he knew inside his head that the other thing that made her seem young was that she was only about eighteen, half his age. She rested her eyes on him with what seemed like puzzlement before speaking.

'You wanna get me a drink?' She half turned her head and a waiter approached.

Easton leaned forward and whispered in her ear. She frowned briefly, then went over to the bar, where a man in a cheap flash evening suit rested one elbow. His hair was greased back black and shiny with oil. His eyes scuttled over the interior of the bar like spiders. The girl spoke into his ear. The scuttling eyes swivelled to Easton, who had ceased to look at anyone while the mechanics of the transaction were put in place. Popular music jingled against the walls of the bar, too loud for the low space.

The man crossed the floor with heavy rolling steps.

He bent down and said, 'It's not a whorehouse.'

Easton stood up immediately and turned to go. He was halfway up the steps before the man, the manager or pimp, walked quickly up behind him and said, 'All right. £200. Half an hour.'

Oddly, it was about the same as Easton charged for his services. He reached into his coat pocket.

The man put a restraining hand on Easton's arm.

151

'Not here. Christ!' He shook his head as if admonishing an idiot.

He led Easton along a dark corridor. To the right stairs ascended to ground level, to the left was a door. They went through the door into a lightless stairwell, and up dim stairs floored in ripped blue lino, like the hidden parts of a run down restaurant. The man led him to a second floor corridor.

'In here.' The man held a door open and jerked his head to the interior. Easton entered the room and the man followed, closing the door behind.

'Two hundred,' the man prompted. Easton was most conscious of operating outside the law. If this man took his money and left him waiting in the room for nothing what could he do? Sue? He was struck how everything fell apart when you ventured outside conventional regulation, how uncertain and unpredictable it was. If this man had produced a razor and slit his throat no body would know where to begin looking for him. It was as if the man sensed his disquiet.

'I'll send her up. She'll be here in a minute.'

Easton took out his wallet and peeled off four fifties.

The pimp scrutinised them by holding them up to the light.

'Cant be too careful,' he said and added, bitterly, 'these days.'

He left Easton standing alone in the room. Eventually Easton had no alternative but to look around. There was a double bed, unmade. He picked up the corner of the crumpled blanket and peeled it back. The sheets revealed were stained, not merely with white, salt bordered dried semen but with blackish smears. Easton imagined these could only be stale blood. There was a bare sink, its filthy pipework exposed underneath. The only other item of furniture was a wooden upright chair. A greasy pink rouched satin blind was lowered over a window. The air in the room closed in rank and thick. Unlike every other area of the building this room was viciously illuminated by a strong white bulb in the cone of a dirty yellow lampshade.

The door opened and the girl entered. She was now wearing a top, a tight red basque like garment. She closed the door and stood before him with an air of what happens now. He didn't know. He had never used a prostitute before. He had no idea if there was some formal procedure to be followed, if he was expected to initiate activity, or set out his requirements ab initio.

At length, after pressing her lips tight in contemplation, she asked, 'How do you want it? You got a half hour, awright?'

He was at a loss.

She went over to the bed, lay on her back and spread her legs. She was wearing no underclothes, only stockings held up by red suspenders. The sinews in her groin stretched hard as she forced her thighs apart. The flesh showing between the tops of her stockings and her shirt was preternaturally white. Around her pubic area she had a thin covering of mousy coloured hair. She looked tiny and bony lying there on the foul ruffled bed.

Easton tried to control his compassion for her.

He couldn't do it in such a way that he could see her face.

'Turn over,' he said. 'Please.'

With an expression of resignation she rolled over onto her knees and bent onto all fours.

'What are you going to do?' she asked, and he felt a quiver of apprehension in her tone. She held herself totally exposed. He understood. She wanted advance warning if he was going to sodomise her.

He put his hand flat on the base of the centre of her spine, in a calming gesture, as one might to a nervous horse or dog. Her white buttocks lifted and he realised he was expected to proceed. A feeling of nausea had travelled to his brain. He looked down at her narrow red slit and he found, incredibly, that he had a strong erection. He touched the end of it to the entrance of her vagina. As he did so he felt her body relax slightly. He had not had sex for over a year and he realised he was desperate. She opened easily. He put his hands against the sides of the prostitute's hips and held her steady

153

as he took her with rapid deep strokes. She made no sound at all, and he barely any, though he was horribly fascinated by the animal grunts held at the back of his throat. It took less than a minute. As he withdrew he noticed his semen seeping out of her, and too late it occurred to him that he ought to have used a condom. The next immediate, involuntary thought was I hope she doesn't get pregnant. The thought flew away into the realms of the ludicrous.

She rolled around and sat on the edge of the bed without looking at him.

'You can wash over there,' she said and nodded towards the sink.

He walked over and looked into the slime streaked basin. On the ledge was a faded bar of old soap ingrained with black curly hairs. Reluctantly he held his fingers under the flow of the cold tap, rubbing the tips together, then shook off the drops and held them briefly against the side of his jacket to dry them. When he turned he saw that the girl was watching him curiously, and realised that it had not been his hands he was expected to wash.

She rose and went to the door and gave it a curt knock. The pimp must have been standing immediately on the other side. A key turned. Easton only now realised he had been locked into the room. The door opened and the pimp entered. Easton nodded a vague acknowledgement to the girl, who seemed neither to comprehend nor care. She walked off down the corridor.

'She's a good ride but thick as pig shit,' commented the pimp, phlegmatically. When he got Easton back to the dark stair to the outside world he said 'Come again,' with no obvious irony.

Later that night, Easton's wife, gambling dangerously, attempted to repeat her mastery. Easton lay still, feeling her hand on him. He lifted himself on to her and went in, closing his eyes and recalling the degradation of the little prostitute.

Immediately he began moving Judith realised she had miscalculated. She pushed his shoulders.

'Get out of me,' she hissed.

He pushed harder to keep her voice out of his ears. The room was in darkness and he couldn't see whom he was fucking so he could pretend anything. He had never wanted to fuck Judith in the light of day. She grabbed his hair with her tight fist and yanked. He pulled her hand off and pinned it and her other hand behind her head on the pillow. She tried to scratch him with her nails but he only used the sharp tearing pain on his wrist to help him achieve what he was doing.

'This afternoon I fucked a whore in Soho, now I'm fucking one in Hampstead,' he said, just before he shot into her. He let her hear his sounds of completion. He had only that week discovered one of her infidelities. While moving her car he had come across a letter in the glove compartment to Judith from one of his colleagues in chambers. It was explicit, about what they did and what Easton couldn't do. He put the letter back where he found it.

When he rolled off Judith's soiled body he got up immediately and went to the bathroom. He turned on the taps to smother the rasps of her hysterical rage from the next room. He knew the moment was seminal. He had released himself from ever having to worry about love. He had strangled love with his bare hands, with his body he had killed it. He had proved that love did not exist.

'I fucked a whore and after that I was able to fuck my wife, even though she didn't want me to.'

Easton found it possible to look straight into Alice's eyes as he told her this. He saw those eyes studying him, while she tried to assimilate her reactions into a structure she could recognise.

Fifth paragraph. 'The Respondent was unable to perform sexually with his wife, although he used to go to prostitutes. However on one occasion he forced himself on his wife, causing her severe distress. He also gave her a sexually transmitted disease.'

That last bit had been unlucky.

'She left the next morning with the baby.'

'You had a child?' Alice found this somehow more shocking than all that had gone before, the presence of a child, a baby, and all that hate going on around it. She made a hard effort to understand the frailties this involved; Easton's and Judith's disgust and the marriage they combined to make. She tried to imagine Judith, but all she could see was a woman putting a baby in a car seat and driving away.

'How old was she?'

'Him. A boy. When she took him, he was two.'

'And now?'

'Seventeen.'

'Do you keep in touch?'

'We lost contact.' Easton raised his glass to eye level and absorbed himself in scrutinizing the base. There was a tiny fault in the transparency, causing a distortion of the image on the other side. It took away Alice's face.

'I didn't see him for a couple of years. When she remarried she started sending him over for occasional weekends. He went to boarding school when he was seven. It was difficult to maintain a relationship.'

She nodded. She could read from his face that there was more. They both understood that she was permitting him to lie. What Alice always found most elusive were words for parents whose children are lost to them, however that loss occurs. The days and nights, hours, minutes, seconds of a lost child tick by and there are no words to alleviate the grief. What did this man do with all his grief?

She wondered if she was right in believing in the safety of the world that Toby offered her. All the Lorettes, all the Garys, Easton, her mother, her father and Easton's boy. None of it had turned out to be safe. She wanted to be told everything to help her understand but she felt the rawness of her lover's scars. She recoiled from disturbing them. There was a time and a place for everything. She was constantly sickened by the results of some of her therapeutic colleagues' failure to get the timing right, ripping open scabs that were not ready, open heart surgery performed by the thickly gloved plumber's apprentice. Alice believed in a very refined version of the talking cure. Sometimes talking was both too much and not enough, a pebble in an abyss.

'I've got something for you.' Easton had thrown the chocolates in the bin at the bottom of East Heath Rd. He picked up a brown paper bag from the sideboard and gave it to her, standing next to her chair.

She took out the box of soap, opened it and held the smooth bar and breathed its scent.

He was still standing near her. She took his hand and kissed the back of it. 'Thank you,' she said, and squeezed his fingers before letting them go. He sat down opposite her again and rested his kissed hand carefully on his thigh.

'Would you like to tell me about your wedding preparations?' He asked because he wanted to tell her he was not going to stand in her way, that he was not asking for anything, that he felt no shrapnel of jealousy, that he did not demand her life to change course for him. He was trying to convey that this was not love, that this was only a fragment of time, and not a whole. He wasn't sure why it was that he felt an actual interest in her wedding plans, why it was that he was seeking an image in his mind of exactly what it would look like.

She shook her head. 'No. I don't want to talk about those.'

They were two parallel strands of her life, or no, she had two lives. That was how it felt. It was only when you put the two together that there were lies and betrayals. Each one of itself was clean.

'Shall we go to bed?' she asked.

He had never taken her to bed.

In the dark he took off her clothes and he undressed and lifted the sheets and got in next to her. The sheets were cold and the body next to him warm. He put his arms around her

157

and they lay together. Her stomach filled the contour beneath his ribs. He realised for the first time that a woman's body and a man's fitted together perfectly. She opened her legs, and he pressed his thigh between them. She moved her lips to his. In the depth of his being he wanted to possess. He covered her mouth with his, kissed her, then took his mouth to her breasts and began to kiss her there, too, moving over the nipple, sucking on it and experiencing the change from soft to taut. He waited until he was sure she wanted him. He knew that once he was inside her he would come. She closed her legs high around him and lifted up. The palms of her hands pressed at the base of his spine, pushing him in. He came, but continued to give her his movements, and then he lay still and she screwed him softly in small stifled clutches, so that he was able to watch the full intensity of her climax.

She came with him in a way that she had never come with Toby. In this parallel life she could be whoever she wanted. There had been only one other man with whom she had been able to open herself completely, and now he was dead. She put her arms around Easton's neck and held on to him.

Easton prayed that the intensity of his need would pass before she left. At one point he felt he would rather kill her than let her go. He thought if he lay still and closed his eyes it would recede, like a tide, in obedience to the painless flow of nature. All he had done was fucked a woman. He had fucked women before and hovered miles away as he did so. Men fucked women all the time and it meant nothing. He turned and lay on his back, to drive a space between them, but the separation felt like tearing skin from skin.

She lifted herself up and sat on the side of the bed. She stood and went to the window. The light in the room had faded to dark and all he could see was the pale silhouette of her face against the outline of the night beyond.

He showered with her. She used the soap he had bought, the water streaming off their one joined body. It was more awkward in the shower, he had to bend his knees and almost lift her off her feet, and he could see her in the bathroom

158

light. Seeing her made him want to explore what he could see, and he put his fingers in her mouth to feel inside.

After she had gone he made himself tea and turned on every light in the house and went to his bright study and sat down to work.

Chapter Sixteen

In children's magic worlds time stands still. But this was no fairytale. Alice crossed the barrier from world to world and found that time had not stopped on the other side. She was late. The hands on her watch told her it was after midnight. She sprinted through the deserted night. The windows in the flat were black, but she imagined Toby lying in the dark, his face turned away, expressionless. She imagined Toby at the moment of suspicion hardening to certain knowledge.

Her heart beat faster than it had when she was coming for Easton. Then it had been slow deep pounding, now she felt the crazy drilling of fear. She realised she was terrified, so frightened she could barely breath.

Silently she let herself into the flat. There were no lights on. She stole through the living room, reaching out blind hands for furniture, navigating by familiarity. She brushed the back of the sofa, felt the tear where it was worn thin. It was there but not the same. Familiarity had been soiled by deception. It would never be the same. You can never go back.

What would she tell him? What would she tell this man in the dark? Suddenly he was no longer Toby, but a man with a right to hate her, but not just to hate her, but to reproach and mortally castigate; a stranger to her.

She stood outside the door of her own bedroom, and wondered if it were worth trying to lie. What were the chances of her being believed? Did it come down to that? A relationship of shared bodies and reciprocal care and mutual experience, did it come down to the chances of having a lie believed? If she said she had unexpectedly met a friend and had supper in the High Street branch of Café Rouge, was it worth the humiliation for both of them of the insultingly obvious lie? She had always thought that the worst element of affairs was the lying, that this, not the bodily infidelity, was more demeaning to the betrayed. It made them look such fools. She had thought she would never lie to Toby. She surprised herself.

She opened the door and crept in.

'Toby,' she whispered, trying to keep the guilt from her voice, still undecided about the possibility of lying.

She sat on the side of the bed and spread out her arm. The bed was empty. She went rapidly to the bathroom and turned on the light. No one was there. She turned on the light in the living room. Toby was not at home. Her first thought was that he had gone out looking for her, and she cast around the tables for a note. He most certainly would have left a note. He was that kind of man. She looked at the remote control. It was where she had put it on the top of the T.V.

She began to hope. Saturday night, now Sunday morning. Toby had gone out on an engagement drinking celebration with his friends. But it was past one. He never went out so late. He always came home to her, dishevelled, relieved to be home, needing her after the absence of a few hours.

In the kitchen there was a disembowelled roll of biscuits straggling untidy crumbs on the work surface, biscuits that she had munched before going out and forgotten to put back in the cupboard. It was all as she had left it. Putting the biscuits back in the cupboard would have been to Toby an involuntary action.

She flipped the answer machine. It was Toby.

'I'm going to a club, sorry about this. I might be late. It's the blokes.' Then there was a crackle, and Alice recognised the voice of Toby's best friend, Eddie, known as Steady Eddie, because of his steadiness, but, like all steady men, having the penchant for occasional exuberant excess.

'Sorry, Alice. Eddie here. We've got your fiancé and we want you to know he's in good hands.' Following which there was an explosion of laughter and the message spluttered out.

'Thanks, Eddie,' said Alice and went to bed.

She was woken by Toby's return. She heard bumping and got up. The clock told her it was a quarter past three. He was standing like a sack of potatoes in the hallway, balancing like a tightrope man. As she watched he took a step forward, or rather his foot reached out, pointed, hovered, missed its stroke and faltered to the side. He staggered.

'I'm sorry I'm late,' he said, from deep in his lungs, slothfully slurred.

She got him under the arm and dragged him, slow footed, virtually a dead weight, into the bedroom. Alcohol fumes wafted from his entire body. She crashed him onto the bed. For a second he lay supine, then, with a grunt of inebriated distress Toby drew up his legs and curled into a ball. A series of discombobulated expressions traversed his face as the room moved uneasily around him.

She had never seen him so drunk. He straightened out and began to snore like a buffalo.

Alice took off Toby's socks and shoes. He was wearing a jacket and rugby shirt. She wanted to get his clothes off. She realised that waking him was not a consideration, so she pulled him around, arms heavy as branches, flopping and falling, and took off the jacket and his trousers. His hairy maleness spread over the bed and it struck her how ugly men were when it came to bodies. She took a couple of towels out of the bathroom and lay them under his head, filled a glass with water and left it on the lamp table next to him.

She stood and looked at him for a long time. Toby. The flat felt normal, her life felt normal. The parallel strands had separated again.

In the night Toby was copiously sick. She heard the sharp attenuated braying and staggered tired out into the bedroom. She had gone to sleep on the sofa with a woollen National Trust blanket Helen had once bought them for Christmas.

Toby was half raised, supporting himself on one elbow, helplessly puking in spraying gouts all over the bed. He had, she saw, had a curry as his last supper. The towels she had placed under him were saturated in bitter stenched brown vomit. Just going in to the room took her breath away.

She grabbed the waste bin and pushed it under his face. To do so she had to kneel on the bed and she realised the wet feeling on her knee was puke. She held his head til he had finished and then stopped him from lying down in the mess. He sat on the edge of the bed trembling in the after shock. She turned on the shower and pushed him into the cubicle. He sank onto his haunches and let the stream of water rinse the puke off his hair and face. He spat.

Alice stripped the bed of sheets, duvet and pillows. She shoved them all in a couple of bin liners for chucking out. The mattress, luckily, had been spared.

'Come on, you poor sod,' she said to the limp figure in the shower. She turned off the water and helped him get out of his wet shirt and underpants. He stood quivering with cold. She wrapped him in a towel and dried him as he sat on the toilet, then put his dressing gown on him.

'How do you feel?'

'I want to die.'

'Going to puke again?'

Toby held his head in his hands. Far away Toby realised things were better than they had been, though in the long distance of his terrible swirling drunkenness he still had the nausea, the agonising splitting in his head, the loss of balance, the absence of limb control and the feeling that he was about to void his bowel.

She made him drink some water. Then she let him sleep.

Fortunately for them, Toby neither crapped nor vomited. Alice had been prepared for both. At nine in the morning she went in with a couple of extra strong paracetamol.

The victim of the night opened his eye a slit and let out a pig's grunt of tremulous remorse. She made him take the paracetamol, opened the window wide and left him again. There was nil chance of his getting up for another ten hours. Thank God it was Sunday and neither of them were on shifts.

She made a cafetiere of coffee and sat in the kitchen looking at the bag of sick drenched bed clothes. The whole flat stank of vomit. She opened all the windows. It wasn't a problem that Toby had been sick. It wasn't a problem that he had got drunk. She felt entirely relaxed about it. She thought it would do him good. She thought people should let it out from time to time. Still she couldn't drink the coffee in the acrid smelling kitchen.

She took her keys, dumped the bin liners in the rubbish hut and walked out. There had been a point in the night, before Toby had got home, that she wondered if anything had happened to him, like a car accident or a mugging. Then what? What if Toby had not merely been out late, but was dead? The flow of mangled heaps into casualty proved the reality of accidents. Stab wounds, broken noses, fractured skulls, torn spinal cords, internal ruptures, glass in eyes. It was one of those worlds. Then she wondered, what if Easton died now, before they had any other of their strange meetings? It would be like discovering that a great iron ship, whose distant lights held the promise of another life, had sunk in the dark cold sea with all hands lost and no trace remaining.

She walked to Easton's door. It was broad day. Birds sat fluffing in the trees and Sunday morning paper buyers were out on the street in slippers and sloppy joggers.

She could tell he wasn't happy to see her. He stared at her as if she were unknown to him.

'Toby is sick,' she said. 'I'm on my own. Do you want to go out?'

'I'm working.'

She had been leaning on the wall next to the door, pretending to be casual.

'That's fine.' She couldn't imagine him 'out' in any event. He existed more really in the space of her mind than in the world

She felt a certain relief flooding in, relief from deception and self-deception and decisions. It was a relationship like any other, one in which you got fucked and then rejected by a man to whom you meant next to nothing. Before Toby she'd had a few of those. She remembered the way Easton fucked her and reflected that in relationships there is always a disparity in the perception of the participants. She was half way down the path when he called.

'I'll get my coat.'

He went into the study and closed the file he was reading.

And now what could he talk about? Had he any passing conversation? Conversation seemed particularly pointless when he had expressed all he had with his body.

He took his coat off the peg and picked up his keys.

'I'm not sure,' he said. 'Why we are going out?'

She thought about it. It was a good question.

'Because you can't have intensity all the time. You need pace.'

He considered her answer. It was the centre of a ripple of ideas. In the meantime he supposed there were the practicalities.

'Where do you want to go?'

'You decide.'

There was an exhibition at the Courtauld he had wanted to see. He had never, as far as he could recall, been to an art gallery with another person. It would be very difficult, like being with a secret lover in the company of those who know you, stealing feelings when no one was looking.

In the cab, she continued.

'The majority of the content of a relationship is padding. But maybe it's essential. Maybe it's the ordinary things people do together that form the bridges over which the extraordinary things cross.'

'I'm not an expert on relationships.'

'But you feel, don't you?' She wondered if he did. She was aware that her own sense of feeling had been cauterized long years ago drifting in the storm beaten boat. Except now with this man.

The cab took them down the back streets of Camden and past Euston, through Bloomsbury.

'Virginia Woolfe's place.' Alice knocked on the window with her knuckle and looked at him expectantly. 'They say, they lived in squares but loved in triangles. I like that, as a thought.'

'Because it reminds you of you?' He was pressed far away in the opposite corner of the seat.

'No. It appealed to me even as a girl. We did 'To The Lighthouse' for A Level. I liked the idea of unconventional loving.'

'So you chose Toby?' He paused and let the sneer hang in the air. 'You're conventional too,' he added.

'Superficially,' she amended. 'Do you know,' she asked, 'what is the record for the length of time a chicken can live headless?'

He turned and stared at her. 'I have no idea.'

'Please guess.'

'I don't know. Twenty minutes?'

'Longer.'

'An hour?'

'Eighteen months.'

'That's ridiculous.'

'It's true. The chicken's name was Jed. His master fed him with a pipette directly into the oesophagus, but he finally choked on a grain of corn in a motel room in Alabama.'

'That is not true,' objected Easton.

'Would I lie?'

After a few seconds of solemn reflection on the chicken's story Easton begin to laugh quietly.

As they walked across the square courtyard, skirting the spouting fountains inlaid in the grey cobbles, she said 'I think this is the most beautiful of the London galleries.'

'It used to be the Divorce Registry. People came here to get their divorces. Where the Hermitage is now, there used to be a corridor of judges' rooms.' Easton remembered the narrow corridor filled with cigarette fumes and bitter disputes.

They stood before an abstract.

'Does it mean anything?' she whispered.

'Not if you have to ask,' he replied and walked off.

He sat on a red banquette, arms folded, in front of angels.

She sat down next to him, her hands flat between her knees. 'Chaos, abstraction, cohesion and form. Meaning. The unarticulated consciousness.'

'Truth and Beauty.'

'You're taking the piss.'

He struggled for a few minutes. He had sat many times in this gallery, many times before this very composition. It was no use.

'I can't do it with you.'

'What?'

'I can't look at the art. It's too…' he broke off.

'Too personal?'

She leaned forward and whispered, 'You can come in my mouth, but you can't look at art with me.'

She suddenly formed an image of the night stars in the boat with her father. He taught her to look at the stars for herself, lying flat on the top of the cabin. There were so many, so many stars and constellations, a billion bright points of light. She asked her father, 'Tell me what you see, so I can see it as you see it.' Edward Christie smiled in the dark. 'You can never see it exactly as another person does.' This had distressed her. 'But I want to,' she pleaded. He moved his head and positioned hers where his had been. 'That's as close as you can get. That's the best you can do.'

'Which do you prefer, Art or Law?' Alice asked Easton.

'They aren't comparables.'

'They serve the same function. They distract. It's all right, Easton. It's how humans operate. Nothing to be ashamed of. Distraction, compensation, transference, suppression. All the little tricks in the box.'

'I don't like you calling me Easton.'

'Why not? Oh, school.'

Shards of memory stuck out in unexpected places like broken glass.

'Have you ever been in therapy, Michael?'

He didn't even reply.

167

'I have. And do you know what? It was complete garbage. It's compulsory for analysts. It's pyramid selling, only less subtle. Most therapists are kept in work by other therapists, thereby proving its worth. I had an old guy with cheese in his beard and fantastically filthy nails. All the time I was telling him about my inmost self I kept thinking, get a nail brush why don't you? But initially I hoped his personal dirt was a sign of his other worldly insights. My first session, I walked in; he had the chairs arranged at disingenuous random and he asked me to choose a seat.' Alice looked around with wide eyes as if replaying the moment of decision. Then her eyes snapped into contempt. 'The seat test. Pathetic.'

'What did you choose?'

'I sat on his knee. I rolled my arse right onto his crotch and gave him a..'

'You did not.'

'I did.'

Easton laughed to himself, the second time that day.

'What did he say, your therapist?'

'He said I was looking for a missing father.'

Easton's face cleared. 'Are you?'

'What? Looking for a missing father? Oh, yes. We're all looking for a missing something, aren't we.'

'Did you fuck your therapist?'

'Only physically.'

Easton turned to her drily.

She said, 'You see, sharing art and time and humour is infinitely more personal than sex. At the moment you can only do sex. Perhaps there was a time when you weren't even able to do that, and I have to say, you do it well. You fuck well. But one day, you may be able to cook spaghetti with a woman.'

As they drove up to Hampstead, she asked him if loving in a triangle made him feel squalid. He said he wasn't the one meshed in a lie. 'The lie makes it squalid.'

This was as she had suspected.

168

'Nothing's good or bad but thinking makes it so,' he reminded her. 'Today you feel squalid, yesterday you didn't. Leave it long enough and you won't feel anything at all.'

'No disgust, no rapture.'

'No.'

She didn't kiss him goodbye.

Alice walked up the left hand side of the street, the bright side, to the Convenience Store and bought some Lucozade. Mrs Patel seized her to talk about the latest break in at the store, an incident that had occurred over three months previously but as a result of which Mrs Patel still suffered nightmares. Mrs Patel knew Alice was a shrink and kept telling her her dream traumas. 'What do you think it means?' she asked, her black irised, dark circled eyes staring with superstitious wonder from in front of the Benson and Hedges.

'It's very good that you are having these dreams,' said Alice. 'It means that you are expelling the poison of anxiety through your subconscious.' Mr Patel, standing holding a box of Walkers crisps raised his shoulders in a cynical, hopeless gesture. All he wanted was not to be broken into again, for the thieves to be caught, prosecuted and incarcerated.

'Oh well. I didn't think of that. That is very good then. Very good.'

Toby was up, lying on the sofa watching The Bridge on The River Kwai, a British war film in which everyone suffered stoically.

'Got you some Lucozade.'

'Where did you go?'

She poured him a glass of the glucosey orange fizz. Lucozade always reminded her strongly of being ill at home, in the living room, covered with a rug, her father popping in from his rounds to see her and touch her perspirant brow, dressed in his pea green tweed jacket. It had brown corduroy elbow patches, soft as a vole.

'I went to a gallery.'

'On your own?' Toby gazed at her in surprise. He hated doing things on his own. He always had to have a companion.

'I went with Michael Easton.'

She sat down and swung her leg carelessly over the arm of the chair. She pretended to be absorbed in the film. 'I rang him to see what he was doing.'

'Oh,' said Toby and she listened acutely while he processed, sorted and evaluated the information. 'Didn't he think that was a bit odd?'

'He didn't seem to. I said you were ill and I wanted to get out. He was quite sweet.'

'Lonely bugger,' commented Toby, sucking the fizzy orange surface of the Lucozade.

'He knows all about Art,' Alice defended Easton, with a clutch of pain at the description.

Toby gave a pitying smile. 'Of course he does, dummy. He's got individual pieces in his house worth more than this flat.' There was a trace of bitterness in the tone. 'A typical gay.'

Alice made some dry toast and gave it to him on a plate.

'Thanks,' he said, and humbly, 'And thank you for rescuing me last night.'

'I'm a doctor. That's what I do.'

Chapter Seventeen

With the days to her wedding growing fewer and fewer Alice, the bride to be, continued her relationship with her lover Easton. Sometimes, sweat entwined between the sheets, they had slight conversations about this aspect of her wedding or that. Alice described Toby's plan for the honeymoon in detail. Easton wanted to know. He specifically asked her, and received the information with apparently unconcerned interest. Alice was alert to hidden or suppressed jealousy, wanting it, not wanting it, then lulled into believing that Easton really did not feel it.

They were still in bed on a Saturday afternoon. Often now she went through Easton's black iron gate when Toby was working and she was not.

Easton was sitting up in bed. She sat with her back resting on his stomach, between his raised legs. She shifted slightly, tickled by the hairs of his chest that coiled so itchily on her skin. He reached around and placed his hand on her thigh. He was trying to drink a cup of tea with the other hand. He had noticed some of the truth about familiarity. He could now drink tea and have a piss in front of her. Once he had read a newspaper next to her. It was, he reflected, odd how these things crept up on you.

She played with the fingers of his hand, drawing it up to her face and examining the nails closely.

'We're doing a tour of the southern Paradors,' she murmured inconsequentially.

Easton knew Spain well. He had travelled in Seville and Madrid and Granada, before Judith. He had been happy travelling alone. In Spring in Spain he knew the rugged landscape would be covered in lines of orange trees, hung with cream clouds of blossom, infusing the blue air with fragrance, and all along the avenues there would be more orange trees and almond and apricot, like soda fountains spilling over, under which you could sit and drink thick dark coffee from small white cups, uninterrupted.

'Spain is a good choice,' he said. He wondered how it might feel to sit on a boulevard in blossom, drinking coffee with her. 'You'll be able to go to the Art galleries and the monasteries.'

'You must give us an itinerary,' she said with innocent cruelty.

She had the back of her head bent over his hand. He looked carefully at that head. 'It's your honeymoon. You'll be busy.'

'We'll still go to galleries, and monasteries. Yes.' She lifted her face, reflecting, thinking of still, shaded cloisters. 'Far away from the world of flesh. In the morning we will fuck and in the evening we will visit the monasteries and speak respectfully with the celibates.'

'And all the time you'll be thinking of me.'

'Of course.'

Only fools think lies can last forever. Neither Easton nor Alice were fools. He let her continue with the examination of his hand. She held his palm covering the back of her fist. Gazing intently she saw each individual hair and pore and the tiny, tiny criss cross lines. She turned his hand over and traced the pattern on his palm, then the blue veins and indigo arteries in his exposed wrist. She ran her fingers lightly over the coloured rivers. The sensation made him quiver. She felt this tiny ripple in him and touched his pulse with the tip of her tongue, tasting the salt of his skin.

'Food and sex,' she mused. 'I think they are very connected. I regularly have dreams in which I'm having sex and it turns into eating, or vice versa.'

'Fear of being consumed,' he said.

'Fear of consuming,' she said.

'Why would you be afraid of consuming?'

'Consuming stands for controlling. I am afraid of becoming a controller. I fear the latent controller in myself.'

She turned so she could see if he was taking it seriously. He was taking it as she gave it, half serious, open to

172

interpretation. Dreams always are, she thought. She asked, 'What about you? What do you dream?'

'I don't sleep enough to dream.'

'Not true,' she corrected. 'The dream state can occur very quickly in a sleep cycle, especially with insomniacs. The dreams of semi wakefulness are often the most powerful precisely because we are so close to consciousness. The worst nightmares appear here. It is often the nightmares that break sleep, and so, a vicious circle.'

He recognised it. His dreams were all nightmares.

'So, tell me your dreams.' She asked him again, but casually, to mask the importance of what she was seeking. She was used to long silences. What she was really doing was training him to trust her. She wasn't sure if he knew this. 'What are your dreams, Michael?'

A whole minute passed while he paced the banks of trust, up and down, up and down.

'School.' He had plunged and it felt icy.

'What happens?'

'It's my first morning at school. I'm on the bed.' He tried to control the way he spoke but the dream was too powerful and he heard his voice crack, and this was humiliating, but there was nothing he could do about it.

Her back pressed against his chest, she felt his heart in her body, beating harder, faster.

'How old are you?' She did not look at him. He had withdrawn his hand from hers and placed it flat against the sheet. She saw that it was trembling, literally shaking.

'Seven.'

She was suddenly afraid that she could not hear what he was about to tell her, that it would change everything, that she should stop him before it was too late.

'There's a master, called Harwell. Harwell is standing over me. He tells me to get up, but I can't get up. He has a cane in his hand. I don't see it. I'm face down. He pulls the sheets off, and my pyjamas and he hits me. He carries on hitting me. There's blood on the sheets. He says, 'Get up, Easton.' I can hear screaming. Then I stop and there's total silence. No sound at all, like deafness. Finally the boy gets up and I see his face.'

She thinks of him, this little boy of seven. She puzzles that the I of the story becomes the boy.

This tells her much and she waits for further clues. No good. He can't continue. He has reached the unbearable. She feels his body force forwards, and press past her because he wants to escape.

He sat on the side of the bed, naked. Now she saw that his entire body had started to tremble. He had his face in his hands. She had shamed herself. If he had been a patient she would have surrounded him with safety nets, mastered his case history, approached him gently and in time, imperceptibly probing the corners of his mind. Instead she had reached straight for the elusive shape hiding in the shadows and made it angry and frightened, all because she was fucking him and fucking someone else and she didn't know why.

He kept his face hidden from her.

She put her arms around his shoulders and pressed her cheek to the muscle of his back.

Her attempt at comfort filled him with rage.

He grabbed her by the wrists and crushed them in his fingers so hard it hurt her bones. She saw, too late, what she had opened up. She had never been physically hurt by a man before, and she knew Easton was going to hurt her now.

'Don't look at me,' he said, and he bent her forward pulling her hair. As he did so his other hand moved between her thighs. He forced his fingers into her.

'No, Easton,' she gasped, trying to take hold of his arm, but in her fear she used the wrong name. She pulled away but he pressed the back of her head hard, face down into the pillow, her high cries deliberately silenced.

Flat on her stomach, her hands held by him tightly over her head, he pushed open her legs with his knee. She felt the power in him and knew that she was powerless. He reached under her stomach and lifted her and rammed himself into her. She shouted in surprise at the pain and shouted again and he pushed her head down harder into the silence. As he thrust on, very fast, he squeezed her hair in his hand. She was unable to move, only to receive and feel. She felt his thighs and groin pounding against her in a beating rhythm, the smacking of sweated skin on skin, she felt red hot burning inside her, she heard his animal rage.

'No. No.'

He gripped her hair tighter. 'Be quiet. Shut up.'

She felt deep inside her the release of his climax.

His hands loosened. She felt his weight heavy on her back. She felt the breath of his mouth by her ear.

'Did you enjoy that?' he asked her bitterly, his damp forehead resting on her neck. He pulled away and sat on the side of the bed. She turned and opened her legs. Blood smeared the sheets and ran down in bright red snakes on her thighs.

'Look at me,' was all she said, and couldn't stop looking at herself.

He tried to remember an area in his head that held the key to this. He reached out and traced a finger down a line of blood. The blood adhered to his fingerprint. He took himself away, as far away as possible. He stopped being aware of her presence. He went to a place where there was absolutely nothing and no one at all. He closed his eyes.

Under his eyelids shutters opened to blinding sunlight. In the far away room violent white heat invaded every corner. Michael turned and surveyed solemnly the effect of the opening of the shutters. The blue of his bed was almost washed away in the whiteness. A fan flipped round and round overhead, distributing air in gusts that dried his throat even as he breathed. After considering the transformation made by the influx of light he crossed the wooden floor to the table on which were his crayon tin and drawing pad. He had drawn the pattern made by sun seeping through the angled slats against the opposite wall. Now he wanted to represent the brilliance, the whiteness. But the page was already white. He sorted the coloured pencils thoughtfully. None of them represented the reality of the room as it was. Finally he selected a pale blue and began to sketch the bed, but as he looked he decided it wasn't blue he needed but yellow. He switched. He had made only a few strokes before putting the crayon down. It wasn't accurate. It did not convey the sense of heat in the room. Disappointed, he realised that the colours in his tin could not describe what he was experiencing. He sat at the table, deflated. The crayon tin lay before him, traitorous. The tin was square, shiny gold on the interior, white round the edges, and the lid was white but covered with butterflies. There was a Red Admiral, a Cabbage White, a Purple Emperor, many others. Michael was mesmerised by the beauty of the tin when he first saw it in its original incarnation as a biscuit box. He had spat out the insipid English tea biscuits (being used to the scented sweet stickiness of date and honey) and took the tin to his room, an object of delight for days, and even now, when he looked at it he was overwhelmed by the way in which the butterflies' gorgeous wings contrasted on the pristine, uncompromised white background.

Distracted from the disappointment of confronting the deficiency of his crayons he held his head close to the tin, absorbed in the tiniest alterations of hue on one part of a delicately veined wing, and the sudden inexplicable blot of dazzling magenta or scarlet, replicated in perfect symmetry on the matching wing. Some of his crayons were made of wax. The tin was flecked on the inside with smudges of melting colour. It gave off a waxy, oily smell. It occurred to him that the view from the window would reflect the colours in his tin. He stood at the open shutters. Cruel sun sparked in a blue languid sky, its rays dropping like knives to the earth below. In the garden, four narrow oblongs of grass were kept, by servants daily hosing, bright emerald, arresting the eye. His mother needed to see the green of grass. She said so

176

as she pressed with longing against the window sill. She pinned her gaze on the grass and said it was all she had to remind her of home.

Michael's conception of England, the mother country to which he was a stranger, entailed rows and rows of thin rectangles of grass.

He was not allowed outside in the midday sun.

He was so terribly, terribly bored. For several minutes he hesitated. The house was utterly silent. He picked up his tin and his drawing pad and carried them carefully clutched to his chest and went out of the room. It was, as far as he could recall, the first time he had ever ventured out of his room between the hours of eleven in the morning and four in the afternoon. He had no clock, but at eleven, after mid morning snack and lessons he was placed in the room by his governess, and at four he was brought out by her, taken to the kitchen, where he was fed soft meat stew and cardamom flavoured rice by servants in bare feet.

He opened the high doors and went into the corridor. The shutters at the end of the hall were closed. A thin line of incredible brilliance showed through the centre where the two doors met, casting a single gash on the lozenge shaped tiles. His room was at the top of the house. His governess had a room next door. It had never occurred to him that this tall, serious, olive skinned, red lipped lady all dressed in black had an existence outside himself. Now he stood at the door of her room and pondered the striking fact that she might actually be behind it. He tried to imagine the governess doing something that wasn't teaching him or walking ahead of him along the stairs or the corridor, in quick tight swaying steps. She wore real shoes. They were black and clicked as she walked. These shoes differentiated her from the servants. Michael knew she was not family, not one of them, because she wasn't English, but he realised she wasn't a servant either. He wondered what it would be like to have no definition, to not be one thing or another. Maybe that was why she never smiled at him. She spoke Arabic to the servants and to him, English to his mother and father. Sometimes he noticed, when she was alone with his father, they spoke Arabic together, softly conspiratorial. His mother spoke only English. When he spoke in Arabic Mother looked at him coldly. Michael sensed that his mother and the governess did not like each other. Michael wondered if he ought to knock on the governess' door. She had no one to be with either. Something told him that she would not welcome his company.

He moved on alone.

On the floor below was the room of his mother. Mother lay down in the afternoons. The heat was too much for her. Michael gazed down the corridor and imagined mother lying on her bed, her face serene and beautiful, asleep. It reminded him of the story of Sleeping Beauty. He had a book in which there was a highly wrought engraving of a somnolent princess, her velvet clad body reclining, her hair and limbs spread in abandon to the spell cast upon her, her lips half open. Michael imagined awakening his mother. He trod softly. He knew without it having been said that waking mother would be a serious misdemeanour.

His object was the garden. Quietly he crept down the stairs. The diplomatic house in which they lived was in the old part of the town, and was very tall and thin. It had four turns of coiled stairs. Michael stopped at the second flight and looked down and up. The stairs had a pleasing shape, ovals within decreasing ovals, perfectly fitting one within the other.

He reached the ground floor. Stepping onto the worn stone he felt as if he were coming onto solidity after descending from a cloud.

To the front was the main door, giving on to steps that led down to the courtyard. Father kept his car there as there was no garage. Father's car was very beautiful, a silver Mercedes with diplomatic plates.

At the rear was the garden, a later addition to the house, attached at the whim of one of the Consuls before the war. A long piece of hard brown dust had been converted to an approximation of an English garden. The roses planted had suffered in the Arab climate and after suffering, losing their colour, wilting, thirsting, they slowly, slowly withered and died. The mid day heat killed everything. Only the grass survived. The grass was Mother's. She strictly ordered its care. In the morning she went outside and stood on it and in the evening she did the same.

Michael opened the door only enough to slide his seven year old body into the garden and then he waited, his back against the door he had just closed behind him. Inside the house was cool and dim. Now he felt the full glare of the noon sun on his face. The wood of the door on his back was hot. He turned and out of interest smelled the door. Then he extended his tongue and licked it. It tasted surprisingly pleasant, almost sweet. The Arab door tasted better than the English biscuits.

A strange sense of elation and curiosity swept through him. In the centre of the four green rectangles there was a stone fountain, its octagonal base bleached pale grey. The water falling from the fountain stem made, he was sure, a sound of silver as it bounced off the surface of the agitated water in the base. He moved around it, so that he was behind it and it was between him and the house.

Beyond the fountain drops he saw a spectrum of colour suspended like waving silk, barely wafting in the still air, the sun's mystical gift for water in the driest of all countries. This was what he had been searching for. He knelt before the fountain and rested the tin of crayons on the stone slabs and the drawing pad on his thighs. Passionately excited, he opened the tin and began to finger through the shades.

Curving his fist inwards he made sweep after rainbow sweep. The whole garden, now that he looked, was curved. Around the walls were curved trunked palms, their great dark leaves curved too. The rainbow was curved, the arc of the falling droplets curved, the shape of the fountain stem ornamentation, curved. He curved the lines of the oblong base. This felt amazing. The lines were not curved but he

179

had made them curved and his curved base was more real and had more validity than the object before which he was kneeling. He felt that in his hands and in his tin he had the power to make anything real.

'Michael?'

He looked up. He saw that one of the shutters in the blank white wall of the house was open. He saw that there was now a tiny figure high up in a square black box. It was his mother, leaning out and staring towards the fountain. She raised a hand and he supposed she was rubbing her eyes. He hoped that the fountain obscured him and that she couldn't really see him. Maybe, he speculated, he looked like a mirage, all wavy and insubstantial and not real. As he watched the figure disappeared. He wondered what to do and decided to stay and pretend she wasn't coming, to block it out. He continued urgently with his picture, his hand sweeping over all uncurved parts of the paper.

'Michael!'

He squinted up at her angry face.

'What *are* you doing?'

'I'm drawing.'

His mother looked down speechless at her small white son with his black eyes. She wished he didn't have such a funny little mouth. He dropped his head, as if the conversation were over.

'You will burn. Don't you understand? This,' she pointed one long accusatory finger upwards to the sun she hated, 'will burn you. Go inside immediately.'

He closed up his drawing pad and put the lid on his crayon tin. His mother let out a sigh of exasperation at the fiddling. He heard it and tried to hurry, glancing up to see if she was displeased and of course she was. She has stopped looking at him. Her lips had drawn into a thin stripe and she was frowning intensely.

He realised at that moment that she did not like him.

He threw down his tin with a clatter and flung his arms around her legs, still kneeling.

She reached down and pushed at his head, not hard, just enough to make him understand that she didn't want him holding on to her legs.

'Stop being silly.'

She took him back to his room.

'You must stay here in the afternoons.'

'Can I open the shutters?'

'No. Please don't be difficult.'

'Why can't I open the shutters?' He felt his voice beginning to crack in desperation. He hated the dark room. He hated being on his own over and over again. He couldn't stand it anymore. He imagined having to be in this room again tomorrow and the next day and the next.

'I really want someone to play with,' he pleaded.

'Well, there isn't anybody. Nobody for you, nobody for me.'

It gave her a certain satisfaction, this spoken confirmation of her own position, and saying something that would hurt her son.

'Couldn't you stay for a while, then? I could show you my pictures.' He held out his sketch book.

His mother reached out and flipped it open. She studied his pictures critically. 'None of them look right,' she observed, wondering why it was that he had drawn things so oddly.

He held out his hand towards the pad, meaning to encourage her to stay by explaining each picture. 'They are right,' he insisted. 'I'll show you.'

She put the pad on the table and pushed it away from her.

'I haven't got time,' she said.

'What have you to do?'

She hesitated. What had she to do?

'I must go to the Club,' she said.

'But you never go to the Club.'

'Today is different.'

Now she affected a tone of insouciance. How pathetic she was, having only a seven year old boy to lie to. She saw his eyes piercing her judgementally and with a sickening lurch realised that even he saw through her. She had nothing to do.

181

There was no reason for her to do anything. She might as well stay in a dark room every day, lying on her bed, waiting, waiting, for nothing and no body. That was her life. Why could she not feel what she was meant to feel for this boy?

'Why are you so unpleasant?' she said, angrily. She felt ill with the heat.

If it were not for him, this boy who sat with his hands on his bony knees and his horribly knowing black gaze, there would be no governess, no indigo haired, olive skinned, full breasted woman in the house.

She knew where she would go today, not to the Club, but to the pearl white house on the harbour with views of the Arabian Sea, where the governess went in the afternoons, in her black dress and black gloves, vanilla scented, to meet with… who? A lover? Should the Lebanese woman imported by her husband have a lover? Was it because the governess' dark face was burnished by the sun but hers drained white and dead? What did she do, this silent governess who taught her son to speak to her in language that she, the mother could not understand? Did she remove her black dress and gloves and lie like deep gold on white sheets, did she undo the clasp in her hair and allow it to fall to her shoulders, did she whisper in Arabic, French and English while her lover made love to her amid the sound of the waves and the cries of the apricot sellers outside the shutters? She would go and see.

'You're going to be like him,' said his mother, leaving.

That evening Michael examined his father anxiously to see what he would be like when he was a man. His father, he sensed, was uncomfortable. He sat on the balcony of the drawing room overlooking the courtyard. To his father's left hand was a small table inlaid with mosaic of lapis lazuli. On the table was a tumbler of water, a glass and a bottle of Scotch. From time to time his father drew his eyes from the news paper he was reading and mixed a little of the water into the whisky and sipped at it. This evening was unusual.

Mother had not arrived for dinner. Michael and his father had eaten dinner alone, for the only time he could remember. He had been sent to bed, but could not sleep. He tried his book, Treasure Island, but couldn't concentrate. He listened for a car.

He got up and walked slowly down the spiral stairs in his night clothes, carrying his book. He had an excuse ready for getting up, that there was a word he didn't understand.

He found his father there on the balcony.

'Has she come back?'

Geoffrey Easton looked at him. 'You say she went to the Club?'

'Yes.'

Michael rather hoped that he would not have small, puffy eyes, a curved nose like a bird's beak, and a square, weary mouth. Maybe Mother was wrong. Maybe he would be different to his father. He would not smoke and drink, he vowed, privately. He watched his father's eyes narrow against the heavy swirling blur of blue smoke as he dragged deep satisfaction from the squat Turkish cigarette he held between his fingers. Michael noticed that the first two of his father's fingers on his right hand were stained yellow.

'What exactly did she say?'

Michael did not reply at once. He traced back in his mind the things his mother had said before she left him. He didn't want to tell.

'I can't remember exactly.'

Just then a car appeared and drove up to the house. It was a taxi. Next to Geoffrey Easton's glinting Merc the taxi looked small and vulgar. Mother stepped out. She opened her purse and took out a coin and paid the man and he drove off.

She didn't look up at the balcony. She walked up the steps to the house. Michael pressed himself to the iron railings to see her. Before she disappeared he thought she looked whiter than usual. He realised that his father was next to him, also pressed to the rail. For one second their eyes met.

'Go to bed,' said his father.

Michael remained on the balcony. The sun was a huge blood red ball far away in a turquoise and black lacquered sky.

Michael picked up his book. He had only just started the first chapter and was finding it hard. It wasn't only the complexity of the vocabulary; it was the alien nature of the descriptions. He tried to picture wind blasted cliffs and a foaming sea, but all he could see were green rectangles of grass. He wondered if the prism of coloured light was still visible in the fountain. He decided to go and see.

He opened the door and made his way down to the bottom of the stairs.

As he stood on the bottom step he heard angry voices from above. He never knew what they were saying. There was his father and there was his mother and then there was a change in tempo and then a shout and then a silence and then something landed on the stone with a dull thump.

As he watched a lake of red spread like magma from a volcano.

Two days after his mother's funeral, a muted affair held hastily because of the rotting power of the Arabian heat, and because the fall had split her like a ripe peach, Michael stood on the steps of the tall, thin diplomatic house in the mid day heat with his trunk next to him.

He had asked his father if he could go by boat.

'No. It's quicker to fly,' said Geoffrey Easton, tersely.

'I want see the sea. I think it would be like being in the desert.'

His father was momentarily surprised. He had assumed the boy was like the mother, afraid and resentful of the desert. Perhaps one day he might take him on one of his trips into the Empty Quarter, the only place, except for the pearl white house, that he felt at home. He had a flash of it in his imagination, the incalculable solitude, the enveloping pitch rotunda of star enamelled night. The child was looking up at him and Geoffrey felt a sudden awareness of missed encounter. Too late.

The servants appeared to put the trunk in the car. A hired Englishwoman was to take him to London. She was small and round and uninterested and stood sweating to one side.

'Try to do well,' Geoffrey said.

For a vile moment he thought the boy was going to spout tears. He looked down into the child's face and saw raw panic. He stepped back, putting his hands in his pockets. The Lebanese governess approached him and stood for a second in front of him.

'You are a clever boy,' she said to him in English. 'You will always do well. Only think of the future. Not the past.'

She smelled of vanilla.

Easton ran the taps on the bath. He had been to the kitchen and brought a box of salt to the bathroom. He poured it into his hand and let the grains fall into the rushing water. He dipped his hand in and swirled the water to make the salt dissolve, then added more until the box was empty. He knew that salt cured wounds.

'I've run you a bath.' He stood in the doorway of the bedroom.

She lay like a wounded animal on the bed. The act of love transmuted into an act of pain. That's what I do, he thought. That's who I am.

He watched as she stood up shakily and walked to the bathroom. She stood by the side of the bath. He put his hand under her elbow to steady her. She allowed him this touch. Slowly she got in the hot water.

'I'm sorry,' he said.

'I know.'

He sat down on the edge of the bath. 'Is it all unconditional with you?'

'Adult love is never unconditional.'

He waited, absorbing the implication of her sentence. He had never mentioned love. How could she speak of love now?

'What are your conditions?' he asked.

She didn't reply. The water was stinging her. Blood drifted through the water between her legs. She watched the river pattern.

'Tell me,' he pressed.

She lifted her head and regarded him out of cracked eyes. 'I can't tell you, Easton, what they are.'

'Please, don't call me Easton.'

'Michael.'

'I don't understand.'

'It's part of the scheme of things.'

'What things?' He needed to understand.

'You and me. It was never going to be simple. What you did is part of it. It's part of who you are. If I accept you I accept all of you, but you can't do it again. You can't ever do it again. It's me, Michael. Me.' She touched her chest lightly, leaving her knuckles against her skin.

She realised now that this was a grown up's game. Her notion of love had been stretched, expanded. She saw it differently. It was much bigger and more complicated and more demanding than she had ever thought. It went on forever.

'Does it hurt?' he asked.

'Yes. You hurt me. How does it feel?'

'The truth?'

'What else?'

'It's not what I did. It's the fact that you're still here.'

A grown up's game. A child's game.

After she left Easton rifled through the stock of basic tools he kept in the cupboard under the stairs. He selected a heavy iron chisel and went into the garden via the kitchen. He had a towel on one hand, and he held this against the glass in the French window, and swung the chisel. To his surprise the glass cracked, but didn't break. He swung the chisel again, harder this time, and the glass splintered inwards, leaving a jagged hole. Shards of glass skittered over the smooth tiled floor, under the table, under the fridge.

He looked down at the York stone beneath his feet. The weather was dry. You wouldn't expect there to be feet marks.

Then he went in and called the police to report a break. They told him someone would come round and investigate, but maybe in about three hours.

Easton went upstairs, took off his clothes and had a shower. As he did so he thought of Alice. At one point he could almost feel the touch of her mouth on his.

After midnight a marked police car purred up to the gate. Two blue uniformed officers, their walkie-talkies continuously crackling, viewed the hole in his window, and looked with ineffable boredom at the glass on the floor.

'This was the point of entry, then.'

'Yes,' He had been prepared for difficult questions. This was not one of them

'Do you know what was taken?'

He showed them into the living room. 'Some silver. Valuable in the right market.'

'And they threatened you?'

'He. There was only one. I only saw one. Yes. With a knife. A big serrated thing.'

The officers exchanged significant glances. Perhaps it was a crime almost worth bothering with. One of the officers, a fattish, middle aged man, wrote in his notebook.

'Could you give a description?'

Easton took them into the hall and picked up a sheet of paper from the hall table.

The two officers surveyed it together. They were like a comedy duo, minus the humour.

'This you, sir?'

'It's him. The thief.'

'I mean, did you draw it?'

'Yes.'

The officers converged over the sheet again. Easton gave them plenty of time. He could be patient when he needed to be.

'You an artist?'

'No. I do a bit of drawing, though.'

'It's good,' said the officer. The other one nodded agreement. 'It's sort of like he's got his expression.'

'He took cash, too. Eighty pounds, which was all I had.'

Easton had gone to the cash point during lunchtime and taken out one hundred, in case they checked. But no one was going to be checking, he realised. That would amount to an investigation.

'Where was the cash? Did you have it on you?'

Easton saw immediately the implications of this question. If there was only one thief then he couldn't have gone upstairs to get the money and hold Easton at knifepoint downstairs.

'It was in my jacket pocket, here.' He gestured at the carved chair in the hall.

The officers gazed around in disinterest.

'Will you be wanting victim counselling, do you think? Only, you'll get a letter about it.'

'No.'

'No. I didn't think so. Right. Well. Anyway. We'll send someone round to dust in the morning. I'm sorry to say,' the officer adopted a final tone of institutional apology, 'That you are statistically unlikely to get your stolen items back. They'll have been sold for what ever he can get and he'll have a load of crack inside him with the proceeds.'

The officer raised his hands palm upwards and shrugged in resignation at the state of the world.

Chapter Eighteen

Tommy hovered around outside the police station. He'd had to go all over to find Chas; Highgate, Archway, Willesden, Kilburn and he hadn't had time to get a hit. The weather was not as cold as Tommy's shivering warranted. He was in a meltdown of panic. He had been in and asked to see Chas and the plod on the desk had more or less told him to fuck off. After the police had picked Chas up Tommy stared open mouthed after the police car on the pavement. He was alone. He had no money, no place to sleep, no idea what to do or where to go. He suddenly needed a crap, but he didn't even have access to a toilet.

He walked to the police station in the area, asking strangers for directions. They didn't want to talk to him and backed off, even though or perhaps because he smiled. The desk sergeant said no one answering Chas description had been brought in. They gave him the addresses of other stations. Tommy walked it. He had no money on him at all. He didn't know whether to try going to the Pig and getting a hit (how without money?) or to persevere with looking for Chas. He chose the latter. Finally they told him they'd got Chas at Kilburn. The duty officer sat behind reinforced glass. Tommy was sweating profusely. It felt as if he has the worst flu in the world. His joints ached. He had a pain in his stomach and he knew that sooner or later he was going to crap all over the place.

He asked if he could see Chas. Confronted by officialdom he used the real name.

'Please can I see Charles Demetriou?'

It was the same officer he had spoken to an hour before.

'I can't talk to you about this. I told you, only family.'

'I'm his brother.'

The officer looked at the skinny blue-eyed fair haired young man in front of him. 'You Greek, then?' he asked, sarcastically.

'All right. I'm not his brother. He hasn't got any family. I'm his friend.'

'Oh, yes?' The officer looked at Tommy with distaste. 'Tuh, all right. He's put in a call to the duty solicitor. After he comes we'll know what we're going to do with your friend.'

'When will that be?'

'Not on your timescale, son.' The officer shook his head. What a mess. He might have been a nice looking kid once. The officer noticed Tommy's accent marked him out as middle class at least. And here he was in a police station waiting all cracked up for some gay boy bit of rough to come out of the cells. The officer, who had his own kids, was disgusted with the family.

'Now go away.'

Tommy stood at the bottom of the station steps. He didn't know which way to turn. He had to get a fix, make all this shit go away. He had no money. He sat down outside the station and put down his hat and waited. Nothing happened. He put his face in his hands. A nun passed by. She said, 'There's a hostel over by West Hampstead,' and she gave him directions and two pounds. She had a sad old face, with very white lips and beautiful blue eyes.

Tommy made his way to the Pig, a squat one storey purple brick building with tiny grimy mottled windows covered in chicken wire. It was the kind of pub no normal person would ever go to for a drink, a stinking, festering hole with thin, sticky black carpets, ripped plastic banquettes, toilets foetid with the stench of diarrhoea and fresh wet vomit. The man who ran it stood behind the bar. His name, Dennis Carroll, was inscribed over the door. Dennis had done six years for beating a man to death with an iron chisel. But now he was out and making a living out of the Pig and Whistle. He watched his clientele carefully, in between pulling pints. He kept a muscular black and tan dog behind the bar with him. Dennis took a cut from the pimps and drug dealers that operated from his pub.

Tommy pushed open the door. He stepped in but had to wait a second for his eyes to adjust to the dark. The interior of the Pig was ill lit with fly blown strip lights, one of them stuttering fitfully, another simply dead. Only one of the strips was fully operational. It was lunchtime but no food was served at the Pig.

Across the bar Tommy saw faces that were familiar, slouched in corners or leaning against the fake mahogany, men with their heels resting on a brass runner attached at the base to the wood. At one of the tables sat a man who sold heroin. Tommy had been with Chas when he had made transactions with this man. He was short, fat and broad shouldered. He wore a leather car jacket, with a thick belt hanging loose. His shape was almost simian, and his calculating eyes held a monkey's alertness. He sat with his legs wide open under the table, his genitalia bulging in tight, black flared trousers. Tommy went over and stood in front of his table.

'Got a wrap?' He used the words he had heard Chas use. It was a formula he had seen working.

'Shut up and sit down, tosser.'

Tommy slid in confusion onto the seat.

'Not that fucking close. Fucking hell!' The dealer shifted. 'Twenty,' he said, looking the other way.

Tommy rubbed his hands over the thigh of his jeans.

'Can I give it you tomorrow?'

The fat dealer turned and fixed Tommy with a stare of incredulity. 'Are you joking or what? Fuck off,' he said, with ineffable bile. Tommy remained where he was, his teeth smiling, his eyes staring in bewildered desperation.

'Go on. Fuck off.'

Tommy stood up and walked to the bar. All his physical symptoms became one congregated mass of anguish. He had to run to the men's where his bowels opened and liquid poured out of him endlessly. The cramps in his stomach were intense but worse, much worse was the utter crushing fear and despair, the psychological opposite extreme of the

191

fantastic rush of well being and sortedness you got on the end of a needle. Tommy pulled up his jeans. He couldn't do the button properly because his hands were shaking so much. He went out into the pub and stood there with tears streaming down his face.

He felt a hand on his elbow. There was a tall, thin, raddled man, in grey slacks a little too short for his spidery legs. His face was badly pocked with acne scars and a clump of brillo pad passed for hair. He wore his shirt open and had a silver chain around his neck. He propelled Tommy into the corridor.

'Twenty,' he said, coming close with his mouth. Tommy caught sight and breath of yellow stained protruding teeth. A slick of saliva hung between the corners of his lips, shining like a spider's thread. He led Tommy to the toilets and into a cubicle.

Afterwards he put twenty quid into Tommy's hand. Tommy went to the dealer, still sitting at the table.

'Got some cash now?' said the dealer with brutal ridicule, having watched it all. Tommy bought his wrap.

Chapter Nineteen

This is a two way mirror. The men on the other side cannot see you.'

Easton stood flanked by two policemen in an airless cell. One of the policemen stank of sweat. An old fashioned radiator pumped out too much heat. Easton still wore his overcoat, not having been invited to remove it.

He faced a rectangular window. The glass was smeared with grease marks. The adjoining room was thus far empty. Easton noted seven yellow dots on the floor in the room. A door opened and a line of men filed in. The two officers glanced at Easton. Most witnesses showed signs of fear and anxiety at this point. Their senses told them that if they could see they could be seen.

The men stood each one on his yellow dot. The eyes, innocent and guilty, stared at reflections in the mirror, wondering if they were going to be selected. Their senses told them that they were guiltless but their twisting guts told otherwise. They all had guilt on their faces.

They stared in silence, dark haired, black eyed, olive skinned silence. Mediterranean in origin, they stood like a row of identical paper men cut from a single folded sheet. Above each man was a number.

Easton made a point of examining them all. He resisted the deep compulsion to study in particular every detail of the man standing under the number four. Number four was a work of art hung on a bare wall, a sucked out bone stick, hollow, sick, hateful.

Easton became conscious of the acceleration of his heartbeat. With conscious control and deceit he pretended to look carefully along the line.

'Take your time,' steadied the sweating policeman and moved conspiratorially closer, bringing with him his stale malodour.

Easton shook his head, left to right, a single swing of surrender.

'I can't be sure.'

'Look at each one in turn. I know it's hot.'

Easton felt the tickle of salt sweat on his forehead. He had spent a lot of time and energy looking for number four.

'Try and concentrate, sir.' There was an edge of impatience in the voice.

Easton decided. He was not going to hand over Number Four. He was going to keep him for his own purpose. It was not merely a question of punishment, or vengeance. It was more complicated than that.

Number Four bore the marks of his adopted way of life, the slick of wet on the upper lip, savage boils on the side of his cheek.

'I can't say which one. They all look the same.' What a lie. He told it with his eyes firmly fixed on the policeman.

'But your drawing?'

'I'm sorry. I can't be sure. I couldn't give evidence on it.'

Easton sensed the policeman's alteration in attitude, a cooling, a withdrawal, even suspicion. Yet another fucking waste of police time.

Out in the cold Easton kept walking. He sucked down air as if he had been held under sewage water. He entered a bar, slick and modern, the kind of place that had a happy hour, the kind of place he loathed. Large imitation leather sofas were grouped around low wooden tables. On one wall was a wide screen TV soundlessly showing gyrating women with swollen lips teasing bulb headed microphones.

Easton positioned himself so that he could see the entrance to the police station. He had to sit right at the bar on a high stool. He ordered tea. For an hour he waited, killing time and listening to the inane conversation of the barmaid as she spoke endlessly on her mobile. Outside on the road traffic cruised by in a river of orange headlights.

Finally he saw what he had been waiting for.

He swung through the glass door of the bar. It was raining. He pulled up the collar on his coat and walked quickly after Number Four. Once he reached a certain level of proximity he held back, slowed down and followed on the same side of the pavement.

Now he had the chance to absorb some of the detail he had been denied in the identification forum.

Number Four moved with rapid, covert, hunched watchfulness. How long had he been in custody? Two weeks? Easton knew from conversations manipulated with Alice that drugs were more easily accessible in prison than on the outside. Still, he assumed Number Four would be looking for a hit as a priority.

Easton came alongside. Number Four turned and pulled up short, first with an expression of alarm, turning quickly to aggression. Easton noticed how aggressive the young man was, how he was always aggressive. It made him really want to destroy Number Four. He hoped it didn't show too nakedly. It wasn't because he was upset by aggression, psychologically speaking. But he realised that aggression was frightening for the weak, the passive, the undefended. He hated Number Four.

'I want to talk to you.' Easton tried to keep his voice clear and level, but not too level. Some degree of tremor might reasonably be expected, in the circumstances.

'Fuck you.'

'Need money?'

Easton placed his hand suggestively in his breast pocket, and waited. He watched with a pleasure that surprised him, the agonising struggle of the emotions flailing in Chas' head as displayed on Chas' face. Easton could afford to wait. He knew what the outcome was going to be. Chas was a one line thinker at this moment. He was patently, pathetically powerless against the drive for smack. Easton had read that the craving for the drug was a whole body and mind pain. He had asked Alice to explain the desire. She said there was no way you could understand it unless you had experienced it, and she said, it would be impossible for Easton to imagine because Easton had no parallels. He had never been addicted. He had never craved anything. To this he had not

195

replied. She said there was no love like the love of a heroin addict for his drug; it swamped everything. She asked him to imagine choosing between his child and anything else.

'All those parents in your court. If they gave up using they could get their kids. But they carry on. They choose the drug. That's how powerful it is.'

Easton knew that parents chose against their children for many reasons, but she had no children, she had no parallels. Nothing was ever simple or true or easy, and love did not exist. He held his own view tightly closed while he opened hers.

'I've got the car, just down here.' He gestured before Chas's face. He was going to prove the non-existence of love.

Chas followed him without speaking. He felt like shit. He trembled and shook. He didn't care what Easton wanted as long as he gave him money for smack. He just wanted to close the distance between him and a wrap. He'd been able to get it in prison, but not in the police station cell, where he'd been all day. Without it he wanted to be dead. He was feeling the slide worse than before.

Easton's car was parked a little way along. He unlocked it with a fob pointed in its general direction. The locking system gave two peeps of obedience. Chas tried not to look at his prospective benefactor, but he couldn't help it. This was the man who would give him the means to his end. As such he was hypnotic. Chas forgot who and what else he was. There would be time for that afterwards. He cast a furtive glance Easton's way. There was no denying the man's purpose.

They got in the car. It was the kind of car Chas hadn't been in before, except to suck someone off for money.

Which reminded him of the job in hand.

Easton had commenced driving.

'Where shall we go?' asked Easton, turning to him, as if they were out for some Sunday afternoon drive with granny.

'Harlesden, yeah.'

Harlesden was where Easton wanted to go. Yes, Harlesden sounded perfect.

They drove in silence, apart from the sound of loose snot rattling around in Chas nasal passages, runny as sea water. He sniffed repeatedly.

'There are some tissues in the glove compartment,' observed Easton, pleasantly. Chas didn't feel any fear. He didn't feel anything other than that he needed heroin. His only terror was that Easton was taking him for a ride, metaphorically rather than physically. The car seemed to move with tortuous slowness through the traffic. Chas wrapped his arms around himself tightly.

'Can you go a bit faster,' he demanded, suspicious that the ride was taking longer than it ought to.

'Bad traffic.' Again there was that light threatening pleasantness of tone.

Easton turned off into a side street and pulled over.

'What the fuck are you doing?'

'I want to talk.'

'I want to score. I mean it.' Chas narrowed his eyes. He wouldn't have cared if he had to break this bloke's head. He would have liked to have done so. That night when he had him on the floor in his house he should have kicked his head like a football. He deserved it. But he realised he was in bad shape and was more likely to get his own head broken.

'I want you to do something for me.'

Chas stared. It took him back, that phrase. And coming from this mouth it seemed more than especially bad. It was only the promise of heroin that held him from lashing out. He would do it, do anything. Even this. He knew it was designed to pay him back.

He reached out towards Easton's crotch and put his hand on it.

'No.' Easton grabbed him by the wrist. 'That's not what I want.'

'What do you want, for fuck's sake?'

They were sitting in a run down residential road where the houses had no front gardens and a few kids played on the street. One of the kids heard Chas shout and looked round.

'I want you to promise never to see Tommy again.'

'No problem. I promise. That it? You're a fucking bastard, you are. Give me the money.'

Easton took out a bank card.

'This is a cash point card. The code is 2878. I've got five hundred in this account. I'll put five hundred in every week but you've got to stay away, not speak to him, not go near him, not contact him in any way, not go the places he goes. If you do see him and he asks you, say you don't want to be with him anymore. Tell him to fuck off. You know how to say that, don't you?'

'Yes. I want cash now.'

'No.'

Tears of anger and frustration dropped from Chas eyes and rolled down his cheeks.

'He said you were a fucking bastard, a cunt. You are.'

I'll drive you where you want to go.'

'Then what?' Chas was screaming at him.

'Then I'll pay.'

Under Chas' direction they drove to an estate of maisonettes. Already Chas was giving Easton what he was buying, his distance from Tommy, so he avoided The Pig. The dwellings formed a concrete ziggurat, one above the other. Chas ran up the stairs. Easton followed. Chas was standing outside a dirty red front door. He saw Easton following and knocked urgently. A man appeared, dressed in jeans and a denim jacket and with a purple bandana tied around his head. He had a straggly moustache and long dry hair wisping out from under the bandana. He looked at Chas and he looked at Easton, chewing his own hair with an air of rueful preoccupation.

'Who's this? You don't bring anyone I don't know to the door.'

'He's a friend. He pays. He'll pay. He's got money,' responded Chas with persuasive eager pleading.

The dealer assessed Easton. It wasn't always the ones you expected. He'd got plenty of middle class professionals on his books. They made good clients, had an investment in keeping their mouths shut. The only thing was they squealed easily if they got caught.

Inside Chas led the way to a room with the curtains drawn. In the dimness Easton made out the figure of a woman slumped against the sofa, a crumpled white faced doll.

Chas stood expectantly. Easton gave him twenty pounds.

He saw the pursed lips of the man in the bandana. 'Got any more?'

Easton produced another twenty from his wallet and handed it over.

The dealer handed a little slip of silver wrap to Chas.

'Want any? Best there is,' offered the dealer.

Easton shook his head.

'What's in it for you? Just the ride?' The dealer went 'heh heh' and walked away to another part of the flat.

Easton watched Chas cook up and fill a syringe with transparent liquid. He watched as Chas, who now seemed oblivious to his presence, undid his trousers and pulled them down. He watched Chas open up his white thighs and press the point of the needle into the crease of his groin, he watched the needle enter, a little ruby drop appearing. He watched Chas sag, and the syringe drop from his fingers, hanging against the side of his thigh. He heard Chas' rush exhale. It lasted a few minutes. Easton knelt down to him. He placed the cash point card in Chas fingers and then searched in Chas' pockets. He drew out what he was looking for and kept it in his hand. It defied and confirmed expectation. Chas rolled his head and opened distant eyes.

'If you see him I'll know. I'll pull the account and I'll tell the police I've remembered your face.'

Chas laughed, high and happy.

'You stupid cunt,' he said. 'He needs me. All right.'

Easton looked down at the needle still in Chas vein then reached down and delicately pulled it out. 'You don't look all right to me.' He held Chas gaze in unabashed scrutiny.

'You know what he'll do to get a score? What I've been doing. Taking it in the arse. Sucking dicks. Everything. I'm used to it. Tommy's not rent, but he will be if he goes on his own. He'll do it in the street, in the pub toilets. That's what he'll have to do. Is that what you want? You want to see the kind of thing he has to do? He's such a beautiful boy. Don't you understand? I've been doing it for both of us. Rent, robbery, anything. He's such a beautiful boy.' The happiness slid away like a fish in the sea.

Chas closed his eyes. When he opened them again Easton was gone. The little plastic friend was in his fingers.

Easton replaced the photograph into a silver frame and put it on the table in his drawing room. The picture had become bent and had a crease over it running like a scar across the middle of the face.

It had been taken while Tommy was at nursery. He was three and smiling. His hair had not recently been cut and fell in blonde strands over his forehead. His eyebrows were blonde too, so blonde that they were nearly transparent, just tiny faint demarcations. He had a baby tooth missing at the front and a few freckles sprayed over the bridge of the nose. He was looking straight to camera, straight at Easton now, with an expression of trust. He had on a blue T shirt and his shoulders seemed small and fragile. He had always had an air of being fragile, of needing to be treated kindly. The smile on his face was an offer, the offer that all children make, to be their best and to love infinitely if only you will like them and love them back.

Chas used his first five hundred in the first week, and realised he was going to need more. These last few days the only way he could cope was by being shot all the time. He went to Easton's house and found he couldn't get in unless he climbed over a big iron gate that had been unlocked before but was now chained. He hung around until late but Easton failed to return. Chas could only see the side of the house. There was one window high up in the wall but that was dark. Chas went down to the off licence and bought a bottle of cider and asked for a piece of paper and the loan of a pencil and wrote a note. He walked back up the hill and put the piece of paper, folded, through the bars of the gate and weighed it down with a stone. Then he wandered over to the Heath and sat on a bench, where he opened the cider bottle and began to take big swigs. He was giving a bloke in Kilburn a hundred a week for a room. He could go to the cashpoint and draw out money and go to the dealer and score without having to do all the stuff in between. He was thinking he could buy a stash and deal it himself. This newfound wealth opened up possibilities. If he could get a client base he could get a flat. He could sell in the clubs, not H necessarily, but E and tabs. It was a good living. Then, when he was established he would go and find Tom.

Since his release from prison ten days had passed and he been held for two weeks prior to release. This meant Tommy had been alone for nearly a month on the street. Chas put his head in his hands. He knew what this meant. He had avoided all the old places, especially the Pig and as time went on the thought of seeing what had happened to Tommy became more and more unbearable. There was only one way of obliterating the guilt. He threw away the bottle and made his way towards the nearest score.

Easton noticed the white soggy paper as he opened his gate to leave the house the next morning. It had rained in the night. He picked it up and peered at the smudgy lettering.

'If you want me to leave him yourll have to put more than five hundred in, I cant live on it. Its very difacult. If you want to find him try the pig and wisle pub. He'll be rent by now.'

Easton sat in his car watching the Pig and Whistle Public House. He saw the comings and goings and the people that went in. There were men and a few women. The women looked like tarts. The tart he had fucked came back into his mind. He saw for a few seconds a perfection of symmetry, looping around like a skein of silk, tying everything together. Then he remembered that there was no symmetry in life. Symmetry implied meaning and design and there was none. It was a peccadillo of the human condition to keep locating pattern in the random, in an attempt to construct meaning. Easton believed that Tommy could only be saved if he wanted to be saved. He had to want it and in order to want it he had to come to the end of the road, to come face to face with annihilation. He had to have a tiny little spark of self-preservation left. Easton wondered, it was so long since he had seen the boy, if Tommy had that spark or whether it had been extinguished by self- loathing. Easton tried to remember Tommy, but all he remembered was the split second that he himself had stopped crying. That was his resistance to annihilation. Some people allow themselves to be annihilated, others fight all the way. Some only start to resist when they are reduced almost to nothing at all, a distant shadow disappearing into a long dark well. Easton thought, it's mainly the decent people that succumb. But he wasn't going to let Tommy go.

He watched for a long time. Eventually he decided it was safe to go inside.

There was a man behind the bar who had the face of a Dicken's villain. He looked up immediately with suspicion when Easton entered, watching his movements. The landlord made a gesture imperceptible to humans and Easton saw an evil looking black and tan dog waddle out from around the bar and stand threateningly poised, its pink silver tongue hanging out across sharp teeth. Easton glanced at it impassively.

He ignored the dog and began to penetrate the thick smoky hostility of the interior. As he passed the tables he looked at the people and they stared back. There was a man fat as a grub sitting at a table on his own. He stared at Easton with a smile curled at his lips and malevolence in his eyes. His white lardy hands lay splayed out on the brown veneer.

Easton took in a long glance. This was his child's life. He went to the toilets and stood holding open the door of one of the cubicles, staring in at the foulness.

His heart was gripped by an inexpressible anger. For a moment he considered going into the main room of the pub and slaughtering the inhabitants. He fantasised a scene of blood, of gaping red throats and burning. He felt the white balanced weight of his razor light in his hand. But he knew that that was not what he would do. The world was much more difficult than that. Horrors cannot just be burned away. They have to be lived with, ignored, distanced, suppressed, rationalised; whatever method was best.

Instead of killing everyone he went outside, got into his car and drove home.

Tommy saw a bag on the back seat of a car. He was standing in a street near a big council block. There was no one around. The flats were a good distance away. Tommy had never broken a car window before. It occurred to him now, standing there, that car windows were thick and resilient. He had nothing but his own hands and he knew he wouldn't be able to break it like that. He walked off along the pavement. He hadn't gone far and he saw a discarded cider bottle in the gutter. It was brown and clear. Tommy picked it up and went back to the car. He drew back his arm, then hesitated. He perceived that glass would shatter everywhere and he would get cut. He hardly really cared, but then he stopped and took off his hat and held it over the side of his cheek before hitting the base of the bottle against the rear window of the car. He heard a huge crash and when he looked the bottle was just a serrated rim in his hand and the window was a smashed warped network of minute intricate cracks. Tommy pressed his hand on the shattered window and it crunched like an ice layer and then fell inwards. He put his arm in and hoiked out the bag.

Two men came out of the flats at a run. Tommy ran. His trainers pounded down the pavement. He lost the track of where he was going, before he realised he was making for the pub. He went down the side of some garages, which is where one of the two men caught him. Tommy was thin and debilitated. He hadn't actually eaten for over three days, and before that had only occasional handouts. He was spending his money on the fat dealer. He wasn't running fast enough.

The two men were delighted to have caught up with Tommy. They were big and fed on burgers and kebabs and had strong views on other people's criminal activities. They kicked him around with the viciousness of school yard bullies towards a flightless pigeon. They actually derived quite a lot of pleasure from it, but towards the end a little bit of latent guilt seeped in when they saw what they had done. They walked off, not running, because running would imply that they had done something wrong or shameful and neither man was prepared to admit that. They crushed the pricking of remorse and didn't talk about it for a while, and when they did the incident had been reborn as a tale of righteous bravura, altered for the consumption of their own consciences and the sensibilities of the pub.

Tommy's body lay under a row of rubber council bins endorsed with the logo of the London Borough of Camden. Some hours later an African man, walking to his garage, discovered the body and called an ambulance. The man knelt down softly. He was a refugee from the Congo. He kept on saying, 'Oh my God, Oh my God,' over and over in a voice full and deep with bafflement. Had he come so far to witness this?

Chapter Twenty

Toby held the boy's arm in his hand. It was thin and blackened and had traces of needle marks under the bruising. 'Has he said anything?' he asked the nurse.

'Nothing.'

A low hampered growl emerged from the mouth. Toby saw the bloody mass of the gums. It looked as if some of the teeth had been pushed up into the nasal passage. The boy kept moaning. Toby delivered an anaesthetic intravenously.

'Bugger,' he breathed in exasperation. 'Veins collapsed.' He finally found a spare space in the groin. The boy was naked on the trolley under a white sheet. Spatters of red dotted the whiteness. Toby examined him and exhaled slowly, talking softly with each new discovery. 'Broken ribs, broken shoulder, dislocated kneecap, broken nose, crushed fingers. At least he won't be injecting for a few weeks. Better scan for internal ruptures. And he'll be going into withdrawal. Great.'

He looked at his watch. Twenty minutes to the end of his shift. Casualty was heaving. Toby knew that if he left now the kid would lie on the trolley for another three hours, unattended.

The mouth with its swollen purple contused lips was moving and a sound was coming out, like a tortured animal.

'What's he saying?'

Toby looked quizzically at the nurse, who made a moue of incomprehension.

'Better give him a local on the mouth, Nurse. I'll try and get the teeth out of his nose first. I'm just going to call home and say I'll be late. Again.'

Toby took the teeth out using a pair of surgical tweezers. Strictly speaking he ought to have done it in the Theatre, but there were no theatres available. Then he sent the boy for a scan. Miraculously there was no internal damage.

'It would be nice if he could be washed,' said Toby to a nurse. The kid had crapped himself profusely and stank.

Toby came back half an hour later and no one had washed the patient. This was the sort of thing that drove Toby wild. Swearing he got a silver dish of hot water and a cloth and cleaned the boy. As he did so the kid came to. Toby saw the boy's blue eyes staring at him.

Toby leaned him onto his back and smiled. 'Hello,' he said. My name's Dr Finch. You've had a bit of an accident. Is there anyone we can contact? Your parents? A friend?'

He wondered if the boy had understood. His eyes looked puzzled, misty and distant. It was hard to tell how old he was, anything between fifteen and twenty. The sound he was making was indecipherable. Toby leaned low and bent his ear to the blood stitched mouth.

Easton and Alice knelt on the bed, him inside her. He held her, naked, with his hands on her arms and moved his lips on her bare skin. He watched her in the mirror, being fucked by him. He touched the contour of her breasts, brushed the nipple with his thumb. He wanted to watch her come. He had been moving, slowly, for a long time and now she was ready. She lifted her face and kissed his throat, and although he wanted to see her he dropped his mouth to hers, keeping himself controlled until the final seconds, when she started to tighten around him, and he felt the quickening and strengthening of the pulsation inside her. Only when he felt those pulses did he lose himself completely, relinquishing to her. He allowed her to see him coming, at the moment in time when he was most exposed. They had no past, no future, and so the moment was all.

They lay on the bed. 'Don't you think it's strange,' she mused aloud, 'that even when a person is most exposed they still have so much hidden?'

He reflected. There were parts of himself that he had discovered still alive only through her.

'I'm honest with you,' he said.

'No one's completely honest.'

206

Easton acknowledged this. 'As honest as I can be. I'm not an honest man.'

'You're defended. Isolated in your fortress, guarding your inner self and all the time it prowls and wants to escape. It's sad and lonely.'

'Everyone is sad and lonely.' He remembered Clive and Mrs Bird. His last statement wasn't true. How hard it was to hit the truth. It was as if no such thing existed.

In the bathroom, Easton filled the sink with water and rubbed shaving cream across the stubble of his jaw.

'Why do you use that?' asked Alice, as she looked at the old fashioned cut throat razor he held between his fingers. Its handle was cold clear Mother of Pearl, its blade straight and bright.

She liked to watch the mysterious ritual of his shaving. She found it intensely intimate.

'It gives a clean shave.' Then, because he wanted to tell her the truth, 'It belonged to my father.'

'Can I do it?'

He turned, holding the razor up, so that its blade shone. 'Have you ever used one of these?'

'I've used a scalpel.'

He found this unpersuasive and wondered if she could see why.

He acquiesced. He sat down on the straight back chair in the bathroom and passed the razor to her.

'It's very sharp,' he said.

She stood behind him and weighed the razor in her fingers. It was heavy, and she had to experiment to balance it. She laid the blade flat against his cheek. He tilted his chin upwards and sideways. The edge of the blade scraped his skin and the perfect white of the shaving cream turned speckled grey. She drew the razor once more over his face, pleased with the pink river of fresh skin revealed below the cream. She shaved the right side of his face and then began the left. This was more difficult. He had to rest his head on her breast and she had to lean over him. She applied the blade in small even

207

drags. She lifted his chin and exposed his throat. She felt his pulse under her thumb and the stretch of the windpipe and she was struck by the miracle of the human body. She had felt the same awe in the surgical part of her training when she had seen during operations the pulsating jellified red interiors of the lungs and heart and gut. And this led to the even more extraordinary miracle of the human mind, contained somewhere in the brain, invisible, intangible, but capable of being shaped, moulded, distorted, damaged, broken and crushed, as fragile as the most delicate of the organs and a million times more inaccessible and complex.

The buzz of her mobile made her jump. She heard his sudden intake of breath and looked down. She had cut him. A bright red slit spread into the whiteness of the shaving foam.

Alice could see it was Toby calling from the number coming up. She picked it up and moved away from Easton, to the other side of the room, watching him as he dabbed a towel over his throat, absorbing the smears of blood.

'Easton's number? Why do you want it?'

Swing doors closed and opened, flipped out and closed again, like the curtain in a crematorium.

Easton went up to the desk in the casualty department. No one could tell him anything. The woman behind the desk asked him to take a seat. After half an hour he approached the desk again. He asked for Dr Finch. It was a different woman. 'He's gone off shift.'

'My son has been brought in.'

'Name?'

'Thomas Easton, but they may not have him listed by name. He's seventeen, blonde. He's a drug addict.'

Easton felt the desire to drop his voice. There were people all around him. No one looked in the slightest interested. There was no sense of privacy.

'There's no one of that name on the record.'

'They didn't know his name when he was brought in.'

The woman looked defeated.

'Well, if they don't know his name…and Dr Finch has gone off shift.' She stopped, helplessly. 'Take a seat. I'll check the record. Mean while could you complete this form?' She handed him a form attached to a clipboard.

Easton sat in his plastic orange chair in the lines of plastic orange chairs. The unit was overflowing with the ill and those who waited with them. Occasionally a name was called and a patient shuffled forward, but the sum total of those waiting only increased.

Easton picked up the pen attached by a length of white string to the clipboard. He began to complete the form. It was the first time he had completed a form about his son. Name? Thomas Adrian Halliwell Easton. Address? Easton put in his own address. Religion? None. Next of kin? There was a cube of blank white to be filled. Easton wrote in his own name. Michael Easton. There was a list of titles to complete. He crossed them all out and where it said 'other' wrote 'Sir.' Occupation? Judge. Relationship to patient? Father. Occupation of patient? Blank. Allergies? Easton tried to think. Had his son any allergies? He couldn't concentrate. He looked over to the reception desk. The woman he had spoken to was conversing with resentful reluctance with an Asian man remonstrating and pointing to a lady in a sari who was sitting bowed, her head deep in her hands, very grey and drawn.

Any previous medical treatment? Tommy must have had some medical treatment, but Easton had no idea what. Inoculations? He passed over the questions one by one, like in the exams that feature in nightmares where one has done no revision and the subject is completely strange. He handed in the form and continued to wait. More sick were brought in, some by relatives or friends, some by ambulance men, some walking, some groaning on stretchers.

'Sir Michael Easton?'

Easton looked up at a stocky robust balding man in a suit under a white coat. The consultant, Mr James Harvey had

209

seen the name on the admission form and come out immediately, appalled that a High Court Judge had been left waiting for two hours. It wasn't a question of snobbery. It was a multiple of considerations. First, the well to do are more demanding and more likely to cause an effective fuss if they are ignored, second, they sue, third they have the potential to become private clients, and fourth they are people like us- our own, we know them and so they matter more.

Mr Harvey led Easton rapidly down a long corridor and to a small consulting room.

'Please, take a seat. I'm so sorry about the wait.'

Easton sat. He was finding it difficult to breath. He anticipated being told his son was dead. The doctor was thinking of his own two teenagers. There but for the Grace of God.

He lifted the admission form and checked the name. 'Thomas was brought in with multiple injuries.'

Easton was confused. He had formed the conviction that Tommy had taken an overdose.

'We'll have to amputate three of his fingers. He has mouth injuries, but the ENT specialist hasn't been able to see him yet. The casualty registrar took out some teeth from his nose, but there's a lot more to do in there, gums split. Plus broken ribs, dislocated kneecap…'

'Wait- what happened to him?'

'We don't know. Casualty Registrar thought he'd been attacked or been in a fight. Doesn't look as if it was a car accident. The police are involved. Also, as you probably know, he's a heroin addict. So he's in the process of withdrawing now, too. Altogether, not a well boy. And,' the doctor paused. He looked at Easton with pity. James Harvey sensed that this was a man who was able to manage bad news. 'I'm afraid it appears that he might have been sexually assaulted quite recently.'

Easton stood up and turned his back. On the wall there was an outline of the human heart, the parts labelled.

'Can I see him?'

'Of course. I understand he's still under sedation. It might be helpful if you could provide a medical history, especially in respect of his drug use. Do you know how long he's been using?' Harvey watched the broad back. He tried to keep his tone brusque, matter of fact.

Easton sat down again. He felt a growing pressure around his temples.

'He was expelled from school for using cannabis.'

'How old?'

'We sent him when he was seven.'

'I mean, when he was expelled?'

'Fourteen.'

The way in which he had found out that his son had been expelled from school was when his standing order for the fees wasn't collected out of his account. He had Clive ring the school to sort it out. Clive said to him 'School wants a word, sir.' The bursar had suggested in haughty disapproval that perhaps the boy's father might like to ring personally, to find out what was happening in his son's life.

The doctor waited for more. 'The mother and I are divorced.' He remembered having to drive to Judith's house, because she wouldn't answer his calls about Tommy. She had married a wine importer called Daniel Sand, and had no more children. Sand had a house in Richmond and a minor chateau in Burgundy, where he and Judith spent a lot of time.

Sand had never met Easton and had never had any interest in hearing about him from Judith. He had been married twice before and was sick of tiresome stories of divorce. He and Judith were extremely emotionally greedy. They fed on each other and complimented each other's dramas; one day he would be peevish and hysterical, the next day they would swap roles, reaching a state of selfish contentment. Sand was astonished and resentful to find a former husband banging on his door. His affected display of pique was brutally ignored. Ordinarily Sand would have enjoyed participating in a

211

dramatic set to, but the former husband was really frightening. For a few minutes Sand listened horrified to the voices from the living room. This was beyond drama. Judith was immediately at fever pitch, but all Sand could hear in response was cold, to the point, contemptuous anger. Judith was beautiful, but Sand left her to fight her own battle. The whole thing anyway was about a boy he frankly didn't like. There was no reason to get involved and every reason to let the parents sort it out between the two of them. He hoped Tommy would go and live with this father of his. He privately doubted it would happen that way. Judith would never let go of him to Easton.

Easton relocated the track of his narrative. 'He started at a college in Central London. The divorce was acrimonious. Tommy didn't really want to see me.' The statement held a certain confined truth. You could do that with fact, Easton knew. If a witness had attempted to lie like this in his court he would have been outraged, not at the dishonesty but at the assumption of his stupidity. But the doctor showed no interest in Easton's lie and it somehow upset him that he wasn't challenged.

'We'll have to keep him a few weeks at least.'

'After that?'

'He'll need looking after. And I suppose it'll depend on Thomas. He may want to continue doing what he's doing.' The doctor paused to allow reaction, but there was none. Easton only waited, presumably for the completion of the list of eventualities. The doctor was beginning to feel his empathy with this man drain away as if a plug had been removed from a sink.

'If he carries on, well, clearly he hasn't been able to live a controlled drug using existence. Some addicts can just about hold it together, have what you might recognise as a life, others just slip further and further away.'

'And die.'

'Yes.'

After his interview with the consultant Easton made his way along overheated corridors to see Tommy. It was a small ward with six beds, two of which were curtained around. Easton never moved among the sick. It was a foreign world. There was a man propped up in one of the beds against a thin stack of cushions. His face was grey. His bony old hands lay like claws on the blue airtex blanket. He had on striped pyjamas and tiny tufts of grey hair showed where the top was not completely buttoned. He slumped slightly to one side. His hair was unbrushed and his eyes were closed, though his mouth was open. The sheets and blanket had jumbled in a twist around him and half of his body was exposed. Easton felt a strong compulsion to go and cover the old man. Instead, he asked a nurse, 'Which is Thomas Easton?'

The nurse consulted her list. 'We've one without a name, it must be him.' She gestured to the curtained bed.

'That man, he needs covering,' said Easton. The nurse looked. She was plainly embarrassed, seeing her ward through different eyes.

Easton approached the hanging curtain and placed a hand on the soft wall. The enclosing rectangle felt to him like a shroud, something intimately connected with death. He stepped inside. Easton was aware of a sound, following a moment of silence. The sound was his own, a deep retarded gasp drawn out of the deepest part of him.

Tommy was not Tommy. Tommy was not a human being at all. His head and face were a huge shiny swollen purple fungus, two tiny red closed slits for eyes, a broken, damaged squidgy mess for a mouth and a white triangle of bandage for a nose. Easton stood and looked at his boy. Thin wires snaked across the blankets and disappeared into his son's nostrils under the bandage. On all sides the bed was flanked by machines.

There was a chair hidden among the electrical equipment, and Easton finally sat down. He found that the monitors were in the way of his line of vision, so he moved the chair a couple of feet so he could have direct visual access.

Easton didn't believe in God. Still this was a shock to something inside him, some barrier of acceptability. He sat and waited.

One morning he had taken Tommy to the shops. It was a contact afternoon. In the morning Tommy had been brought over by the au pair, a Danish teenager with exceptionally blonde hair, fair skin and broken English. They were early and Easton had been working in his study. He arrived at the door with a feeling of resentment that they were early and exasperation that he had had his work interrupted. He remembered no response of joy or of welcome. Tommy was wearing bottle green corduroy trousers and a green cardigan with a picture of Winnie-the-Pooh on one side. The cardigan had brown buttons that reminded Easton of chocolate buttons. The girl trilled her goodbye and made a quick get away for her anticipated day in London.

Tommy stood awkwardly in the hallway, unaware of time, being only six, unaware of his father's work commitment and of trial starting on Monday, aware only that he was visiting his father in obedience to some distant adult law that dictated his movements in the coming and the going of the world. Easton supposed he had no idea, had never wondered why it was that every month he was brought to this man's house and left for six hours at the end of which he was taken away again. Over the seventeen months of continuing contact visits on a monthly basis Easton had tried various activities; the park, which had the advantage that he could read some papers while sitting on a bench nearby; he had tried the cinema, appallingly boring, children's theatre, marginally worse, the swimming pool, a ghastly rigmarole of dripping puddles of clothes, awkward changing rooms, limbs that wouldn't be pushed into clothing, wet, chilly and tedious. He went through the motions of snap and snakes and ladders, but motions do not a relationship make and Easton could not make it work. If anything they were becoming more distant. He had no idea what was happening in his child's life. He didn't know how to talk to a child, nor how to listen to a child. He didn't know how a child thought or felt. The problem was, he couldn't open the place in his mind or heart where love grows.

Easton remembered exactly the case he was preparing. He even recalled the point in the construction of the argument he had reached when the door bell summoned him. If he had had this minute to put the argument again he could have done so. The abstract was clear and pure, supported by a beautiful interlocking of documentary evidence. He put Tommy in front of the TV. An hour slid by into an hour and a half. When he went into the living room Tommy was sitting impassively exactly where he had been put watching the screen, Racing from Goodwood. He was sucking his thumb. A line of dribble had accumulated on his chin and his sleeve was wet with it.

'Don't suck your thumb.' Why was a six year old sucking his thumb? Easton thought of boys at school who had sucked their thumbs, lonely ones, mainly, or scared. Easton turned away and examined the grey gathering clouds from his window. The Heath would be no good.

'Do you want to go to the park?' There was a little park with swings and slides and a sand pit down at the end of the road. 'If you do.'

'Me? I don't want to go to the park.'

The child dropped his eyes. 'What do you want to do?'

'You tell me.' Easton had tried to make his voice sound kind and cheerful. He tried to make his voice feel kind and cheerful, because now that he looked at the boy in his green little outfit, his small feet in their small shoes hanging down the side of the sofa a sense of immense tenderness began to well up, accompanied by a flood of other more dangerous flotsam.

'I think you'll say no, but I'd like to buy some shoes.'

Easton was surprised by how offended he was. 'Why would I say no?'

Tommy shrugged, unable to answer the question.

The shoe shop was Saturday afternoon busy. There were only two assistants, one kneeling at the feet of a girl who was trying on pink boots, the other fetching boxes of black school shoes for a chatty brown haired boy and his equally chatty mother. Other mothers and children milled about, waiting to be served. The store was decorated for children with a giant multi striped bumble bee pinned to the wall by gossamer wings. Each time the shop door opened the bee's wings shimmered delicately in the draught. Easton saw Tommy looking at the bee with pleasure.

'You like it?'

'Yes. It's so stripy.'

Tommy examined the shelf of little boy's shoes. There was a particular pair, navy blue with a Velcro strap. On the strap was a sewn in design of a tiger.

He picked them up and held them reverently.

But he didn't know his size.

Easton looked around. He had no idea about the time required to purchase a pair of shoes for a child. After twenty minutes he was incandescent with frustration at the waste of time. Time and the cost of time were the lodestones of his professional life. Finally it was their turn.

'He doesn't know his size,' said Easton.

'Better measure you, hadn't we,' said the overweight girl. She gave Tommy a wink and tickled his ribs. 'Oh, get on with it,' screamed a voice in Easton's head.

The yellow tape went around Tommy's foot.

'One F,' declared the girl. 'What? You like these? The tigery ones.' She did a pretend roar and Tommy laughed. She went off to the back and the minutes crept by in a slow torture. Easton thought he was going to explode with tension. The girl reappeared with a stack of white boxes.

'Now in these,' she opened a lid to reveal a pair of Tiger shoes, 'we've only got a one C, so I'm not sure if they'll be wide enough. Otherwise there's these.' She pulled off the lids and displayed a selection of shoes, all of which seemed to Easton to be entirely similar.

'Poke your toe at me. Where did you get all those freckles? Ooh, tickly toes.'

After the endless trying on, foot squeezing, walking up and down, all accompanied by mindless banter that caused Easton particular irritation, and which Tommy seemed unaccountably to enjoy, the shoe girl pronounced regretfully that the size one C were too tight. 'Why not try some of the others? No. You like these little tigers, don't you?'

She raised her head to Easton. 'Hunters at the top of the hill have these, just the same. They might have one F. It's always worth a try, isn't it?'

'We'll just take those,' replied Easton, nodding tersely at the one C's on the chair. More than anything in the world he wanted to terminate this process. It was closing in on him, the stuffy shop, the breathtaking slowness and inefficiency, the pointless chatter, the waste of time. He had a dim presentiment that he was moving towards something he wouldn't like.

'But, they don't fit,' pointed out the girl.

'They'll be alright.'

'They'll give him blisters, why not...'

'Look, it's only a pair of shoes. Who cares?' snapped Easton back.

The fat girl rose with dignity from her knees and packed the shoes in eloquent silence. When Easton paid at the till she handed the shiny bag to Tommy. Easton caught her glance of pity for the child and contempt for him. He saw that Tommy had seen it too.

He was mortified and humiliated, that this common shop girl had demonstrated an intrinsic compassion and decency that he, in all his intellectual hauteur, lacked. It was a glimpse into a world where patience, good nature and simple kindness to a child mattered, a world in which his deficiency was just that, and could not be hidden nor transformed into a vanquishing weapon.

Easton took Tommy to a café to feed him. The boy maintained the distressing silence of a child that has been hurt and is trying not to show it. Tommy sat at the table with his box of wrong sized shoes on his knee.

'Do you want to put,' for some reason Easton was unable to use the words 'your shoes' and instead said, 'the bag on the floor?'

Tommy raised an anxious face.

'Do you want me to?'

Easton controlled his exasperation. He manufactured a smile, which he realised was compromised by the expression in his eyes, and replied, 'I really don't mind.'

When the croque monsieur arrived, arranged on the plate with a drab salad and a superfluity of chips, Tommy was rather too far from the table and as he ate, he dropped pieces of food onto his shoe bag. As each piece fell he cast increasingly panicky glances at his father, who pretended to himself and to his son that he wasn't noticing the mess or the panic. Finally, Easton reached over and removed the box from Tommy's knee and put it on the floor.

Tommy lay down his knife and fork. 'I think you wanted to do that all the time. But you didn't say so.' After a few seconds Easton saw that his son was crying slow quiet tears.

He swallowed hard and felt the edges of his teeth grit. He lifted his tea cup and took a sip, averting his eyes.

'Don't cry,' he said, using the tone that he himself recognised as the manifestation of extreme anger, suppressed. Outside he was completely still. His hands rested loosely on the table. He watched Tommy trying to stem the tears, but they got worse. Easton was forced to sit in the café on his bamboo seat in a public place with a child who was crying. He leaned across the table so that he was close to Tommy's face and whispered, 'Stop crying.'

Both man and boy probably realised at the same moment that something terrible and shocking would happen if Tommy did not stop crying. Tommy stopped crying.

They left the café and walked down the hill, Tommy carrying his plastic bag.

Easton lifted his head. He had been sitting forward in the chair, his hands joined, his face lowered, like a man in a church, not quite religious enough to kneel, but aware of the respect of the people around him praying.

A nurse twitched through the curtain like a magician appearing suddenly on stage.

'We're taking him to Theatre,' she said.

'What are you going to do?'

'Who are you?'

'I'm his father?'

'They are going to amputate three of his fingers. On the right hand. And they are going to extract some of the broken teeth from his gums. Also reset his knee and he needs internal stitching.'

At first Easton was unclear what this last meant. But then he understood.

In the clerk's room Clive told the Clerk of the Rules that the judge was not able to come to court today. 'Sir Michael cannot come in today,' he imparted, confidentially to the red nailed lady, who peered over the top of her thin framed glasses in irritated bemusement.

'What's wrong with him? That's not like him. Must be serious, whatever it is. Bloody hope he's in tomorrow. List's horrendous.'

Easton did not go home. He could not be in the space of his own silence. He went to the home he knew best, the cold, high towers of the court. As he entered, Clive rose to greet him. He brought the judge his papers and laid them on the desk.

'As full a list as ever, Sir.' He scoured his judge's face. Easton looked up and saw compassion and had to turn away.

219

'We can arrange a series of short matters, if that might be best.'

'Yes, that might be best. Thank you, Clive.'

He felt, sitting there in his chambers, with Clive, as if it were the only arrangement of place and person he could trust. Absolute safety. If only he could stay in this room, in this moment forever and nothing else ever be. He let his eye rest on the pink tied bundles.

Then he remembered Alice. He thought of her lying on his bed, the contour of her naked body, waiting for him, the touch of her hand on his arm. He knew it could not be only bundles of papers any more. He had slept with her, he had been inside life, tasted her salty wetness. He had allowed her to come near. She had asked for nothing back, no promises, no commitments, no death us do part. He had shown her the worst parts of himself. In return she had shown him a different way of being.

Chapter Twenty One

Alice went to see her lover's son.

She looked at the boy, as fragile and damaged as a kicked bird. His wounds were healing, four weeks after his operations. Some semblance of his face was returning. The back of his skull was shaped like a swan's head, oval and curved. His hair, which had been shaved, was re-seeding in tiny gold prickles. His eyes were very deep cobalt blue. She thought, with surprise, he must be Judith's child. She realised this boy was, under his damage, beautiful. There were no traces of Easton in him. Perhaps, when he recovered, he would show the little mannerisms, the speech patterns, gestures, the tilt of the chin, all the arresting manifestations of coincident DNA, replicating over the generations, marking out one human being as an offshoot of another. Tommy showed nothing of his paternity as far as Alice could see.

What she did see was years of work for her and her profession. It is not possible to unpick childhood's experience and start with a blank page. Childhood is like one of those pictures composed of millions and millions of other tiny pictures. From a distance there is just the one image, and as you come closer you see the detail of the components, until all you see is the individual picture among the millions, which, if it were changed in shade or position would alter the appearance of the whole. There it is, with the parts presented to you and all you can do is turn up the focus in some areas and down in others, to make the picture comprehensible and manageable.

His eyes were open. He watched her silently. She introduced herself. She explained she was on the DDT, the drug dependency team. No one had spoken to him about his life.

She leaned forward and brushed the sores on his arms where the needles had left sceptic holes. So many red punctures along the purple paths.

'How are you?'

'Fine.' Then after a thoughtful pause, 'Thank you.'

'Will you tell me your history? In terms of usage? It'll help us to get your treatment right while you're here, however short a time that is.'

It had to appear unthreatening. She took in his battered body. She knew he had been sodomised. He had been raped and beaten up. It would be a miracle if he ever spoke to anyone again. What does that mean? Raped and beaten. It means that nothing is the same again. Perceptions are permanently altered.

'When did you start taking drugs?'

'When I was fourteen. I went to a boarding school.' His eyes, which had been focused on the ceiling while she spoke to him, dropped quizzically to her. She sat next to him and waited. She knew she had the knack of drawing people out. She listened. Alice understood that being listened to satisfies a basic human social need; to be valued.

Tommy had no memory after taking the bag from the car. He had a lot of gaps in memory, great big hours that formed holes. He remembered the Pig and the people in it. He remembered Chas. All the time since returning to sentience he worried about Chas. He missed Chas. He longed to hear his voice. He longed to see him. He longed to hear him. He felt as if there were an essential piece of himself missing. He began to cry and he brought up his hand to hide his tears but it was the wrong hand and throbbed painfully where the fingers had been amputated.

'Tell me,' said Alice.

'I had a friend. But I don't know what's happened to him.'

'Was he with you when you were attacked?'

'No. I lost track of him before then.'

'What's his name?'

'Chas.'

'Is that short for Charles?'

She smiled. She sensed that Chas was more than a friend. People want to talk about those they love. People's talk gives so many indicators; who they talk about and how tells you so

222

much. The more talk the better. It is also possible to detect absences in talk. The first person Tommy mentioned was Chas. Most people talk first about themselves. That was an absence. Tommy was an absence in Tommy's talk.

'Where did you meet him?'

'At the college. I was expelled from school for dealing cannabis, and my mother arranged for me to go to a college. It was one of those that took you if you couldn't fit anywhere else. There were a couple of boys like me, who'd been expelled from school, a couple who'd had breakdowns, and the care boys.'

'Were there girls?'

'Oh, yes,' he replied, in a way which indicated they hadn't any meaning for him. 'Chas was a care leaver. He was sixteen. I liked the college. It was better than school. Everything at school was about beating someone else; at maths, running, rugby, in looks, social status, the entire essence of life was beating the other boy. There was no such thing as a free standing relationship or even a free standing personality. It was all subsumed into the conventionality of outstripping your neighbour.'

It was bizarre hearing this analysis from the bandaged addict half upright on the bed. Alice recognised what it was that Tommy had inherited from his father; intelligence.

'Drugs were everywhere; unsurprising really, as there were a lot of wealthy, self indulgent, stressed teenagers. It must have been a field day for the dealers, sitting there in the local pub in the middle of an affluent market town, all green pastures and Jerusalem and dope. That was where I was smoked, actually, in the Chapel. I loved dope. It was so calm and heavenly. The others used to send me into the town to buy it for them. I didn't care. Of course, when one of them was caught taking it he blamed me immediately. He squealed. His father came down to plead and bribe them to keep him.'

'What about your father?'

'He didn't materialise.' Alice envisaged some spectre hanging in the ether. Tommy paused. 'I don't talk about him.'

'Why not?'

'If you knew him... I expect you will meet him. He comes every day. He scares people.'

'Does he scare you?'

'Yes.'

'The casualty officer said you asked for him, your father, not your mother.'

'I named him. Like an incantation. It was the only thing I could think of more powerful than the drugs, or the pain of losing Chas, or even what had happened to me.'

'When you were on the street, who did you talk to?'

'I didn't. There was no need. There was Heroin and there was Chas.' He arched his back. Alice helped him to move, to readjust himself to a position in which there was marginally less discomfort.

'My mother and father hate each other. Or rather, she hates him. She's capable of hating. He's not capable of having any emotions, apart from anger, and he doesn't even let that out. It hovers, under the surface. He controls it. When he's most angry he speaks very, very softly.'

'Is he angry now?'

Toby paused to reflect. 'He seems different.'

'In what way?'

Could he tell, this intuitive boy? For once Alice felt the one who was at risk of being seen through. He was scrutinising her.

'Not so much angry as sad. Maybe there's always been that and I haven't been able to see it. Parents have secrets from their children, I suppose.'

'Not always.'

'Everyone has secrets.' He paused. 'When will I be able to leave here?'

'Three weeks, depending if there's anyone to look after you on discharge. If you go back to the drugs in this condition you'll probably get septicaemia.'

'That's why I need Chas.'

'Do you have housing?'

'No.'

'You can't go on the street. You'll die.'

Tommy considered this statement with dislocated interest. Would it be better?

'You don't want to die, Tommy. I think you want to live.'

'But what for?'

'Someone once described suicide as a terminal solution to a temporary problem.'

'They've never been suicidal, then.'

'Things change. In ten years time I imagine you will be a good looking seven fingered man living with a boyfriend in a flat and doing drug counselling or writing successful novels.'

Tommy looked surprised. He had never thought of himself in this way.

'We could ask your father if you could stay in his house, to recover. Then at least you have options. Or if you can't be with him, what about your mother? '

The thought of his mother made Tommy feel nauseous. The thought of his father made him feel panic. Many times Chas had told him to fuck it and forget it; told him his father was a waste of space and a cunt. Chas' feelings about his own parents were so strong that they were literally and actively killing him. In care Chas had had counselling and he knew that his parents were at the root of it. Sometimes Chas used to cry and scream in his sleep, like a shell shocked war veteran with vacant eyes staring at nothing.

It was touching Chas that Tommy missed, comforting him in the night shadows, lost in the woods together.

'We haven't told her I'm here.'

'Who's we?'

Tommy realised with a spasm of amazement that he had unified himself into a pronoun with his father.

'Mother's awful. I can hardly bear even to think about her. Critical, controlling, emotionally selfish, manipulative, hysterical, needy. And her husband. You couldn't imagine two men more different than my father and my step father. Anyway, she and Daniel virtually live in France. They only come back for wine fairs. If she knew my father were seeing me she'd be back, though. She wouldn't be able to resist the chance of conflict. When I was little she played games with contact between me and him. If he wanted a week in August he could have four days in June. If he wanted two til six he could have ten til two.'

'How do you know?'

'She kept the letters in a folder and used to pull them out and read them to me. It wasn't difficult to put him off. Then she hated him for it, because she'd manoeuvred herself out of spite into a position where she had all the responsibility. After getting kicked out of school I lived with her and Daniel. Daniel didn't like having a third party in the house. He liked it even less when I started stealing his wine. And his money. And when Chas came to stay.' Tommy gave a private little smile, remembering Judith and Daniel's fear of Chas. Their world of safe and selfish pseudo drama was overwhelmed as a much more brutal drama was played out in their home. Judith kept telling Tommy with tearful resentment that he wasn't the boy she knew. She meant of course that he wasn't the boy she wanted. And she was truly bereaved. She longed for a charming handsome clever son who would adore her and take her to restaurants. The death of this image child was heart breaking and all she had left was a boring self obsessed husband who wore soft Italian loafers and a blazer, whom she did not love. Each time Judith looked at Tommy it was torture.

'Chas says you have to cut them off completely and start again. Never contact them, never think about them.'

'And so that's what you did?'

'Well, you can't, can you?' said Tommy with an air of ancient weariness. Thoughts of his parents hovered about him like a bad dream, always there in the dark.

Alice knew he was right.

'I loved my father,' she said. And then she stopped, astonished that this had come out. She stood up quickly. But it was too late. Tommy was already processing her bald statement. He looked at her curiously.

'You would make a good therapist,' she told him truthfully and to divert attention from her mistake. 'You have intuition. That's something that can never be taught. You've either got it or you haven't. You'll be out of here in a few weeks, detoxed. Why don't we get you on a programme?'

'What about Chas? I can't leave him.'

'Maybe you can help him by getting clean.'

'Too simple.'

'It's a consideration.'

Tommy nodded. He knew that left to his own devices he would just go back onto the street. Tommy thought of the sick in the sinks at the Pig. He thought of what Chas did to get them money, thought of what had been done to him. Here in hospital, for the first time, he was able to feel a little pity for himself. He wondered why. Maybe it was being treated like a person by the psychiatrist. She treated him as if he were worth something. This was a very new, indeed novel experience. He recognised it as good.

'Would you be able to see Chas as well?' he asked Alice. 'Get him on a programme?'

'Definitely,' she replied, and she smiled at him. She realised he was checking her eyes for signs of lying. She left him to rest.

Tommy, weighed down with hospital drugs, couldn't move his body much, but he could move his mind and through all the hours he lay there he had for the first time in years the capacity to think in a continuous line.

Chapter Twenty-Two.

There had been a delay coming out of Boston and the plane had sat with a full compliment of exasperated passengers for over an hour before take off. Marion had left the kids with her best friend in Connecticut and taken off and now she felt liberated and fun. She imagined that people were looking at her and thinking that this woman looks like a lot of fun. She had bought a couple of new novels from the terminal and was anticipating getting her hand round an ice cold gin and tonic in a little plastic cup. She was flying First Class on David's air miles. As the gin and tonic went down, her exasperation with the delay melted and a feeling of relaxation and anticipation grew. She followed with a couple of glasses of champagne and flirted a bit with the man sitting next to her, a good looking advertising exec, originally from New York, now Boston based, who had a house in Martha's Vineyard. Marion wanted David to buy on the Vineyard. She could see herself in a wood clad run down house overlooking the beach inviting her many friends to visit and chill out on the hippest Island. Marion always enjoyed sharing her success. She wondered what Helen would think of Martha's Vineyard. She concluded that Helen would like it but only as much as she would like a caravan in Newquay. Toby and Alice could come. Marion imagined Toby in his socks and sandals, swim shorts and formal checked shirt. The Americans in Martha's Vineyard would be baffled by Toby. Marion grinned to herself. She wondered if she could persuade him to wear a knotted handkerchief and a tank top over his shirt.

Alice waited in the crowd at the exit point for arrivals from Boston. Taxi drivers hung around holding up cards with the names of strangers written in felt pen. Kids rode on baggage trolleys and the ping pong of the tannoy system preceded obscure droning announcements. In dribs and drabs passengers began to trail through from the burrow of the customs tunnel, blinking in release from flight repression. Marion screamed when she saw her sister. 'Oh my God, you look great. Being engaged really suits you.'

'Being rich really suits you,' Alice observed, noting her sister's healthy, glowing skin and auburn tinted hair.

Alice passively accepted Marion's big hug.

'Tell me all your news,' squealed Marion, digging her sister in the ribs.

'I haven't got any news.'

'Apart from wedding plans.' Marion faked shirtiness, which Alice knew concealed real shirtiness. Marion was here to have a great time, to run about excitedly in a tizz of vicarious pre wedding girldom. She wanted it and she was going to get it.

'Oh, wedding plans. Helen's looking after those.'

Marion immediately adopted a serious confidentiality and put her arm through Alice's arm. 'Is that a problem, Hon?'

Marion was ready for family drama, with her at the centre of it. If Alice needed someone to fight her corner Marion would be the one to do it.

'No, I don't mind.' Alice examined this for truth. It was a good job Helen was managing the wedding. Her affair with Easton had deactivated her capacity to make any wedding arrangements. She could do the wedding, she could do the marriage, but she could not do the wedding plans. Each step would have seemed dishonest. Initially Helen had checked things with her over the phone and had endless catalogues sent, with pictures blue pen starred for approval. However as it became more and more apparent that Alice was totally pliable Helen simply went her own way, feeling that she had a brief to do it all. Although it was exhausting her she was incapable of stopping herself finalising the tiniest details. Whether to have pink and white sugared almonds or silver and gold? Whether the shoes of the bridesmaids have straps or not? Whether the order of service be printed on square cards or oblong? When her husband asked her, what does Alice think? She replied with an indulgent smile that Alice couldn't be expected to manage a psychiatric ward and a wedding.

Marion pressed on. 'Helen can be really bossy; if there are things she's doing you don't like you have to stand up for yourself. Like I did.'

Marion saw herself as a trail blazer. First she married a Jew and converted, which was big bucks at the time, or Marion made it so. Second she got married in the synagogue in London and had a huge reception. It was this that had caused the real problem in the family. The whole idea of converting to Jewry was too odd for the family to get their heads around, like the ancients not realising that the great earth they stood upon was round not flat. No, it was the reception. More precisely it was the cost of the reception. Marion hired a Central London hotel that cost a fortune. Alice's mother simply wasn't in the market for paying that sort of money. But it was the family tradition that the girl's parents paid and organised the detail. By booking a wedding that Maria couldn't buy, Marion offended her mother into mortified silence. On the weekend of the wedding the two families met for the first time. David's mother was unbelievably glamorous and exotic, his father an insignificant looking man with a wispy moustache, a breast surgeon by trade. Marion joked that each of the tiles in their bathroom represented the financial fruit of a surgically improved nipple. Eighty seven of David's relatives had come from The States or from Israel and it was wild. The bride's mother had danced backwards out of the synagogue, her arms weaving like serpents, her long jewelled fingers clicking. Maria had to be rescued lots of times at the wedding and encouraged to enjoy herself. Her eyes filled with tears when she saw David's mother and father embracing at the reception. It had been therefore a difficult wedding for Alice.

'If you want to do something just do it,' said Marion forcefully in the cab as they went along.

Alice shrugged with indifference. 'I'm happy with Helen doing it.'

'You are so weird,' said Marion. 'If it's about upsetting Mum, I mean, she's got a lot to get over.' Marion stared at her with meaning.

'What about you? Still doing the therapy?' Alice diverted the conversation.

'Not so much now. Once a week only. You should try it. It really helps.'

'I do my own therapy,' said Alice, allowing it to be half a joke. 'It's cheaper.'

'That's bollocks. You can't do your own therapy.' Marion was a therapy aficionado. She knew her Freud from her Jung, her Gestalt from her Transactional.

'I know, but it doesn't have to be formal.'

Marion didn't like being called formal. 'It's about insight,' she responded.

'I've got quite enough of that, thank you. Anyway,' Alice couldn't allow Marion's definition of therapy to go without examination, now that it had come up. 'It's also about acceptance, absolution, recovery, change. In the past these things were provided by religion, or by storytelling, by ceremonies, by work, philosophy, mysticism, meditation, art, nature, friends, death, suffering or sex. They still are. The talking cure is only one way.'

'So what have you chosen?'

'I have chosen…' she mused, 'letting Helen arrange my wedding.'

'Your problem is you never confront emotions,' complained Marion, disgruntled that her sister was refusing to talk. 'You don't do feelings. You have to make everything an intellectual exercise. No wonder you're good with all that stuff you do at work. It just becomes academic, doesn't it? Witnessing other people's pain doesn't upset you. You don't feel it. You're so detached you're almost heartless.' Marion looked at her sister for a reaction.

'That's just not true,' said Alice. Marion knew that Alice was right. Her analysis of her sister was off centre, but Marion couldn't put her finger on it. She groped around for an improvement. 'It's not that you don't feel other people's pain. Its more…' she was going to say, 'That you don't feel your own.' But she stopped. The family never talked about that.

They disembarked at The Portobello Rd and wandered to the restaurant on Kensington Park Rd, where they were meeting Toby. Marion put her arm around Alice's waist as she strolled. Alice envied Marion her capacity for sincerity and warmth.

Marion was saying, 'It's so exciting you getting married. I was worried you never would. And Toby's such a lovely guy. He'll make a fantastic father. You thought about babies? You're no spring chicken. Oh my God, there he is.'

Toby was walking towards them along the pavement. He was in his hospital outfit, check shirt, brown cords and jacket. Marion ran to him and jumped into his arms.

Next day Alice had taken time from work to amuse Marion. Marion had a huge wad of English notes and peeled them off like Monopoly money. She wanted to go to Harvey Nichols to buy presents for the kids and her friends back in Connecticut.

They went up to the fifth floor restaurant for coffee.

'I'm not eating. I've lost a stone since Cornwall,' Marion lifted her blouse and showed Alice her stomach, which was a bit saggy and had stretch marks, but not fat.

'You were never fat,' said Alice.

'Yeah, I know but with three kids you have to be careful. It's no so much fat as flab. If you get flabby your husband leaves you.'

'There's always going to be someone thinner.'

'You can talk. You're looking really thin. Men don't like women who are too thin.'

'I doubt Toby notices,' said Alice and ordered two coffees and a Banoffee Pie and Ice Cream.

The waiter brought the order.

'You're so lucky to be getting married. I had such a great day on my wedding day. It's a day you remember all your life.'

'And do you have a great marriage, too?'

Back in Connecticut the condition of everyone's marriage was the rock that underpinned all other subjects. Marion had sat on numberless sofas sipping coffee and chatting intimately about the shortcomings of the husbands. But that was a part of the social scene, as much as Cookie Sales and Halloween.

Marion put down her fork, which she was using to spoon up the main part of the Banoffee.

'No body has a *great* marriage. You have to put things in perspective.'

'What things?'

'There are always grumbles. That's family life.'

'The minutiae?'

Alice watched Marion stir her milk into her coffee. The milk disappeared into the black liquid, changing its colour to homogenous light brown.

Alice asked, 'But are you happy? You're always moaning at David.'

'That's just me. The perspective is this; marriage is to secure stable structures for raising kids. No more, no less.'

'That can't be true.' Alice recoiled from her sister's image of marriage as a bare function.

'Can't it? You wait til you have children. What you need from a husband is obviously kids, then money to look after them properly, and commitment to not fucking off with some bimbo half your age. So he travels, so he works late, so he forgets to tell me my dress looks nice, or ask me how I feel. But he's on the phone asking twice a day are the kids alright. He doesn't have affairs, he doesn't leave.'

'So *are* you happy?'

'I'm not unhappy. Listen, romance is no good if you can't pay the bills and he doesn't care when their first tooth comes through. Toby's not the kind of man who is going to make you unhappy. He's good husband, good father material. Why have we got onto this?'

Alice was sitting opposite her and gave no response. Marion felt a cold chill clutch her stomach. 'You're not sure? Oh my God, Alice. You'd better bloody be. You're getting married in a week's time.' Bright red triangles of emotion flushed onto Marion's cheeks. 'Does Toby know?'

'No.'

'Don't you love him?'

'Things are not that simple.'

Marion gasped. She recognised the phrase her husband so often used and felt her pleasure in the weekend turning to ashes. She tried to get things right.

'Will you marry him?'

'Yes,' replied Alice.

Marion weighed whether this was enough to salvage her weekend. She decided to settle for it.

'If you let Toby go you are fucking mad,' she warned, to seal it.

Chapter Twenty Three.

Tommy entered the house like a nervous horse in a burning stable. Easton observed him carefully. He looked so pale and ill and uncertain. The next day he was going in to the Priory. This was his one night in the care of his father. Tommy was on a high dose methadone programme.

Is it me? Easton asked himself. Did I put this in to him?

'Do you want something to eat?' he asked.

Tommy shook his head. The night he had burgled his father he had been blinded with the need for a hit. He hadn't noticed his surroundings. He had barely registered being at his father's house.

Now he looked around. He remembered being brought here by the au pair for contact sessions.

He shook his head. 'No, thank you.'

He noticed changes. There was still the same table in the hallway, still the same brass lamp, still the same mirror, still the same colour walls. But there was a difference. There were more paintings, hangings, screens, sculptures, prints, rugs; more art. The house was full of it, as if it had become an obsession.

'Do you want to go and sit down?'

His father was treating him like a child. Tommy acquiesced. There was nothing else to do. His father followed him through and watched him sit on the sofa. The arrangement of the furniture was the same, with one sofa facing the other. Tommy's heart began to overbeat; it seemed to Tommy that the two terracotta coloured pieces of furniture were locked in confrontation. He hoped his father would not sit opposite him, but he did.

Silence hung in the air between them.

'I've got some chocolate if you want it.'

Tommy grasped at the straw. Anything to move the man off the sofa and away. 'Yes. Thank you.'

Easton kept bars of Lindt in his cupboard. He kept them for Alice. As he took one out the smell of the confection reminded him of her.

One day she had shown him how to melt chocolate over a bain-marie. The melted chocolate shone velvety in its silver dish. When it cooled she dipped her finger in and licked it. She dipped again and her finger slid into his mouth and he sucked. She undid the buttons of her blouse and touched the chocolate onto her breast leaving a tiny pointed curl and he had bent and taken the curl and the nipple into his mouth.

Easton held the chocolate bar out to Tommy. Tommy kept his bandaged hand on the sofa and raised the one with five digits still remaining. Easton recalled holding the fingers new born, when thin pink miniature nails were like transparent coral, feeling them tighten around his own. Those fingers had been torn out at the roots by the bone.

Easton broke the chocolate and lay a square neatly on top of the bar and gave it to his son.

Tommy ate the piece ruminatively and then the rest in large thoughtless bites. 'Thank you,' he said, again. Easton sought in vain for something between them that was not politeness.

Tommy, as he deliberately averted himself from the man standing by him, was amazed to be able to identify pity, alongside anger and fear. When he stopped thinking of this man as his father he was able to feel sorry for him.

'Were you in court today?' He looked up and as he expected he saw his father's body lift.

'Yes.'

'A big case?'

'Small cases.'

'Why small?' Tommy felt a prickle of indignation.

'While you were in hospital I asked them for short matters.'

'But you usually hear big cases?'

'Yes.'

'I was sorry about what happened.'

'What?'

'When we took the silver. Chas was frightened. That's why he hit you.'

'It doesn't matter. I was back in court the next day.'

'Did you report it to the police?'

It was brilliant, the kind of cross examination Easton would have been proud of. It caught him completely off guard.

'No. I didn't want to.' He had to get away from the lie.

'Shall we watch the television?' No more need to talk.

Easton flicked the remote. On the TV a blonde young woman was followed with ludicrous seriousness by a reporting team as she pursued a career in modelling. Its banality repelled Easton. He switched a fast glance at his son whose face had cleared into impassive vapidity. The girl was stupid and had nothing to say but said it anyway in a loud insistent American nasal tone. A five minute interval passed infinitely slowly. Easton realised his son was drifting into sleep. His eyes were closing and his breath had become slower and deeper. He no longer saw his father and Easton took the opportunity to look at him. He waited until the breathing had settled to a somnolent regularity then approaching Tommy, Easton leaned down and inhaled the smell of his son's scalp, face and breath. He sat gently next to him and examined skin, hair, ears, eyelashes, mouth in close detail. The boy slept on, oblivious. At length Easton touched his shoulder.

'You can't sleep here. Go to bed.'

With the vacancy of a dream walker Tommy stood. Easton followed him up the stairs. Tommy went to his room, the one in which he had slept as a child, without any prompting. He lay supine, and closed his eyes, motionless. He had not slept in that bed for seven years.

Easton had not even chance to turn on the light. A pale yellow line of light from the hallway fell on the bed, slanting across Tommy's face.

Tommy had left his bag in the hall. Easton carried it into the kitchen and took out his son's things, not that there was much, a paperback of crossword puzzles, semi completed, pyjamas, underwear, a T shirt, a notebook with scrawly, virtually indecipherable writing in it. Easton glanced at the kitchen door, and thought about reading his son's diary, but there seemed something horribly intrusive in that, and he put the blue backed book down. There were a few phials of tablets- Easton read the labels but they were meaningless, apart from the valium bottle. He assumed they were painkillers.

Easton locked the front door with a Chubb key and put it in his pocket and locked the iron grill on the French windows in the kitchen. He hoped Tommy didn't start a fire in the night. For all he knew his son could be a pyromaniac. Easton had no idea what existed in Tommy's head. He went to bed and lay listening to the house.

He must have fallen asleep because his next conscious idea was that there was movement in the hallway. He quickly looked at the ghostly hour illumined in green on the face of his watch.

Tommy was in the hall at the door trying to get out.

'I want to go.' There was a hard edge to the voice that Easton had never heard before.

'No, don't be…'

'I want to go.' This time it pierced the silence of the night as a scream, loud as a monkey in a rage.

Easton hid his shock and said 'Go to bed.'

Tommy suddenly stopped. He went to his father. Before Easton's eyes the boy's body began to quiver and tremble with something long suppressed.

'Cunt,' he shouted and spat into Easton's face. 'I hate you, you cunt.'

He lashed out and caught Easton on the shoulder, and again with his bandaged hand. Easton caught it at the wrist, and in his mind at the time was the thought that if Tommy hit with that hand it would bleed and there would be open wounds seeping red onto the white bandage. He saw the spread of colour, red, in his mind's eye and it seemed to drench everything. It covered the bandage, covered the film of the glass ball of his eye. He allowed his son to hit him with the other hand, though he did raise his arm in involuntary defence. Some of the blows which rained down fell on his arm, some went to his head and face, and with each blow he heard his son's grunts and the words his boy had for him.

Finally Tommy stood back. Then, with a look of sheer hatred he went up the stairs. Easton wiped the dripping, bubble flecked froth of saliva from his face, waited, then followed softly. He could hear sobs of outrage from the bedroom.

He went downstairs, feeling the heavy beat of his heart inside.

He called Alice and she came. She came as a doctor. He wasn't sure how he had called her, or what role he wanted her to play. Was she there for him or for Tommy?

She climbed the stairs and opened the door into Tommy's room. The boy was occupying a small space on the floor next to the bed. His face was distorted, more than just with the broken teeth and healing mouth. The stitch scars were still red and sewn, like a monster in a Hammer movie, the mummified fist raised and furious. Out of his mouth issued grunts, and 'Fuck off,' loud and full of energy as Alice entered. His chest panted like a dog dying of thirst. His face shone with smeared tears. He turned and saw who it was and said, 'Nice Dr Christie.'

She saw the mural, the wall's bright rendering of Rousseau's tropical storm. Striped fronds gathered pace and strained in violent wind. The tiger's feral growl echoed in a terrified jungle. Black and amber muscular power quavered before the onslaught of nature unbounded.

'Who painted this?' she asked.

Tommy raised his eyes and saw the direction of her gaze.

'Him,' he said. 'When I was little.'

'Did you like it?'

'Scared of it.'

'Did you tell him?'

'No.'

239

'What would you prefer on the wall?'

'My version of stripes.'

'What colour?'

'Black and white. I'd paint it all black and white.'

'Take this.' She poured a small top up of methadone for him. He swigged it down in a gulp. 'And this. Just a mild sedative.'

He took it.

'Why don't you lie on the bed? Look at the ceiling. Look at it then you can close your eyes. Look at what's behind them.'

Tommy lay. As she spoke he fell into an unfathomable relaxation. Her voice came to him through the swell of the sea, as if his ears were bunged with foam, lighter and lighter until it was no more than a faint pah pah, like the opening and closing of a fish's mouth and the words merely bubbles vanishing in the deep solitude.

'He should sleep til morning.' She walked down the stairs, Easton following. He had been waiting outside the door.

She turned to him. She thought about him in the son's room painting the mural. It must have taken many hours. She thought of him waking in his son's night and lifting him from the cot and feeding him, the two bodies in one bed, father and son, tiny baby.

She stood away with her bag symbolically in front of her.

'Toby and I are getting married on Saturday.'

He nodded. He needed to feel her touch. He needed her to want him to touch her. He put his hands in his pockets.

'I don't know what it was between us,' she said. Living. The sensation of being alive.

He watched her walk down the path, then closed the door and the parallelogram of white light falling on the garden grass disappeared.

The rehab unit into which Tommy was booked was a large Victorian red brick building in parkland. The house had belonged to a man of letters, whose family had made a fortune in the slave trade. It was now used by the wealthy to restore to health their drug addicts, alcoholics, good old fashioned neurotics, kleptomaniacs, obsessive compulsives, gamblers and so on. Easton's car crunched with smooth superciliousness up the long gravel drive. All around the building's parameters were high walls and high green trees.

Tommy sat white in the passenger seat, looking out of the window.

'What shall I say about my hand?' he asked.

A brief reflection, a riffle through the filing cabinet of his mind brought the reply from Easton, 'Septicaemia.'

Tommy laughed softly.

'What?'

'Septicaemia,' he repeated and stopped laughing and looked sad.

The woman on the desk in reception was buttoned up in a twin set and looked like a headmaster's secretary. She took them to a large drawing room with leather sofas and low coffee tables, an ornate plasterwork ceiling and two grand fireplaces. From the window there was a vista of green manicured lawns and trees swaying in the breeze. Easton half expected to see playing fields, rugby goals, cricket nets and boys covered in mud.

A dapper middle-aged man in a three piece suit strode in. His brogues made a hard clack on the wooden floor as he approached them, his arm outstretched. He had a gold watch on a chain looped through his waistcoat.

Even before he reached them he was announcing his name. 'Philip Barley,' he called. He was short and thick-set like a rugby player and had faintly reddish thin hair. Ginger haired men often look like each other. Easton recoiled but had no alternative but to shake the man's hand. When he touched it, it was surprisingly soft and round. Barley looked from Easton to Tommy.

'How was the journey?' Barley's manner was bluff. He was a psychiatrist. He had been working with addicts for thirty years. He was going to be in charge of Tommy. Easton felt a

241

tensing of the muscles in his hands and shoulders. 'The journey was fine, thank you,' replied Easton.

'Beautiful grounds, aren't they? The place was built by Laurence Thyne. During the war it was used as a boy's school. Shall I lead on?'

Barley went ahead of them at a leisurely pace, turning constantly as he spoke as he walked, pointing out the various rooms and facilities. He described the regime. Tommy seemed barely to be listening. They came to a wide white corridor, with white doors and a beige carpet.

'Number eight,' announced Barley in a jaunty manner and opened the door. 'I'll leave you to say goodbye to Dad, then perhaps we could have a talk. I'll be in my room. It's off the corridor in the reception area. The receptionist will point you in the right direction.'

He closed the door and left them alone.

All his life Easton had kept on fighting. He wanted to transfer some of that fight to his boy. Tommy stood with his arms hanging limply by his side. Maybe if he'd been less passive it wouldn't have been so easy to bully him. Now, for the first time, Easton attached a name to what he'd done.

Tommy noticed with curiosity that his father was sweating. Rivulets were dripping from under the hairline down to his eyebrows.

'Are you all right?' asked Tommy.

Easton turned away and looked out at the grass fields. 'I don't like these institutional places very much.' He forced a self-deprecatory laugh, which sounded false and said, 'You don't have to stay.'

'I thought you wanted me to.'

'I want you to get clean. But…'

'What?'

'Not if you're frightened.'

Tommy looked aside and considered this, and gave a small shrug.

'Are *you* frightened?' he asked, in reply.

Easton couldn't answer the question. It hovered on his lips to say something along the lines that everyone is frightened of some things sometimes. It would be normal and human to admit fear, but he couldn't admit it and Tommy had a warning look in his eye.

Tommy held a vision in his head of a man who was never frightened. He beheld his father. He had a horrible feeling that the man before him might have fears, hopes, and disappointments. He rejected this interpretation rapidly and said, 'I'm not frightened of being here, if that's what you mean.' He paused and then asked, with his head cocked in a gesture of curiosity that seemed to Easton almost theatrical. 'Are you ever frightened at court?'

'Never,' Easton replied instantly. The tenor of his voice and in the involuntary twist of his lips conveyed contempt for fear and all those who might be afraid. Tommy felt a flush of satisfaction. He pushed it further.

'Are you afraid of Judith? Or were you?'

'No.' Here was the ring of truth. But Easton recalled his son's surprising capacity for the wide bowled question.

'What about failure?' pursued Tommy.

With a sensation of despair like being pressed into a dark corner, Easton gave his son what he wanted to hear, at the expense of truth. 'Everything I've tried at I've succeeded at.'

Tommy nodded, satisfied. For a few seconds the truth of Easton's life hovered just behind his lips. He watched Tommy for a sign, the slightest softening. 'Just put it on there,' said the boy, and turned to the window.

Easton put Tommy's bag on the bed and started unpacking.

Alice had come with him to buy Tommy's things shortly after Tommy had been admitted to hospital. They walked to the High Street and went into Gap. Pop music played in the shop. Alice riffled efficiently through the racks and pulled out three pairs of jeans, a handful of T shirts bearing logos, a couple of sweatshirts, a hooded fleece, and a blue jacket with a zip. She picked up some packs of boxer shorts then stood at a shelf of trainers and asked 'What size are his feet?'

Easton shook his head, and she picked out three sets of shoes. Then they went to the Oxfam shop, (it struck him that this was the place their relationship had begun, and now it book ended, the last of the places they had gone together). He had no idea what seventeen year old boys read, more particularly, what his son read. He saw a copy of Treasure Island and picked it out. Alice watched him with no comment. She selected a book called Junk, about teenage drug addicts she said, and he accepted it, as he had to accept it all. Also she added A Clockwork Orange, Catch 22, Lolita and The Bell Jar. She commented that there was a gap in the market for teenage homosexual boys. He had not thought of his son as a homosexual. Alice brought the obscure into focus, in her casual laying out of the truth, in the buying of a second hand book, in a word, or a look, or a touch. Her absence now was like an actual physical pain.

As he rolled his car up the drive away from the building in which he had left Tommy, he slowed and turned his head. He saw his son still at the window, watching his departure.

Easton notified the Clerk of the Rules that he was available to sit as emergency judge over the Christmas period, not only Christmas Eve, but Christmas Day, Boxing Day, the three subsequent days, New Year's Eve and New Year's Day.

'Poor sod,' laughed one of the junior girls in the office overlooking the roof tops of Fleet Street. She had a tight schedule of fun and parties over the Christmas. She was too young to know what loneliness meant. The Clerk of the Rules was an older woman, whose secret was that she could feel sympathy.

'No body calls Mr Justice Easton a sod in this office. Any judge who covers the entire holiday schedule for us is my best friend, so shut it.' The Clerk of The Rules tapped her rapid red fingertips absorbedly over the keyboard and filled in the schedule.

The court was cleared at five on Christmas Eve.

Easton retired into his chambers. Clive followed.

'All finished, then, Mr Easton?'

'You go, Clive. I'm going to sort out some matters to look at home.'

Easton had driven in so that he could fill his car with bundles to read over the vacation.

'Yes, sir, I'll be off.' Still Clive hesitated. 'Mrs Bird and I always do Christmas at our place,' he said. Easton looked up at him without knowing what he meant. 'Always more than we can eat or drink, endless people dropping in, you know how it is. Still, the more the merrier, I suppose.'

'Yes,' nodded Easton.

'So if you were in our neck of the woods, if you were passing, well, don't think twice.'

'About what?'

'Dropping in, sir.'

Easton finally comprehended. His clerk was telling him he didn't have to be alone on Christmas Day. Had he become that pathetic? He was the court, he was chambers, he was the Family Law Bar; he was the committees that he chaired, the functions he attended, the legal books to which he contributed. No one knew him as a man. For a moment he glimpsed himself as he imagined others might see him. He wondered if his isolation was that obvious. They would never know who he really was. He really was the man he was with Alice and when she was gone what would he be? The Christmas judge? The prospect opened before him of life on his own again.

When he got home he dropped the bundles on his desk in the study. The cleaner had left him a Christmas card. He frowned. He hadn't realised that was how she spelled her name. He twisted the card up and threw it in the bin. She had also arrayed on the table in the kitchen a plate of home made gold iced biscuits, her Christmas offering. Easton ate one, but it was too dry. He tipped those in the bin, too.

He wandered into Tommy's room and lay on the bed.

When Judith left he could have applied for an order giving him the custody of Tommy. It was possible he might have won. Judith was under a psychiatrist, on pills, emotionally wrecked. But it would have exposed him as a prostitute using sexual inadequate with a venereal disease and while that didn't bother him in itself it would have been bad for his career. Having the care of a child would have been bad for his career.

He lay on the bed and stared at the ceiling.

Early on Christmas Day he had a visitor. He went to the door because it could have been Alice, but his visitor was Chas.

Easton let him in. He showed him in to the living room deliberately.

'What do you want?'

'Tommy.'

'He's not here.' He paused, rapidly calculating. 'He's in rehab.'

'He won't last. Not without...' Chas squeezed his shoulders up to his jaws and stopped short, compacting his features balefully. He didn't want to share anything about Tommy with this man.

Easton waited. He wanted to know what it was that Tommy couldn't rehabilitate himself without.

Chas was wearing clean clothes. Easton wondered if his money was changing Chas' life in any other way. It occurred to him that he was paying as much to keep this boy on smack as he was paying to get Tommy off.

'Not on the street, now?' he asked.

'What the fuck do you care? You'd like it if I died.'

Easton acknowledged to himself the truth of this insight. There was no point denying it. He was deliberately bringing about Chas' death with the use of money. Chas looked at him with resentment glowing in his face. It troubled Easton momentarily that here was someone's child being handed the ultimate rejection, fuck off and die.

'I want you to leave my boy alone, that's all.' No vengeance? He pushed the question back to the shadows.

'I need more money.'

'Of course you do.' He supposed Chas would find out the hard way that there was a limit to what the body could accept. Chas was already on the way out, Easton could see it. He was startled by how much weight Chas had lost. Where before he had been thin, now he had become skeletal. The skin around his nose was pulled tight and his eyes stared unnaturally. His neck reminded Easton of the decapitated chicken who had lived out his final days in motel rooms being fed by a dropper directly into the oesophagus. With Easton's help Chas had become a terminal grotesque.

'I'll give you more if you write a letter for me.' It occurred to Easton that Chas probably couldn't write. 'If you can.'

'Yes, I can write.' Chas brought his brows together fiercely. Easton saw a flint of pride in those black eyes.

'I just want a few lines. Tell him you don't want to see him anymore.'

'He won't believe it.'

'That's my problem.'

Easton watched in morbid fascination as Chas engaged in a final struggle between love and dignity on the one hand, betrayal and degradation on the other. Love lost.

Easton got paper and a pencil and watched as Chas curled his bony knuckles clumsily around the pencil.

'What shall I say?' he asked.

'Tell him you don't love him.' A sense of vindication tingled deep down in Easton.

'What, though?' Chas insisted on being given the words.

'Say it as you'd say it.'

'I wouldn't say it. It's not true.'

'You know how to lie.'

Chas shook his head, at a loss.

'Say, "Dear Tommy, I've got someone who'll pay for me. I've got money now. I don't want to go back to the way it was. You and me will kill each other. Don't try and find me." '

Chas wrote the words with effort. Easton looked at it. It was barely legible and laughably mis-spelled.

Chas accepted a further one hundred pounds there and then and Easton promised to double his money through the account. Looking at Chas he wondered how much longer he would need to keep making the payments.

Chas was Easton's only Christmas caller.

Chapter Twenty Four.

The church bells, having pealed in the New Year, now rang for a wedding. The weather could not have been more awful. A bleak wind howled off the sea, wrenching the ribbons that secured silver balloons to Toby's car. The cream foam lettering that the best man and the ushers had sprayed in fun across the rear window, 'Just married,' was blown away into the thunder fuelled air. Rain lashed down, obliterating any residual foam.

'At least Toby's car's going to be clean,' commented David, with the ironic phlegmatism of the Jews. One of David's favourite expressions was 'No body died.' It was an expression he rolled out in the middle of most of Marion's dramas. Marion didn't understand that this was a reasonable bottom line for a man whose paternal uncles, aunts, cousins, grandfather and grandmother had been wiped out in the war.

David stood at the window. He felt uncomfortable in the clothes they had made him wear, a hired tail coat and white shirt and pinstripes. He came from a culture of expensive casual.

He and Alice were the only ones left in the house. The rest had gone to the church. David was giving Alice away. Helen's husband Paul had been considered and rejected by Helen. Helen had formed the view that as David was coming from a great distance (both geographically and ethnically) it would be the thing to do to indicate his full acceptance into the family. She thought this was the sort of thing that might bother David. David couldn't care less. His certainty in his own heritage, in his identity, was absolute.

They waited for the wedding car. David wondered if she was thinking that her father should be there. He turned and assessed her. She stood in the centre of the room, as she had been ordered, so as not to wrinkle the silk of her long Regency dress and, David thought, this is a woman who is absent.

'Looking good,' he observed. Yes, she was a stunner of a girl, in her cream and rose skin, oil dark hair, wide grey eyes that looked right in at you. David experienced a male stirring, and reminded himself that she was fatherless, and that this was her wedding day. He could never have married this sister. There was something held back, depths under the surface. With Marion what you saw was what you got, she was right out in the open, every little glitch and glimmer of feeling came bursting out one way or another. Marion ran the house, ran the kids, O.K a little chaotic, but she was a good mother, a good daughter in law. These things were important. He never had to worry about her, about what she really wanted. Marion ran along under the steam of her own contrived dramas. But Toby was going to have to work real hard with this little sister.

'You're on,' David called, as the silver Rolls swept onto the front pavement. A little group of gawpers had gathered under umbrellas, elderly neighbours and women with toddlers from down the road.

The car had silver ribbons tied in a V shape to the bonnet. One of the ends had come loose and was flying in the wind. The disgruntled chauffeur was trying to tie it back on. Rain dripped from his peaked cap. The ribbon on the bonnet had snapped too short to be repaired so for the sake of symmetry the chauffeur yanked the other side off too.

He took the car in a purring loop down onto the coast road to the village. Alice looked out at the sky. The car wipers lurched insanely from side to side. Streams of water obliterated the driver's straining vision as the car proceeded slowly to the church.

'Look at the sea,' said Alice, her hand flat against the window, leaning forward transfixed.

'They said at the bakers it was the worst storm since '87.' David liked imparting factual information. It was only after the words were spoken that he remembered Alice's father had died in '87.

250

The church was at the end of the road, right in the centre of the village. Helen had tied a spray of flowers to the wooden gate so stoutly that the petals had blown off but the stalks remained. The grassy verge was a swamp of mud. The chauffeur had to park in the middle of the lane and help the bride step into the storm.

At the lych gate a pool of brown water had formed in the trodden hollow. Alice's shoes were silver silk. She felt almost intoxicated with the intemperance of the weather. She looked up at the grey spire and its anchor shaped vane, a memorial for all the seamen who rested below, and then down at the granite graves, some partially overgrown, rising like rickety teeth from the green gum of the ground. Her father was buried at the rear of the church. She had a sudden urge to go to the grave and not go to the wedding at all. What would he say to her if it were him at her side now? He would say, 'Leave it. Let's go out on the boat. Let's sail.' But you cannot sail forever. You have to come to land sometime. Only he hadn't. He was still at sea. If he had lived would it all have been different? In the pointlessness of his death she felt the pointlessness of life and, at the same time, the magnitude of life.

The church was early Victorian, built on the plot of a much earlier edifice. There were graves that went back two hundred and fifty years. One of Alice's childhood games was to discover the oldest incumbent of the church yard. The outright winner was Emily Goose, relict of Frdk Goose, of the parish of Porth, born 1735, died 1827. Her husband had died in 1775. Emily had lived as his widow for fifty two years. The youngest incumbent was Susan Mannis, who was three hours old when Jesus took her to himself. Alice had loitered here in the long ago, imagining the lives of the dead in detail. She had created mental pictures of them, and their families and homes, their losses and joys, burials and weddings and loves.

The church portal was mock Norman, a pointed arch with decorative surrounding stonework. The heavy wooden door

251

stood open, but the second interior door had been shut to stop the storm entering. Helen and the bridesmaids and pageboys were waiting in the porch, a cold stone area, with an old swallows nest on one rafter, and adverts for Christian Aid and the toddler group pinned on a damp wall.

'This weather,' lamented Helen and set to work straightening and adjusting. She caught sight of the stained silk shoes. 'Oh, look at your shoes! Oh, no. What a pity!' And then as she finished poking and plucking, 'Ready? Don't be nervous. I'll give them the nod,' and Helen disappeared, slipping through the door.

Alice heard the sound of the organ's preliminary notes, and the door was thrown open by Toby's two ushers. The rising howl of the gale swept like an unbidden guest down the aisle, announcing the bride's arrival. Heads turned. Alice placed her hand on her brother in law's arm and stepped into the church. The little bridesmaids and the pantalooned pageboys moved forward.

The Vicar waited robed in the centre of the altar, Toby and his brother joined shoulder to shoulder. Toby turned. His face glowed. He was so near, only ten yards away from having her as his wife. There were some people on the left she barely recognised. They were Toby's side. The church was bursting at the seams. What the family had lost on Marion's wedding they were amending for here. Hats and faces, men's bald pates and clean shaved chins, Auntie Rose's crimson lipstick, bridesmaids' frothing satin, posies of purple spraying from the end pews, veils and fluttered mascara, and her strangely quiet heart.

Alice began to close the gap, step by step. Faces loomed towards her, eagerly beaming from either side, urging her on. Only one head rested downwards, as if in slight disinterest, the shoulders heavy, mid way down the aisle, on her side, face averted. As she drew level he turned and raised his eyes, there in the congregation, in the heart of her family. He had done this terrible thing. He had come to her wedding, converging the two strands of her life, imprinting one over the other so that she could never, ever forget. His presence was to her shocking, like a sin committed in church in full view.

Alice felt her hand tighten on David's arm. She felt Easton's eyes on her.

'Who gives this woman to this man?' called the Vicar and smiled a man of the cloth's smile.

David delivered Alice to her groom.

The vicar's robes were white as swan, the Book of Prayer black in pink hands.

'Welcome, everybody,' he boomed in child like delight. 'Welcome to the wedding of Alice and Toby, two people who love each other very much.'

And they were married. Man and wife. Toby kissed her tenderly and chastely. Alice wondered whether Easton could see how Toby loved. Toby's love was made of an entirely different material to anything that Easton's heart held.

The organ thrashed at Vidor's Toccata. The notes flooded out, one on top of the other, falling over themselves in joyfulness.

He did not look at her. She wondered if he had expected some miracle, some sudden sea change from the altar. Had he come to sweep her away?

No. He had come merely to see her married, no more, no less. She and Toby walked to the back of the church.

Then Easton rose from his pew, excused himself for stepping over legs and came forward. Alice stood at the entrance to the church, with her husband, leaning on his arm. She was in the circle of her sister and her mother and her sisters' children. She saw him coming. She arranged her face. Then Helen leaned forward. As Easton approached Helen took him by the wrist. Alice knew how he would hate this touch of a stranger.

'Sir Michael has kindly agreed to be a witness,' said Helen, her eyes twinkling with the happy notion of a title on her little sister's entry of marriage for all the village to see.

253

Toby reached forward and held out his hand. Easton took it without any hesitation.

'Congratulations,' he said to Toby.

'I didn't think you could come,' Alice said. He was about to reply.

'Sir Michael called me yesterday evening,' intervened Helen, 'I forgot to mention it, so much going on.' Helen hung on to Easton's wrist as if he might fly away. 'Always room for one more, I say.'

'Excellent,' cried Toby. 'I'm glad you could make it.' Toby was drunk with happiness. Everything was excellent, everything marvellous. He just wanted to share, share, share.

Easton was given a place at the reception next to Aunt Clara. She was Alice's father's older sister. She was a lecturer in Medieval History at Exeter University. Her hair was thick and wiry grey, long and drawn into a bun, secured with a wooden clasp. She introduced her self to Easton and shook his hand as a man would. Helen had made a good choice. Aunt Clara was an astute woman who never bored.

Easton poured wine for her.

'And so you know Alice…?' she opened.

'Through work. She was a witness in one of the cases I heard. And they live very close to me.'

Aunt Clara nodded, thinking it was rather an odd basis for acquaintance. She waited for further elucidation of the friendship, but none came. Instead he asked her about herself, her job, discoursed intelligently about Medieval art, and drew the conversation finally to her brother.

'He was a doctor?'

'He was top of his year at Guy's. He was offered some very good jobs in London. But he wanted to come back here. He loved Cornwall, and the sea.' Her eyes slipped across the room as if trying to get away from the eventuality of fate. Aunt Clara had the same grey eyes as Alice.

'I've never seen a photograph of him. Is Alice like him?'

'Very, in appearance and in disposition. I'm surprised she hasn't chosen to settle in Cornwall. I suppose she might have if things had happened differently.'

'Meeting Toby?'

'No, although that too, possibly.' Aunt Clara winced as if she had kicked her toe on a sharp object. 'I mean,' she sighed, 'Edward's death. It was a very complicated time for Alice.' Clara glanced with restrained resentment across the crowded room to the top table where Maria sat in her salmon pink bride's mother's outfit.

'Maria took it extremely hard. I'm sorry, I don't mean to sound heartless. We all took it hard. Edward was an exceptional man. I'm not saying that because I'm his sister. I hope I have more objectivity than that. But he was truly unique, a completely free spirit and hugely independent thinker. He attracted people. He was a restless man, in some ways. I'm not sure marriage was really right for him. I don't know if you are a married man, oh, divorced, then you'll appreciate what I mean when I say that marriages are not always made in Heaven. He loved his girls totally, but he had a particularly special relationship with Alice. To be honest having a third was Maria's choice. Alice came some years after the others, cementing Edward, as it were. I don't think Maria had anticipated that the two would be so close, nor so similar. Sometimes, I notice, Maria has difficulty just looking at Alice. The memory, I suppose. Well, when he died...you see, there'd been warning of the storm, but Alice so wanted to go. It turned like this, just as the weather is now.' Clara raised her hands palms upwards in resignation. 'He was a very competent sailor. He would run over to Brittany or round the Lizard, even to La Coruna. But the sea...' She paused and turned to Easton. He was listening intently. 'I'm running on,' she said.

'Please continue.' He made a flowing gesture with his hand, to soften the demand.

Clara noted the man's interest to be unusual, but she was immersed in her story, the story of her brother's death. 'A storm hit them. It seems that Alice fell from the boat. Edward went in to rescue her, and did so, but he couldn't get back into the boat himself. After he'd...gone, Alice drifted in the dark for hours. They didn't pick her up until the morning. She was freezing cold, soaked to the skin and the boat had taken in a lot of water. It was slowly going down, with her in it, and she knew it was sinking. It was a miracle she survived. Any other girl would have been hysterical, but she was very calm.' Clara paused, reflecting. 'Not so Maria. Maria lived through Edward. She defined herself by him. She'd married him young, not more than nineteen. Helen was on the way. Edward was only twenty three. Edward was Maria's raison d'etre. After he was lost, Alice came to Rex and myself for a few months, so that Maria could recover. I wasn't sure she'd be able to go back. But she did. Well, she had to. It would have looked odd otherwise, and Maria doesn't do odd. And, I suppose,' added Clara doubtfully, 'She loves her.'

'Maria blames Alice for Edward's death.' This stranger weighed the words.

'I wouldn't exactly say that.' Clara's backtrack was contingent. 'These things are complicated. Parents and children are complicated.'

She could take the explanation no further. 'Not a propitious subject at a wedding,' she concluded. 'Edward wouldn't have liked it. He was a superstitious person in some ways. He certainly believed in the power of dreams. He said dreams were essential for understanding oneself and others. I suppose he was a bit of a Freudian at heart. Perhaps that's why Alice became a psychiatrist. I wish he hadn't died.'

Easton scrutinised her obliquely for tears. There were none. Clara's handsome features belied only profound regret. 'I hope she's happy.'

Easton looked over at the top table with its starched white cloth, now cluttered with posies and small dishes of silver coated sugar almonds, bottles of wine, ice buckets, glasses and champagne corks, all the paraphernalia of celebrated nuptials.

'It's funny,' Clara added, 'how the tradition of wedding has barely changed in essence since the medieval period, when marriage had changed so much. People like to hold on to the outward show, whatever happens to the substance. Look, they could be twelfth century lovers, tying the knot.'

Alice and Toby sat in the middle of a long table, flanked by family on either side, drinking and eating and laughing. Alice's veil was made of ivory lace inlaid with black stitching, and over it, like a crown of thorns, she wore a circle of tiny fresh white snowdrops, pale green shoots woven together with dark laurel. 'She could be a pagan bride. In some ways, I think that's what she really is.'

'And Toby?'

'The adoring husband.' Easton noted a slightly disparaging curl of the lips. 'Oh, no,' said Clara. 'Speeches. One tradition we could do without.'

Joel, Toby's brother went first, thankfully quite shortly, unhindered by the usual Best Man obscenities. Clearly not a natural speaker, he confined himself to words from a cue card about his senior brother, thanked all the persons whom he was required to thank and sat down to heartfelt applause that reflected gratitude for its brevity.

Marion replied for Alice. She made a speech about her little sister. 'Isn't she looking beautiful?' she demanded and the guests howled 'Yes!' 'Have you all had enough to drink?' and the guests howled 'No!' 'Well drink some more, then.' And, 'I am so, so happy finally to be able to get her married; we were all starting to worry we had a spinster on our hands.'

The spinsters in the room looked down at their nails, and laughed in humiliation but Marion was in full flow. 'It's about time Toby made an honest woman of her. As you know this is what you might call a traditional family, apart from our Helen, of course, who loves to buck convention.'

Helen chuckled, secure in her conventionality.

257

'But of course, as any psychiatrist will tell you, there's no such thing as normal. And my little sister definitely isn't normal. You can see that from the boyfriends she's had in the past.'

Alice pulled a face and Toby pushed himself to be amused as this, after all, was his wedding day.

'Who remembers Dean?' Marion held out a blown up photograph of a scowling schoolboy with a satchel. They laughed. 'Or Trevor?' Trevor was a crew cut blonde boy on a beach with a surf board at a priapic angle to his body. 'No wonder she liked Trevor. And then she got serious. Does anyone remember Mr Pryor?' This last with a wicked wink. 'Mr Pryor taught Latin in the sixth form to my sister and went out with her in the summer holidays. How wrong was that?' The old, old friends whooped shared recollection. Mr Pryor appeared as a blow up, a short bespectacled monk of a man. 'University brought Bill the hippy.' An incredibly hirsute man in an Afghan and beads was displayed. 'And this was the nineties, not the sixties.' Marion shook her head sorrowfully. 'Phil the Welsh motorcycling Mathematics PhD.' A thickset Celt on a Harley. 'And possibly worst of all, who remembers Mercer?' Mercer squinted insecurely through long brown hair, biting his nails in front of the Taj Mahal. 'What the hell was she looking for?' Marion's voice rose in shrill mystification. 'So I say thank God for this man.'

The final blow up was a photograph of Alice with Toby on the beach in front of the rock, the wind whipping Alice's hair across her face.

Then it was Toby. He stood up to rapturous applause. He was a well liked man.

'I think if I had known about my predecessors I might have had some doubts. But fortunately Alice has seen the light and here we are today. I hate other people's speeches so I'm not going to inflict one on you, my friends and family. All I wish to say is thank you to the lovely bridesmaids and page boys.' He held out parcels and the children came forward. He

258

kissed the girls and Sunny threw her arms around him desperately.

'What can I say about my marvellous sister in law, Helen, without whom none of this would have been possible? You ought to be for hire, Helen, for the organisation of lives generally.' A huge bouquet was carried on by the kids and Helen simpered and twinkled. Toby turned to the guests. 'Obviously Alice is far from perfect. Her abysmal taste in music, her shocking disregard for couture, her worrying reliance on chocolate, her debilitating lack of tidiness and her tendency to forget to wash up, despite these deficiencies, incredibly, I still love her.' He smiled. The guests made rowdy comment. He looked at her, as if to say, you know it's a joke. He put his hand on her bare shoulder and realised something.

'All of my life has been moving to this point.' They stared at him. 'All of my life I have been waiting for this.' Toby found himself expressing the thought that had just overpowered him. 'I am a lucky, lucky man.'

'Ahhh,' rose from the tables.

'He means it,' murmured Clara, and shook her head.

Easton stared at the golden haired, pleasant young speechmaker and recognised a sincere man, a man who was not afraid of feeling. Is this what Alice wanted? Is this what she was choosing? The good, honest emotions? Straightforward affection, the frank gaze, the supporting arm; amiable familiarity; easy companionship; the declaration of love, of dependency, need, trust? A steady shoulder to cry on?

It enraged him that he could not give these things. What had taken these capacities away from him? What had he to give?

'Kiss the bride,' shouted fat Uncle.

Easton sat and watched Toby put his arms around Alice and raise her up so her face was towards his. He watched their lips touch, he watched her mouth open for Toby. He watched intricately. He saw that Toby had his tongue inside her, that he was really kissing his bride, eyes closed in passion and

259

possession. Everybody clapped. She knew he was there, but she kissed and allowed herself to be kissed.

No knee in the groin had felt like this, no sharp slash of a stick. It felt as if he had been slit open, left to hang in the wind, disembowelled and abandoned.

Perhaps, without the kiss, Easton might not have done what he did.

The three tiered wedding cake was carried in. The cake was Helen's masterpiece. She had iced it herself in thick white and lilac, icing pink rosebuds around the edges with real roses scattered on the virgin surface, frosted sugar petals covering the base. Someone put a silver knife in Alice's hand. She looked up and saw Easton's face.

Toby placed his hand over hers. The blade rested on the perfect surface. Toby's grip was surprisingly strong. She looked at the cake and felt that to cut into it would be an act of desecration. Toby's hand pressed down. For a moment she resisted. The serrated edge merely tapped the surface, then the pure white cracked open; the knife slid into the soft black interior. Toby pulled out her hand and forced it down again, making another deep hard incision.

Coffee was lingering affair. Easton drank four cups, black. A waiter placed a plate before him, on it a dark rich square of yellow and white rimmed wedding cake.

The bride and groom had come down from their pedestals and were making their way around the tables, mingling in with the guests.

Easton had eaten little of the main courses and dessert. He abjured the anaesthetic of wine. Now, he broke the cake in his fingers and ate it, piece by piece, until it was all gone. He washed away the sweetness with bitter dregs of the last coffee.

'Excuse me,' he said, the old inculcation of manners innate, almost involuntary.

He left the table and walked out of the hotel.

The storm had blown itself out during the wedding reception. A stiff wind blustered in sea borne from the West.

Easton could smell sea. He wasn't used to this cold salt on the wind. All he could remember was hot sea, the lazy rippling air over the Gulf, the wavy palms, the sweet, sticky date aroma, the warming fresh fish in wicker baskets.

He wanted to stand by the side of the sea now.

The road from the Hotel wound through high banks of rhododendrons past the outer houses of the village. He noticed a row of terraced cottages, set at an incredibly steep angle, their slate roofs gleaming black. A slice of sun attempted escape from a formulation of iron coloured clouds. Its cold winter rays gave the afternoon a watercolour brilliance. Lower were a few badly planned bungalows, under rising cliffs. The road fell and fell and then he was at the beach. There had once been a harbour, but the waves had been too strong, sweeping the walls down. To the left hand side of the beach massive granite blocks had been pushed by the tide into a jagged breakwater. A hump backed bridge crossed a stream that opened onto the beach, glazing the rocks with smooth icy rivulets.

Along the slipway two cafes were padlocked for the winter. The tide was low, exposing the sands. The beach stretched in a long sea bounded ribbon to the far cliffs. Easton walked onto the beach. He was wearing a suit and looked improbable. His shoes sank in wet sand. As he approached the sea's edge puffs of brown flurry made wave patterns on the shore. He was absorbed for a while in the purity of the shapes. Alice had once said, 'The sea is a sculptress.' Now the carved granite outlines brought back her words and the moment that they had been spoken, her hand loosely in his. The rocks of the cliff were made of swirling layers, heaved up by unimaginable geological pressures. He breathed in clear ozone.

Easton had never had a seaside holiday. He had never explored rock pools with a fish net and bucket. He watched two children, a brother and sister, industriously companionable, squatting by the edge of a black ridge of rock, pointing. The mother stood at their side. He couldn't

261

hear what she was saying, only her tone of cheerful enthusiasm and encouragement.

He crossed the beach laterally to its farthest point, stood and faced the tide, watching it roll and crash, and then walked back the way he had come.

A little blue and white boat sat grounded on rusty wheels on the slipway. He wondered if this was where Alice and her father had commenced their fateful voyage. He looked at the craft and he looked out at the stone grey sea. He imagined the waves, high as houses, and the head of a drowning man dipping below the surface between vast swells. He imagined a rain soaked, freezing child clinging to the side of a boat and watching her father disappear in the waves, sinking slowly herself.

The sea was like the desert. Over both the sky was huge at night and star studded. He understood what it was that had brought Edward Christie back here and kept him here. He instinctively understood the space and the solitude and the sense of absolute indifference of the landscape to the human condition. In the sea and in the desert only the essentials mattered.

He left the beach and went back up the hill to the Hotel.

People had moved off into fragmented groups, lolling on soft sofas and armchairs, standing in drinking circles, still some in the dining area around tables, old family members meeting again, old friends reuniting. Some of the men were in the billiard room watched by giggling women in heels.

A huge log fire crackled in the main lounge. A few were outside, smoking in the rose garden.

Easton saw Toby with his brother and other men in the lounge, holding wine glasses. Toby had taken off his jacket and was standing with his arm around his brother's shoulder.

A bridesmaid sat on the stairs, a glum little crazy haired girl. Her swirls of lilac satin made a peony of her knees.

Easton bent towards her.

'Where is the bride?' he asked.

'She's in her room with a headache.' The little bridesmaid curled her lip in contempt. She watched the man's nod, and sensed somewhere his meaning. After a while of deliberation she went to find her mother.

He knocked. The corridor was quiet. The room was on a floor of its own, a bridal suite, secluded from prying eyes. There was no reply, so he knocked once more.
She came to the door in her wedding dress. She had taken off the veil. Without the veil she seemed denuded.
He looked past her into the room. There was no one else.
'Michael.' She used his name. He pushed past her and closed the door.
'Has Toby been in?'
'In where?'
'In here, with you.'
'No.'
He laid his lips hard on hers, forcing her against the door. She felt the need in him that would not go away. She felt his loneliness. She would rescue him now from this moment. She would give him something to take away with him that would always be his.
She moved his head away, and indicated with her look and gesture that she would take him, that she wanted him. For her to refuse now, to play the wife, would have left him dead and empty. She had to want him. She did want him. She held on to his body. She rested her fingers lightly on his shoulders and opened her mouth under his. She stroked the familiar pattern of the hairs at the back of his neck. She touched his earlobes between her fingers. She kissed him under his jaw, and scraped the bristle of his throat with her tongue. She loved him. She loved his body. It was the body she loved above all others, the body that excited her above all others.
He pulled up the hem of her wedding dress. Under it she wore white stockings. He pulled her to the bed and lay down between her legs. He heard her small catches of stolen breath. He began to move and as he moved he held his face

263

over hers. The sounds she made went to the centre of his being. She wanted him. He wanted to watch her wanting him. He pressed back the urgency in his stomach. He wanted his consciousness now, more than at any time in his life. He wanted to watch her come. Her mouth opened, her head tilted back, her body lifted. He felt the signs of her drifting to orgasm, the tensing around him like a hand squeezing and relaxing, in waves. She said, 'I love you.' He concentrated, listened, felt, inhaled the experience so that he would remember each second. The waves grew and grew, she clung around him. He fell into the deepest pit of consciousness, where all there is is feeling, an immense feeling of the heart and the body. He knew instinctively that this was the main experience of his life, the moment he would hold on to in his dying hour. She held his head as he reached his climax. He gritted his teeth against the huge pressure that had built up inside.

As soon as he felt the last pulses fade, he pulled out and stood up. He turned away to zip his trousers, a little private intimacy withheld. Now was the time to show he didn't need her. Now was the moment to damage.

There was a knock on the door.

He leaned against one of the posts of the bed, a canopied bridal bed and folded his arms. 'I wonder if that could be your husband?' he asked. As Alice began to move past him he grasped her arm hard and said, 'You married him. You fucked me. On your wedding day. There's a word for it. It's not love.'

'Go into the bathroom and wait.' She looked at herself from a far distance, a huge agitation welling in her heart, trapped.

He said, 'It's fucking. That's what they call it. Did you fuck your dad? Is that why your mother's jealous? Is she angry because you fucked him then you let him die in the sea? Why didn't you throw him the life jacket, Alice?'

Easton crossed the carpet and opened the bedroom door. For a second Alice couldn't see who it was in front of him.

Easton stepped back and held the door wide.

It was Marion. She walked into the room and stood still. Easton leaned forward and whispered something in her ear. He took one glance behind him. Alice stood in her wedding dress, her fingers loosely linked. He noticed, with a wrenching stab of pity, that her shoes had got stained and were dirty. Dirty white stained wedding shoes. He felt a burst of fury at them all. Why had they not taken more care of her?

When he left Marion stood in the doorway facing her sister.

'Is it true?' she demanded.

Alice remained silent.

'You bitch. You stupid, stupid bitch.'

They sat in Alice's mother's sun room. Wedding presents lay in a jumble on the table and on the floor. Some were already unwrapped, some still to be done. Helen sat cross legged on a hard chair making a note of who had given what. Alice knelt on the carpet, next to Toby's legs. Maria watched, from behind the table. The cousins noisily competed to be allowed to rip off packaging.

Marion sat in the other room. She had a headache. A woman who was unable to contain the slightest emotion now contained this one great secret. Very soon she would tell her husband. Very soon she would tell her friends, her sister, her brother in law.

Marion's daughter rested like a pining puppy comatose against Toby's body. His arm wrapped around Sunny. Sunny longed for him to kiss her. She had decided she would kiss him back, properly. Alice knelt close enough for Sunny to kick her with her toe, and she did, then smiled, pretending it was a joke.

Alice opened her wedding presents. She had opened her legs for her husband in her wedding bed when Easton's semen was still inside her. Her husband had told her he loved her, again and again. He had kissed her lightly on the brow of her head before going to sleep.

265

'Why do people stray from the list?' asked Helen in frustration. 'That's another fondue set, now, and both in brown. You'll have to put them aside for gifts, Alice.'

'We'll keep them until Sunny gets married. You'd like a fondue set, wouldn't you.' Toby gave a conspiratorial grin, and Sunny in the sunshine of that smile turned and slapped him, sharp enough to elicit a cry. She would slap him and kiss him. Both were exciting.

'Let's unwrap this one,' pleaded Gabby.

'We're keeping that until last,' said Toby, enigmatically. 'It's from a very important guest.'

'Oh no, please, now,' cried Sunny, jumping off his side and standing breathlessly before him.

'Go on then, but carefully.'

'Why not let Gabby help,' suggested Alice.

The gift was not wrapped as such. It had been delivered by a discreet black van and carried in with respect by two men who had driven from London. It stood against the wall, large and rectangular and covered protectively with thick brown cardboard. On it was a red sticker with the words 'Christopher Mc Fadden Gallery, Mayfair.'

The cardboard was stapled as well as taped and it needed force to rip it off. Under the cardboard exterior were layers of opaque bubble wrap. The younger boys grabbed it and began popping the bubbles with their heels, each bubble exhaling tiny truncated screams of termination.

'Who's it from?' asked Gabby.

'It's Easton's present,' said Alice.

'Why do you call him Easton? The poor man has a name,' chivvied Helen. 'Sir Michael Easton,' she finished with a flourish, so that Gabby would remember. 'He was so polite. Clara thought he was charming. I think they got on quite nicely, maybe there's hope there.' Helen twinkled naughtily. Uncle Rex had died of renal cancer three years before. Helen had a vague feeling that it was time for Clara to be getting over it and getting on with life.

Toby removed the last sticky fronds of bubble wrap. The present was clearly, had clearly been all along, a painting. But of what? There remained a final layer, a layer of felt like substance over the face of the canvas. Theatrically Toby stripped it away.

'It's quite modern,' observed Helen, critically. Helen liked knowing what she was looking at. She liked the straightforwardly representational. 'Or is it?' She frowned.

'Venice,' said Toby.

'Istanbul, surely. Those are minarets,' said Paul, who had once been to Istanbul on a tour.

'Looks like Manhattan Island to me,' observed David, glancing from behind the pink tent of his FT. 'Whatever it is, it's good.'

'Really?' said Helen and stopped frowning and started admiring.

Maria said, 'It's Moscow. This is a river of ice.' She pointed a finger at the foreground.

'That's not ice, its sand. It's the desert,' asserted Sunny and looked at Toby for support in her theory. 'It can't be ice. It's not white. It's not any colour. It's all colours merging. You can't tell what it is because you can't see where things start and finish. There aren't any proper lines. You can't sort of see it properly.'

'I suppose it's where ever you want it to be,' said Gabby with a self deprecatory shrug.

'What does the note say?'

Toby had peeled an envelope off the front of the packaging before opening it.

He slit the seal and read. The others watched in anticipation of discovery.

'It's called 'View,' by an artist called Eduardo Para.'

'Doesn't ring any bells,' said Helen, doubtfully.

'He's sent an insurance valuation.'

'How much?' asked David.

'Twenty three thousand pounds.'

There was a collective silence.

'Twenty three thousand pounds?' queried Helen. 'It can't be.'

'It is.'

'But that's ridiculous.'

Alice, without looking, could see Toby thinking.

'I expect,' he said, slowly. 'It's because I was casualty officer when his son had had an accident. I stayed and bandaged him up. I suppose he's grateful. It's funny. He doesn't strike you as very feeling. I suppose he is, underneath.'

'Still waters run deep,' commented Helen, pleased for Clara.

Chapter Twenty Five

'What do you want me to say?' Tommy was trying his best to comply.

'I don't want you to say anything.' The therapist sat cross legged in one corner of the triangle. He was middle aged, but had a silver stud in one ear, wore Doc Martens, cream chinos and a navy jacket over a T shirt. His hair was a razored white pig bristle, shorter than the grey stubble that grew on his chin. He kept rubbing his chin with his fingers, making a rasping noise. But now he was still and silent.

It was a cold white room, though not cold in temperature. There were a couple of black and white posters on the walls, no desk, only the three necessary chairs facing in to a vanishing point. There were white walls and a white blind on the window. The carpet was blue. A blue and white Arctic scene.

'Why do you think I want you to say something?' queried the therapist.

Tommy looked to the other corner where his father was sitting.

'Does your father make you uncomfortable?' The therapist was quelling the discomfort in himself.

Tommy glanced with rapid anxiety at his father again. 'Sometimes.'

'If you could put him where ever you wanted him to be, where would he be?' The therapist would have put Easton a long way away.

'He'd be in court.'

'Why?'

'Because that's where he wants to be.'

'And Michael,' (Easton had agreed that this stranger should use his Christian name. What else could he suggest? Sir Michael? Mr Easton? Not on any account plain Easton.) 'Where would you put Tommy?'

Easton hated this game of make believe. The world was not make believe.

'In a safe place.'

'And where is that?'

'Not on the street. Not here. Not injecting heroin. Not with people who inject heroin.'

'What would he be safe from?'

'Drugs. All that goes with it.'

'He means rent,' said Tommy, as if explaining a minor mistranslation between two foreigners.

'Not just that.'

'Say what you mean, Michael.'

'Safe from people.'

'Doing what?'

'Beating him, fucking him, degrading him, making him an outcast. Making him feel like nothing.'

The therapist was staring over at Easton's hand. It was mesmerising. He'd never seen it before. The client was pressing his nails so hard into the fleshed part of the ball of his hand that blood was oozing out. When he shifted position a small smear of blood was left on the pale brown of the arm of the chair.

'Tommy, when you get clean, and leave this place, what will you do?' The therapist found it hard to drag his eyes away from the stain on the chair.

'I'll get Chas clean too.'

'Where is Chas right now?'

'In prison, I think.' Distress covered Tommy like a blanket. 'He was arrested.'

'What for?'

'Stealing, I suppose. Burglary, or robbing, or mugging.'

'Did he do that a lot?'

'Yes. To get money for smack.'

'Did you do that?'

'I robbed from a car. I burgled once. Not really a burglary. It was him.' He gestured vaguely in Easton's direction.

'You burgled your father?'

'It wasn't a real burglary.'

'How did that feel?'

'Bad, when I saw him on the floor.'

'On the floor?'

'Chas hit him. He had to. He didn't mean to hurt him.'

'When you saw your father on the floor, what did you feel?'

Seconds dripped by.

'Very bad.'

'Sorry?'

'No. Shocked. It was shocking, to see him on the floor.'

'If you could have said something to your father when he was on the floor, what would it be?'

'I'd say, 'Get up. Get up, now. Stand up.' ' The boy's high voice took on a hectoring tone.

'Did you feel angry with Chas, for knocking your father down?'

'I felt angry with him.'

'Chas?'

'No. Him.'

'Your father?'

'Yes.'

'Why?'

'For not getting up.'

'What do you feel about your father?'

'Fear.'

'What do you feel for Chas?'

'Love.'

They both looked at Easton. He was laughing.

Chapter Twenty Six

'I love you.' Toby whispered the words in her ear as he reached across to the breakfast tray. The hotel room was cool and dark. It was part of a castle that looked as if it had come straight from Don Quixote. Heavy wooden shutters, engraved intricately with the heads of deer, blocked the bright light from entering. Such light as there was filtered in through the crack between the shutter and the side of the wall to which it was attached. The bed clothes lay in disarray. When they had arrived the sheets were stiff and starched, white as snow. Now they had surrendered to the couple's will. The room was citrus scented by a bowl of green stemmed oranges that stood on a sideboard.

They had left the honeymoon until April. Married at Christmas, honeymoon at Easter. Toby thought it sensible. The weather would be warmer, and it could double as a summer holiday. He was untroubled by the dictates of romance. They had gone back to London three nights after the wedding. The original plan had been to have two nights at Rick Stein's in Padstow. Then Toby thought, why actually stay at Stein's hotel, which is expensive, why not stay somewhere more reasonable, and just eat at Stein's? Then he thought, why not just eat at Stein's once, not both nights? Then he decided not to actually book, as he was sure there would always be tables in January. Then when they stood outside the restaurant and looked at the prices it seemed almost mad to spend so much on one meal and Alice never minded where she ate anyway, so they had chips on the harbour.

Since they were married, he thought, she had become like a married woman; more sober, more restrained. He wondered if she were preparing for motherhood.

Alice lay naked on the sheets. Toby traced a finger down the long curve of her spine, starting at the top and finishing at the coccyx. She rolled over and lay on her side, supporting her head with her hand, one knee forward. Toby saw the black triangle of her pubic hair, the slight undulation of her stomach.

'Open the window, Tobe,' she asked.

Light flooded in.

She lifted herself and gazed out over the flat interior of Spain. They had hired a little car and were driving from Madrid to the Southern coast, taking in the sights on the way. Here there were no sights, only the plain where Hannibal had fought a battle, ochre under strong sun. The flat table receded into opaque distance. It was Spring and the earth was fertile. They had driven past furrowed groves of wild Mediterranean flowers under rows of burgeoning orange trees, white heavy with blossom, and past pale green waves of olive bushes.

This morning the maid had brought them a tray of breakfast; small sweetly sticky cakes, springy fissiparous hard shelled bread, dates, coffee, chocolate and watermelon. Toby wasn't keen on Spanish breakfast. He couldn't get a proper cup of tea. The pale liquid they gave him was insipid and unendurable.

'Abroad is all very well,' he said. 'But it has its drawbacks.' Toby would cheerfully have holidayed in Cornwall every holiday. It was fortunate, he reflected, that they could stay with family and never more have to worry about hotels.

They were about twenty miles inland from Granada. Toby thought it would be better to stay outside Granada as it would be less crowded and they could drive into the town in an hour.

They had lain in too long. It had been a slightly unsettled night. In the darkness Alice had woken to a sound. She listened. From next door came a rhythmic tap tap tap against the wall at her head. She realised that someone was having sex, the bed rocking against the wall. As she focused her ears she heard mingled moans of pleasure. Toby woke too.

'You'd think they'd keep it down,' he grumbled.

273

And then of course they could not get back to sleep. The compulsion to listen was too great. In the end Toby was fascinated. The tapping went on and on, altering in tempo, first fast, then slow, frenzied, then lazy.

Toby went to the lavatory and stuffed damp loo roll in his ears.

'Revolting,' he said, into his aurally dimmed world.

Alice looked at the figures on the digital clock. The fucking continued for an hour and a half.

'Perhaps they are real honeymooners,' she said to herself. 'Perhaps they have waited and this is their first time.'

She lay in the dark trying not to think too hard. Whenever she had space to think she became upset. The space filled with impressions, tumbling over themselves and she tried to rearrange them, to sort them, to make sense of them, to form valid structures for understanding. It takes a lot of work, to gather up a lifetime's worth of random experience, and elicit coherence. It was as if the outer shell of her life were in stasis, while this inner process whirred on. In the night, against the background sonata of the lovemakers, she thought of the eye. The eye takes in messages. The brain interprets the messages. In order to do this it utilises all the past experiences of the body and the senses to construct predictive hypotheses. Memory, past experience, analogy, categorisation, perception, interpretation; the mind a series of perpetually reflecting mirrors, explaining to us who we are and where we are and what it all means. Alice had the feeling that she was in a house where all the mirrors had blind spots where she herself should be.

When Alice and Toby stepped out of the hotel room after showering and dressing in cool holiday clothes, coincidentally the neighbouring door opened. Alice and Toby both waited, intrigued to behold sight of the rutting pair.

From the room came, with enormous dignity, a grave and elderly Spanish gentleman, exquisitely attired in dark slacks, gold buckled belt, immaculately pressed open necked shirt and tailored jacket hung over his shoulders in the fashion of a cape. He had beautiful shiny chestnut coloured shoes and a fastidiously groomed moustache. By his side walked a solemn lady of similarly advanced years, wearing a tailored navy dress and low square heeled court shoes. Her hair was shoulder length, shiningly clean and held in shape by a silver brooch and pin. This lady inclined her head fractionally towards the young English couple, before stepping in feline manner alongside her husband, resting her hand on his arm.

'Unexpected,' murmured Toby.

'Real love endures,' thought Alice.

In a church in Granada Alice stood before an image of crucified Christ, typically Spanish in tenor, the emphasis all on torture and agony. The ripped plaster body raised sinewy arms outwards, ribs strained, pierced feet twisted. They had given him a wig, so that a curtain of hair fell from blood soaked scalp.

'All that unnecessary suffering,' observed Toby in distaste. 'How Catholic.'

Toby would have described himself as Anglican, though he never went to church.

'Through suffering we are purified,' suggested Alice, in the flickering of the candle rows.

'Rubbish,' said Toby, with elemental simplicity.

Alice tended to agree. Suffering had its place, but not right in the centre, as a benchmark for all that follows. Suffering was just another memory in the room, another refraction of the light.

She bought a postcard. The picture on the front was a portrait of a stern Spanish Inquisitor, heavy lidded black burning eyes, a hooked nose, a hard, cruel set to the lip, his hand raised to his chest, fingers curled around a furl of papers sealed with red wax. The Inquisitor's black ruffed cloak blended with the shadowy background so that the face stood out with startling intensity. On the reverse she wrote, 'Orange blossom heavy on trees. Very beautiful here,' and posted it to Easton.

275

She also bought cards for the family. On the card to America she just wrote, 'Weather fine. All well.' On the bottom of that card Toby added, 'Hello, Sunny. Missing you,' and signed his name.

'You know Sunny's in love with you,' said Alice.

'She's a child.'

'You know it, don't you? And you like it.'

'Infatuation' said Toby. He experienced slight discomfort, but couldn't have identified why. 'Next year she'll think I'm a foul, smelly old man.'

'But until then you are content to be a God.'

They went to the Alhambra. Its intense beauty made Alice feel terribly lonely.

As they lay on loungers next to each other later by the hotel swimming pool, a glinting oblong of blue against dust hot terracotta tiles, Toby said, 'Deceptive.'

'What?' She squinted at him in the glare.

'This pale sun. You ought to be careful, or you'll burn.' Toby had smeared thick yellow blobs of cream all over his chest and thighs.

She left Toby by the pool and walked from the cool of the hotel lobby into the sun filled road. Nothing much was happening. Alice wanted to find a chemist for calamine lotion. Toby was right. She had failed to protect herself and she had burned. The pain was turning to a dull ache in her shoulders already.

She was angry with herself for being such a fool. Perhaps, she mused, she was forcing punishments on herself. She sat down at a metal table in the hot shade of a café canopy. She just wanted to be by herself for a while. She admitted that her analysis of her sunburn was ludicrous. She had burned because she had misjudged the heat of the sun. That was all.

She ordered a Cerveza and it came in a glass beaded with ice cold droplets. Though Toby was only a short stroll away she felt entirely alone. She believed, suddenly, under the striped red and white canopy, with old women in black passing by and a cage of dying rabbits casually left on the shadeless part of the street, that the most essential part of a relationship, including the relationship with ones self, is honesty. Deceit in her thoughts, words and actions; this was her wedding present to Toby. All around her marriage she saw lies piling up, like mounds of bodies.

Her gift to Easton had been partial emotional resuscitation, just enough to let the pain in. She allowed herself really to remember Easton, to bring him right into the forefront of her mind, and suffer the consequences. He used to have her lie on the bed with her legs wide open so that he could see her. He wanted, he said, really to see her; to look at her when she was most exposed. They had each pursued each other's boundaries of trust. It was he who had let go first.

Chapter Twenty-Seven

The therapist suggested, 'You are avoiding your father.'

'Yes.'

The therapist and Tommy were physically alone in the room, but the therapist could feel the presence of the absent third.

Tommy had asked that he do no more of the therapy sessions with his father.

'Why?'

'To avoid what he makes me feel.'

The therapist left a silence. Tommy was one of the most intelligent clients to sit in the white room. The therapist thought Tommy would make a good therapist, if he didn't relapse into heroin.

'He makes me feel useless, disappointing, inadequate, a failure.'

'Do you think he is right?'

'It isn't what I think that counts.'

'Do you think your father has ever failed in any area?' The therapist thought about Easton. Privately the therapist had formed the view that Easton was permanently emotionally cauterised. He would have loved to do an intensive case study of the man.

'He's a winner. You only have to look at him. He believes in himself. He's strong. He's almost impregnable.'

'But when Chas knocked him down...' The therapist kept returning to this incident.

'If you break someone's fingers and kick them hard enough in the bollocks they fall,' retorted Tommy. The therapist noted with interest Tommy's vent of anger. 'Any way, he was back in court the next day. He told me so.'

'Do you think he grieves over the loss of his marriage?'

Tommy laughed carelessly. 'No. I can't believe he married her in the first place.' He stopped laughing and frowned thoughtfully. 'Though she was very beautiful. So it was suitable in that way.'

'He was clever and rich and successful, and she was beautiful,' reflected the therapist.

'Yes. Superficially, they made a suitable couple.'

This was more like it. The therapist reached for the key he had been handed.

'Superficially?'

'I know where this is leading. They both have damaged interiors. I know that. Her damage has made her ridiculous and awful. But his damage has made him invulnerable. I mean, what does it matter that you can't keep relationships going if relationships aren't important to you? If all that's important is professional success? You get to the end of your life and you measure what you've achieved against what you wanted to achieve, and you've won. He's won. He's impregnable.' Tommy's voice rang with pride. 'The only area he hasn't won is me. I'm his only failure. He won't admit it, but it's true. No wonder he hates the sight of me. Look at me.' Tommy lifted up and showed his amputated hand and began to cry.

'It is not your fault,' reiterated the therapist, wearily, and closed the session.

Tommy returned to the Pig within three hours of the expiry of his eight week treatment at the Residential Unit, which had cost his father forty thousand pounds. He had had extensive orthodontic treatment. He had gained six kilos in weight, the eruptions on his skin had cleared, he had a haircut and he was wearing clean new clothes.

'You been polished up, then?' asked the dealer, still fixed at the same table in the corner. His fat shoulders heaved up and down in mirth. He sat wide legged, each thigh a slug in trousers, his knees protuberant and melony. 'Looks like you come into a few quid. You got some ponce looking after you? Want somtfink?' The dealer held out a little silver wrap.

Tommy asked, without taking the goods offered, 'Seen Chas?'

The dealer sniffed the air suspiciously. 'Might have. Might not.'

'Well, have you?' pressed Tommy. There was something a little more forceful, even a little contemptuous in Tommy's tone that surprised the dealer and caused his small brutal eyes to snap upwards.

'He's not been around. I don't know where he is and I don't give a fuck.' He bared his teeth in an evil smile.

Tommy moved over to the bar and asked his questions and got the same answer. No one knows anything in the Pig.

After wandering around some of the old places looking for Chas Tommy went back to his father's house, where he was staying. He had told his father he would stay for a bit, an open ended intention. It was still his plan to find Chas and to see what happened after that.

When he got back he listened as he entered the hall. His father had brought him home from The Priory and then gone out to buy some Coca-Cola. Tommy had asked for Coke as he knew there was no possibility of his father having any in the house. While he was out Tommy had left.

There was no sound. There was never any sound in the house, no talking, no music. Tommy deliberated. He wanted to go to his room and avoid seeing his father. But he had to check in, as it were. He banged the door, thinking this would bring his father to the hall, but it didn't. He found the living room empty. Of course, Tommy knew where he would be; the study.

His father was working at the computer. He looked up.

'Hi,' said Tommy. In Tommy's head his father had only one expression. It was a singular expression, one he had never seen on any other face. Tommy had thought about that expression many times and tried many words to make them fit it; unforgiving, threatening, critical, contemptuous, frightening. None were adequate.

Now his father wore a completely different face. It was peculiar, a shock, seeing a different face. In all his reconstructions Tommy had never seen a face like this one. None of them had ever scared him as much as this one. His stomach turned.

'I'm just preparing a judgement.' Easton touched the keyboard and saved his work and stood up. 'Your Coke's in the fridge.'

'Thanks.'

'It's late.'

Tommy had no idea of the time. Time wasn't a concept he needed.

'You must be tired.'

'No.' But when Tommy said it he realised he was tired. More than tired.

'Did you find him?'

'Who?' Tommy pretended.

'Chas?'

'No.'

'You're missing him?' Easton had learned all about missing.

'I don't know where he's gone.'

'You'll get used to it.'

'I'll find him, sooner or later.'

Easton calculated. He sensed he was at the right time. He allowed Tommy to see him hesitate.

'I've seen him. He came here, to the house, while you were in the unit. I didn't want to tell you because I thought you'd leave.'

'What did you tell him?' Tommy seemed aghast.

'I told him you were in rehab. He gave me a letter for you.'

'A letter?'

Easton sensed his son's incredulity. He trod carefully. He needed Tommy to believe what he was putting to him. At this moment what was required was a precisely measured solution of truth and untruth.

'He wanted to see you.' True. 'I wouldn't tell him where you were.' True. 'He was upset.' True. 'I told him you were lucky to be alive.' Also true. 'He asked me for some paper and he wrote you a letter.' Literally true. No lies there.

Easton pulled open a drawer and brought forth the second letter that Chas had written, the one Easton had dictated.

Tommy scrutinised the shape of his name on the envelope. Easton watched him carefully as he read it. It was the content of the letter that was the lie.

"Dear Tommy, I've got someone who'll pay for me. I've got money now. I don't want to go back to the way it was. You and me will kill each other. Don't try and find me."

Easton knew that people are most likely to believe in a lie if it is told to them by someone they love. He knew his son would not believe his lie, so he had used Chas.

'Have you read this?' asked Tommy.

'Yes'

'It's not true.'

Easton didn't contradict. It was Chas's lie, not his. Easton wiped his prints from it.

He gave Tommy his Coke in a long glass. Tommy sat labouring over the letter, reading and re reading, the one precious object from his lover, literally the only keepsake he possessed. Eventually Tommy said 'Would you put Chas into rehab?'

Easton understood but it served his purpose to be confused.

'I can't put him in.'

'I mean, would you pay for him to get clean?' Tommy' face was suffused with painful expectation. Easton thought it was incredible that Tommy could really imagine that he would pay for the rehabilitation of the man who had destroyed his child. Could anyone be so naive?

What had Alice told him? Once they got to a certain level of usage it was almost impossible to stop, and when you did stop it would kill you, one way or another. That was the level that Easton had been paying for Chas to reach.

'I think that's something I'd have to consider.'

'You have to consider now. I can't tell Chas we'll rescue him if it's not true.'

'Rescue?' Easton was taken off guard by the use of the word. He tried to wipe the incredulity off his face. 'What makes you think you can do that?'

'We love each other.'

'That isn't enough.'

'How would you know?'

'I see it every day in court.'

'Yes, but you've never loved anyone.'

Tell your son you love him, Alice had said. But he hadn't and he couldn't. He hadn't told Alice he loved her, he hadn't told his mother, his father, or his wife; Alice had told him she loved him as he fucked her on her wedding bed. Believing you love someone is a dangerous mistake. Every day in court he had his belief confirmed. Why else did he devote his life to this boring, squalid jumbled mess of human emotion? Love is not enough, and if it's not enough what use is it? Clearly it was the same for everyone. Love wasn't something that happened to other people, it didn't happen to anyone. It was an illusion.

'Tell Chas whatever you want. I'll do whatever it takes.'

'You promise?'

'Yes.'

'Thank you.'

Tommy searched for Chas every day. He had a routine. He went to the chemist in the morning and, watched by the careful Indian chemist, swigged back his methadone. He went each day to the clinic and did urine samples. He attended therapy three times a week at the clinic with a lady called Monica. Alice was no longer his treating psychiatrist, she had signed him over to her colleague Dr Richards, but Tommy regularly bumped into her when he was sitting on the sofas waiting to do his sample or for his therapy session. He liked Dr Christie. He thought she was funny. She always sat down and had a chat with him. He didn't mind telling her things. She looked him in the eye and was interested in what he said. He found her interesting, too. It was nice to talk to interesting people who weren't competing with you, only being friendly.

The rest of the time he looked for Chas. He went to the Pig most days, only for a few minutes, to sweep the interior with his eye, not really to go in. He had told Alice what he was doing and she had suggested he take something along with him when he was going around the old places and faces to remind him that he had moved on, something that he could actually touch. He hadn't got anything, so she gave him a key on a chain. It was the key to her first flat in London. She told him whenever he touched it to think of how good it was going to be when he moved out of his father's place and into a place of his own, with his own work and his own friends, and maybe Chas too. So when he moved around the drug haunts looking for Chas he took Alice's key with him and held it in his hand. It worked.

She recommended a group for him to attend, a bit like AA, but for young people. He had to travel to East London for it, so it used time. She also sent him to the Hampstead Oxfam to volunteer, and so he started working in there on Saturdays.

'Do you remember Dr Christie? From the DDU?'
Easton was standing at the sink rinsing out the teapot. Tommy was sitting at the kitchen table, dunking jammy buttered croissant into hot chocolate. He dipped his head in the rapid turning motion of a diving cormorant in order to wrap his mouth around the soggy patisserie before it decomposed back into the cup. Easton had had to start having food delivered. Even still he would come home and find the refrigerator gaping at him hollow mouthed. Tommy ate. He ate and ate. It was as if he were compensating for years of semi starvation. He also cooked. He concocted elaborate dishes from cookery books he had bought from the Oxfam shop and the cleaner had shown him how to make samosas and bhajis. He cooked these dishes and then

demolished them from the pan, standing up at the work surface.

'Dr Christie asked me if I could do some painting at her flat. She says she'd pay me. But I don't like to charge her. She's been really good to me. She's trying to sell.'

Easton moved his hand around the flaky interior of the teapot, assiduously ridding it of wet leaves.

'She's moving out of London. Her husband's got a job in Bath.' Tommy looked up expectantly and waited. He prompted, 'Remember Dr Christie? She came here once.'

'Yes. I remember.'

It was as good a way as any of telling him she was leaving. It was where she put the level of his entitlement. How could he object to that? She didn't mean anything to him and he didn't mean anything to her. It wouldn't matter if she was no longer just down the hill, if there was no longer any prospect that he might encounter her by accident; see her across the street occasionally. She was no longer a part of his life. It was over and it had meant nothing. It was a mistake and it was over.

Although he had just cleaned the teapot he put the kettle on the boil again for a fresh pot.

He did remember. When he remembered it came as a sudden mental stabbing and he had to recoil urgently, crushing her out. Sometimes, even in court, he might be hearing argument, referring to a bundle or the wording of an Act and there she would be, unconjured, not her face or her body, but the sensation of her, close to him. And then there would come a desire so real he could feel the touch of her, the smell of her, like an amputated limb. He saw her face, and her body, the cross of her knees, the lift of the head, the spread of her fingers on the table. He wanted to be able to stop her coming like this. Her leaving London, her total physical absence, would feel conclusive, like a death after a long illness.

'What did you do today?'

'Chemist, clinic, stuff.'

'Looking for Chas?'

Tommy shrugged.

'Chas knows where you are if he wants you.' He phrased that sentence carefully. Tommy's face closed up.

'Why do you think he's not getting in touch?' Easton asked, subduing the ring of victory. So much for Chas and his love, bought off for a thousand a week. Easton speculated that it could have been less if he had lowered himself to haggle over the price of this thing. The more you looked at the idea of love the more it diminished. If you could buy it and sell it, if it could be there one day and gone the next, extinguished by a momentary gust of physical revulsion, if it could wither with separation, dehydrate with boredom, if it could metamorphose slyly into the sludge of routine, if it is a temporary commodity, if it comes wrapped in possession and jealousy, demands, disappointment, deals and quid quo pros, is it love at all? To these questions Easton knew the answer.

'I think he must be dead.'

'Dead?' echoed Easton, bemused. Did Tommy truly believe that the end of love could be accounted for only by death. Easton wanted to explain it all to him. Your boyfriend's exchanged you for hard cash. He wanted Tommy to understand the way the world worked; he knew it would hurt and at that moment he wanted inflict hurt. But Tommy had already begun to cry.

'Don't,' said Easton. But Tommy carried on. Easton raised his hand palm forward in a gesture of prohibition. 'No.' It was a command, a word to a dog, and at the sound of the command Tommy remembered and tried to stifle his cries, but he knew Chas was dead, or he would have come to him. The tears swelled and flowed.

'Stop…' Easton couldn't use the verb. It was blocked behind an immense weight.

Easton turned the lock in the French windows with frantic fingers so he could get away from the sound of tears. He fumbled with fingers that did not seem to belong to him. He

286

threw open the door and stepped into the garden. It had recently rained. The heavy branches bent to him, lachrymose also. The earth smelled wet and decaying.

He had stood with her here in the garden. He had wanted her then, before he had even touched her. What force had driven him to her on that night? What if he'd been the kind of man who proclaimed love? But he wasn't. She would move out, she would live in a house with a garden, she would have toast in the morning with her husband, pay the gas bill, go to the supermarket, put her clothes in the washing machine, have marital sex, get pregnant, give birth, worry about her kids, watch them build sandcastles. She would be a mother. She would have a life; seconds, minutes, hours, passing into days and years. Her memory of him would diminish to inconsequentiality, a speck in the distance. If a tragedy occurred and she were mown down by a bus, already her obituary would hold no trace of him at all, only her sister had her piece of shocking knowledge, a grubby fragment unfit to be mentioned. Alice had a life and he was not in it. He longed to get away from the pain, newly rekindled.

He went back to the kitchen.

'He's not dead.'

Tommy stared at him from reddened eyes.

'I know he's alive.'

'How?' asked Tommy.

'Because I'm giving him money.'

'What do you mean?'

'To stay away from you. He said he'd stay away if I paid him. I've been giving him thousand a week. I know he's alive because the account goes down.'

Easton watched his son, curious as to his reaction.

'That's not true.'

Easton's kettle had boiled. He unscrewed the lid from the tea caddy and used the little ornate spoon to put three heaps of leaves into the tea pot.

'That's not true,' repeated Tommy.

'It's true.'

287

Tommy sucked in his breath. His father's voice had sunk so softly it was frightening. 'I tell you what. I'll stop the payments this week and we'll see how fast Chas turns up on my door.'

He had his back to Tommy and couldn't see the boy's face. He no longer wanted to see the effect. He was sick of love and all its pain.

'He loves me.' Tommy whispered the words, as if they were the only words in the world that mattered.

The caddy slammed into the sink. The leaves spilled out.

'He doesn't love you. It's not love.' Tommy's father, who never shouted, was shouting now. He had his face so close, Tommy could feel the heat of his breath. 'There's no such fucking thing.' Each word was slow and separate and carried its own emphasis. Finally he slapped his hands hard together, as if love were a mosquito in between. Tommy's father strode out and ransacked his desk, threw a piece of paper at Tommy, then snatched it up again. 'Let me help you read it.' He held out the little note. He hadn't got his glasses. He didn't need them. He knew what it said. He looked directly at Tommy.

'If you want me to leave him yourll have to put more than five hundred in, I cant live on it. Its very difacult. If you want to find him try the pig and wisle pub. He'll be rent by now.' He let Tommy see the note, holding it out before his eyes.

'He can't really spell can he?' Easton finished, with a small derisive laugh.

Tommy took the note into his fingers and looked at it for a long time.

Chapter Twenty-Eight

The house Toby had seen was situated in a village about two miles outside the city. It was a modern house, erected on a plot that had once been a beautiful meadow, spreading buttercups in summer. The house sat with its four siblings on the brow of a slope. Below, the hill swept down to a valley, then rose again to an incline that had not yet been desecrated with further housing.

'I know the house itself is plain, but the view's magnificent,' said Toby, standing behind Alice, and hoping that she would like it. He had been down to the area on a number of sorties to view appropriate accommodation for them. The choice of location was a mingle in his head of good work opportunities for him and secondarily for her, nice clean air, a convivial city and relative proximity to the family in Exeter and Cornwall. He wanted his wife to be happy.

Two dun horses lazily cropped the grass beyond the creosote fence.

'We could put in some decking. We could sit out here in the summer and have breakfast. Orange juice and croissants.' Toby had it all in his head.

The house already had its white goods installed. There were four bedrooms, one of them so minute as to be a cupboard in any respectable old house. It was described, manipulatively Alice thought, as a 'cot room'.

Toby had done the maths and it added up. He had the job at the Bath Infirmary confirmed. Alice still had to make enquiries about work. He was a touch put out that she hadn't managed to get round to it yet. It had occurred to him, however that at twenty nine his wife might well have her mind on higher matters. Once this idea entered his head he could almost hear the tick tick of the biological clock in bed next to him. He ascribed any behavioural aberration to broodiness, and was particularly careful to humour her. He had noticed signs, a certain distance, a certain preoccupation; he might almost describe it as nerviness. It wasn't a peaceful

289

mood. She wasn't sleeping very well, and had acquired a sort of reckless sexuality. He did his best. She seemed to want more, though she never actually said this. It was in the way she moved, making him go deeper, so deep it was almost as if she wanted him to hurt her. Sometimes he found it secretly exhilarating that his wife should be so potent, but he was also slightly disconcerted. Sex for Toby was a becoming more and more what you did before reading the Sunday papers. This was what he wanted from marriage. This was what he had to give. Toby ascribed her abandon to the raging of an empty womb.

He had hoped for a few more years of saving before they had children, so he didn't actually broach the subject in case it came falling down on his head.

That night after they had returned from the West Country, as they lay in bed he said, 'You must look in the BMJ.' He meant look for jobs.

'Yes. I must do that.' She saw the years stretching away.

'Alice.' She could hear from the sound of his voice that he was going to raise something loaded. 'Have you argued with Marion?'

He received his reply in her silence.

'What about?'

'Sister stuff.'

'You ought to write. Or call.'

Oughts and shoulds. Toby spoke in the language of duty. He was a very well matched addition to the family.

'It would be nice to go out and see them in the autumn, now they've bought that place on Martha's Vineyard. They say its best in autumn.'

'Maybe,' said Alice and turned over.

'You'll have to make up at some stage. You can't never speak to your sister again, now can you? Not over some trivial thing. Family's too important. What ever it is, as David says, no body died.'

Chapter Twenty-Nine

Easton went in to chambers in the usual way. Unusually the Clerk of the Rules was waiting for him there.

'Sorry, sir. There's bad news.' She was the kind of woman who took life and shook it, no matter what it held. If there was bad news there was no point pretending it wasn't there.

In the Clerk's room the girls had been sad. They were fond of quiet, kindly Clive.

'Poor Clive. What a life. Looking after her in the wheelchair *and* looking after that Easton; making him work like a dog and knowing all what he had to do at home. See him, poor old bloody Clive piling great heavy piles of bundles in the boot of the judge's car every night. I mean, what does he do with it? Work all night?' Sammy pulled a sneer and flicked back her raven black hair.

Donna said, 'Nothing else to keep him up, is there?' leaning over her keyboard with folded arms. 'Yeah, like fucking the living dead. Imagine. Bloody Nosferatu.'

'Poor old Clive.'

'It's about Clive, sir.'

Not wholly unexpected. Easton lowered the bundles to the desk. 'Is she dead?' He had wondered if Mrs Bird's end would come suddenly, or whether she would stay out her final days, weeks maybe in hospital, wasting away. He thought of the tiny body that had been Mrs Bird. Surely it couldn't have taken long?

'Not Mrs Bird, sir. Clive. He had a heart attack this morning. I'm afraid he's very poorly.'

'What did he say?' asked Sammy, pruriently interested.

'He was upset.' The Clerk of the Rules returned to her desk and flicked on the computer screen. Her lips tightened. She wasn't the sort herself to let it out when she was bothered. She could sense the judge was bothered, in his way. These girls, they didn't know anything. You had to get on with it.

Even when the worst happens, you have to get on with it. 'We'll have to find him a new clerk. I can't have my best judge with no clerk,' she said.

Clive and Easton had come as a package. Easton had brought Clive with him when he was appointed. The man at the LCD, the employer of court staff, hadn't really wanted Clive to come in. They'd got enough of their own people. But Easton wouldn't leave without Clive. They had been a package. That was Easton's condition.

'Are you family?'

'No.'

The young black nurse waited for elucidation.

'Friend?'

'We work together.'

'Oh.' The nurse seemed unimpressed.

They were standing in the corridor of the Intensive Care Unit.

'I'll tell the family you're here.'

Easton waited. He tried to make himself unobtrusive. He could see through a wide glass window into the Intensive Care Ward. The wheels of a wheel chair poked out from behind a curtain closed around a bed.

The curtain opened and a man appeared and made his way across the ward. He was like Clive, only younger and pinker. He wore glasses and pushed them higher up the bridge of his nose in a distracted gesture. He looked like a man containing grief. He came around the corner of the ward and approached Easton, hand outstretched.

'I don't mean to intrude.' Easton wasn't even sure why he had come. They had told him Clive was very ill. Was it some old notion of paying respects?

'Mum says to come in.'

Behind the curtain the family of the dying man was assembled. Mrs Bird's wheel chair was at the top of the bed by Clive's head. She sat, a twisted little sparrow in her chair, legs of incredible thinness poking out from her brown flowery skirt.

Easton absorbed the tableau.

The man who had come out to greet him was the son, Matthew. Matthew resumed a position at the end of the bed, sombre, head of family in waiting. His wife sat on the bed, his sister, Anna weeping silently next to her mother. Anna's husband, a burly, reliable builder stood arms crossed, waiting grimly.

All focused on Clive, Clive as Easton had never before seen him; lifeless, bluey- white, ventilated by a pair of bellows heaving and puffing from a machine by his head. The bellows seemed to regulate Easton's breath, too, in the dense intimacy.

Mrs Bird turned her neck and looked at him. Her head bent at a bizarre angle. She made a sound. Matthew bent forward to catch her series of rapid noises. Easton saw her eyes flick his way again. It was clearly about him that she was speaking.

'She's saying she's glad you made it.'

Easton had no idea what her capacity for movement was; sparse, by the look of it. He said, 'I am so sorry,' and kept his hands loosely linked in front of him, not risking offering his hand to her. Mrs Bird's head perpetually nodded, but all the time she kept her eye on Easton. The evenings he had kept Clive late came back to him. Why had Clive let him do it?

He felt he ought to say something.

'What do they say?' he asked, meaning the medical opinion.

'We've given consent for the ventilator to be withdrawn. We're waiting for the vicar,' said Matthew. As he spoke, Easton detected a crack in the son's voice.

Easton was appalled. Mrs Bird spoke again, her unique language, interpreted by her son. 'We're going to leave you with dad for a few minutes. Mum says he'd want to see you alone.'

'I don't want to take you away from him,' Easton protested, horrified.

'It'll be only for a few minutes.' Easton could see Matthew was reluctantly obeying instructions.

As he watched, Mrs Bird stretched out a quaking hand and raised Clive's inert fingers to her lips and kissed them.

The family withdrew, leaving him alone with Clive. He found himself expected to talk to the ventilated body of his clerk. Easton glanced at the screen monitors. Various flickering graphs proclaimed the basic functions of the brain and heart. The brain was a line. The heart still pounded pointlessly, nothing more than a shining pink blancmange without the input of the superior organ. Clive was dead, and Easton revolted from participating in this macabre and elaborate pretence.

He sat on one of the chairs pulled up to the bed. He noticed Clive was still wearing his wedding ring.

As he looked at the body, the lump under the blankets, the wires like entrails from nose, mouth, arms, a listening silence seemed to grow over the puff and whirr of the machines, a silence that became more and more lambent until Easton felt the gigantic rebuke of nature. There was something here that was alive and completely outside him, sternly rebuking him that he had nothing to say to this man who had attended him every day for twenty five years. Easton did not believe in Heaven or Hell, or any kind of afterlife. He believed that Clive was dead and could not hear him anymore. For a moment, out of the corner of his eye he thought he saw a movement on Clive's face.

The sensation made him jump internally and watch with no breath the detail of his clerk's features. No. If there had been any sign of life it was the corpse of Clive fooling him.

Easton reached out and touched Clive's hand. It was surprisingly warm. He had expected it to be cold. He leaned forward.

'You know how I feel,' he said experimentally to Clive's body.

The chest rose and fell artificially. Easton scoured the dead face for a response. There was none. Twenty five years of good faith, loyalty and care, and a bottle of whisky every Christmas. He had never had a drink with the man, never invited him to his home, never visited him or his sick wife, never crossed the barrier of his own rank and superiority and unrelenting aloofness. Now that Clive was dead he suddenly saw himself as Clive must have seen him. Clive knew the value of friendship, kindness and family. The image of Mrs Bird's kiss revealed its meaning. Easton finally understood what Clive's assiduous care of him had been based upon.

'Goodbye, Clive,' he said.

His father said; 'In the desert you can wake up one morning and get out of your tent and the entire contour of the landscape has changed from what it was the night before. That is, if you haven't been buried alive.'

Geoffrey Easton had married again, late in life, a widow who had no interest in him nor him in her. She was blonde and still had a neat figure at the age of fifty four, and she liked the life of being waited on by servants.

One day, as Geoffrey drove his shiny black sedan along the wide palm-fringed boulevard in Muscat there was a clear hard crack and the car slewed gently into a crowd of jalaba clad men drinking tea outside a café. When the wailing and arm shaking subsided Easton's father was transported to the American hospital. Here, he was X rayed, tested and told by a young Texan that he had bone cancer, secondary to lung cancer, so advanced that there was no point even in giving up smoking. He had about three months.

Geoffrey sat on the verandah of the English club with his broken bone set in a sling and carried on smoking and drinking Johnnie Walker and talking to his friends. When he could he got them to drive him out to the desert, but they didn't really like to because his cough was so bad they all thought he might die any moment, and what an embarrassment to have to come back with a cadaver slumped next to you in the passenger seat.

Someone said, 'Hasn't he got a son? Oughtn't you to let him know, Irene?'

Irene had never met her husband's son. Geoffrey never really spoken about him and he never came out to visit. Geoffrey wrote and told him they were married, but, as far as Irene knew, there had not been a response. Irene had two children of her own. Her daughter had married an American and was living in California. Her son was an accountant in London. She had no interest in Easton's son, except to wonder how she could find out whether he was the main beneficiary in Geoffrey's will.

Geoffrey had money from family. He certainly didn't earn much as a diplomat, but Irene knew there was money, because people said so at the club. Geoffrey didn't look as if he had money. The first time she saw him he was in a seedy Arab restaurant surrounded by desert types, that is, men who made it a bad habit to go out under the sun and trek pointlessly about the wilderness with camels and indigenous guides. Irene and her acquaintances had gone to the place for a little local colour but had soon left. She had seen him again at the club. She made enquiries; first wife dead, nasty accident; son at school in England; bit of a drinker, but bright if you caught him sober; ex- Harrow school, big house in Hampstead. Word was that the diplomatic service would give him a nice little pension soon as seemly, and he'd retire in a pretty good state back home. Irene could see herself in a house in Hampstead. She had aspirations. Her first husband had been employed by a date importer. It wasn't a very prestigious job. He had died, and she had had an unsatisfactory relationship with a man who kept failing to marry her. She married Geoffrey Easton out of boredom, pique, and greed. There are worse reasons. No one quite knew why Geoffrey married her. Probably the same reason he didn't seem to care about dying.

Finally Irene conceded she would have to get in touch with the son. It might at any rate shed some light on the testamentary arrangements. Her continuing hints to Geoffrey were irritatingly avoided. She wrote to the college in Cambridge. Basically she wrote that his father was dying and that if he wanted to see him he ought to come now.

Easton was three weeks away from Finals. He hadn't seen his father since the day on the steps at the diplomatic house. He threw away the letter and carried on working. When his exams finished he booked a flight to the Gulf.

During his years at school in Oxfordshire his long holidays had been passed at the nearby home of his Aunt Grace, a terminal hypochondriac, who was actually his father's paternal aunt. Grace's brother, Easton's grandfather, had died. He occasionally met his grandmother. Even when he was quite old she used to give him peppermints from her bag and recite to him 'The Owl and the Pussycat'. Young Easton formed a morbid dislike of elderly ladies. Aunt Grace wilted. Everything was a terrible effort. She had a bad back, and debilitating palpitations. She gazed at him with long suffering brown eyes, though her indifference never descended to actual unkindness. Her torture was boy Easton. His torture was the lavender smell and slow unendurable boredom of Aunt Grace's home. All there was to do was read and work, read and work. Within walking distance was only a dull village. When he got a bit older he used to get the bus into Oxford, an hour's ride away, and walk around the Ashmolean and the book shops.

For many years however Easton forgave Aunt Grace and even tried to feel gratitude, because she held the honour of being the only person in his life who had offered him care of any sort. It was only later that he realised that she had been paid, and paid a lot, for sharing her home with him. This realisation was accompanied by strong unexpressed feelings, and he left the house forever shortly after and never got in touch with Aunt Grace again, eradicating her from his life. Instead, during school and university holidays he used the allowance from his father to travel in European cities, unhampered by the need for companions.

When he stepped out of the aircraft the ferocity of the summer Gulf temperature swamped his breath. His first thought was that the heat was coming from the whirling turbines of the engines and that he ought to move away as fast as he could. It was only after ten or eleven steps on the sweating Tarmac that he realised that the heat was actually the heat of the day. He remembered it and stopped suddenly, right there in the column of travellers making its way to the airport building. Tutting, they parted and walked around him, a boulder in a stream. The heat, the colours drained of their potency by the invincible power of the sun, the sweltering, glinting sky. The Gulf. It resumed its place in his memory as if it had never been gone.

He took a cab to the house.

It was not as he remembered it. Modernisation had occurred. New building was going on everywhere. Shiny big hotels, dual carriageway roads, long flat ugly industrial sites scarred the desert, for that was still what it was; desert sand with buildings on it.

The driver took him to the old town. He didn't recognise any of it. He had been seven when he left. He didn't recognise it, but the smells came back and stirred in him. The language stirred him too, hearing it as the spoken language of the street. At the time of his leaving it would be fair to say that his Arabic was as good as his English, and it was the one thing his father had taken care to provide for. He had specified to the school that his son have lessons in Arabic. An impoverished old don had to be brought from Oxford each week just for Easton.

The words, the intonation, the guttural back throated sounds were the sounds he had heard when being bathed as a baby, dressed as a toddler, fed as a child, and taken out to market on the food buying sorties of the servants.

When he got to the house he stood outside the main door for a while before ringing the bell. He was wearing a shirt and jacket and was perspiring badly under the arms. An Arab servant in a white jalaba came to let him in. He stepped through into the courtyard and looked involuntarily up to the second floor balcony. His eye was held by the shape of the ironwork of the bars. Memory flashed back. The courtyard seemed to have shrunk.

There was no one in to greet him. He was not expected. He ascertained that his father was not yet dead. No indeed, he was at the Club. Mrs Easton was visiting friends. The Arab servant offered him mint tea, speaking broken English. He was very surprised when the young man in such unsuitable clothes replied in Arabic. It was an old fashioned Arabic, not exactly the stuff of everyday use, formal and convoluted, but comprehensible.

Easton accepted the mint tea, and asked if he could see the house. He didn't say that he had once lived there.

The servant led him hospitably from room to room. The mosaic of the hallway floor under the stairwell had not been changed. The garden at the back of the house no longer possessed its rectangles of green. The fountain was still there.

Easton had no desire to meet his step mother. He was relieved that she was absent. The drawing room betrayed her personality, with its slightly showy artefacts and prominently displayed photographs of her blonde children. He noticed and immediately obliterated the fact that there were no photographs of himself, nor of his mother. When he had been sent away, they had not packed for him a picture of his mother.

He decided not to wait. The servant called a car to take him to the Club.

It was like all the Clubs in all the dusty, sweaty corners of the globe. It had a lobby and a reception, and beyond these, a bar and a verandah. Upstairs there were rooms that could be rented out for a month or a single night.

The floor was tiled in terracotta lozenges, the walls cream painted plaster. In corners stood high palms in pots.

'Do you know a man called Geoffrey Easton?' he asked the lazy doorman.

He was directed to the verandah.

An Arabic arch led through to a dim, air conditioned room with low sofas and circular brass tables arranged in huddles. It was late afternoon, and there were several men sitting at the tables, Arab and European, taking tea. Beyond this were a series of doorways leading to the verandah, which was more like a cloister, enclosing a shaded courtyard with a small plashy fountain at its centre. Around the parameter, under four joining sloping roofs, were set out chairs and inlaid tables.

Easton looked about. The sun was still high. There was no one out there. Then Easton noticed a person in the corner to his left. It wasn't his father.

He went back in and walked through the inner room, trying to examine faces without being noticed. It was only as he traversed the room that realisation dawned upon him, and he turned back.

The mental detail of his father's appearance had faded like an old sepia photograph. Fifteen years had passed. The man was sick and dying. Easton went back to have a look at the person sitting in the corner by himself.

As he watched, the wrinkled, emaciated figure raised a glass in a shaking hand and drank. On the table by his side was a bottle of Johnnie Walker.

Easton made himself go forward. It had struck him to withdraw, quietly, go back to England, or Paris, or any place on the earth other than the one he was now in. He approached his father and stood in front of him.

Geoffrey Easton looked up. His eyes were bright yellow, and leaking at the sides. It looked as if he were crying, but it was only an involuntary emission.

'Yes?' he said, suspiciously. 'Who the hell are you?'

300

The ice broken, Easton sat down. The man opposite seemed to have shrunk inside his suit. The collar stuck out like a yoke, the trousers were pulled tight around fleshless hips by a belt in which extra holes had had to be pierced in order to be small enough. Easton saw under the flannel trousers the shape not of legs, but of sticks. His father's weeping eyes struggled for focus.

'Who are you?' he repeated, indignantly.

'I'm Michael.'

'Michael who?'

'Michael Easton.'

The eyes showed puzzlement. Then he said, testily, 'I don't know what they've brought you here for.'

'They said you were dying.' They had told the truth.

Geoffrey looked at his son and astonished himself by feeling interest.

'So this is you, is it?'

There seemed to be no reply required.

'Light me one of those, would you.'

A bony claw indicated a packet of Turkish cigarettes on the table. Next to the pack was bronze ash tray, containing a heap of low smoked butts.

Easton lit a cigarette, putting it between his own lips first, to get it going. He had smoked a little at school, but hadn't liked the effect. He passed the cigarette to his father. The fingers that plucked it away from his, delicately, like a bird picking up a crumb of bread from the grass, were orange with nicotine. Geoffrey took a long drag then exhaled. A sound like a running gutter came up from his lungs.

'I'm sorry I didn't write,' he said, almost peevishly. 'I suppose I should have. Didn't really feel like it, you know, after what happened. Seemed such a long way away, England.'

'Out of sight, out of mind.'

'Something like that. Anyway, you don't look as if you've suffered too much. What are you doing?'

Easton didn't have opportunity to reply. A slow rattle began deep down somewhere inside the man, gurgled, grew, rose and broke as a violent coughing fit. The bones inside the suit juddered and shook with the assault, it went on and on. Easton looked around to see if there was anyone who might help. They were alone. Finally Geoffrey Easton turned his head and leaned forward and emitted a great, slow green gob of thick mucous from his lips. It hung, shining like an emerald for a second or two then dropped with a soft plop.

Easton noticed a brass spittoon next to his father's chair. The sound the phlegm made as hit the surface indicated that the vessel was already fairly full. Easton felt a wave of nausea in the pit of his gut. He became aware of the overpowering stench coming from his father's rotting lungs.

'How long have you been like this?'

His father gasped for air, raised his hand, which still held on to the cigarette and took another long drag.

'Too bloody long.'

His skin was the texture of dry pastry. Easton had the impression it would flake off if it were touched. As the lips parted to receive the cigarette end Easton saw that the teeth were stained butterscotch brown. He stared at the dying man; literally dying. How many days to go? They would take him to the hospital eventually.

'Where's your wife?'

'I told her, I'm not going back. I don't want to die in the house.'

'What happened to the governess?'

Geoffrey Easton's eyes closed. He was much too tired to reply. The involuntary emission at the eyes resumed. So long ago, but he could smell the apricots from the street and the vanilla she used to rub into her hair. Could it have been the same life?

'She went back to the Lebanon. She was upset. Blamed herself. She was that sort of woman. Thought too much.'

The dying man opened his eyes. He said, 'Doesn't do any good to think too much.'

Another fit of rasping, ending as before.

The Club found Michael a car and a driver.

When he lifted his father out of his cane seat there was only lightness, like carrying a bundle of desiccated twigs. He put Geoffrey in the back seat of the waiting car and got in afterwards. The car slid away from the town along the new straight road, as the afternoon closed and the sun descended and turned tangerine.

He had to prop the weightless frame against his own shoulder to keep it semi upright. His father coughed often. Easton caught the slime in the ashtray he had brought from the club, and each time tossed the dripping mucous out of the window.

They drove along the sea board for a long time, with the sun behind them, getting lower and lower, a glowing ball balanced on the horizon, then turned North and began to head inland, into the heart of the desert. Perhaps they didn't need to drive so far; the desert was always there, all around. But Easton wanted to be far, as far away as he could go and he wanted it to be night.

Night came suddenly, a hand over the eye.

He made the driver stop, and he got out of the car.

He went round and opened the other rear seat door and took his father out. The driver watched, perplexed, but accepting. It was not his father, not his business.

The sand rose in dunes on either side of the tarmac road. Easton walked up one of the dunes. His shoes sank in the shifting sands. It was higher than it appeared. When he got to the top all he could see was black night and stars, immensely bright points of light in the distant universe. The sky looked so smooth, so clear, velvet and diamond and the air of the desert hung soft as silk in the dark.

He took a few steps down the other side, so that the car was lost to sight. There was no sound at all. There was utter silence, only the laboured breaths of the man he was carrying.

Easton laid his father down on the sand and sat down next to him. The sand was gentle and dry under his hand and still quite warm from the sun. Where ever you looked there were stars and silence, and the pale luminosity of the white moon shining.

Easton looked down at his father. The man had his eyes open and was looking fixedly upwards to the sky. His lungs churned and wheezed.

Easton supposed he was on medication. It would probably be wearing off. He wouldn't let it go too long, now.

The driver stood outside the car, resting against the bonnet, smoking a cigarette. He had smoked one, two, before he saw the black outline coming down from the desert.

The driver could see that the body the younger man carried was dead.

The driver threw away his cigarette and got back in the car.

The son put the body in the rear seat and got in next to the driver.

The car returned to the city, an infinitesimal dot on the road that stretched away into nothingness, sand for mile after mile and sky above.

When Easton arrived home from Clive's bedside he heard voices from the living room.

When he opened the door he saw Tommy and Chas. Chas was in the corner of the sofa, and Tommy was kneeling on the sofa, facing and over his friend, like a guardian angel.

Chas had suffered a change. Where before he had been thin but properly dressed, and relatively composed, now he was not. His clothing was filthy and he stank. Globules of perspiration stood out on his fore head. He was grubby and unshaven and grey. His arms were wrapped tight around himself.

Tommy said to Easton, 'This is what you've done.'

Easton closed the door slowly behind him and looked at Chas. 'It's what he's done to himself. I told you he'd come.'

Easton had stopped making payments in to the Chas account. He had been expecting Chas' visit. In fact he was surprised it had taken so long. He had considered it possible that Chas was dead. They might never know, because it wasn't a death that anyone was going to notice. There wasn't exactly going to be a Times obituary.

Still kneeling Tommy rounded on him. 'He hasn't come for money.'

Easton was struck by the ridiculousness of it, teenagers naively taking on the world and thinking they could win. 'He's addicted to heroin. He's come for money.'

'No. He's come to say goodbye.' Tommy clambered off the sofa and stood facing Easton in a pose of triumphal confrontation.

'Really,' said Easton.

Chas grunted and bent over.

Tommy was immediately by his side, a protective hand on his friend's back.

'Cramps,' He looked up and met his father's eye. He saw contempt, where he had expected compassion. He had genuinely assumed his father would feel pity. He could imagine no other response to what was in the room.

'He's really bad.' But the sense that everything would be alright was gone. The world, as manifested in his father, did not care. Tommy was momentarily bewildered.

Was this how things were, then?

Chas lifted himself up. 'I'm off.'

'No, no.' Tommy held him in an embrace.

'Don't do that,' grimaced Chas, not wanting to be touched. 'I don't want your money, or his.'

'A social call, then?' hazarded Easton, sardonically.

Chas ignored it. 'I see him clean. I see how he looks. I thank you.'

Easton looked at Chas. Words eluded him.

Chas turned to Tommy.

'Your dad's right. You won't stay clean with me. There is no life together. It was just hopes, not real.'

'I'm not letting you go.'

'You can't stop me.'

'I'm going to look after you.'

'Too late.' Chas cast a bitter glance at Easton. 'It's the way things are. Now don't fucking follow me.'

'No, Chas, listen. He's going to put you in the Priory, where I went. It's good. It can work.'

'Is that what you told him?' Chas looked at Easton, derision in his eye.

Tommy pulled Chas' reluctant face to his between the tender palms of his hands.

'I do love you. I always will.'

Easton looked away. Shame mingled with disbelief in this child's version of love.

'You will pay for him,' Tommy demanded.

'If he wants it.' Easton couldn't look at Chas

Chas spat, 'He's playing games. I'm past it. He can see it if you can't. Now fuck off, Tommy.'

'No.' Tommy put his arms around Chas and held him. Chas looked over his shoulder helplessly at Easton.

'Leave him alone, Tommy,' ordered Easton, sharply. If it had to be done, let it be done. He was on Chas side in the escape from the terrible deception of love.

Tommy let go.

Chas walked to the door. Easton followed him and held it open. Chas didn't look back. Easton watched the wretched stumbling as Chas turned the corner and vanished from view.

When Easton returned to the room Tommy was standing in the middle of the room. He had the appearance of being in profound thought. 'You've never loved anything or anyone, have you?' Tommy asked slowly, as if groping towards understanding. 'Apart from your job, that is.'

Easton stood silent. Where was the point in responding? Alice's touch on his skin. Was that love? The things she told him, the voice that listened. The telling of truths. Feeling whole. Feeling alive. But in the end she had married another man and he had done his best, from the centre of his heart, to bring down on her humiliation and disaster. The final interpretation of love.

He still had his coat on. He went into the hall and took it off and hung it on the peg.

Clive's wife kissing a dead hand. Changing Tommy's nappy and putting him in his vest in the cold dawn, and carrying that small warm body into his bed and sleeping with him until the morning. Listening to baby breath in the dark. Letting his child be taken away and doing nothing.

'I want you to be well.' Easton articulated the feeling closest to the surface.

'Why?'

Easton went through the range of possible replies in his head and tested them out. There was only really one that felt true. But he couldn't say it. No one would believe it, least of all himself. He remained silent.

His son shouted, 'Look at you! You're pathetic. The things you say and believe are pathetic. It's not being best in your profession that counts, or getting a First, or winning, or having more money, or a title, or higher status. That's just compensation for being hollow. You've got no friends. No one loves you. You're entirely alone. You're always going to be alone, and the worst thing is, you don't care. That's why you're pathetic.'

Easton filled the kettle and heard the door bang as Tommy left.

Chapter Twenty Nine.

There he was, on a Tuesday morning on a dull cold day, sitting in the interior of an old fashioned East European coffee shop. The pavement outside the shop smelled of coffee. Alice never went in because it was sufficiently old fashioned still to be a smokers haunt.

The shop was in a narrow little alley off the main High Street. She was going to the florists. She was on her way to buy fresh flowers for the flat to persuade potential buyers that it was the home of their dreams. The flat was proving hard to shift at the price Toby wanted. Soon the job he had at the Bath Royal would start. They would have to bridge and rent. Toby was getting very stressed and was bad tempered a lot of the time. She had found a job, too. She was moving on. Fresh flowers, no clutter and the aroma of baked bread; this was the advice of the estate agent. The estate agent was a sharp fellow in a sharp suit, a caricature of his profession. Being an obedient sort of girl Alice went out twice a week to make the purchase of flowers. She wasn't sure what she was going to do about the baked bread. The estate agent had conceded that coffee might be an acceptable alternative smell, although, he said, it had become hackneyed as a concept, so much so that punters now felt suspicious of the smell of coffee, like an obvious duplicity perpetrated upon them as if they were stupid.

'What about fish?' she asked. 'I could bake some mackerel.' The estate agent didn't think it was funny. 'Fish,' he said, 'is the kiss of death.'

Alice liked that expression. The kiss of death. She turned it over in the background of her thoughts all day. She was thinking of it as she passed the window of the Kondetorei and absently glanced in to look at the chocolate cakes and saw him sitting there.

She passed on and went to buy her flowers. She bought some purple iris', streaked in the cup with lines of yellow.

They had never discussed times in the future. Easton didn't like time. Time was merely a factor in the measurement of productivity. It was not the past, not even the present and certainly not the future. Alice was now the same. He had bequeathed her a dislike of the consideration of time. The future had become a no man's land, full of mines.

She used to ask him, 'How do you think you'll end up?'

'Dead, like everyone else.'

He wasn't being morose. It was his sense of humour.

'I mean, before that. Will you carry on being a judge for ever?'

'Yes. Court of Appeal. Law Lord.'

'Until some sex scandal brings you down.' She toyed with him. 'And are you going to stay in this house for ever?'

'Yes. For ever,' he mocked her.

She mocked him back. 'Alone?'

He didn't reply.

The times they spent together were situated outside time.

She opened the door of the Kondetorei and went in. He was wearing his suit and tie, and was reading a newspaper spread out on the table. By his elbow was a cup of half drunk brown tea, and a stainless steel pot, and a plate with the remnants of a sweet cake in small crumby boulders.

He had the air of a man who had been there for some time.

'What's new?' she asked.

He looked up, startled, and then dipped his head and returned his gaze to the newspaper. She thought, with surprise, that he was blanking her. It wasn't the kind of thing he did.

He creased the paper into folds as if he had just come to the end of it anyway.

'Do you want to sit down?'

She noticed that he avoided meeting her eye.

'What are you doing?' It was a weekday at ten o clock.

'I'm going to a funeral.'

'Whose?'

'Clive Bird. He died.'

'What happened?'

'Heart failure.'

'I'm sorry.'

No one had told him they were sorry for him that Clive had died.

'Do you miss him?'

'Yes.' He missed Clive. Answering her question revealed the truth to him. 'Would you like some tea? Or coffee?'

'No, thanks.'

He wanted to ask her how she was. He could hardly ask her how she was. He said, 'How's Toby?' Oddly he cared what the answer was. Easton knew that Toby was a good man, whatever that meant.

She didn't reply at once. She looked sad. 'He's worried about selling the flat.'

'Ah.' Easton nodded.

Alice's hand rested on the table. She was rubbing her thumb absently against her index finger. Her fingers were capable and business like. She never had manicured nails. They were cut short. These were hands that cleaned up sick and opened obstinate jam jars. These were hands that did things and by passed the fripperies of ornament and flipped impatiently at insincerities.

The portly middle aged middle European waitress waddled over.

'The end?' She raised her pudgy hands in imprecation. The man had been sitting there for two hours now and she was getting irritated. No one normal spent two hours in the Kondetorei eating a slice of cake and drinking two pots of tea. What was he waiting for?

He nodded and she cleared and put the bill down next to him and went away.

'Tommy said you were moving out of London.'

'Toby thinks its best.'

She detected his inquiry. Did the fabric of their marriage already require the clean wind of change? And was it as a result of his words, his actions?

'In terms of quality of life,' she added.

They say that in relationships there is always the one who loves and the one who condescends to be loved. It's not so between Easton and me, thought Alice, as she sat with him. Lies and truth mattered. They would always matter.

'I threw the life jacket. But he couldn't catch it.' The waves were too high and he was too far away too quickly, too far to rescue, but not too far for her to see him drown.

And he didn't fuck me. He loved me. And I loved him. Always will. I killed him and he still loved me.

She realised she had spoken aloud. She hadn't meant to do that. Michael waited and absorbed the answer. The unconditional love of a father. He thought of Tommy. He thought of Tommy almost all the time, Tommy, Alice, Tommy, Alice.

'Are you still seeing Tommy?' he asked her.

He waited in expectant hope for the only crumbs of information he could get about his son, his attempt at contact having been rejected. He had not pursued it. Tommy had reason, more than reason, to reject.

Alice reflected. What harm could it do? She wasn't Tommy's treating doctor. She had kept in touch with Tommy because Chas was assigned to her, because she liked them and the courage of their love for each other. The shock of detox had nearly finished Chas off.

'Tommy's clean. They're in a little flat. Tommy's looking after Chas now. He's a wreck.'

'Is Chas clean?' He hoped Chas was clean. He indulged himself by picturing the two of them in a sort of childlike domesticity, but Tommy was no longer a child, he was an adult, stepping out on his own. Easton wished Tommy knew how much he wanted him to succeed, against all the odds. He wished he had had the opportunity to begin making amends. 'Do they need any money?'

311

'Do you think they'd accept it?' He read her meaning. She knew about his former generosity to Chas, but here she was still, talking to him.

She said, 'I've got a new job in Bath. We're leaving next week.'

'Tommy will miss you. You've been a good friend to him.' He would have liked to say more, but instead sipped his cold tea.

She realised that she had not managed to bring him home safe. He was still at sea.

'Do you want me to come to the funeral with you?'

'To hold my hand?' He raised an ironic brow.

'When did you ever need your hand holding?' She wanted more than anything to hold his hand.

'It makes no difference,' he said. Life would go on.

'Do you want me to? I'm not going to come if you don't want me to.' She had never put up with games.

'Yes. I want you to come.'

In the car it occurred to him that he could take advantage of the unexpected presence of a doctor. He kept his eyes on the road, and recollecting the tablets he had unpacked from his son's bag he asked, 'Do you know a drug called Zidovudine?'

She knew immediately and horribly where the question had come from. She had continued to scrutinise Tommy's medical notes. She bought time.

'Why do you ask?'

'Something to do with a case I'm doing.'

He knew she'd know it for a lie, but also knew that for once she would let him have his lie.

'Why don't you look it up on the net?' she said.

'Since you're here.' He wanted it to come from her. Alice always made things clear for him.

'Since I'm here I might as well answer your questions. I think that might be where we came in.'

312

She looked through the window. They were on the North Circular. It was a particularly depressing section. The houses reflected the states of aspiration of those who dwelt within. The only life worth living is the examined life. She had once believed this blithely, without understanding the true cost of honesty.

She answered, 'It's an anti-retroviral. It's usually taken in combination with other anti-retrovirals.'

He didn't say anything. She could sense him thinking. She helped him along. 'They control the progress of HIV.'

The words fell upon the epidermis of his perception, quivered momentarily, broke the surface and sank.

The church had a long spire, visible for miles from its bed of trees. It was set on a common surrounded by oak woods. The inhabitants of the houses around the edge of the common had the right to collect kindling and graze pigs on the land. To the best of Easton's knowledge, Clive had no pigs to graze. But still, it was a family place, the kind of place you went to to raise children. Toby might have been happy there if it were not for the tarnishing clichés that hung about the county's neck.

Clive had been happy there.

They arrived early. Easton had never been to Essex and he overestimated the time it would take. The journey, in the middle of the day, had been relatively flowing. Clive's son, Matthew, had churned out on his computer very detailed maps of how to get to the church.

It was easy to park. St Michael's was down a small wooded lane that led nowhere but to a bridle path onto the common and to the church.

'Shall we go in?' Alice asked him.

'Not yet.'

Easton sat at the driver's wheel and watched the first of the mourners enter. The hearse drew up and parked by the church gate. The coffin inside was laden with flowers. It reminded Alice that she had the irises still in the back seat. They'd be dead by the time she got them back to the flat.

The undertakers' black limo purred gently down the lane and drew up behind the hearse. Matthew emerged, in a dark suit. The driver opened up the boot and Matthew went round and pulled out his mum's wheel chair and flipped it open expertly. He lifted Mrs Bird out of the car and into the chair.

Soon she was surrounded; her son, her daughter, her in-laws, grandchildren, sisters and brother, Clive's brother and his wife, so much family that she was obscured by the milling crowd.

Easton saw a delegation from his and Clive's old chambers, 12 King's Buildings. There were the barristers, Desmond Bagley Q.C, Sonia Grimmond, Paul Marshall, and the clerks Richard and Gavin. Easton watched their folding of arms and shaking of heads. More people arrived. The Clerk of the Rules was there. She lived in Essex herself, so it was a trip down the road for her. The group from 12 King's Bench greeted her. Desmond Bagley risked a kiss on the cheek of this powerful woman, calculating that it was a presumption excusable on the grounds that it was an occasion for grief and support.

Alice observed. 'They're going in.'

Easton pulled himself out of the car and made a show of locking up. Out of the corner of his eye he noticed the circle of his chambers colleagues break and open as they saw him. He couldn't bring himself to go and join them. He could hear their muttering in his head.

All he needed to do now was what he had always done; maintain his outer face.

The doors of the church surrounded a tunnel of darkness.

Chambers had turned and was looking his way.

The pallbearers gathered like bluebottles around the back of the hearse. One of them opened the rear doors and slid the coffin out a little way, so it protruded over the edge. Then they bent and with sublime professional grace swung Clive's heavy wooden cocoon up into the air and on to their shoulders, so smoothly that the body hardly stirred in its satin bed.

Easton hung at the side of the car pretending to sort the keys on his fob.

A burning sensation like molten lead slowly leaking grew heavy under his temples and converged around the eyes.

He was aware of Alice standing next to him.

'Are you alright?' she asked.

'I've got a headache.'

It struck him that he might have been here alone and how unbearable that would have been.

She put her hand on his arm and steered him towards the maw of the church. As he passed the Chambers group he nodded and looked straight ahead, offering nothing. No one spoke to him. He realised he was protected by the presence of Alice.

Alice saw the colleagues watch her with ravenous curiosity. There was one strikingly dominant woman in a black trouser suit and brown jumper. Her eyes were hard green, under big arched brows. She had a strong, long nose and wore her lipstick and nails red. The members of Chambers passed in behind Easton. He stood back to let them go ahead and the QC led pompously straight to the front pews of the church. As the green eyed woman passed Easton she murmured with tight sarcasm, 'What's that about the first shall be last?'

She was looking forward to telling the girls that Mr Easton had turned up with a babe. That'd shut their nattering little faces for a while.

The pews were full.

Easton and Alice stood at the back with the other overspills.

The singing of a hymn about eternity rose up to the church's high beams. A woman next to Alice passed her a hymn book open at the page. Alice was at home in the Anglican tradition and sang. She held the verses between her and Easton. He, out of age old habit, echoes from the benches of the school chapel, aligned his head with the book and mouthed the phrases. Since leaving school he had been to church twice;

once for Alice's wedding and now, for his clerk's funeral. His own wedding had been a registry office affair. Judith had been married twice before.

He lifted his eyes to avoid the words of the hymn.

Very close to him in silver veined marble was a sturdy baptismal font in which the sins of infants were absolved. He had never had Tommy baptised. Since God didn't exist, where was the point? Easton wondered if he could get him baptised now, his dying, HIV infected boy. He clasped his hands together to stop them from shaking. God did not exist but God seeped in at the edges under high pressure.

The singing gathered to a crescendo.

Heads turned, daffodils in the wind. Alice turned too. Easton returned his eyes to the page in front of him, the lesser of two evils.

The six men stood in two rows, Clive's coffin hoisted between them. Of the six one was his son, one his son in law and one his younger brother. They proceeded with their heavy load, in slow unison of step, down the aisle. As they passed by, Easton looked up at the casket and at the men supporting it, their faces against the polished wood. On the coffin was a red cross shaped wreath, and as the entourage passed the soft, passionate scent of roses filled the air.

They laid the coffin on a table before the altar.

The organ and the singers shuddered to a lingering halt. There was a shuffle and the congregation sat down with an air of anticipation.

'This is the funeral of Clive Bird,' announced the vicar.

Because they were standing, Alice and Easton could see him. He was robed in black and white, a shrewd pock marked Northerner, the kind of vicar that visited the sick not just to listen but to do the ironing and washing up as well, a social work vicar who lived the message and drank with the flock. The vicar raked bright cobalt eyes along the rows, searching for the possibility of engagement. The vicar kept up a constant war with human despair in an empty universe.

316

'I'm not going to say that Clive Bird was a decent man; a kind, thoughtful, patient friend; a loving father and husband, because you know that already.'

The vicar paused, allowing the silence to fill.

'I'm not going to give you a reason as to why Clive died, aged only fifty five. There is no explanation. The world is a place of tragedy as well as joy. I'm not going to get into a theological discourse about pain and free will being flip sides of a coin. I'm not going to tell you the meaning of Clive's death. No, I'm going to tell you the meaning of Clive's life.'

The vicar moved to the lower step of the altar, closer to the people. He stood with one hand loosely linked around the other, speaking from the head, no notes.

Easton appreciated a man who could speak from the head. He found himself listening for the next words.

'Clive loved people and people loved Clive back. What do I mean by love? I suppose it's as hard to define love as it is to define God. Love and God are bigger, much bigger, than any human definition. There are as many different interpretations of love as there are of God, ranging from the sublime to the not so sublime. St Paul gave us some guidelines. Love suffers long and is kind. It doesn't show off and it isn't puffed up.' (Desmond Bagley Q.C shifted in his pew.) 'Love doesn't seek out its best interests, it bears adversity, it hopes and it endures. Some people say it's the doing of good works. Some people say it's about making sacrifices but, St Paul tells us, none of this is worth a brass farthing if it's not done with love. In other words, the outer show, the trappings of love, the worldly structures we spend so much energy erecting are no good unless love is at the centre.

'You can't see it. You can't touch it, or sell it or own it and you can't substitute something else in its place or make an artificial model. But you can feel it and you can feel, very powerfully, its absence. The absence of love is Hell. That's my take on it because I'm a religious man. I know that there are those of you here today who don't believe in God. But I don't imagine that there are many of you who don't believe in love. We all need love. Love makes us whole.

'Some people in Clive's place might have felt angry or bitter. He and Susan lost their little boy Andrew when he was only two years old. Susan developed MS when she was thirty six. But Clive never closed his heart, and neither did Susan. They transformed their lives and the lives of their children and of the people they came across day to day, friends and colleagues. I know that Clive was especially fond of the man he called 'his judge.' But it was Clive's family that sustained him, believing in each other, trusting each other, tolerating each other's weaknesses, forgiving and understanding because, God knows, human love is never perfect. We have to take each other as we are, to take ourselves as we are, to love others and ourselves, to know that we and others are worth loving. We all need to be loved. But we must love in return. It's only then that life is worth the effort.'

The vicar gave a nod. He had finished. A collective stirring, as of dreamers awaking, rustled among the congregation. The organ trembled into life, the preliminary chords of 'Abide with me,' rousing the mourners to their feet.

'Abide with me; fast falls the evening tide,'

The pain in Easton's head had intensified, spreading a hideous pressure to the very back of his skull, to his throat, almost as if someone was pulling a rope immensely tightly around the neck. The words on the page that he was looking at began to dissolve. At the front of the church Easton saw Matthew, the eight pint a night Essex man, the careful interpreter of his mother's crippled language, the sombre watcher by the hospital bed, the pall bearer, Clive's son, head bent, tears streaming wet on his cheeks.

Alice followed the words of the hymn, though she had them in her head, her own father's valedictory, his sailor's farewell.

A movement and there was an empty space beside her. She looked. The hymn drew to a close. Easton had left.

The tightness in his head had forced him out into the open air. He stood on the gravel path and took his bearings. The wind in the trees rattled twiggy branches. He had a horrified idea of what was coming. He moved like a hunted man.

He bore off to the right, around the side of the church, past the standing headstones with their bright forlorn posies, past lumpen beds of thorn stemmed rose bushes. Thankfully no bereaved lingered. He turned the corner of the west transept and finding himself alone and enclosed on two sides at least rested his forearm against the brick wall of the church.

He could feel it coming. He put his forehead on his arm and closed his eyes. It was rising in him like nausea. He inhaled the smell of the brick, impregnated with a light pale coating of damp furry lichen.

He tried to concentrate on the physical sensation of pain; he imagined the point of a heated blade pressed between his eyes.

The first sounds were constricted, twisted, animal. The sounds intensified. The pain spread from his head to his throat to his chest to his stomach. It became an entire body pain. He tried to imagine he was somewhere else and that the man crying, not just crying, but almost literally vomiting tears, was not him. It went on and on and he could not control it. He was a puppet. He surrendered utterly, for there was no choice. He simply cried a harsh, hot, unending river of tears.

He was crying when she found him. She supported him to the car. In the car he continued to cry for some time. She drove them both back to London. He sat in silence and gazed through the window at the M25 and at nothing at all.

'Will there be anybody home?' she asked him, outside his house, lowering her face to look at his.

He shook his head.

No body.

She took him into his living room. Around the walls, on the surfaces, were the works of art he had collected. These gave him some comfort, the comfort of being around the one unhindered manifestation of his natural inclination. It was he, Michael, who had chosen them for no reason other than that they made him feel something. They made him feel as if he still existed. Everything else of him had been taken away and killed.

She took his fingers in hers.

'Come upstairs,' she said.

He did not want to know when she was leaving. In ignorance there would be no morning when he would wake and know she was gone, no morning when he would feel the absence of love.

What did he say to the hopeless women whose children he ordered to be taken from them? That he hoped they would be able to give their blessing as they said goodbye for the last time; be happy in your new life.

He understood now. He had never before understood anything. He had never understood the miracle of love. Chas had been abused and abandoned but he loved. Clive with his dead baby and crippled wife had loved. His beautiful little Tommy, negated and degraded, loved. The woman with him now had offered the opportunity of love and in return he had given her the bile of his hubris and now it was too late.

They lay on the bed fully clothed. She lay behind him, her shape moulded to his back. Her hand encircled his shoulder and chest. He held tight to her fingers in his palm. The wedding ring was hard and unfamiliar.

He felt wrung out, drained, frozen.

The light, which was grey, faded to no colour at all and rain began to spatter on the window.

The pieces of the last minutes crumbled away.

Eventually she moved. She sat on the corner of the bed, bent over and kissed his temple, placed her hand on his head for one second. When she looked at him he didn't stir and he didn't say anything as she left the room. He had his eyes closed. She hoped he would sleep for a while.

He heard the front door close. After she'd gone he continued to lie there. There were things he ought to get up for, matters to attend to. He had cases to prepare. In the iris of his eye he could see the very page upturned on his desk. He had papers to read, a judgement to finalise. There were cases waiting for him to hear; he was in the middle of a two week trial. He had only had the morning off for the funeral. Life had to go on. Life was going on, all around him. He had pieces of work that were half finished and he would get up and do them, and go to court and come back and on the way home he would call in to the store and pick up some bread and maybe some wine, yes, he would start to drink wine, and he would resume his life.

Time stretched away, day after day, over and over. He imagined having to be empty and alone again tomorrow and the next day and the next.

Lying there on the bed was a continuation of being with her. He could sense the indentation in the mattress where she had been. She had left behind the scent of vanilla. Her presence lingered fragile as a snowflake.

Lying there was better than stepping out into the mechanical wilderness, the arid nothing, the artificial substitute for love.

When I get up, he thought, I will be alone and from that moment I will be alone. Isolation bore down on him like a wall of water, poised just before falling. In the second that the image formed he actually held his breath and his heart accelerated, so great was the anticipation of sinking into a vast, frozen solitude.

He recalled his mother's face appearing through the fountain; and her dead, staring, dislocated eyeball, inches away from her fractured cheekbone, connected only by a shiny red cord to the socket and her blood spreading out over the floor; his father's step back away from him as he said goodbye on the sun drenched steps of the Embassy house; he recalled parchment dry, nicotine stained fingers scraping at a

321

son's suffocating hand while yellow eyes drank panic from the final starlit sky. The boy who rose from the bed in his dream had his son's face and Harwell in the dream was Easton.

He sat up.

He felt strangely at ease with leaving his work unfinished. It gave him a sense of time standing still forever.

He went the bathroom and ran the tap in the sink.

He could not come home to the empty house any more. He longed for Alice. He ached for his child.

He bent and washed water over his face and looked at himself in the mirror of the shaving cabinet. He had never seen himself looking so ridiculous. His eyes were ludicrously red and swollen. He opened the cabinet with a click. Inside were his shaving cream and his father's razor. He took them both out, and opened the razor and laid it on the porcelain sink. He was still using shaving cream Alice had bought him. He took the top off the bowl and inhaled its citrus scent. It had lasted surprisingly well. He rubbed a little on his wet hand and cupped it over his nose, breathing deeply.

'Where've you been?' Toby remonstrated. 'The agent said there was no one in for the viewers. What are those?'

She put the withered flowers on the table.

'I didn't get here in time.'

Toby waited for a deserved explanation. None came.

She sat down on the sofa and pressed her hands together.

The familiar objects of their existence seemed to be the objects of the distant past.

'I was with Michael Easton.'

Toby knew. He had had no warning, no conscious inkling, no suspicion, no clue. But he knew immediately in the centre of his being what she meant. So he said simply, 'No,' and shook his head in an involuntary gesture of denial. He wanted to put it where bad dreams go, but he could not do this because it was true. Fear cut through Toby like a knife.

'I've been seeing him for over a year. Seeing him and sleeping with him.'

'Still?'

'No. The last time was our wedding day. I slept with him on our wedding day and then not again.'

In a moment everything that Toby had believed, and the way in which he believed it, dissolved.

'Michael Easton?'

'Yes.'

'But he's old enough to be your father. In ten years time he'll be drawing his pension. Christ, Alice. There'll be no normality, no children, your family won't ever accept it. It's insane.' Toby's brain kicked in, arranging feelings into shapes that could be comprehended even though they were unfamiliar. Toby's brain automatically sorted through the billions of former perceptions and predictive hypotheses and recognised betrayal. His throat felt very dry. He fought against the panic setting in.

'You and Michael Easton?' He asked again, incredulous. There would be time for the details, the when and the how. 'Why?'

'Because when I think of myself, I think of him. He makes me feel alive. With him, I am myself. I can't explain any better than that.'

She stood up. It didn't seem there was anything more to be said, nothing at any rate that Toby would understand.

'The thing is, Toby, that I didn't want to hurt you. But I have hurt you and you will not want me as a friend. And there is nothing I can say.'

'I think there's a lot we can say.'

'It's over.' She knew this with merciless certainty.

'We are married. We have been married for six months.' His voice had sunk to an incredulous whisper. His face had creased in a way she had never seen before. He stood by the fireplace that she had resurrected. It now held no significance for her. The past and the future were broken forever.

323

'You're not what I need. It was a mistake. My mistake. I tried so hard, but I can't leave him.'

Toby straightened as if he had been shot.

She saw anger; she saw indignation and disbelief. Most of all she saw pain. It was written all over his face, and it was just a beginning.

'I'm going to go now.' She felt a surge of emotion for Toby, for his unhappiness. But she did not want to hold him. 'I'm not coming back.'

Reality had been harder than she had ever imagined. Outside on the street she trembled with the stress. She stopped for a moment, just to marshal some sense of direction in the confusion. She had no map of reference now. It was like drifting at sea on a vast and lonely tide. She walked to the Heath and lay down, closed her eyes and imagined she was on the beach at Chapel Porth, with her hand on the smooth rock's surface and the sound of the waves in her ears. There were always these, always the sea, always the rock, the elementals that made her whole. Her father, Easton, they were elemental, too. She had promised she would never go so far away that she couldn't come back. Now was the time to return.

Easton went to look at his son's room.

The tiger in the storm was lost under many coats of thickly applied paint. Tommy had covered the tiger with black and white stripes. It had taken him a day and a half and the boy kept applying the paint over and over until there was nothing to be seen of what his father had created underneath and only then had Tommy been satisfied.

It was odd. He had made two incisions but the blood was coming very slowly. He was entirely calm. There was a trail up the stairs and a bright red pool in the bathroom. He realised he would have to make a third incision, this time harder. He raised the sharp blade and held it to the existing cut. He had to admit he felt surprised. He thought he would have made a ruthless suicide. Instead it was dripping relatively slowly. Not the best way, he thought, wryly.

The round window in his son's room faced the world. It was the only one that did. He happened to look out at the Heath. He certainly didn't mean to because the world as he was draining of blood felt just as indifferent as it had been during his life. He saw Alice standing on the slope opposite the house. Even from a distance he could see she was alone. She turned very slowly. He wondered why she was just standing on the Heath. It was like one of the mirages he had seen in the desert when he was a boy. Instinctively he put his hand over the slit in his wrist. The blood slid hotly. For the first time he looked down and realised that he had made quite a mess.

He began to go down the stairs, feeling light headed. For some reason he saw himself living in a lighthouse, and winding and winding down circular stairs. A lighthouse would be good. Why had had never thought of that before? It was a good thought. He felt euphoric. He and Alice would live in a lighthouse. He fumbled with the door, leaving long smears of red on the woodwork, and went out into the day, and along the path. His iron gate was padlocked. He couldn't remember the code. He couldn't get out. He put blood soaked fingers around the black bars. His thoughts were dancing now. He couldn't see too much. There were bright spots of light like sun reflecting on water. He saw Alice coming towards him out of the spots, very real, very clear, walking on the light as if she were walking on the sea. He reached out, through the gate. There was so much he wanted to say to her, everything in his heart. He felt a heavy pain in his wrists and around his chest. She came towards him as a transparent ghost. He could hear her voice, calling him. He was at the lighthouse. She was on the waves. Her hands stretched out to him. He began to swim.

THE END

325

HENRY V

Henry VIII was one of England's most unforgettable monarchs. He was at once inspiring, menacing and perplexing to his contemporaries, and his reputation remains both impressive and enigmatic. Henry was a Renaissance prince whose court dazzled with artistic display, yet he was also a savage adversary, who ruthlessly destroyed all those who opposed him. He defied the Pope, destroyed England's monasteries and devastated much traditional religion. Yet he also gave us the English Bible, the palace of Whitehall, cathedrals, castles and colleges, a reconfigured Church and a political legend. Musician, sportsman, theologian, tyrant, humanist scholar and chivalric warrior, he continues to evade easy characterisation.

Lucy Wooding's timely study provides an insightful and original portrait of this larger-than-life figure, and of the many paradoxes of his character and reign. Building on significant advances in recent research to put forward a distinctive interpretation of Henry's complex character and remarkable style of kingship, Wooding locates him firmly in the context of the English Renaissance and the fierce currents of religious change that characterized the early Reformation.

Complete with colour illustrations, this compelling new biography gives a fresh portrayal of Henry VIII, cutting away the misleading mythology in order to provide a vivid account of this passionate, wilful, intelligent and destructive king.

Lucy Wooding is a lecturer in early modern history at King's College, London. Her research interests lie in the political, religious and cultural history of the fifteenth and sixteenth centuries, in particular the history of the Reformation. She is the author of *Rethinking Catholicism in Reformation England* (2000).

ROUTLEDGE HISTORICAL BIOGRAPHIES

SERIES EDITOR: ROBERT PEARCE

Routledge Historical Biographies provide engaging, readable and academically credible biographies written from an explicitly historical perspective. These concise and accessible accounts will bring important historical figures to life for students and general readers alike.

In the same series:

HENRY VIII

Lucy Wooding

LONDON AND NEW YORK

First published 2009
by Routledge
2 Park Square, Milton Park, Abingdon, Oxon, OX14 4RN

Simultaneously published in the USA and Canada
by Routledge
270 Madison Ave, New York, NY 10016

Routledge is an imprint of the Taylor & Francis Group, an informa business

Typeset in Garamond by Saxon Graphics Ltd, Derby
Printed and bound in Great Britain by CPI Antony Rowe, Chippenham,
Wiltshire

British Library Cataloguing in Publication Data
A catalogue record for this book is available from the British Library

Library of Congress Cataloging in Publication Data
Wooding, Lucy E. C.
Henry VIII / Lucy Wooding.
p. cm. — (Routledge historical biographies)
Includes bibliographical references and index.
1. Henry VIII, King of England, 1491–1547. 2. Great Britain–Kings and
rulers–Biography. 3. Great Britain–History–Henry VIII, 1509–1547. I. Title.
DA332.W64 2008
942.05′2092–dc22
[B]
2008011255

ISBN10: 0-415-33996-0 (hbk)
        0-415-33995-2 (pbk)

ISBN13: 978-0-415-33996-4 (hbk)
        978-0-415-33995-7 (pbk)

For Alyosha

CONTENTS

LIST OF PLATES
(Between pages 208 and 209)

Acknowledgements

I would like to thank my colleagues at King's College London for their good will and forbearance during the writing of this book, and in particular Ludmilla Jordanova for her support and inspiration in the final stages. Robert Pearce has been a wonderful editor, both astute and benevolent, and Elizabeth Clifford at Routledge has been very patient and helpful. George Bernard was good enough to read the book in manuscript and I have benefited immensely from both his generous encouragement and his sharp eye for detail. The colour illustrations in this book were made possible by a grant from the Scouloudi Foundation in association with the Institute of Historical Research, and I would like to acknowledge gratefully the generosity of both institutions. I would also like to thank any number of students who have discussed Henry VIII with me over the years, and from whom I have learned so much. I was thinking of them as I wrote this book.

The gestation of this biography coincided with the arrival of Misha and Vanya in our lives. I am thankful for their stoical acceptance of the time Mama spent frowning at the 'piancooter', as well as for the happiness they generated all the rest of the time. I am also very grateful to Agnieszka Woloszyn and Monika Tesarova for keeping the children happy, safe and fed whilst I was struggling with Henry. I must thank my wider family too, and the many stalwart friends who have kept me going. It has been a challenge, trying to combine part-time work as a historian with full-time work as a mother, and one that is only achievable with a lot of allies. This book is dedicated, with all my love, to my husband, who makes all things possible, and who is so entirely unlike Henry VIII.

CHRONOLOGY

1485   Henry of Richmond wins the Battle of Bosworth and becomes Henry VII.

1491   Henry VIII is born, second son of Henry VII and Elizabeth of York.

1502   Prince Arthur dies, and Prince Henry becomes heir to the throne.

1503   Henry's mother, Elizabeth of York, dies.

1509   Henry VIII accedes to the throne and marries Katherine of Aragon.

1511   Henry and Katherine's first son, Prince Henry, is born and dies within weeks. Henry joins the Holy League against France.

1513   Henry leads his army into northern France to the 'Battle of the Spurs', and the capture of Thérouanne and Tournai. Scots are defeated at the Battle of Flodden and James IV of Scotland is killed.

1514   Peace with France. Princess Mary (Henry's younger sister) marries King Louis XII of France. Wolsey is made Archbishop of York.

1515   Louis XII dies and Mary marries the Duke of Suffolk. Wolsey is made cardinal and lord chancellor.

1516   Erasmus publishes his new Latin translation of the New Testament. Princess Mary is born.

1517   Martin Luther publicizes his '95 Theses'.

1518   Treaty of London.

1519   Election of Charles I of Spain as Charles V, Holy Roman Emperor. Henry Fitzroy is born, Henry VIII's illegitimate son by Elizabeth Blount.

1520   Field of the Cloth of Gold.

1521   Duke of Buckingham is executed for treason. Henry writes *Assertio Septem Sacramentorum* in answer to Luther.

1522   Charles V visits England. War with France is declared.

1525   Failure of the 'Amicable Grant'. War with France ends.

1526   Henry becomes involved with Anne Boleyn.

1527   Henry begins to seek an annulment of his marriage. French embassy concludes Anglo-French peace treaty at Greenwich.

1529   Legatine court at Blackfriars fails to grant Henry an annulment; case is recalled to Rome. Wolsey is deprived of the chancellorship and exiled to York. 'Reformation Parliament' meets and passes anti-clerical legislation. Henry acquires York Place from Wolsey and begins planning the Palace of Whitehall.

1530   Wolsey dies while travelling south to stand trial for treason. Clergy charged with *praemunire*. Convocation submits to Henry's authority.

1532   Act in Conditional Restraint of Annates. Commons also submits the Supplication against the Ordinaries. State visit by Henry and Anne Boleyn to Calais; meeting with Francis I; Anne becomes pregnant.

1533   Henry marries Anne Boleyn in January. Thomas Cranmer becomes Archbishop of Canterbury. Parliament passes the Act in Restraint of Appeals. Cranmer annuls Henry's first marriage and confirms his marriage to Anne, whose coronation takes place with her six months pregnant. Princess Elizabeth is born.

1534   Break with Rome and Royal Supremacy confirmed by parliamentary legislation. Elizabeth Barton is executed.

1535   John Fisher and Thomas More are executed.

1536   Act for the dissolution of the smaller monasteries. Ten Articles promulgated. Anne Boleyn is tried and executed. Henry marries Jane Seymour. Lincolnshire rebellion is followed by the Pilgrimage of Grace. Henry Fitzroy dies. First Royal Injunctions attempt to expunge superstitious religious practices.

1537   Prince Edward is born and Jane Seymour dies. *The Institution of a Christian Man,* or 'Bishops' Book', is published.

1538   Trial and execution of John Lambert and burning of John Forest for heresy. Nonsuch palace is begun.

1539   Act of Six Articles. 'Great Bible' in English is published.

1540   Henry marries Anne of Cleves but the marriage is soon annulled. Thomas Cromwell executed. Henry marries Katherine Howard.

1541   Royal progress to the north of England.

1542   Katherine Howard tried and executed. War with Scotland; Battle of Solway Moss.

1543   Act for the Advancement of True Religion. Henry marries Katherine Parr. *A Necessary Doctrine and Erudition for a Christian Man*, or 'King's Book', is published.

1544   Henry leads his army to war in France; Boulogne is captured.

1545   South coast is fortified against threatened French invasion.

1546   Anne Askew is burned for heresy. Peace with France. Duke of Norfolk and Earl of Surrey imprisoned.

1547   Surrey executed. Henry VIII dies and is buried at Windsor.

ABBREVIATIONS

Bernard, *King's Reformation*
G. W. Bernard, *The King's Reformation: Henry VIII and the Remaking of the English Church* (New Haven and London, 2005)

Bernard and Gunn, *Authority and Consent*
G. W. Bernard and S. Gunn (eds.), *Authority and Consent in Tudor England: Essays Presented to C. S. L. Davies* (Ashgate, 2002)

BIHR
Bulletin of the Institute of Historical Research

BL
British Library

Burnet
G. Burnet, *A History of the Reformation*, ed. N. Pocock (7 vols, Oxford, 1865)

Byrne, *Letters*
M. St. Clare Byrne, *The Letters of King Henry VIII: A Selection* (Newcastle, 1936)

Carley, *Books of Henry VIII*
J. P. Carley, *The Books of Henry VIII and His Wives* (British Library, 2004)

Cavendish
George Cavendish, 'The life and death of Cardinal Wolsey' in *Two Early Tudor Lives*, ed. R. S. Sylvester and D. P. Harding (New Haven and London, 1962)

Colvin, *King's Works*
H. M. Colvin (ed.), *The History of the King's Works 1485–1660*, parts 1 and 2, (vols iii, iv, London, 1975,1982)

CS
Camden Society

CSPS
Calendar of State Papers, Spanish, ed. G. A. Bergenroth *et al.* (13 vols, 1862–1964)

CSPV
Calendar of State Papers, Venetian, ed. Rawdon Brown *et al.* (9 vols, 1864–98)

CWE

> *Collected Works of Erasmus* (Toronto, 1974 –)

EETS

> *Early English Text Society*

EHD

> *English Historical Documents, vol. v, 1485–1558*, ed. C. H. Williams (London, 1967)

EHR

> *English Historical Review*

Elton, *Constitution*

> G. R. Elton (ed.), *The Tudor Constitution: Documents and Commentary* (Cambridge, 1962)

Fortescue

> Sir John Fortescue, *On the Laws and Governance of England*, ed. S. Lockwood, Cambridge Texts in the History of Political Thought (Cambridge, 1997)

Fox, *Letters*

> P. S. Allen and H. M. Allen (eds.), *Letters of Richard Fox, 1486–1527* (Oxford, 1929)

Foxe

> *John Foxe, Acts and Monuments*, ed. S. R. Cattley and G. Townsend (8 vols, 1837–41)

Hall

> *The Union of the Two Noble and Illustre Famelies York and Lancaster*, ed. C. Whibley (2 volumes, London and Edinburgh, 1904)

HJ

> *Historical Journal*

HR

> *Historical Research*

Inventory

> *The Inventory of King Henry VIII*, ed. D. Starkey, vol. i (Society of Antiquaries of London, 1998), 56–7, 13

Ives, *Life and Death*

> E. Ives, *The Life and Death of Anne Boleyn* (Oxford, 2004)

JBS

> *Journal of British Studies*

JEH

Journal of Ecclesiastical History

LP

Letters and Papers, Foreign and Domestic, of the Reign of Henry VIII, 1509–47,
ed. J. S. Brewer, J. Gairdner and R. H. Brodie (21 vols, 1862–1932)

Lloyd, *Formularies*

Formularies of Faith put forth by Authority during the Reign of Henry VIII, ed.
C. Lloyd (Oxford, 1825)

MacCulloch, *Cranmer*

D. MacCulloch, *Thomas Cranmer: A Life* (New Haven and London, 1996)

MacCulloch, *Reign of Henry VIII*

D. MacCulloch (ed.), *The Reign of Henry VIII: Politics, Policy and Piety*
(Basingstoke, 1995)

Muller, *Letters*

J. A. Muller (ed.), *The Letters of Stephen Gardiner* (Cambridge, 1933)

NA

National Archives

ODNB

Oxford Dictionary of National Biography

Original Letters

Original Letters Relative to the English Reformation, ed. H. Robinson (2 vols,
Parker Society, Cambridge, 1846–7)

PS

Parker Society

P&P

Past and Present

Roper, *Life of More*

William Roper, 'The life of Sir Thomas More', in *Two Early Tudor
Lives,* ed. R. S. Sylvester and D. P. Harding (New Haven and London,
1962)

RSTC

*A Short-Title Catalogue of Books Printed in England, Scotland and Ireland,
and of English Books Printed Abroad, 1475–1640* (2nd edn, ed. W. A.
Jackson, F. J. Ferguson and K. F. Pantzer (2 vols, 1976, 1986)

Scarisbrick, *Henry VIII*

J. J. Scarisbrick, *Henry VIII* (London, 1968)

SP

   State Papers

Thurley, *Royal Palaces*

   S. Thurley, *The Royal Palaces of Tudor England* (New Haven and London, 1993)

TRHS

   Transactions of the Royal Historical Society

Walker, *Writing Under Tyranny*

   G. Walker, *Writing Under Tyranny: English Literature and the Henrician Reformation* (Oxford, 2005)

INTRODUCTION

... the prince is the life, the head and the authority of all things that be done in the realm of England.[1]

Henry VIII is easy to caricature as a monarch, hard to understand as a man. His reputation was extraordinary while he was still alive, and became even more lurid after he was dead. From the first, his character was depicted in terms of extremes and often opposing extremes, and whether we look at the man himself or the legend he engendered, a mass of contradictions immediately appear. Henry was often labelled a tyrant and, most unusually, was called a tyrant by some of his subjects even while he was still alive.[2] He pushed through Parliament an array of unprecedented legislation giving him powers never before held by an English king. Yet much of his behaviour demonstrated only too clearly that at times he felt a deep sense of insecurity. He was obviously painfully aware that his father had put only a tentative stop to the civil wars of the fifteenth century, and his fears of Yorkist conspiracy never went away, heightened over time by his crushing inability to secure the succession before 1537 and the birth of Prince Edward. Even then, for the last ten years of his reign his security was pitifully dependent on the life of this sole male child.

Henry also reconfigured England's religion, and in so doing made lasting and important changes to the lives of every single one of his subjects. Religion shaped Tudor society as profoundly, if not more so, than royal authority, and for Henry, as well as for a great many of his subjects, the two were inextricably intertwined. Yet Henry's religious convictions and intentions continue to defy categorisation. This unlikely hero of Protestant tales was the lecherous villain of Catholic histories, but he always insisted on his Catholicism, defending the mass even as he dissolved the monasteries, resisting the central Protestant doctrine of 'justification by faith alone' even as he pillaged Catholic shrines and poured scorn on the 'superstitious' nature of much traditional devotion. As historical debate has ebbed and flowed over the issues of his reign, his character has been redrawn time and time again: as a tyrant swayed by his unholy passions for a series of inappropriate women; as an early Protestant with true enthusiasm for the Bible only hampered by a lack of consistency in the application of his ideas; as the playboy king who went hunting and left Cardinal Wolsey to control his affairs; as the sporadically attentive ruler who instigated the modernisation of government under Thomas Cromwell; as the bloated Machiavellian who played power games with the lives of his queens and courtiers. There is still no consensus over who was really in control during Henry's reign – the king himself, or those who revolved around him in the dazzling mixture of luxury and brutality that was the Tudor court.

The true nature of Henry VIII, then, remains a problem for historians, and there are few records that provide any uncomplicated assistance; few written declarations that lead us straight to the man's soul. Yet there is a wealth of archive material which sheds light obliquely onto the king. Through state papers, diplomatic records, legislation, chronicles, the records of his courtiers, and a wealth of published literature, it is possible to piece together many facets of his character. Above all, we can judge him by his deeds, by his relationships, and by the image he sought to project, particularly if we can grasp the circumstances in which he ruled England. The start of the sixteenth century was a time of unprecedented possibilities, when the boundaries of human knowledge and experience were opening up in both material and conceptual terms. As the voyages of discovery uncovered uncharted regions of the earth, so the intellectual journeys of Renaissance scholars and artists revealed new pathways of knowledge, channels of understanding to both the classical past and the exciting future that was believed to lie ahead. Desiderius Erasmus, possibly Europe's most famous scholar, whom Henry liked to consider a friend, wrote of the 'age of gold' he saw dawning:

> I feel the summons to a sure and certain hope that besides high moral stand-
> ards and Christian piety, the reformed and genuine study of literature and the
> liberal disciplines may be partly reborn and partly find new lustre; the more
> so, since this object is now pursued with equal enthusiasm in different regions
> of the world, in Rome by Pope Leo, in Spain by the Cardinal of Toledo, in
> England by King Henry, eighth of that name who is something of a scholar
> himself.[3]

This vision was both a genuine statement of humanist idealism and a ploy to engender patronage through flattery, and as such it expresses very well the mingled idealism and pragmatism of the age. Henry VIII was intensely involved in both this vision of regeneration and the exploitation of such ideals to advance his own ambitions and glorify his own kingship. This does not mean he was guilty of cynical manipulation of the Renaissance ideal. The truth was more frightening than that, for Henry was convinced that he embodied the divine will for the rebirth of the English church and the consolidation of the English crown. For him there could be little variance between his own will and that of the God who had placed him on the throne. The 'godly prince' of Renaissance literature was at the same time the vengeful prince whose persecutions shocked all of Christendom, for a vigorous and suspicious ruler is never so devastating as when invigorated by ideological fervour.

This blend of private ambition and principled zeal was a potent mix, and a potentially successful one. The first twenty years of Henry's reign saw the king largely secure, expansive, inventive, and capable of commanding the loyalty and often the love of his subjects. The king's imagination and energy, guided and refined at times by Thomas Wolsey and other gifted councillors, bore fruit in the diplomatic achievements of the Treaty of London in 1518, and the Field of the Cloth of Gold in 1520, which aimed at international security, an unusual and impressive initiative, although one that was ultimately unsuccessful. The same vigour produced a ringing condemnation of Luther's heresy, the building of royal armouries and palaces, the patronage of all that was most forward looking in literature and education, and above all the development of a brilliant and sophisticated court. It was during these years that Henry VIII developed a style of kingship which aimed at the splendour and pretension of his French and Habsburg contemporaries, and in the first twenty years his leadership won him respect at home and abroad.

It was the developments of the late 1520s, when the king became convinced that his marriage was a sham, that were to reconfigure the nature of his rule. For Henry insisted that his deeply felt convictions must be shared by his subjects, particularly his most important and influential subjects. Before 1527, his convictions had been largely unremarkable, and this insistence had not been so problematic. But with the 'King's Great Matter' came an evangelical reincarnation for Henry as his understanding of his God and his divinely appointed role as monarch underwent a rebirth. His struggles to rid himself of Katherine of Aragon and his determination to marry Anne Boleyn were inspired by his private emotions, but their public ramifications were huge. When Henry rejected his first wife he rejected too a set of assumptions about church and state, national and international power, and with his second marriage he instituted a new understanding of England, the English Church and the place within both of the English king. And since Tudor society was arranged in pyramid form, with the king at the summit, Henry's redefinition of his own kingship was to mean the reordering of his entire world; the reconstruction of king, court, church and state alike.

To observe Henry's responses to both the insecurities of his dynastic position and the glittering possibilities of his intellectual world is to come one step closer to the man himself. He was energetic, often impatient; curious, frequently suspicious; his reactions moved rapidly, sometimes wildly, between extremes. In good times, he could be generous, gregarious and cheerful, and his many physical gifts and intellectual talents were clear. In bad times, he compounded fear with anger and the result was usually savage retribution against real or perceived enemies. In human relationships he demanded total devotion and obedience, and although there were times when a streak of independence proved appealing to him – in Katherine of Aragon's queenly dignity, in Anne Boleyn's spirited nature, in the committed and principled public service offered by Thomas Wolsey, Thomas More or Thomas Cromwell, in the evangelical notions of Thomas Cranmer and others – he always found it necessary to curb that independence, sometimes by annihilating the wife or servant concerned. He demanded efficiency from those about him, and showed little mercy towards those who failed. Wolsey was unable to extricate him from his first marriage; Anne Boleyn failed to produce a son; Cromwell was held responsible for the fiasco of the Cleves marriage; the Earl of Surrey was tainted by military ineptness in France. All four of these figures suffered spectacular falls from grace, and although their failures were not the immediate cause, these did mean that Henry had lost respect for them, which left them vulnerable to other charges. In particular, the king took any sign of convictions which differed from his own as an appalling betrayal, and frequently as an offence against God as well as man, and he exacted the brutal, derisory, flamboyant revenge of a man both convinced that he was always right, and terrified lest his glory collapse around him like a house of cards.

Particularly sickening, but also highly significant, is the way Henry staged and celebrated the deaths of those he had formerly loved, and then 'discovered' to be traitors. When Katherine of Aragon died, he and his new queen dressed in bright yellow and danced the night away; when Thomas Cromwell, who had faithfully advanced his wishes and his authority for many years, was ignominiously deposed and executed, Henry chose the day of his death for his wedding day, as he married Katherine Howard with extravagant celebration. These sudden reversals of fortune left his courtiers and subjects shaken, and as he grew older and more anxious, and the number of betrayals accumulated, Henry's swift turns from ebullience to savagery became more and more frightening. As a young king, he had delighted in scholarly debate, and had received graciously the many treatises of political advice written for him. As he grew older, men guarded their thoughts, and surrendered their hopes of shaping the king with their sage advice. Disillusion was expressed covertly, in ambiguous sonnets, and treatises full of twisted irony.[4] As a young king, he had promoted men of great talent, and indulgently tolerated the excesses of some of his subjects, permitting or pardoning recklessness in those whose mettlesome spirits might serve him well. As he grew older, Henry grew more angry and intractable; in the last years of his reign, perhaps only those buoyed up by evangelical aspirations could still hope to see the reign end in triumph as a victory for Protestantism, and they too were to be disappointed.

Thomas More, it was said, once cautioned Cromwell against revealing to the king the scope of his potential power:

> If you will follow my poor advice, you shall, in your counsel-giving unto his grace, ever tell him what he ought to do, but never what he is able to do. ... For, if a lion knew his own strength, hard were it for any man to rule him.[5]

Yet in the 1530s, Henry had truly discovered his own strength, and ever after there was a new level of unpredictability to his government. As a young king he had been respected, even loved; as a mature king he was more feared. At the same time, his expanding powers, and in particular his initiatives in the realms of religious policy, had energised the forces of resistance at home and abroad. The price of the lion's new-found strength was a loss of stability. The kingship which had drawn on idealism and enthusiasm was to find itself sliding towards moral confusion as well as literal bankruptcy. If Henry had learned how to extend his authority in the 1530s, he had not realised that there could be limitations on his powers. In his later years, he was to find, to his frustration and annoyance, that he could not compel his subjects' consciences any more than he could coerce the Scots into submission or the emperor into friendly alliance. With his last three marriages he discovered that he could not even expect his wives to be attractive, faithful or submissive to his opinions; qualities which he had previously taken for granted. Yet to the last, Henry continued his energetic, ambitious, dominant style of government, refusing to admit defeat even as he refused to countenance the diminishing capabilities of his diseased body, with its huge girth and weeping ulcers.

This study will argue that, for Henry VIII and his subjects alike, the business of kingship was an intensely personal matter, and the character of the king was central to all the key developments of the reign. This is not a history of that reign, but an attempt to uncover the true nature of the king by unravelling the key events and relationships of his life. It will touch on many of the central historical events of that time precisely because this was a king who lived his life on the public stage, and played out his emotional dramas in the court, the council, in parliament, in the tilting-yard, on the battlefield and in the streets of his capital city. Tudor kingship was by nature theatrical, a display that attempted to persuade, a demonstration of princely traits which sought to convince. The Tudors as a dynasty were consummate actors, and none more than Henry VIII, whose rapid intellect, energy and passion could deliver a startling and outstanding performance. Yet he was not alone in this;

there were other key players in this drama, and like most members of the Tudor elite, their language and understanding was rich with classical allusions, chivalric pretensions and religious symbolism. In piecing together their interactions, aspirations and expectations, it is hoped that the elusive character of Henry VIII will take on more tangible form.

It must be asked why another biography of Henry VIII is necessary, or how one can be optimistically attempted when five centuries have failed to secure a definitive answer. The reply to this is that history is never a definitive answer to a single question, but a continuing dialogue where the questions we ask are always a little different with each successive generation. Meanwhile, the histories we write reveal as much about the age in which they are written as about the age they seek to elucidate. For a while in the twentieth century, the lives of kings ceased to have central importance, and a fuller picture of Tudor society, its economic foundations, its cultural aspirations and its religious convictions, all emerged. Yet we keep being brought back to the lives of kings precisely because they were so obviously of central importance to Tudor society: all social history is at some level also political history.[6]

For this present generation, in continuing to evaluate those royal lives, it has become possible to discover new truths about the interaction between those who govern and those who are governed. In the twentieth century, with its unavoidable anxiety about totalitarianism, Henry VIII often appeared as a Tudor Stalin. More recently, it has perhaps become easier to see how much his authority rested on popular validation and was shaped by popular expectations. If Tudor kingship was theatre, it could not impress and move the audience if it did not also seek, at least some of the time, to please the crowd.

It is also important to realise that the writing of biography evolves with each successive age. The two greatest biographies of Henry VIII in the twentieth century were written by A. F. Pollard in 1902, and by J. J. Scarisbrick in 1968. Pollard's work is eloquent and confident. He lived in an age which tended to believe that the Reformation in England was inevitable, progressive and popular, and that Henry VIII was ruthless, but brave in embracing the new rather than clinging to the old: 'Surrounded by faint hearts and fearful minds, Henry VIII neither faltered nor failed.'[7] For Pollard, Henry was 'Machiavelli's *Prince* in action', not exactly admirable, but definitely effective and impressive.[8] For Scarisbrick, the Reformation may have been unavoidable, but it was also wanton destruction, and Henry's acknowledged dynamism was self-ish and damaging: 'rarely, if ever, have the unawareness and responsibility of a king proved more costly of material benefit to his people.'[9] With the twenty-first century, a more variegated understanding of religious change has emerged, matched with a deeper sense of the complexities of political authority.

This life also seeks to explore, albeit tentatively, the material and physical world of Henry VIII. Alongside the unarguably crucial themes of high politics, ecclesiastical authority and dynastic strategy, it is important to recognise that Henry was a man shaped by his physical environment, his relationships, his palaces, books and possessions. Our knowledge of his material environment has been vastly expanded by two important projects in particular: the survey of the king's building works and the publication of the inventory of his material possessions.[10] Recent work has also encouraged us to explore his ideas, to seek after his under-standing of the world around him, to uncover his mentality. Henry lived in palaces and castles, stayed in country houses and abbeys, hunted in forests, travelled by royal barge up and down the Thames. He was obses-sive about jousting and tournaments, in which the celebration of physical prowess in the fighting was matched by the exuberance of costly display in the costumes worn. He was passionately fond of music, writing it himself and ensuring that the most skilled performers available belonged to his Chapel Royal. These material realities are as much a part of his history as the more conceptual aspects to his rule, and they tell us much about his personality and the way he chose to shape his kingship.

This attention to Henry's environment is essential precisely because we know that Henry himself was unusually interested in his material surroundings. He inherited a dozen palaces: by the end of his life he owned fifty-five. He also owned over 2,000 tapestries, over 150 paint-ings, over 2,000 pieces of plate, and nearly 1,500 books.[11] These were prodigious numbers of possessions for an English king but Henry was aware that such objects could be symbolic of the majesty he sought to project. He also appreciated the value of symbolism in much of what he destroyed. The dissolution of over 800 religious houses was a more elo-quent rejection of papal authority and the doctrine of purgatory than anything he commanded into print or declared in parliament. His destruction of images, shrines and relics from the 1530s in his campaign against superstition and the perversion of religious truth was a visual war, in which Henry annihilated any symbols that might compete with his own. When in due course the crucified Christ was taken down inside the parish churches and replaced by the royal coat of arms it was the clear fulfilment of Henry's understanding of Reformation.

In 1538 Henry VIII burned a papalist friar named John Forest for heresy. His commissioners saw to it that the bonfire contained the wooden image of St Dderfel Gadarn from the Welsh pilgrimage site of Llandderfel. Contemporaries explained that a prophecy had foretold that this miraculous image would one day set a forest on fire – in this case John Forest.[12] Henry, in this gruesome piece of theatre, was not just executing a papalist – and perpetrating a dreadful pun – but was attacking a whole network of beliefs in sacred objects, miraculous symbols and powerful popular saints.

In another execution, almost his last act as king, he had the Earl of Surrey executed for the crime of displaying the arms of Edward the Confessor.[13] Surrey had voiced the opinion that his family should control the young King Edward once Henry was dead, but equally incriminating was this heraldic mistake, by which Surrey was taken to be aiming at the throne; it was visual treason.[14] Surrey was a proud man; he was even to tell one of his less aristocratic judges, 'Thou hadst better hold thy tongue, for the kingdom has never been well since the King put creatures such as thou into the government.'[15] Thus his arrest and trial were designed to humiliate this aristocratic pride as he was taken on foot, like a commoner, to the Tower, and tried not at Westminster as befitted a peer but at the London Guildhall. These are just two examples of how Henry's politics were visual politics, and how the language of symbolism spoke just as powerfully as any other at this time.

In encountering the life of Henry VIII we are required to learn a new language, to decode systems of meaning which were second nature to his contemporaries, but which have only partial resonance today. Another justification for a new biography, therefore, is that to write about Henry's life is to provide, however imperfectly, a way into the mental world of the sixteenth century, through the life of an extraordinary individual who helped to reshape that world. As historians, we now understand much better than before how human experience is shaped by economic developments, gender relations, trade networks, poverty, disease, printing and an array of other realities. Yet we must also allow that the ideas, actions, and interactions of individuals could be just as important in shaping the experience and understanding of those now dead. We need to resist that historical determinism which leaves no place for human agency. Henry's own conviction of his supreme importance was unshakeable, and more importantly, it was shared by his contemporaries; his pre-eminence is therefore a crucial part of the historical landscape of the sixteenth century.

Henry himself was deeply interested in the examples given by the lives of kings. One of his first acts as king was to commission a biography of Henry V, his predecessor as king a century before. This was a translation of an earlier life, but the translator included so many interpolations of his own opinions that it made of it a new work of political advice as well as hagiographical inspiration. In particular, the anonymous author delivered an oblique warning to his young monarch, reminding him that he was under a stern obligation to benefit his subjects. His praise of Henry V was an implicit admonition to the new King Henry:

> Oh how great was the constant love of the public weal in this Prince that desired rather to die than to be unprofitable to the realm. Certainly this is a special note to be remembered of all Princes, and especially of them that court more their singular pleasure, honour, and profit than the universal advantage and wealth of his people and countries, whose blind affection th'example of this noble Prince utterly condemneth.[16]

The relationship between a Tudor monarch and his subjects was a family affair, a relationship at the same time emotional, financial, coercive, volatile, unequal and unbreakable. Like all intense relationships, it left indelible marks on the characters of those involved. Tudor men and women knew this only too well, and they paid close attention to the characters, convictions and actions of kings and queens both present and past. In our attempts to understand Tudor society, we would do well to follow their example.

1

THE EDUCATION OF A
CHRISTIAN PRINCE, 1491–1509

As God set up a beautiful likeness of himself in the heavens, the sun, so he
established among men a tangible and living image of himself, the king.[1]

Henry VIII was born in 1491, almost six years after his father, Henry
VII, had become king. He was the third child and the second son produced by Elizabeth of York, Henry VII's queen, since their marriage in
January, 1486. With a new regime to render secure, the need for royal
offspring was paramount. In the matter of producing children the Tudor
dynasty was often to be blighted by disappointment, but it began
remarkably well, since Henry's older brother, Arthur, was born just
eight months and a day after his parents' wedding.[2] The eldest girl,
Margaret, was born in 1489, and Henry followed two years later. He was
born in the royal palace at Greenwich on 28 June and baptised by
Richard Fox, Bishop of Exeter, in the church of the Observant Franciscans,
whose religious community was based at Greenwich.

Everything about this prince's birth spoke of his father's hopes for the
future. Greenwich was given special status by Henry VII, and was greatly
embellished between 1500 and 1504, becoming the favoured abode of the
new king. In this, as in so much else, Henry VII sought to sanction his
royal profile with material display of the most fashionable sort. The new
redbrick palace he constructed was in the modern Renaissance style,
inspired by the example of the more stylish French and Burgundian

courts. It had no moat, but a river frontage, with plentiful provision of windows. Its outward elegance and light-filled interiors marked the rejection of dark medieval castles and the attempt of the fledgling dynasty to embrace the kind of cultural sophistication which dignified royal courts abroad.[3] Greenwich was to retain its importance throughout Henry's life, even though it was surpassed by the new Palace of Whitehall from the 1530s. It was at Greenwich Palace too that Henry VIII was to marry Katherine of Aragon, and where he insisted that Anne Boleyn give birth in 1533, when he so confidently expected a son, and was instead presented with his daughter Elizabeth.

The religious sanction bestowed upon the new baby also had resonance for the future of one who would one day be 'Supreme Head of the Church in England'. Richard Fox, who baptised the small prince, was Lord Privy Seal as well as Bishop of Exeter, eventually to become Bishop of Winchester; a churchman and courtier on the Renaissance model. Fox was to follow the trend set by other erudite reformers, including Henry VII's own formidable mother, in dissolving decayed monastic houses and with the proceeds founding a new university college, Corpus Christi College in Oxford. Such educational establishments were dedicated to fostering the Renaissance learning with which Henry VIII would seek to adorn his royal pretensions, and which in due course he would use to reconfigure English kingship and launch a religious revolution.

The Observant Franciscans were also symbolic of new currents in religious thought, 'observant' because they followed a reformed and ascetic Franciscan tradition. As an elite religious order they were often associated with royalty; the venerable Spanish primate, Cardinal Ximenes, belonged to their order and was confessor to Queen Isabella, Henry VII's prized ally and Henry VIII's formidable future mother-in-law. Henry VII made sure there were Observant Franciscans close to both his major palaces of Richmond and Greenwich, and the Franciscans at Greenwich were to provide confessors to the king and queen until Henry's break with Rome. This emulation of continental trends in court architecture and religious life was symptomatic of Henry VII's careful construction of his royal image. Spain was at this time a formidable European power and a centre of religious learning and reform, and Henry VII's achievement of an alliance with Spain's royal house for his eldest son was another attempt to add lustre to the new regime. When Henry VIII decided to marry his dead brother's Spanish wife after Henry VII's demise, it was a continuation of his father's aspirations. Comparisons are often drawn between the imposing and majestic figure of Henry VIII and the more shadowy figure of his father, but in the matter of furthering their dynastic strength and security, father and son were at one.

To understand the significance of Henry's birth and the objectives behind his upbringing, it is necessary to know something of the political world into which he was born. The glories of Tudor kingship, despite appearances, were built on shaky ground, and the reputation of this flamboyant dynasty often obscures its fragile and precarious origins. Henry VII had an uncertain claim to the throne, founded on two very unlikely marriages. In 1396 John of Gaunt, Duke of Lancaster, third son of Edward III, had married his long-term mistress, Katherine Swynford, and had their already adult children legitimated by act of parliament. These were the Beauforts, and although they and their descendants were key political figures in the dramatic events of the fifteenth century, their legitimation had barred them from claiming the throne. It was Margaret Beaufort who gave birth to the future Henry VII, when she was 13, and already a widow. The second unlikely marriage was when Henry V's widow, Queen Katherine, the French princess won by the king after his victory at Agincourt, had fallen for a handsome Welshman of the royal household, Owen Tudor, and married again. Her son, Edmund Earl of Richmond, was Margaret Beaufort's first husband, and father to the future Henry VII, the child he never saw. Edmund was admittedly half-brother to Henry VI, but through his French mother, which made Henry VII's claim to the English throne far from obvious.

The fifteenth century had been a time of unparalleled political instability. From Richard II in 1399 to Richard III in 1485, five kings suffered deposition, three of whom were murdered, with one dying on the field of battle. The explanation behind these events, which were unhelpfully labelled 'the Wars of the Roses' (the phrase was first used by David Hume in 1762), remains complex. There was a genuine dynastic problem, as it was unclear whether the Yorkist or the Lancastrian line had the better claim to the throne, but this problem had only surfaced because of the profound failure of Henry VI to fulfil the obligations of kingship.[4] Thus Henry VIII's grandfather, Edward IV, had won the throne in 1461 only to lose it again in 1470. He regained it a year later, but when he died, leaving two underage sons, they vanished in the Tower and their uncle, who had ironically been appointed Protector, usurped the throne as Richard III. That these events gripped the imagination of the time is clear from their prominent place in the history plays of Shakespeare a century later. There could not have been a more vivid warning to any future king of the absolute necessity of maintaining royal dignity and popularity, and of securing the succession with healthy adult children.

The situation after 1483, when Richard III's usurpation of the throne from his nephew left the Yorkist camp divided and in distress, had provided unexpected opportunity for Henry of Richmond, soon to be Henry VII, who was the only person close to a Lancastrian candidate for the throne. His pledge to marry Elizabeth of York, eldest daughter of Edward IV, secured him the support of those Yorkists who could not bear to serve Richard III, and who seem to have known that the princes in the Tower were now dead. French backing brought him to England, and victory at Bosworth secured him the rest. He defeated Richard III, was crowned, married Elizabeth, and saw the birth of their first son, all within thirteen months. Victory in battle, an important dynastic alliance and the birth of an heir: this succession of events might appear fortunate to the modern observer, but to fifteenth-century eyes it confirmed that God had blessed the new king. In the early modern period Providence was a valuable ally. The birth of a second healthy son in 1491 strengthened Henry VII's position still further. When Henry VIII became king, he had only to turn to the immediate past to gain piercing insight into the potential within kingship for both triumph and disaster.

The perpetuation of the new regime remained a constant struggle and it is important to realise how the fifteenth-century difficulties cast a long and menacing shadow over Tudor rule. It would be wrong to characterise the fifteenth century as an age of anarchy, where power-hungry magnates could topple kings and private feuds could escalate into civil war, although that analysis has proved an easy one for many commentators.[5] In fact, fifteenth-century politics were capable of great sophistication and political protest nearly always made emphatic appeals to clearly understood principles.[6] The system depended, however, on personal supervision by the monarch, and where the monarch failed to understand the rules by which his kingship was expected to work, instability resulted. Most famously, the reign of Henry VI saw a failure of kingship which precipitated civil war. Such was its level of drama that it produced three plays by Shakespeare, when most reigns merited only one.[7]

Such experiences rendered the English increasingly introspective on the subject of kingship. By the time Henry VII came to the throne, there was a particularly acute longing for peace and strong, steady government by a wise and balanced king; there was also a lot of intellectual activity being devoted to the question of how best to secure good governance. Henry VIII's reign was to see both the development of the cult of personal kingship and the introduction of new institutions and methods of government; both were a response to the problems that had gone before.[8] Yet there were also many loose ends that had yet to be tied up. Where the sixteenth century was to suffer from the lack of royal progeny, the later fifteenth century had been burdened by too much royal issue, and Henry VII and Henry VIII were both to remain wary of the Yorkist nobility whose claim to the throne might have challenged their own. Henry VII fought off a Yorkist challenge in 1486. In 1487 he defeated Lambert Simnel, who had been crowned king in Dublin. For most of the 1490s he battled the threat of Perkin Warbeck, who claimed to be Richard, Duke of York, the younger of the two princes in the Tower, and who could command support in Ireland, Scotland, France and Burgundy. Warbeck was executed in 1499, as was the long-imprisoned Earl of Warwick, but it was not until 1506 that the Earl of Suffolk was handed over by Burgundy and imprisoned in the Tower.[9]

Henry VII was always conscious of a potential challenger waiting in the wings. One report of a potentially treasonable conversation from the later years of his reign records a conversation in Calais where the deputy-governor and others speculated on what might happen at the king's death. Some spoke of Buckingham, some of Edmund de la Pole; none of them mentioned the Prince of Wales.[10] It was to take many long years before the Tudor dynasty was firmly established.

Henry VII's attempts to ensure the safety of himself and his heirs established some patterns of government which his son would continue to follow, even as he rejected others. Henry VII fostered tight security, kept a strict rein on any potentially subversive nobles, and pursued a foreign policy geared chiefly towards defence, the elimination of Yorkist pretenders and the reinforcement of his dynasty through advantageous royal marriages. At home he played the part of the Renaissance monarch, building and beautifying palaces, patronising Italian and Burgundian scholars and artists, and developing the ceremonial importance of the royal court. He was the first English king to establish a royal bodyguard, one of his first actions on coming to power, and Henry VIII never saw the need to disband these 'yeomen of the guard', who have been with us ever since. Characteristically, the idea was taken from the French court where Henry VII had lived in exile; father and son alike were to borrow ideas from more established royal houses on the continent, playing their parts to the hilt in the hope that as many people as possible would be taken in by their performance.

Henry VII's reputation has suffered from his falling between two historical eras, at the end of the late medieval period and the beginning of the early modern, with neither side paying sufficient attention to his reign.[11] There is also a traditional caricature of Henry VII as mean, guarded, defensive and rapacious, which is taken from Francis Bacon and Polydore Vergil. Bacon lived a century too late to know the king, but Vergil, an Italian scholar commissioned to write the history of the reign, knew him quite well, and it should be noted that Vergil's criticism was in fact far outweighed by his praise of his patron:

> In government he was shrewd and prudent. ... He was gracious and kind and was as attentive to his visitors as he was easy of access. His hospitality was splendidly generous

These were virtues appropriate to kingship.

> He well knew how to maintain his royal majesty and all which appertains to kingship at every time and at every place. He was most fortunate in war, although he was constitutionally more inclined to peace than to war. He cherished justice above all things; as a result he vigorously punished violence, manslaughter, and every other kind of wickedness. ... Consequently he was greatly regretted on that account by all his subjects.

Vergil's portrait, quite unfairly, is only remembered for the last indictment, that:

> all these virtues were obscured latterly by avarice, from which he suffered ... in a monarch indeed it may be considered the worse vice since it is harmful to everyone, and distorts those qualities of trustfulness, justice and integrity by which the State must be governed.[12]

It seems clear that Henry VII did become overly exacting in his later years, in particular through the use of recognizances, extracting fines from law-breakers in a manner which was not illegal, but was certainly immoderate. In Henry's defence, the use of bonds and recognizances was also a policy for securing good behaviour, and it was after the devastating loss of his wife and eldest son in 1502–3, when the survival of the dynasty hung on the person of Prince Henry, that the use of recognizances became so extraordinary.[13] Henry VIII was to make ostentatious renunciation of his father's exacting ways, and brought about the judicial murder of his two most disliked financial agents in an early bid for popularity. But he must also have been powerfully aware of his father's achievements, as a dynamic and successful pretender to the throne, who after fourteen years in exile launched a successful invasion of England, and swept to power and success as an established and internationally respected monarch known for his strong and prosperous government.

History has generally contrasted father and son, and emphasised the difference between Henry VIII and Henry VII; the picture has been of the flamboyant, expansive but dangerous heir replacing his secretive, miserly, over-cautious predecessor. As we have seen, this demonstrates an abject failure to understand the true character of Henry VII; it also fails to grasp a fundamental underlying anxiety about the succession which shaped the reigns of all five Tudors. As a family, they were never free from the worry that they might be usurped by another noble family claiming royal blood. There was a perpetual suspicion of those who married anyone with royal associations. For example, Lord Thomas Howard died in the Tower in 1537, imprisoned for marrying the king's niece, Lady Margaret Douglas, without permission, and thirty years later Elizabeth I was to imprison the Earl of Hertford and his bride Lady Katherine Grey, her cousin, for marrying in similar fashion. Many executions for alleged treason were hastened by the noble lineage of the victim. This was a policy established by Henry VII, for example with the execution of the Earl of Warwick in 1499 for alleged treason. Another possible Yorkist claimant, William de la Pole, was imprisoned in the Tower by Henry VII in 1501, and stayed there until he died in Henry VIII's reign, thirty-eight years later.[14] When it came to safeguarding dynastic security, there was a distinct family resemblance between all the Tudors.

Henry VIII's reign was to be thick with examples of such royal unease, which often mounted to the level of paranoia, given that his nobility were in reality very loyal and showed a strong commitment to the royal service that was expected of them by contemporaries.[15] The literature of the time made many appeals to the nobility to follow their duty and do service to king and commonwealth, petitions which were resonant with the ideals of chivalry.[16] This kind of idealised appeal reflected the very real dedication to royal service manifested in so many of the nobility. Much of the time Henry VIII was to recognise this dedication, and indeed his government, and in particular the furtherance of his wars, relied on it. Occasionally he even seemed to like the high-handed flourishes of noble pride and recklessness. In 1518 a group of his favourite courtiers, his 'minions', had rioted through the streets of Paris: 'They, with the French King, rode daily disguised through Paris, throwing eggs, stones and other foolish trifles at the people.'[17] At times, Henry could relish this kind of arrogance as a fit preparation for the ostentation of the tournament and the recklessness required in battle.

Whenever the king felt threatened, however, noble lineage could readily heighten his suspicion of treason. In 1521 the Duke of Buckingham perished, convicted of treason, condemned by the Duke of Norfolk who wept as he passed sentence on the man whose daughter was married to Norfolk's own son. In 1538 another suspected conspiracy led to the execution of members of the Pole and Courtenay families, noble houses with obvious Yorkist associations. The very old and the very young were not exempt. Edward Courtenay, son of the executed Marquess of Exeter, was imprisoned in the Tower at the age of 12, and would not see the light of day again for fifteen years. Even more strikingly, Henry's savagery finally extended in 1541 to the execution of the oldest member of the Pole family, the frail Countess of Salisbury, who in her seventies had to be carried to the scaffold in a chair. In an age where any high-level political trial or execution was emphatically a piece of theatre, this betrays Henry's venom, born of the fear for his infant son's future. These, and many other such deaths, were a testimony to the profound disquiet that haunted Henry throughout his life. It was a direct inheritance from his father.

Henry VIII grew up in an atmosphere which outwardly emphasised the crucial importance and extent of royal authority, and which made an extravagant display of royal dignity. Yet his father's style of government as much as the recent history of his realm made it quite clear that a terrible price would be demanded of the monarch who failed to maintain his kingly estate. This background must in large part account for the striking combination of huge political ambition and severe political anxiety which characterised Henry's regime. 'Uneasy lies the head that wears a crown', wrote Shakespeare of a sleepless Henry IV, pacing the palace of Westminster in his nightgown, envying his lowliest subjects who could sleep in peace at night.[18] Whilst not precisely an historical source, as a Tudor commentary on the trials of kingship, it is no bad reflection on the burden Henry was to carry as king.

THE EDUCATION OF A PRINCE

If Henry VIII grew up in a family which was facing a profound political challenge, it was one which he was to meet with energy and optimism, at least for the first half of his reign, and at many points thereafter. He was armed to meet that challenge with all the ideological arsenal of the late medieval and Renaissance world. It was, of course, not Henry but his elder brother Arthur who was intended to take on the responsibilities of government, and so, devoid of any obviously untainted and proud lineage to bestow upon his eldest son, Henry VII named him after the mythical King Arthur to sanction him by means of chivalric legend instead. One of the first fruits of Caxton's printing press, established in Westminster in 1476, was the very popular edition of Sir Thomas Malory's *Le Morte d'Arthur,* which suggests that many of the little prince's contemporaries knew the Arthurian legends. If this seems a fragile legacy, this endowment of his son with a fairy tale, it must be remembered that where modern government relies on institutions, fifteenth and sixteenth-century English government relied far more on ideas. Without a standing army, civil service, police force or prison service at its disposal, Tudor government was instead able to call its subjects to obedience and loyalty on the basis of chivalric and Christian codes of conduct, and feudal notions of obligation. Myth, legend and the examples of literature and history had very real political force.

Tudor education was therefore an attempt to equip boys, and a few noble or royal girls, with an array of *exempla*, literary or historical models and sayings, with which they could respond to any event or contingency. In effect, the young were taught how to reenact the past, and take on the guise of heroes, philosophers, orators and saints, as the occasion demanded.

Tudor children were taught Latin, and sometimes Greek, by having to memorise, repeat and translate classical authors until they could speak and write as elegantly and eloquently as Cicero, Quintilian or Demosthenes. Memory and repetition were the foundation of learning; Erasmus, in his work *On Education for Children*, commented that 'nature has equipped children with a unique urge to imitate whatever they hear or see; they do this with great enthusiasm, as though they were monkeys, and are over-joyed if they think they have been successful'.[19] This power of imitation enabled them to amass many pieces of classical wisdom:

> What is to hinder them from learning delightful tales, witty aphorisms, memorable incidents from history, or intelligent fables with no greater effort than that with which they pick up and absorb stupid, often vulgar ballads, ridiculous old wives' tales, and all sorts of tedious womanish gossip?[20]

To grow in wisdom and virtue was the aim of Tudor education, and it was to be achieved by following the examples of the past. The education of Henry's own eldest child, Princess Mary, was in part entrusted to the Spanish humanist Juan Luis Vives. One of his many works, *The Education of a Christian Woman*, produced a wealth of role-models for the young princess, classical, mythical, biblical or drawn from the early years of Christian history. Cornelia, mother of the Gracchi; Cassandra and Chryseis, priestesses of Apollo and Juno; Catherine of Alexandria, and Catherine of Siena, both Christian saints: these were the female figures the princess was to emulate.[21] Indeed, Vives gave an example of the educational methods he had in mind when he described Hortensia, daughter to the orator Hortensius, who:

> so matched her father in eloquence that as a woman worthy of honour and respect, she delivered a speech ... that later ages read not only in admiration and appreciation of female eloquence but also for imitation, as they would the writings of Cicero or Demosthenes.[22]

This kind of instructive mimicry relied as much on pictures as on words. When in 1538 Henry began to build a palace for his son at Nonsuch, the decorative panels in its inner courtyard were designed to be an education in pictures, depicting Henry VIII and Prince Edward presiding over figures from classical history and mythology, representations of the liberal arts and cardinal virtues and vices.[23] Equally, many of Holbein's sketches and portraits found their way into the portfolio of over eighty pictures owned by John Cheke and used in his education of Prince Edward.[24]

This kind of education produced someone whose mental processes were inevitably accompanied by a host of literary and historical allusions, whose language evoked past philosophies and whose conduct aimed at recreating the triumphs of the past. This was, of course, particularly pointed in the education of a prince. Although we know little about the details of Henry's education, we do know that it produced an impressive specimen of Renaissance learning. We also know that the examples Henry was encouraged to follow stayed with him throughout his life. He played the part of a series of princes, prophets and legendary heroes. All who read classical texts were encouraged to imagine themselves within the landscape they read about; in the case of a future king, this must have meant that he appeared to himself as the hero of every epic, romance or historical event. The models beloved of Henry VIII were military heroes such as Alexander the Great or Henry V, luminous figures of Christian history such as the Emperor Constantine, Old Testament kings like King David or King Solomon, or chivalrous and romantic characters like King Arthur.

We know a fair amount about the education of Henry's older brother, Arthur, whose tutor, Bernard André, educated him in both classical and Renaissance texts, from Augustine's *City of God* on which André wrote a commentary, to the fifteenth-century Italian scholar Lorenzo Valla who had helped initiate the radical reform of Latin grammar and rhetoric, and who in 1440 had also revealed the *Donation of Constantine* to be a forgery. This document had purported to be the grant of supremacy from the first Christian Emperor to the papacy: it held a central place in the arguments for papal supremacy, and the revelation that it was a fake had profound implications for Renaissance ideas about the rights and privileges of the Pope. This educational programme could therefore both embrace time-honoured tradition and cutting-edge scholarship. It was also a lively and inventive kind of education: André composed speeches addressed to the young prince by imaginary envoys from ancient Athens and Sparta. To base an educational programme upon the wisdom of the past was not to rule out the possibility of innovation and reform.

It was, of course, the fashion of the time to urge classical ideals and models upon a young prince, and it was not merely for his own good.

When Henry's tutor, John Skelton, compared the young king to Alexander the Great, it had the fortunate corollary of turning Skelton himself into a second Aristotle.[25] Yet we know that these role-models had an enduring significance for Henry VIII because of the way they kept recurring at important moments. In his early years as king, Henry longed for military success in France, and it was then that he commissioned a translation of the life of Henry V.[26] Ten years later he was still pursuing military glory, and this time he commissioned a translation of Froissart.[27] Later still, as we shall see, Constantine was the part he played in enacting the royal supremacy, while King David was the model for his stance as he undertook religious reforms.

The education which Henry VIII received, and which he clearly relished, made him a beacon of hope for the humanists who thronged his court and government. 'Humanism' remains a difficult concept to define, being at the same time so variegated, so self-referential, and productive of so many different religious and political convictions. Yet even if it continues to frustrate modern historians, it is clear that it was a real and powerful ideological force in England as the sixteenth century dawned. Humanism was the intellectual, linguistic and literary aspect of the Renaissance, running alongside the developments in art, architecture, music and science. In some it emerged with a more secular set of preoccupations, focusing on classical ideals of philosophy, education, literature or politics. Here the key texts experiencing a 'rebirth' would be Latin works by such as Cicero, Livy or Pliny, or Greek works by such as Euripides, Plutarch or Thucydides.

It was rare for Renaissance preoccupations to be purely secular, however, and for many the most important development was the 'rebirth' of the Bible, supplemented by the revived enthusiasm for ancient Christian fathers like Augustine, Cyprian, John Chrysostom and Origen. The Bible too, after all, was an ancient text, a contemporary of some of these classical works, and to understand the Bible it was necessary to acquire knowledge of neglected languages, particularly the Hebrew and Greek of the original texts. For many humanists, then, their interest in classical and biblical scholarship were deeply interwoven. Scholars such as Erasmus, Thomas More, John Fisher and John Colet were to be leading lights in Henry VIII's world. They were variously laymen, priests and politicians, but all of them had a burning desire to reform their world through the renewal of Scripture, classical learning and the theology of the early church fathers, and all of them were prodigiously well educated in Latin, sometimes Greek and occasionally Hebrew too, seeking the true message of the ancient texts they studied, edited, translated and published. As well as this industrious excavation of the texts of the ancients, they also wrote themselves – letters, religious and political treatises, poetry, plays, and works which defy categorisation, such as More's *Utopia* and Erasmus's *Praise of Folly*.

Henry supported the endeavours of the humanists throughout his reign. In return he demanded from them their unqualified approval and support, and could be fiercely indignant if this was not forthcoming, as the fate of Thomas More was to demonstrate. More was appointed chancellor at a critical point in 1529 when Henry was seeking to deploy all the weight of humanist scholarship in support of his claim that his first marriage was invalid. More's refusal to act as Henry wished set him on the path to his execution in 1535.

In his youth, however, Henry's relationship with the humanists seemed harmonious, and promising. It is worth noting that of the only two letters which survive from Henry's childhood, one was to Erasmus, in 1507. It was headed by the pious exclamation 'Jesus is my hope'. This was a nod to the evangelical piety which Erasmus was propagating across Europe, and an echo of the cult of the Name of Jesus, famously encouraged by Henry's formidable grandmother, Lady Margaret Beaufort. The letter was short, consisting chiefly of elegant compliments to Erasmus, and a lament over the death of the King of Castile, but it is notable that Henry here was attempting to compose the kind of stylish letter commonly exchanged and frequently published by humanist scholars.[28]

When Erasmus or Thomas More hailed Henry's accession as the dawn of a 'golden age', therefore, there was a wealth of meaning implied by their rejoicing.[29] They were expressing their hopes and expectations that Henry would be lavish with his patronage of learning, that he would encourage their scholarship, press for changes in schools and universities, foster debate among the educated and the privileged, and endow his court with the combination of books, international scholars, learned preachers, and even educated women that together symbolised the Renaissance idea of civilisation.

Yet this explosion of scholarly and artistic activity which we term 'Renaissance' was also stirring up anxiety. Fundamental assumptions about the place of God and monarch in the world order were still unchallenged, but different aspects of both religion and politics were becoming the subject of increasingly heated debate. Henry VIII was born into a world where authority rested not just on force and coercion, but also upon consensus, theology and a strong sense of moral obligation. Yet that authority had been shaken by civil war, and was now being laid open to question by humanists, all reinforced by the swift development of printing and the widening of intellectual debate which followed.

POLITICAL THEORY

Underlying the celebrations of 1509 and the hyperbole, the panegyric and the predictions of glory, there could also be found a sense of wariness and even anxiety. The intricate combination of optimism and anxiety which characterised humanist thinking was particularly evident in the political theory of the age, and this too provides a necessary backdrop to Henry's accession. To the modern mind, which expects politics to serve as an arena for conflict, the political ideas of the late fifteenth and early sixteenth centuries display what might seem a naive hopefulness that all men will work together to procure peace and prosperity. This should not be dismissed as pious but empty rhetoric, however; the political theorists of this age bear witness to important features of Tudor society, in particular the level of social integration in the business of government. It was understood that the commonwealth and the king were one and the same in their interests and objectives. There was no perceived conflict between ruler and ruled, and reverence and respect for the law went hand in hand with deference and obedience to the royal prerogative. The task of upholding peace, justice, order and prosperity was one shared by king, lords and commons, a triumvirate formally reflected in Parliament, but given informal expression in a wealth of obligations. As the king undertook to protect the Church, dispense patronage, defend the realm and uphold the law in his realm at large, so the nobility and gentry participated in the same undertaking in their particular areas of influence. At local level, sheriff, bailiff, priest, parish constable and churchwarden all pursued the same ends as their overlords.

This shared sense of obligation was given emphatic reinforcement by religion and history, which were both powerful authorities in an age where moral sanction had as much force as economic sanction has in the modern world. Fear of damnation was a compelling influence, and God's favour or displeasure could be read in the events of history, as well as in natural phenomena, and the amplification of both by popular rumour, song, commemoration and – increasingly – literature, put forward a moral tale for society at large to absorb.[30] The approval of God and the endorsement of history were avidly sought by kings and nobles no less than the strange portents of storms, fires, comets and monstrous births were feared by humbler folk. Henry VII published the papal bull which confirmed the legitimacy of his claim to the English throne; he decorated the great hall at Richmond Palace with portrayals of past kings, including King Arthur, 'many noble warriors, and kings of this royal realm, with their fashions and swords in theire hands, visaged, and appearing like bold and valiant knights', with his own portrait at the highest point of all.[31] These visual declarations were of weighty importance.

Numerous works of the time illustrate how politicians of the age thought about the business of government, how they conceived of their society, or 'commonweal', and how they saw true religion and an awareness of the lessons of history as central to good kingship. One example comes straight from the heart of the Tudor administration. Edmund Dudley had served Henry VII as a lawyer, and was well known as one of his most effective tax collectors. One of Henry VIII's first acts as king was to imprison him and his colleague Richard Empson, the living symbols of the dead king's parsimony, as an indication that the new king intended to condemn the errors of the previous reign and pursue a path of reform. It was an early example of the kind of political theatre for which Henry VIII's reign would become notorious. Confined to the Tower, Dudley wrote *The Tree of Commonwealth*, which was his summary of contemporary political theory. He took it as self-evident that:

> every man is naturally bound not only most heartily to pray for the prosperous continuance of his liege sovereign lord and the increase of the commonwealth of his native country, but also to the uttermost of his power to do all things that might further or sound to the increase and help of the same.[32]

He also made it clear that the ties of obedience bound ruler and ruled together in a harmonious mutuality:

> His wealth and prosperity standeth in the wealth of his true subjects, for though the people be subjects to the king yet are they the people of god, and god hath ordained their prince to protect them and they to obey their prince.[33]

The lessons of history were also central, and compelling, showing that the three offences of cruelty, worldliness and lustful appetite were always punished. 'For the first, who was more rigorous and cruel than Harald, sometime king of this realm?', asked Dudley. 'Verily none. What was his conclusion? A short reign and a cruel.' Worldliness was exemplified by Henry III, who was 'so insatiable that he lost thereby the hearts of his subjects, in so much that all his realm rejoiced his death.' And Dudley noted solemnly that the lusts of Richard II had left the king without heirs, and the realm in disarray. And he asked:

> also is it not like that the punishment that the late king of noble memory, king Edward the fourth, had in the fair flourishing issue of his body, his sons I do meane, much for loving his flesshly appetite?'[34]

In contrast to these unworthy kings, who met a miserable fate, models such as Edward the Confessor, Charlemagne and King David were upheld as worthy of emulation. Significantly, given Henry VIII's later history, Dudley also opined that:

> For keeping his body clean and chaste to his wife and queen god shall send him plenty of fair issue which shall succeed him in honour and virtue, and over that shall crown him in heaven with the holy king and confessor, St Edward.[35]

Likewise, the life of Henry V which the young king had translated in 1513 contained a key passage where the aged Henry IV warns his son, the future Henry V, that all good fortune in life is to be ascribed solely to the generosity of God:

> My Son, thou shalt fear and dread God above all things, and thou shalt love, honour and worship him with all thy heart. Thou shalt attribute and ascribe to him all things wherein thou seest thy self to be well fortunate, be it victory of thine enemies, love of thy friends, obedience of thy subjects, strength and activeness of thy body, honour, riches, or fruitfull generations.[36]

The idea that good fortune, success, and in particular 'fruitfull genera-tions', were a clear indicator of God's especial favour was to be a crucial foundation for Henry's understanding of his place in the divinely ordained pattern. Sexual morality was a key ingredient to this pattern of virtue, and children were its reward. The biographer of Henry V laid particular emphasis on the king's continence, and how 'from the death of the King his Father until the marriage of himself he never had knowledge carnally of women'.[37] It was firmly established in contemporary thought, that the king who produced no children to inherit his throne must in some way have offended God; that sexual sins committed in private would have public and catastrophic implications. This idea was to return to haunt Henry with extraordinary persistence as his years unfolded.

This level of consensus provided the foundations of political thought at this time; on to this root was grafted the political debate. In fact, the humanist scholarship which flourished around 1500 meant that Henry came to the throne in an age of particularly intense debate, which centred in particular on the role of the monarch.[38] It seems likely that he was aware of much of this thought, because several of the key works on the subject were presented and sometimes also dedicated to him, including some by Erasmus.[39] Others, such as Machiavelli's *The Prince*, published in 1532, were sufficiently famous (in Machiavelli's case notorious) to be the object of discussion among the educated. All of these works, despite being wildly different in their conclusions, shared the understanding that the good of society at large required the best sort of monarchical rule.

If society was a single integrated whole, then the person of the king was the keystone which held all together. On its most basic level, this meant there was widespread alarm at any damage or disease which threatened the king's physical body. Hall records how at a royal joust 'every man feared, lest some ill chance might happen to the king, and fain would have had him a looker on, rather than a doer', whilst at the same time glorying that 'his courage was so noble that he would ever be at the one end'.[40] Dudley on the basis of this same understanding warned the young Henry to avoid 'dangerous sports' for fear of casualties, impressing on him that 'in your only person dependeth the whole wealth and honour of this your realm'.[41] If the king's bodily health was the source of all security, then his moral health acted as the guarantee of jus-tice in his realm. However, were his moral health to be called into question, then the stability of the kingdom was at risk, almost as much as if the king's life was at risk. And as Henry ascended the throne, the debate over how to avert political instability was acquiring a new level of sophistication.

In general, the political debate of the time veered between different extremes of idealism and pragmatism, and different extents of optimism or pessimism about the chances of godly rule. More's *Utopia*, for example, published in 1516, presented an idealised world ruled on the basis of rationality alone, which appeared to mock and reproach the Christian commonwealths of his own day. It also contained an unresolved debate between two characters as to whether it was possible to be a good and moral statesman, or whether the true philosopher should shun the sordid pragmatism of the political world in favour of pure contemplation. The figure of Morus says to the traveller Hythlodaeus:

> surely it would be quite in keeping with this admirably philosophical attitude if you could bring yourself, even at the cost of some personal inconvenience, to apply your talents and energies to public affairs? Now the most effective way of doing so would be to gain the confidence of some great king or other, and give him, as I know you would, really good advice. [42]

But the philosopher is not to be persuaded.

In this was contained much of the anxiety about political processes which was common to Henry VIII's day, and in particular the concern over how the king should be advised. The literature of the time reveals much debate about the conflicting influences on kings and princes: good counsel opposed to flattery, true religion opposed to hypocrisy or heresy, genuine loyalty opposed to the discord between factions.

It was a central belief of the age that good rule depended heavily on good counsel. Erasmus's translation for Henry VIII, 'How to distinguish between flatterers and friends', outlined a recurrent theme, namely the Tudor unease as to whether a court could be purged of sycophants in favour of good honest advisors. Certainly, whenever political process was deemed to have failed, it was the king's advisors who took the blame, a necessary response in an age when the king could not be openly attacked for fear of plunging the country at large into chaos. Those who were both commentators and active participators in the political process often expressed ambivalence as to whether honesty could or should be applied at court, and others besides More seemed unsure whether they should try to serve in a court full of duplicity or seek a more high-minded exile with purer morals, but lonely isolation.[43] It was agreed that a better solution to the early modern political dilemma was to start with the education of the prince. Erasmus's tract, written for the young Charles V, advised that 'the main hope of getting a good prince hangs on his proper education, which should be managed all the more attentively, so that what has been lost with the right to vote is made up for by the care given to his upbringing'.[44] Here too, the key figure was the counsellor, this time in the role of tutor.

The mention of the 'right to vote' by Erasmus underlines another important consideration of the time, namely the impact which Renaissance thought had had upon ideas about the foundations of political authority. The medieval notion of the community as a body, with the king as the head or heart, but with every individual integrated into the whole, was here developed to a more mature understanding of how popular consent was needed for good government. Erasmus made a clear statement of this.

> A state, even if it lacks a prince, will still be a state. Vast empires have flourished without a prince, such as Rome and Athens under democracy. But a prince simply cannot exist without a state, and in fact the state takes in the prince, rather than the reverse. What makes a prince a great man, except the consent of his subjects?[45]

The study of the classical world had opened up new political possibilities to Tudor statesmen and scholars. As Henry's reign continued, new forms of political debate and advice would develop, fostered by the king himself, who loved to encourage debate. Yet all of the political theorising of his reign was destined to circle around the single fundamental point that on the king depended all hopes of security, justice and prosperity. The consent and loyalty of a king's subjects were necessary to him, but these in turn would primarily be a response to the ruler's character and personality.

EARLY LIFE

The fragments of evidence which survive for Henry's early life do not tell us much, but what they tell us is significant. In particular they indicate a fundamental difficulty with the exercise of royal authority which would plague Henry throughout his life. Early modern kingship had constantly to grapple with the problem that loyalty to the monarchy was predominantly personal loyalty. This meant that when the king turned up in person he could command great devotion and enthusiasm; personal appearances could put an end to riot and rebellion, as with Richard II and the Peasants' Revolt, or Mary I's appearance at the Guildhall during Wyatt's rebellion. But when the king was absent, his subjects did not respond in the same way to his delegated authority.[46] Royal progresses were one answer to this, or a peripatetic style of kingship like that of Emperor Charles V, who had a life of constant travel and abdicated in weariness when only 55.

Letters could do some good too: in 1513 Thomas Howard, finding low morale within the army, wrote to Wolsey to say that the captains were discouraged, and to beg for a favourable letter for them from the king. Within the week he was writing to thank the king for having written, reporting that the captains 'marvellously rejoiced' to receive his letters.[47] Another answer was to co-opt the royal family, who in themselves reflected the magnificence and the sanctity of the anointed monarch, to shore up the realm at its weakest points.

It is appropriate, then, that Henry's first position, aged less than 2, was that of constable of Dover Castle and warden of the Cinque Ports, an echo of the future for a king who was to be so preoccupied with the chances of conquest in France, and with the risk of invasion from his European competitors. A year later, already Earl Marshal of England, he was made Lieutenant of Ireland, Duke of York, and Warden of the Scottish Marches. To the modern mind it appears either ridiculous or irrelevant to load a child with such offices, but to contemporaries it was a clear signal that he was being groomed to join the family business and help take responsibility for the outlying and border areas of the realm which were frequently so troublesome. Scottish raiding over the borders was endemic, and the English hold on Ireland was always insecure. Prince Henry's titles were a small but important gesture toward strengthening the dynasty's authority there. In 1494 he was also invested with the Order of the Bath, and a year later he received the Order of the Garter. In highly elaborate ceremonies, with a large number of the nobility in attendance, Henry was given the chivalric status which would enhance his royal nature, and fit him to hold sway over his father's subjects on his father's behalf. In the same way, his elder brother Arthur, as Prince of Wales, was to be sent to Ludlow, to personally head the royal presence in the Marches of Wales, a border region which could also prove problematic.

Before Arthur left for Ludlow, however, he was to get married. Henry's first major public appearance was as a 10-year-old, during the festivities surrounding his older brother's marriage to Katherine of Aragon. In November 1501 Henry headed the procession which accompanied the Spanish princess from Baynard's Castle, the royal palace on the Thames, to St Paul's Cathedral. He escorted the princess both in and out of the cathedral, and like the bride and groom, he too was dressed in dazzling white, sparkling with diamonds. In the ten days of festivities which followed, Henry played his part in the pageantry, devised by his father to give a triumphant endorsement of Tudor authority and to celebrate the extraordinary achievement of this alliance with such a great European power. The excitement and glamour of this match was transitory, however, and Arthur's apprenticeship in power at Ludlow was tragically brief; after just four months there he died, aged 15, in April 1502.

Before Arthur's death, Henry had lived a sheltered life, brought up with his sisters, in part at Eltham Palace, where More and Erasmus encountered the young prince. Eltham Palace was close to Greenwich; when Henry's daughter Elizabeth was born in 1533 an establishment was made for her at Eltham, in emulation of Henry's own childhood. After Arthur's death, Henry's life was equally quiet. Prince Henry's survival was now the sole guarantee of the future of the dynasty, and although he too became Prince of Wales in 1503, he was too precious to risk. He was given no formal or informal role in government, but kept close by his father. This did mean living at court, however, and some of the grandeur of this is reflected in an inventory of Henry's jewels from 1504. He possessed many religious images, including a gold cross with five table diamonds and three good pearls, given by his mother, and an image of St Michael opposing the devil, wrought of gold and diamonds, given by his father. He had received gifts from a wide range of courtiers, including the Lord Chamberlain, the Bishop of London, the Abbot of Westminster and Edmund Dudley. He also had a collar of gold 'of th'order of Tosaunde' given by the 'King of Castile' at Windsor, which was the order of the 'Toison d'Or', or Golden Fleece, the chivalric order which was the Burgundian equivalent of the Order of the Garter.[48] This glimpse of the prince's jewels is a quiet foretaste of the magnificent jewellery he was to possess as king.

Henry VII had been severely shaken by the death of his eldest son, and even more by the death of his wife in 1503. His third son Edmund had already died, aged 16 months, in 1500. It was at this time that Henry's mounting anxieties led him to impose increasing restrictions on some of his subjects, generally through the use of the system of large suspended fines known as bonds. The escalation in his use of these from 1502 onwards suggests a man increasingly apprehensive about security. After Henry VII died, his minister Dudley produced a great list of the unjust exactions he had helped perpetrate in a bid to right some of the wrongs done in this way and secure 'relief for the dead king's soul'.[49] It is clear that the last years of Henry VII's reign had been full of unease. The opinion of the Spanish envoy who visited in 1508, that Henry was as protected as if he were a young girl, may be another indication of the father's nervousness over the fate of his sole surviving heir.[50]

It also appears that Henry VII vacillated over the crucial question of whom his son should marry. This was not unusual since the alignment of European allies was always changeable and frequently unpredictable, but Henry had previously been very successful at securing promising alliances for his children. He had married his eldest daughter Margaret to James IV of Scotland in 1503, helping to shore up the contested northern borders, and his daughter Mary was in 1507 betrothed to the Archduke Charles, the Duke of Burgundy, and future King of Spain and Holy Roman Emperor. He was unable to secure for Prince Henry, however, anything that equalled the triumph of Arthur's match with a daughter of the Spanish royal house. Katherine of Aragon was still living in England as Dowager Princess of Wales, and in the wake of Arthur's death Prince Henry was initially betrothed to her. But the death of her mother Queen Isabella in 1504, which undermined the union of the Spanish crowns of Castile and Aragon, meant Katherine's status was considerably lessened. In 1505 Prince Henry took a solemn vow renouncing his betrothal, whilst Katherine struggled with poverty, her dowry from her parents unpaid, and at one point, her allowance from her father-in-law suspended. Meanwhile Prince Henry was included in the proposed alliance with the Habsburgs, provisionally to be married to Eleanor of Castile as his sister Mary was betrothed to her brother the Archduke Charles. There was even the proposal that their father would be married again, to Margaret of Savoy, Charles and Eleanor's aunt.

These proposals came to nothing. The last years of Henry VII's life had been troubled with ill health, and he had been expected to die in the spring of 1507, and again in the summer of 1508. By March 1509 he was despaired of, and he died at Richmond on 21 April, his son – as ever – by his side. The anxieties of the closing years of the reign were reflected in the fact that the death was kept a secret for two days, with a number of people, including the future Henry VIII, maintaining the pretence that Henry VII was still alive. The young Henry went to evensong and supper on St George's day still pretending he was a prince; it was only after supper that the court was told he was in fact their new king.[51]

Henry VII's funeral was held at St Paul's Cathedral, and the funeral sermon preached by John Fisher, Bishop of Rochester, and printed at the request of the late king's mother, the formidable Lady Margaret Beaufort. His body was laid to rest in the chapel at Westminster Abbey which he had begun to build, and which still bears his name. The tomb carries effigies of Henry VII and Elizabeth of York, lying side by side, sculpted by Pietro Torrigiano. It was a dignified funeral, a magnificent tomb, and a safe handover of power, reflecting all the most important objectives of the dead king.

For the new king there was much to emulate, and much to reject from his father's reign. Henry VIII is often portrayed in 1509 as the boisterous, pleasure-loving, irresponsible young king, discarding the tedious but reliable policies of his father along with the men who had served him. But the new king was far from stupid. He could appreciate the extraordinary achievements of his father, who had established his kingship and ensured that it remained respected, prosperous and effective. Perhaps he even gloried in the memory of the young Henry VII who had risked everything in a daring invasion of England and been sanctioned by God and military glory at Bosworth. It would be unlikely that Henry VIII, so vividly aware of military skill and accomplishment, would have forgotten this foundation for his rule.

In 1537, Henry commissioned Hans Holbein to adorn his privy chamber with a mural depicting himself and Jane Seymour, with his parents standing behind and above them; a visual demonstration of the dynasty unfolding (see Plate 1). The figures stand either side of a monument on which is inscribed a Latin verse, which praises both father and son. This iconic image was placed at the symbolic and actual heart of Tudor government in the king's own chamber, and was of central importance to Henry's self-perception and self-portrayal. The verse, then, is worth quoting in full.

> If you find pleasure in seeing fair pictures of heroes,
> Look then at these! None greater was ever portrayed.
> Fierce is the struggle and hot the disputing; the question
> Does father, does son – or do both – the pre-eminence win?
> One ever withstood his foes and his country's destruction,
> Finally giving his people the blessing of peace;
> But, born to things greater, the son drove out of his councils
> His ministers worthless, and ever supported the just.
> And in truth, to this steadfastness Papal arrogance yielded
> When the sceptre of power was wielded by Henry the Eighth,
> Under whose reign the true faith was restored to the nation
> And the doctrines of God began to be reverenced with awe.[52]

This leaves us in no doubt as to Henry's view of his own central achievements. Yet it also shows that Henry had a healthy respect for his father's skills and success.

Much then was to remain from the previous reign. Henry VII had picked a set of councillors who served him with extraordinary longevity. Richard Fox, for example, had joined the young Henry of Richmond in 1484, fresh from university in Paris; he served Henry VII for the entirety of his reign, and remained in office as Lord Privy Seal to the new king until he retired in 1515. Even then, he only withdrew from the scene once he had trained his protege, Thomas Wolsey, to take over from him. William Warham, Archbishop of Canterbury, was also Henry VII's Lord Chancellor from 1504, and remained in this post until 1515. The Speaker of the House of Commons in Henry VIII's first parliament was Sir Thomas Englefield, who had also served as Speaker in the parliament of 1497. Henry VIII was far too intelligent to throw away the experience and expertise of the previous regime.

Yet there were also many new initiatives begun in 1509. Within hours of his accession, Henry VIII had determined the downfall of Richard Empson and Edmund Dudley, who were imprisoned in the Tower on just his second day as king. Henry astutely appreciated the propaganda value of distancing himself like this from the unjustly repressive exactions of his father's later years. He had also, within a few months, made it clear that he intended war on France, in a return to the chivalric past and the grand ambitions of the Hundred Years War. This was an idea all his own, which necessitated a painstaking redirection of diplomatic effort to bring about a major realignment of the European system of alliances.

It is the tomb by Pietro Torrigiano which provides the most lasting image of Henry VII. The king had wanted a Renaissance tomb, since he brought Guido Mazzoni to England to work on the commission, but the tomb he ended up with was Henry VIII's doing. Torrigiano signed the contract for the tomb in 1512, and for the High Altar in the same chapel in 1517. He was paid £1,500 for his work, but a greater commission, for £2,000, was to be the tomb of Henry VIII and Katherine of Aragon, commissioned in January 1519, clearly envisaged as being along the same lines, only grander.[53] It might stand as a metaphor for the relationship between father and son. So much that Henry VII achieved was to be taken up and raised to a new pitch of achievement by his son. In everything that he did, however, Henry VIII had to be sure to exceed his father. And in much of what he did, Henry was to take things to excess.

ENVIRONMENT

To understand a man's life, it is necessary to have some knowledge of his environment. We need to know, therefore, what the world was like into which Henry VIII was born, and what it meant to be King of England in 1509. We need to explore, as far as we can, what were the parameters of his existence – the geographical boundaries, the social limits, the economic framework, the linguistic structure. Knowing too the material objects which the king handled on a daily basis, and the small concerns of his daily life, can help enhance our understanding of this complex character. This is especially important since Henry was so interested in his surroundings and his possessions, building and decorating palaces on an unprecedented scale, and filling them with beautiful and expensive objects. He also brokered his relationships with the exchange of gifts, from the formal gift-giving at court which marked each New Year, to the steady trickle of small informal bequests granted throughout the year. And his subjects pledged their loyalty through gifts also.

His Privy Purse records show that he received an array of small, useful presents: pheasaunts and partridge, wild boar, wild fowl or baked lampreys are examples of edible gifts from the nobility and gentry.[54] The servants who conveyed these gifts would be rewarded with a payment of several shillings: five shillings, for example, was given 'to a servant of Sir Giles Capell in rewarde for bringing Cheeses to the king's grace'; in the same month, the Earl of Westmorland sent a servant to take 'a spaniel to the king's grace'.[55] It was not just his wealthy subjects who proffered presents: in 1532 six shillings was given 'to a poor woman in Reward for bringing a present of Apples to the King's grace'.[56] Meanwhile the king's amorous intentions also took material form: in the autumn of 1529, when he was deeply in love with Anne Boleyn, we find over forty shillings expended for 'a yard and a quarter of purple velvet for mistress Anne'.[57]

England in 1509 had a population of between 2 and 3 million people, of which perhaps 6 per cent lived in towns, including the 3 per cent who lived in London. This was far less than there had been before 1348, and the first onslaught of the plague, or the 'Black Death'. Population figures are notoriously difficult to extract from the records of this period, but it seems likely that the plague reduced England's population by a third, maybe more. Certain communities were particularly hard hit; in some religious houses, we learn, only two men of every twenty survived, and some contemporaries thought mankind would be wiped out altogether.[58] Moreover, the plague became a constant fact of life, with recurrent epidemics; a series of major outbreaks between 1464 and 1479 meant the horrors were still within living memory when Henry came to the throne. There were also epidemics during 1493, 1499–1500, 1505 and 1521, during Henry's own lifetime, which helps put his dread of disease and his anxieties for the succession in perspective.

Much of England was still covered by forest. This was not wild forest, for England had already been cultivated for centuries. Tudor forest was a mixture of elements: trees, scrub and fen; coppice-woods and pollards for the harvesting of wood; grassland which fed cattle as well as deer. Hatfield forest today gives some idea of the forests of Henry's day, as do the New Forest and the Forest of Dean.[59] 'Wild boar pie' was still a favourite dish of Tudor monarchs, but the last wild boars had been killed in the Forest of Dean in the thirteenth century: the pies were made from animals reared in parks.[60] Farmland, towns and villages would have looked not unlike rural England today. Hedges were created from plants dug up in the local woods, or from 'quickset' thorns grown especially for the purpose, and oak, ash and elm trees were the most common non-woodland trees.[61] Some of the land previously cultivated had been abandoned after the Black Death, many villages had been abandoned, and more had shrunk, but this tended to mean better conditions for the peasantry that was left, as holdings grew in size and peasants obtained better conditions of tenure.

Climate change in the later Middle Ages had led to lower tempera-tures and increased rainfall, which created problems farming in certain areas, but on the whole there was increasing prosperity through the late Middle Ages, with a fair degree of enterprise within rural communi-ties.[62] This was reflected in the buildings of the time: church buildings like at Lavenham or Louth, church houses, guild halls, or the handsome stone bridges that can still be seen in Barnstaple, Wakefield, Monmouth and Stratford-upon-Avon. Communal buildings such as churches were frequently paid for by collective fundraising within the parish.

There were around 9,000 parishes in Henry VIII's England, and sev-enteen dioceses, to which he would be responsible for adding another six, converting important abbeys into the new cathedrals of Oxford, Peterborough, Chester, Bristol, Westminster and Gloucester. London was huge, with around 60,000 inhabitants, but in the provinces, other cities were a tiny fraction of the size: Norwich and Bristol had about 12,000 and 10,000 inhabitants respectively, and York, Exeter, Newcastle, Coventry and Salisbury had populations of around 8,000 or less. There were about 100 incorporated towns with populations of between 1,500 and 5,000, and about 500 small towns with populations of less than 1,000. In Wales, Carmarthen had about 2,000 inhabitants, and other major centres about 1,000 to 1,500. In the 1520s, a quarter of the property in Coventry lay vacant, and many other urban centres still bore the visible marks of abandonment and decay after the plague.[63] Yet other urban centres were flourishing, such as Walden, which became known in the sixteenth century as Saffron Walden in tribute to the crocus which was the foundation of its wealth.

By modern standards, England would have been unspoilt, and very beautiful, but to the Tudors land was defined by its function, with man's dominance over the natural world confirmed by God; weeds, pests, venomous creatures and the stubborn natures of recalcitrant domestic beasts were all the consequence of human sinfulness.[64] The world had been designed as a paradise for man, and by his folly and error he had made life in it a struggle. All natural creatures were designed to answer human needs; one Elizabethan noted approvingly that the lobster answered multiple requirements, since it provided man with food, exercise in cracking it open, and an object for wonder in its armour.[65]

The brutal treatment of animals was a source of much enjoyment: bear-baiting and cock-fighting were considered suitable entertainment for royalty and nobility, and Henry VIII made a cockpit the centrepiece of the recreation grounds in his new Palace of Whitehall. The 1560 map of London from the Guildhall Library shows the two great arenas for bull-baiting and bear-baiting on Bankside, which would in due course compete with Shakespeare's Globe; indeed, it has been suggested that theatres often doubled as bear-rings or cockpits.[66]

Henry would have been familiar with the English landscape, because he travelled constantly between his different palaces, castles and houses. Winter was spent predominantly in the five great palaces which were strung along the Thames, from Windsor, Hampton Court and Richmond in the west, to Whitehall (which the king acquired in 1529) just west of London, and Greenwich to the east. Summers were spent hunting, and going on progresses, staying in smaller royal palaces, houses and hunting lodges, or in the great homes of the nobility and gentry. Henry's palaces were all surrounded by parks, emphasising the extent to which even by 1500 man had shaped the landscape of England. Deer parks were a status symbol dating back to the Norman Conquest: at their peak around 1300 there were well over 3,000 in England, accounting for about 2 per cent of the territory, pleasure grounds for royalty, nobility and gentry, monastic houses and university colleges. By Henry's time their usage was declining, but he revived the practice, confiscating the monastic parks, taking the seven great parks which traditionally belonged to the Archbishop of Canterbury away from Cranmer, and surrounding his new palaces with them. In 1539 he created Hampton Court Chase, with 10,000 acres including four villages.[67] Like Henry's endorsement of chivalric orders and motifs, there was a self-conscious appeal to the medieval past at work here, but there was also an element of Renaissance display, with the landscape artfully shaped with groves and avenues to create an idealised backdrop to the royal ostentation that was the hunting expedition. It is to Henry too that we owe the great London parks: he bought up St James's Park, Green Park, Hyde Park and Marylebone (later Regent's) Park through the 1530s and 1540s to provide space for hunting, partly for entertainment and partly for food. St James's Park was walled, with ponds for fish and waterfowl to feed the king's table.[68]

The king would have been most familiar with the urban landscape of London, where he could reside in the Tower, or the Palace of Westminster, or his palace at Baynard's Castle. There were problems here, since the Tower accommodation was cramped until reorganised by Cromwell in the 1530s, and the living quarters of the Palace of Westminster burned down in 1512. The king's response to this was first to develop Bridewell in the city, creating a palace from a collection of ecclesiastical properties bordering Fleet Street. This palace faced the great priory of the London Blackfriars across the river Fleet. Blackfriars was sufficiently grand to be used for important state occasions, most infamously the divorce trial of 1529. Bridewell Palace had the long gallery which was characteristic of Tudor palaces, and which ended in a watergate, for travel was nearly always by water.[69] After he inherited York Place from Wolsey, Henry turned it into the Palace of Whitehall, which was to be the chief of all his residences. In the 1530s he also built St James's Palace and the second half of his reign was to see a great proliferation of building work.

The population of London was growing steadily, but Tudor London was a very different city from the one we know today. Westminster and Whitehall, for example, lay outside the city walls, and Covent Garden (as the same suggests) was still the garden which sustained the community of Benedictine monks at Westminster Abbey. The city began at Temple Bar, and stretched east, although settlement outside the city walls was well established, reflected in the parish names of St. Botolph's without Aldgate or St Martin-in-the-Fields. John Stow's *Survey of London* gives us a good idea of Tudor London; Stow was born in Threadneedle Street in 1525. We find a city crowded and often filthy, yet with fine ancient buildings, some dating back to the eleventh or twelfth centuries. The population was unusually young, given the depredations of disease and the influx of hopeful transients, and apprentices in particular were inclined to drunken revelry which often became violent, after football matches, or on Shrove Tuesday when they raided the brothels, or on 'Evil May Day' in 1517 when foreigners and their houses were attacked.

When the king travelled within London, he nearly always went by water, in the gilded and carved royal barges. These barges could be sumptuously decorated. When Anne Boleyn made her ceremonial entrance from Greenwich into the city as queen in 1533 there was a splendid procession, led by the mayor's state barge hung with flags and tapestries, with trumpets sounding, and a floating stage where 'a dragon pranced about furiously, twisting his tail and belching out wildfire'.[70] To travel by land was unusual; in the winter of 1537 Hall recorded that: 'the Thames of London [was] all frozen over wherefore the king's Majesty with his beautiful spouse queen Jane, rode throughout the city of London to Greenwich.'[71] In general Henry would have lived at one remove from the more offensive aspects of the city.

Henry VIII spoke English to his wives, courtiers and councillors, but he also spoke Latin, French, and some Italian. Being married to Katherine of Aragon for twenty-four years, he also learned to speak some Spanish. The English language had a distinctive, slightly precarious, newly aggressive quality at this time, since it was less than 100 years since royalty and nobility would have automatically spoken and written in French, and official records were only recently turning to English as their customary tongue. When translating into English, or writing in the vernacular, there were often no precedents to follow. The translator of a devotional work published in 1530 for the Brigittine nuns of Syon, the royal foundation near Richmond Palace, wrote a little plaintively, 'It is not light [i.e. easy] for every man to draw any long thing from latin into our English tongue. For there is many words in Latin that we have no proper english according thereto.'[72] The editors of the *Complete Works* of Chaucer in 1532, commissioned by and dedicated to Henry VIII, saw their work as a patriotic act, a proud statement of the glories of the English language and its literature, while admitting that English was still undergoing a process of 'beautifying and bettering'.[73]

Henry VIII and his court were sharply delineated from the rest of Tudor society simply by what they ate. This was an age in which the nobility probably spent a third of their total income on food and drink, because providing for a large household and demonstrating wealth were both crucial aspects of the political process. For this reason the diet of the nobility was much less healthy than the diet of the reasonably prosperous peasant. Where peasant diet involved butter, cheese and other dairy produce, and vegetables such as beans, peas, onions and garlic, a noble diet involved largely meat and fish, and was extremely deficient in fruit, vegetables or dairy products. Fresh meat and fish could be obtained all year round; the predominance of spices in the food of the nobility was not to disguise the taste of poor-quality or salted produce, but to demonstrate luxury and sophistication. Nevertheless, most noble and gentry households ate reasonably humdrum creatures: cows, sheep and poultry, or herring, cod and haddock on the fish-days every week and throughout Lent. [74]

By contrast, the diet of the royal household was ostentatiously exotic, full of game birds, venison and unusual fishes. In 1513 was published *The Boke of Kervynge*, which gave instructions to the carver, butler, chamberlain and other officers of a royal or noble establishment. The list of correct terminology used for dissecting the different creatures gives an idea of the range of foodstuffs. The 'Termes of a Kerver' include: 'unbrace that mallard ...dismember that heron, display that crane, disfigure that peacock ... wing that quail, mince that plover, thigh that pigeon ... chine that salmon, string that lamprey, splat that pike, sauce that plaice ...' and end with 'barb that lobster'.[75] The royal palaces all came with parks and pheasant yards which could provide the fresh meat for the court; Hampton Court had its own warren. Most houses had ponds too, to provide the fish that was eaten on Fridays and throughout Lent; in York Place fish were kept alive in piped running water just prior to consumption.[76]

Food at this time was served not on plates, but on trenchers, carved from loaves, ideally for ease of carving bread that was four days old. Henry VIII, however, probably ate from trenchers made of silver or gilt: his inventory includes many such, often with a place for salt at one end or in the corner, and he had one trencher of solid gold.[77] The wine and ale for the king and queen were kept separately from the 300 casks of wine drunk annually by the court, which also consumed around 600,000 gallons of ale. These vast quantities of alcohol were kept under careful guard: at Hampton Court the cellar door had two locks, with the two different keys kept by two different household officials. After he had dined, the king might repair to the banqueting house for the evening. 'Banquets' at the time were a kind of after-dinner party with sweet wines and confections. Food for banquets might include quince paste, quince cakes, jelly, gingerbread, spice cake, marchpane (marzipan), conserves and baked and dried fruits, with hippocras, which was spiced and sweetened wine, to drink.[78] Instructions 'For to make Ypocras' were another section in *The Boke of Kervynge*. When Henry built Whitehall Palace he included a banqueting house at the southern end of the formal gardens.

In one sense it is difficult to imagine a typical day in the life of Henry VIII, since he was so constantly on the move between palaces, great houses and hunting lodges, and his surroundings were always changing. Even when resident in one palace, he enjoyed going visiting, particularly in London when a short river journey would take him from Greenwich to visit Archbishop Warham at Lambeth Palace, Chancellor Thomas More in Chelsea, or Cardinal Wolsey at York Place, ostensibly impromptu visits which in fact usually necessitated the careful preparation of lavish entertainment by his hosts. Wolsey's biographer, George Cavendish, describes the luxurious provision made for the king's delight

> Such pleasures were then devised for the King's comfort and consolation as might be invented or by man's wit imagined. The banquets were set forth with masques and mummeries in so gorgeous a sort and costly manner that it was an heaven to behold.[79]

Cavendish also gives a detailed account of one of these 'surprise' visits, with Wolsey and his entourage feigning ignorance of the king's identity until Henry delightedly declared himself.[80] This rather heavy-handed kind of charade seems to have brought Henry a lot of pleasure, since he often dressed up and acted the part of a stranger, only to reveal himself with a melodramatic flourish, to general – and presumably well-simulated – surprise and applause. Later in the reign, when York Place had become Henry's own Palace of Whitehall, he would travel from there by boat to Winchester Palace in Southwark, where Bishop Gardiner entertained him, or to the Dowager Duchess of Norfolk's house in Lambeth where he was to court Katherine Howard. His private expenses contain a great many payments to boatmen, for example, 'to the king's watermen for waiting five dayes and three nights'.[81] In modern parlance, Henry liked to keep a taxi waiting at all times.

On the other hand, if the king was constantly on the move, still court ritual was replicated according to the same pattern in every place he went, and most of his household servants and his prized possessions travelled with him, including his bed. The bed even went with him to France when he was leading an army, and sleeping under canvas, albeit canvas of the most sumptuous and extensive sort. It was an innovation when the new Palace of Whitehall was provided with a permanent collection of furnishings and artefacts in the later part of the reign. It is possible to envisage Henry's daily routine, therefore. He would have woken in his bedchamber but probably not alone, as there would be a gentleman of the privy chamber sleeping nearby, perhaps on a pallet on the floor, or possibly in an ante-chamber. He would then have been shaved and clothed, sending down for clothes from the royal wardrobe, which at Whitehall was below the privy lodgings. *The Boke of Kervynge* instructs the chamberlain that he should warm the king's shirt and other clothes, and after helping him to dress, combing his hair and washing his hands, that he should kneel to ask what robe the king wanted to wear. Breakfast was also eaten in the privy lodgings, prepared in the king's private kitchen, and followed by mass. The chamberlain, having dressed the king, was instructed to go to his closet in church or chapel and there place carpets and cushions, and lay out the king's prayer book.[82] Henry VIII attended mass at least once a day, and clearly other noblemen were expected to behave similarly. A mid-Tudor tract on healthy living instructs the reader to every morning:

> wash your handes and wrists, your face, and eyes, and your teeth, with cold water; and after that you be apparalled, walk in your garden or park, a thousand pace or two. And then great and noble men doth use to hear mass.[83]

After mass, the king was free until dinner, to attend to business with his councillors, or to hunt, play tennis or practise some other kind of sport. The Palace of Whitehall was built with four tennis courts, two of them indoor. When they were not required by the king they could be hired by courtiers for two shillings and sixpence per day.[84] In general the king dined twice a day, once around noon, and then again in the late afternoon. These meals would be served in the privy chamber, with the king seated alone under his canopy of cloth of estate, and even on ordinary days his food would arrive with much ceremony and a fanfare of trumpets.[85] After dinner he might go to the queen's apartments to relax in a slightly less formal atmosphere, with music and dancing, and if he spent the night in the queen's apartments there would be no household officials sleeping on the floor, although they would be close at hand in the next chamber.

Henry was constantly surrounded by company in his private apartments, from his more lowly private servants to the gentlemen of the privy chamber who combined in one the role of body servant, close friend and important political figure. The chief gentleman of the privy chamber was the 'groom of the stool' who attended on the king as he used his lavatory, or close stool, which was a portable wooden box containing a pot. This close stool would be handsomely cushioned and decorated with trimming. The king's inventory records, for example, one such close stool 'of black velvet embroidered with cloth of gold and venice Silk and gold with the king's arms fringed with black silk and venice gold', after which sumptuousness is more prosaically recorded 'with two broad tin basins and a conduit of tin for the same'.[86] Any tribulations the king might suffer whilst employing this device would be solemnly recorded for his physicians. Thomas Heneage, groom of the stool in 1539, related to Cromwell that after some medical treatment, the king:

> slept unto two of the clock in the morning and then his Grace rose to go to the stool, which, by working of the pills and glyster that his Highness had taken before, had a very fair siege.[87]

His closest attendants were to all intents and purposes Henry's family. It is significant that despite the many changes of his reign, Henry had only four grooms of the stool: Sir William Compton, who had served him as prince, held the post until 1526, then Henry Norris until 1536, Sir Thomas Heneage until 1546, and Sir Anthony Denny for the last year of the reign. Henry had to take care of his immediate attendants: in 1530 there was a payment of fifteen shillings 'for fifty-two pair of hose for master Weston', and a month later over twenty-four shillings was paid 'to black John the hardwareman for bonnets for young Weston, And other children of the private chamber'.[88] There were other small concerns, including payments to the 'keeper of the beagles', and ten shillings for someone who brought hens to feed the king's hawks, whilst a stable hand received forty shillings towards his marriage.[89] The master of the beagles and the stable hand are both mentioned by name in the accounts, suggesting a host of small acquaintances among the king's more lowly subjects. Henry also regularly dispensed ten pounds a month in alms, and would give presents of money to his daughter, or his niece Lady Margaret Douglas, who was largely brought up at court.

For Henry, private life and political life merged. The men who helped him get up in the morning might equally be those who fought beside him in battle or who were sent as ambassadors to foreign courts. His privy councillors who formed his government on the basis of their education and administrative skill overlapped with the nobility who controlled the localities on the basis of heredity. The women who adorned his court might be married to either, and most unusually, four of them were to be married to the king himself. It was almost unheard-of for the king to marry a subject, and Edward IV had caused grave political instability when he had done so in 1464, but Henry was confident enough to defy convention, and the court he was creating was new in several respects.

If for Henry private and public merged, so too did secular and sacred. As we have seen, the king heard mass on a daily basis. Sometimes this was in his private chapel, called the king's closet or privy closet, next to his privy chamber, from which he could see, through a grille, the liturgy being celebrated by one of his royal chaplains. On Sundays and important holy days, however, he went in solemn procession to the main palace chapel, where the liturgy was celebrated with great pomp by the dean, chaplains, master, gentlemen and choristers of the Chapel Royal. The master, gentlemen and choristers were the best that money could buy, and although much of the sacred music of the time was plainsong, great occasions provided an opportunity for polyphonic mass settings, or 'pricksong' as it was known, since it required that the notes be actually written down, or pricked out, for the singers to follow. When Henry went to France in 1520, he took 115 members of the Chapel Royal with him, which helps demonstrate the scale of this ecclesiastical spectacle. The star of the show was, of course, the king himself, although there were variations in the pageantry according to season.

One of the most important feast days, from the court's point of view, was Epiphany, when the king – like the Magi arriving to venerate the infant Jesus – wore his crown. At Easter, Whitsun, Christmas and All Saints, there was the 'wearing of the purple', involving the same gorgeous robes, but no crown. Purple was a colour restricted to the king and his immediate family, as the sumptuary law of 1533 reiterated. There were also 'Days of Estate', on the feast days of Candlemas, the Assumption, the Nativity of the Virgin, the Circumcision of Christ and the Nativity of St John. On these days the king probably wore the red velvet robes of state. He processed to the 'Holyday Closet' on the first-floor gallery from where he could look down upon the chapel. This piece of theatre was performed every Sunday, and on the forty-seven feast days in the year.[90]

Religion and politics were inextricable in Henry's lifetime, and just as his processions to the Chapel Royal were an opportunity to make an important political statement, so too they were an occasion for political business. Letters and petitions could be pressed into the king's hand as he walked through the palace, and important discussions often took place in the privy closet or the Holyday Closet. Wolsey, writing to Bishop Fox in 1509 about the likelihood of the Pope's imminent death, said 'Yesterday at mass I broke with the King in this matter.'[91] In 1521 Richard Pace brought the papal bull and brief announcing the excommunication of Luther, he reported to Wolsey that the king was very pleased with the papal brief and 'read it every word at his second mass time'.[92] The sources give the impression that this was an excellent time for getting an exceedingly energetic and impossibly busy man to sit still and concentrate on something.

As Henry embarked on kingship in 1509, much of his future was already shaped by the expectations and assumption of Christian piety, chivalry, Renaissance learning and display, but a great deal of Henry's self-fashioning as king was to be unlike anything that had gone before.

2

THE FOUNDATIONS OF KINGSHIP, 1509–1518

But when you know what a hero he now shows himself, how wisely he behaves, what a lover he is of justice and goodness, what affection he bears to the learned, I will venture to swear that you will need wings to make you fly to behold this new and auspicious star. ... If you could see how all the world here is rejoicing in the possession of so great a prince, how his life is all their desire, you could not contain your tears for joy.[1]

Henry VIII acceded to the throne of England peacefully, and was both healthy and solvent, and this in itself was rare enough to bring general rejoicing. In addition, he was young – still only 17 – and he was also vigorous, handsome and cultivated. He had had very little experience of wielding authority under his father's anxious and rigorous control, but those who surrounded him were immediately impressed by his confidence, his princely demeanour and his energy. Their ecstatic comments were of course exaggerated, but there is sufficient consensus in the accounts to suggest a good basis of truth in their descriptions. The new king's accession was greeted with bonfires and celebrations, and from the more educated classes, a combination of Renaissance panegyric and carefully phrased advice. From the first, it was clear that Henry looked the part, an immensely important feature of leadership in Tudor society. It should be noted, for example, that – unusually for the time – he was over six foot tall. His father's historian, Polydore Vergil, listed his attributes:

his handsome bearing, his comely and manly features (in which one could discern as much authority as good will), his outstanding physical strength, remarkable memory, aptness at all the arts of both war and peace, skill at arms and on horseback, scholarship of no mean order, thorough knowledge of music and his humanity, benevolence and self-control.[2]

For Vergil, and his contemporaries, attributes emphasising strength, authority and skill were clearly most important. In appearance, therefore, Henry seemed the epitome of kingship. In 1518, when the Treaty of London was being celebrated with ecclesiastical pomp in St Paul's, the king's secretary Richard Pace preached a sermon in which he praised Henry's longing for peace, all the more remarkable since, the preacher observed, Nature seemed to have shaped the king for war:

He who looks closely upon you cannot but see that the beauty of your splendid body, the incomparable aptness and compactness of your limbs, all breathes war: you are tall, brave, active, powerful, and so strong that you leave far behind you all who seek to display their bodily strength in earnest or in play.[3]

This personal description might seem curiously out of place in a sermon, but it indicates how closely intertwined was the physical strength of the king with the moral, material and military strength of the kingdom.

It is clear that the testimonies of Vergil, Pace and others were not merely flattery (although they were that too). Henry VIII's feats of physical prowess were legendary, and contemporaries rejoiced that he could hunt from dawn until dusk without tiredness, or dance until dawn with such vigour and grace. When hunting he could tire out eight or more horses; at home he played tennis, or practised wrestling, with equal verve. He loved to joust, despite the risk, and the score cards or 'cheques' kept at tournaments show that Henry really was a brilliant jouster.[4] The political use he made of his physical attributes and skills show that Henry understood quite clearly the value of his talents. When he interrogated the Venetian ambassador about the King of France's height and build, and heard that his legs could be described as 'spare', the ambassador reports that 'he opened the front of his doublet, and placing his hand on his thigh, said 'Look here! And I have also a goodly calf to my leg.' This needs to be seen in the context of the later anecdote in the same despatch, where the king, having toppled his opponent in a tournament, came over to laugh and chat with the ambassadors as they watched events from a window, 'to our very great honour, and to the surprise of all beholders'. Henry was sending a clear message about his political and military strength to observers on the continent.

Henry's first important decision as king was to marry Katherine of Aragon. All his life he was to be preoccupied with questions of family and – ironically for a man largely known for his marital excesses – it seems that he had a deep abiding reverence for the married state, and a longing to be happily and successfully married. Perhaps he had taken to heart the extent to which his mother's hand in marriage had consolidated the royal status of his father, who might otherwise have remained a penniless exile and adventurer. Vergil, describing how the people flocked to Henry's coronation, noted that 'their affections were not half-hearted, because the king on his father's side descended from Henry VI, and on his mother's from Edward IV', and whether we view Vergil as historian or royal propagandist here, the implications for Henry's own perception of the situation are equally clear.[5]

Marriage consolidated kingship, and if Henry's enthusiastic espousal of Katherine of Aragon was a reaction against his father's caution, as has been suggested, he nevertheless chose to marry the woman who had secured his father's most important diplomatic achievement. He claimed that he married her in fulfilment of his father's dying wish, which may well be true; although he reacted against many aspects of his father's rule, he was careful to build on Henry VII's most solid achievements, and shared more of his father's preoccupations than he might care to admit.[6] Equally importantly, it seems that he was attracted to Katherine, and that, initially at least, he loved her. As a boy of 10, he had escorted Katherine to the altar in St Paul's to marry his elder brother, in a glittering ceremony, where perhaps he had envied the lot of his elder brother as future king as well as new-wedded husband. Now finally taking his brother's place as king, he completed the transformation by marrying Katherine. It was his first clear affirmation of his own adulthood, and as such it may even have helped that Katherine was over six years older than he was.

This marriage was not the extravagant public display that Arthur and Katherine's wedding had been: like all of Henry's marriages, it took place quietly and privately, at Greenwich Palace on 11 June. The political message of this alliance was unambiguous. Katherine may have spent the previous seven years as the impoverished Dowager Princess of Wales, but she was the daughter of Ferdinand and Isabella of Aragon and Castile, whose status, wealth and European influence far exceeded that of the Tudors. Her parents were both monarchs in their own right, who had united Spain by accident of marriage and consolidated its territories with their conquest of Granada, the last Muslim kingdom in Spain. Given the title of Their Catholic Majesties, they were champions of the faith, the leading power in Europe, and rulers of the New World discovered by Columbus. It was also a point worth noting that Katherine's mother was the great-granddaughter (twice over) of John of Gaunt, and that this alliance would add some Plantagenet respectability to the Tudor line as well as a goodly amount of wealth and glory.[7] Finally, Katherine's father (her mother had died in 1504) was an obvious ally for anyone seeking to make war on France.

Katherine is usually remembered now for her painful struggle with her primary responsibility as queen, to produce sufficient children to secure the succession. In all other aspects of the role, however, she was a formidable figure, and an important aspect of Henry's kingship is reflected in the piety, the erudition and the political weight of his queen. His choice of Katherine illustrates his ability to surround himself with people of extraordinary intelligence, resourcefulness and loyalty. As a daughter of Isabella of Castile, she had a powerful role model as mother, for Isabella was a brave and forthright military leader as well as a pious and intelligent ruler. Katherine had handled the political awkwardness of her years in England as Arthur's widow with dignity and courage. As queen she displayed the same characteristics, and complemented her husband's religious fervour and his intellectual enthusiasms. Erasmus was not flattering her unduly when he remarked that 'The queen is astonishingly well read, far beyond what would be surprising in a woman, and as admirable for piety as she is for learning.'[8] Books were dedicated to her and Henry together, including biblical translations and the *Res gestae Alexandri Magni*, or 'Deeds of Alexander the Great', which brought together two of the king's particular enthusiasms.[9] Katherine herself had been given a good humanist education; her mother's patronage had led to a flowering of the Renaissance in Spain. Katherine was fluent in Latin, and familiar with classical and early Christian authors, history and law.[10]

It is highly significant that for her sole surviving child, Princess Mary, she commissioned the Spanish humanist Juan Luis Vives to draw up a plan of education. He published the result, *De Ratione Studii Puerilis*, or 'On the right method of instruction for children' in 1524, and his forthright recommendation of political texts by Plato, Thomas More, Erasmus and other biblical, patristic and classical authors suggests that he was preparing the princess to wield worldly authority.[11] In the same year, Vives also produced *De Institutione Foeminae Christianae*, or 'The instruction of a Christian woman', in which the dedication to Queen Katherine began:

> Moved by the holiness of your life and your ardent zeal for sacred studies, I have endeavoured to write something for Your Majesty on the education of a Christian woman, a subject of paramount importance, but one that has not been treated hitherto by anyone among the great multitude and diversity of talented writers of the past.[12]

Like her husband, Katherine could embrace both traditional piety and the radical ideas of the humanists.

Katherine's identity as queen was closely involved with Henry's own emerging identity as king. In their early years together he seems to have been genuinely and exuberantly enamoured of her, always putting her at the heart of the elaborate festivities of courtly life. When the king felt like playing at Robin Hood, or dressing up as a Saracen, Katherine's presence was essential as he peacocked and displayed his beauty, his athleticism and his inventiveness. The New Year revelry for 1516, recorded by the faithful chronicler, concludes, 'the Quene heartily thanked the king's grace for her goodly pastime, and kissed him.'[13] Henry also slept with Katherine on a regular basis; a fact apparent to his court, since it meant he spent the night in the queen's bedchamber rather than his own. This affection for his wife did not prevent him taking mistresses, the first in 1510 when Katherine was occupied with her first unsuccessful pregnancy. Henry's affections tended to be dependent on the ability of those around him to fulfil his desires. When on New Year's Day 1511 the Queen gave birth to a prince, Henry's jubilation was unmatched. After the baptism at Richmond the king went on a pilgrimage of thanksgiving to the shrine of Our Lady at Walsingham. He returned to take part in the celebratory joust at Westminster which he had announced on the day of Prince

Henry's christening, adopting the guise of 'Sir Loyal Heart', with his blue trappings decorated with gold 'K's, and hearts, and the word 'Loyal'.

When God seemed to favour him, Henry's love, generosity and valour overflowed, and Katherine was at the centre of this pageantry, her status secured by her success as the mother of his heir. Characteristically, Henry behaved as the model of piety at Walshingham, and the model of chivalry at Westminster; the image of perfect kingship, complete with adored wife and precious child. Ten days later the baby was dead. It was the first of many cruel reversals, in which Henry's vision of his own magnificence, closely interwoven with divine favour and dynastic security, was shattered. In 1511 he was young, and he picked up the pieces again readily enough. As his reign wore on, these disappointments would take him each time a little deeper into fear, anger and suspicion.

In considering the life of Henry VIII, it is important not to rush too far ahead to the years when conflicts and difficulties twisted the king's nature and the more anxious and vengeful sides of his character emerged. For the first twenty years of his reign, there was a great deal that was deemed successful, and the promise of 1509 was in many ways fulfilled. Throughout those twenty years Katherine of Aragon was at his side, and she was a popular and revered figure. Their mutual affection was also a source of security for the realm at large, since the stability of the dynasty had clear political and material benefits for the king's subjects. When Henry was reunited with Katherine after his first campaign in France, the chronicler records that after landing at Dover, 'he with a small company rode to Richmond in post to the queen, where was such a loving meeting, that every creature rejoiced.'[14]

Henry VII had died on 22 April 1509. Two months later, on 24 June, with the new king already married, there took place Henry and Katherine's joint coronation, a magnificent and triumphant celebration for Midsummer's day. Katherine's dress, her horses, the litter in which she was carried, were all white, and her coronal was set with pearls. Her auburn hair was worn loose, in traditional style. Henry's clothes were stiff with jewels – 'Diamonds, Rubies, Emeralds, great Pearls, and other rich Stones', and the pageantry was lavish: 'for a surety, more rich, nor more strange nor more curious works hath not been seen than were prepared against this coronation,' wrote the chronicler.[15]

A coronation was a hugely important occasion, involving vast expense, as everyone who participated was dressed at the crown's expense: the goodwill of the capital could in large part be taken for granted, since London's merchants must have made a handsome profit from the ceremony.[16] If the enthusiasm of the mercantile sector was secured by these straightforward means, the loyalty of the nobility was reinforced by more arcane, chivalric customs. Two days before the coronation, the ritual began in the Tower, where overnight twenty-six new Knights of the Bath were created, including Thomas Boleyn and Thomas Parr, whose daughters would one day be queen in place of Katherine, unthinkable as that would have seemed at the time. Ritually cleansed, these knights spent the night in prayer, their vigil underscoring the necessity of divine sanction for all temporal authority. A king did not stand alone, but had to be surrounded by knights whose nobility and wealth enhanced his own status, whose loyalty underscored his strength.

The royal procession through the city the next day to Westminster followed a route hung with tapestries and cloth of gold, where all the livery companies stood solemnly arrayed in order of precedence. The Goldsmiths put on a display 'with Virgins in white, with branches of white Wax: the priests and clerks, in rich Copes with Crosses and censers of silver, with censing his grace, and the Queen also as they passed'.[17] White symbolised both luxury and purity, and censing with incense indicated the presence of something holy, here according king and queen the same status as a priest or a holy relic. The occasion was thick with symbolic meaning. In front of the King rode two men, carrying the arms of the Duchy of Guienne and the Duchy of Normandy respectively, and behind him came nine children clothed in blue velvet with gold fleurs-de-lys, proclaiming Henry's claim to England, France, Gascony, Guienne, Normandy, Anjou, Cornwall, Wales and Ireland. This helped to underline Henry's claim to the French crown and the former English lands in France.

The day after that, which was Sunday and Midsummer day, the procession moved to Westminster Hall, then on to the Abbey for the ritual of coronation. As the royal couple walked to the abbey, the cloth they had traversed was cut up by the crowd, who took away the pieces as relics of the occasion, another indication that in the eyes of their contemporaries, Henry and his wife were holy objects. The crowns used at the coronation were believed to have belonged to Edward the Confessor and his wife, and were kept in the saint's shrine itself. Henry was anointed and clothed in vestments like those of a bishop, indicating that as king his authority was as much sacred as temporal. The city of London was again honoured at the coronation banquet, since the king made the lord mayor a knight before he sat down, and at the end of the meal accepted Hippocras – sweet spiced wine – from him in a gold cup, which cup the lord mayor was allowed to keep. This too was fully in accordance with tradition. But at the jousts which followed the coronation banquet, king and queen sat in a pavilion surmounted by 'a great Crown Imperial', a departure from usual practice.[18] Imperial power exceeded royal power, in particular because it claimed sovereignty over church as well as state. At this first entrance onto the political stage, then, Henry was hinting at an authority which exceeded that of his predecessors.

THE MENTAL WORLD OF TUDOR KINGSHIP

Henry had inherited the throne, married, and been crowned, all within two months: throughout his life, he moved swiftly to secure what he wanted. In many of his actions, he was guided by the customs and precepts of established tradition, and in particular by the need to obtain and demonstrate religious sanction. Henry seems to have been a genuinely religious man, although on first sight, this seems a deeply implausible statement. After all, this was the man notorious for having six wives, and for cruelly rejecting the first, and beheading the second, both on highly specious grounds. This was the man who high-handedly reorganised the church in England, rewrote Christian doctrine, and could not even be said to have done so in the service of Protestantism, since he persecuted Catholics and Protestants alike. His religious policies were at different times a vehicle for his greed, his paranoia and his egotism. Nonetheless, the fact remains that he was deeply committed to his faith, that it formed a central part of his existence, and that his relationship with God was all important to him, although at times it seemed like Henry dictated its terms. Like all important relationships, Henry's involvement with his maker consumed quite a lot of his time.

As we have seen, Henry attended mass every weekday, not just on Sundays, and sometimes heard mass more than once a day. It is true that he often talked to his councillors and courtiers and arranged business during mass, but ideas of church-going at the time focused more on the importance of being physically present, rather than concentrating on the words that were said, or in Henry's case, largely sung. Henry went on pilgrimage, he venerated shrines, he gave alms to the poor on a daily basis. The Venetian ambassador recorded in 1531 that the king 'gives many alms, relieving paupers, orphans, widows and cripples, his almoner disbursing annually ten thousand golden ducats for this purpose', and although the figure may be questionable, the practice is not.[19] The king's confessor was an integral part of the community of the court, and like the priests and musicians of the Chapel Royal, went with him as he travelled.

In part, this was no more than the understanding of the age he lived in. Life was so precarious, danger and disease so widespread and formidable, that a fervent belief in a benign and powerful deity was one of the few safeguards against fear. The speed with which Henry fled from the plague, or the sweating sickness, during their repeated outbreaks, shows he was not foolhardy when it came to such menaces: Bishop Gardiner, in a letter of August 1529 wrote of an outbreak of sweating sickness, 'the only name and voice wherof is so terrible and fearful in his highness' ears that he dare in nowise approach unto the place where it is noised to have been'.[20] Henry's pilgrimages to Walsingham seem to have been in thanksgiving for surviving an epidemic, or as in 1511, for the survival of his wife and baby in childbirth. To uphold the Christian faith was more than just an attempt to placate unkind forces, however. It was the philosophy, the rhythm and the emotion of the age encapsulated in a single system of belief, and a rich and intricate pattern of devotional practices.

The very passing of time was understood with reference to the Christian year, in which the life of Christ was relived; conception, birth, death, resurrection and exaltation; from Lady Day to Christmas to Easter and Ascension, interspersed with Candlemas, Pentecost, Corpus Christi and many other feast days. The lives and deaths of the saints also helped mark time; legal and university terms were called after St Michael, St Hilary and the Trinity, and the great festivals of All Saints and All Souls in November commemorated the massed ranks of the blessed and the great army of the dead. Day-to-day life encapsulated an abiding sense of the holy – holy days, holy places and things, holy prayers and people.

Henry's court always celebrated the great feasts; on royal progresses the king and his cavalcade would stop at abbeys, cathedrals and shrines to pray, and among Henry's elaborate and expensive possessions were his rosary, his psalter, his crucifix. He was sufficiently familiar with the liturgy of the mass to write five-part musical settings for it, and he patronised many religious houses, particularly the Observant Franciscans at Richmond and Greenwich, the Carthusians at Sheen near Richmond Palace and, across the river from Sheen, the Brigittines at Syon. This close association between palaces and religious houses was no accident; Sheen and Syon were both foundations of Henry V, and Henry VII had brought the Franciscans to his two main palaces.

In other words, the modern division between sacred and secular did not apply in the England of Henry VIII's day. Not everyone was equally pious, but the obligations of religion were universally recognised and they touched every aspect of life. Those who left money in their wills for good works might equally well instruct that a road be mended, or a bridge built, as much as an altar gilded, or a statue set up in their local church. Monasteries were schools, hospitals, farms, fortresses and places of refuge for the poor as well as houses of prayer. Bishops served as diplomats, lawyers and courtiers as well as being responsible for good order and piety in their dioceses. Hospitality was as much a duty of the clergy as prayer. Usually the balance was maintained reasonably well, although Richard Fox, Bishop of Winchester, who was a mainstay of Henry VII's Council and perhaps the chief minister of Henry VIII before Wolsey rose to that place, longed for release in 1516. He wrote to Wolsey of his anxiety at neglecting his diocese, and his hope to retire from court 'whereby I may do some satisfaction for twenty-eight years negligence'.[21] Fox was a man of unusual piety, however, and a humanist who sought reform within the church. For most of Henry VIII's contemporaries, their working life and their religion were closely integrated.

Religious observance was not something which happened at a distance, on a single day in the week, among a minority of the population. It was a part of the household, a part of everyday life. Children learned to read by spelling out the Paternoster; songs and plays, festivals and fairs, art and music all revolved around religious themes, occasions and places. Tudor men and women belonged not to Europe, but to Christendom; the crime of heresy was more heinous than murder, and punished by the most terrible sentence of being burned alive. As late as 1543, money was being raised by voluntary donation to help the inhabitants of the Holy Roman Empire resist the infidel by launching a crusade: the fear of the Turks was not prejudice alone, but the response to a real political threat, since in 1526 the Turkish armies laid siege to Vienna.[22] The most important of human experiences, namely birth, marriage and death, all required religious protection and sanction, and religious beliefs and practices were constantly being developed and diversified to meet the needs of the communities who upheld them.

There was an added dimension to Henry's religion, however, which was a central part of his kingship. Kings were appointed by God, and their strengths and successes were a sign of God's favour: these beliefs were universally upheld in the sixteenth century. The extraordinary and unexpected success of Henry VII in establishing his rule; Henry's own exceptional ability, intelligence, strength and beauty: all this was a clear mark of divine blessing, as commentators of the time were quick to point out. The euphoria and exuberance of Henry's early years surely reflected his own and everyone else's conviction that he was especially beloved of God. Kings at this time were believed to have healing hands: Henry VIII performed ceremonies of the laying on of hands to cure a disease known as 'the King's evil', another piece of royal theatre which underlined his close link to God. There was a darker side to providentialism, however, for God could take away as easily as he could give. Thomas Elyot in his famous treatise on government had this warning for those who held authority:

> First and above all thing, let them consider, that from god only proceedeth all honour, And that neither noble progeny, succession, nor election be of such force, that by them any estate or dignity may be so established, that god being stirred to vengeance, shall not shortly resume it, and perchance translate it where it shall like him.[23]

With the memory of the reversals, usurpations and royal disasters of the fifteenth century still strong, this was a warning Henry did not need to have reiterated. He had seen how little the laws of succession mattered if God decreed otherwise; his own father owed his throne not to succession rights, but to the divine favour shown at the battle of Bosworth. Henry's relationship with God was thus all-important, and the chief guarantee of his kingship. Dudley's treatise of 1509 describes the triumphant outcome of good kingship as almost the deification of the righteous king, where God is heard to speak in the first person, saying:

> come now to me and reign with me as my glorious knight and Christian king, my dear son, my good and singular beloved brother in manhood, my very

fellow in creation of thy soul. I shall anoint thee a king eternall with the holy oil that issueth out of the bosom of my father, and crown thee with the crown of mine own immortal glory and honour. And now shall thy subjects, thou also and I, be made as one thing, and shall always be together glorified.[24]

These words would have spoken directly to Henry's heart. No doubt Dudley, under imminent threat of execution, was counting on them to do so.

In the early years of his reign Henry's religious observance appeared to be in tune with that of his father and other late medieval kings. Yet there was always a clear sense in Henry's faith that his relationship with God was that of an especially favoured son, far above and beyond the experience of ordinary believers. The corollary of this was that as divinely appointed monarch, the church should be subservient to his wishes. This view was to form the basis for the royal supremacy in the 1530s, but it is important to realise that Henry held that view from far earlier in his reign, probably from the very beginning. It reached its most outspoken statement in 1515, in the wake of the Hunne case. The infamous death in custody of Richard Hunne, who had accused the church of *praemunire* (the offence of appealing to a power outside the realm), and had himself been accused of heresy, roused up great feeling concerning the extent of clerical authority and privilege. Henry presided over a conference called to settle the disagreements because they had spiralled to the point where the royal prerogative was being questioned. He crushed the arguments of those who upheld clerical independence from secular law, and bluntly asserted his own authority over church and state alike:

By the ordinance and sufferance of God We are King of England, and the Kings of England in time past have never had any superior but God alone. Wherefore, know ye well that we will maintain the right of our Crown and of our temporal jurisdiction, as well on this point as on all others, in as ample a way as any of our progenitors have done before our time.

In answer to their demand that the privileges of the clergy be recognised, he answered 'we will not consent to your wish any more than our progenitors have done in times past!'[25] These were defiant responses, but it is clear that Henry also regarded them as historically validated by the actions of past kings. The single greatest innovation of his reign, the monarchy's supremacy over the church, was to be founded upon an appeal to ancient tradition.

If religious belief underlined the mental world of Henry's time, the physical world was, by contrast, dominated by the king's own physical prowess. These were not unrelated preoccupations: religious devotion and military skill, unlikely companions from a modern perspective, were in fact deeply entwined in the chivalric tradition which remained a constant feature of Henry's reign. Although Henry also exploited classical themes, and enjoyed assuming the part of a Renaissance prince, he never rejected the older tradition of chivalry. Indeed, he probably saw the two as complementary: the 'nine worthies' who were regarded as the embodiment of chivalric valour from the fourteenth century onwards comprised three classical, three Old Testament and three later Christian figures, so Hector, Alexander the Great and Julius Caesar kept company with Josiah, David and Judas Maccabeus, and with Arthur, Charlemagne and Godfrey of Bouillon.

The images which surrounded Henry in his palaces reinforce the suggestion that for the young king, classical, biblical, medieval and mythical scenes were all blended together to provide an inspirational, if historically indistinct, background to his daily life. The tapestries at Greenwich Palace variously depicted Hannibal, Romulus and Remus, hawking, an allegory of the love of God, Solomon, the prodigal son of the New Testament, Saint Paul, King David, Samson, Joshua and the Passion of Christ.[26] Similarly, the hangings in Windsor Castle included portrayals of everything from the siege of Jerusalem and the siege of Troy, through theological themes such as the Trinity and the Assumption, to Old Testament stories of Assuer and Hester (Xerxes and Esther) or King David, to pagan gods and goddesses and the medieval Emperor Charlemagne.[27] Chivalric notions were reinforced by heroic tales from other eras.

At the heart of Henry VIII's chivalry lay the Order of the Garter, centred on St George's Chapel in Windsor Castle, where the saint's heart lay enshrined. The Order had been established by Edward III, who had also instituted St George as England's patron saint. Other kings had fostered the cult of St George; Henry VII had processed into London in 1505 preceded by the relic of the saint's leg, encased in silver.[28] Even as a prince, Henry had possessed four images of St George, more than of any other religious figure.[29] Henry VIII, as ever, went one better than his father and gave new preeminence to the order, whilst also changing the oath taken by knights of the Garter: rather than swearing to defend the college of St George's Windsor, new knights now undertook to defend the 'honors, quarrels, rights, dominions and cause' of their king.[30] To be invested with the Order of the Garter was the highest honour imaginable; the knights followed immediately after the peers of the realm in Henry's table of precedence.[31] It is also clear that the duties of Garter knights were taken very seriously. Henry, like his father before him, used the Order to create a loyal body of young, noble warriors who were close to him. They prayed together in St George's Chapel, and they rode together in tournaments, and were thus tied together by bonds of both sanctity and military skill.

In an extension of the same idea, Henry also took the company of 'the King's Spears' instituted by his father, and expanded it into a company of fifty or more, dedicated to attending on the king. The objective seems to have been to train the young nobility in feats of arms whilst reinforcing their bonds of loyalty to their king. The company had to be abolished in 1515 because it was too costly, but this early initiative reflects many of Henry's preoccupations. Hall described the company, noting that it did not last long because 'the apparel and charges were so great, for there were none of them, but they and their Horses, were apparelled and trapped in Cloth of Gold, Silver, and Gold Smiths worke, and their servants richly apparelled also'.[32] This glorious setting, of sumptuously clothed noble youth, armed for battle, was the one Henry wanted to set off his young and dashing kingship. This emphasis on the visual impact of his authority was never to waver; even when old and sick he was to travel on horseback, richly dressed, and surrounded by a glittering retinue, like the kings and knights of chivalric legend.

Hunting, hawking, all forms of sport, and whenever possible, jousting, were the central passions of Henry's early life. Whenever there was a pretext, there was a joust; to celebrate the Coronation, Twelfth Night, St George's day, May Day, Pentecost, or as a display for visiting dignitaries. Jousts and tournaments brought together military prowess, chivalrous display, fabulous ostentation, masculine daring and feminine adulation. They required enormous stamina, courage, and skill, and they were an outstanding showcase for the physical strength and theatrical kingship of a young and ardent king. Henry was addicted, and jousted constantly, although this was far from traditional. There are luscious descriptions of the gorgeous costumes worn by the king and his followers, as this example from 1517:

> The king ... and his company were apparelled horse and all in purple velvet, set full of leaves of cloth of gold ... with fine flat gold or damask, embroidered like to Rose leaves, and every leaf fastened to other with pointes of damask gold, and on all their borders were letters of gold bullion. And on the king waited five lords fourteen knights in frocks of yellow velvet, guarded and bound with rich cloth of gold, and thirty gentlemen were in like apparel on foot, and forty officers in yellow satin edged with cloth of gold: thus with great triumph they entered the field.[33]

More important than the jewels, velvets, silks and cloth of gold and silver were the king's achievements. 'The king being lusty, young, and courageous, greatly delighted in feats of chivalry', wrote Hall, who was also clearly delighted by his monarch's prowess, gleefully noting when 'the king broke more staves than any other'.[34] 'Every man did run twelve courses, the king did bear away the ring five times, and attained it three'; this punctilious record concerned a display for the Spanish ambassadors, who made a flattering request to take away some of the king's badges, only to strip him of them all when they discovered them to be real gold.[35]

Not everybody welcomed the young king's enthusiasm. Hall records the mixed feelings of 1512: 'The king ever desirous to serve Mars, began another Joust the fifteenth day of the said month. ... There was good running and many a spear brast, but for all the sport every man feared, lest some ill chaunce might happen to the king ... and spake thereof as much as they durst', although the king would not be persuaded into carefulness.[36]

For Hall, admiration seems to have outweighed the need for caution, but Edmund Dudley had warned the king about the importance of preserving his own person. Henri II of France was to die as a result of a jousting injury in 1559, precipitating much political instability and in due course civil war in France. The dangers were very real, and eventually, after a fall in 1536 which left him unconscious for two hours, Henry would give up jousting. For twenty-five years, however, it was one of his favourite pastimes. It was also a direct route to his favour: the skill of Sir William Compton, with whom he first entered the lists incognito in

1510, helped fit him to be groom of the stool, the most important officer of the Privy Chamber, for Compton was of unremarkable social origin. Charles Brandon, Henry's most frequent tilting partner in the early years, was as skilled as the king, and his appointment as military commander, his elevation to the dukedom of Suffolk, and his eventual marriage to the king's sister, were all based on the bond with Henry established in the tiltyard.

Henry's love of tournaments, and attendant activities like hunting and hawking, has frequently been misunderstood by more modern commentators as inattention to duty, or irresponsible risking of his own life. Such observations have failed to grasp that the risking of his own life was a required part of Henry's kingship, essential to ensure his success as a ruler. Historians preoccupied with administrative or institutional history have been unable to see that for his contemporaries, Henry's authority was not founded on the workings of his Privy Council or his control of his JPs nearly as much as it was secured by his courage and daring as a military leader. To joust, or hunt, was to rehearse the skills of horsemanship, agility, athleticism and daring on which a king's prowess as a warrior relied. It was also to form a bond with those who jousted with him, forging a brotherhood that could survive, when the time came, even in the thick of battle. In the expectations of the sixteenth century, a king must be a champion, and the definition of political service was the ability to fight at his command, and in his defence.

Sir John Fortescue, in a discussion of government from the fifteenth century, a work inspired by the painful necessity of healing civil conflict, took a king's dedication to military prowess as a given. *In Praise of the Laws of England* was written to instruct Henry VI's heir, Prince Edward, and is cast as a dialogue between the chancellor, and the prince he is instructing.[37] He gives his chancellor words with which to advise the prince to study law which encapsulate the dual obligations of kingship:

> I do indeed rejoice, most fair Prince, at your noble disposition, perceiving as I do with how much eagerness you embrace military exercises, which are fitting for you to take such delight in, not merely because you are a knight but all the more because you are going to be king. 'For the office of a king is to fight the battles of his people and to judge them rightfully', as you may very clearly learn in I Kings, chapter viii. For that reason, I wish that I observed you to be devoted to the study of the laws with the same zeal as you are to that of

arms, since, as battles are determined by arms, so judgements are by laws. This fact the Emperor Justinian carefully bears in mind when ... he says, 'Imperial Majesty ought to be not only adorned with arms but also armed with laws, so that it can govern aright in both times of peace and of war.'[38]

The bitter irony that Fortescue served, and perhaps wrote for, Henry VI, a king who could neither win battles nor administer laws, makes his opinion all the more powerful. There could be no greater glory than victory on the battlefield, and it was the glory of military success and the adulation of men and blessing of God which accompanied such success, which best secured a throne. Henry VIII, whose own father had secured his throne almost by battle alone, was only too aware of the need to succeed as the heroes of the past had done. Moreover, he was a gifted sportsman and warrior, seemingly destined by his Maker to be just such another leader. His hours on the tournament field, or spent hunting, were not hours wasted; they were at the very heart of his identity and purpose as king.

Henry's displays of military skill at the tournament were of vital use in binding him ever closer to the nobility, on whose loyalty and service he was dependent if he was ever to secure success overseas or stability at home. In an age where there were few formal institutions of government, a king relied on the informal ties of obligation. The nobility were his conduit to the provinces of his kingdom, through which his authority was channelled to those who might never set eyes upon their monarch. Henry's relationship with his nobility was a complex one. In return for their loyalty, he was under obligation to show good lordship to them. This meant that he had to honour their dignity, reinforce with his patronage both their social status and their wealth of land and goods, act as arbitrator in their quarrels, and keep a close eye on their alliances. Historians sometimes write as though a king's sole concern was to limit the might and ambition of his nobility, lest it threaten his own position: this was important, but a meek and chastened ruling class was of no use to Henry either. His father had sought to suppress the self-aggrandising instincts of the nobility, particularly in his later years when with wife and five out of eight children dead, his security seemed so fragile. Henry had less anxiety to begin with about the dynasty: he wanted men to fight at his side in the French wars. The chronicler notes his encouragement of other young men: 'the king delighting to set forth young gentlemen ... lent to them horse and harness to encourage all youth to seek deeds of arms'.[39] The rationale of the sixteenth-century nobility was still at root to provide a king with an army. When Henry V rode to war in France, one of his advantages was the group of young noblemen of his own age who went with him: as friends and comrades, not just king and subjects, they fought together. As Henry VIII appeared time after time alongside the higher nobility he was seeking the same common tie, reinforcing the bonds of brothers in arms, even before war in earnest had been achieved.

Much of the King's activity in these early years was simultaneously a preparation for government and a preparation for battle, since to display his strength whilst associating with the nobility was to promote both ends. It was also necessary to spend time forging links with the country gentry, and for this the annual summer progress was invaluable. Hall's *Chronicle* describes the king, still a teenager in the second year of his reign, going on progress:

> exercising himself daily in shooting, singing, dancing, wrestling, casting of the bar, playing at the recorders, flute, virginals, and in setting of songs, making of ballads, and did set two goodly masses, every of them five parts, which were song oftentimes in his chapel, and afterwards in diverse other places. And when he came to Woking, there were kept both Jousts and Tourneys: the rest of this progress was spent in hunting, hawking and shooting.[40]

In other words, progresses had many important purposes. We know how central they were to the queenship of Henry's daughter Elizabeth, but he himself made intelligent use of them. It has been suggested that the great rebellion of 1536, the Pilgrimage of Grace, did not spread from the north to the West Country precisely because Henry had visited the area on an extended progress in the preceding summer.[41] Showing himself to his courtiers and his lowlier subjects, and showing himself to advantage as he hunted, wrestled, sung and danced, was the most immediate way of displaying – and ramming home – his royal authority. Bestowing his royal presence as houseguest on a series of courtiers greatly enhanced their standing in the locality, and incidentally gave the king the opportunity to observe them in their native habitat. It is possible that the lavish hospitality of the Duke of Buckingham during the progress of 1519 helped fuel the suspicions that led two years later to his execution for treason. On the whole, however, royal progresses reached out not to the highest lords of the land, but to the next layer down of nobility and county gentry. Hunting, which was the chief occupation whilst on progress, fulfilled the same purpose as the joust but was open to a far wider number.[42] In the west country in 1516, the king 'visited his towns and castles there, and heard the complaints of his poor comminalty, and ever as he rode, he hunted and liberally departed with [i.e. gave away] venison'.[43] The intention was to leave behind a glow of satisfaction, based on a newly formed or refurbished personal relationship with the king.

Alongside their very real political value, the energetic revelries at court were meant to be enormous fun. Since political credibility was so closely linked to personal charisma and chivalric display, this is no contradiction. Hall's description of Henry's first year, after the excitements of the coronation, is instructive. He describes the king behaving as a chivalrous king should. Henry pardoned the innocent in the person of Henry Stafford, brother to the Duke of Buckingham, making him Earl of Wiltshire; he expanded the company of the King's Spears; he sent relief to Calais, which was afflicted by the plague; he held Parliament, in which the traitors Empson and Dudley were condemned. And then, after Christmas at Richmond, the king took part in his first ever joust at Twelfth Night, appearing in disguise, and winning much acclaim, until someone cried out 'God save the King'. Hall reports how, 'with that, all the people were astonished, and then the kyng discovered [i.e. revealed] himself to the great comfort of all the people.' The court soon after moved to Westminster, where one morning the king, with the earls of Essex and Wiltshire, and other companions, erupted into the queen's chamber one morning, dressed as Robin Hood and his companions. It may have taken the queen a moment to appreciate the honour: Hall reports that 'the Queen, the Ladies, and all other there, were abashed, as well for the strange sight, as also for their sudden coming, and after certain dances, and pastime made, they departed.' A few weeks later, and there was a banquet at Westminster, where the king made the queen preside, since 'he would not sit, but walked from place to place, makyng cheer to the Queen, and the strangers.' Then suddenly the king disappeared, only to reappear, again with the Earl of Essex, dressed:

> after Turkey fashion, in long robes ... powdered with gold, hats on their heads of Crimson Velvet, with great rolls of Gold, girded with two swords, called Cimiteries [scimitars], hanging by great baldricks of gold.[44]

Hall was an MP, and a lawyer, but he was not a member of the court: here he reflects the London gossip of the time, the public perception of the young, exuberant, confident king, the splendid propaganda that Henry's behaviour generated.

WAR WITH FRANCE

The constant jousts, tournaments, progresses and hunting expeditions of Henry's early years as king were politics in action, but they were also preparation for war, and it soon became clear that Henry intended war sooner rather than later. Military achievement and military defence were perhaps the most weighty preoccupations consistently sustained by Henry throughout his reign, and the reign began with a clear indication that the king intended war with France, the traditional enemy, whose kingship the kings of England would continue to claim for years to come.

The Tudor age is often described as though 1485 marked a clear break with the medieval past, and historians have been much preoccupied with finding 'new', 'modern' or 'revolutionary' elements to Tudor rule, particularly under Henry VIII. To the king himself, it was vitally important that 1485 was *not* seen to be a break with the past; the new dynasty needed the sanction of the past, and the sanctity of royal ancestors to reinforce its initially shaky hold on power. We might use the label 'Tudor', but to Henry and his contemporaries, his family was a union of the Lancastrians and Yorkists, as celebrated by Polydore Vergil, or later in the title of Hall's *Chronicle*. Even when Henry assumed the role of Renaissance king, which involved many new ways of thinking and behaving, it must be remembered that this was based on the Renaissance ideal of a 'rebirth' of ancient wisdom and culture. The notion of what we would call 'progress' was always, to the Tudors, looking backwards to some golden age that was past, and which they sought to revive.

For Henry, the most immediate objective was to recapture the glories of the Hundred Years War, and revive the chivalrous and military exploits of his Plantagenet and Lancastrian forbears. In particular, he longed to follow his namesake, Henry V, and win his own magnificent victory to rival that at Agincourt. Shakespeare's inspirational portrayal of Henry V shows the place this legendary king occupied in the Tudor imagination. He was seen as the epitome of chivalrous prowess, by turns daring, merciful, ruthless or devout, but always a figure of majesty. This was the way that Henry VIII sought to present himself.

It was in 1513 that Henry V's life appeared in print, commissioned by the young king. From the first weeks of his reign, Henry VIII had made it clear that he too had ambitions in France. It was reputed that the king 'swore ... immediately after his coronation to make war on France'.[45] The Venetian ambassador also recorded how a fat French abbot, arriving as envoy from the French king, announced that he had come to confirm peace and friendship in answer to a letter from Henry hoping for such amity. The king indignantly denied all knowledge of this letter, declaring sarcastically 'I ask peace of the King of France, who dare not look me in the face, still less make war on me!' This fine flourish was compounded when the abbot arrived at the tiltyard to find he had not been given a seat; he departed in indignation, although in the end the king, relenting, had him recalled, and given a cushion.[46] Henry was clearly aiming at a dramatic flourish, although the incident also had a touch of the comical.

The Venetian ambassador concluded, 'In short, King Henry holds France in small account.'[47] This was what the Venetians wanted to believe, since the League of Cambrai of 1508 had brought together France, Spain, the Empire and the papacy in an offensive against their small but temptingly wealthy state, and they were desperate for allies. It was not all wishful thinking, however, since there are other signs that Henry VIII intended war against France from the very start of his reign. In 1509 he appointed Christopher Bainbridge, Archbishop of York, as envoy to the papacy. This was meant to prepare the way to war, for Bainbridge loathed the French, and shared the king's enthusiasm for war; indeed his aggressive tendencies were later to prove an embarrassment when the king sought peace instead.[48] It has been thought that Henry's Council, divided over the wisdom of such a course, prevaricated, with one more peaceable faction securing the treaty signed with France in March 1510. This view belongs with the old interpretation of Henry as being subject to manipulation by his councillors. It seems more likely, however, that Henry's Council responded with respect to the unequivocal intentions of their new ruler, and that any delays or detours along the path to war were part of the complexities of the diplomatic game. Henry VIII was not foolish enough to think he could go to war against France without allies; his councillors spent the first year of his reign working to secure him those allies, not trying to blunt his purpose.

In May 1510 the treaty with Spain was signed, which meant Henry had secured his most important ally, whilst the European powers generally were regrouping for an attack on France. The linchpin of the new alliance was the papacy of Julius II, known then and since as the 'Warrior Pope', who sought to expel the French aggressors who had been dictating developments within Italy since 1494. Warned of papal intentions, Louis XII of France called first a Council of the French Church to criticise the papacy, and then summoned a schismatic General Council to meet in Pisa in May 1511. It can be seen that a bold and direct challenge to papal authority was by no means to be an innovation of Henry's. On this occasion, these actions by Louis provided exactly the basis for war against France which Henry and his allies needed, since the alliance could justly be termed a 'Holy League' which sought to defend the holy father; ironically, therefore, considering Henry's later actions, he first went to war to defend the successor to St Peter and Christ's Vicar on earth.

Despite the centrality of warfare to early modern ideas of kingship and nobility, it was unacceptable to contemporaries to make war merely for purposes of self-aggrandisement. Broadly speaking, there were three acceptable justifications for war: self-defence against foreign aggression, the pursuit of dynastic claims to territory or titles, or the defence of true religion. The war which was looming from 1510 onwards could lay claim to all three of these. Henry was claiming ancestral lands in Normandy and Aquitaine, he was defending the Pope, and he was responding – with his allies – to French aggression in Italy. Julius sent Henry the golden rose (along with 100 Parmesan cheeses) as a mark of papal gratitude and favour.[49] The king gloried in his role as the loyal son of the papacy and the defender of the church. The arrival of a baby prince on New Year's Day 1511 must have seemed further confirmation of the divine blessing upon Henry's enterprise, heightening the king's anticipation of a glorious victory to rival Agincourt.

Yet little Prince Henry lived only a few weeks, and military success was no more easily arrived at than dynastic security. In May 1511 a force of 1,000 men was sent under the command of Lord Darcy to Cadiz, to help Ferdinand on an expedition to North Africa against the Moors. This first small blow in the name of religion and in support of the new alliance ended in humiliation. Darcy arrived in Cadiz only to find the venture had been cancelled; his troops created an unfortunate impression by their drunken brawling in Cadiz, and then they sailed home. A similarly sized small force sent to help Margaret of Savoy against the Duke of Guelders had better fortune, and acquitted itself well; its commander, Sir Edward Poynings, warden of the Cinque Ports, would later prove useful to Henry in other campaigns. Henry had to wait another five months until the Holy League was formally signed in October 1511. By November it was agreed that an offensive should be launched against Aquitaine, with English and Spanish forces fighting together, and the next five months were devoted to making ready for war. This put Henry in his element; he loved martial preparation. One of his first acts in 1509, as we have seen, was to establish a personal band of warriors known as the 'King's Spears', who were to be reformed in 1539 as the Gentleman Pensioners. Between 1511 and 1515 he had armouries established at Southwark and Greenwich, as well as buying many hundreds of suits of armour from the continent. He also spent almost £3,000 on ordnance between 1509 and 1512.[50] He was determined to make England a major military power within the European arena.

In April 1512 war was formally declared on the French, and the fleet set sail. Land troops were despatched at the start of June, 12,000 men under the command of the Marquis of Dorset. When the army arrived, the Spanish failed to provide the horses and ordnance they had promised. Ferdinand's real objective was to use the proposed attack on Aquitaine as a smoke-screen whilst he captured Navarre; at first he insisted that the English join him, and when Dorset protested, he attacked alone, leaving the English to fester in their camps. Four months later, weary and diseased, they left for home, betrayed by Ferdinand, who nevertheless took their departure as an opportunity to disparage the English, and make peace with the French using their departure as his justification. It was a humiliating beginning to Henry's military career, softened only by the fact that he had not been personally present in this fiasco.

It seems clear that Henry was furious, since he held an audience with the Spanish ambassadors at which the officers were publicly condemned.[51] A second attempt at invasion was then organised, this time in northern France, with the Spanish agreeing to attack Aquitaine. After much diplomatic effort, Emperor Maximilian was also persuaded to join the League, and attack from the north-east, and the papacy promised a fourth line of attack from the south-east. It is an indication of Henry's involvement that the newly enlarged League took its formal oath at St Paul's in London in April 1513. Moreover, this time the young king led his troops to war. It is perhaps significant that Henry had not wished to lead the force in Aquitaine, but rather chose to head an army in northern France, in emulation of Henry V. Security must also have been a consideration; leaving the kingdom was a risky business, and Henry had the last available Yorkist, Edmund de la Pole, Earl of Suffolk brought out of imprisonment in the Tower and beheaded before he went. Polydore Vergil imagined the King arguing down the anxieties of his councillors, explaining that it was necessary to:

> create such a fine opinion about his valour among all men that they would clearly understand that his ambition was not merely to equal but indeed to exceed the glorious deeds of his ancestors. Moreover, he recalled the many triumphs over their enemies won by his ancestors when they were leading their armies in person.[52]

The conversation may have been imagined, but the evidence suggests that the sentiments here expressed were genuine.

For Henry this was a holy war, and as such, one blessed with every chance of success. His newly forged cannons were named 'the Twelve Apostles', reflecting the religious underpinnings of his war propaganda. Pope Julius II had promised him that if he were victorious, he should take the title of 'Most Christian King' which had previously belonged to the Kings of France. The printing presses produced new editions of works by John Lydgate, who had been Henry V's favourite poet, including *The Historye, Sege and Dystruccyon of Troye*, this edition commissioned by Henry VIII.[53] Songs were composed for the campaign: the 'Henry VIII manuscript' which contains music by the king himself, as well as Fairfax, Cornish, Dunstable and others, includes ballads for the war; one such begins:

> England, be glad! Pluck up thy lusty hart!
> Help now thy kyng, thy kyng, and take his part!
> Against the Frenchmen in the field to fight
> In the quarrel of the church and in the right.[54]

The religious justification for the war was further emphasised by the king taking the Chapel Royal with him to France, just as Henry V had done, when they had sung mass at dawn before the battle of Agincourt.[55]

More prosaically, extensive practical preparations were under way to convey Henry VIII and his entourage overseas, largely overseen by Thomas Wolsey, whose talents were being given their full expression in the appalling task of transporting, housing, arming and feeding the army Henry demanded. That Henry realised Wolsey's capabilities is shown by his rapid promotion, from royal almoner and chaplain under Henry VII, to registrar of the Order of the Garter in 1510, to Dean of York in February 1513.[56] We also have seven letters written by Wolsey's mentor, Bishop Fox of Winchester, who as lord privy seal and veteran of the French campaign of 1492 was heavily involved, but whose age and dubious health made him less burdened than Wolsey, for whose health under this 'outrageous charge and labour' he was much concerned. He wrote that if Wolsey's work was not soon done, he 'shall have a cold stomach, little sleep, pale image and a thin belly *cum rara egestione*: all which and as deaf as a stock, I had when in your case'.[57]

The maintenance and provisioning of Henry's huge army was an extremely complicated and awkward business. The state papers from this time are full of anxieties and instructions about beer and biscuits, fish and flesh. From the West Country, it was reported in May 1513 that the soldiers billeted there did not like the local beer, and that although they had consumed twenty-five barrels of it during their twelve days in Plymouth, they were now refusing it because the beer arriving from London was so much better.[58] More solemn testimony came the same month from the fleet at sea, where it was reported that many were sick and wounded after engagements with the French, and many dead of the measles. One captain who escorted the victualling ships to meet with the fleet at Brest recorded his ecstatic reception:

> And then I trow there was never knight more welcome to his sovereign lady [than] I was to my lord Admiral and unto all the whole army, for by [cause that] I brought the vittlers with me. For of 10 days before there was no [man] in all the army that had but one meal a day and once drink.[59]

For the king, campaigning meant travelling with enormous pomp and ceremony and very little diminution in his usual luxurious standard of living. Living under canvas meant living in tents draped with cloth of gold and sleeping in his usual vast, carved and ornate bed, which was laboriously transported everywhere he went. For the rest of the army, essential provisions and equipment could not be relied upon, and once the army had landed on the continent, constant vigilance was needed to try to protect the supply lines from across the Channel.

When Henry landed in Calais, on 30 June 1513, the sea was black with ships, and the sound of the guns thundering in celebration of his arrival could be heard in Dover. He was accompanied by hundreds of members of his household, including over 100 clergy and musicians from the Chapel Royal, ten minstrels, eight trumpeters and nearly 300 household staff.[60] His first action on disembarking at Calais was to ride in procession to the church of St Nicholas to implore God's blessing on his venture. He wore a tunic of cloth of gold over his armour embroidered with the red cross of England, and a brooch of St George in his hat. Hall records how on a later mission to France 'the Englishmen had ever on their apparell red crosses to be known for love of their country', and the king was here displaying a symbol whose resonance still endures.[61] Henry's Spanish allies had betrayed him, since Ferdinand had again made a truce with the French, but he still had the emperor on his side, and more important than that, he clearly felt he had God on his side also.

In the last military expedition to France in 1492, Henry VII had taken an army of about 13,000 men, but Henry VIII's force was nearly three times that number. These were drawn from the retinues of leading courtier peers such as Henry Stafford, Earl of Wiltshire, Henry Bourchier, Earl of Essex, and Thomas Grey, Marquis of Dorset, accompanied by the household men who had proved their skill in jousting with the king, like Sir William Compton, Sir Henry Guildford and Sir Charles Brandon. George Talbot, Earl of Shrewsbury, who was both territorial magnate and steward of the king's household, provided around 4,500 men. The territorial magnates who were not a usual presence at court also supplied large numbers of troops, men like Edward Stafford, Duke of Buckingham and George Neville, Lord Bergavenny.[62] The nobility were not merely in attendance out of a sense of chivalric honour, although this intermingled with the more concrete rewards of giving loyal service to the monarch, such as titles and gifts. There was also good potential for looting whilst on campaign, and for capturing important men from the French forces who could then be ransomed for substantial amounts of money; such financial incentives were recognised by Henry and his contemporaries as being a useful encouragement to his soldiers.[63]

After much preparation in Calais, Henry's army set out to do battle on 21 July. In expectation of an engagement the following day, the king went round his camp to encourage his men, just as Henry V had done before Agincourt. Henry's demeanour often recalled the legends about Henry V which would eventually be immortalised by Shakespeare: in 1512, the hanging of a favoured yeomen of the guard for murder recalled the hanging of Bardolph, where principle was seen to triumph over favouritism.[64] But despite Henry's heroics, the French did not want to do battle, and apart from one or two minor incidents, there was no fighting until the English army laid siege to the small town of Thérouanne. Here, on 16 August, a body of French cavalry accidentally came face to face with the enemy, and after some exchange of fire, turned and fled. This unimpressive encounter and pursuit did at least result in the capture of some important prisoners and six standards: it was to be known as 'the Battle of the Spurs', and rather pathetically, seized upon as a notable success, solemnly commemorated in prose and paint. The pictures and engravings of the battle give it all the dignity of a major battle in a Renaissance landscape, showing how badly the king needed some such success. The engraving shown in Plate 2 was one made by the Netherlands publisher Cornelis Anthoniszoon in 1553, showing the extent to which propaganda had managed to establish this battle in European memory. Inconveniently, Henry himself had not taken the field, but directed from the rear. The fall of Thérouanne followed, and the king's musicians were deployed to sing *Te Deum* in the town church in celebration. The town was immediately handed over to the emperor, who destroyed all of it but the church, but it too acquired an iconic status as a royal victory. When in 1527 Henry signed a treaty with France, he celebrated the occasion with as much pomp as he could muster, including a specially created set of chambers at Greenwich, where a triumphal arch leading from the banqueting house was decorated with Holbein's depiction of the siege of Thérouanne.[65] This may have been a quiet reminder to his new French allies that they should remember his strength, but possibly it had just become such a favourite theme that nobody thought to wonder if it might offend the French.

A second siege of the city of Tournai, which succeeded in late September, brought more real glory, all the more since Edward III had failed to capture the city long before. This was a far more splendid prize than Thérouanne, being a handsome walled city and an episcopal seat. It has been noted how Henry VIII's declarations of sovereignty over the city, and his insistence that Wolsey hold the bishopric of Tournai despite later papal opposition, prefigure his later ideas of imperial sovereignty and royal supremacy.[66] These gains were also the first victories against the French since the 1440s.

It is hard not to feel the sense of irony, however, that the real victory of the summer of 1513 belonged to Katherine of Aragon, left at home as regent, whose army had defeated the Scots at Flodden on 9 September. It had been expected that the king's absence from the realm would result in a Scottish invasion. Under the command of Thomas Howard, Earl of Surrey, the English slaughtered a large proportion of the Scots nobility, and King James IV himself died in battle. Surrey had been speechless with grief when left behind in England; 'the Earle could scantly speak when he took his leave, for the departing from the noble prince his sovereign Lord and king, and from the flower of all the nobility', but after Flodden he brought the dead body of James IV to the queen at Richmond, and in due course he was rewarded with the dukedom of Norfolk.

War at this time was seasonal, and after the fall of Tournai Henry came home. He had been moderately successful, but it was not enough to convince the Pope; the promise of the papal title and a coronation at Rheims, where all French kings were crowned, remained conditional. The war was not over; Henry and Maximilian had agreed to resume the campaign the following summer, and also to marry Henry's sister Mary to Maximilian's grandson, Charles of Burgundy (the future Charles V). In the triumph of hope over experience, Ferdinand was also included in the plan. But these plans were all to come to nothing. Julius II had been replaced in March 1513 by Pope Leo X, who sought peace with France, and duly achieved it when the French abandoned their schismatic Council at Pisa and submitted to the Fifth Lateran Council. Ferdinand again deserted the alliance, signing a treaty with the French in the name of Henry and Maximilian as well as on his own behalf. Henry was furious, but Maximilian was content to leave a Holy League which was fast losing credibility. Henry talked of continuing the campaign with his Swiss allies, and indeed in June an English army landed in France. The tide was turning against war, however, and Henry was in particular unable to withstand the papal pressure for peace when his whole rationale for war in the first place had been built on papal support.

Papal demands for peace were sustained through the early months of 1514, and Fox and Wolsey also seem to have been urging the king in that direction. On 21 May Henry received the sword and cap of maintenance as a papal gift in St Paul's, although the cap, not being meant for actual use, hung down over his face and looked ridiculous. The event suggests that Henry was bowing to pressure, and in August he concluded a peace with France. It was an honourable peace, since it was based on papal initiative, involved French payment of the pension arrears owed from the 1492 Treaty of Étaples, and was dignified by the marriage of Henry's sister Mary to King Louis XII of France. It also repaid Ferdinand for his disloyalty by making common cause with his enemy, and indeed there were soon suggestions that this peace treaty might become the basis for a joint attack on Spain. The only immediate fruit of this was that Charles Brandon, Duke of Suffolk, who had been sent to witness Mary's coronation as Queen of France and to discuss the possibility of aggression against Ferdinand, was still in Paris when Louis XII died. Mary had been married only eleven weeks to the aged king, three times her age, when she was set free to marry her true love. It is a mark of Henry's sense of brotherhood with his long-time jousting partner that although initially angry, he soon accepted the match. Unusually for a Tudor, Mary was able to live what appears to have been a happy married life as the Duchess of Suffolk.

PEACE

The conclusion of peace with France had been as much a statement of Henry's royal magnificence, then, as the warfare which had gone before. Having dignified the peace treaty with ceremony, symbolism and the gloss of Renaissance learning, Henry turned to other projects which might also serve to enhance his kingship. One of these was building works. Construction work which had been begun by Henry VII at Hanworth, Woking, Wanstead, Ditton and Leeds Castle was continuing under the new king's auspices, but he sought to further enhance his reputation with bricks and mortar. In this, as in war, he was able to profit from Wolsey's expertise and initiative. One immediate problem was the lack of a royal palace after Westminster Palace had burned down in 1512. Wolsey had in 1510 acquired land in the City of London, next to the Fleet river, a garden and a rectory which had previously belonged to the disgraced minister of Henry VII, Richard Empson, and begun building there. But in 1515 Wolsey became entitled to use York Place, the London residence of the archbishops of York, and Henry took over the new house by the river, which became the Palace of Bridewell. This palace was built of brick, three stories high, arranged around two courtyards with a long gallery leading to the watergate onto the Thames. Unusually, there was no great hall, but a grand processional staircase leading up to the king's apartments.[67] So although much of Bridewell resembled Henry VII's palace at Richmond, the absence of a great hall signalled a move towards greater royal privacy, a concept which Henry would use in all subsequent royal palaces to enhance the aura of majesty.

If Henry's building endeavours remained on a relatively modest scale at this point this was because he already had a new and impressive palace at Greenwich, which was barely fifteen years old, and which he was still completing. His additions in these early years of his reign were focused upon making proper provision for the tournaments that were at the centre of so many royal occasions, and where he gave such spectacular displays of his own prowess. He built stables for his stud horses and for his coursers, and a viewing gallery with towers overlooking the tiltyard. He also seems to have rebuilt the chapel, and built a library, with a gallery overlooking the Thames.[68] According to the inventory made after Henry's death, this library contained 329 books. Those making the inventory rather regrettably described them mostly by the colour of their binding, but some descriptions were recorded such as 'a great book called an herbal' or 'two great bibles in Latin'.[69]

The building of this library is significant because Henry was always keen to maintain his reputation as an enthusiastic patron of scholarship. The intellectual world of Henry's early years as king is often given insufficient attention in the rush to understand the momentous changes of the 1530s. The excitement among humanists which greeted Henry's accession was in part just hopeful flattery, but it was also partly based upon the King's reputation as someone who loved learning. When Lord Mountjoy wrote to Erasmus and urged him to come to England, he proffered evidence of Henry's enthusiasm:

Our king's heart is set not upon gold or jewels or mines of ore, but upon virtue, reputation and eternal renown. Here is a mere sample: a few days ago, when he said that he longed to be a more accomplished scholar, I remarked, 'We do not expect this of you; what we expect is that you should foster and encourage those who are scholars'. 'Of course,' he replied, 'for without them we could scarcely exist.' What better remark could be made by any king?[70]

This anecdote is interesting because it suggests that even as a young king, Henry sought to exceed expectations. To begin with, however, he followed the more usual path suggested here by Mountjoy, and confined his activities to patronage.

Henry's patronage extended beyond the court to the universities. In large part the Renaissance was being spearheaded there by his close associates, in particular by Bishop Fox's 1517 foundation of Corpus Christi College, Oxford, and then by Wolsey's Cardinal College, founded in 1525. When Fox, his father's eminent councillor, founded Corpus Christi it was with the intention to make it a hive of Renaissance learning: the foundation statutes repeatedly used the metaphor of a bee garden. In this garden the study of Greek and Latin through classical texts was paramount: Greek was to be studied through the works of Euripides, Aristophanes, Sophocles, Hesiod, Demosthenes, Thucydides, Aristotle and Plutarch, whilst works by Cicero, Sallust, Pliny, Livy, Virgil, Ovid, and Terence formed the basis for Latin studies. The first president of Corpus, John Claymond, another friend of Erasmus, wrote a commentary on Pliny's *Natural History* which was an early contribution to the history of science.[71] When Wolsey founded Cardinal College, he ensured that the professors of theology and humanities were paid £40 per year, twice as much as the other professors. The humanities professor was to give two lectures each day, with rhetoric at eight o'clock in the morning, and Greek after lunch. The king could also intervene directly; in the early 1520s he sent his astronomer, Nicholas Kratzer, to lecture at Oxford in astronomy and geography. In 1518 he backed Thomas More in his attempt to defend the new drive towards learning Greek in the universities. A group at Oxford who christened themselves 'Trojans' had openly deplored the humanist enthusiasm for Greek, even preaching against it. More wrote from the court, then at Abingdon, making it clear that Greek studies had the support of the king, as well as of Oxford's chancellor, the Archbishop of Canterbury, William Warham.[72]

The king was surrounded by others at court who shared his enthusiasm for humanist learning. Many of these had also served his father, such as Archbishop Warham, who was also Erasmus's patron, and to whom Erasmus dedicated his translations of Euripides' *Hecuba* and *Iphigenia*. That Warham's classicism was not merely Erasmus's wishful thinking is suggested by the opening sermon he preached to parliament in February 1512, with the humanist theme *'Justicia et pax osculatae sunt'*, appealing to Roman history to support his insistence on the necessity of frequent parliaments.[73] There were also foreigners such as Polydore Vergil, the poet Pietro Carmeliano who stayed on as Henry VIII's Latin secretary, or Bernard André, the blind Austin friar who had been Prince Arthur's tutor and *'poeta laureatus'* to the old king, but who remained in the service of the new king until his death in 1522. André wrote the inevitable celebratory verses commemorating Henry's victories in France and Scotland in 1513; his earliest surviving New Year's gift to Henry and his queen, a psalm commentary, was an acrostic with the first letters of each line spelling out Henry and Katherine's names and titles.[74] In ways like this scholarship and royalty were able mutually to sustain one another.

Henry VIII's accession saw a new wave of appointments and patronage which showed that he endorsed humanist learning even more than his father. There was a vibrant community of Renaissance scholars in England at this time, who had often complemented their education at Oxford or Cambridge with time spent in Padua, or elsewhere in Italy. Thomas More and John Colet were part of a network of friends including Cuthbert Tunstall, Richard Pace, William Latimer, William Grocyn and Thomas Linacre. All of them were friends and correspondents of Erasmus: Tunstall and Latimer both helped him with his new translation of the New Testament; Pace was commissioned by him to write a handbook of rhetoric for Colet's new school at St Paul's. All helped promote the study of Greek and Latin on the classical model: Grocyn gave the first Greek public lectures at Oxford in the 1490s; Pace published Latin translations of Plutarch and Lucian; Linacre taught Greek to Thomas More and published three works on Latin grammar. It was men such as these that Henry chose to serve him: Tunstall was sent abroad on diplomatic missions from 1515, and in 1516 became Master of the Rolls; Pace served Bainbridge, Henry's envoy to Rome, from 1509, returning to become Henry's principal secretary in 1516; Linacre became royal physician in 1509, and founder and first president, by royal permission, of the College of Physicians in 1518.[75]

It was in 1515 that Thomas More sat down to write *Utopia*. The intellectual excitement of the age is given full expression by the classical erudition, satirical force, imagination and humour of this work. There was a close connection between the world of these humanist scholars and the court where they served, or longed to serve. In 1517 Erasmus sent a hand-illuminated copy of his *Education of a Christian Prince* to Henry VIII, hoping to secure royal patronage in England and a convivial home within this community of his friends. In the carefully phrased accompanying letter he noted that:

> amidst all the business of the realm and indeed of the whole world, scarcely a day passes in which you do not devote some portion of your time to reading books, enjoying the society of those philosophers of old who flatter least of men, and of those books especially from whose perusal you will rise more judicious, a better man and a better king.[76]

Erasmus was flattering with intent to secure a royal stipend, but his remarks had to have a basis in truth to be acceptable. In the same year, Richard Pace said of Henry: 'He is so well disposed to all *eruditi* that he hears nothing more willingly than conversations about scholars and books.'[77]

When Henry travelled, as he did all the time, his possessions went with him in vast quantities. When he died, the coffers containing these moveable possessions were stored in the Tower of London's Jewel House. One of these coffers was dedicated to books on music and surgery, a small insight into the king's interests. Henry's health had troubled him for some time, but even when he was young and healthy, the king's alarmed response to infection was a recurrent feature of his life. At any sign of illness he would flee with alacrity, taking only a small number of attendants and moving rapidly between houses. The Tudor court seldom stayed more than a few months in any given location, since the accumulation of dirt and the shabbiness caused by a household of several hundred required constant renovation. In times of illness, however, Henry rarely stayed a matter of weeks in any given location. Even when deeply in love with Anne Boleyn, he kept his distance when she was ill. One letter, which lamented the news of her illness, equally deplored that their separation would now be all the longer, and generously avowed that he desired her health 'as much as mine own', declaring, with equally measured generosity, 'the half of whose malady I would willingly bear to have you healed thereof'.[78] Even at the height of passion, Henry could not rank another's well-being higher than his own.

More cheerfully, the books of music which travelled with the king gave testimony to a lifelong love. Flattery aside, it seems clear that Henry was a reasonably talented musician, and a very ardent one. He loved to sing, and played both lute and keyboard. He also loved to collect instruments; his inventory shows that at his death he possessed seventy-two flutes and seventy-six recorders, some of them ivory, or decorated with gold and silver. He also owned twenty-five viols.[79] Where possible, he also collected musicians, poaching gifted singers from other households and institutions for the Chapel Royal, which also boasted some of the greatest composers of the age: William Cornish, who served there until his death in 1523, and Robert Fairfax, who died in 1521, had both been recruited by Henry VII. Where his father had kept nine trumpeters, Henry raised the number to fifteen for his coronation, and by the end of his reign had eighteen. By maintaining the musical reputation of his court and household Henry also managed to attract foreign musicians; the organists Benedictus de Opitis, from the Netherlands, and Dionisio Memmo, from Venice, both arrived in 1516. He also recruited Philip van Wilder, the Flemish lutenist, and in the 1540s he imported a viol ensemble of Sephardic Jews from Italy.[80] Famously on one occasion in 1517 he listened to Memmo play for four hours, and a year later was delighted when the infant Princess Mary, aged 2 and on display for the Venetian ambassador, saw Memmo and cried out 'Priest'! until he played for her.[81]

The British Library contains a manuscript called *Henry VIII's Songbook*, with thirty-four of the 109 pieces, mostly of secular music, attributed to the king.[82] One at least seems to have been a cover version of an earlier work, but there is no reason to doubt that the king had considerable skill as a composer. He is also known to have written five-part Mass settings. Music was considered an important part of the Renaissance skills required of a courtier: Sir Thomas Elyot in his *The Boke Called the Governour* devoted an entire chapter to music, whilst warning that it was only seemly for a nobleman to play in private. But the court, although it was so populous, was Henry's private household, as the architectural developments of the reign were to emphasise. So the king could often be found making music there. The life of one of his courtiers, Sir Peter Carew, soldier, adventurer and gentleman of the Privy Chamber, records how Carew and the king sang together.

> For the King himself being much delighted to sing, and Sir Peter Carew having a pleasant voice, the King would very often use him to sing with him certain songs they called fremen songs, as namely 'By the bank as I lay', and 'As I walked the wood so wild', etc.'[83]

The best of European musical skill was to be found at Henry's court. When in the 1520s the Florentine republic sought Henry as an ally, they put together a gift of music, thirty madrigals and thirty motets, selected (and in large part written) by Philippe Verdelot, as a present guaranteed to appeal to the king.[84] And one motet by Josquin des Pres, perhaps the greatest composer of the age, survives in a presentation copy given to Henry and Katherine of Aragon sometime between 1516 and 1522. It reflected the new trend of drawing on Hebrew scriptures, and was a setting of the lament by King David for his dead son, Absalom. The translated text runs: 'Absalom, my son, would that I had died for thee, my son, Absalom. Let me live no longer, but descend into hell weeping'.[85] It was not perhaps in Henry's nature to desire to die on someone else's behalf, but the anguish at the death of a son was something both he and Katherine must have known.

From his many different interests and accomplishments Henry put together a pattern of life at court which both legitimated and amplified his authority. To read any account of the day-to-day life of Henry VIII and his court is to be overwhelmed by the levels of sheer ostentation and luxurious display. The modern observer needs to appreciate the very real political meaning conveyed by all this posturing. At its most basic level, this was a display of wealth, and therefore strength. It was also a display of civilisation, and therefore of subtlety, intelligence and honour. A civilised monarch could be trusted as signatory to a treaty, or in a marriage alliance. When in 1519 the papal legate Campeggio returned to Rome after a sojourn at the English court, it was reported that his praise of the king had greatly increased Henry's reputation in Italy. 'He extols the balls, music and tournaments, and the wonderful splendour of the English court'.[86] Such a summary of Henry's regime, even from a churchman, was not considered inappropriate. Henry's status was communicated by the magnificence of his life and his entourage. When in 1530 Wolsey was sent north after his fall from power, he asked for money to pay for the journey, and the Council debated this. Some were against giving him anything, according to Cavendish, but others:

> thought it much against the council's honor, and much more against the King's high dignity, to see him want the maintenance of his estate which the King had given him in this realm; and also hath been in such estimation with the King and in great authority under him in this realm; it should be rathe [ie. quickly] a great slander in foreign realms to the King and his whole council to see him want that lately had so much and now so little.[87]

Courtly display was not a series of empty formalities as it might seem to a modern observer. It was the daily reenactment of the ideological framework upon which political and social stability depended.

FACTION

In all the developments discussed in this chapter, it can be seen that Henry himself has been viewed as the motivating force behind all important policies, decisions, fashions and trends in these early years of his reign. This runs counter to an older view which portrayed Henry as manipulated by his Council, by Wolsey, and by his wives and their backers, blustering and bombastic but ultimately vacillating and unreliable; in Geoffrey Elton's famous words, 'a bit of a booby and a bit of a baby', who was 'almost consistently inept' in his judgements, and owed all his success to wiser councillors.[88] This view is still upheld, or partially upheld, by more recent commentators, and the historical debate seems likely to remain unresolved on this score for some time to come.[89] This biography, however, takes the view that there are many things wrong with portraying Henry as open to manipulation, and with characterising the workings of Tudor politics as being defined by factional conflict. The portrayal of Henry which emerges from such an emphasis is a false one, a misconceived notion of a king who paid only intermittent attention to politics, who was easily distracted and seduced by entertainments and pretty women, and who was not very clever, but who could be covertly directed and controlled by others who were more intelligent.

This interpretation does not fit the available evidence. Henry was clearly highly intelligent, and extremely interested in the business of government. It needs to be remembered that such an interest did not leave the same kind of paper trail produced by modern methods of government, but was evidenced in the personal interactions of the king. Henry talked politics all the time. He also kept a close eye on the correspondence through which much of the business of government was conducted; the letters of his secretaries repeatedly record the king's sharp enquiries as to why expected responses from Wolsey and others had not yet arrived. We know from the reports of foreign ambassadors how detailed was his understanding of European events, and how lengthy and acute was his discussion of these events with foreign envoys. It is also clear that when the issue was of particular importance to Henry, his scrutiny of policy was intense. The detailed debates over religious doctrine in the 1530s and 1540s are perhaps the best example. Cranmer replied at great length, and with some forceful criticisms, to the king's notations on the 'Bishops' Book' of 1538; it is notable that the king's opinion prevailed, despite the archbishop's best efforts. This is not to say that factions did not exist; as in any political sphere, they were a fact of life, and the contentious religious and foreign policy issues of Henry's reign gave the factions of his time a particularly energetic agenda at times. It is also not to say that Henry could not be influenced; he was fond of debate, interested in different opinions, and often receptive to new ideas. He was also impressed by efficiency, just as he was annoyed by failure. But there is no convincing evidence to suggest that Henry could be manoeuvred into making decisions solely through factional pressure.

Apart from the problems of evidence, there are some conceptual difficulties with characterising Henrician politics as dominated by factional conflict, and it is probable that the differing historical opinions on this point reflect a conceptual disagreement. This study will argue that the view of Henry VIII as the puppet, or at least the pawn, of Wolsey or Cromwell, or Anne Boleyn and her family, rests on a mistaken notion of early modern kingship. Henry is described as the victim of faction, as though the existence of kinship and interest groups at court and within the nobility were a blight which any more responsible king might have eradicated. In fact, faction was a fact of sixteenth-century life which was politically neutral, which could be used to destabilise or which could be used to enhance and impose royal authority. Tudor courtiers frequently banded together according to family ties, religious sympathies, military comradeship or geographical origins. The mere existence of these groups, however, did not mean that Henry was open to manipulation. It is probably true that he was open to encouragement, if one or other faction could make a suggestion which suited his needs and could advance his existing objectives. It is certainly true that he canvassed opinions widely, asking diplomats, councillors and churchmen their opinions on the issues of the day: apart from anything else, it is quite clear that Henry loved to talk. But it is also true that he silenced, or reprimanded, those who gave unwelcome advice. Queen Jane was told to be quiet when she made an appeal for the monasteries, and Queen Katherine Parr got into trouble by debating religious questions too freely with her husband: both accepted the admonition meekly. To be open to discussion is not nearly the same thing as to be open to manipulation. Henry had strong opinions, and he shaped and pursued his policies with authority and confidence. To assert that he was manipulated is fundamentally to misunderstand his character and his role within the royal court.

Much of the case for faction has rested on making connections between changes in personnel and changes in policy. Thus Anne Boleyn's years as Henry's love, and then as his wife, are associated with an interest in evangelical ideas and the advance of some religious reform policies. It is also true that Anne's own interests inclined towards evangelical literature, although she was not the Protestant she is sometimes made out to be. The *correlation* is there between an important person in Henry's life, and her associates who might be termed a faction, and Henry's policies. But the *causal connection* is not. There is no evidence that Anne and the Boleyn faction actually changed Henry's mind about anything. It is a lot more plausible to suggest that Henry's enthusiasm for evangelical ideas came from the fact that they had helped to release him from his first marriage and bring about his second, and that a shared enthusiasm for fashionable evangelism brought him and his second wife together. Factions of a particular ilk are discernible at court and associated with certain royal policies because Henry gave them that position at court, and often employed them to implement his policies. In other words, it was Henry making use of factions, rather than factions making use of the king.

There is also a problem with understanding the factions themselves. It is easy to talk about a 'Boleyn faction', and probably accurate, since family fortunes were closely interwoven and bonds of loyalty were tight. But even so, Anne Boleyn and her brother, Lord Rochford, were sent to their death partly on the evidence of Lord Rochford's wife. Even family ties were not reliably secure. Other factions are defined as 'conservative' or 'evangelical', and these groupings are far less tight. For one thing religious loyalties could be countered by familial, regional, occupational or other loyalties pulling the other way. For another, religious identities were in a state of flux throughout Henry's reign, and plenty of people blithely identified as 'Protestant' or 'Catholic' in the past cannot now be held to fit the more cautious definitions of 'evangelical' or 'conservative' that we tend to use today. Finally, it is important to understand how his subjects, even his most important subjects, viewed the king. To them he was divinely appointed, his role a partly sacred one even before the royal supremacy; his power over them was huge, and could (and frequently did) extend to imprisonment or death. He was not someone to be pushed around as cabinet colleagues might attempt to lobby a contemporary prime minister. He was someone to be approached with caution and reverence, to whom ideas might be suggested, but with humility and in anxious hope of approval. Cranmer's description of Cromwell, written in surprise and sadness after Cromwell's fall from grace, is a good description of the place of a minister in Henry's government:

> he that was so advanced by your majesty; he whose surety was only by your majesty; he who loved your majesty (as I ever thought) no less than God; he who studied always to set forwards whatsoever was your majesty's will and pleasure; he that cared for no man's displeasure to serve your majesty.[90]

Henry's closest advisors, Wolsey and Cromwell, as well as many others, were entirely dependent on the king's favour for their very livelihood, and their chief concern was always to advance the king's will, not to subvert it.

It is true that contemporaries often discussed developments and reversals in royal policy as if they were the consequence of pressure from one or other kinship or interest group. In part this was the consequence of pride: Tudor courtiers rather liked to think of themselves as important, and both the Duke of Buckingham and the Earl of Surrey were executed for having views about their own importance, in particular with regard to the succession, since Buckingham seems to have advanced his own chances of inheriting the throne before his fall in 1519, and Surrey seems to have considered that his own family should control the realm during the anticipated minority of the future Edward VI. It is important to note, however, that Henry had both these men executed for their presumption.

On a lesser scale, the question of counsel was central to the political debate of the time. Good counsel was an important element of government, and one which was all the more talked about since it was one of the few forms of political influence which was theoretically open to the populace at large. The fact that it was widely discussed does not mean that counsel could hold sway over the king. To use modern terminology, Henry VIII preferred a presidential style of command to cabinet government. This was why Wolsey, and later Cromwell, were so important, and why contemporaries were so nervous. Discussions of how to influence the king were in large part wishful thinking.

Another explanation for some of the misleading emphasis on faction in contemporary documents is the way in which people regarded the person of the monarch in the sixteenth century. Since the king was divinely appointed, sanctified by his coronation, and since his royal dignity was not only continually reasserted but a major safeguard to the stability and prosperity of his subjects, it was almost unthinkable to criticise him directly. Tudor rebellions never attacked the king by word or deed, but constantly reiterated their loyalty to the person of the monarch whilst directing all their ire and indignation at his counsellors. Thus many of the complaints of the Pilgrimage of Grace were aimed at Cromwell, who was blamed for the dissolution of the monasteries and a range of other unpopular policies. This rhetoric was applied more subtly in other contexts too, including the accounts of ambassadors who had to uphold the dignity of their own rulers, and this has frequently been misinterpreted by more modern commentators who have no inhibitions about criticising the actions of royalty. In particular, the frightening vengeance with which the king destroyed Thomas Wolsey, Anne Boleyn, Thomas More and John Fisher, Thomas Cromwell, the Earl of Surrey and others was sufficiently appalling to observers then as now, to make it very difficult to blame the king directly. Factional explanations were advanced for these spectacular falls from grace, for it would have been unthinkable to bluntly state that the king himself was responsible. Even Henry himself sometimes employed this kind of rhetoric, as when he lamented Cromwell's death and blamed others for his downfall.

One final reason for this very political judgement, that the king was at the mercy of faction, actually lies in the field of religious rhetoric, and the contested history of the English Reformation. The first offender here is John Foxe, whose *Book of Martyrs* became a defining text for English Protestants, arguably as important as the Bible itself when it came to shaping the English Protestant mentality.[91] Foxe's work was a history of the Protestant Church in England, but one rooted firmly in a sixteenth-century Protestant mindset which brought together a number of prejudices with an otherwise reasonable degree of historical accuracy. Faced with critics who sneered at Protestantism as a modern invention, Foxe set himself the task of showing how Protestantism was the direct descendant of the religion of Christ and his apostles, with the torch of true faith being carried through every age, despite persecution from Rome, by a small band of loyal followers. He is best known for his moving descriptions of the martyrdom of Protestants under Mary I, but he had described too those who kept the flame alight in earlier reigns, including that of Henry VIII. Since some, but not all, of what Henry VIII had achieved fitted into Foxe's narrative of the inexorable progress of English Protestantism, he could not decry Henry's achievement, but nor could he praise it whole-heartedly. Instead, he chose probably the only way out of his dilemma, which was to describe Henry as a monarch easily led by those about him. He could not admit, probably he could not even accept, that Protestantism in England in the 1530s and 1540s was diverse, even divided, and uncertain in its objectives. It made more sense to him to explain that Henry had brought in some 'good' Protestant initiatives like an English Bible, and the Dissolution of the Monasteries, but had also clung to some 'bad' aspects of the past such as the Latin mass, not because he had a religious outlook which defied Foxe's categories, but because he listened first to Protestant advisors, and then to Catholic diehards:

> Even as the king was ruled and gave ear sometimes to one, sometimes to another, so one while it went forward, at another season as much backward again, and sometimes clean altered and changed for a season, according as they could prevail, who were about the king.[92]

Foxe's opinion, deprived of its religious context, has helped shape subsequent ideas about Henry's style of government. Historical assessment of Henry's own religion has now reached the point, however, where it is possible to make sense of Henry's policies in the context of the 1530s without suggesting he brought together an indigestible mixture of Protestant and Catholic ideas. This is particularly evident when it is realised that neither 'Protestant' or 'Catholic' bore their contemporary meanings during Henry's own lifetime. This will be discussed at much more length in later chapters, but the removal of this religious bias from our assessment of Henry has left the way clear to understand him as a king who pursued policy with much more determination and consistency than Foxe or his successors could allow.

The historical debate over faction is open to caricature, when in fact there is a degree of subtlety to the argument which is often overlooked. As one supporter of factional interpretation has commented:

> There is no contradiction between a dominant Henry and a Henry dependent on others for information and advice, whose courtiers staked a lifetime and sometimes life on the conviction that he was vulnerable to pressure.[93]

His opponent has asserted:

> To claim, as I do, that Henry was very much the dominant force in the politics and policy-making of his reign is not to claim that he could do whatever he liked. That would be a caricature of the arguments of those who have made that case. My argument is directed against those historians who have claimed that Henry was manipulated by factions. It is not my claim that Henry was somehow totally immune from influence.[94]

There is considerable sophistication within this discussion. Unfortunately, this is often lost in transit, and many commentators lapse into explaining every policy decision of the reign in terms of faction, for example, that 'at the start of 1533, the Boleyn faction was in the ascendant', or 'in the summer of 1540, the conservatives controlled the Court'. In this way, a restrained and multifaceted analysis is warped into a monocausal explanation.

Henry was only human, and he was of course open to influence from those about him. But it was Henry who decided who should live in close

proximity to him. He was responsible for choosing his wives, his councillors, his gentlemen of the privy chamber, and he rejected them – with
unusual forcefulness – when they ceased to please him. His close associates mirrored his own interests, and were frequently as athletic, musical,
dynamic, literary, bellicose or religious as the king himself, and so in the
way of friends and family, they no doubt exerted gentle sway over the
King, and encouraged him down one or other path. They could not have
done so, however, without him noticing, or without him agreeing. It is
also the case that when Henry was considering some major policy decision in a contentious field such as religion, he liked to listen to those
with opposing views before committing himself. And it is notable that
'the policy of balance, of Janus-like impartiality' which he liked to
present in matters of religion, involved imposing compromise on precisely those people who were most disposed to offer him principled
resistance.[95] The subjects who most consistently and intelligently
opposed and sought to influence the king were bishops like Cranmer,
Latimer, Gardiner and Tunstall, all of whom were brave enough to question the king at different times. Yet Henry continued to carve out the
religious policy he himself wanted, producing formulations like the
'Bishop's Book' which 'contains something to please both evangelicals
and traditionalists, and something to annoy them both'.[96]

The two servants who served him longest and most faithfully were
Wolsey and Cranmer, and neither managed to influence him away from
policies which they were convinced were misguided. In particular if
Cranmer, whom he loved and trusted, and knew to be a man of integrity, could not persuade the king, then it seems unlikely that anyone else
would have succeeded. This theme will continue to recur, in this book
no less than in wider historical discussion of Henry's reign, but in these
pages Henry's mastery of his own government is not in question.

The debate over faction and manipulation emerges only a few years
into the reign of Henry VIII in response to Thomas Wolsey's rise to
power. Even the very origins of Wolsey's pre-eminence, it has been
argued in the past, were based on his calculating nature, which fitted
him to establish his sway over the young, pleasure-loving king even as
he undermined Richard Fox, Bishop of Winchester, his former mentor,
and usurped his place in government. We now know that Wolsey
remained on good terms with Fox, who gratefully sought retirement
whilst fostering his protégé's career at court.[97]

Thomas Wolsey came to power because of his extraordinary intelligence, his facility as a communicator and mediator and his outstanding administrative ability. His biographer, Cavendish, tells us that he first came to Henry VII's attention when commissioned to take despatches to the Emperor Maximilian; leaving immediately, he made the journey there and back in three days, to the wonder of all.[98] This efficiency coloured almost everything he did. Yet Wolsey has been peculiarly unlucky in his reputation. In part, this is built upon the resentment of his contemporaries at his spectacular rise to power, coupled with a certain snobbery about his lowly origins. Two leading chroniclers of Henry's reign, Polydore Vergil and Edward Hall, both disliked Wolsey intensely. The effects of this are compounded by the Tudor tendency to blame the chief minister for unpopular royal policies, and by the fact that Wolsey was the last pre-Reformation cardinal, and as such has been used as a symbol of all that was corrupt in the pre-Reformation church. These components have been fused into a modern interpretation which sees Wolsey as the power behind the throne, manipulating Henry to his own ends, and aggrandising himself to an obscene extent, as simultaneously cardinal, papal legate, Archbishop of York, Bishop of Winchester, Abbot of St Albans. These hostile assessments of Wolsey have also contained a kind of distaste that a churchman should in any case be so heavily involved in politics.

Much of this indicates the extent to which we have so readily misunderstood the past. As recent scholarship has pointed out, Wolsey was an impressive example of the kind of churchman who was also a leading statesman, a political animal vital to the successful working of the early modern state.[99] Since churchmen more than most had the best education, it was only natural that bishops should end up in government, and since they provided for curates and others to attend to the cure of souls, their episcopal duties were not neglected. Moreover, in an age when the business of politics was seeped in religious belief and inextricably bound up with religious practice, it was not considered odd for bishops to take on political responsibilities. Henry's first chancellor had been the Archbishop of Canterbury, William Warham, and indeed he spent quite a lot of time staying at the archbishop's palace at Lambeth in the early years of his reign, to expedite government business. Incidentally, Warham is someone else whom Wolsey was said to have elbowed out, since it was to Wolsey that Warham resigned the chancellorship in 1515. Thomas More, however, told Erasmus that Warham was glad to retire from this post, and relations remained cordial between the two men: in 1522 Wolsey sent Warham a jewel for Becket's shrine in Canterbury, and in 1523 he invited him to convalesce at Hampton Court.[100]

If the extent of Wolsey's benefices was unprecedented, then so were his political duties, and the expenses he incurred in pursuit of them. Henry gave Wolsey the abbacy of St Albans, England's wealthiest abbey, in 1521, because he estimated that Wolsey's last embassy to the continent had probably cost him about £10,000. It is also clear that Wolsey was a skilled and diligent statesman, who made every effort to benefit his country, perhaps particularly in his efforts to maintain peace in Europe. He was also a reformer, the founder of two important educational institutions in Ipswich School and Cardinal College (later Christ Church) in Oxford. He had a mistress, called Mistress Lark, and two children, Dorothy and Thomas. Contemporaries did not necessarily set much store by clerical celibacy, however, as long as a priest was faithful to his partner, and not a fornicator, which Wolsey cannot have been, or his critics would have discovered the salacious details.[101]

As to Wolsey's central relationship with Henry VIII, again there has been a failure to appreciate the way in which early modern kingship functioned, and Henry's own particular style of government. Cavendish made it clear that Wolsey's swift advancement was because 'he was most earnest and readiest among all the Council to advance the King's own will and pleasure without any respect to the case.'[102] This suggests that on his way up the ladder Wolsey was not worried about the consequences as long as the king was pleased. Henry was an intelligent individual, however, and was unlikely to be pleased by anything which by its corruption or folly weakened his authority. Chiefly Wolsey seems to have come to prominence by organising the campaign against France in 1513, and although the wisdom of warfare might always be debatable, it seems clear that Wolsey could not have opposed the king in his desire to make war at the start of his reign. As we shall see, he made an impressive case for peace later in the reign, with the king's cooperation and approval, but his freedom of action was always to be constrained by Henry's own policy decisions, which were often clear and emphatic. As Cavendish said of 1513, Henry was 'fully persuaded and resolved in his most royal person to invade his foreign enemies with a puissant army', and Wolsey's involvement was because 'it was thought very necessary that this royal enterprise should be speedily provided and plentifully furnished in every degree of things apt and convenient for the same.'[103]

Wolsey's greatness lay in taking Henry's often impulsive desires and helping to fashion them into a majestic, impressive and successful royal policy. He was also astoundingly versatile, dealing with kings, ambassadors and the vagaries of international politics on the one hand, whilst resolving petty disputes, arranging housing and victualling for armies, appointing to church offices, promoting Renaissance art, architecture and learning and devising entertaining dinner parties for the court on the other. A random selection of documents from 1519–20, when he was at the height of his powers, shows Wolsey arranging an Anglo-French summit, seeking how to strike the best bargain over German silver for the Royal Mint, receiving thanks from Oxford for endowing lectures there and giving advice about their stagnant marshes and watercourses, being asked for help by the Bishop of Ely to quell his unruly clergy, being asked for support by Erasmus against critics of his New Testament translation, receiving warning from an agent about the level of popular discontent at the king's proposed visit to France, and being granted papal permission to eat meat that Lent.[104]

And if Wolsey had an extraordinary role in Henry's regime, then this was in part because they shared so many convictions about the right way for the king to rule. Wolsey was as anxious as Henry to advance his dignity and gave him any number of opportunities for magnificent display. They shared a love of Renaissance learning and an inclination to promote humanist reform. Wolsey perhaps was more cautious than Henry, as befitted a servant. When commenting on Campeggio's mission in 1519, they both praised the papal envoy, but whereas Henry lauded his 'splendour, skill and assiduity', Wolsey praised his 'moderation and prudence'.[105] Where necessary, however, Wolsey cast aside moderation, and if he conducted himself with all the pomp and ostentation he could muster, this was not just because it was appropriate to his office, but also because it reflected well on his master. Cavendish records how he went in procession 'with two great crosses of silver borne before him, with also two great pillars of silver, and his sergeant at arms with a great mace of silver gilt'. But he also record the splendour and pageantry of his visit to Charles V, after which 'he returned home again into England with great triumph, being no less in estimation with the King than he was before but rather much more.'[106]

Wolsey's magnificence enhanced Henry's own. Moreover, they seem to have liked one another. Certainly Henry would play his favourite trick of making surprise appearances in disguise at Wolsey's house, a stunt which otherwise he tended to reserve for his queen. And Wolsey went to great lengths to entertain his king. Cavendish describes some of the lavish entertainment, explaining that:

> this matter I have declared at large because ye shall understand what joy and delight the Cardinal had to see his prince and sovereign lord in his house so nobly entertained and pleased; which was always his only study, to devise things to his comfort, not passing of the charges or expenses.[107]

The correspondence between Henry and Wolsey is vast, but all of it bespeaks their closeness, and Wolsey's dependence upon the King's will. He was not incapable of annoying Henry, but any minor transgression always ended in Wolsey's submission and Henry's gracious forgiveness. There is little to suggest that Wolsey was an independent operator: Henry confided in him, but equally read letters addressed to him, and consistently treated him as a valuable, and valued assistant, but no more.

In 1518, for example, Henry wrote to Wolsey from Woodstock, unusually in his own hand, but then his reasons for writing were 'so secret that they cause me at this time to write to you myself', namely that he thought Katherine was pregnant again. He continued as follows:

> the chief cause why I am so loath to repair to London were, because about this time is partly of her dangerous times, and because of that I would remove her as little as I may now. My Lord I write this unto [you] not as a ensured thing, but as a thing wherein I have great hope ... and because I do well know that this thing will be comfortable to you to understand, therefore I do write it unto you at this time.[108]

Henry was worried that Katherine might miscarry at the same point in the pregnancy as she had previously. This private confidence shows the depth of the trust he had in Wolsey. As to whether Wolsey, or any one else, might manipulate Henry on the basis of such trust, another illustration is given by a letter from Richard Pace, the king's secretary, to Wolsey in 1521, clearly protesting at the suggestion that he had in some way misrepresented Wolsey to the king. Pace pointed out that the king 'readeth all your letters with great diligence, and mine answers made to the same not by my device but by his instructions'. He described Henry reading Wolsey's letters, marking the places he wanted to respond to, and giving clear instruction as to what that response should be. Pace protested that he could not misrepresent the content of Wolsey's letters to Henry:

> without great shame and to mine own evident ruin, for his grace doth read them all himself, and examine the same at leisure with great deliberation, and hath better wit to understand them than I to inform him.[109]

Even given the fact that Pace was seeking to clear his name, it is clear that Henry kept a close eye on the workings of government, and paid close attention to the correspondence which conveyed his wishes to the wider world.

Henry's first decade in power had provided him with a wealth of experience at home and abroad. He had learned the business of ruling, and brought together an impressive collection of men to serve him at court, as diplomats abroad, and on the field of battle, and in Wolsey he had found a royal servant of extraordinary skill. He had fashioned an image for himself as king which was multi-faceted, inspiring and sophisticated. The future of his dynasty remained uncertain, however, for he still lacked a male heir.

3

THE LURE OF EMPIRE, 1518–1527

Then the king of England showed himself ... in beauty and personage, the most goodliest Prince that ever reigned over the Realm of England: his grace was apparelled in a garment of Cloth of Silver, of Damask, ribbed with Cloth of Gold, so thick as might be ... of such shape and making, that it was marvelous to behold.[1]

PEACEMAKING

Henry VIII had begun his reign by seeking glory in war, but after nearly ten years on the throne, he had decided to seek an alternative and equal glory as the peacemaker of Europe. 1518 saw the construction and consolidation of the Treaty of London, designed and orchestrated by Wolsey but entirely in tune with his master's ambitions. The treaty brought together the great European powers and over twenty smaller territories, in an anti-aggression pact. Any attack upon a member state was to result in a collective demand for withdrawal, to be followed by a collective declaration of war within a month, and active campaigning by land and sea within two and three months respectively. If to the modern mind this suggests an early version of the League of Nations or NATO, to Tudor minds it might have been more reminiscent of Arthur's round table, and a chivalric undertaking to preserve an honourable peace.

From England's point of view, this was also a new solution to the always problematic question of relations with France. The Anglo-French element to the wider treaty was made central to the inauguration of the treaty in the first week of October, with other great powers signing up to it some time later. Tournai was restored to France for 600,000 crowns, whilst the infant princess Mary was betrothed to the Dauphin. These were both important concessions from England, and although with hindsight it is easy to be sceptical about a treaty which did not last, it is clear that at the time it was at the centre of Henry's policy, and Wolsey's preoccupations. The Pope, who had being trying unsuccessfully to launch a scheme of his own, to unify Christendom and recapture Constantinople, duly ratified the Treaty of London in December 1518. Despite enjoying his status as a loyal supporter of the Holy See, Henry was not prepared to let Leo X set the agenda at this point. The papal legate Campeggio, who had arrived in England in April 1518 to promote this cause, had only been allowed into the realm after the Pope had granted Wolsey's request to be made *legate a latere* also, that he might have equal status with Campeggio.

The peace plan and the rhetoric of the Treaty of London all bore the stamp of Wolsey's humanist enthusiasm and learning, something which Henry approved of and was proud to flourish as an ornament to his kingship. As in so many things, Henry assumed the mantle of leadership, while Wolsey worked hard to finalise the details. The desire for peace was a central part of humanist thought at this time; it was in 1517 that Erasmus published his *Querela Pacis,* or 'Complaint of peace', and the adages called *Dulce bellum inexpertis*, or 'War is sweet to those who know it not', and his ideas were echoed by other humanists across Europe.[2] More's 'Utopians' had loathed and despised war: 'They say it's a quite subhuman form of activity, although human beings are more addicted to it than any of the lower animals. In fact, the Utopians are practically the only people on earth who fail to see anything glorious in war.'[3] More's characters had been ostensibly respectful about the behaviour of European princes, although this may well have been heavy irony on his part. Erasmus spoke out more bluntly against contemporary practice:

> I am ashamed to recount the disgraceful and frivolous pretexts Christian princes find for calling the whole world to arms. One discovers or invents some mouldering, obsolete title to support his claim, as if it really matters

much who rules a kingdom so long as there is proper concern for the welfare of the people. Another pleads some trifling omissions in a treaty covering a hundred clauses, or has a personal grievance against his neighbour over the interception of an intended spouse or a careless word of slander.[4]

This was at least in part intended for Henry, who had gone to war in 1513 in support of his ancient claim to the French throne, and who was to make war on France in 1523–4 on the pretext that the French had not paid the pension they owed him. Erasmus's work was meant as an oblique attack on Henry, and a straightforward denigration of the conventions of warfare.[5] In 1518, however, Henry and Wolsey were both treading the dignified path of peacemakers, using Christian humanist rhetoric to justify their actions and hallow their reputations.

Again it is worth remembering how much ideas could matter to Henry, and how much he sought the approval of learned men. Just before his last war, on Good Friday 1513, with preparations under way for the French campaign, John Colet had preached to the Court at Greenwich on the need to follow Christ rather than classical heroes. According to Erasmus, he had declared an unjust peace better than a just war. Henry had been so concerned by this, especially the effect it might have on his troops, that he had a long private discussion with Colet, although he had apparently emerged from their talk in high spirits, with Colet's blessing on his enterprise. Colet was a humanist scholar, Dean of St Paul's, founder of St Paul's school, renowned for his personal piety and asceticism, who for the first eight years of Henry's reign gave the Good Friday sermon at court.

It is significant that the words of a scholarly cleric, however renowned in his own field, could have such resonance for Henry, and that sermons were believed to have such resonance for soldiers. It was also entirely characteristic of the king not to rest until he had secured Colet's acquiescence. Similarly, it seems to have been important to Henry's self-perception that he retained the approval of scholars like Erasmus and More. As a young prince of 15 or so he had written to Erasmus, using the exaggerated rhetoric of scholarly deference:

> But wherefore do I determine to laud your eloquence, whose renown is known throughout the whole world? Nothing that I am able to fashion in your praise can be enough worthy of that consummate erudition.[6]

Ten years on, the deference was gone, but Henry still cared about the opinions of Erasmus and his like. He did not care enough about such opinions to refrain from fighting when he wanted to make war. But he cared enough to dignify his attempts at peace with the scholarly rhetoric of the age, and to persist in his efforts to win the support of men like Colet, Erasmus and More.

The inauguration of the Treaty of London was marked with a solemn high mass at St Paul's, where 'there was made from the West door to the choir door of the church equal with the highest step, a hautepace [high walkway] of timber of twelve foot broad, that the king and the Ambassadors might be seen.' Important occasions at St Paul's often merited this kind of raised walkway, driving home the importance of public witness when it came to an alliance. The sermon was preached by Richard Pace, the king's secretary, who quoted Erasmus as he enumerated the horrors of 'tearful and ruinous war', and praised the kings of England and France for inaugurating a new era of peace.[7] Mass was sung by Wolsey, who was particularly careful of his state since his fellow papal legate Campeggio was also present. Both legates processed solemnly at the ceremony of inauguration, but it was Wolsey who celebrated the high mass, with every possible form of ostentation: he 'had his cloth of estate of Tissue: his Cup board set with basins all gilt covered: his place was five steps high'.[8] Henry would not have tolerated the glory of his treaty, or his cardinal, being outstripped on his own native soil and Wolsey was careful of both his own and his master's reputation for grandeur.

The events of 1518 underline the precise nature of the very important role which Wolsey played in Henry's affairs. The sermon given by Richard Pace praised Wolsey's part in the peace process, and addressing the king, quoted Erasmus again as he said 'it was the Most Reverend Lord Cardinal of York who, as they say, stuck the spur into you when you were running hard already.' Attempting to flatter both men at once, Pace did a reasonable job of describing their relationship.

Henry's ambitions were fierce, but indistinct; Wolsey was a master of detailed organisation. The king wanted glory, and Wolsey made sure he gave it to him, on terms which the king would find acceptable. It is probable that there was a large amount of Wolsey's own inspiration in conceiving the Treaty of London; as churchman, humanist, chancellor and papal legate he would have appreciated the lure of this peace treaty on several levels. Its Christian and scholarly rhetoric was irreproachable, contemporary pressure towards it was strong, the exalted status it bestowed on Henry was guaranteed to please the king, it would save him the ruinous cost of further campaigning and it would please the Pope. It is important to realise, however, that these motivations which convinced Wolsey were the same as those which persuaded Henry. Wolsey's initiative was acceptable where it advanced the broader aims of the king, who left him to work out the details and arrange everything with his usual efficiency. Wolsey could not spur the king in a direction that Henry did not want to go, and he would not have been foolish enough to want to do so.

The year 1518 had seen several reversals of fortune. It had begun badly, with outbreaks of the 'sweating sickness', a new and alarming disease which caused heavy sweating for a brief period between four and twenty-four hours, culminating in either speedy recovery or swift demise. The latest outbreak saw Henry travelling hastily between one residence and the next, anxious to escape infection as he moved between Windsor, Reading, Abingdon and Woodstock.[9] It was at the last residence that he left Katherine in the early and dangerous stages of pregnancy; when he returned in July to find her with a reassuringly large belly, he ordered that *Te Deum* be sung at St Paul's, but also at Woodstock where she had been kept safe. After Mary's safe arrival in 1516, Henry clearly hoped for a son with renewed optimism, and arranged for Katherine's lying-in at Greenwich. The child, born in November, was a girl, and soon died. It was another in a series of crushing disappointments.

The Tudor dynasty still lacked the male heir Henry so badly needed, but in all other respects Henry's estate as king was becoming increasingly majestic. The St George's day festivities for 1519 were kept with great solemnity, and the banquet was 'like the feast of a coronacion'. At the requiem mass in St George's Chapel were offered the banner and hatchments of the Emperor Maximilian, who had died that February, and who had been a Knight of the Garter.[10] As solemn obsequies took place, the manoeuvring began for his replacement.

The head of the Holy Roman Empire, which covered a range of territories in central Europe, including much of modern day Germany, Austria, Switzerland, Poland and the Netherlands, as well as parts of France, Italy, Slovenia and the Czech Republic, was traditionally elected by a motley assortment of electors from these different territories. Historically the succession had been well established in the Habsburg line, but this was by no means secure, particularly as the Habsburg heir, Charles I of Spain, had been raised in the Netherlands, made King of Spain in 1516, and had no obvious personal association with the Empire. Francis I made it clear that he would contest the election, and initially the English envoys dutifully made encouraging noises to both camps, until in May 1519 Henry VIII suddenly began campaigning on his own behalf. The idea had been raised before, when Maximilian had advanced a plan for declaring Henry as his son and heir, but then Maximilian was known for advancing wildly improbably and grandiose schemes, including one wonderful and peculiar plan to have himself made Pope and saint together.[11] Henry was sufficiently interested in the prospect of imperial election to send Richard Pace as an envoy to the electors, but whereas both Charles and Francis handed out lavish bribes, Pace merely promised money in the event of Henry being elected. From this it seems that even Henry did not expect his candidature to be taken very seriously. Nonetheless, it is another hint of the attractions of imperial status for him, a precursor of the imperial dream which was eventually to take shape in the 1530s with the royal supremacy.

It used to be thought that the idea of Henry as emperor was something which came to Cromwell in a flash of inspiration in the early 1530s. In fact it had much longer roots. In a study of the iconography of the imperial crown, it is no surprise to find that it first appears on the chantry tomb of Henry V in Westminster Abbey. The life of Henry V which Henry VIII had had translated in 1513 also described him as emperor and Henry V's claim on the French throne had an imperial subtext.[12] If Henry VIII was inspired by the idea of imperial status, this model may have helped. Certainly we find him giving the title of 'imperial' to two of his ships from about this time, and his excitement at meeting a real Emperor when he fought alongside Maximilian in 1513 is palpable from the sources, betrayed not least by the way he dressed so gorgeously in honour of the occasion.[13]

As Hall records, despite being occupied with the siege of Thérouanne, when news of Maximilian's approach reached Henry he 'prepared all things necessary to meet with th'emperor in triumph', his noblemen 'gorgeously apparelled' and he himself 'in a garment of great riches in jewels'.[14] The emperor himself had been slightly less careful of his estate, perhaps because he was more confident of it; since the English were paying him and his troops for their efforts, he condescended to wear their colours: 'Th'emperor as the king's soldier wore a Cross of saint George with a Rose.'[15] Perhaps Henry was gratified to see an Emperor so arrayed; it is hard in retrospect not to see the irony of Maximilian's gesture towards an alliance based not on mutual strength and respect but on hard cash.

One tangible opportunity to lay the foundations for empire presented itself around this time, although it was Wolsey who best appreciated its potential. Henry VII had sponsored John and Sebastian Cabot to lead the first English expedition to the New World, and Henry VIII continued to employ Sebastian as a cartographer at Greenwich. In 1517 John Rastell, chiefly known as the printer and writer who was married to Thomas More's sister, launched a bid under Cabot's direction, and with royal backing, to find and colonise new territory across the Atlantic. He and his ships got no further than Waterford in Ireland, where the sailors abandoned him and left to sell their cargo in Bordeaux. Rastell, who was clearly an adaptable individual, stayed in Ireland for two years, and wrote a play, a moral work which seems to have been the first English printed work to give the New World the name of 'America', and which by including a song, was the first to incorporate a printed musical score.[16] Three years later Wolsey was devising another plan to have Cabot lead a voyage in search of the North-West Passage to the Far East. Cabot, in Venice, declined the commission, so Wolsey turned to the merchants of London instead. They too were reluctant to take such a gamble, and although some money and ships were put together, the expedition never sailed. During the rest of Henry's reign there were occasional flickers of interest, but no real commitment to the exploration which was bringing the Spanish and Portuguese such riches. When Sebastian Cabot sought royal patronage in 1537 he was refused. The kind of empire which Henry had in mind was based on classical and medieval precedent; he did not envisage the empires which were to come.

While Henry was imagining himself as Maximilian's successor abroad, he was also adjusting his image at home. In the same month as Pace was despatched abroad to explore Henry's imperial prospects, reform was under way at Court. His 'minions', Carew, Bryan and the others, who had served him, hunted, danced and jousted with him, were banished from the court. Hall reports that the Privy Council 'perceived that certain young men in his privy chamber, not regarding his estate nor degree, were so familiar and homely with him, and played such light touches with him that they forgot themselves', and that this was 'not meet to be suffered for the king's honour'.[17]

More sober individuals took their place in the privy chamber. The significance of this has been debated. For some it is a mark of the power struggle between Wolsey and this Francophile group of courtiers, with Wolsey resenting their closeness to the king, their extravagance and their ability to prejudice the king in considerations of foreign policy.[18] It was accompanied by a raft of proposed reforms suggesting that the king 'in his own person' should adopt the practice of closely and regularly scrutinising financial and administrative affairs.[19] The fact that these proposed reforms failed to materialise, and that the 'minions' – suitably chastened – soon found their way back to favour, perhaps suggests that it was not Wolsey's initiative, not least since Wolsey's plans tended to come to fruition. It is probable that the Privy Council did indeed express their anxieties, and that Henry himself, perhaps spurred on by the attractive idea of himself as emperor, sought to add a new weight and seriousness to his role in both court and Council. It is implausible to suggest that Henry was not the decision-maker here, particularly in something which touched his daily life so closely.[20] Yet like many attempts at self-improvement, it did not come to very much.

The various initiatives from the years between 1518 and 1521 seem to suggest that Henry at this time was hungry for glory, but that he was not sure where it might best be found. In the summer of 1519 he made a startlingly enthusiastic avowal to the Pope of his readiness to go on crusade, seemingly persuaded more by the idea when it was his own initiative than he had been a year earlier when it was Leo X's proposal. In part, this must have been an attempt to mollify the Pope in order to secure the permanent confirmation of Wolsey's office as legate. It is significant, however, that Henry VIII's ambitions during these years were all enfolded in the reassuring garb of religious sanction. It is true that such sanction was negotiated on his terms, rather than those of the papacy, but it still made for an impressively devout effect. It suggests that throughout his lifetime Henry was inclined to see the endorsement of religion as a route to self-glorification, even though the nature of the religion employed for this task was to vary.

As the idea of a crusade was left on one side, another plan for glory took shape with the proposal that Wolsey be elected as Pope. It was vital to Henry that Wolsey's ecclesiastical authority was of the very highest;

this way he could ensure that all his policies retained the aura of divine sanction as well as the detailed organisation that came from the cardinal's more secular skills. When Leo X died in 1521, the tempting possibility arose that Wolsey might replace him, and the ever-reliable Richard Pace was once more despatched, this time to Rome, to push Wolsey's case.

This plan to make Wolsey pope has been ascribed to the cardinal's own fierce ambition, as part of the general caricature of Wolsey as all things reprehensible. It seems fairly clear, however, that the scheme to make him pope was Henry's idea. Wolsey was ambitious, but his stage was England; he made no attempts to work his influence at the papal court, and in so far as he sought to make an impression in Europe, it was always for the sake of Henry's diplomatic efforts, not through involvement in church politics. He worked hard to charm Charles V and Margaret of Savoy, but did not waste his efforts on the Italian cardinals. Henry seized on the idea with enthusiasm, however, again illustrating the role that Wolsey played in his affairs. To have his chief servant and minister placed as the Vicar of Christ might rather pleasingly suggest that Henry VIII and Christ were on an equal footing; at any rate, it would make Henry's prestige even greater and his control over the church absolute. Henry never seems to have feared that Wolsey would follow the path of that other royal servant, Thomas à Becket, who did not in the end prove as biddable as his king had hoped.

There were two chances at the papacy: one, when Leo X died in 1521, and another two years later when Adrian VI died after his brief pontificate. If anything, the fact of Charles V's old tutor (formerly Adrian of Utrecht) becoming Pope, rather served to encourage Henry's hopes. It had proved that it was possible to elect a non-Italian Pope, and one previously distinguished by his royal service; Adrian was also, like Wolsey, a scholar, a reformer and a peacemaker. Wolsey made self-deprecating comments when faced with the possibility, and several remarks to the effect that he would do the job only if the king wished it, but he seems to have been neither hopeful nor particularly enthusiastic. His reading of the situation was a lot more shrewd than that of Henry who had the tendency to get carried away with his own visions of glory. Giulio de Medici, as Wolsey had expected, was made Pope Clement VII. Since he was Cardinal Protector of England, and believed to be sympathetic to the regime, this was seen as a good result. There would not be another non-Italian pope until the election of John Paul II in the twentieth century.

Other attempts to enhance the aura of the young king took more material form. Building work continued, and at Newhall in Essex the 'costly mansion' of Beaulieu took form; it was at Henry's instigation that the house was rechristened Beaulieu, although such sophistication seems to have been stolidly resisted by the locals, who persisted in calling it Newhall. The supervisor of the work was William Bolton, who had overseen the completion of Henry VII's chapel at Westminster Abbey, and who had since been employed by Wolsey in charge of building work at Hampton Court.[21] Henry was clearly happy to trust the architectural preferences of his father and his new cardinal, as being representative of the most modern trends.

It was at Beaulieu in the autumn of 1519 that the king welcomed the queen and the French hostages to a splendid banquet. The French hostages were four members of the French court who were in residence at the English court as guarantee of Francis I's promise to pay 600,000 crowns for the return of Tournai. Their presence guaranteed a display of courtly magnificence. The banquet at Beaulieu was the culmination of a lengthy summer progress where the court had been entertained by a succession of the nobility and gentry, including the Duke of Buckingham, who may have spent up to £1,500 in his attempt to provide worthy hospitality.[22] The queen had also entertained in her own right at her manor of Havering-atte-Bower in Essex, before bringing the French to Beaulieu. Henry was happy to have his courtiers play at the politics of ostentation too, but it was understood that the most magnificent court occasions had to be under his own roof; thus the banquet at Beaulieu was the climax of the summer's activities.

The most outspoken statement of Henry's pretensions during these years, however, was to be a temporary construction in northern France. After the brief and rather unconvincing attempt to secure the Empire in 1519, the preparations began to intensify for the more established plan of a meeting between Henry and Francis I. The best guarantee of any royal policy, as we have seen, was always the king's own physical presence, and it follows, therefore, that in the wake of the Treaty of London there was much effort devoted to bringing Henry and Francis together. The meeting was initially planned for 1519, but postponed. After this deferment, Henry expressed his dismay and gallantly promised not to shave until the meeting had been accomplished, a touching vow which Francis seconded. Katherine of Aragon protested, however, not liking her husband bearded, and after it was agreed that the love between the two kings lay in their hearts rather than their beards, the promise was amended.[23] This individual touch shows just how much international treaties had to be cast in terms of personal friendships, however insincerely; it also perhaps shows how important Katherine still was in Henry's life at this time. The growing public affection between the two kings roused Charles I of Spain, who from 1519 was also Charles V, Holy Roman Emperor, also to seek a meeting with Henry. Such face-to-face encounters could give a degree of strength to an alliance which to the modern viewpoint seems disproportionate.

Charles V was able to beat his rival and was first to meet with Henry, landing at Dover in May 1520. He only just managed to squeeze in his visit before the king's departure for France, which Henry delayed as long as possible in hopes of Charles's arrival. Wolsey went out to meet the emperor in his boat as he headed for shore, and Henry hurried to Dover when news came of his arrival. When the king reached Dover Castle in the early hours of the morning he rushed straight to meet this most important visitor. As the chronicler recorded it:

> the Emperor hearing the king to be come, came out of his chamber to meet with the king, and so met with him on the stairs ere he could come up, where each embraced other right lovingly: then the king brought the Emperor to his chamber, whereas their communing was of gladness.[24]

This informality, with the two kings hugging on the stairs to the bedroom, was a more telling endorsement of the union than any formal reception could provide. Henry might use pomp and magnificence to their utmost, but to treat Charles in this way was to proclaim the emperor to be part of the family, and that was more important than anything. On the following day there was a formal and splendid reception at Canterbury with the queen, who really was family since Charles was her nephew. The ratio of dining, dancing and display to what the modern mind might class as actual 'business' is instructive; one afternoon was spent in political discussion, but the rest of the three days was devoted to celebration. It is important to remember that the spectacle of Henry riding, dining and talking with the emperor was of equal importance to any cabinet discussion when it came to securing the alliance, and the mutual credit of both rulers.

As Charles V departed, so too Henry made ready to leave for France, and the long-awaited meeting with Francis I. The quite extraordinary levels of preparation and expense involved in this demonstrate the huge significance of this Anglo-French summit, as well as testifying to Wolsey's remarkable organisational ability. Over 5,000 people went with Henry into France, including most of the higher nobility and much of the royal court. The richest jewels, the costliest clothes, the most imposing suits of armour and an extraordinary quantity of food and drink all contributed to an event which made contemporaries marvel. A temporary palace had been built outside Calais, in English territory, to house the English court. Hall's chronicle recorded that 'This palace was set on stages by great cunning and sumptuous work', before going on to list in great and admiring detail the workmanship and rich decoration of the palace, the pageantry, ceremony and display of over two weeks' festivities.[25] The resourceful John Rastell, back from his time in Ireland, was brought in to decorate the roof of the royal pavilion. The French court was housed at Ardres, just inside French territory. The valley between the two, carefully reshaped so neither side should seem to have the geographical advantage, was the arena for equally stylised displays of affection and strength by the two kings, and for ostentatious display by the two bodies of nobility and courtiers.

The famous picture which records this historic event, here seen as a later engraving (Plate 3), shows both palaces – the English one in the foreground at the right, the French one beyond the river. Prominence is given to Henry VIII's arrival in procession at the front left, but also to the fabulous fountains which 'ran to all people plenteously with red, white, and claret wine'. It also shows the tiltyard in the far right-hand corner, for what is often forgotten is that the 'field' referred to in the 'Field of the Cloth of Gold' was of course a jousting field, where the two kings jousted together, not against one another, but as 'brethren in arms'. This explosion of pageantry and splendour was the apotheosis of Henry VIII's love of the tournament, a resounding celebration of that curiously symbolic, restrained, enthusiastic violence by which Renaissance kings declared their personal and dynastic strengths, kept in training for war, and showed their mettle to both supporters and potential enemies. Notably enough, the first encounter between the kings took place on 7 June, which was Corpus Christi day, a church feast day in honour of the holy Sacrament of the Altar, which was in itself the most revered symbol of unity.

In the religious imagination of the time, just as many grains of wheat came together to make bread, and many grapes were pressed to make wine, so the people came together at the moment of consecration, achieving a mystical union with Christ, the angels and saints, the living and the dead, in a miraculous moment of unity. On this day, Hall recorded, 'the king of England showed himself ... in beauty and personage, the most goodliest Prince that ever reigned over the Realm of England', clad in rich fabrics and jewels.[26] On the last day the tiltyard was transformed into a chapel, the viewing galleries became pews, Wolsey 'sang an high and solemn mass', and Richard Pace preached a sermon on peace, as he had done nearly two years before at the signing of the Treaty of London. The stage-management behind the Field of the Cloth of Gold was well-nigh perfect.

Hall's *Chronicle,* which recounted all these details with so much awe, also recorded the level of tension in the English camp, the doubts, the anxieties about being outnumbered by the French, all the latent hostility and distrust which bore witness to the long years of rivalry and conflict between the two nations. The tense moment which came when Francis threw Henry during a wrestling match was swiftly covered up by every side insisting how evenly the kings were matched. The moment of their first encounter had seen the kings face one another across the artificial valley, their followers drawn up in what might as well have been battle array, only for Henry and Francis to ride towards one another and embrace. These details underscore the achievement of this meeting, not an empty parade of amity, but an energetic attempt to achieve all the same ends of glory and security as warfare but without leaving many thousands dead and maimed. Erasmus had urged his readers:

> if you have ever seen towns in ruins, villages destroyed, churches burnt, and farmland abandoned and have found it a pitiable spectacle, as indeed it is, reflect that all this is the consequence of war.

And he had addressed both Francis and Henry by name as he called the princes of his own time to account:

> The majority of the common people loathe war and pray for peace; only a handful of individuals, whose evil joys depend on general misery, desire war. Whether it is right or not for their wickedness to prevail over the will of all honest men is for you yourselves to judge.[27]

Within three years the two nations would again be at war, but before we dismiss the Field of the Cloth of Gold as an entirely empty charade in an enduringly brutal age, we might muse on the continuing relevance of these words by Erasmus, whom Henry VIII counted as his friend, and observe the frequency with which modern states espouse the cause of peace and yet so frequently find themselves at war.

HERESY AND TREASON

Henry always sought to be pre-eminent in the world of ideas as well as in feats of arms. He also continually sought the approval of the Church in his early years as king, seeing this as the best way to cement his own control over the Church in England. A unique and particularly exciting possibility to prove himself as the loyal son of the Papacy arose in the years after 1517 as the events unfolded in Saxony, and other parts of the Empire, which would one day be described as the beginnings of the Protestant Reformation. In 1517 the Augustinian friar and humanist scholar Martin Luther had raised ninety-five objections to the practice of selling indulgences, and his ideas had caused an unprecedented popular reaction. Official condemnation and scholarly opposition had led him to refine and develop his ideas to the point where in 1520 he attacked the doctrine of the seven sacraments, the Catholic understanding of the process of salvation, and the worldly and spiritual authority of the papacy. The European response to these events was complex, volatile and resonated through all layers of society. Henry VIII's response was outraged, articulate, theologically intelligent and politically shrewd. He did what no English king had ever done before; he published a book, *Assertio Septem Sacramentorum*, or 'In defence of the seven sacraments', in 1521.

Henry's book does not seem to have been entirely his own work. As was second nature to him, it seems likely that he delegated the detailed work to others while the broad conception of the work remained his own. The book has not been hailed as possessing any great literary or theological merit, but it was a short, vigorous, capable response to Luther, and most importantly, it had a divinely appointed king as author. In keeping with his role as devout and godly prince, Henry dedicated the work to Leo X, and in keeping with his usual flair for political theatre, he marked its completion with a solemn mass at St Paul's, when Luther's works were publicly burned and John Fisher delivered a sermon against heresy. Luther had acknowledged the resemblance between his own ideas and those of the Bohemian heretic Jan Hus, who had contributed to the growth of the Lollard heresy in England a century before. Now Henry VIII proclaimed his determination to stamp out Lutheranism just as Henry V had stamped out Lollardy. The reward for his labours was the papal title for which he had been angling since 1512. Leo X was finally prevailed upon to draw up a shortlist, and Henry chose *Fidei Defensor*. This title, initially granted to him alone, he was to enshrine as a perpetual title by statute law in 1543, ten years after rejecting the papal authority which had granted it, and by strange historical accident it remains a royal title to this day, proclaimed on every coin by our now firmly Protestant royal dynasty.[28]

Henry's book was hugely popular throughout Europe and translated into several languages. Two German editions were published the very next year, prompting Luther's response. At this point Henry preserved a dignified distance from the theological fray, and it was John Fisher and Thomas More who replied to Luther's venomous response, whilst on the continent Luther's former disputant John Eck wrote a defence of the king's book. The fact that Henry's first foray into theological debate was so eye-catching and so successful probably helped fashion his existing interest in theology and church politics into an even more important part of his kingly identity. Here too the stage was being set for the future.

At the same time as Henry was battling with Luther on paper, he was also battling with murkier possibilities that threatened him much closer to home. Some time in 1519 or 1520 he wrote Wolsey a letter, commanding him to keep watch on a clutch of the highest nobility, the dukes of Suffolk and Buckingham, the earls of Northumberland, Derby and Wiltshire, 'and on other which you think suspect to see what they do with this news'.[29] We do not know what the 'news' was, but it is clear that Henry was harbouring suspicions of even Charles Brandon, the Duke of Suffolk, his former comrade-in-arms and now brother-in-law.

Since Suffolk's marriage brought him one step closer to the throne, and made his children potential heirs, it is perhaps inevitable that his new closeness to Henry brought attendant dangers. It cannot have helped that Suffolk's wife, Henry's sister, had produced three healthy children since their marriage in 1515, including a son, perhaps inauspiciously named Henry.[30]

It is not clear whether there is any connection between this episode and later developments, but certainly the king's misgivings were soon to find some concrete grounds for anxiety in the activities of the Duke of Buckingham. On several occasions and in several different contexts, Buckingham was found to have discussed, even boasted about, his chances of taking the throne. One source of concern was his connection with a Carthusian prior who specialised in prophesy, and who had predicted his future kingship on several occasions over the years. He had also talked of murdering Henry VIII. In a modern context these scraps of gossip do not, perhaps, sound very convincing, and some commentators have concluded that Buckingham was the unfortunate victim of Wolsey's plot to oust him. He definitely disliked Wolsey, and made it clear that he would execute him once he became king. But there is evidence to suggest that this information was not invented, and indeed not even sought by Wolsey, but the genuine testament of Buckingham's disaffected associates. Futhermore, it is important to understand that in the world of 1521, this kind of evidence was utterly damning.

Buckingham's trial and execution can only be understood in the context of his proud and awkward character. It did not help his case that he was an old-fashioned model of a magnate, immensely rich, propertied, and arrogant, with a fierce sense of his own breeding and importance, and a clutch of Yorkist relations. His mother was sister to Edward IV's queen and his paternal line descended from Edward III. Yet other Yorkists, other magnates, even other dukes, managed to serve Henry peaceably enough without arousing his suspicions, let alone providing grounds for accusations of treason. Buckingham's claim to the throne was probably about as good as Henry's own claim, and that would always give pause for thought. The chief problem was, however, that Buckingham's loyalty does seem to have been questionable. This was probably exacerbated by his ostentatious wealth, and his sense of his own nobility. He stood out in Hall's description of the meeting with the Emperor in 1513; all the English noblemen were splendidly arrayed:

but in especial the duke of Buckingham, he was in purple satin, his apparel and his bard [i.e. his horse's trappings] full of antelopes and swans of fine gold bullion and full of spangles and little bells of gold marvelous costly and pleasant to behold.[31]

The swans and the antelopes both made reference to his royal ancestry; it probably did him no good to stand out in this way. The story at the root of his quarrel with Wolsey is that he was once outraged to see Wolsey wash his hands in the bowl of water just used by the king; furious at this presumption by someone so lowly in origin, he seized the bowl and emptied it over Wolsey's feet. He was known for such arrogance and for being wilful and vengeful. Entertaining the king lavishly at Penshurst Place, building a huge castle on his estate at Thornbury, insisting that his family had a hereditary right to the office of Great Constable of England and bringing his case to law – all these underlined his pride and consciousness of his own heritage. But there is no sign that he was in trouble much before 1521; he attended at court when required, participated grandly in the Field of the Cloth of Gold. Far from conspiring against him, Wolsey seems to have warned him to be careful how he behaved towards the king.[32] The evidence suggests that he was probably guilty, not of actively conspiring against Henry – this was never alleged – but certainly of holding the Tudors in comparatively low esteem and thinking that he should rule in their stead. His fate was sealed by his own folly.

We might draw several conclusions from examining Buckingham's fall, but on the whole it chiefly seems significant as providing an exception to the rule. In general, Henry had good relations with the higher nobility, at least in the first twenty years of his reign, and this applied even to those of Yorkist blood. Buckingham had, however, proved only lukewarm in his willingness to participate in the affairs of Henry's regime, and clearly had been unpersuaded by Henry's magnificence. There is little evidence to suggest that there was any animosity between him and Wolsey. Like most of the nobility, he was on a civil and business-like footing with the cardinal, seeking his intercession with the king, and apparently respecting his office. It should be noted that many of Henry VIII's other bishops were of lowly or indifferent origin; 92 per cent were non-noble, with nearly 50 per cent coming from the yeomanry.[33] It was well established that clerical office could raise men high above the level of their birth, but this does not seem to have been a major problem, perhaps because they could have no legitimate offspring to inherit after them; several nobles sent their children to be trained in Wolsey's household, for example, which was treating him like a fellow member of the nobility. It was Buckingham's treasonous ambition which had caused his downfall, and in this too he seems an exception. Henry VIII faced few real challenges to his kingship, and compared with the constant anxiety about pretenders to the throne which had dogged his father, his success seems striking. Buckingham was the sole reminder of the wayward magnates of the previous century. For most of his subjects, Henry VIII's constant attempts to impress and convince worked quite well.

THE RETURN TO WAR

In 1521 came the first serious trial of the Treaty of London. It is notable that Henry had upheld the spirit of the treaty and refused a series of requests from a less scrupulous Charles V to enter in to some kind of alliance against the French.[34] As relations between France and the Empire became more acrimonious, Wolsey, with Henry's full support, urged temperance, moderation, restraint. In May a French attack on the Empire, after a series of border incidents, led Charles V to appeal to Henry VIII for support. Henry's natural sympathies seem to have been with the emperor, which made good strategic sense. England's economic ties to the Netherlands were of crucial importance, whilst anyone attempting to rule both Spain and the Low Countries needed to guarantee a friendly power on at least one side of the Channel, if communications were to stay open. We need to remember that at this time travel by sea was swift and reliable compared with travel by land, and the union of the Habsburg lands with Spain in 1519 meant that an alliance with England was to remain of central importance for much of the century. Historically, too, English enmity with France was well established, and not to be overturned by just a few years of energetic pro-French diplomacy by Henry.

Yet Henry did his best to uphold the Treaty of London. Backed by his Council, he proposed that England attempt mediation, and Wolsey was despatched accordingly. It is true that the end result of this prolonged visit to the continent was the failure of the Treaty, since ultimately Wolsey concluded a pact with Charles V at Bruges, and war with France followed. But the events of 1521 should not be dismissed as a cynical ploy to cloak preparations for war with an hypocritical attempt at peace-making. Wolsey was sent on this mission with papers empowering him to bring about a wide range of possible outcomes, from peace between France and the Empire, to closer amity with France, to a range of different pacts and alliances with the Empire.[35] He was also sent with a magnificent entourage and a vast array of talent in terms of his diplomatic team, which included Thomas More, Cuthbert Tunstall and Sir Thomas Boleyn. When Wolsey made his entrance into the city of Bruges to meet with the emperor it was with around 1,000 horsemen, and he maintained his state there with great splendour. He also seems to have done his level best to procure peace, while restraining by letter Henry's emerging enthusiasm for sending military aid to Charles V sooner rather than later. Moreover, although in the end he had no choice but to agree an alliance with the Empire, he bought England time.

The joint invasion of France – if French hostilities continued – was not to take place for nearly two years, in May 1523. Wolsey battled on with negotiations for months, returning exhausted in November, having spent a small fortune on the mission, never quite giving up hope. Right to the end, the English continued to talk of peace. But war had already broken out in Italy, and in May 1522 Charles V arrived in England to cement the Treaty of Bruges. England had maintained peace with France for eight years, but this had now to end. A 'Great Enterprise' against France was mooted, although it was agreed that they should stall until 1524 to give time to prepare for the assault.

So war began gradually, with some action in 1523, but more meditated for a year hence. In time, the 'Great Enterprise' was postponed again, talked of this time for 1525. And in this conflict, the king was not to lead his army into the field, probably because it was not the incarnation of all his hopes, as in 1513, but the consequence of a Habsburg initiative into which he had been brought rather reluctantly. He gave the Earl of Surrey command, but apart from some destructive forays into Brittany and the region around Calais, little was achieved in 1522 before it was time to go home again for the winter. There was also trouble with Scotland to divert England's attention northwards. Then the antagonism of the Duke of Bourbon, determined to keep his lands from being swallowed up by the French throne, offered new hope for the anti-French alliance. A more convincing alliance of Charles V, Henry VIII, the Duke of Bourbon, the Swiss and the Venetians was lined up, and Henry talked of making Bourbon acknowledge him as the rightful King of France. Old memories and ambitions were beginning to stir again.

In 1523, then, ten years after the first assault on France, the second was launched, with the Duke of Suffolk leading an army of about 10,000 men across the Channel. The immediate aim was the capture of Boulogne, but Wolsey urged Henry to aim for Paris instead, and astoundingly, Suffolk's army got within fifty miles. By then, however, it was October, and the army was suffering acutely from cold, hunger, disease, the desertion of the imperial troops and the failures of its allies on other fronts. The army retreated back to Flanders. Henry was at first outraged, then began again to plan. But his objectives were continually shifting in line with the fluctuating fortunes of his allies. As Bourbon's hopes increased, so too did Henry's optimism, although it did not match the enthusiasm of Richard Pace, writing from Bourbon's camp and much impressed by his potential. Then Bourbon's fortune deserted him, and the secret peace talks which had been going on with the French seemed like a better bet.

International relations at this time were a fiendishly complicated blend of different elements, competing strategies and interests, with all plans contingent on loyalties that might easily turn treacherous, and military success which could evaporate overnight. In the early 1520s England on the whole inclined towards the Habsburgs, but was always open to other possibilities. The delicate balance of power could be decisively and rapidly altered by events. In February 1525, for example, outside the walls of the city of Pavia, the French suffered a devastating defeat at the hands of the imperial troops. Francis I was held prisoner. Henry and Wolsey had been contemplating a rapprochement with France, but after such a disastrous defeat this could only be folly. The Habsburg alliance once more appeared to be the way forward. Henry reportedly told the messenger who brought him the news that he was like the Archangel Gabriel at the Annunciation, bringing news of Christ, which if it is true, shows the alarming confusion of theological and military triumphalism in the king's mind. Moreover, the last Yorkist claimant, Richard de la Pole, had been killed. Henry ordered bonfires and *Te Deum* to be sung, and Wolsey celebrated a Mass of thanksgiving at St Paul's. The 'Great Enterprise' could now go forward, clearly blessed by God, and preparations for an invasion of France were once more under way. This time Henry was to lead his army again, and once more the crown of France was his objective.

The undertaking might have been blessed by God, in Henry's eyes, but his subjects were to take a more jaundiced view. Henry requested an 'amicable grant' of the money needed for the campaign. Despite its soothing title, this was a considerable financial exaction that he was demanding: clerics were to pay a third of their income if it was more than £10, a quarter if it was less; the laity were to pay a sixth of their income.[36] Taxation had been heavy in recent years and rebellion threatened. Popular enthusiasm for the war was minimal and the tactics of the commissioners trying to raise the money were of questionable legality. Concessions were made, but they differed according to area. An uprising threatened in Suffolk, and there were rumours elsewhere. Meanwhile Charles V was sounding far from enthusiastic about a possible invasion of France. Henry performed a masterly reversal, announcing to a great council 'that his mind was never, to ask any thing of his commons, whiche might sound to his dishonour, or to the breach of his laws'.[37] The demands for money were rescinded, whilst the king declared that he had had no knowledge of the level of the exactions. A touching scene was enacted where Wolsey begged the king to rescind it, and the general impression was given that Wolsey was to blame.

This episode is of singular importance in showing where the limits of royal authority lay. Popular opinion mattered far more than we might imagine. Royal exactions were usually accepted, but there had to be a reason for them, and that reason had to be convincing. That is not to say that popular reaction was organised on an entirely logical basis: the protesters in Suffolk were by and large too poor to feel the burden of the amicable grant directly, but were using it as a focus for their anxieties about the cloth trade, which was suffering at the time. Resistance in other places was more intelligent, however.

Hall, whose knowledge of London affairs was usually good, reports an encounter between the mayor and aldermen of the city and Cardinal Wolsey, after the grant had been commuted to a 'benevolence'. The city fathers objected that there was a law against such a practice from the time of Richard III, also that 'some persons comming before your grace, may for fear grant that, that all days of their life they shall repent, and some to win your favour, will grant more than they be able to pay of their own.' And when Wolsey protested his amazement that they should appeal to the acts of Richard III, a usurper and murderer, the reply came that there were good acts made during his reign 'not by him only, but by the consent of the body of the whole Realm, which is the parliament'.[38] Perhaps particularly among the wealthier and more educated layers of society there was knowledge of the law and a determination to see it upheld, although it is also possible that Hall himself was interpreting the affair in this way with hindsight. There was also an expectation that a king divinely appointed should rule in a manner at least roughly consistent with morality and justice. When his government appeared to be behaving badly, Henry had to distance himself from their proceedings, and assume the mantle of magnanimous superiority, whilst the blame fell on his closest servants. Henry certainly knew all about the amicable grant, and Wolsey was aware of this, but for the sake of Henry's kingship appearing untainted, they played out their little drama of penance and forgiveness, whilst backing down from their unreasonable fiscal demands.

There were two ways of responding to Charles V's victory at Pavia, and the Habsburg superiority in Europe which it confirmed. Henry's initial impulse seems to have been to ride upon his ally's success and participate in the dismemberment of French territory. But it was not just Charles V's reluctance and the failure of the amicable grant which made this untenable. Pavia had made Charles V look sufficiently powerful to render his former allies uncomfortable. He had achieved his success without any major English input, so it was unlikely that the English alliance would henceforth mean enough to the Empire for Charles to respect English interests. He was beginning to look too powerful, which made the thought of an alliance with France perhaps more tempting in the long run. It was also the case that by 1525 Henry's marriage to Katherine of Aragon had ceased to have any practical value, as she was clearly not going to bear him any more children. That particular Habsburg link had proved infertile, and if Henry were to marry again, a range of alliances lay open to him, including one with a French princess. Meanwhile Charles V had reneged on his solemn vow to marry Princess Mary and was now courting a Portuguese princess. In August 1525 a treaty was signed at Wolsey's residence of the More (subsequently Moor Park near Rickmansworth) which ended the war with France which had been limping on since 1522.

The alliance with France which was slowly constructed from 1525 onwards was to form the basis of English foreign policy for the next ten years. It is usually credited to Wolsey's inspiration, but it is clear that it had Henry's wholehearted sanction. Wolsey was particularly adept at diplomacy; he was also committed to the cause of European peace, to which Charles V now seemed to be the chief menace. These interests were always secondary, however, to his fundamental task of preserving the king's reputation and estate, and he pursued the French alliance because it was what Henry wanted. This policy was also to pay dividends as Henry became increasingly antagonistic towards the papacy, for France was traditionally critical of papal pretensions and inclined to preserve its distance from Rome. Wolsey seems to have wanted a French wife for Henry to replace Katherine, where in fact the king became increasingly enamoured of Anne Boleyn, but since Anne had been educated in France and had friends in the French court the inclination towards the French was still fostered, though not as Wolsey had envisaged. The crucial years of 1526 to 1527 seem to be when Henry fell in love with Anne, and finally decided to end his marriage to Katherine. It was in these self-same years that a new and weighty alliance with France was forged which would keep England and France at peace until 1543; in terms of sixteenth-century diplomacy, almost a lifetime.

Informal steps towards peace with France had been under way since 1524, with Wolsey acting for Henry VIII in negotiations fostered by Francis I's mother, Louise of Savoy. Progress had been halted after Pavia, when it seemed the 'Great Enterprise' might resume, but began again in the summer of 1525, when by the Treaty of the More Henry agreed to work for Francis I's release from captivity and France undertook to pay England 100,000 écus a year for the next twenty years. In May 1526 the Holy League of Cognac was signed between France, the papacy, Venice, Florence and Milan, and Henry agreed to be 'Protector' of this league, while in August 1526 the Treaty of Hampton Court bound England and France not to treat independently with the Empire. The following spring the Treaty of Westminster was signed, and celebrated with great magnificence at Greenwich. Then in August Wolsey went, also with much splendour, on an embassy to Francis I and signed the Treaty of Amiens. By this stage, Henry's desire to annul his first marriage was at the centre of policy considerations, and it was imperative that the papacy be kept close to the French who might support Henry rather than to the Habsburgs who would inevitably oppose his attempt to reject his Spanish wife.

The Treaty of Westminster in 1527 was another embodiment of the humanist ideals of peace-making which had first found expression in the Treaty of London. It envisaged that if war broke out between the Empire and the new Anglo-French axis, then Princess Mary would marry Francis I's son, the Duke of Orleans, and Francis I would marry Charles V's sister Eleanor.

The celebrations of this treaty were fabulous.[39] The tiltyard at Greenwich which had been one of the first of Henry's building projects was further adorned with a new banqueting house, richly decorated with heraldic devices and classical imagery. Hall describes it in glowing terms, particularly the triumphal arches at the rear of the hall, 'upon three Antique pillars all of gold burnished swagged and graven full of Gargoyles and Serpents' whilst the splendour of the meal actually defeated him. 'The whole supper was served in vessel of gold: to rehearse the fare, the strangeness of dishes, with devices of beasts and fowls it were too long, wherefore I will let pass over the supper with songs and minstrelsy.' There was also a 'disguising house' for masques, laid out like an amphitheatre, with a painted ceiling showing the planets and the signs of the zodiac, the work of Holbein and the king's astronomer. Statues of Hercules, Scipio, Julius, Pompey 'and such other conquerors' set the tone. The speeches and masques which followed were full of praise for the peace and the peacemakers, and contained various elaborate displays, including one where Princess Mary came out of a cave with seven ladies, 'all apparelled after the roman fashion in rich cloth of gold of tissue and Crimson tinsel bendy and their hairs wrapped in cauls of gold with bonnets of Crimson velvet on their heads, set full of pearl and stone', which ladies paired up with other masked figures and 'danced lustily about the place'.[40] The imagery and allegory might at times have proved puzzling, and indeed the prominent display of a picture of Henry's siege of Thérouanne was perhaps an odd choice – Hall says they were more pleased by the skill of the picture than by the remembrance of the event – but the general effect was unmistakeable. Henry's magnificence and unassailable status as a leading Renaissance prince were here loudly proclaimed.

A week after the Treaty of Westminster was signed, Charles V's troops sacked Rome. This was a shocking and devastating development; a terrible affront to the papacy and an insult to the Church, but also an alarming confirmation of Charles V's dominance in Italy. The importance of the Anglo-French alliance increased accordingly, and Henry agreed to help fund the French army that was setting off for Italy. Wolsey left for France, with a grand entourage, many of whose faces still look back at us from the portraits sketched by Holbein. The Treaty of Amiens, agreed in August, ensured that the marriage of Mary and the Duke of Orleans would go ahead, and France and England agreed not to participate in any General Council while the Pope was still Charles V's prisoner. This was an acknowledgement of the problems Charles was facing with Lutheranism in the Empire, which he hoped might be solved by a General Council. These two treaties were followed in November 1527 by a sumptuous display of chivalry as Henry was invested with the Order of St Michel whilst across the Channel in Paris Francis I was given the Order of the Garter.[41]

FAMILY MATTERS

In the first two decades of his reign, Henry VIII's own performance as king was an impressive one, on almost all counts but one. Nearly twenty years after his accession and marriage, he still had no male heir. Princess Mary, born in 1516, was being carefully groomed for high office by her mother, who saw no difficulty with the idea of a queen regnant, since her own mother – the legendary Queen Isabella – had ruled Castile in her own right, with strength and success. Katherine directed her efforts towards preparing her daughter to rule. Enormous care was taken over the appointment of Mary's household and over her education. To begin with her lady mistress was Lady Bryan, who was to take charge of the nursery for Princess Elizabeth and Prince Edward in due course. When Mary was about 3, the Countess of Salisbury was given this office, a noblewoman of impeccable if Yorkist pedigree, and immense learning. The countess's chaplain, Gentian Hervetus, was responsible for publishing translations of learned and pious works, including a sermon by Erasmus. When Mary was a little older, Katherine commissioned Juan Luis Vives, probably the greatest Spanish humanist of his age, to draw up a plan for her education. Vives came to England to prepare what he probably saw as its future monarch for the business of ruling; at the same time he took the post of reader in rhetoric at Oxford.

In many ways this kind of education was a radical innovation. Thomas More had educated his three daughters according to the best humanist models; one of them had even published a translation of Erasmus's *Treatise on the Paternoster*. When she was grown up, Mary too would have a translation of Erasmus's *Paraphrase on the Gospel of John* published. Vives drew up a list of works she should study, with heavy emphasis on the Bible, including readings from the New Testament night and morning, also St Cyprian, St Augustine and St Jerome, arguably the architects of the early Christian church, and important authors such as Boethius, Cicero and Plato. More's *Utopia* was also included. He emphasised, however, that the woman educated according to this plan should turn out as modest, biddable and obedient as any other. In a sense this kind of education, which became standard for Tudor royal women, promised an extraordinary intellectual freedom, but Vives was careful to insist that there would be no breaking of social convention involved. Princess Mary might still make a dutiful and submissive wife, as her mother had.

The Spanish example was not calculated to inspire widely, however. The English had no such model of fierce queenship to inspire, and Mary was viewed by most of her father's subjects as a potential bride for an important European ruler – indeed she was betrothed to nearly every one available – but not as a potential ruler. Once a king ceased to be young, the strength of his regime in part always depended on whether he had secured the succession. Thus the repeated bids for greater glory in these years were accompanied by sporadic reminders of Henry's potential insecurity. None of these were as poignant and as painful as the deaths of his children. Indeed, other causes of anxiety, such as Buckingham's alleged treachery, could all be traced back to this single source of unease.

Katherine's failure to produce the longed-for heir was all the more frustrating in that she was so often pregnant; at least seven pregnancies continued long enough to be reliably witnessed by courtiers and ambassadors. Their failures also coincided with other reversals often enough to drive home the point that Henry was peculiarly unlucky when it came to having children. The peace with France in 1514 had given rise to rumours that Henry might repudiate his barren Spanish wife. Katherine was seen to be visibly pregnant about the same time, but at just this point when the diplomatic advantages of a Spanish queen were evaporating, she gave birth prematurely to a dead child 'through grief, as it is said, for the misunderstanding between her father and her husband'.[42] After Mary's birth in 1516 Katherine was not pregnant again until two years later; the rate of her conceptions was slowing down. As we have seen, the high hopes which Henry entertained of this pregnancy were dashed. Katherine would not conceive again. Although Henry had no way of knowing this, his hopes of his queen were fading, and it was just at this point that another arrival compounded his disquiet.

In 1519, Henry's mistress Elizabeth Blount – or Bessie Blount, as she was called – gave birth to a baby boy. He was named Henry Fitzroy, and raised with as much care as if he was a legitimate prince. After ten years of marriage, the king's ability to sire healthy male children had been confirmed, which focused Henry's anxieties even more on Katherine's inadequacies. The day after the child's sixth birthday, he was made Earl of Nottingham and Duke of Richmond and Somerset. It was especially telling that Henry had given him the title of Richmond which had been carried by Henry VII before his accession to the throne. Moreover he was immediately despatched north, as lieutenant-general north of the Trent and warden-general of the Marches. This was to give Fitzroy the same symbolic importance as a legitimate prince; royal children were often used in this way to secure the troublesome borders of the realm. Henry's older brother Prince Arthur had been sent to Ludlow as Prince of Wales, and at the same time as the new Duke of Richmond was given his appointment, Princess Mary was sent to head the Council in the Marches of Wales. It was an indication of Henry's desperation, that he should apparently be grooming his bastard for the throne. Katherine understood the implications and was reportedly extremely upset: three of her ladies were banished from court for supporting her. These developments of 1525 indicate some of the anguish Henry must have been feeling about the succession. Buckingham's fall too might not have been so dramatic had the king felt at ease about the future of his dynasty. 1525 was the year that Katherine turned 40 – Henry was still only 34 – and there remained little hope of a legitimate male heir.

It was at this point in Henry's reign that he fell in love. We cannot be sure of the exact date, but it seems probable that by 1526 he was emotionally involved with Anne Boleyn, and by 1527 he obviously envisaged her as his future wife, because it was in August of that year that he sought papal dispensation for this eventuality. Seventeen of the king's love letters survive, ironically enough in the Vatican, but they are undated. At first they suggest no more than the usual type of courtly flirtation. Then Henry's tone becomes more serious, and also uncertain, 'not being assured either of failure or of finding place in your heart and grounded affection'. They had been involved in at least some sense for over a year by the time he wrote to her, and made an astounding forthright avowal:

> If it shall please you to do me the office of a true, loyal mistress and friend and to give yourself up, body and soul, to me who will be and have been your loyal servant (if by your severity you do not forbid me), I promise you that not only shall the name be given you, but that also I will take you for my only mistress, rejecting from thought and affection all others save yourself, to serve you only.

Anne's biographer has suggested that what Henry was offering was the post of 'official mistress'.[43] It appears that Anne refused, and underlined her refusal by staying away from court. Whether she did not relish the idea of being the king's mistress, only to be eventually cast aside as her sister was, or whether she hoped to marry somebody else, we cannot know. It seems unlikely, however, that she was playing a calculating game that aimed to make her queen. With the sole recent exception of Edward IV, kings did not marry their subjects. Anne probably thought that the best she could hope for was to follow the path of her sister, who had been Henry's mistress, and it was not an inspiring possibility. Her refusal, however, made Henry begin to appreciate the possibilities. His marriage to Katherine was now worthless. If she were to be replaced, then perhaps she could be replaced by this woman who had so beguiled him, and who continued to elude him.

Shakespeare's Anne Boleyn was a pure and high-minded maiden taken entirely by surprise at the king's interest in her, and importantly, not aware of this interest until after his marriage with Katherine had already foundered. It was necessary that Elizabeth I's mother should be painted in the most sympathetic way possible, but the attempt at white-wash is painfully obvious. Other commentators were less indulgent. Nicholas Sanders, who wrote a Catholic history of the break with Rome, portrayed her as promiscuous, ambitious and scheming:

> At fifteen she sinned first with her father's butler, and then with his chaplain, and forthwith was sent to France. ... Soon afterwards she appeared at the French court, where she was called the English mare, because of her

shameless behaviour; and then the royal mule, when she became acquainted with the king of France.[44]

Sanders also described her following not only her sister, but also her mother, into the king's bed. The appealing story that when Henry VIII was confronted with this rumour he reportedly answered rather guile-lessly, 'Never with the mother', was almost certainly invented by the man who boasted of it.[45] Yet the essentials of this story were correct.

The trouble with trying to disentangle any truth about Anne Boleyn is that she, like Wolsey, was blamed for some of Henry's most unpopular policies, then and since. Henry's reasons for seeing his marriage to Katherine as invalid were complex and most people's opinion was little touched by them, being straightforwardly repulsed by his attempt to put away his faithful, pious, gracious and popular queen of nearly twenty years' standing. It was also frightening how deeply Henry was devoted to Anne. People in love often act wildly out of character, and Henry's rejection of formerly favoured men who had served him loyally, most notably Thomas Wolsey and Thomas More, underlined how this king-in-love was perilously unpredictable. The hours spent dancing attendance on Anne, lavishing her with gifts and titles, designing palaces to house her, all undermined the solemn dignity of Henry's kingship. To many, Anne made Henry look a fool. And in retrospect, to many with strong Catholic loyalties, Anne was the woman for whom Henry deserted the Catholic Church, leading to the destruction of Catholic England, and she was and sometimes still is reviled as a dangerously free-thinking, sexually threatening, selfish and ruthless marriage-wrecker.

This tangle of prejudices has led to some obvious mistakes. She is often portrayed as a woman of fairly lowly origin, since Tudor society liked to revile people by sneering at them as social climbers. In fact she was firmly rooted in the higher nobility of the realm; her mother was daughter to one duke of Norfolk and sister to another, and the dukes of Norfolk were the foremost magnates of the time. Her father was only slightly less exalted, a descendant of the Butler earls of Ormonde, and he earned himself an important place at court long before his daughters had come to the king's attention, and indeed before Henry VIII himself had come to the throne, since he first rose to prominence under Henry VII. She is portrayed as a Protestant, when the truth is much more nuanced and interesting. She was clearly interested in the ideas of religious reform current at the time, but more as an Erasmian humanist than an early Protestant, reflecting the ideas that were in favour at both the French and the English courts.

Anne has also been portrayed as a scheming woman, which in our allegedly enlightened age still rouses a fury of condemnation, withholding her sexual favours until she was guaranteed the throne of England. This traditional view dovetailed neatly with the picture of Henry as someone easily manipulated, and particularly susceptible to sexual attraction. But the idea that Henry could be pushed around in this way is highly unconvincing, and never more so than in the matter of the annulment. It is clear that he was the leading figure in the campaign, that the sense of urgency came first and foremost from the King, and that his passion for Anne, spontaneously conceived, was interwoven as it developed with the rational conviction that she would make a suitable wife. A recent study has even suggested that Henry and Anne may have been lovers at first, around 1526, but that thereafter it was Henry who urged chastity on an initially reluctant Anne until his marital problems were sorted, and they could be properly married.[46] His love letters certainly contain references to sexual restraint. Furthermore, in 1527 he sought a papal dispensation for a future marriage, should his first marriage be successfully annulled. This is clearly a reference to Anne Boleyn, since it describes someone who may have been previously engaged, and with whose sister he had had intercourse. It has been pointed out that it also refers to someone with whom the king had already had intercourse, although this may have been Henry allowing for all possible contingencies, and perhaps hoping to sleep with Anne quite soon.[47] Yet there is good evidence to show that they were not having sexual relations from 1527 until the end of 1532. It would be unlike Henry to subordinate his political objectives to sexual or emotional whim. In any case, the decision to remain chaste and to aim at matrimony could only have been sustained through six long years of campaigning if it had had their mutual agreement.

Henry always had an exalted ideal of marriage and he was convinced from about 1527 onwards that he was rejecting his former offences against divine law and vowing himself to a more Christian future. It was also obvious that his case would have seemed less convincing, both in Rome and at home, if Anne had been pregnant. It seems much more likely that Henry and Anne together took the romantic, high-minded, and prudent approach of deciding to remain chaste until they were married, all the more likely since in 1527 Henry seemed to think that this would soon be achieved. The curious mixture of passion, idealism and political ambition at work here gives some insight into Henry's character.

Anne must have signalled her willingness to be Henry's wife by the summer of 1527, for it was then that he despatched his secretary, William Knight, to Rome, to request papal dispensation for their marriage, in the event of his first marriage being declared invalid. The irony was that Henry's previous relationship with her sister Mary meant the same degree of affinity existed between Henry and Anne as between Henry and Katherine. Henry was not to be daunted by this, however, all the more since his rejection of Katherine was to be based on the literal interpretation of the Bible passage which forbade marriage to a brother's wife. The Bible made no mention of a former mistress's sister. Still, he knew what he was doing was ill-advised. Anne's biographer has noted Henry's reference to 'my so great folly' as 'a highly perceptive remark from a man not given to much self-analysis'.[48] Even more significantly, Henry was keeping this a secret from Wolsey. Indeed, since Knight was to travel via Compiègne, where Wolsey was embroiled in peace negotiations, Henry went to elaborate lengths to conceal the true purpose of his secretary's mission to Rome. Always before, Henry's wishes had been fulfilled, and often elaborated, by Wolsey's skill. The king's desire for an annulment of his marriage to Katherine was known to the cardinal, and was a difficult but entirely understandable request. But Wolsey would not have wanted Henry to behave so irresponsibly as to marry a lady of the court, whose status so clearly fitted her to be nothing more than his mistress. The reason we know this is that Henry acted so covertly; he must have known what Wolsey's response would have been. He must in his heart of hearts have known, too, that what he was doing went against everything he and Wolsey had worked for over almost twenty years. The majesty, grandeur and European reputation they had so carefully constructed was being threatened by an affair based on no obvious consideration of political advantage or prudence, but largely on the king's powerful emotions.

Anne was undoubtedly intelligent, attractive, spirited. Even Nicholas Sanders, who viciously outlined her flaws – sallow face, a projecting tooth, a sixth finger on the right hand, and a large wen under her chin – was unable to avoid admitting that she was 'handsome to look at, with a pretty mouth, amusing in her ways, playing well on the lute, and ... a good dancer'. He also said that she was 'the model and the mirror of those who were at court, for she was always well dressed, and every day made some change in the fashion of her garments'.[49] Most importantly, she was ten years younger than Henry, where Katherine had been six years older, and thus much more likely to bear him children. Still, 27 was hardly the best age, in Tudor eyes: if his sole concern had been fertility, Henry could have chosen a lively teenager, a bride more like Katherine Howard. It is clear that he was genuinely, abjectly and energetically in love with Anne, and it seems probable that she returned this love, particularly when it became clear that it might have an honourable future. Henry in 1526–7 was in his mid-thirties, still handsome and vigorous, majestic and powerful, a seductive combination. Anne was tall and fashionable where Katherine was short and stout; Anne had allure and sophistication after her education in France, but none of Katherine's infuriating foreign peculiarities and loyalties. They both loved music, dancing, display; they were both cultivated, interested in religion and literature; it was unsurprising that they found one another attractive.

By the end of 1527 Henry VIII was contemplating a range of possibilities, all of them demanding the best of his wisdom and leadership. On the continent, the dominance of Charles V in Italy, and his control of the papacy, was a menace against which the new Anglo-French treaty offered only partial reassurance. At home, Henry's desperation concerning the succession was mounting, he was facing the worrying prospect of having to forcibly reject his first wife, and he was emotionally committed to the woman who would replace her. His reliance on Cardinal Wolsey was also in question, since unusually his chancellor saw no clear and immediate way to give the king what he wanted. The years that followed were to bring Henry to the height of his maturity and develop his abilities as a ruler to a new pitch of achievement. They were also to expose his vulnerability as never before, and show the savage undertow of fear and vengeance which could underpin the magnificence, eloquence and learning of this extraordinary king.

4

DYNASTY AND SUPREMACY,
1527–1533

Where by divers sundry old authentic histories and chronicles it is manifestly declared and expressed that this realm of England is an empire ... governed by one supreme head and king having the dignity and royal estate of the imperial crown of the same ... he being also institute and furnished by the goodness and sufferance of Almighty God with plenary, whole and entire power, pre-eminence, authority, prerogative and jurisdiction.[1]

The years from 1527 until 1534 were the pivotal years of Henry VIII's reign. Perhaps more than anything else they underline the extent to which kingship at this time was personal kingship, because Henry's chief objective during these years was to reconfigure his family, but in so doing, he made major changes to kingship itself which would have profound and shocking implications for the country at large. The question of how his marriage to Katherine of Aragon might be annulled as illegitimate, and how he might be able to marry Anne Boleyn, on whom his heart was set, was known to contemporaries as 'the King's Great Matter'. This marital problem was the catalyst which prompted a cascade of developments which would challenge papal authority, set the king up as virtual pope within England, bring the English Bible to every parish in the kingdom, destroy the monasteries, vastly increase royal wealth and authority, and ultimately render England a Protestant country for the next five centuries.

Modern historians have questioned the old notion that single individuals can have any very great impact upon the world at large, and yet Katherine of Aragon's pitiful failure to produce a son, and Henry's passion for Anne Boleyn, were to have very large consequences for Tudor England. That said, much of what Henry VIII brought about between 1527 and 1534 was far from being entirely new, or even entirely unexpected. He had always had a leaning towards the humanism which vaunted the authority of the Bible, and he had always been attracted by the vision of himself as emperor. He had long dominated the church in England through Wolsey, and the idea of dissolving monasteries to fund other ecclesiastical institutions was not unprecedented: both Henry's pious grandmother, Lady Margaret Beaufort, and Cardinal Wolsey had done the same. Above all, Henry had constantly sought to exalt his majesty and authority as king. Yet the repudiation of Katherine and the Pope and the construction of the royal supremacy gave unprecedented scope to all of these ideas, and from these established notions and preoccupations, all the time vehemently claiming the sanction of antiquity, Henry was nevertheless to produce something shockingly innovative.

THE KING'S GREAT MATTER

It seems probable that Henry VIII ceased sleeping with Katherine of Aragon from about 1525 onwards. This was the year he raised his illegitimate son to the title of Duke of Richmond, as if admitting that this was the only son he was likely to have. Pictorial evidence from medals, busts and portraits, although a bit patchy, does suggests that he adopted the fashion of wearing a beard from around the mid-1520s, which reportedly was something the Queen disliked.[2] Katherine was in her forties, and she had lost her looks some time before. As early as 1515 she had been described as 'rather ugly than otherwise', and by 1519 Francis I commented how Henry, himself 'young and handsome', nevertheless had 'an old deformed wife'.[3] By 'deformed' he meant she had run to fat, which is hardly surprising after at least seven pregnancies, but this was perhaps all the more noticeable given that she was less than five feet tall. Beside her younger husband, who was over six feet tall, and who seemed to retain all his youthful energies well into his thirties and forties, she cannot have looked good. And as we have seen, the Tudors could be as mercilessly critical of physical failings as any modern audience; physical health, strength and beauty were held to demonstrate strength of character, moral excellence and divine approbation, so to be old, fat and ugly was to suffer a serious loss of status.

Had Katherine been the mother of sons, any physical failing could have been eclipsed by this greater sign of God's blessing. Their absence was an aching void at the heart of Henry's world. It seems likely that Katherine viewed it as slightly less of a problem. She certainly gave Princess Mary the training of a future queen. Henry seems to have encouraged this educational plan; indeed, it would not have been possible without his approval. Moreover, as well as raising Henry Fitzroy to the peerage, he gave Mary all the estate she might wish as Princess of Wales, and in many ways treated her like his future heir. But this did not prevent him referring bluntly to the fact that he was 'childless'. It seems too that the consequences of leaving a female heir to the throne had been carefully considered. In 1532, Henry was to publish a work called *A Glasse of the Truthe* which explained the king's justification for thinking his marriage to Katherine invalid. The preface to this work pointed out that his need for a male heir was far more significant for the country at large than for Henry himself:

> For his lack of heirs male is a displeasure to him but for his life time: as lacking that which naturally is desired of all men. ... But our lack shall be permanent so long as the world lasteth: except that god provide.

The point was that:

> if the female heir, shall chance to rule, she cannot continue long without a husband, which by god's law, must then be her governor and head, and so finally shall direct this realm.

This would indeed be the problem that in time both Mary I and Elizabeth I would face; women were subject to their husband's authority. The work went on to spell out the difficulties for such a female ruler in choosing a husband, making it clear how important popular consent was to the successful implementation of authority. Such a choice would be problematic if a female ruler married a foreign prince, and perhaps even worse if she married a subject:

And as touching any marriage within this realm, we think, it were hard to devise any condign and able person, for so high an enterprise, much harder, to find one, with whom the whole realm would and could be contented to have him ruler and governor.[4]

There was a lot of wisdom in these observations, as both Henry's daughters would one day discover.

It was still a big jump from lamenting having only a single living daughter, to defying the Pope's authority over the church. That Henry made this leap says much about his character and convictions. Like most of his contemporaries, he knew that the blessings of life, including children, were gifts from God. Unlike most of his contemporaries, he demanded such blessings as of right. His extraordinary good fortune in 1509, when he inherited the throne peacefully, and found that he was young, healthy, handsome, talented and beloved, had left him with the conviction that this was what he deserved. Rather than accept any reversal of fortune, he looked for an explanation elsewhere, and a course of action which would restore his position as the favoured son of God. The authority which he maintained with such state was far from automatic, and Henry shows every sign of having known this well. If power had to be negotiated between king and subjects, then it was essential to brandish obvious proofs of divine favour. Henry was always physically impressive, vigorous and intelligent. The trappings of kingship could be bought; Renaissance display could be constructed. Military or diplomatic success, however, was less easily secured, and the crowning glory of a male heir continued to elude him. Henry seems always to have been convinced, however, that he could achieve anything he might want. Every problem he ever encountered produced a forceful response, and this one was no exception.

In later life, when reversals of fortune came more swiftly, Henry became more insecure, more prone to swift acts of revenge, more inclined to suspect others of betraying him, more savage and shrill in his assertion of his own dominance. In this first attempt to make sense of his personal misfortune, he moved much more slowly and carefully. His chances of having a son with Katherine had declined markedly by early in the 1520s but it was not until 1526 or so that he produced an explanation why he had not been blessed with the sons whom he thought, as a godly and virtuous prince, he deserved. The explanation lay in the

Bible, in the Old Testament book of Leviticus, chapter 18, verse 16: 'Thou shalt not uncover the nakedness of thy brother's wife: it is thy brother's nakedness.' This was reinforced even more specifically by Leviticus chapter 20, verse 21: 'And if a man shall take his brother's wife, it is an unclean thing: he hath uncovered his brother's nakedness; they shall be childless.' It soon became clear, to use Wolsey's words, that 'as this matrimony is contrary to God's law, the King's conscience is grievously offended.'[5]

The interesting thing about this argument is the spin which Henry put upon it. The idea that a marriage could be rendered invalid by some previous relationship to close kin was hardly new; the papacy was constantly issuing dispensations allowing people to marry in this way. The papacy was also well used to manipulating church law in order to allow the rich and influential to marry whomever they desired. Henry's conviction that his marriage was unlawful, and his determination to have it recognised as such, and to marry again, was entirely unremarkable. But the fact that he made this sentence from the Bible so central to his case was unusual, interesting and potentially explosive. It also tells us a great deal about Henry himself.

It used to be thought that Henry turned first to his advisors for a solution to his problems, that they tried a series of different strategies, and that the argument from Scripture was only deployed when other strategies had proved unsuccessful. We now know that the biblical arguments were at the heart of the king's case right from the beginning, and that it was Henry himself who put them there. In a series of documents drawn up to outline and argue the King's case, the biblical argument is of central importance.[6]

The campaign for the annulment is one more piece of evidence which shows how much Henry was in control of policy when it came to the most important issues. More than anything else he did during his life, Henry was deeply involved in every stage of the process. He wrote, and read, and debated and harangued at great length, and with enormous energy. It was not a divorce he sought, although it is often referred to as such, inspiring the mistaken assumption that the breach with the Pope came because of Catholic opposition to divorce. Rather, he insisted that his marriage to Katherine had never existed in the first place, that they had been living in sin for nearly twenty years, and that this explained their failure to produce a son. And since he had made this decision himself, on the basis of scripture, he was setting a precedent that in a way rivalled Luther's attempts to do something similar. The new interest in the Bible at this time was producing an array of unexpected results. Luther, of course, was after doctrinal truth, whilst Henry was attempting, in his own eyes at least, to right an injustice. Luther was also a consummate and gifted scholar, whilst Henry took an entirely partial and prejudiced approach to his sources. Yet they both demonstrated how reading the Bible could unleash a revolution.

Henry was therefore anxious that everyone of importance should appreciate that his cause was a matter of religious duty, not merely a marital problem. He worked hard to create the impression that the personalities of the two women involved were of lesser importance than the necessity of obedience to the word of God. Wolsey, instructing the ambassadors at Rome in 1528, wrote that he 'dare put his soul' upon the fact that the king's wishes were:

> grounded upon justice, and not from any grudge of displeasure to the Queen, whom the King honours and loves, and minds to love and to treat as his sister, with all manner of kindness. Also as she is the relict of his dearest brother he will entertain her with all joy and felicity.

This may well have been largely true, since Henry's animosity towards Katherine seems to have been only in response to her refusal to accept quietly his repudiation of their marriage. Wolsey had to struggle rather more with the truth to depict Anne as the quintessence of virtue, but he tried hard to stress her attractions:

> the purity of her life, her constant virginity, her maidenly and womanly pudicity, her soberness, chasteness, meekness, humility, wisdom, descent of right noble and high thorough regal blood, education in all good and laudable [qualities] and manners, apparent aptness to procreation of children, with her other infinite good qualities.[7]

The official line, only partially unconvincing, was that Henry's chief motivation was his realisation of his offence against God through his supposed marriage to Katherine. His love for Anne was cast as a moderate, prudent, obvious choice, when in reality it was something far more irresponsible and uncontainable. The idea that he was bound by his duty to God to repudiate Katherine, however, was clearly of equal importance in Henry's mind.

Thus the 'King's Great Matter' was to be cast as a conversion experience: Henry's road to Damascus. He had been wallowing in sin and ignorance, but the true light of scripture had penetrated the darkness and the repentant king would now make due restitution, and put away the woman with whom he had lived unlawfully. The Word of God had saved him. The depth of Henry's conviction on this point is underlined by his admonitory letter of 1527 to his sister, whose own marriage (her second, to the Earl of Angus) had just been annulled by the papacy, bastardising her daughter and freeing her to marry Henry Stewart, with whom she was already living. Clement VII had granted her an annulment on the spurious grounds of an alleged pre-contract by the Earl of Angus, and the ludicrous assertion that her first husband had not, in fact, been killed at the Battle of Flodden, but had stayed alive long enough to render her second marriage bigamous. Henry wrote to her with pious exhortation to observe 'the divine ordinance of inseparable matrimony', urging her 'to turn the sight of your soul unto God's word, the lively doctrine of Jesus Christ, the only ground of salvation'. He also warned her:

> what charge of conscience, what grudge and fretting, yea, what danger of damnation should it be to your soul, with perpetual infamy of your renown, slanderously to distain with dishonour so goodly a creature ... namely your natural child, procreate in lawful matrimony, as to reputed baseborn.[8]

It is quite clear that Henry's own attempts to separate from a former partner, thereby rendering his daughter 'baseborn', were to be considered as in a quite different league.

BIBLICAL TRUTH

Henry, in his letter to his sister, had rested his case on evangelical truth, citing the New Testament as he asserted that: 'no man can lay none other foundation than that is laid [al]ready, which is Jesus Christ, he is the Rock.'[9] In the 1520s, when Henry's scruples of conscience reached this pitch of apparently unbearable anxiety, the Bible was undergoing its own especial Renaissance. For many long years, the text of the Bible in everyday use was that translated from Hebrew and Greek into Latin by St Jerome in 382 AD. This text was known as the Vulgate, on account of it being in the 'vulgar' tongue, a description which was by 1527 obviously inappropriate.

Meanwhile, the Renaissance which had begun in Italy and spread throughout Europe had as one of its key aims the rediscovery of ancient texts through the use of ancient languages newly acquired. Churchmen, scholars, intellectuals, and many courtiers, nobles and princes who sought the prestige of being accounted learned, were all turning to the study of a purer form of Latin, to the study of long-forgotten Greek and occasionally even to the study of Hebrew. Equipped with this expertise, they turned again to the Bible, and began to reassess the various translations available. Inevitably, this kind of study focused attention on the biblical text with a renewed zeal, where for years the study of the Bible had largely focused on medieval commentaries on the actual text.

The consequences of this were electrifying. It was like the difference between reading Shakespeare, groaning with boredom, in a class at school, and going to see a play enacted on stage for the first time, brilliant and immediate. For many – although perhaps not as many as we once thought – it was like encountering their religion for the first time. The noted scholars of the age started giving lectures based on the actual words of the Bible, rather than what medieval commentators had said about them, from John Colet in Oxford, to Luther in Wittenberg, both of them lecturing in particular on St Paul's epistles to the early Christians. Many people felt they were going back to that age, when the life of Christ was held in living memory, when the Church was young, vigorous, full of excitement. Debates sprang up about central points of Christian belief, and many traditions were questioned. Traditionalists were quick to defend established ways, but the old certainties were under review. One character in a work by Erasmus reports that he has heard a sermon telling people to shun anything new, but another replies: 'The man ... deserves never to change his socks and dirty underwear, forever to eat rotten eggs and to drink nothing but soured wine.'[10] New ideas were in vogue, and a new understanding of scripture was spreading across Europe.

That said, those who embraced this new approach to the Bible were quick to emphasise that they were still sanctioned by the past. They argued that they were trying to return to an accurate understanding of scripture which had been lost in the Middle Ages; the term 'Middle Ages' had itself been invented by a Renaissance humanist.[11] They pointed out that Jerome himself had denied that making a new translation implied any disrespect to former translators.[12] Henry and others were to echo this justification for their biblical studies. Many of the early translators also sought papal sanction for their efforts. However, the Bible was also a serious rival to papal authority to anyone who saw the teachings of scripture diverging from the teachings of the Pope. Even the successor of St Peter, Christ's Vicar on earth, could not claim greater authority than the Word of God itself.

For many, papal interpretation and church tradition remained a necessary adjunct to the true understanding of scripture. But for many others, caught up in evangelical excitement, the Bible needed no further interpretation or explication, but could speak for itself, or so they claimed, although this did not prevent reformers from issuing new translations of the Bible which were heavy with glosses and explanations.

It was hugely significant, therefore, that Henry VIII based his appeal to the Pope on a direct quotation from the Bible, and an appeal to divine law. He could have asked for his marriage to be annulled on the grounds of a mistake in the original dispensation; this was a well-trodden route, and would have preserved the dignity of both king and Pope, and indeed this was one of the alternatives explored at the time. By repeatedly locating his case in biblical exegesis, however, and emphasising the importance of the words from Leviticus, Henry was tapping in to all the new and exciting ideas of the age, and arguing that he was following not his own base passions, but divine inspiration. He was also, crucially, calling into question many long-established assumptions about papal supremacy. If people were to rely more and more on the Bible, then they would have less and less need for the papacy.

All religions require a source of authority, to establish what is true belief and what is heresy, to govern, adjudicate, arbitrate and inspire. Given that the Renaissance papacy was notorious for its violence, luxury, sexual immorality and political ambition, the idea of relying on a text transcribed by saints and dictated by God himself was a lot more tempting. There was an immediate affinity, therefore, between many of those engaged in the revival of scripture, and many others who were critical of the papacy. Older criticisms of the papacy were revived to make the point anew. Marsilius of Padua, who had written an attack on papal power in 1324, was one of these: his *Defensor Pacis* was published by royal approval in 1535 in English translation. It explained what had gone wrong:

> With our schools, glosses, comments, and interpretations, we have taken away and destroyed well near all the whole scripture of god. Scripture is not peradventure overturned and destroyed, but being as it were dumb, in a manner speaketh no more.

All the troubles of the modern world were laid at the door of this neglect of the Gospel, and the translator's marginal gloss emphasised the same point: 'The despising and setting at nought of god's word: is the cause of all the present evils in the world.'[13] The return to scripture was cast therefore as the cure for the ills of the age. Henry had always been drawn to this idea, and had backed its exponents ever since his childhood. But now that it looked like the way to cure his own particular ills, he put the full weight of his majesty behind the concept.

This was an approach which appealed to Henry's own vision of himself as king. In his earlier correspondence with Luther he had outlined his view of a king's responsibilities: the English version of this made a timely appearance in print in 1527. He wrote:

> It hath seemed to us always, that likewise as it appertaineth to the office and estate of a king diligently to procure the temporal wealth and commodity of his subjects: So doth it of duty more especially belong to the part and office of a christian king ... far yet more fervently to labour, travail and study ... how he may surely keep establish and confirm ... the hearts and minds of his subjects in the right religion of god ... by whose high providence ... they were for that purpose chiefly committed unto his governance.[14]

In his debate with Luther, Henry had of course been defending the papacy, and now he was questioning its authority. Yet this apparent inconsistency needs to be seen in the light of Henry's ideas about his own kingship, which remained constant, merely intensifying as the struggle for the annulment unfolded. Whether upholding or undermining papal supremacy, the important point was that Henry was taking responsibility for the religious welfare of his subjects. In the first half of his reign, Henry had seen the Pope as an ally, a valuable source of religious sanction for his kingship. From 1527 the tide was turning in the other direction.

DEALINGS WITH THE PAPACY

In turning to criticism of papal authority Henry was able to draw on many well-established ideas. Many of the humanist scholars of Henry's time were already highly dubious about papal pretensions. This was by no means a new argument, but one which had been rumbling on for centuries. The process by which the Bishops of Rome had exalted their status to the point of declaring themselves the Vicars of Christ, the representatives of God on earth, had been largely accepted by Christendom, the lands of Christian Europe which were under their sway. Sceptical voices had been raised in recurrent declarations of criticism and challenge, however, intensifying with the first stirrings of Renaissance sensibility. The biblical revival had added a new twist to an old set of tensions. The more people considered the first Christians, their simple lives, their passionate faith despite the oppression they faced, the more the popes, cardinals and bishops of the sixteenth-century Church, with all their splendour and corruption, seemed offensive. Equally, the more nation states began to emerge as coherent and centralised political entities, the more the papal assertion of authority over secular princes seemed untenable. Papal claims to spiritual headship and moral sanctity seemed appalling hypocrisy when seen against the lawlessness and impiety of Rome and the aggressive foreign policies pursued by the Pope; papal demands for secular obedience seemed unfounded and unworkable.

The most entertaining expression by far of this anti-papal feeling was a short work by Erasmus (though he never openly acknowledged he had written it), a kind of Renaissance 'pearly gates' joke, called *Julius Excluded from Heaven*. Here the self-same Julius II with whom Henry had negotiated the Holy League, whom contemporaries called the 'Warrior Pope', is described arriving at the gates of Heaven with his usual magnificence and a huge entourage, only to be met by a dubious St Peter. Julius trumpets his wealth and power, while Peter asks bemusedly about his glittering robes, his battle-scarred followers 'all stinking of brothels, booze, and gunpowder', his catamites and his much vaunted achievements. 'Were you eminent in theology?' asks Peter, 'Were you famous for your miracles? ... Did you pray simply and regularly?... Did you mortify the flesh by fasting and vigils?' Julius expounds instead on his worldly achievements, his battles, his extortions, his self-aggrandisement. Equally, he boasts of having ornamented the church, and Peter asks hopefully what ornaments he means – 'Warm faith? ... Sacred learning? ... Contempt for the world?' – but Julius thinks Peter hasn't grasped the point, and lists the ornaments he means:

> Royal palaces, the most handsome horses and mules, hordes of servants, well-trained troops, dainty courtiers ... gold, purple, taxes; in fact, such is the wealth and splendour of the Roman pontiff that, by comparison, any king would seem a poor and insignificant fellow.[15]

Perhaps the most telling point of this work is the way Julius just cannot understand what Peter is talking about; it underlines Erasmus's conviction that much of the institutional church of the time was so far away from Christian truth they couldn't even recognise it, let alone follow it. The encounter ends with Peter barring the way into heaven and Julius laying siege, and vowing to enter by force. This wonderfully satirical work expresses all the rage, scorn and disappointment felt by many about the papacy of Henry's day.

This is not to say that Henry began his case against his marriage with an outright attack upon the Pope. He had always relished being the devout and loyal supporter of the Papacy, in the Holy League of 1513, answering the papal call to peace with the Treaty of London in 1518, or defending the papacy against Luther's attacks in 1521. Moreover, Pope Clement VII was not particularly hostile to the idea of Henry's first marriage being declared invalid; his sole concern was not to antagonise Katherine of Aragon's nephew, Charles V, too badly.

In the early stages of negotiations, it did appear that the 'special relationship' between Henry and the papacy might yet prevail and produce for Henry the result he so badly wanted. He had a particular affinity with Medici popes: Leo X had been Giovanni de' Medici, and as Pope from 1513 to 1521, he had observed and applauded Henry's consolidation of his kingship. Giulio de'Medici, his cousin, was elected Pope Clement VII in 1523, and seems to have viewed Henry with especial favour. The first Golden Rose of his pontificate was sent to Henry, and in 1524 he confirmed the title of *Fidei Defensor*. In February 1527, Henry had sent the beleaguered Pope 30,000 ducats, which 'restored his holiness from death to life'.[16] Then three months later, just before Henry became finally convinced of the need to be rid of Katherine, with painfully unfortunate timing, unpaid Imperial troops ransacked Rome, and imprisoned Clement VII.

Even then, there were hopes that Clement VII's goodwill might be enough to get Henry his annulment. Bishop Gardiner, sent to Rome as Henry's envoy, reported back:

> that his Holiness hath, in mine opinion, a fast and sincere love towards your Grace, not grounded upon his necessities, but upon such devotion as he hath perceived and doth daily understand to be in your Majesty towards this see.[17]

This was of course what Henry wanted to hear, but it may well be an accurate description too. As Charles V's predominance in Europe remained unassailed, however, Clement VII continued to stall. Henry was impatient to marry Anne and begin siring a dynasty, twenty years later than he had expected and intended, so a dithering Pope was a severe aggravation. Nine months on from the above observation, Gardiner was commenting less optimistically, that the Imperial camp still had the upper hand, not least because 'for that it lieth in them to stop the access of vittles and so famine this country'.[18] And in April 1529, he sent another description of Clement VII's state:

> His Holiness is in a great perplexity and agony of mind, nor can tell what to do. He seemeth in words, fashion, and manner of speaking, as though he would do somewhat for your Highness; and yet, when it cometh to the point, nothing he doth.

It seems likely that Clement would have wanted to help Henry, had he dared, but his overriding emotion seems to have been a deep longing to have the problem go away. Gardiner reported that the Pope had said to him, 'that he would, for the wealth of Christendom, the Queen were in her grave.'[19] Such an incautious observation has the ring of genuine feeling about it.

The longer that Rome proved unwilling to provide a satisfying solution, the more Henry was inclined to question whether Rome really needed to be involved in what seemed to him a straightforward act of obedience to a clearly stated divine law. He did of course consider other alternatives; indeed, he was open to any suggestion that might help him. In the early stages he put considerable pressure on Katherine to become a nun, which would have had the convenient effect of terminating their marriage without anyone having to decide whether it had been lawful or not. Katherine, however, was proud, devout and passionately defensive of her daughter's rights. To admit Henry's case was to declare her own beloved daughter, groomed for the throne, a bastard, and this she would never do. There were other possibilities too for those who grasped the extraordinary complexities of canon law; Wolsey saw some of these.[20] For Henry, however, it was the argument from Leviticus which entranced him, and the idea that it was clearly and straightforwardly an offence against divine law to marry your brother's widow.

LEGAL POSSIBILITIES

A great deal hinged on whether the divine law in question really was this obvious. Henry turned to the academics and churchmen at his disposal for an answer, every inch the Renaissance prince in his ostentatious deference to scholarly learning as well as in his scepticism about traditional papal claims to authority. The first formal exploration of this case came in the summer of 1527, when a treatise by John Fisher, arguing for Katherine that her marriage had been legal, was answered by Robert Wakefield, the Cambridge university lecturer in Hebrew. Henry had been responsible, in his guise as a patron of humanists, for promoting Wakefield and the study of Hebrew; now he reaped the intellectual harvest he had sown. Wakefield's treatise argued – conveniently enough – that the proper translation of Leviticus 20:21 should be rendered not 'he will be childless' but 'he will be without sons'. This improvement on the Vulgate was characteristic of what humanist biblical scholarship was doing at the time, only this time it paid less attention to the real meaning of the Hebrew than to the king's own interests.

The preface to the treatise was written by Henry himself, rebuking Fisher for advising his king to remain in a godless marriage. Henry pleaded in his own defence that he had not known he was doing wrong, that he had not had as good an understanding of scripture and scriptural languages when he was young, but that now he had he intended to discover the truth from learned men.²¹ Significantly, he did not intend to discover the truth by asking the Pope. Already Henry was implying that the Pope was not the real authority in this matter.

Henry was clearly excited about his own arguments, and thought they outweighed any possible opposition. More objective commentators were not so sure, and Fisher in particular had some powerful arguments on the other side of the case. For one thing, there was a passage in Deuteronomy, another Old Testament book, which expressly commanded marriage to a brother's widow. Henry's supporters dismissed this as Jewish ceremonial law, and therefore not binding, or tried to interpret it allegorically, with the same effect. But as Fisher argued, even if it was a commandment applicable only to the Jews, could God have commanded something, even temporarily, which was contrary to natural law? Henry's supporters were arguing that this was what marriage to a brother's widow was – contrary to natural law, in other words fundamentally wrong, but this was by no means clear. Fisher also suggested that the Levitical prohibition against marrying a brother's wife was meant to apply in the case of both brothers being still alive; a simple and devastating objection to the king's case.²²

Another possible problem was that the passage from Leviticus could only apply if Katherine's marriage to Arthur had been a *real* marriage, that is, if it had been consummated, which Katherine denied. Henry and his team dredged up a mass of gossip over twenty years old to suggest that she was lying. But Katherine had some formidable supporters. Henry had allowed her a defence team, for it was vital that he be seen to act graciously and fairly, and she had Bishop John Fisher, Juan Luis Vives, Bishop Cuthbert Tunstall, Archbishop William Warham, Bishop John Clerk and Bishop George Athequa all ranged on her side. She also had a strong conviction that she was rightfully Henry's wife, that Mary was their legitimate daughter, and that it was her moral duty to uphold this truth. If Henry was suddenly carried away with a vision of himself as moral crusader, he met resistance from a woman in every way as passionate about her religion. She was a worthy opponent, and an exceptionally brave one, and perhaps even more importantly, she was a staunchly devoted mother.

If Henry's case against his existing marriage, and his proposal for how the matter should be sorted out, seemed to him entirely clear, logical and forcefully persuasive, this was in large part because of their strong emotional foundations. He had fallen in love with the woman who would replace Katherine as queen, and he was convinced that at long last he had found his rightful consort. Like most people in love, he was carried forward by boundless enthusiasm, and became entirely ruthless in his determination to possess the beloved object. Even so, he proceeded with a measure of caution. In this momentous undertaking Henry's bravado is evident, but so is his wariness. Even his choice of Anne was in one sense dictated by caution; her older sister, Mary, had been his mistress between about 1522 and 1525, so the likeness between the sisters might help reassure him. It seems probable that, despite his reputation for sexual voracity, Henry VIII was relatively hesitant with women. His first two wives were women he had known for some time; his later wives were either very meek or very young, and the one time he married a stranger it was a fiasco. By the standards of the age he was a faithful and loving husband, in general only taking mistresses when his wives were made unavailable through pregnancy. His liaison with Anne Boleyn was clearly the most passionate and most reckless love affair of his life, but for all that, it was relatively controlled.

The king's marriage first went on trial in May 1527. Significantly enough, the court which Wolsey set up by virtue of his authority as papal legate, was a secret one. It called Henry to answer the charge of having lived for eighteen years in an unlawful union with his brother's wife. This was a court which would never reach a verdict, however. The complexities of the case itself were compounded by the news arriving of the sacking of Rome by the Imperial army. Charles V now controlled Rome, and held the Pope a prisoner in all but name in the Castel Sant'Angelo. The prospect of Katherine appealing to Rome in these circumstances was enough to halt the activities of Wolsey's tribunal. It is clear that at this early stage even Henry did not envisage solving his problem without papal approval and consent. Meanwhile Wolsey set off to the continent with a grand plan to take over the running of the Church whilst the Pope was out of action. This seemed to promise a simpler way of sorting out the annulment. Wolsey already had the document drawn up which gave him the power to adjudicate the king's case; all it required was the Pope's signature.[23]

In Wolsey's absence, Henry broke the news to Katherine, in June 1527, that their marriage was a sham. If this was a terrible shock, it was also a spur to action, and Katherine was a fighter, who swiftly began to rally her supporters. Meanwhile, it was in September 1527 that Henry applied to the Pope for the dispensation already mentioned, that in the event of his first marriage being declared invalid, he should be permitted to marry Anne. The document did not give her name, but described a woman previously betrothed (as Anne had been to Henry Percy) and related in the first degree of affinity from 'forbidden wedlock', which was a reference to her being the sister of Henry's former mistress.[24] He did this without Wolsey's knowledge; indeed he seems to have deliberately concealed the mission from his cardinal. There were signs that Henry was beginning to question Wolsey's ability to help him in this all-important manner.[25] Wolsey was statesman enough to perceive that Katherine had to go, but by the same token, he would have seen the proposed marriage to Anne as at best a waste of time, at worst a serious political blunder. Henry was astute enough to realise how Wolsey probably viewed the affair. There was no wisdom in a king marrying one of his subjects. Nevertheless, there is no sign that Wolsey tried any less hard than usual to fulfil Henry's will, directing all his efforts towards securing the Pope's acquiescence. This time, however, Henry had set him an almost impossible task.

Henry was taking command of the situation. His conviction that he was pursuing the right course of action strengthened his resolve, but was also something of a liability. The dispensation he applied for in 1527 shows how narrowly he was focusing on getting rid of Katherine. In fact, because Anne was the sister of his former mistress, she was related to him in the same degree as Katherine was. This was passed over, but it could be argued that Henry sleeping with Anne's sister barred the way to future marriage just as much as Katherine sleeping with Henry's brother. However, the king was always more impressionistic than precise in his reasoning when he felt himself to be in the right. Henry's confidence that he was acting in obedience to divine commandment meant he seemingly had no worries about whether his future marriage might not be lawful. It seems highly likely that he viewed his powerful emotions for Anne as being as providential as his discovery of the crucial passages in Leviticus. In any case, there was no direct biblical commandment against marrying a mistress's sister; the bull he was trying to extract from Clement VII allowed him to marry any woman who was not his brother's wife. Henry was preparing the way for his future wife with total conviction, before his existing wife had been dismissed; he was that confident that God was on his side.

The 'King's Great Matter' gave rise to an enormous academic research project. Already, Fisher and Wakefield between them had laid out the cases for and against, and now Henry had begun to recruit his team of scholars, including Richard Pace his chaplain, Edward Foxe, the Cambridge theologian who was Wolsey's secretary, and John Stokesley, dean of St George's Windsor and later Bishop of London. Significantly, Wakefield was Hebrew tutor to both Pace and Stokesley; it was men of a particular ilk whom the king sought to support him. He was clearly convinced that anyone loyal to the cause of biblical renewal must see the justice of his case. In this, he was oversimplifying a very complex intellectual and devotional movement.

In the autumn of 1527 Henry had a long talk in the gallery at Hampton Court with Thomas More, and explained his case to him. More would remain famously unconvinced by the king's approach. Others were more persuadable. In November a group of bishops and other learned men was brought together at Hampton Court, and later at York Place. A book emerged from these gatherings, which presented the arguments on both sides of the case. It was another of the books from Henry's reign to be known as 'the King's Book'. A copy of this work was presented to the Pope in March 1528, with another copy going to Cardinal Campeggio. It was more cautious in tone than the earlier work by Wakefield, perhaps in order to avoid alienating the papacy, perhaps because of Wolsey's influence. Wolsey himself seems to have been reluctant to take the more challenging line based on Leviticus, when other less contentious options were open to the king.[26] Since the cardinal had no emotional investment in the case, he could take the more objective view, and probably concluded quite sensibly that if Fisher, Tunstall, Vives, Warham and others thought the king had no real case, they were probably right. Henry might be full of the conviction that humanist scholarship was on his side, but the more formidable band of humanist scholars was behind the queen. Nevertheless, the research work went on in England and it continued to focus on the argument from scripture.[27]

At the same time, in Rome, a painfully slow and unrewarding diplomatic effort was under way. Stephen Gardiner and Edward Foxe were sent to the papal curia in 1528 to extract papal permission to have the king's case decided by Wolsey in England. This was not an unreasonable or even particularly unusual request, and the Pope was not in principle particularly opposed to the idea. The menacing presence of Charles V and his armies, however, and the fluctuating nature of Italian politics, meant that Clement VII may have wanted to say yes, but could do little more than look encouraging and say nothing. Henry VIII, meanwhile, was impatient for a swift solution. The luckless ambassadors were caught between the two. By agonisingly slow stages, they secured the papal commission they sought, the appointment of Campeggio as papal legate to hear the case with Wolsey, and Campeggio's departure for England, arriving in September 1528. The Pope had empowered his legate to act, but urged him to keep stalling, reflecting Charles V's continuing dominance of the European scene.

At a crucial point, Katherine produced a key document – hitherto kept in Spain – which if genuine would have rendered the papal commission to Wolsey and Campeggio invalid. This was an alternative version of the original dispensation which had allowed her to marry Henry in 1509, differently worded. Since the King's case against the original dispensation had been carefully based on the details of the wording, Katherine's revelation undermined an already shaky legal case. Henry, furious, insisted it was a forgery, but others were not so sure. All of this took many months more than it should have done. And upon his arrival in England Campeggio moved equally slowly, weighed down by the burden of his contradictory instructions, by anxiety at the huge political tensions created by the case, and afflicted by chronic ill-health.

Meanwhile, Henry began to face the unwelcome truth that his desire to be rid of Katherine was extremely unpopular. This was not easy for a man who often tried to deal with unwelcome truths by ignoring them, and this aspect of the 'King's Great Matter' was to have some profound effects upon Henry's character. It would turn him into a consummate propagandist, determined to preserve the love and adulation which he had been accustomed to command when he first came to the throne. It would also turn him into an angry and vengeful persecutor of those who opposed him. He seems to have been psychologically incapable of recognising that some of his former friends and servants were genuinely unconvinced by his arguments. His conviction of his own importance led him to conclude that those who would not accept a viewpoint so dear to him must have some fatal flaw, must be at heart traitors. His behaviour during these years became increasingly erratic. There were some masterly and majestic displays when he was expounding his moral scruples and his determination to submit to divine law. There was a fair deal of ebullience when he thought things were going his way, and a lot of extravagant love-making towards Anne. There was also some extraordinary cruelty, some casual and some calculated, towards those who stood in his way.

Edward Hall, whose account of Henry's reign is perhaps the most vivid, was persuaded by the king's case. He wrote of how Henry:

> was in a great scruple of his conscience and not quiet in his mind, because the divers divines well-learned secretly informed him that he lived in adultery with his brother's wife to the great peril of his soul, and told him farther that the court of Rome could not dispense with God's commandment and precept.[28]

He also gives an account of a speech Henry made in November 1528 at Bridewell to a gathering of the nobility, judiciary and councillors, explaining it as a direct response to popular gossip, for:

> the common people being ignorant of the truth and in especial women and other that favoured the queen talked largely, and said that the king would for his own pleasure have another wife and had sent for this legate to be divorced from his queen.[29]

It underlines a point often neglected in accounts of Henry's kingship, namely that his greatness as a monarch rested in large part upon popular acceptance, admiration and obedience, and – even more importantly – that Henry was aware of this fact. In his speech at Bridewell he protested that:

> as touching the queen, if it be adjudged by the law of God that she is my lawfull wife, there was never thinge more pleasant nor more acceptable to me in my life both for the discharge and clearing of my conscience and also for the good qualities and conditions the which I know to be in her. For I assure you all, that beside her noble parentage ... she is a woman of most gentleness, of most humility and buxomness, yea and of all good qualities appertaining to nobility, she is without comparison, as I this twenty years almost have had the true experiment, so that if I were to marry again if the marriage might be good I would surely chose her above all other women.[30]

Given that less than a month later Katherine had been despatched to Hampton Court, and Anne installed in her rooms at Greenwich, such protestations by the king seem like rank hypocrisy, and yet such was Henry's ability to play a part, and more importantly, to believe in himself as a godly prince above all reproach, that he may well have been persuaded by these words as he spoke them. His praise of Katherine would have been at least in part genuine; they had been a devoted couple, and the only charge he could lay against her – until she began to resist his plans to declare their marriage void – was that she had not given him a son. Equally, he had begun the speech with a blunt reminder of the Wars of the Roses, and the damage that a disputed succession could do. Hall reports him, highly significantly, as saying that 'we think that all our doings in our lifetime are clearly defaced and worthy of no memory if we leave you in trouble at the time of our death.'[31]

In all the machinations surrounding the 'King's Great Matter', many of them disreputable, it has to be remembered that Henry was fundamentally doing his duty, and for all that he sought to improve his own situation, and marry his sweetheart, his main concern was what would happen once he was dead and gone. It is overly simplistic to dismiss his actions as those of a selfish and greedy megalomaniac. He was also working for the greater good, and if he identified that greater good as inextricably entwined with his own personal good, that was the consequence of living in an era of personal monarchy.

This approach also meant that Henry viewed with justifiable indignation anyone whom he perceived to be working against him. Their personal disloyalty was also, as he saw it, a threat to national security and an insult to God. This may help explain the ferocity of his reactions. When, for example, Katherine produced the evidence of the 'Spanish brief', the alternative version – safely in Charles V's keeping – of the original dispensation from Julius II, threatening the whole basis of the king's case, Henry's anger knew no bounds. He sent Warham and Tunstall, two of Katherine's supporters, to tell her she was not to see her daughter any more, that the Council thought it unsafe for her to come near the king, that she was torturing Henry out of hatred and that she was trying to drum up popular support with too many public appearances. She was now an outcast. But the king's fury was because he perceived her opposition as the height of selfishness, when political necessity and moral law alike were on his side; so, at least, he saw the matter. By this stage – the end of 1528 – a touch of desperation was entering into Henry's pronouncements. His next embassy to Rome was sent with a host of complicated instructions, including the task of sounding out the idea of Henry committing bigamy with papal approval. Although this sounded 'right rare, new and strange', precedent could still be found in the Old Testament.[32] If Henry was still open to a range of possibilities, he did keep coming back to the Bible.

THE BLACKFRIARS COURT AND THE FALL OF WOLSEY

The legatine court finally met at Blackfriars in June 1529, presided over by Wolsey and Campeggio. Not surprisingly, Campeggio continued to be plagued with illness and depression throughout this venture, secretly pleading with Pope and Emperor to get the case recalled to Rome, whilst also pleading with Katherine to take the veil. Wolsey, who was having a hard time satisfying his master at this point, kept Campeggio under constant pressure, reiterating the threat that if the marriage was not annulled, England would reject her allegiance to Rome.[33] There were too many conflicting interests at stake, many of them passionately upheld. At the opening session, the queen made an unexpected appearance, to protest formally against the holding of such a court, and to make a public appeal to Rome. Katherine's stance on this was to edge Henry further and further towards an outright break with Rome; he had been working for two years towards this court hearing, and he was optimistic that his objective lay within his grasp. He had thought, back in 1527, that he might be married to Anne within months, and already the wait had stretched into years. To be told by Katherine and a chorus of European opinion that such a case could not be tried on English soil was a severe aggravation. It is little wonder that his animosity towards papal authority was increasing, and his respect for his first wife was turning to hatred.

Meanwhile, at the second session of the Blackfriars trial, Henry and Katherine both appeared, and a courtroom confrontation unfolded which made compelling drama even before it made its way into Shakespeare's *Henry VIII*. Katherine, called to answer to the court, ignored the officials, and made her way to Henry under his cloth of estate, where she knelt before him, and in broken English made her heart-rending plea:

Sir ... I beseech you for all the loves that hath been between us and for the love of God, let me have justice and right; take of me some pity and compassion, for I am a poor woman and a stranger, born out of your dominion. I have here no assured friends and much less indifferent [i.e. impartial] counsel. I flee to you as to the head of justice within this realm. Alas, sir, wherein have I offended you ...? ... I take God and all the world to witness that I have been to you a true, humble, and obedient wife, ever confirmable to your will and pleasure, that never said or did anything to the contrary thereof, being always well pleased and contented with all things wherein ye had any delight or dalliance .... I loved all those whom ye loved only for your sake. ... This twenty years I have been your true wife (or more) and by me ye have had divers children, although it hath pleased God to call them out of this world, which hath been no default in me.

She then vowed that she had come to him a virgin, promised that she would obey if there were any true cause that proved the marriage invalid, but pointed out that what had pleased King Ferdinand, King Henry VII and all their learned councillors at the time was unlikely to be in error. Stating that the court assembled there could not be impartial, she asked to be excused from it, ending 'And if ye will not extend to me so much indifferent favor, your pleasure then be fulfilled, and to God I commit my case.'[34] She then rose, curtseyed, and departed, ignoring the attempts of the court to call her back. It was a performance like none other. Katherine had been an impressive consort and a worthy match for Henry for twenty years, and at the end she showed that she was his equal when it came to the moral drama that was so central to majesty.

Katherine's passionate and moving plea shows what an extraordinary ideological conflict was unfolding. It would be wrong to cast the queen as the pious and wronged victim of Henry's calculating self-interest. Henry too had a moral case, which hinged on scripture, in which the future security of the kingdom was at stake. From his point of view Katherine's stubbornness was both selfish and destructive. To her supporters, however, it was truly courageous. John Fisher's equally passionate speech on her behalf declared his willingness to lay down his life like John the Baptist in this cause – which, in time, he did indeed do. Since John the Baptist had died for criticising King Herod's unlawful marriage (ironically to his brother's wife, Herodias), this was to label Henry as the murderous Herod, not a biblical figure he wanted to emulate.

Katherine's defiance was poetic, dignified and a brave moral stand, but its result was to harden Henry's resolve and suspicion. More practically, her appeal reached Rome, and Clement VII revoked the authority of the Blackfriars court, which Campeggio had already, to Henry's fury, closed down for the summer, not to reopen until October.

In the summer of 1529, it was clear that Henry had suffered a major defeat, and that a new approach was needed. New blood, it seemed, was also wanted. The first casualty of the debacle at Blackfriars was Wolsey. Formerly adept at bringing the king everything he wanted, particularly when it came to ecclesiastical and diplomatic affairs, Wolsey had spectacularly failed to bring Henry the thing he wanted more than anything else. This underlines a crucial point about Wolsey's place in Henry's life: he did not dominate the king, as some have suggested; he served him, and when he ceased to serve him to Henry's satisfaction, he fell from power. This has been represented as a victory for faction, a confirmation of Anne Boleyn's personal vendetta against the Cardinal. In fact, it seems that Henry bore very little animosity towards Wolsey as an individual, and treated him quite kindly in his newly reduced state. The act of removing Wolsey from power was more political than personal. It was also an indication of how Henry intended next to proceed. To attack the papal legate was to attack the Pope he represented. Henry's threats against the papacy had already made it clear that Wolsey's ruin might be the king's first step in repudiation of Rome.[35] He was now beginning to fulfil those threats.

The Church had failed the king; the Church was now to feel the force of his wrath. Wolsey was found guilty of *praemunire*, the offence of appealing to an outside authority in a matter that was under the jurisdiction of the realm. This was the traditional charge for those who put the claims of their Church above those of their king. He was replaced as lord chancellor by Thomas More. This was a hugely significant choice. More had an international reputation as a man of extraordinary learning, but he was equally known for his piety and integrity. Henry clearly planned an intellectual and moral crusade, and would not hear More's initial refusal to accept the post, nor take account of More's refusal to give an opinion about the 'King's Great Matter'. Henry was convinced that right was on his side, and that all right-thinking people could be brought to see the matter from his own viewpoint. A week after More took office, in November 1529, Parliament met. This was the Parliament that would, highly unusually in time of peace, remain in existence (if not in session) until 1536, and would one day be christened the 'Reformation Parliament'. The power of popular acclaim and Parliamentary consensus was now to be brought into play too. Henry had assembled his forces for the next stage of the assault.

PARLIAMENT AND PRESSURE

Almost the first objective of the new Parliament was an attempt to curb the powers of the clergy. This was a grievance separate from Henry's own particular problem with ecclesiastical authority, but it chimed in rather well with his increasing desire to bring the Church under his own control. It can be described under the umbrella term of 'anticlericalism', although this can be as misleading as it can prove helpful. It used to be thought that there was a straightforward groundswell of popular opinion against the medieval church at this time, in which indignation was focused at the clergy for their ignorance, superstition, immorality and the way they deceived and extorted money from their vulnerable congregations. Anticlericalism, therefore, used to be seen as a stepping-stone to Reformation, and the rejection of medieval Catholicism in favour of the simpler, more biblical, educated and popular faith that was Protestantism. We now know that this is a very partial and prejudiced account, that the medieval church was popular, and successful, and that the Reformation came slowly to England, and was to many extremely unwelcome. 'Anticlericalism' as a concept has fragmented, and although some of those who urged reform of the clergy were genuinely working for Protestantism, we can now appreciate that many who urged reform did so out of their commitment to the existing Catholic faith, reflecting its vibrancy, its intellectual capacity and its levels of piety.

There was a particular strand of anticlericalism, however, which was highly critical of the clergy, and continued to deplore and condemn their failings and their avarice, and this strand was especially strong in London, where the clergy were a lot wealthier than elsewhere, and common among lawyers and merchants, and even some courtiers. It had flared up in the wake of the death of Richard Hunne, a London merchant, probably with Lollard sympathies, who had been involved in a notorious dispute with the Church, been found hanged in prison, and was widely believed to have been murdered, and his suicide then faked. Hunne's case had been a rallying point for those who were critical of the clergy. Similar sentiments were given erudite expression by William Tyndale in *The Obedience of a Christian Man*, who argued that:

> our holy prelates and our ghostly religious, which ought to defend God's word, speak evil of it and do all the shame they can to it, and rail on it ... and teacheth the people to disobey their heads and governors, and moveth them to rise against their princes ... and to make havoc of other man's goods.[36]

The same idea took a more forceful, populist form in *The Supplication for the Beggars,* addressed to the king by Simon Fish, a London lawyer who was also a Lutheran, and who argued that poverty within England was the direct result of the clergy's extortion, 'this idle, ravenous sort, which (setting all labour aside) have begged so importunately that they have gotten into their hands more then the third part of all your Realm'.[37] He was right that the Church owned a large part of England at this point. He also alleged that the clergy were responsible for turning honest people into beggars and whores, and that they were so powerful the king could not oppose them in Parliament. These were exaggerated claims, but the House of Lords did contain a large contingent of bishops and abbots, so again he had a basis in truth. It was said that Anne Boleyn was responsible for showing both works to Henry; even if this is apocryphal, it does reflect the current of ideas at the time that the king was able to channel to achieve his own purposes.

It was this kind of anticlericalism – angry, scornful, and partially inspired by evangelical influences – which moved Parliament in 1529 to begin by discussing their grievances against the clergy. The fees charged for probate of wills, and mortuary fees paid for clerical services attendant on a death, were both decried, as was non-residence, pluralism and the holding of secular appointments and involvement in husbandry and trade.[38] These complaints were voiced by the Commons; some of them were accepted by the Lords, but others raised anger and antagonism; Hall says they called the Commons 'heretics and schismatics'.

Events in Germany, where the Reformation begun by Luther was now well established, had given new edge to criticisms of the clergy at home. Henry did not encourage these debates in Parliament, but he watched developments carefully. In a conversation with the imperial

ambassador in October 1529 he had ostentatiously deplored the luxurious and immoral lives of popes and prelates and expressed the pious and
significant wish that they would live more in accordance with the Bible
and the early Church. He said Luther had been right to criticise them,
although wrong to then attack the sacraments. He said it was Charles
V's duty as emperor to tackle Church abuses, and that he as king of
England intended to do the same. Conversations with ambassadors are
never casual. This was tantamount to Henry making a policy declaration. Meanwhile Parliament passed three acts against clerical abuses.
Three bishops who appealed to Rome against this legislation seem to
have been briefly imprisoned: two of them, John Fisher and John Clerk,
were significantly among Katherine's chief supporters.

It was unusual for clerical misdemeanours to be tackled in such
depth by Parliament; usually this was the responsibility of Convocation,
which was a kind of parliament for the Church in England, divided
into two houses, North and South, according to the two archdioceses of
York and Canterbury. When Convocation did meet, and drew up a list
of reforms, the king went over the list and made corrections.[39] The
traditional autonomy of the Church was being slowly undermined. In
May 1530 Henry announced that he would sponsor an English translation of the New Testament. He was taking an extraordinarily close
interest in ecclesiastical matters, and moving ever closer to the idea of
the royal supremacy. In practice, this was not a new departure. One of
the many benefits of Wolsey as servant was that Henry had effectively
ruled the Church in England through his minister. Wolsey's seat in
London, York Place, had been the conduit for a kind of informal royal
supremacy. Now Wolsey was disgraced, and soon he would be dead,
and York Place belonged to the king, and was rechristened Whitehall.
It was a kind of architectural metaphor. Government of the church was
increasingly to rest in the hands of the king.

Nonetheless, it would be easier to control the Church with the blessing of the papacy than by defying Rome. It is easy to caricature English
politics at this point by implying that there were two parties at work –
Rome versus London, traditional Catholics versus humanist free-thinkers,
Katherine's supporters versus the king's. In fact only the last of these
was true, and even these two groups were not clear-cut. Nor did Henry
and his supporters ever actively seek a break with Rome; they would
have much preferred the Pope to give his permission, have the case

settled in England, and move on. The arguments which Henry mobilised to put pressure on the Pope, however, increasingly pointed the way
towards the arguments which would one day justify the rejection of
papal authority altogether.

Strenuous efforts were still being made to devise new initiatives. In
the summer of 1529 a young Cambridge don named Thomas Cranmer
was working as tutor to two boys in Waltham. The king was staying at
Waltham Abbey, and by chance Stephen Gardiner and Edward Foxe
were billeted at the house where Cranmer was living. He suggested to
them that the opinions of Europe's universities be canvassed as to
whether Henry's marriage to Katherine was valid or not; not perhaps a
new suggestion, but a timely one. The accidental nature of this encounter shows how eagerly Henry was casting around for any possible helpful
suggestions. This was the beginning of Cranmer's meteoric rise to power;
he had managed to get his first foot on the ladder by proving so in tune
with Henry's own thinking at this time. Henry was being increasingly
drawn to the idea that formerly unassailable truths were now open to
debate and discussion. Where before he had sent repeated embassies to
Rome, now he also sent out his agents to the universities. The men he
chose were themselves noted for their humanist scholarship, including
Reginald Pole, the king's own cousin, and Cranmer himself, and
although their efforts were vigorously combated by those of Katherine's
supporters, by 1530 they had the decisions of several universities in
Henry's favour.

In the wake of the failure of the Blackfriars court, therefore, Henry
was now waging a propaganda war. He was convinced that he was right,
but he needed others to be convinced too. This worked several ways – it
might serve to pressurise the Pope, it might win him allies abroad which
would do the same, or then again it might stir up popular opinion at
home to such a pitch that it gave him justification to act unilaterally. At
this point in 1530–1, it seemed that anything might happen, but the
scale of the public relations exercise now under way was an interesting
indication of Henry's determination to act only to popular acclaim.
Adulation and approval were necessary to him as an individual; they
were also essential to the political process. He needed the backing of his
kingdom, or at least of his more important subjects. One example of this
is an extraordinary document which was intended to be signed by every
important person in the realm. It was a letter to the Pope, despatched in

the summer of 1530, demanding that the Pope confirm 'what so many learned men proclaim', and signed by both archbishops, four bishops, twenty-five abbots, two dukes, forty peers and several others.[40] Henry seems to have decided to put as much pressure on the papacy as possible to secure the result he wanted, whilst reserving the possibility that he might take even more dramatic action if it was not forthcoming. Clement seems to have received this message as it was intended, describing it as a threat that unless papal approval was forthcoming, the English might take the matter into their own hands.[41]

The case which Clement VII had recalled to Rome after Katherine's appeal was finally being heard, but Henry's thinking had advanced considerably in the three years since he first began his campaign for annulment, and the always implied criticism of papal authority which stemmed from the case built on Leviticus was now becoming more explicit. Despite the huge amount of academic endeavour which was going into building his case, at root its inspiration lay in Henry's conviction that anything which seemed to constrain his own authority must be wrong.

When the papacy had set the seal on his ambitions in France in 1513, or hallowed his role as peacemaker in 1518 or confirmed him in his papal title in 1521, its authority had been acceptable to Henry. Now it was taking his all-important court case out of English hands and claiming that it should be settled in some distant Italian setting, it was clearly an offence against his royal dignity. Arguments in support of this followed. Helpfully, in the summer of 1530 the great research project which had been rumbling on since 1527 came to fruition. The collection of biblical, patristic and historical evidence needed to back Henry's case was completed, and the *Collectanea satis copiosa* was now deployed in the battle.

CONSTRUCTING THE SUPREMACY

From this point onwards, the struggle to secure the annulment was also the foundation for the Royal Supremacy. Henry's case was now increasingly circling around the idea that the king could not legally be summoned to Rome, that there was no higher judicial authority in the realm than the king himself. He began to claim that he had authority over spiritual and secular matters alike within England; that he was head of the Church as well as head of state. This was a new and astounding idea. The conflict between civil law (the law of the state) and canon law (the law of the Church) had rumbled on for centuries, but this was a radical solution to the problem. It was by no means a Protestant idea; Luther thought Henry was merely assuming the powers of the Pope for himself, which is not a bad assessment of the situation. It did, however, draw on humanist and evangelical ideas about the Bible, and it used the kings of the Old Testament in particular as a model. It also drew on imperial ideas and imagery, since the early Christian emperors had set a helpful precedent by wielding both spiritual and secular authority. In fact, Henry picked up ideas, precedents, examples from scripture, history and legend, and any other possible support for his theory with boundless enthusiasm and a distinct lack of scholarly rigour. His propaganda campaign, for all the academic research underpinning it, was distinctly journalistic in flavour. It didn't matter where the material came from, as long as it looked good.

Some of the propaganda published at this time was in Latin, clearly aimed at an intellectual and international audience. The decisions of the universities were published in both Latin and English, to reach as many as possible: *Gravissimae censurae* appeared in April 1531, and the English version was published in November of the same year: *The determinations of the moste famous and mooste excellent vniuersities of Italy and Fraunce, that it is so unlefull for a man to marie his brothers wyfe, that the pope hath no power to dispense therewith*. In fact less than a tenth of this work was occupied with the testimonies from just a handful of universities, and the rest of the book was a lengthy and detailed treatise explaining the king's case. Seven chapters of dense argument, loaded with citations, concluded that:

> the prohibition ... we should not marry our brother's wife ... is not such a prohibition, as standeth by constitution of man, but as nature first did plant in man's mind ... and our lord showed it unto his chosen people by Moses, and such as the custom of christian men ... hath from the beginnine of the christian faith many years followed and observed, which hath so often been renewed by councils, received and confirmed by later laws. And finally we have proved, that the Pope's auctority cannot stretch so far that he may dispense with such marriages.[42]

This was the king's justification, that natural law, the Old Testament law of the Bible, and the tradition begun by the primitive Church and reinforced by the General Councils of the Church were all more than the Pope had authority to overturn.

Other works were just published in English, and very obviously aimed at a readership nearer home. *A Dialogue betwene a Knyght and a Clerke Concernynge the Power Spiritual and Temporall* was published by Berthelet, the king's printer, in 1531. It was a revision of an older anti-papal work which took the form of a debate between a priest and a knight, on the question of whether the king has equal authority over both. It is interesting that this included such a forthright statement of the case against the king: the priest begins by saying:

> I wonder sir noble knight that in few days, times be changed, right is buried, laws be overturned, and statutes be trod underfoot.[43]

But it is equally interesting that the priest is cast as a fretful, whining intellectual, his respondent is depicted as a plain man, who responds bluntly:

> These words pass my capacity, I am a lewd [ie. uncouth] man; and though I went to school in my childhood, yet got I not so profound learning that those your words can of me be understood. And therefore worshipful clerk, if you desire to have communication with me, you must use a more homely and plainer fashion of speaking.

When the priest protests that laws must be made by the 'bishops of Rome', the knight gives a business-like answer:

> Whatever they ordain, or other have ordained in time past of temporality, may well be law to you, but not to us. For no man hath power to ordain statutes of things, over the which he hath no lordship. As the king of France may ordain no statutes upon the empire, neither the emperor upon the King of England. And likewise as princes of the world may ordain no statutes of your spiritual-ity, over the which they have no power; no more you may ordain no statutes of their temporalities, over the which you have neither power nor authority.[44]

In other words, it came down to a plain question of authority. And the King of England must surely be in charge of everything within the boundaries of his kingdom. This view, the work suggested, was seconded by the Bible, which also gave a satisfyingly straightforward example: 'it is evident and plain, that the bishops of the Hebrews were subjects to kings, and the kings deposed the bishops': although the respondent then added with pious caution, 'but god forbid that they should so now', the point was made.[45] The same idea was given legal expression by Christopher St German, in another dialogue printed in 1530, this time between a doctor and a student, which argued that nothing could fall outside the king's jurisdiction.[46] The simplicity of these dialogues was meant to appeal to the reading public; it seems likely that Henry himself thought in terms this simple much of the time.

The propaganda of the time also made the point very emphatically that this was not just a problem for the king and a few other elevated individuals, but something which touched every one of his subjects closely. Yet another dialogue, this time between a churchman and a lawyer, published in 1532, discussed the moral obligation Henry's subjects were under, to support him in his campaign. It asked

> how can we be so bold to desire his grace of his most high goodness and favour to assist us in our righteous causes: when we do not frankly assist him, yea and offer us to live and die in this his just cause and matter?[47]

The implicit contract between ruler and ruled was here being made explicit. A practical suggestion was also given by this work, when the churchman asked how the problem could be solved, and the lawyer replied:

> I think that the way might be found well enough, if the whole head and body of the Parliament would set their wits and good wills unto it. For no doubt but that it ought to be determined within this realm.

The churchman then agreed, 'me thinketh, the succession of this realm, ought not to be ordered by foreigners'.[48] It was necessary to keep underlining this point; twice in 1530 Henry had asked a council of notables whether they would agree that he should disregard Rome and settle his case in England, and twice they had refused.

By 1531, then, Henry knew what he wanted, namely public backing for the idea that he had the authority to judge his own case, and indeed any other contentious cases, within England. He wanted the political nation to stand behind him in his claim to rule the English Church. It took until 1534 for this to be finally achieved and encoded in statute law, but in the meantime he bullied, coerced, cajoled and persuaded his nobility, gentry and clergy, at court, in Parliament and in Convocation, to agree with him. He was also keeping up the pressure on Clement VII, as his agents in Rome went on relentlessly arguing his case. Had there been a reconfiguration of European powers which enabled the Pope to agree to his demands, no doubt Henry would have accepted gladly, although it is likely that he would have even then continued to press for some measure of religious reform. As the Pope remained in thrall to the emperor, however, the king's vision of a rival form for the English Church was solidifying.

The emergence of the legal argument, that Henry alone had jurisdiction within the realm, facilitated the extraordinary accusation of 1531 when the charge of *praemunire* was extended to implicate the entire body of clergy of the Church in England. This had worked well when it was a case of bringing Wolsey down; now Henry broadened his approach. It was like a parent accusing its child of disloyalty for obeying its other parent; absurd and undeniable at the same time. Henry was accusing the clergy of treason just by virtue of their being clergy within a hierarchy which had the Pope at its pinnacle. Convocation could not offer a defence; the clergy, as a body, submitted, apologised, and pressed £100,000 upon the king, who graciously pardoned them. The fundamental point was made, that he had the right both to accuse and to forgive in this way.

It would be a mistake to imagine that the progression towards the Royal Supremacy during these crucial years was in any way steady or consistent. There were some underlying continuities. Henry was convinced that his first marriage was invalid, determined to marry Anne, and in the process make a point of elevating scriptural authority, undermining papal claims to supremacy, and insisting on his right to rule the Church in England. These were, however, broad indicators, rather than a carefully worked out policy. Henry was used to having Wolsey to hand to transform his desires and ambitions, grandly conceived, into a plan of action, or into concrete and workable legislation. His rejection of Wolsey in 1529 had left him without that standby. Progress since 1529 had been erratic, and it was by no means clear where exactly it was leading, or by what route.

By 1531 Henry had ousted Katherine from court, and asserted his authority over the clergy in Convocation, but much of 1531 was spent waiting. Parliament was prorogued at Easter, which was usual, but rather than reconvening after Easter, it was prorogued until October, and in the autumn its recall was postponed again until the following year. According to the imperial ambassador, this was because Henry was waiting for word from Rome and his ministers were unsure how next to proceed.[49]

By the end of 1531 Henry had replaced Wolsey. Edward Lee became Archbishop of York and Stephen Gardiner became Bishop of Winchester. Both had been key players in the 'King's Great Matter', as scholars, propagandists and diplomats. More importantly, Thomas Cromwell, who had joined the Council at the start of the year, was by the autumn increasingly prominent in government. Cromwell, significantly enough, was a former member of Wolsey's household, and equipped with many of the same skills as his former master. In particular, Cromwell seems to have taken over the administration of business concerning Parliament, appropriately enough since he was himself a former MP. He was making elaborate preparation for the new session, and he was also the privy councillor from whom permission to be absent from Parliament was sought.[50] The third session of the 'Reformation Parliament', which began in January 1532, saw Cromwell's involvement at every turn. It also saw opposition. It was not just the absence of Wolsey that made the progress towards the royal supremacy so slow. It was the fact that what the king was trying to do was unprecedented, alarming and widely unpopular.

Henry could not proceed with confidence unless he had most of the ruling class behind him. This is why, for example, behind the scenes of the 1532 session of Parliament, the Duke of Norfolk called a council of influential men and put it to them that matrimonial cases should not be judged outside the realm, but belonged within the jurisdiction of the king as emperor within England. The reaction was clearly one of dismay. The nobility were not used to being asked to adjudicate on ecclesiastical causes, and in this all-important case it is easy to see why their responses remained noncommittal. The anxiety and caution among his more influential subjects may have been one reason why Henry recommended the attack on the papacy by bringing the question of annates to the fore.

Annates, or 'first fruits', were the chief source of papal revenue from England, comprising most of the first year's income for any newly-appointed bishop or archbishop. Any attack on annates was bound to catch the Pope's attention, and might even provide sufficient leverage to change his mind. Meanwhile an attack on English money going to Rome was more likely to prove an immediately popular cause than the more complex question of spiritual authority. When this campaign finally took form as statute law, it emphasised 'that great and inestimable sums of money be daily conveyed out of this realm to the impoverishment of the same'.[51] Even so, this act was only passed conditionally in 1532. Henry VIII still held back from taking the last shocking step towards severance from the papacy, despite the fact that he had been threatening this now for years.

Convocation had already submitted once to the king in 1531, after the accusation of *praemunire*. In 1532 this same drama was played out again, but this time for higher stakes, and in Parliament as well as Convocation, with the new principles established being codified in statute law. The *Supplication against the Ordinaries* was a long list of grievances against clerical failings and exactions submitted in the name of the House of Commons. It is unlikely that this was Henry trying to put further pressure on the Pope. It seems far more likely that this was the king establishing the basis of authority with which he intended to supplant the Pope.

The *Supplication* attacked the clergy because 'in their Convocations ... [they] have made and daily make divers fashions of laws and ordinances concerning temporal things; and some of them be repugnant to the laws and statutes of your realm.' In other words, the clergy were under attack for wielding authority, not for their religious failings. Indeed, the preamble noted that the combination of the 'uncharitable behaviour and dealing' of the clergy with 'new fantastical and erroneous opinions' creeping into the realm through the medium of 'seditious' books, had led to great 'discord, variance and debate'. If anything, this *Supplication* was seeking to protect the traditional faith. The only hint of religious reform it contained was a plea for the number of holy days to be reduced, since many were kept 'with very small devotion', encouraging vice and getting in the way of the harvest.[52] The right of the clergy to proceed against sin and heresy was respected, even encouraged. At this point Henry's sights were set on the Church's temporal authority only; his interest in its spiritual authority would develop later.

The *Supplication* was presented in April 1532 to Convocation, who returned a spirited rebuttal through the hands of the king. A month later, Convocation was told by the king to submit to his authority: all future legislation was to be subject to royal assent. The clergy resisted, trying to prove from scripture their right to legislative autonomy; by this stage, they understood the rules of the game the king was playing, and knew that any claim not based on biblical authority would have little success. But Henry fought back and this time with menace, suggesting to Parliament that they examine the oath taken by bishops to the Pope, and subdue this treasonous clerical independence by statute.

In the end, a battered and depleted Convocation submitted; Fisher was ill, seven other bishops were absent, and only three gave their full consent.[53] Such a shallow victory, however, was enough to give Henry the aura of legality he needed. He took Convocation's submission back to Parliament, where the 'Submission of the Clergy' was then enshrined in statute law, a formal admission that 'the Convocations of the same clergy is always, hath been, and ought to be assembled only by the King's writ', that canon law 'prejudicial to the King's prerogative royal and repugnant to the laws and statutes of this realm' was to be abolished, and that nothing henceforth was to be done without the king's permission.[54] By this point in 1532 it could be argued that Henry had won. Now all he had to do was convince as many people as possible that he had won fairly.

KATHERINE AND ANNE

The situation of Henry's queens – his rejected queen, and his queen-in-waiting – during these years was perhaps equally unenviable. Until the campaign for the annulment had achieved some kind of resolution, Henry was compelled to go on according Queen Katherine his usual respect, and include her in all official occasions. Katherine presumably hoped that the king's plans for an annulment would come to nothing, and that her best strategy in the meantime was to go on playing the part of the loyal and devoted wife. Pathetically, the queen was still making Henry's shirts as she had always done; we know this because Anne made such a fuss when she discovered it.[55] King and queen also continued to exchange messages every three days when not able to meet, as had been their habit throughout twenty years of marriage.[56] Anne had her own set of apartments at Greenwich, and her loyal band of supporters. In 1529, her father was made Earl of Wiltshire and Ormonde, and at the feast in celebration Anne took pride of place. Yet Christmas 1529 was celebrated in the usual fashion, and with Katherine in her accustomed place. Henry sent her away in early 1530 to reside elsewhere, but the customary summer progress in 1530 saw king and queen travel together as was normal. Katherine's strategy of playing the loyal wife left Henry the option of acting as though nothing was wrong between them.

As well as her rather touching attempts to preserve the marriage that was now under such threat, Katherine continued to act, rather more aggressively, to motivate her allies abroad. In particular she stayed in regular communication with her nephew, Charles V. As a Spaniard, she continued to think in terms of European realities, which set her apart from Henry and much of his court, for whom English preoccupations were paramount. Indeed, this difference in perspective explains much of the dealings between 1527 and 1533: Katherine was outraged at the proposed slur to the papacy, the Habsburgs and the daughter she had groomed to be a queen regnant, just as Katherine's mother Isabella had been. Henry, for his part, was outraged that his barren wife did not realise that a queen regnant was an unprecedented and unwanted possibility in an England context, that she was endangering the kingdom by refusing to stand aside, heightening the risk of civil war, and that her opposition was an affront to the pre-eminence of his own authority within his realm.

Anne Boleyn's position in these years was peculiar and precarious. Undoubtedly Henry loved her: he lavished gifts upon her, and constantly sought her company. Officially, however, she was a court lady of little standing, and since she probably turned 30 in 1530 or 1531, she was an old maid by Tudor standards. If her hopes of marrying Henry were to be disappointed, she would be a pitiful figure indeed. Significantly, the imperial ambassador reported that she had complained to Henry in 1529 that by waiting so long she had sacrificed her chances of marriage and children elsewhere.[57] Living at court was necessary if she were to be near Henry, but this also necessitated being near the queen, who behaved as she had done with Henry's former mistresses, as if nothing untoward was happening. It seems likely that this was particularly galling for Anne. Both she and Henry seem to have seized upon the chance offered by York Place, soon to be rebuilt as Whitehall Palace. Since it was the traditional home of the archbishops of York in London, it had only one official suite of private rooms, and was therefore not an appropriate dwelling for both king and queen. Just two days after Wolsey pleaded guilty to the charges of *praemunire*, in October 1529, a party of just four, comprising Henry and Anne, Anne's mother and a gentleman of the Privy Chamber, came to look round York Place.[58] The rebuilding of Whitehall was a joint project for Henry and Anne, and one which must have comforted her, as they planned their future marital home. It was at Whitehall that Anne's coronation feasts and jousts were held in 1533; her hopes of this presumably sustained her during her long wait for recognition.

The wait for the marriage she had been promised must at times have seemed unbearable. Henry seems to have expected to carry opinion with him, and was obviously furious and resentful at the level of support Katherine could command. An unpleasant event occurred in March 1531, when several people fell ill after a dinner at Bishop John Fisher's London house, and his cook confessed under torture that he had put poison in the food. There was public horror, and the unfortunate cook suffered death by being boiled alive, a punishment which was held to fit the crime.[59] Popular rumour blamed the Boleyns. Even if they had not been involved, it was popular recognition of the level of impatience and antagonism that Anne might be expected to feel in her awkward situation.

In all the reversals and hesitations of these years, whilst the king waited to see what might be forthcoming from Rome, and whilst he applied pressure to the Church at home, Anne's chances slowly improved. In July 1531 the king left Windsor, early one morning, to go hunting, with Anne at his side. He would not see Katherine again, and he did not make any formal farewell. When he returned to Windsor, he first made sure that Katherine had moved to Wolsey's old palace of the More. He instructed that she should seek some permanent place of retirement, and most unkind of all, he gave the command that she was not to see their daughter. Henry had not been her husband for over twenty years without learning what would hurt Katherine most deeply. She loved her daughter, and she also pinned all her hopes for the future on Mary. No doubt Henry knew that if anything could persuade Katherine to relent, it was the pain of separation from her child, yet had she relented, it would have consigned Mary to bastardy and destroyed her chance of inheriting the throne. Katherine remained obdurate, and that year Christmas was celebrated at Greenwich without a queen.

Hall reported that there was popular unease at the separation of king and queen. 'Wherefore the Common people daily murmured and spake their foolish fantasies.' This must also have been a source of unease for Henry. Hall went on to assert that 'the affairs of Princes be not ordered by the common people, nor it were not convenient that all things were opened to them.'[60] This was wishful thinking, however; Tudor authority could not operate beyond a minimal level of popular disaffection.

1532 began, therefore, in an atmosphere of tension. Henry was poised to make the break with Rome, but a great deal had to be achieved if it was to be done convincingly, dragging with him as much of the political nation as he could. Events in Parliament moved slowly. The king sought some solace in building for the future, in this case literally, as work proceeded on the new palace of Whitehall, which was to house his new family. To make room for his building work he had bought up a substantial amount of Westminster and levelled it, paying over £1,000 in compensation to the unfortunates who were evicted from their homes there.[61] It was in 1532 that he bought what subsequently became St James's Palace and Park as an adjunct to Whitehall, and to provide fish and waterfowl for his new palace. Hall describes this as a crucial part of the transformation of Whitehall from bishop's house into royal palace:

> Ye have heard before how the king had purchased the Bishop of York's place, which was a fair Bishop's house, but not meet for a king: wherefore the King purchased all the meadows about saint James, and all the whole house of St James, and there made a fair mansion and a park, and builded many costly and commodious houses for great pleasure.[62]

In due course, St James's Palace was to be viewed as the ascribed dwelling for the heir to the throne, a royal nursery in a satellite palace, just as Eltham had been a satellite to Greenwich, and Henry's home as a child. It seems likely that this was already in Henry's mind when he bought the Palace, and gave directions for its alteration.

By the summer of 1532 Anne was clearly about to become queen, in Henry's mind at least, which was increasingly the only one that mattered. The king had brought the Church at home to the point of submission, which was in the eyes of Thomas More the point of no return. Once the Parliament which had secured the Submission of the

Clergy had been prorogued, More resigned, returning the Great Seal to the king. He was replaced with Thomas Audley, which put one of Anne's sympathisers at the heart of government, to augment her brother's place in the privy chamber and her father's position as Lord Privy Seal. Audley had also been speaker of the House of Commons during the first three sessions of the Reformation Parliament, and Henry was evidently grateful for the work he had done promoting royal interests there.

When William Warham died in August 1532 he was replaced as Archbishop of Canterbury by Thomas Cranmer, another telling mark of Henry's determination, for not only was it highly unusual to elevate an archdeacon directly to the rank of archbishop, it was also unusual to make a direct appointment rather than letting the crown enjoy the income of the vacant see for a year first. It had been expected that Gardiner would succeed Warham, but his outspoken protest against the Submission of the Clergy had blighted his chances: there was general astonishment at the news of his replacement.[63] Cranmer, however, had a proven record of loyalty to the Boleyns, one which would endure beyond Anne's eventual disgrace. It is typical of Henry that he did not inquire further into Cranmer's circumstances, but assumed that his loyal service to date was an indication of his future obedience to Henry's will. In fact, Cranmer was in Lutheran Nuremberg in the summer of 1532, where he had just married the niece of Osiander, the Lutheran pastor there. For an English cleric to marry at this stage was an unequivocal gesture of commitment to the evangelical cause. Henry's decision to make him archbishop seems to have been an unpleasant shock.[64] Cranmer would spend the next fourteen years struggling with conflicting loyalties to his faith and to his king. Henry, as ever, would be slow to understand that those who served him could still hold opinions which differed from his own.

In September, Cromwell was already drafting the Act of Appeals which would the following year enact the decisive break from papal authority by declaring that the marriage question could be settled within England. Meanwhile, Anne was preparing to accompany Henry to France for a meeting with the French king. She was to travel as queen in all but name, and symbolically, Katherine was forced to surrender her jewels so Anne could wear them on this visit. Unusually, Katherine had at first resisted the king's wishes in this, compelling him to make a direct request through a gentleman of the privy chamber, which was almost as bad as making the king turn up in person. Perhaps for

Katherine this seemed like the point of no return; it was certainly an extraordinary humiliation. And on Sunday, 1 September, at Windsor Castle, Anne was made Marquess of Pembroke, to give her sufficient status to meet the King of France as something other than the woman Henry wanted to marry. Henry himself put the crimson velvet mantle on her, and placed the gold coronet on her head. Anne wore her hair loose, and her dress was stiff with jewels. It was a coronation in miniature, only symbolically enough it was not a bishop, but the king himself who performed the ceremony.

The visit to France took place in October. Slightly awkwardly, the Queen of France was a niece of Katherine of Aragon, but the English angled for the attendance of some royal ladies to emphasise the solemnity of the occasion. French reluctance on this point emphasises the oddity of Anne's presence, and it was concluded that no ladies would be officially present, but that Francis and Anne would meet unofficially.[65] Anne's own household was small compared with the 2,000 or so in Henry's entourage, and although she was everywhere at Henry's side during the first ten days in Calais, she was left behind when the king went to Boulogne to visit Francis. However, Henry then brought Francis back to Calais for the weekend, and it was at the climax of the chief banquet that Anne made her entrance, costumed and masqued with six other ladies. She claimed the hand of the French king and danced with him incognito until Henry himself removed her disguise. To impartial observers it might have seemed a strange, awkward affair, a royal visit that was not quite dignified, a queen substitute who was not the genuine article, but to Henry and Anne it was a glorious occasion. It also marked a highly significant point in their relationship. At some point on the return journey, after many years of waiting, they slept together. Within a matter of weeks, Anne was to fall pregnant. For Henry and perhaps for Anne too, this must have seemed like the divine seal of approval on all their endeavours. It meant that the final repudiation of Rome was all but unavoidable. In January, Henry and Anne were finally married; Cranmer later reported that the date was around 25 January but the ceremony, for obvious reasons, was kept secret.

The break with Rome was given legal definition by the Act in Restraint of Annates, passed conditionally in 1532 and confirmed in 1534, and by the Act of Appeals of 1533. The Act in Restraint of Annates, which withdrew revenue from Rome, and effectively put appointments of abbots and bishops into the hands of the king, was the opening salvo. The Act of Appeals made the break complete, and it is the one Parliamentary act that should be required reading for anyone seeking to understand Henry VIII, for it enshrined the mature argument that he and his advisors had been working towards for the last six years. It passed through several drafts between September 1532 and April 1533 when it became law.[66] The crucial opening passage – which heads this chapter – was probably of Cromwell's devising, and was present from the very first drafts. It began:

> Where by divers sundry old authentic histories and chronicles it is manifestly declared and expressed that this realm of England is an empire, and so hath been accepted in the world, governed by one supreme head and king having the dignity and royal estate of the imperial crown of the same.

This preamble was enough to show the essentials of Henry's victory; vague and impressionistic but unassailable. England was an empire: everybody said so, everybody had always said so, which meant Henry was in charge of everything. The act also stated firmly that the English Church, under his authority, was able to decide and adjudicate disputes and administer itself 'without the intermeddling of any exterior person or persons'.[67] This meant that Henry's marriage could be annulled at home; it also meant that henceforth, he ruled the Church in England. It was an extraordinary achievement.

Yet if the break with Rome was given formal expression by Parliament, it was given actual expression for the king and most of his subjects by the coronation of Anne Boleyn as queen in June 1533. The questionable nature of her status as queen, given that Queen Katherine was still alive, was strengthened considerably by the fact that she was six months pregnant at the time. The ceremony and celebration was spread out over four days. It began with a triumphant progression from Greenwich to the Tower by river, then followed ceremonies within the Tower where Henry created eighteen Knights of the Bath and nearly fifty knights bachelor, ensuring that Anne's triumph was reinforced with the gratitude of the political elite. The repairs at the Tower and the renovation of the royal apartments had been hastily completed in readiness for this occasions. On the third day there was a procession through the city to Westminster, with pageants along the way, and on the fourth day the coronation took place in Westminster Abbey followed by the traditional banquet in Westminster Hall.

The spectacle made sure that everybody, from foreign envoys to the court to the merchants and apprentices of the City, witnessed Anne's apotheosis as queen. Anne had become Henry's wife in the face of public opinion, and by highly dubious means. The coronation, therefore, was an emphatic endorsement of political correctness as it was understood at the time. It was also a group effort which involved so much financial outlay, and participation by all layers of society, that was intended to have a bonding effect upon the new queen and her new and perhaps suspicious subjects. Henry was setting the seal upon the new order in the most ostentatious way he could find.

5

THE GODLY PRINCE, 1533–1539

Be it enacted by authority of this present Parliament that the king our sovereign lord, his heirs and successors kings of this realm, shall be taken, accepted and reputed the only supreme head in earth of the Church of England called *Anglicana Ecclesia*, and shall have and enjoy annexed and united to the imperial crown of this realm as well the title and style thereof, as all honours, dignities, preeminences, jurisdictions, privileges, authorities, immunities, profits and commodities, to the said dignity of supreme head of the same Church belonging and appertaining.[1]

With the royal supremacy, Henry had recast his kingship in an even more glorious form. He had reinvented himself, as spiritual as well as political leader, and he had a new queen, a new seat of government in Whitehall Palace, a new Archbishop of Canterbury to bless his endeavours, and a new style of discourse which shaped everything from Acts of Parliament to the interior decorations produced by Hans Holbein. What he did not yet have, although he craved it, was approval, either human or divine. His subjects were variously mystified, alarmed, outraged and sceptical concerning his new claims, particularly as they related to their queen – to either queen – and to their Pope. At the same time, divine sanction had not yet been granted in the form of the son he longed for. The child carried by Anne Boleyn at her coronation was so confidently expected to be a boy that the letters announcing his birth had already been prepared. Holbein, who more than any other artist gave material form to Henry's new conception of majesty, designed an appropriately splendid cradle. The boy was to be called either Henry or Edward. Henry insisted that the birth take place at Greenwich, with Anne enthroned in a sumptuous bed; as ever, he created the right dramatic setting. Then, on 7 September 1533, the new queen gave birth to a girl. The pre-prepared letters, thanking God for giving Anne 'good speed in the deliverance and bringing forth of a prince' were amended with an additional 's' to announce the unexpected princess.[2] Henry might be able to bully most of his subjects into submission, but he had found that he was not able to intimidate God into granting his most heartfelt desire.

The sense of dramatic irony is strong, but in fact Elizabeth's birth was not too serious a blow.[3] After all, she had been conceived swiftly, born without difficulty, and was healthy, so sons should soon follow. In giving her the name of her paternal grandmother, Henry perhaps remembered his love for the mother who had died, aged only 37, when he was not quite 12. In her early years, the king made several open demonstrations of his affection for his little daughter. In the meantime, Henry set about securing popular approval for his initiatives, and for his queen. Those who did not realise that he had struck a blow for true morality by rejecting his adulterous liaison with Katherine, or that he had endorsed a purer vision of the Church in his rejection of the papacy, must be enlightened and convinced of this. He wanted his subjects to share his exultation at his new marriage, and his confident expectation of an heir at last. And those who continued wantonly, faithlessly and inexplicably to oppose him, must be punished. The rhetoric of government which unfolded in the years following the enactment of the royal supremacy was thus at the same time exalted, inspirational, and menacing.

It was also quite difficult to understand. Historians have struggled with the 1530s more perhaps than with any other decade of the sixteenth century. Henry's endeavours, and those of his leading advisors – Thomas Cranmer, Thomas Cromwell, Stephen Gardiner – have been subjected to cyclical reinterpretation and remain the focus of much debate and disagreement. Did Henry embrace Protestantism, only to draw back when new dangers threatened? Was there any consistency to his policies, or were they an arbitrary selection of preferences, or a reflection of constantly shifting influences about the king? Was a new style of centralised and rational government emerging under Cromwell's direction? These and many other questions have preoccupied commentators.

It is important to realise that Henry's motivations and objectives remained equally opaque to most of his contemporaries. Many, including both Cranmer and Cromwell, thought the king was heading in a Protestant direction, but they were to be proved wrong. Gardiner was perhaps more astute in realising the kind of reformation that Henry had in mind, but it is unlikely that he found it entirely convincing. Arguably Anne Boleyn came closest to appreciating Henry's vision, which was at once evangelical and Catholic, reforming and traditionalist, and above all aimed at the exaltation of his own majestic authority. But Anne failed him in other respects, and Henry's subsequent wives never came as close to understanding him in this. For much of the decade Henry thought he had an ally in Cromwell, and deployed his skills to the full in pursuit of his chief aims, only to discover in 1540 that he had been duped. The ferocity of Henry's response would show the extent of his sense of betrayal. His pursuit of a new style of godly kingship in these years from 1533 to 1539 was then energetic, innovative, ruthless and never totally successful.

KINGSHIP REDRAWN

With the enactment of the royal supremacy and the Anne Boleyn's coronation as queen, a new era began in Henry's kingship. His energetic attempts to enforce, justify and defend the new order were to lead to kingship itself being redrawn. Tellingly enough, it seems to have been about this time that Henry redrafted the coronation oath. The traditional phrase, where the king swore that 'he shall do in his judgements equity and right justice' was altered to 'he shall *according to his conscience* in all his Judgements [ad]minister equity'.[4] Justice had become a much more subjective matter since the king's conscience had moved to him to declare his first marriage invalid, to repudiate papal authority, to take control of the Church and crown Anne as queen even while Katherine still lived. The traditional phrase where kings swore to 'keep and maintain the right and the liberties of holy church of old time granted by the righteous Christian kings of England' was altered to specify that those rights and liberties were 'not prejudicial to his Jurisdiction and dignity royal'.[5] Henry's new understanding of his own royal authority was neatly encapsulated in these two alterations; it was both more assertive of his individual majesty, and more defensive against possible outside encroachment.

This transition in Henry's self-image is evident in the portraits of the king. To walk around Room 1 of the National Portrait Gallery is to appreciate the point very well. The earliest known portrait of Henry from 1511 shows Henry in the stance adopted by his father and his other fifteenth-century predecessors; it is a portrait of just the upper half of his person, his hands held in front of him, fiddling with a ring just as Henry VII had fiddled with a rose (Edward IV and Richard III had also held rings). The king's dress is rich, embroidered and bejewelled; he wears a heavy jewelled collar and a rich ornament in his black hat, but there is nothing to make this portrayal significantly different from others in the same genre that had preceded it.[6] Other portraits from the 1520s followed this model. The new conception of kingship which began to dawn in the 1530s had its outstanding chronicler in Hans Holbein, who came to Henry's court in 1532 and stayed to immortalise it.[7] His creation is the iconic image of Henry from 1536, here as a preparatory sketch, which is still the most famous portrayal of the king today, and which was initially enshrined at the heart of government itself as a mural on the wall of the king's privy chamber in the palace of Whitehall (see Plate 1).[8] The king appears life-sized, in the first ever full-length portrait of an English monarch, in a tableau which declared his dynastic confidence, his personal majesty, his relationship with wife and parents, his Renaissance pretensions, and his physical magnificence. It was a virtuoso declaration of Henry's self-fashioning as king, significantly enough commissioned after Queen Jane's pregnancy was confirmed, and intended to reinforce the king's own understanding of his role as well as conveying a sense of that identity to the governmental and diplomatic elite who were granted admittance to the privy chamber. In the 1540s Henry opened the chamber up to wider access on important occasions and took rooms in the gallery beyond for his private use, perhaps seeking to maximise the effect of this powerful piece of iconography.

Holbein's image of the king is all the more telling because the painter was an important person at Henry's court and someone whose activities lay close to the king's keenest interests. As we have seen, Henry had a consistent appreciation of the power of the visual image, and was well aware of his good fortune in securing Holbein's services. He said to a nobleman, 'I could make seven earls from seven peasants if it pleased me, but I could not make one Hans Holbein, or so excellent an artist, out of seven earls.'[9]

Holbein was deeply enmeshed in the humanist world which so appealed to Henry; he had painted Erasmus in 1523, and Erasmus had given him letters of introduction to Thomas More, and when he had produced his famous portrait of More's learned household he went on to paint several members of the Boleyn family and faction. His return to Basle in 1528 was brief because he was not sufficiently Protestant to be accepted there, and when he returned to England in 1532 as 'royal painter' he became a key mythmaker for the regime. He painted nearly all the key figures at court, including Cromwell and the young Prince Edward. He designed cups and jewellery for the queens, designed new insignia for the Order of the Garter, produced the woodcut for the title page of the Coverdale Bible, and in his miniature of *Solomon and the Queen of Sheba* produced an allegory of the submission of the Church to Henry VIII.[10] He was thus connected with almost everything that was of central importance to the king.

The Holbein portrait of Henry which is by far the best-known image of the man is a statement of kingly magnificence, a visual assertion of his majesty, Holbein's direct communication of Henry's new conception of himself as king. It has been pointed out that in this portrait Henry carries none of the usual trappings of kingship; no crown, orb or sceptre, no symbol beyond the Garter.[11] His unadorned figure is in itself a sufficient statement of royal dominance. The mature king had taken on the aura of sacred majesty and was as recognisable as the depictions of Christ in Majesty which also require no further elaboration.

From this image on the wall of the privy chamber, which lay at the heart of government, Henry's concern with his self-presentation radiated outwards. This was both a private and a public matter. In private, Henry used a Latin psalter produced by the Frenchman Jean Maillart, who arrived from the court of Francis I in 1539. Four key illustrations to this depicted Henry as King David, wearing his distinctive court dress (in particular the feathered black and white cap of the Holbein portrait) as he prayed, read, played on the harp, and – most incongruously of all – confronted Goliath (see Plate 4). We know that Henry used this psalter because he wrote in the margin, commenting on the parallels between his life and that of the Old Testament king.

In public, the new order was given triumphant and concrete expression in the new palace which Henry built to house himself and his new young wife. Whitehall Palace was a redesigned and much glorified version of the former York Place, the London palace of the archbishops of York, which Wolsey had reluctantly surrendered. Its construction was a continuing project during the tense years when Henry was working towards the fulfilment of his 'Great Matter'. James Needham, the king's master carpenter, was promoted to be surveyor of the king's works, and at every stage of the design and building process submitted plans to Henry and Anne for approval, beginning long before she was queen, though some time after Henry had made the decision that she would be. Possibly it gave the king some much-needed relief, and Anne some much-needed reassurance, to be able to build a palace for their future life together. If so their hopes were misplaced, for building work at Whitehall was to last a lot longer than Anne herself. But the importance of the palace would remain even as Anne died an ignominious death: an Act of Parliament in 1536 gave it official status as the king's chief residence, and formally (and rather confusingly) reabsorbed it within the Palace of Westminster.

This palace, which we shall continue to call Whitehall – perhaps so named because of the light-coloured stone used for its construction – was divided by King Street, the forerunner of today's Whitehall, on which stood the so-called 'Holbein Gate', its architectural style both modern and triumphalist. In line with Henry's own eclectic style, however, the buildings were decorated with a combination of classical motifs and heraldic devices. On the north side of King Street, between the road and the newly-acquired St James's Park, around which Henry had set a high wall, there was a tiltyard, with viewing gallery, a collection of tennis courts and bowling alleys, and a cockpit. The main body of the palace was on the south side, with great hall and privy lodgings, and gardens where today the Ministry of Defence sits.

This new palace covered over twenty-three acres compared to the six occupied by Hampton Court.[12] Henry filled it with treasures, as was demonstrated after his death by the inventory which took eighteen months to catalogue his possessions. By that time some of them were broken treasures: among the items in the 'secret jewelhouse' were 'a table of bone with Imagery broken', 'an instrument or a thing to roast puddings in of Silver gilt lackinge a piece of the foot', and 'the length of the haft [handle] of a dagger of green stone … the lower part being broken'.[13] Many of the items pertained to the king's varied leisure activities: in the study at the end of the long gallery was to be found a cabinet with twenty-three pairs of hawks bells, a coffer of chessmen, five instruments of astronomy, a great wooden sailor's compass and two spectacle cases.[14] In the king's 'secret study called the chairhouse' were found a case with four rackets 'covered with crimson velvet and Satin embroidered with gold', three horns to put gunpowder in, a green angling rod in a case of leather, two coffers containing silk, samplers and other materials for embroidery, and a long box containing two dozen visors to be worn at a masque.[15] Some of this recalls the assorted items depicted in Holbein's portrait of *The Ambassadors*, although without the artistic embellishment. It makes the point that this great palace was not only a distinctive political statement; it was also Henry's home.

New work was also undertaken at Hampton Court, where from 1529 to 1533 Henry had been content to use the palace as Wolsey had left it. Renovations after 1533 abandoned the old principle of 'stacked' lodgings, with the king's apartments on the floor above those of the queen, and instituted a new principle of royal apartments side by side on the same floor, with shared use of a grand processional staircase. These developments mirrored those in the French court around the same time. There was also a greater emphasis on royal privacy, with the provision of privy lodgings which were to become more and more the focus of the king's day-to-day existence. Greenwich Palace was also reconfigured to provide both sets of royal apartments on the same level, with larger privy lodgings for both.[16]

The 1530s saw a vast expansion generally in Henry VIII's building works. Between 1535 and 1545 he was to acquire thirty-two new houses and palaces.[17] Some of these acquisitions were a consequence of the dissolution of the monasteries; Henry had always used abbeys as places to stay on his progresses, and he acquired several of those on major routes in the south-east, such as Dartford, so he could continue using them when travelling.

Henry's palaces were also provided with parks. This was all the more important since in January 1536 Henry sustained a heavy fall from his horse which left him unconscious for two hours. This incident, at the age of 44, seems to have had a profound effect upon him. Certainly after this the king never jousted again, and hunting became his main form of exercise and entertainment on horseback. The creation of the great London parks belongs to this decade, and it was one of the many benefits of Henry's headship over the Church that he was in a position to acquire the seven Kentish parks of the archbishops of Canterbury in these years.

SUPREMACY AND OPPOSITION

If Henry's reconfigured kingship was given most immediate and personal expression in his new life with Anne, it received its most emphatic public expression in the flood of legislation, implementation and propaganda which sought to secure the Royal Supremacy. Henry's new role as Supreme Head of the Church of England was the ideological foundation of his new self-image; it was also the source of new channels of communication and coercion which employed the pulpits and the ecclesiastical hierarchy to impose his revamped authority; finally, it was a useful source of wealth. The importance of the Supremacy resonates, therefore, through most of the official pronouncements of the 1530s. It was made clear that:

> this your Grace's realm, recognising no superior under God but only your Grace, hath been and is free from subjection to any man's laws but only to such as have been devised, made and ordained within this realm for the wealth of the same.[18]

It was a defiant statement of England's independence, and the untouchable authority of its king. It was also to become an article of faith in the English Church no less than any article of salvation. The first item of the Injunctions issued in 1536, for example, was that the clergy should:

> faithfully keep and observe, and as far as in them may lie, shall cause to be observed and kept of other, all and singular laws and statutes of this realm made for the abolishing and extirpation of the Bishop of Rome's pretensed and usurped power and jurisdiction within this realm, and for the establishment and confirmation of the king's authority and jurisdiction within the same, as of the Supreme Head of the Church of England.[19]

Leaving nothing to chance, these injunctions then went on to spell out the necessity of preaching on the subject, once every Sunday for the next quarter of the year, and thereafter at least twice every quarter.

The supremacy was a political statement, and it owed its existence to a largely political problem, but it was also a religious declaration, and its religious consequences were as ambiguous as its political clout was unmistakeable. The Act quoted above, which set about the meticulous dismantling of papal power within England, also included a caveat:

> Provided always that this act nor any thing or things therein contained shall be hereafter interpreted or expounded that your Grace, your nobles and subjects, intend by the same to decline or vary from the congregation of Christ's Church in any things concerning the very articles of the Catholic Faith of Christendom; or in any other things declared by Holy Scripture and the word of God necessary for your and their salvations; but only to make an ordinance by policies necessary and convenient to repress vice and for good conservation of this realm in peace, unity and tranquillity.[20]

Henry wanted to remain free from the taint of heresy; he wanted England to remain within the unity of Christendom; he wanted to uphold the primacy of scripture as the source of religious authority – both because he believed this to be true, and because he could control the interpretation of scripture, or at least thought he could. In the same year, the Act of Supremacy gave him 'authority to reform and redress all errors, heresies and abuses' within his Church. Henry clearly thought that all these desires were mutually compatible. Not all his subjects were as easily persuaded.

Against the new initiatives of these years must be set the constant criticism of the king's actions to be heard from many different levels of society. The most well-known of these were voiced by his more eminent subjects, but there was antagonism at all levels of society. In the summer of 1533 it was recorded that:

> the 23rd day of August were two women beaten about the Cheap naked from the waist upward, with rods, and their ears nailed to the Standard for because they said queen Katherine was the true queen of England, and not queen Anne: and one of the women was big with child: and when these two women had thus been punished, they fortified their saying still, to die in the quarrel for queen Katherine's sake.[21]

Henry was to discover that his subjects could prove remarkably courageous, and obdurate, in refusing to accept his new policies, and his justification for them.

One of the earliest and most interesting challenges to the new order was the affair of the 'Nun of Kent' which was perhaps the first major challenge to Henry's new dignity and authority, apart from the resistance of Katherine and her supporters. This episode showed the extent of Henry's vulnerability to popular dislike, and was particularly instructive because it constituted opposition from a cross-section of society, from the higher clergy and nobility down to more ordinary folk. Elizabeth Barton was a servant woman who had been miraculously healed of illness in the 1520s, and had then become a nun at St Sepulchre's in Canterbury. Already in the 1520s she was in the habit of going into trances and having visions. These were acceptable, if unusual, manifestations of religious devotion at this time; visions and miracles were perhaps on the extreme end of mainstream piety, but they were much respected, underlining the difference between the Tudor age and our own. Barton was uneducated, with an intense sort of religious zeal, but she was given the approval and blessing of the Archbishop of Canterbury and gained a considerable popular following. As a channel of popular piety, it is unsurprising that she then began to channel popular dislike of Henry's attempts to reject Queen Katherine. She claimed an angel had told her to go to the king and warn him to desist, promising that if he married Anne Boleyn terrible vengeance would be exacted.[22]

Rather startlingly, Elizabeth Barton did as the angel commanded; she is recorded as having had at least two meetings with Henry. She also spoke with the Archbishop of Canterbury, Bishop John Fisher, Thomas More and a fairly large number of monks in Canterbury, Observant Franciscan friars from Greenwich and Richmond, and Brigittine nuns and priests in Syon. That she was taken this seriously says a lot about the importance of religion at the time, and the extent to which the miraculous and providential could be accepted as genuine communications from God. Henry swiftly decided that the woman was a fraud, however, and the tool of those who sought to undermine him. She was denounced, and executed. The manner of the denunciation is interesting: not only her predictions concerning the king were attacked, but every aspect of her supposed piety was exposed as fraudulent, allegedly on the basis of her own confession. The description of how she had faked her visions in the 1520s, how she had been healed naturally, not miraculously, and the suggestion that she had enjoyed sexual relations with her chief sponsor, all gave indications of how later attacks on the monasteries and other religious 'superstitions' would proceed. Barton herself had said that the king, once married to Anne Boleyn, ceased to be king: this was tantamount to treason. But her significance went wider than that. Henry did not attempt to try her: she and her associates were condemned by parliamentary Act of Attainder, a sure sign of nervousness. And with her was condemned an entire religious outlook. Henry was jealous of his newly acquired spiritual dominion, and resentful of powers, particularly providential ones, which sought to challenge his position.

Barton and her associates were executed at Tyburn in April 1534. This paved the way for another execution, which was also an act of vengeance. John Fisher had been an irritant to Henry since the inception of the campaign for the annulment, all the more since he was a figure of incontestable integrity. Eventually canonised in 1935, his reputation even before his death testifies to his deep and sincere piety. His opposition enraged Henry, perhaps it also secretly appalled him. To take on a distant Pope was one thing, but Fisher was a home-grown saint-in-the-making, and his moral stature was redoubtable. Fisher had been confessor to the king's formidable and pious grandmother Lady Margaret Beaufort; he had preached the funeral sermon for Henry VII; he had been Bishop of Rochester since 1504, refusing further advancement to remain in England's poorest see; he was a scholar of international repute, vice-chancellor of Cambridge University, responsible for bringing Erasmus to Cambridge; he had helped lead the campaign against Luther in the 1520s. He had also been the leading voice among Katherine's supporters, and a tireless campaigner on her behalf. Holbein's portrait of him suggests both the sanctity and the strength of purpose. He was a redoubtable opponent. He was attainted for treason with the Nun of Kent and her followers, but not executed; perhaps Henry's nerve failed him at the thought of the judicial killing of someone so respected. In the same month as she died, however, Fisher refused to swear the Oath of Succession. He was deprived of his bishopric, imprisoned, and treated harshly. Old, ill, cold, with only ragged clothes, he was in the Tower for a year. In May 1535 the Pope made him a cardinal, perhaps thinking to save his life, but in fact hastening his end, such was Henry's fury at this honour. He was convicted of treason, and executed on 22 June 1535, two days before his patronal feast day of St John the Baptist. Since St John had also been beheaded for criticising a king on his second marriage, the parallels were easily made. Fisher had foreseen laying down his life like his patron saint at the Blackfriars trial six years before, and now his foresight was proved accurate. Since this analogy cast Henry in the role of Herod, it is clear that this particular death was not one of Henry's most successful ventures when it came to constructing an image of the godly prince.

John Fisher was canonised as a Roman Catholic saint in company with Thomas More, and the two have been linked together in the popular imagination ever since they died in the same year for opposing Henry's self-aggrandisement. Yet More was a very different opponent. He had not agreed with Henry's rejection of Katherine, nor with the royal supremacy, but he had sought refuge in silence, rather than actively opposing him, resigning his chancellorship and attempting to retire from the political scene. Henry's desire for approval and adulation went far beyond securing political assent, however. He wanted to be seen as the moral guardian of his kingdom, and the opinions of men like More were important to him, no matter what official post they might hold. Moreover, he had always expected More to be on his side.

Thomas More was exactly the kind of councillor who suited Henry's idea of himself: educated, devout, humorous; a talented author, lawyer, and diplomat; a man who could simultaneously entertain and instruct Tudor society by writing *Utopia,* but who could also be ruthless and terrifying in his opposition to heresy. Perhaps that last point should have given Henry more pause for thought. More's polemical works against William Tyndale in the 1520s demonstrate the extraordinary wrath he was capable of feeling against those who endangered innocent souls. Some have been at a loss to explain how the same man could write the gentle and humane satire of *Utopia*, and also write against Tyndale with every disgusting image and epithet that could be dredged from the teeming waters of Tudor prose. But More saw Tyndale and his like as jeopardising the salvation of thousands, and responded with the same ferocity as a modern-day campaigner might use who saw thousands of lives threatened.

More clearly thought that silence might save his life, and the lives and possessions of his family and friends. Here he failed to appreciate the character of his monarch. Henry could not rest until he had secured compliance. More was in the Tower for over a year, refusing to swear the oaths required of him, refusing to explain why he would not do so. During this time Henry repeatedly harried him for answers. The absence of outspoken opposition was not enough; the king wanted More's submission.

Here again we have a distinctive facet of Henry's character; partly through arrogance, partly through fear, he required his subjects to make open protestation of not just their loyalty – More openly protested that he was 'the king's true faithful subject' – but of their entire agreement. More's treason was no more than a difference of opinion. His defence at his trial was a masterly display of his legal skill, and it may well be that it took a dishonest witness to provide false evidence with which to convict him.[23] Given the new imperatives unleashed by the break with Rome, however, it was unavoidable that More should die. He died not for the papacy so much as for the 'common faith of Christendom'. Tellingly enough, his chief concern seems to have been the kind of unity of faith which Henry was to spend the rest of his reign pursuing in vain.

REFORMATION

Henry's persecution of his opponents was always vicious, partly because he was always convinced that he had right on his side, partly because he seems to have had a strong emotional reaction against any who opposed him. This was heightened to extremes during the campaign to enforce the royal supremacy, because more than at any other time, Henry saw himself as leading a moral crusade. And this was not merely a matter of ecclesiastical authority.

The 1530s saw Henry launch his own unique and distinctive reformation. Rejection of the papacy was one of the foundation stones on which this was built, but it was only one. Equally important were Henry's appeals to the Bible, and the primitive Church. This foundation stone took its inspiration more from the reforming ideas of Erasmus and his friends. It was on these two rocks of anti-papalism and biblicism that Henry set out to build his Church. Both were given eloquent expression in the painting commissioned from Girolamo da Treviso around 1542 (see Plate 6), which is still in Hampton Court. In this picture, the four Evangelists, Matthew, Mark, Luke and John (each identified by name on the stone they are holding) stone the Pope who lies sprawled at their feet alongside his companions Hypocrisy and Avarice. Da Treviso was in Henry's service when this picture was produced; he was to die in Henry's service in 1544 as a military engineer at the siege of Boulogne.[24] It was a clear representation of the king's religious policy.

Throughout the campaign for the annulment and the subsequent separation from Rome, Henry VIII had justified his actions by appeals to scripture. From the passage of Leviticus which had first proved to him the unlawfulness of his marriage to Katherine, to the Old Testament kings who became his model for supreme head of the Church, the Bible had proved his most powerful ally. Alongside this, Henry had repeatedly reinforced his view that he bore responsibility for the spiritual welfare of his subjects. He had also referred constantly to his desire to see religious reform and spiritual regeneration within his realm. A letter to Erasmus in 1527 gave high-minded expression to this noble aim:

> For we have felt for several years, and now feel, that very thing: our breast, incited without doubt by the Holy Spirit, is kindled and inflamed with passion that we should restore the faith and religion of Christ to its pristine dignity ... so that ... the word of God should run freely and purely.[25]

It was, of course, entirely characteristic of Henry VIII to feel that his impulses concerning religion were 'without doubt' inspired by nothing less than the Holy Spirit. His separation from Rome was consistently cast as a rejection of corruption and an attempt to restore the spiritual purity of the English Church. At first, this largely took the form of attacking the alleged abuses of the English clergy and the false claims to jurisdiction of the Pope. There was also a broader agenda at work, however, based on the idea that the papacy had led believers away from the purity of life and doctrine enshrined in the early Church. As the royal supremacy became assured, Henry sought to evaluate, and to improve, the condition of the Church which was now under his sole authority.

Nothing in Henry's reign has proved more contentious than his religious policies in the 1530s and 1540s. The so-called 'Henrician Reformation' has been reinterpreted many many times, each with a slightly different understanding. One key problem is the extent to which it genuinely was Henry's own Reformation, to what extent he instigated policies. Those who tend to think that Henry was dominated by Wolsey in the first part of his reign tend to suggest that he was controlled by Thomas Cromwell and Thomas Cranmer during these years, with contributions too from Anne Boleyn and his last wife, Katherine Parr. This thesis remains problematic for several reasons. As well as being at odds with the king's nature, and the mechanisms of power within his court, it fails to explain the way in which policies unfolded, and in particular the way in which attempts to spur reform were matched by attempts to restrain reform from progressing too far, or becoming too uncontrolled. It could be argued that the religious policies of these years were random, arbitrary, the consequence of a range of different impulses and the king's ill-assorted preferences, or it could be maintained that the fluctuations in religious policy reflect fluctuating alliances within Europe. There is a small amount of truth in both of these views. Henry's enthusiasms could flare up swiftly, only to be equally swiftly constrained by new developments. It was also the case that diplomatic isolation, as France and the Empire drew closer together, helped spur Henry's interest in negotiations with the Schmalkaldic League, the union of German Protestant states. These explanations provide only a very partial illumination, however, of what was unfolding in these years of religious change.

Henry's interest in religion was deep and abiding, and although it had been heightened by the circumstances of the 'King's Great Matter' it did not originate then, but stretched back to his youth. The young Henry had corresponded with Erasmus, promoted humanist study in the universities; he had heard mass daily, and taken his religious responsibilities seriously. He had also always seen his own kingship as a religious role, and his success as king as a mark of divine favour. These were constant elements in his character and outlook. The royal supremacy led him down the path of religious reform, and although there were hesitations and reversals along that route, there was also a degree of consistency in the policies he pursued. That they seemed incoherent to later commentators has a lot to do with the origins of Reformation in England. Henry's objectives in the 1530s made sense at the time, but were to be quickly rendered obsolete as religious division in Europe hardened. By the 1550s, Protestant and Catholic doctrines and identities were well on the way to reaching a settled and structured form. The institutional churches and formulations of faith which resulted are still recognisable today, which makes the modern terms of 'Catholic' and 'Protestant' inappropriate to Henry's lifetime, when religious identities and beliefs were still in flux. We do better to use the terms 'conservative' and 'evangelical' of Henry's contemporaries, and even those are not foolproof.[26] The Henrician Reformation is still contested ground for modern churches, since modern Anglicanism continues to debate its own origins, and modern Catholicism continues to debate its own identity, particularly over the issue of papal supremacy. Taken out of a modern context, and divested of modern religious prejudices, however, the religious policies of the 1530s and 1540s do have a fair amount of coherence, and they cast a fascinating light on Henry himself, and his preoccupations as king.

At the centre of this reform programme were Henry's plans for the Bible. As early as 1530 he had announced his intention to secure a vernacular translation of the New Testament. This commitment to an English Bible helps place Henry in the convoluted religious landscape of the time. The desire for an English Bible does not, despite later developments, mean that he had Protestant leanings. In fact, one of the few clear traits of Henry's own religious outlook is his suspicion of Protestant theology, which in the 1530s largely meant Lutheran theology, since those were the ideas which found clearest expression in England. There was, however, a general feeling among religious thinkers of the time that reform was necessary, and in particular, that ordinary people needed better access to the Word of God – *Verbum Dei* was a phrase which was much used at the time. In fact it became so much a part of Henry VIII's persona that during Mary I's coronation procession a picture of him holding a Bible labelled 'Verbum Dei' was used in the decorations; it was at Bishop Gardiner's prompting that this would be painted out, and a pair of gloves hastily substituted instead. Yet even Mary would support the idea of an English Bible (though not one with a Protestant bias in its translation of certain words and phrases) because most educated Catholics did at that time.

Henry's plans for the Bible, then, were of a piece with his general approach to religious reform. He wanted evangelical fervour, a cleansing of past errors and corruptions, but he didn't want Protestantism. It was unfortunate, therefore, that the only good translations available in the 1530s were by men with Protestant convictions, and all of them were based on the 1520s translation by William Tyndale. It was not just that Tyndale's marginal notes were clearly anti-Catholic, but he had challenged traditional belief by his use of certain words. Thomas More charged him with causing particular mischief by replacing the words 'priest' with 'elder', 'church' with 'congregation', and 'charity' – with all its connotations of good works – with 'love', which involved no such implication. Yet Tyndale's translation was to remain the basis of the English Bible, and the editions published in the 1530s all owed a debt to him, although efforts had been made to cover up the more obvious signs of authorship and introduce a greater air of neutrality. The 1535 version by Coverdale was still predominantly Tyndale's version, and the 1537 Matthew's Bible had some controversial Protestant features which rendered it problematic. Miles Coverdale was put to work again, and the final version was the Great Bible of 1539, substantially revised from Tyndale's version, using in particular the work of Sebastian Munster on the Old Testament and Erasmus when it came to the New Testament. This version came to replace all others.

It is clear that what Henry wanted, regardless of what was actually available, was a Bible which mirrored his moderate reformist views on religion. This is made evident by the prologue which appeared in 1540 in the second edition of the Great Bible. It was written by Cranmer, but had been submitted to Henry for approval first, and the tenor of it suggests that this time the king read it before he gave it his sanction. It explained that such a preface was needed for 'two sundry sorts of people', and went on to reprove both those who were too conservative and those who were too radical:

> For truly some there are that be too slow, and need the spur: some other seem too quick, and need more of the bridle. .... In the former sort be all they that refuse to read, or to hear read the scripture in the vulgar tongues; much worse they that also let or discourage the other from the reading or hearing thereof. In the latter sort be they, which by their inordinate reading, undiscreet speaking, contentious disputing, or otherwise, by their licentious living, slander and hinder the word of God most of all other, whereof they would seem to be greatest furtherers.[27]

Henry wanted people to read the scriptures in English, but not to reach any independent conclusions from doing so. He wanted to maintain both evangelical enthusiasm and deference to authority in the same national Church. Like many of his objectives, this was to prove too ambitious, but as ever Henry was fairly clear about what he wanted.

This campaign for an English Bible has also left us one superb visual representation of how Henry conceived of his role as king and Supreme Head of the Church. The illustrated title-page of the Great Bible (see Plate 5) tells us much of what we need to know concerning Henry's mature kingship. The title at the centre emphasises that this Bible has been 'truly translated after the verity of the Hebrew and Greek texts, by the diligent study of diverse excellent learned men, expert in the foresaid tongues'. As ever, Henry sought to stress the humanist erudition on which his reformation was founded. At the head of the page, Henry sits enthroned, in a pose which was a clear echo of the many depictions of Christ in Majesty which decorated English parish churches at this time. One can imagine the effect as the reader in the parish church in the 1540s looks up from this title-page to behold God in a similar stance on the west wall of the church, or above the chancel arch, where Last Judgements were often painted. In the illustration, Henry is handing out vernacular bibles to right and left, with suitable exhortations drawn from scripture. On one side Cranmer receives his copy on behalf of the clergy, and further down the page we see him handing it on to others; it should be noted that the bishops' mitres are on the floor at their feet, in deference to the king's presence. As a secular mirror to this, on the other side it is Cromwell who receives the volume, and further down the page he appears to be handing it on to other learned layfolk. To the populace at large, the king declares, in Latin, 'My commandment is, in my dominion and kingdom, that men fear and stand in awe of the living God,' a quotation from the Book of Daniel.[28] At the bottom of the page, the populace at large is rejoicing at dissemination of the Word, including a mother and her children, and the preacher in his pulpit takes as his text the opening verses of Paul's first epistle to Timothy:

> I exhort, therefore, that, first of all, supplications, prayers, intercessions, and giving of thanks, be made for all men; For kings, and for all that are in authority; that we may lead a quiet and peaceable life in all godliness and honesty.[29]

To balance the pulpit on one side, on the other there is a small prison; in the illuminated version, one of its inmates is wearing a red cap, so may be intended to depict Cardinal John Fisher.[30] Meanwhile, small ribbons issuing from the mouths of the people enlighten us as to what they are saying. In anyone else's reformation, we might expect them to be praising God. But this is Henry's reformation, and we see that they are saying 'Vivat rex!' and 'God save the king!'

Alongside the campaign for an English Bible, Henry also used his new role to purge belief and define true doctrine. If the progression towards this seems at points rather erratic in the mid-1530s, that was partly because the king's ideas seem still to have been coalescing. Personnel was also a problem. Cromwell dutifully drafted in preachers to defy the Pope and assert the royal supremacy; whatever else they chose to include in their sermons was rather less subject to government control. There was also a lack of consensus as to how the clarification of doctrine should best proceed. When the Ten Articles of 1536 were put together, the preamble stated that it was as a consequence of the king's own 'pains, study, labours and travails'. Henry had convened a rather motley group of bishops and scholars, and had pressurised Convocation into formulating the result of their discussions.

The Ten Articles were one of the first fruits of Henry's new style of kingship, and they remain something of an historical oddity. They were not an Act of Parliament, like the Six Articles three years later. They were not the foundation stone of English Protestantism, either, as some have implied, although they showed some signs of Protestant influence. They were a reflection of the curious times in which they were drawn up, the fruit of much debate and some strife within Convocation. They were made up of two quite different halves: the first half dealt with matters concerning salvation, and reflected the agreement reached with the German Lutherans in the spring of 1536, the seventeen 'Wittenberg Articles'. The second half dealt with ceremonies, and had altogether less doctrinal significance, but possibly more of an impact on religion at parish level. It used to be thought that the first five articles involved a scaling down of the traditional seven sacrament to three, much closer to the official Lutheran tally of just two sacraments, baptism and the Eucharist.

The intention of the Ten Articles is in fact not so clear. Only three sacraments are mentioned, but there is no explicit rejection of the other four. With similar lack of clarity, the article on salvation used language which was clearly reformed: some have seen it as unambiguously Lutheran, whilst others see it as a compromise.[31] It definitely spoke the language of 'justification by faith alone', emphasising that it was 'not as though our contrition, or faith, or any works proceeding thereof, can worthily merit or deserve to attain the said justification'. But it supplemented this with an insistence on the equal importance of good works for salvation, stating that 'our good works be necessarily required to the attaining of everlasting life.' It also insisted that bishops and preachers should teach the people 'that God necessarily requireth of us to do good works commanded by him'.[32] Subsequently Henry was always to oppose the doctrine of 'justification by faith alone', so it seems likely that he did not view the Ten Articles as Protestant on this point, allowing ambiguity perhaps under pressure from his archbishop, and with a view to keeping his options open. The fact that the true meaning of the Ten Articles is so hotly disputed still today indicates how much room for variation there was in the early years of Reformation.

The second half of the Articles followed the lines of more Erasmian reform. They sought to promote a more intelligent, and less superstitious, use of images. Traditional devotions such as prayer to saints and use of holy water were commended, with the clear reminder that they could not promote salvation: saints were only intercessors and ceremonies could only 'lift up our minds unto God'. Purgatory was emphatically denied, as being an invention of the Bishop of Rome, but prayers for the dead were held to be laudable. This was a careful and cautious statement of reform which did not challenge the central doctrines of the pre-Reformation church even if it tried to modify some of its habits.

Arriving at the final version of the Ten Articles involved conflict between evangelicals and conservatives, with Cranmer heading the evangelical grouping, and Cuthbert Tunstall, Bishop of Durham, seeking to protect more traditional religion. It also necessitated personal intervention by Henry himself, and showed just how difficult it was being Supreme Head of the English Church. Henry never tried to use Convocation in this way again: all future doctrinal settlement was to be worked out by private committees of churchmen and scholars.[33] All this shows how fiercely contested Henry's Reformation was. There were so many different objectives at work. Henry himself wanted the Supremacy upheld; he also wanted to appear as a godly and reforming prince, but he was not entirely sure how best to achieve that, which left him open to suggestions. His doctrinal convictions were clear, but not total: he was consistent in his dislike of certain key Protestant doctrines, including justification by faith alone, the marriage of priests, and the abolition of confession and he thought the Catholic doctrine of the mass should remain inviolable. His archbishop, Thomas Cranmer, had a more decided commitment to Protestantism, but in 1536 this had yet to evolve into its final form, whilst he had an equally burning desire to please his king. The potential conflict between these two objectives was to be the burden of his life. Others, of a more conservative persuasion, such as Tunstall or Gardiner, could embrace ideas of an English Bible or Erasmian reform with approval, albeit sometimes cautiously, but were emphatic that the royal supremacy should not be the first step on the road to what they saw as heresy. That any doctrinal formulations managed to emerge at all out of the range of conflicting objectives was impressive; that they were more consistent than not seems to argue that Henry himself, despite persistent lobbying, remained largely in control of what was being worked out.

The Ten Articles were deployed by the Royal Injunctions of 1536, issued in Henry's name by Cromwell as vicegerent. These were instructions sent out to every parish priest, and were a slightly odd bundling together of all of Henry's objectives as supreme head of the Church. The most important point to be hammered home was the supremacy itself, and the 'abolishing and extirpation of the Bishop of Rome's pretensed and usurped power and jurisdiction within this realm'. Henry had already instructed the bishops the year before that they and their clergy were to declare the royal supremacy every Sunday, which doubtless speedily made the subject familiar, if not popular, among his subjects.

The Injunctions also commanded that the Ten Articles be maintained, and preached upon. There was then an attack upon holy days, pilgrimage was decried as a waste of time and money, and the basics of the faith – the Paternoster, Ave and Ten Commandments – were to be taught to everyone in English, which did not prevent the Lord's Prayer being still referred to by time-honoured tradition as the Paternoster. There was to be dutiful administration of the sacraments; priests were to stay away from taverns and ale-houses, and 'not give themselves to drinking or riot', or to idleness; money was to be given to the poor, to those who sought education, and in order to keep the church buildings in good repair.[34] In other words, the Church was to be put in order, from top to bottom. From the pretended authority of the 'Vicar of Christ' to priests who played cards in the local tavern, corruption and wrong-doing were to be driven out.

THE FALL OF ANNE BOLEYN

As Henry's increasingly weighty vision of himself as the godly prince was perpetuated, the royal family was once again cast into turmoil.

Indeed, it may well be that Henry sought refuge from the scandal and frustration of his married life in the soothing vision of himself as supreme head of the Church. Anne Boleyn's early promise had not been fulfilled, and two years after their marriage, the all-important son and heir, the ultimate sign of God's favour, had not appeared. After the six-year struggle for the annulment, and having faced down opposition from all sides, Henry expected to be vindicated by God. Yet Anne's second pregnancy had ended in miscarriage in 1534. Popular discontent at his new queen and the new direction of his policies continued to fester. In the summer of 1535, with the king in Hampshire hunting, there was a demonstration in support of Princess Mary at Greenwich, staged by London women and backed by some of the women from the court. Abroad, the papacy had finally decided in Katherine's favour in March; nearly five years after she had made her appeal to Rome. The threat of intervention from Charles V was intensifying, and he was fresh from his successes in Africa and the Mediterranean, where he had taken Tunis and defeated the Turks to great acclaim. The Pope even proposed an alliance between France and the Empire which would enable them to invade England together. Henry's efforts had not been blessed with the success he felt he so deeply deserved.

The cause of all of this opposition, Katherine of Aragon, who was generally so passive in her dealings with Henry, had herself by 1535 decided that the time was ripe for more active intervention. She appealed to Charles V to act. She also appealed to the Pope, in terms which make it clear that she saw it as her religious duty to protect her adopted country:

> Your Holiness knows, and all Christendom knows, what things are done here, what great offence is given to God, what scandal to the world, what reproach is thrown upon your Holiness. If a remedy be not applied shortly, there will be no end to ruined souls and martyred saints. The good will be firm and suffer. The lukewarm will fail if they find none to help them, and the greater part will stray away like sheep without a shepherd.[35]

But Charles V had other more pressing commitments, and Katherine herself was far from well. By the end of the year, she was dying. Chapuys came in haste to see her, and to note her pitiful requests, that she be buried in a convent of the Observant Friars, that her daughter have her furs and the few jewels left to her. There were no Observant Friars left in England by this point; Katherine clung to the past she remembered, just as she clung to the idea that Henry was her husband. The morning of 7 January 1536, the day she died, she dictated a letter to him, urging him to safeguard his soul, telling him that she forgave him everything, beseeching him to be good to Mary. The letter closed with a heartfelt sentence that embodies the tragedy of this woman's life. It said, 'Lastly, I make this vow, that mine eyes desire you above all things.'[36] But she had not seen her husband for five years, and she died disappointed, in this as so many other things. She was buried, with the honours appropriate to a dowager princess, in Peterborough Abbey.

Henry greeted Katherine's death as a piece of good fortune, with wild, and tasteless, shows of delight. 'You could not conceive the joy that this king and those who favour the concubinage have shown,' wrote the imperial ambassador, disapprovingly.[37] The next day both Henry and Anne were dressed in bright yellow, and so was Princess Elizabeth, who went with them to chapel, and later was taken into the great hall at Greenwich by her father and proudly displayed to the ladies there. He ordered a joust, too, a sure sign of high spirits. But in the tiltyard just over three weeks later, he suffered a serious fall, and was unconscious for two hours. It is possible that Anne was overcome by terror at the thought of what might happen next. On 29 January, just as Katherine was buried in Peterborough Abbey, Anne had a second miscarriage, producing a foetus which appeared to be male.[38] After all that he had gone through with his first wife, Henry could not fail to take this as a sign. Two miscarriages in quick succession were too much like a clear message from God. His cold response to his wife's distress was to say, 'I see that God will not give me male children.'[39] Something was wrong with this marriage too.

Anne's fall from power was spectacular and terrifyingly swift. It had taken over six years to make her queen, but it took less than three weeks to bring about her disgrace and death. Within those three weeks she was accused of multiple adulteries, including incest with her own brother. Bewildered, at times hysterical, she was imprisoned in the Tower, which only three years before had been refurbished in honour of her coronation. She wrote in desperation to Henry, 'Your Grace's displeasure and my imprisonment are things so strange unto me as what to write or what to excuse I am altogether ignorant.'[40] Nothing she could say or write was able to persuade her husband, whose fervent love for her had turned to equally passionate hatred, and the conviction that she had betrayed him in the most horrible fashion. She was to meet her death on the scaffold on 19 May 1536. The five men convicted of being her lovers – including her brother – had already been executed. The day after she died, Henry was betrothed to his new love, and ten days later, he would marry again.

It is hard to understand quite how this appalling succession of events came about. Some commentators have seen preparations for legal and parliamentary business at the end of April as intimating that her enemies – with Henry's connivance – were planning to bring her down, but it seems probable that nothing more than routine legal and parliamentary business was envisaged. Anne's destruction seems to have taken even her detractors by surprise. However, tensions had clearly been mounting for some weeks before the fatal May Day weekend on which her fate was sealed. Anne had been deeply unhappy at Henry's infatuation with Jane Seymour, which seems to have been an established fact at the start of 1536, and the miscarriage at the end of January would have heightened her misery, as well as giving her enemies at court the opportunity to attack her further. That jealousy had corroded their relationship was suggested in Anne's letter from the Tower, when she could not resist making a reference to one 'whose name I could somewhile since have pointed unto, your Grace being not ignorant of my suspicion therein'.[41]

When Henry was in love with Anne, she had been able to treat him as an equal; now that his love was waning, it seems that he expected her to treat him as a king, and not dare to reproach him. The miscarriage was a terrible blow, and it had come just a week after Henry's accident in the tiltyard; it is possible that Henry, shaken by the incident and perhaps reminded of his own mortality, felt a renewed compulsion to secure the succession. It also came at a time when Henry's religious policies were entering a new stage of development. Supporters of traditional religion, who tended also to be supporters of Princess Mary, were alarmed by the moves against the monasteries. With Anne out of the way, Henry might be persuaded to acknowledge Mary as his legitimate daughter; Katherine's death made such an admission possible. If she could be replaced by Jane Seymour, this might perhaps halt the progress of religious reform. Henry was, of course, to prove their suppositions wrong in this last point, but it was a reasonable enough hope. These machinations need to be seen against the background of religious turmoil; horror at the executions of More, Fisher and the Carthusians, and apprehension at the campaign against the monasteries which was just getting under way. Later that year, when rumoured dissolution had become established fact, the strength of feeling would lead to major rebellion.

One extraordinary indication of the level of feeling at court was given by a sermon preached by Anne's chaplain, John Skip, on 2 April. In part this seems to have been a veiled attack on Cromwell, and all those who 'rebuke the clergy ... because they would have from the clergy their possessions'. More alarmingly, it seems also to have been meant as a rebuke to Henry and his infidelities. Skip spoke of how Solomon in his later years 'defamed himself sore by sensual and carnal appetite in taking of many wives and concubines', and it was quite clear what he was talking about. Anne knew what her enemies were saying, and she was outraged and distraught that her husband had, apparently, ceased to love her. Had she still been pregnant, the malice directed against her would have been less outspoken. Gossip could not bring her down, and Henry could not be influenced by spite alone; indeed, he continued to treat her and her family with respect and favour. Henry and Cromwell were both endeavouring in the same month of April to secure official Imperial recognition of Anne as queen, so whatever the levels of bad feeling, it seems unlikely that Henry had decided to get rid of her. But the atmosphere at court was fraught with enmity, and both the conservative faction and the Seymours were seeking any possible opportunity to move against Anne, who no longer had the king's undiluted attention or affection.

It seems that the suggestion that Anne was adulterous came neither from Henry nor from Cromwell, but once he had had the idea suggested to him, the king began to consider it likely, and was soon brought to consider it to be true. It is probable that he was compelled towards that conclusion by the strength of his longing for Jane, his disillusion concerning Anne, and his desire for a wife whose legitimacy nobody could doubt, who would not miscarry of his sons. But the events which followed must indicate that he believed Anne to be guilty. To a more dispassionate observer it seems unlikely that she was, although Henry's levels of conviction have convinced some commentators that she must have committed adultery in a desperate attempt to conceive the son who could save them both.[42] To this author it does not seem plausible that she was guilty as charged. But it is clear that Henry believed that she was.

Henry was not, therefore, responsible for creating – or compelling others to create – the case against his wife. That is perhaps the single point in mitigation of Henry's conduct in an otherwise terrible affair. It may be that the first suggestion that Anne had committed adultery was nothing more than a throwaway remark made during the course of a family argument. Sir Anthony Browne, another gentleman of the privy chamber, seems to have reproved his sister, the Countess of Worcester, for her loose behaviour, and she responded that she was no worse than the queen, mentioning Mark Smeaton and Lord Rochford.

Mark Smeaton was a groom of Anne's privy chamber, who had secured this position through his musical skill; Lord Rochford was her brother. It seems likely that nothing more than flirtatious behaviour was under discussion here, although some contemporaries had darker suspicions, but it was enough to start a train of thought.[43] The next development, on 30 April, was the arrest of Mark Smeaton, the only commoner accused of adultery with Anne. His confessions, probably extracted under torture, seem to have been the basis of the whole flimsy case against her. It was also on 30 April that Anne and Henry quarrelled, and Anne requested Henry Norris to go to her chaplain John Skip and swear that she was 'a good woman'.[44] Henry Norris was a gentleman of the privy chamber, and thus effectively a member of the family to Henry and Anne. It is clear that Anne and he were on familiar terms, even that they used to flirt as was conventional at court. But suddenly, some piece of information that Henry was fed by Anne's detractors had made the king see that relationship in a new light. He clearly began to suspect that she had been unfaithful, an idea which had obviously never occurred to him before; probably because it was such a ludicrous concept. Apart from the fact that Anne genuinely seems to have loved him, her life revolved around him. Yet the idea took hold with all the immediacy that conspiracy theories often possess, all the more because it must have offered an explanation for the absence of sons which in no way involved Henry, and because it offered such a speedy solution to the king's difficulties. Henry had the kind of impatient, impulsive nature which could seize upon a rapid solution and push it through without second thoughts. Once his suspicions were aroused, it was a matter of days until Anne and her bewildered 'accomplices' lay dead.

On 1 May, Henry departed suddenly, causing much comment, from the May Day jousts at Greenwich, and travelled back to Whitehall not by water, as was usual, but overland, giving him the chance to question Henry Norris on the way. The following day Norris went to the Tower; so too did Anne Boleyn and her brother George, Lord Rochford. Two days later they were followed by Brereton, Weston, Page and Wyatt. Within a week the commoners had been found guilty. Anne and her brother were tried in the Tower on 15 May; the stands erected to seat the 2,000 spectators who attended were still there in the eighteenth century.

Anne denied all charges, as had all those accused with her, save Smeaton, who pleaded guilty to the adultery he had confessed under torture. She was found guilty, and so too was her brother. The jury had been carefully selected by Cromwell to secure the desired verdict, although the Earl of Northumberland, who had once hoped to marry Anne himself, collapsed after declaring her guilty. Smeaton, Norris, Brereton and Weston were also to die. They were executed almost immediately, and although they died the good death expected at a Tudor execution, Norris, Brereton and Weston broke with tradition in making no admission of their guilt.[45]

Anne was the last to die, on Friday, 19 May. When she had first been taken to the Tower, she had asked Sir William Kingston, the Constable of the Tower, 'Master Kingston, shall I die without justice?' and he had replied, 'The poorest subject the king hath, had justice.' Anne had laughed. Just over two weeks later, when the same Kingston was trying to prepare her for her death, he had reassured her that the execution would not be painful. Anne said 'I heard say the executor was very good, and I have a little neck', and she put her hands to her throat and again began to laugh. Perhaps it was hysteria at the thought of dying, but perhaps too it was a recognition of the absurd folly of the whole affair.

Anne died with the dignity which was required of every Tudor criminal. A good death was a badge of honour, and held out some hope of salvation in the next world. It was important to have left behind all anger and recrimination, and to embrace death with humility and obedience. It is jarring to consider how far it was a public spectacle; perhaps

1,000 spectators had assembled to see her die, and at the front, gathered around the scaffold, were members of the Council and court. She wore a grey damask gown lined with fur and an ermine mantle; dressed like a queen, she was escorted by four waiting-women and the Constable of the Tower. Less than three years before she had come to the Tower as a prelude to her coronation, leaving it to make her solemn progress through the City to Westminster. Perhaps it seemed surreal, that she should be leaving those same royal apartments now to face her execution. Her speech was a model of gravity and grace:

> Good Christian people, I have not come here to preach a sermon, I have come here to die. For according to the law and by the law I am judged to die, and therefore I will speak nothing against it. I am come hither to accuse no man, nor to speak of that whereof I am accused and condemned to die, but I pray God save the king and send him long to reign over you, for a gentler nor a more merciful prince was there never, and to me he was ever a good, a gentle, and sovereign lord. And if any person will meddle of my cause, I require them to judge the best. And thus I take my leave of the world and of you all, and I heartily desire you all to pray for me.[46]

Anne could not have protested her innocence; it would have offended against all the conventions of the time, imperilled her soul and endangered the baby daughter, now to be declared a bastard, whom she left behind to an already uncertain fate. But she did not admit her guilt. And perhaps, in her generous words about Henry, she showed the extent to which she had loved him.

The fall of Anne Boleyn has given rise to a huge amount of debate and some of the details remain obscure. There were several reasons why, with such frightening speed, she was accused, tried, and executed within a matter of weeks. One reason, perversely, was Katherine's death. With his first queen alive, there had always been doubt as to Anne's status, and Henry had been forced to realise that he could not cajole or coerce this doubt out of existence. With Katherine dead, if he could also be rid of Anne, he might make a new marriage which would be beyond reproach. Equally importantly, he had found his third wife. Jane Seymour was young, meek, respectable, and the king was in love with her. There is good evidence that his relationship with Anne had always been fiery; this was in part what had attracted him, but now she had so bitterly disappointed him by failing to give him a son, he found it repulsive, and turned instead to a woman who had a gentle, dignified demeanour more like that of his first wife. Moreover, the volatility of Henry and Anne's relationship seems to have fuelled his eventual conviction that she must have betrayed him; to the end, this was a relationship characterised by extreme emotions.

Finally, the rise of the Boleyns to dominance at court had unnerved and outraged any number of the political elite, who were poised to engineer their downfall if that was what the king seemed to want. And Anne herself, clever, funny, daring, outspoken, had said too many things that were unusual, unnerving, open to misinterpretation. She had flirted with those about her, she had gossiped with her brother. Damagingly, she may have confided in her brother, Lord Rochford, that Henry was not always able to maintain an erection. At his trial, which took place after his sister had already been condemned, Rochford was handed a piece of paper that he might read in silence this damaging accusation concerning the king's sexual performance; scornfully, he read it aloud. From these frail threads of jealousy, misfortune and gossip was woven together just enough of a case to bring about the death of the queen, her brother, and four other men.

Had circumstances been just a little different, Anne Boleyn might still have lived. Had she produced a son, Jane would have been a passing distraction, Anne's enemies would have been silenced, and her fiery character might again have seemed, at least at times, beguiling to Henry. During the course of their brief marriage, which lasted just over three years, there had been many fluctuations. After the final miscarriage, Anne fought back, saying she had been frightened by Henry's accident, but also brokenhearted at his paying attention to another woman. This kind of criticism was not something Henry was prepared to tolerate in a wife; one of Katherine's strengths, as she herself acknowledged, was that she had never shown any sign of animosity or distress in response to the king's infidelities. Henry and Anne's relationship had been a genuine love-match, however, and the volatility which had helped bring about the extraordinary events of the break with Rome remained a part of their relationship ever after.

All the signs are that Anne's feelings for Henry remained passionate, and uncompromising, but that he had ceased to think of her as a lover, and begun to think of her as a wife. For that role, defined by Katherine's patient dignity over the course of twenty years, Anne's character was ill-suited. The words she is supposed to have said at her trial may well describe the reality of their marriage:

> I do not say that I have always borne towards the king the humility which I owed him, considering his kindness and the great honour he showed me and the great respect he always paid me; I admit, too, that often I have taken it into my head to be jealous of him. ... But may God be my witness if I have done him any other wrong.[47]

She had been proud, wilful, strong, defiant; all these qualities had attracted Henry to her in the first place, and sustained their relationship through years of difficulty. She had almost certainly not been unfaithful to him.[48] But it was in large part the distinctive character which had helped bring her to the throne against such powerful odds, which also brought about her downfall.

The savage end of Anne Boleyn marks the more sinister transformation in Henry VIII's kingship which underlay his solemn protestations of spiritual headship and godly reform. Nobody now could call him to account in the sacred or the secular realm, and although it goes too far to say that his will was law, since some respect was still due to the judicial process, the legal travesty of Anne's trial and execution shows what his unchecked authority could now achieve. It also illustrated the forces which Henry had unleashed by breaking with Rome. From this point onwards, political division would be matched by a level of ideological division previously unknown. Anne had been backed by those who supported religious reform and sneered at papal pretension; her fall was hastened by the efforts of those whose loyalties for the most part lay with Princess Mary and the Catholic past. Cromwell had slipped adeptly – and temporarily – from the former group to the latter, and such political reinventions were to remain common, but many continued to be fired by strong religious convictions, allowing religious division to exacerbate political tensions to a dangerous extent.

The Henrician court of the 1530s had become a dangerous place. The lasting epitaph to this tragic affair must be the sonnet in which Sir Thomas Wyatt expressed his sadness. Accused as one of Anne's lovers, he had escaped the block, but the slaughter would always haunt him thereafter:

> These bloody days have broken my heart.
> My lust, my youth did then depart,
> And blind desire of estate.
> Who hastes to climb seeks to revert.
> Of truth, *circa Regna tonat*.[49]

Henry married his third wife on 30 May 1536. It had taken less than a month to replace one queen with another. The marriage took place in the queen's closet (that is, her private chapel) at Whitehall, which Henry and Anne had planned together. Henry's indecent haste was an indication of just how desperate he still was to produce an heir whilst there was still time. The death of Henry Fitzroy, Duke of Richmond, just weeks after Anne Boleyn's death, would have underlined the sense of urgency. The king knew how bad it looked; the official line was that he had only married Jane because he had been begged to do so by 'all his nobles and council upon their knees'. But Jane proved popular. She fitted the Tudor ideal of womanhood much more than pale, proud, impetuous Anne Boleyn. She was gentle, kind, not very bright, and had a quiet dignity. She was nothing like the challenge that his previous wife had been. On one of the few occasions that she annoyed him, by pleading for the monasteries, he told her sharply not to meddle, because her predecessor had died in consequence of meddling too much with state affairs.[50] In general, she was all meek amiability. As one courtier wrote to his friend:

> she is as gentle a lady as ever I knew, and as fair a Queen as any in Christendom. The king hath come out of hell into heaven, for the gentleness in this, and the cursedness and unhappiness in the other.[51]

In particular, Jane's gentleness extended to the king's first unhappy and rejected daughter. Princess Mary, though still 'the Lady Mary', returned to court, partly at Jane's instigation. The ritual humiliation of serving her baby half-sister was ended, since by the second Act of Succession, passed in the summer of 1536, Elizabeth was rendered a bastard too. The French envoy reported that 'Madame Marie is now the first after the queen, and sits at table opposite her, after having first given the napkin for washing to the king and queen.'[52] Henry's magnanimity was strictly limited, however. Before Mary was readmitted to his favour, she was forced to beg his forgiveness for her obduracy, and take a solemn and unremittable oath that her mother had never truly been his wife. At the same time she applied secretly to the papacy for dispensation from such a terrible vow, but her life in England was unsupportable without this capitulation. Henry would not now tolerate evasion, let alone opposition, on this issue of the supremacy. His commitment was to be deepened by the events which unfolded in the autumn of 1536. The king's domestic life might have reached calmer waters, but his new policies were about to prompt an eruption of protest and antagonism in the country at large.

DISSOLUTION OF THE MONASTERIES

Despite the fall of Anne Boleyn, who with her family had embodied the new spiritual enthusiasms shaping Henry's ideas, and her replacement by the much more conservative Jane Seymour, there was no interruption to Henry's pursuit of religious reform. Henry's interest in humanism and reform had not been a result of Anne's influence; rather, his existing interests had led him to find her intellectual leanings all the more beguiling. His desire to reshape the English Church remained constant, even if his ideas on how it should be done sometimes varied.

During 1536, when so many other dramas were being played out at court, another aspect of his reform programme was set in motion which would have more profound consequences for the country than perhaps anything else attempted by Henry. A bill was passed by Parliament for the dissolution of the smaller monasteries, and its implementation began soon afterwards. The houses in question were swiftly surveyed, and over the summer the monks and nuns were dispersed, their livestock sold off, their precious metals melted down, and tenants installed in their place. Church bells became cannon and lead from church roofs was melted down for shot. By the autumn of 1536 much of the work of this first wave of dissolution was done.

In part Henry's motivations here were purely acquisitive. As soon as Henry had established his authority over the Church, he had taken steps to discover precisely how much it was worth. The *Valor Ecclesiasticus* was a detailed valuation of all ecclesiastical incomes, a huge task which had not been attempted since 1291. The figures which were obtained perhaps made it all the more evident that Henry's next target would be English monasticism, yet this too was not a straightforward initiative.

As the accompanying rhetoric made clear, Henry saw the monasteries as morally suspect, and spiritually lax. The opening words of the statute bluntly insisted that 'manifest sin, vicious, carnal and abominable living' was the daily practice of the 'little and small abbeys'. It swiftly moved on, however, to rather ambiguous criticism of the governors of these abbeys, who were said to:

> spoil, destroy, consume and utterly waste as well their churches, monasteries, priories, principal houses, farms, granges, lands, tenements and hereditaments, as the ornaments of their churches and their goods and chattels to the high displeasure of Almighty God, slander of good religion, and to the great infamy of the king's Highness and the realm if redress should not be had thereof.[53]

The implication seemed to be that the abbeys were proving inadequate managers, and that all this property, land, goods and chattels would be far better off under royal management. It does not seem that the king intended more than a radical reform of monasticism at this point, and the confiscation of property from houses too small and unimportant to put up much of a fight. Certainly he retained the right to grant exemptions from dissolution, and more importantly, the religious men and women of these houses could request permission 'to be committed to such honourable great monasteries of this realm wherein good religion is observed as shall be limited by his Highness, there to live religiously during their lives'.[54] Henry wanted to prune monasticism, but not to uproot it altogether.

Monasteries had many characteristics to inspire the king's dislike. They were often wealthy and powerful landowners with a tradition of remaining independent of royal control. In this, they were like the papacy in miniature, and the fact that many of them had strong papal loyalties confirmed this impression. They were full of relics and images, and those who went on pilgrimage to these – as Henry had done to the shrine at Walsingham – could earn indulgences freeing them from time in purgatory. Relics, images and purgatory were all tokens of superstition in Henry's eyes, and indulgences were granted by Rome, and thus were doubly repellent.

The different monasteries and priories had been founded at different times over hundreds of years, and they were under the control of a range of different authorities, often either independent of episcopal control or answering to a bishop outside the diocese in which they were geographically situated. This was less obviously offensive, but it did make for a lot of administrative confusion. Finally, many of them commanded great popular loyalty, and as Henry faced the unwelcome truth that his popularity had been severely damaged by his rejection of Katherine, he became increasingly jealous and suspicious of rivals for his subjects' allegiance.

Some of the monastic houses threatened in 1536, therefore, had earned Henry's particular and personal enmity. For one thing, many of them posed a serious ideological challenge to the king, who wanted no competitors when it came to spiritual leadership and who had already come to blows with many of the religious orders over the royal supremacy. He faced the most steady and principled opposition from the orders which were widely accepted as being the most ascetic and dedicated: the Carthusians, the Brigittines, the Observant Franciscans. These orders had great moral stature at the time, which is no doubt why these were the very orders which the 'Nun of Kent' seems to have targeted. Henry knew that these orders commanded great popular loyalties, not least because until recently he had been equally loyal to them himself.

The Observant Franciscans had been an integral part of life at the palaces of Greenwich and Richmond: Henry himself had been baptised in their church at Greenwich and the order continued to supply royal confessors and chaplains. Henry's first son had been baptised at the Richmond friary church in 1511, and both Mary and Elizabeth were baptised in the friary church at Greenwich. These royal associations had reinforced the status of such communities; they had also given them confidence to speak out. On Easter Sunday, 1532, William Peto, the head of the order in England, preached an extraordinary sermon to the king at Greenwich, urging him not to divorce, and comparing him to King Ahab, who listened only to false prophets but let the true prophet Micah languish in prison.[55] On the most important Sunday of the Church's year, to stage such a denunciation was a singular act of resistance. Peto was not the only Observant Franciscan to speak out, and in 1534 the order were required to swear a special form of the Oath of Supremacy. Since a large number resisted, Henry abolished the order in England by the subtle ploy of transferring their houses to the Conventual Franciscans. This was even though the dissolution proper had not yet begun.[56] There was a level of personal animosity at work here.

This animosity was perhaps even greater in the case of the Carthusians. They too had close associations with the court: the Charterhouse at Sheen was close to the Palace of Richmond. The London Charterhouse, in the heart of the City at Smithfield, was a focus of piety for Londoners, and where Thomas More had sought spiritual refuge. Many of the monks complied with Henry's demands for submission to the royal supremacy, but a substantial minority resisted. They were imprisoned, intimidated, starved, and ultimately seven were executed, whilst another nine died in their chains in prison. Given that Henry was perfectly prepared to act this brutally, it is notable what enormous efforts he made to convince as many monks and friars as he could that his new marriage was genuine, his supremacy over the Church a fulfilment of God's will. That there was intimidation by the king's agents is unsurprising; that there were such concerted attempts to persuade as many as possible is more striking. Henry did not want merely to be unchallenged; he wanted to be approved, praised and admired.

Since Henry had had such an unsatisfactory experience of English monasteries when it came to securing their loyalty to the royal supremacy, it is unsurprising that plans for dissolution proved attractive. Henry's justification for his actions in dissolving the smaller monasteries made perfect sense within the context of reform ideology at that time. There was a well-established precedent; the king's own most saintly grandmother, Lady Margaret Beaufort, had dissolved religious houses in order to found St John's college, Cambridge, and Wolsey had also used dissolutions to fund his Oxford college. There was also a great deal of humanist criticism of monastic folly and corruption: Erasmus had mocked monks in his *Praise of Folly*, noting their ignorance, superstition, debauchery and their predilection for being at war with one another, one order against another. He described those 'who shrink from the touch of money as if it were deadly poison, but are less restrained when it comes to wine or contact with women'.[57] This intellectual cynicism fed into a more robust dislike of monastic wealth and acquisitiveness, and a sense that monasticism was an outdated form of religious observation, which was being replaced by more educated and austere alternatives. Cromwell, to judge from both his patronage and his rhetoric, was deeply influenced by these intellectual trends, both the humanist and the anticlerical.

Even so, the wholesale abolition of monastic life in England was not a carefully planned policy; rather it evolved over time. It was in the summer of 1535, as the last contributions to the *Valor Ecclesiasticus* were coming in, that Cromwell sent out his commissioners to enquire into the condition of the monasteries. His commissioners were predisposed to find corruption and immorality, but they were not entirely blinkered. Their reports are full of heavy sarcasm at the idiocies and blatant hypocrisy which they managed to uncover, but they do sometimes bear witness to honest individual monks or friars, and well-ordered pious houses. There is particular sneering at relics, and a kind of patronising delight at the sexual misdemeanours uncovered. Richard Layton wrote to Cromwell concerning the prior of Maiden Bradley:

> where is an holy father prior, and hath but six children, and but one daughter married yet of the goods of the monastery, trusting shortly to marry the rest. His sons be tall men waiting upon him, and he thanks God he never meddled with married women, but all with maidens the fairest could be got, and always married them right well [ie. found them husbands afterwards]. The Pope, considering his fragility, gave him licence to keep an whore.[58]

This might seem incontrovertible proof of degradation, and yet there is good evidence that contemporaries were more forgiving of such behaviour. Ordinary people seem to have felt some sympathy with clerics who maintained a family, seeing it as a reasonable and natural impulse, reserving their criticism for those who did 'meddle with married women', or committed more serious sexual misdemeanours, and resenting those who failed in their duty to provide the sacraments and dispense hospitality. Not everyone thought that being a good prior was incompatible with having children; but undeniably, this kind of thing did not look good in an official report. On the other hand, John Tregonwell, another of Cromwell's agents on a journey through the Cotswolds, found at Godstow 'all things well and in good order'; at Eynsham discovered that 'the abbot is chaste of his living and doth right well overlook [supervise] the reparations of his house', and at Bruern found that the abbot was 'not only virtuous and well learned in holy Scripture, but also hath right well repaired the ruin and decay of that house, left by his predecessors' negligence'.[59]

The condition of the monastic houses was at best varied; this provided Henry with enough justification to begin the work of dissolution. As ever, he required enough evidence only to make his case look plausible, not to make it watertight. At this stage, perhaps few thought that monasticism would go altogether, and this probably included Henry himself. The preamble to this first act was aimed at houses with fewer than twelve occupants, but the act itself specified religious houses worth less than £200 per year. Some creative accounting resulted: the Augustinian priory in Cartmel in Lancashire was initially valued at £91.6s.3d., but the priory protested, and a second survey recorded a valuation of £212.12s.10½d. It seems that both criteria were applied in the subsequent dissolution. Cartmel had a community of only ten canons, so despite its income it suffered closure nonetheless.[60]

That Henry did not intend from the first to destroy monasticism completely is shown by his careful arrangements for the transfer of religious to larger monasteries. It is also suggested by his two foundations of Stixwold and Bisham in 1537. Stixwold was a Premonstratensian house which replaced an earlier Cistercian foundation, and Bisham was a wealthy Benedictine foundation using the endowments, and the monks, of the Abbey of Chertsey, which was dissolved for the purpose. Both projects were instigated in July 1537, as Jane Seymour's pregnancy was in its sixth month, and seem to have been intended to provide for the souls of king, queen and unborn child in the usual manner.[61] Henry had not therefore rejected the principle of monasticism; the rhetoric that he sought to reform (rather than to destroy) clearly had some basis in truth. As the dissolution unfolded, however, and the carts laden with gold, jewels, rich textiles and other loot rolled into London, there was a powerful incentive to extend the campaign.

Even more importantly, in 1536 Henry was faced with a catastrophic outbreak of popular opposition, which took the form of the Pilgrimage of Grace. This was the largest rebellion faced by any member of the Tudor dynasty, and the grimmest indication yet that Henry's policies were violating profound popular loyalties and threatening religious beliefs and institutions which were of fundamental importance to the commonwealth. The Pilgrimage of Grace began in Lincolnshire, but swiftly spread across the seven northern counties of England, and it was a comprehensive indictment of Henry's new policy initiatives. It was founded on the consternation at this first Act of Dissolution, but significantly many of Henry's subjects strongly suspected he would not stop there. Rumours abounded that the next attack would be on parish churches, that many of those – though like the monasteries, not all – would be closed down, and that the precious church possessions would be seized.[62] The rebels had a fairly clear appreciation, it seems, that the dissolution was part of a wider policy initiative, and what Henry might have called reform they more bluntly labelled 'heresy'. Several statements made at the time gave a precise identification of the 'heretic bishops' whom they associated with the new policies, and Cromwell's name was also frequently mentioned. As was traditional in early modern rebellions, criticism could not be aimed at the king himself, so his close associates were targeted.

There has been much debate over the motivations behind the Pilgrimage of Grace, and for a while it was fashionable to stress the social and economic motivations which, it was claimed, underlay protests about religious change. Henry's own initial response was to deny that he meant to denude the parish churches of their treasures, but also to deny that he intended to impose extra taxation.[63] Possibly his experience with the amicable grant meant his first reaction to this rebellion was to assume that money as well as parish loyalties was at the root of the problem. The first set of rebel articles addressed to the king protested against both the statute of uses, and a proposed tax on sheep and cattle, but they began by lamenting the dissolution, and the damage it had wrought upon both the service of God and the community, and they ended by deploring the suspect religious beliefs of the king's most recent bishops at Canterbury, Rochester, Worcester, Salisbury, St David's and Dublin. These last were Cranmer, Hilsey, Latimer, Shaxton, Barlow and Browne, and their identification as 'heretics' was fairly shrewd, since most of them were Protestants in the making.

In general, the language used by the rebels makes it clear that religion was their chief concern. It may be that a problem of categorisation is to blame for part of the historical debate. The Pilgrimage of Grace was about religion as a way of life and a part of the community. The pilgrims protested about the loss of religious houses that had not only maintained the cycle of prayer which was held to benefit all, and administered the sacraments, but which had also provided hospitality, healing for the sick, alms for the poor, refuge for travellers, and employment for many as lay brothers and sisters as well as choir monks and nuns. To separate these functions out and isolate some as 'social and economic' factors is to fundamentally misunderstand religion as an early modern phenomenon.

If the Pilgrimage of Grace, which was a collection of different uprisings, can be said to have had a leader, then it was the lawyer Robert Aske, who in October 1536 issued a proclamation to the city of York which made it clear how religious loyalties and loyalty to community and society – in Tudor terms, to 'the commonwealth' – were inextricably involved. He declared that 'evil disposed persons' in the king's Council had moved him to 'many and sundry new inventions, which be contrary [to] the faith of God and honour to the king's majesty and the commonwealth of this realm, and thereby intendeth to destroy the church of England and the ministers of the same'. He also pointed out how the council 'hath spoiled and robbed, and [is] further intending utterly to spoil and rob the whole body of this realm'. It seems clear that he regarded this spoliation and robbery as being of treasures both secular and sacred, material and spiritual. Aske concluded by declaring that:

> this pilgrimage, we have [under]taken it for the preservation of Christ's church of this realm of England, the king our sovereign lord, the nobility and commons of the same, and to the intent to make petition to the king's highness for the reformation of that which is amiss within this his realm and for the punishment of heretics and subverters of the laws.[64]

The defence of Church, realm, king and community were all inextricably interwoven.

The Pilgrimage of Grace proclaimed its loyalties with banners of the Trinity and the Five Wounds of Christ. The pilgrims marched to York Minster, and there made offering in the traditional manner of pilgrims returning home. They restored some of the monasteries which had recently been dissolved and they did so having sworn an oath 'for the love that ye do bear unto almighty God, his faith, and to holy church militant' to uphold 'his faith, the restitution of the church, the suppression of these heretics and their opinions'.[65] If they also protested against the king's councillors, describing in the Lincoln articles those 'persons as be of low birth and small reputation' who had profited from the dissolution, and in their oath vowing 'to expluse all villain blood and evil

Plate 1 Remigius van Leemput's copy of Hans Holbein's *Whitehall Mural*.
The Royal Collection © 2007, Her Majesty Queen Elizabeth II.

Plate 2 The Battle of the Spurs by Cornelis Anthoniszoon, 1553. Amsterdam, Rijksmuseum (Prentenkabinet).

LE CHAMP DE DRAP D'OR.

TO EXHIBIT THE ENTREVUE OF THE KING OF ENGLAND AND THE VERY KING, FRANCIS I OF FRANCE, WHICH ARE VERIFIED IN THE MONTH OF JUNE 1520

Plate 3 Field of the Cloth of Gold, c.1774 (engraving) by James Basire (1730–1802) Yale Art Center for British Art, Yale Art Gallery Collection/Bridgeman Art Library.

Plate 4 'David and Goliath' from the Psalter of Henry VIII. © British Library Board. All Rights Reserved 72518

Plate 5 Title-page of The Great Bible, published 1539. © British Library
Board. All Rights Reserved 64968

Plate 6 The Four Evangelists Stoning the Pope: a Protestant allegory, by Girolamo da Treviso the Younger, c.1542. The Royal Collection © 2007, Her Majesty Queen Elizabeth II.

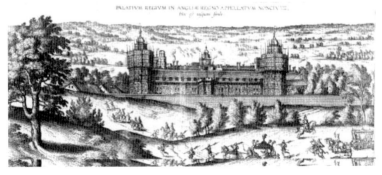

Plate 7 A late sixteenth-century view of the Nonsuch Palace. *Elizabeth I's Procession Arriving at Nonesuch Palace and Illustrations of Social Hierarchy*, 1582. B/w photo of an engraving by Joris Hoefnagel (1542–1600). Private collection/Bridgeman Art Library.

Plate 8 Portrait of Edward VI as a Child, c.1538 oil on panel by Holbein the Younger (1497/8-1543) National Gallery of Art, Washington DC/The Bridgeman Art Library.

Plate 9 King Edward VI (1537-53) and the Pope, c.1570 oil on panel by a 16th-century English School painter. National Portrait Gallery, London/ Bridgeman Art Library.

Plate 10 The Family of Henry VIII: an allegory of the Tudor succession, c.1570-75, attributed by Lucas de Heere (1534-84). © National Museum and Gallery of Wales, Cardiff/Bridgeman Art Library.

councillors against the commonwealth from his grace and his privy council of the same', this was because they were sufficiently politicised to understand that the king's policies were part of a general policy advance employing a number of officers of greater and lesser social origin.[66]

This rebellion was located in the north of England, but reports of uprisings in such disparate parts of the realm as Cornwall, Buckinghamshire and East Anglia were taken very seriously by the government; clearly they made no assumptions that this protest could be contained in the north.[67] The pilgrims themselves seem to have had some sense of northern identity: a ballad written for them by a Dominican friar from York saw them as providentially chosen to defeat the 'southern turk'.[68] It is possible that monasteries had continued to play a large part in the life of those who lived in the more scattered settlements of northern England, whilst the religious life of the southern regions may have focused more on the parish church, and the chantries, gilds and confraternities whose activities were centred there. It is also possible that being at a distance from the centre of power in the south-east made a difference: the northern counties were not accustomed to feeling the immediacy of royal authority or to being exhilarated and impressed by royal display.

The Pilgrimage of Grace was a profound challenge to Henry's authority and his new policies. Its seriousness for the regime is shown by the fact that Henry, despite his desire to crush the rebels, was forced at first to negotiate with them. He promised them that the dissolved monasteries could stand again until the following year, when everything might be decided at a new parliament called to York, where the coronation of the queen would also be held. He also promised them a pardon; or so they thought, such were the terms of the compromise agreed at Doncaster by the Duke of Norfolk, in the king's name, in December 1536. It is clear that Henry never intended to fulfil these terms, however, and others in the north seem to have appreciated as much, prompting further outbreaks of dissent which in turn gave Henry the excuse to renege on his promises and crush the rebellion as brutally as possible. In a peculiarly unpleasant twist, he gave Robert Aske safe conduct to London, where he spent Christmas at court, clearly trusting in the king's assurances, advising him on the government of the north, and returning to the north as part of Norfolk's entourage.

When Aske eventually returned to London in March 1537, to his arrest, imprisonment and conviction for treason, it is probable that this was the fate Henry had intended for him all along.

If the Pilgrimage of Grace was based on widespread popular loyalty to religious tradition, of which monasticism was only a part, Henry in his response chose to blame the monasteries. The loyalty shown by Aske and others to the monasteries was particularly held against them.[69] In October 1536, when news first reached him of trouble in the borders of Lancashire, Henry had given instruction to the Earl of Derby that if he found the Abbot of Sawley and his monks restored to their former abbey:

> we will that you shall take the said abbot and monks with their assistants forth with violence and without any manner of delay in their monks apparel cause them to be hanged up as right arrant traitors and movers of insurrection and sedition accordingly.[70]

From the savagery of this language, it seems that Henry had taken the rebellion personally, and was exacting a very personal revenge. Many abbots were to be hung from their own church towers in consequence, and Aske was hung in chains at York. This particular outburst of opposition had enraged the king beyond all measure. In part this was because the Pilgrimage had understood so well the scope of his policies from 1532 to 1536. The Pontefract Articles issued by the rebels in December 1536 upheld monasticism and attacked heresy, but they also attacked the royal supremacy, and called for Princess Mary – now just Lady Mary – to be made legitimate again. This was a sweeping attack on all Henry's most dearly held beliefs and objectives.

The repression after the Pilgrimage of Grace was brutal. Norfolk cut a swathe across northern England with arrests, confiscation of property, and ostentatiously cruel executions. Henry's instructions to him were to proceed 'without pity or circumstance', to ensure 'such dreadful execution upon a good number ... as shall be a fearful warning', and to 'cause the monks to be tied up without further delay or ceremony'.[71] For some idea of the misery that resulted from the persecution, we might look to the tiny village of Cartmel, in Lancashire North of the Sands. Cartmel had housed just ten Augustinian canons, all but one under the age of 42, and three in their twenties, suggesting a community which still had some spiritual vitality.[72] Cromwell's commissioners had found no evidence of evil living there, though they alleged that one of the canons had fathered five children. As well as its religious duties, the priory had provided guides to those negotiating the potentially lethal quicksands of Morecambe Bay. Closed down in the autumn of 1536, it had been restored by the locals soon afterwards, and was incited to violence in the early weeks of 1537, albeit with a local focus, attacking one of the beneficiaries of the dissolution. This involvement in the second rebellion had terrible consequences. Four of the canons, and ten of the villagers were hanged in Lancaster Castle. At Easter their families, mostly their womenfolk, came to steal the decomposing corpses away, hoping to give them Christian burial; some died from the infections they caught as a result.[73] The death count of fourteen is not so far short of the sixteen who died in the First World War, which so ravaged English society. By rare chance the priory managed to survive, since it was also the parish church, but most of it fell into decay as the parishioners clung on to just the south aisle for their own use. All over the country, and particularly in the north, other communities were facing the same kind of fate.

The Pilgrimage of Grace sealed the fate of the remaining monasteries. Henry could not now leave any potential focus for resistance, and he was also disinclined to be merciful, betrayed and outraged as he was at the level of popular antagonism. A second Act of Dissolution, passed in 1539, made this clear. It is striking, too, that Henry seized monastic lands from abbots who had been found guilty of treason, much as he might confiscate the land of an attainted noble, although abbots had never owned monastic lands and goods.[74] Their opposition had robbed them in his eyes of all religious credibility. In his indignation and revenge Henry chose to treat the remaining abbeys very much as he had treated the papacy, as combining illicit secular authority with spiritual corruption and religious superstition. Yet even now, the language he employed was significant.

The second Act of Dissolution did not give a justification for Henry's actions: it merely confirmed his possession of former monastic property and ensured the dissolution of all that was left. It was accompanied, however, by an Act creating six new bishoprics. The government had considered founding as many as fifteen, and the king felt strongly enough about the accompanying propaganda to draft the preamble to the act himself.[75] This preamble explained Henry's vision for the reuse of monastic wealth:

> it is not unknown the slothful and ungodly life which hath been used amongst all those sort which have borne the name of religious folk, and to the intent that from henceforth many of them might be turned to better use ... whereby God's word might the better be set forth, children brought up in learning, clerks nourished in the universities, old servants decayed to have livings, almshouses for poor folk to be sustained in, readers of Greek, Hebrew, and Latin to have good stipend, daily alms to be ministered, mending of highways, exhibition of ministers of the church. It is thought therefore unto the king's Highness most expedient and necessary that more bishoprics collegiate and cathedral churches shall be established, instead of these aforesaid religious houses.[76]

This deployed all of Henry's favourite ideas: the reform of corruption, education, charity, humanist learning in the universities. It was not a total rejection of the past, but a reconfigured Church, with superstition excised, learning exalted, and control firmly in the hands of the monarch. Instead of a rabble of monasteries and priories, with their random array of allegiances, there would be six new dioceses, under a single episcopal hierarchy appointed by the king, and schools, hospitals and almshouses to answer the various social needs. In many ways this was the logical extension of fifteenth-century trends in religious endowments. A shift from monasticism to the endowment of collegiate foundations and charitable institutions was already underway; Henry just brought it to a brutal conclusion.

The dissolution of the monasteries was to prove perhaps the single most destructive act of any English monarch. A large part of England belonged to the monasteries, and monastic institutions were deeply embedded in the lives of rural and urban communities alike. They performed multiple functions, as houses of prayer, petitioning for the souls in purgatory; as hospitals and almshouses; as landowners with a host of tenants and peasants dependent upon their overlordship; as centres of learning and education. There were houses which served as mausoleums for noble families, such as Thetford Priory, where the Mowbray and Howard Dukes of Norfolk were entombed; there were houses which could serve as hostels, such as Whalley, on the difficult journey over the

Pennines. Robert Aske, in his most famous utterance, left testimony to the place of the monasteries in popular loyalties. He related how 'the abbeys in the north parts gave great alms to poor men and laudably served God', and how:

many of the said abbeys were in the mountains and desert places, where the people be rude of conditions and not well taught the law of God, and when the said abbeys stood, the said people not only had worldly refreshing in their bodies, but also spiritual refuge both by ghostly living of them and also by spiritual information and preaching.

He lamented the fate of their tenants now the abbeys were gone, as well as the blow to religious life.

Also the abbeys was one of the beauties of this realm to all men and strangers passing through the same; also all gentlemen much succoured in their needs with money, their young sons there succoured, and in nunneries their daughters brought up in virtue.

They had even maintained the sea walls, bridges and highways.[77] When in 1538 Evesham Abbey petitioned that it might be allowed to survive as an educational establishment, it grounded its request on a number of considerations. The wholesome air, the well-kept buildings, the fact that it was on the route into Wales, and its reputation for hospitality were all emphasised; so too was the fact that many poor people were dependent on it for daily help.[78] The monasteries had answered many needs.

If the monasteries were an integral part of English society, however, they were also hugely diverse in composition, integrity and levels of piety, and the response of monks, nuns and friars to Henry's divorce and supremacy was extremely varied. There were many heroic individuals who opposed and criticised Henry, but they did so for a range of reasons: loyalty to Queen Katherine, loyalty to the Pope, opposition to the royal supremacy, opposition to Anne Boleyn, dismay at the dissolution, anxiety at the broader drift of Henry's religious policies. These were reasons that were interconnected, but still different, and which made any united opposition unlikely. There were also many, particularly among the friars, who were excited by the new ideas reaching England, and who helped lay the foundations for English Protestantism: Robert Barnes, John Bale, John Hooper and Miles Coverdale being among the best known.[79] And although many houses maintained reasonable standards, only a few achieved the levels of asceticism which contemporaries acknowledged as the epitome of the religious life, and many were known for immorality, corruption and extortion.

Like so much about the Henrician Reformation, nothing was black and white; the monasteries were not entirely blameless, nor entirely opposed to reform, and nor were Henry's policies entirely destructive. Meanwhile, the piecemeal nature of the dissolution meant that only with hindsight can we appreciate just how much was swept away.

BIRTH AND DEATH

The winter of 1536–7 had contained both magnificence and menace. It was the first festive season which Henry and Jane had spent together since they married, and there was much celebration, but the threat from the rebellion in the north was still serious, and the king was forced to tread carefully, much against his wishes. Henry and his new queen had celebrated Christmas at Greenwich, arriving on horseback, since the Thames was frozen over that year. The journey through London from Whitehall to Greenwich was made the excuse for much pageantry. Henry had not been able to have Jane's coronation in the autumn because of the plague, and his promises to have his new queen crowned in York had probably always been insincere. Moreover, since Jane had become his wife only ten days after Anne had died, perhaps even Henry felt it would be seemly to wait a while before celebrating her coronation. This journey through London had the feel of a ceremonial occasion, however; it reminded one commentator of the emperor's visit, fifteen years before. In Fleet Street the king and queen were greeted by all four orders of friars – Dominicans, Franciscans, Augustinians and Carmelites – and at St Paul's they were received by the Bishop of London and two abbots as well as the choir. These monks and friars who played so prominent a part in the procession were soon to be removed from the English landscape altogether, and their fate had already been sealed by the Pilgrimage of Grace. Another reveller at the Court for Christmas was Robert Aske, who accepted a present of a crimson satin jacket from the king, and believed that he was there to advise his monarch on how best to appease the north of England. In fact, he was a pawn in Henry's game, and within months would be dead, hung in chains in the city of York, where he had led the 'pilgrims' to make their offering. 1537 would be remembered for its long list of dead: beheaded, hung, drawn and quartered, or hung in chains. In a final and significant act of royal defiance, Cromwell – singled out by the Pilgrimage of Grace as the author of so much destruction – was made a knight of the Garter. Henry made his northern subjects pay for the indignity he had suffered of being brought to negotiate with rebels.

1537 would also be remembered for a happier reason. As Henry manoeuvred to quell resistance in the north, one much longed-for and all-important blessing was confirmed. Jane fell pregnant, and by the end of May the news was public, celebrated with *Te Deum* at St Paul's. In mid-September she withdrew for her confinement at Hampton Court; it was perhaps a conscious choice to keep away from Greenwich, where both Mary and Elizabeth had been born to disappoint their father. The plague threatened; Henry withdrew to Esher so the human traffic around Hampton Court would be less. Jane had a long labour, and a procession was staged at St Paul's; lengthy and elaborate prayers with procession were Henry's usual response to danger. But Jane, unlike both her predecessors, did not disappoint.

After nearly thirty years of waiting, Henry was presented with a son, born on 12 October. This was the eve of the feast of St Edward the Confessor, a saint beloved of England's kings, all the more since he had been a king himself. Three days later he was christened in the chapel at Hampton Court, and named Edward in honour of the saint. His godfathers were Cranmer and the Duke of Norfolk, and his godmother was Lady Mary. Already it was reported that he suckled well, a healthy child. The mother recovered well from her labour, and preparations were made for her to be 'churched', the ritual by which she would be welcomed back into the Church after the experience of childbirth. Henry, and the realm at large, rejoiced.

The rejoicing was soon to be blighted by anxiety. Jane fell ill. She lingered for a few days, and then died, less than two weeks after Edward was born. She suffered some kind of discharge before she died. It has been suggested that she probably had retained some portion of the placenta, and died after the resultant haemorrhage. Experienced midwives would have known to check that the placenta had been expelled, but Jane, in consequence of her being queen, was attended by the royal physicians, all of them men who had little practical experience of childbirth.[80] Her royal status may well have killed her, therefore, just as surely as it had ended the lives of her predecessors. She was buried in the chapel of St George at Windsor, with every solemnity, and the king ordered that hundreds of masses be said for her soul. Henry was stricken by the blow. Hall recounts that 'of none in the realm was it more heavlier taken than of the king's Majesty himself', and that he retired to Whitehall, 'where he mourned and kept himself close and secret a great while'.[81]

FURTHER REFORMATION

Henry may have mourned his third and most dutiful wife, but he did not step back from his programme of reform. As violence swept back and forth across the north of England, the work of doctrinal reformulation continued in the south. The follow-up to the Ten Articles and Injunctions of 1536 was the 'Bishops' Book' of 1537, followed by the Injunctions of 1538. The 'Bishops' Book' was more properly entitled *The Institution of a Christian Man*, and as the authors rather nervously explained in the preface, 'your highness commanded us now of late to assemble ourselves together, and upon the diligent search and perusing of holy scripture, to set forth a plain and sincere doctrine.'[82] It was issued, however, without the king's express approval, no doubt since the rebellion in the north, closely followed by the birth of his son and the death of his wife, had required his first attention. A letter to the commissioners explained that he had not really had the time to study it, and gave only the rather vague explanation that he had 'taken as it were a taste of this your book'.[83] When he did find time to read it, he felt it had gone too far, and ordered a revision.

The king's annotations on the 'Bishops' Book' were the basis for some extensive comments by Thomas Cranmer, and an examination of their different views on this particular text exposes the different mentalities which were at work over the religious policies of this decade. The king had entrusted the commissioners with the work of extracting from Scripture a clear explanation of basic Christian doctrine. It does not seem to have occurred to him that their study of the Bible might lead them to conclusions different from his own. There was a kind of stupidity to Henry here, but it was not so much a case of intellectual or academic limitations; rather, his reliance on the idea that his own will was, and always should be, paramount had warped his perception. He was frequently surprised, as well as often enraged, when people he had hitherto trusted were found to hold ideas which challenged his own.

In the case of the Bishops' Book, the chief variance was a simple one. Cranmer, and many of the other commissioners, had been persuaded by the fundamental Protestant belief of 'justification by faith alone'. They did not believe that human beings had their own free will, that they could perform good works out of conscious choice. Instead, they thought that human nature was entirely corrupt, and could only be lifted out of its degradation and sin by God's grace, freely given, which justified and made men and women elect, sanctified and saved, through no effort or merit of their own. This was a view which glorified God, and took a very lowly view of human nature. Catholics, and on this matter Henry himself was always a Catholic, took a more hopeful view of human nature. They believed that humans did have free will, that they could choose to do good works, and that this would contribute to their chance of being saved, even if most of the work of salvation was still the free gift of God. In particular, they tended to emphasise the mutual effect of man trying his best and Christ's death on the Cross; it was a joint effort, in the Catholic view, that could win someone a place in heaven. And those good works were closely tied to the seven sacraments of the Catholic faith, which encouraged people to be good and which gave them doses of divine grace to help transform them.

Cranmer had long since rejected this view of the world by the time he wrote his answers to Henry's annotations, and a comparison of what the two men wrote shows how far they belonged to different worlds. To the phrase, 'I am his servant and his own son by adoption and grace, and the right inheritor of his kingdom', Henry added 'As long as I persevere in his precepts and laws'. Where the 'Bishops' Book' spoke of salvation 'by this passion and death of our Saviour Jesus Christ', Henry doggedly added 'I doing my duty'. Cranmer retorted to this rather sharply, 'We may not say that we do our duty ... no man doth do all his duty, for then he needeth not to have any faith for the remission of his sins.' Cranmer's focus was on the moment of salvation, which he ascribed only to God – good works might follow, but they were only a consequence of man's salvation, never a cause. Henry, on the other hand, had a mindset in which the attempt to be good, to obey divine law, remained important. Where the original text spoke of justification 'not for the worthiness of any merit or work done by the penitent, but for the only merits of the blood and passion of our Saviour', Henry altered it to read 'not only for the worthiness of any merit or work ... but chiefly for the only merits ... of our Saviour'. Cranmer wrote emphatically in response, 'These two words may not be put in this place in any wise', but he was fighting a losing battle. For Henry, salvation came through a combination of God's grace and man's good works, and he would never believe otherwise.[84]

Cranmer's view was never to prevail, even though Cromwell was probably sympathetic to it too, because Henry's view had always to remain paramount. That said, Cranmer never gave up hope of persuading Henry, and in every theological discussion he patiently put forward the more reformed understanding. He also prepared for the future by diligently appointing men of his own way of thinking wherever he could, and as Archbishop of Canterbury he had many benefices in his gift. The only way in which the evangelical cause was significantly advanced during these years, however, was when Henry's aims and those of the reformers happened to coincide. There was a fair amount of shared ground: the rejection of papal authority, the introduction of an English Bible, the attack upon the monasteries, the introduction of prayers in English, the attack upon idolatry and the promotion of education.

Often evangelicals misread what Henry intended, and many remained hopeful to the end that the king would embrace the Protestant faith. Yet every time their hopes were raised, the king would implement another piece of religious policy which failed to satisfy expectations. He allowed the English Bible, but not the overtly Protestant translation; he attacked images that had been improperly venerated, but allowed other images to remain; he allowed a new emphasis on salvation through faith, but would never allow salvation through faith *alone*. To be a true Protestant under Henry VIII was to endure continual frustration.

One piece of religious policy which raised evangelical hopes was the Injunctions of 1538. These are sometimes called Cromwell's Injunctions, but they were no more Cromwell's, and no less the king's, than those of 1536. These reissued the command that an English Bible be placed in every church, this time with no mention of the Latin version.[85] They also reiterated the command:

That ye shall discourage no man privily or apertly from the reading or hearing of the said Bible, but shall expressly provoke, stir, and exhort every person to read the same, as that which is the very lively word of God, that every Christian man is bound to embrace, believe and follow if he look to be saved.[86]

They also added weight to the commandment of 1536 that everyone be taught the basics of the faith in English, by ordering that priests put this to the test every Lent when the faithful came to confession.[87] The campaign against images was pushed forward too, as it was commanded that any which had been 'abused with pilgrimages or offerings' should be taken down, and that no candles or lights should be allowed in church before any other image than those on the rood-loft, whilst a light before the sacrament or the Easter sepulchre was also permitted. This injuction was to have a devastating effect upon the traditions of worship in the parish. Every church had its local or patronal saint, and images were loved and venerated, with little groupings within the parish raising money for the different lights which were maintained in front of them. In the small Devonshire parish of Morebath, there were statues of Jesus, the Virgin, St George, St Loy, St Antony, St Sunday, St Anne and St Sidwell, most of them with lights burning before them, maintained by a series of devotional funds, or 'stores', of which this one small parish had no fewer than eight.[88] The changes of 1538 struck a profound blow against traditional worship. Lights went out, the communal activity which had sustained them ceased, and few new images were henceforth to appear in parish churches.[89] Evidence suggests that these changes were not popular: pious giving was reassigned to maintain the lights which were still permitted, rather than drying up altogether. The new official view of images, so carefully calibrated, that as 'books of unlearned men' they were still permitted, was probably understood more directly: the king had made war on images.

DEFENDING THE THRONE

The rhetoric of the 1530s was so grand, it is important to remember that it was a statement of intent rather than a reflection of reality. Many of his subjects continued to find Henry's claims – to supremacy over the church, to imperial authority – either incomprehensible or outrageous.

They were also unconvinced by the way he had demoted his daughters to the status of bastards, and rewritten the laws of succession. The Act of Succession of 1534 was an important piece of statute law, and also a model piece of propaganda. It purported to be a plea from the Parliament, that Henry's marriage to Katherine should be 'definitely, clearly and absolutely declared, deemed and adjudged to be against the laws of Almighty God', and his marriage to his 'most dear and entirely beloved wife Queen Anne' should be 'established and taken for undoubtful, true, sincere and perfect ever hereafter'. It contained so much special pleading, however, that the defensive edge to its language is clear to see. In mentioning Katherine's marriage to Arthur, it specified 'which by him was carnally known'; a pointed reference to the central point at issue in the case for annulment. The marriage with Anne, moreover, was described as true:

> according to the just judgment of ... Thomas, archbishop of Canterbury, metropolitan and primate of all this realm, whose grounds of judgment have been confirmed as well by the whole clergy of this realm in both the Convocations, and by both the Universities thereof, as by the Universities of Bologna, Padua, Paris, Orleans, Toulouse, Angers and divers others, and also by the private writings of many right excellent well-learned men.[90]

To ground the legitimacy of the marriage on this array of authorities was to give a hint of desperation to the claim, when in day-to-day life the legitimacy of a marriage might be expected to be self-evident. It could be argued, too, that a combination of a highly partisan interpretation of the 'laws of Almighty God' with the agreement of a subservient archbishop, an intimidated body of clergy, and a random bunch of academics, did not really outweigh the age-old authority of the Pope. So, indeed, many others thought.

For much of the 1530s, therefore, it could be said that royal authority was on the defensive. The more outstanding changes brought about by Henry VIII during the 1530s were accompanied by a series of new statutes in Parliament which served to redefine his authority. These reflected a new double-edged reality: first, his newly exalted understanding of his own kingship, and second, the extent to which he had not only aroused opposition, but provided it with an ideological foundation. Subjects had resented, even opposed, their monarchs before, but Henry had given them the possibility of seeing him as a heretic. Unsurprising, then, that one of Henry's first legal initiatives after the royal supremacy was to rewrite the law of treason. He had inherited a definition of the offence from 1352, which made it treason to attempt the king's death, make war upon him or assist his enemies. This definition had been stretched at times to include treason by words, but it was not until 1534 that a new statute gave this formal definition, extending the protection of law not just to the queen, but also to the king's headship of the Church. Traitors, said the new law, were those who:

> do maliciously wish, will or desire by words or writing, or by craft imagine, invent, practise or attempt any bodily harm to be done or committed to the king's most royal person, the queen's or their heir's apparent, or to deprive them or any of them of the dignity, title or name of their royal estates, or slanderously and maliciously publish and pronounce, by express writing or words, that the king our sovereign lord should be heretic, schismatic, tyrant, infidel or usurper of the crown.[91]

In other words, Henry was determined to track down those who said that Anne Boleyn was just his mistress, or that he was a heretic for rejecting the Pope, particularly those who preached or published their views, as many were prepared to do. The inclusion of the word 'tyrant' is particularly telling, for this is what many were beginning to whisper, or insinuate.

Henry was never straightforwardly a tyrant; the importance of common law, the partial independence of the judiciary, the involvement of Parliament in the legislative process and the centrality of religion to sixteenth-century thinking all made this impossible. But as his reign advanced, there were definite signs of unease at the way in which he was wielding his authority. One of the most important books on government from the time was Sir Thomas Elyot's treatise of 1531, *The Book Named the Governor*. Ostensibly a work rooted in the tradition of 'mirror for princes' literature, urging education and morality as a basis for ruling and emphasising the importance of good counsel, closer study has suggested that its emphasis on mercy, patience, affability, prudence and circumspection were all, in the context of 1531, attempts to restrain Henry's excesses.[92] Perhaps the most telling analogy for kingship was the parallel of the beehive, with the king at its heart.

This was an example taken from Seneca, and used by Erasmus among others, the important point being that this 'one principal Bee ... excelleth all other in greatness, yet hath no prick or sting, but in him is more knowledge than in the residue.'[93] The idea of Henry depending upon wisdom rather than coercive power was already becoming attractive by 1531. Elyot's later work was less hopeful in tone, dwelling more on the evils of flattering counsellors and their evil influence upon a headstrong prince, criticising those who pretend holiness while cherry-picking Bible verses to justify their own interests, and exploring the contention that the true philosopher is morally obliged to confront a tyrant.[94] By the end, Elyot was very firmly advocating restraints upon royal power.[95] Clearly Henry's new initiatives in government were making even his loyal subjects nervous.

Much of the legislation of the 1530s shows Henry's impulses being channelled and given precision by the legal creativity of Thomas Cromwell. It may have been his tidy mind which suggested to the king that a more formal definition of his kingship over Wales and Ireland might also be helpful. Certainly by statutes of 1536 and 1543 Wales was brought into line with English law and administration, with the marcher lordships reorganised into shires. Then in 1541 Henry was given the title 'King of Ireland' where before he had been just Lord of the island. These changes meant something to those in Wales, since they did make a difference to how the country was governed, and brought what had formerly been the principality of Wales far closer to English practice. In Ireland, the new title confirmed the growing sense of alienation between the English king and the Irish. A rebellion by the Fitzgeralds in 1534 had suffered a devastating defeat by English forces, and left the balance of Irish politics destabilised. Following this Henry sought to implement his Reformation, and the first suggestion was made as to the wisdom of plantation, as a way of 'civilising' the Irish. Monasteries were dissolved in the Crown territories, but remained in the territories of the Irish lords. Further rebellion followed in 1539, which paved the way to Henry's declaration of kingship. The Irish lords were compelled to surrender their lands to the new king, and receive them back as feudal grants.[96] Henry had a measure of crude success with these policies, but he was stirring up currents of resentment and antagonism which would have profound future consequences.

DEFENDING THE TRUE FAITH

In 1539 Parliament passed the Act of Six Articles. In many ways this appeared to be a reassertion of traditional Catholic beliefs, and it has often been interpreted as a reversal of Henry's earlier policies. It insisted that Christ was really present in the bread and wine consecrated during mass, and that it was not necessary to receive both bread and wine during communion, but that either would do, since both contained Christ's flesh and blood together. It also insisted that priests must not marry, that vows of chastity were binding, that private masses (where priests celebrated mass on their own) were a good thing and that auricular confession (that is, confession to a priest) was a necessary part of religious life. In other words, this Act upheld the traditional Catholic doctrines of the mass, confession, and clerical celibacy.

If the Ten Articles and the 'Bishops' Book' are taken as indicating a step towards Protestantism, then the Six Articles might be taken as a step back towards Catholicism. However, it is probable that Henry VIII did not mean the Ten Articles to indicate a step towards Protestantism, even if Cranmer and others had hopes of such a progression. Those with genuinely Protestant objectives took the Six Articles as a great blow: Hugh Latimer, Bishop of Worcester, and Nicholas Shaxton, Bishop of Salisbury, resigned their sees in protest. Henry, on the other hand, seems to have seen no contradiction in this piece of legislation.

In the Ten Articles, Henry had been indicating the furthest extent of the reform he was prepared to envisage for his Church. In the Six Articles, he was indicating the fundamental points on which he was not prepared to compromise. He was also responding to the 'great discord and variance' which had arisen 'as well amongst the clergy of this ... realm as amongst a great number of vulgar people'.[97] None of the key doctrines in the Six Articles had previously been attacked or undermined, so Henry was not going back on earlier policies, he was merely underlining a different set of priorities. The preamble to the Act spoke of 'variable and sundry opinions and judgments' which had arisen in reaction to the Ten Articles, and explained how this Act was meant to achieve 'a full and perfect resolution of the said articles' and thus produce 'a perfect concord and unity generally amongst all his loving and obedient subjects'.[98] Clearly the measured amount of reform which Henry had intended to introduce in 1536 had got out of control. The Ten Articles had been misunderstood, and the 'Bishops' Book' had given an impression of Protestant leanings which the king had not intended. The Six Articles were an attempt to set the record straight. They were not a step backwards, merely not the step forward which the evangelicals had been hoping to see. Their enthusiasm had got the better of them, and led them to cast their king in a role he was not prepared to play.

The charge of inconsistency in religion is one frequently levelled at Henry VIII and the debate about its accuracy remains vigorous, even acrimonious, not least because hotly contested questions about the identity and doctrine of modern Anglicanism continue to refer back to its sixteenth-century foundations. The influence of John Foxe is again to be felt, who depicted Henry as vacillating between Protestant and Catholic alternatives according to who had his ear at any given time. For some historians, this is still the best explanation. Henry is seen as wayward, inconsistent, easily influenced, whilst his religious policies can be described as a 'rag-bag of emotional preferences'.[99]

There is an element of truth in nearly all the mainstream opinions of Henry and certainly his approach to religion appears to have been an emotional one. There was more consistency to his overall objectives, however, than this last description allows. He may have vacillated at times over the smaller details, but he did have a vision of the Church which he steadily pursued once the royal supremacy was in place and – crucially – once the campaign for that supremacy had educated him in the potential of biblical, patristic and historical justification. Between 1527 and 1533 Henry learned that the Bible and other sources could be used to reshape religious belief and practice; between 1533 and 1546 he put that realisation to work.

Henry's vision of the Church had certain non-negotiable elements, of which his own spiritual authority was paramount. Every proclamation, set of injunctions or religious publication reiterated that he was head of the Church, and rehearsed the necessity of rejecting papal power, often attaching the list of reasons for this. If his subjects really did get to hear this every Sunday, they must soon have become well-versed in the idea. After this, another key element was his idea of himself as an Old Testament king, with all its implications for the defeat of idolatry.[100] This intersected neatly with the ideas on church reform he had absorbed from Erasmus and other humanists, that traditional practices were allowable once they had been purged of superstition. This explains, for example, the ideas about saints and images in the Ten Articles: allowable as intercessors and books for the unlearned, but offensive if made the focus of false, ignorant and inappropriate devotion. These inclinations all have a reformed spirit, but Henry combined them with an unshakeable devotion to the Latin mass which was at the heart of traditional religious practice. The doctrine that Christ was really and bodily present in the bread and wine of the Eucharist was something on which he never wavered. Similarly, the priests who administered this sacrament he expected to remain celibate.

In part, Henry was steering here between extremes. This was something he liked to do, appearing as the impartial arbitrator above the rank-and-file who were so fiercely opposed. Several key pronouncements of his reign emphasised the idea of steering a middle course, most notably the parliamentary speech of 1544 where Henry attacked his subjects for the fact that 'discord and dissention beareth rule in every place', and attacked radicals and conservatives alike.[101] Recently the idea of a Henrician *via media* has been proposed, with some persuasive evidence in support of the notion.[102] Yet the contention that he was taking a middle path between Rome and Geneva, or Rome and Zurich, is problematic too, since it was not clear in the 1530s quite what Geneva or Zurich stood for, or indeed quite which strain of Catholic thought would remain dominant in Rome.

'Protestantism' at this stage was still in an embryonic form. In particular, the question of whether Christ was really present in the bread and wine at Mass, was contested with great bitterness between different groups, as, for example, between Lutherans and Zwinglians. The most definitive Protestant doctrine was justification by faith alone, and even this gave rise to conflict within the evangelical brethren. It has to be remembered that Protestant identity at this point was still mostly understood as a *political* identity: 'Protestant' in the 1530s was a term applied to a small group of German principalities in the Schmalkaldic League. Henry was not going to endorse a religious position which he saw as chiefly defined by a political entity. If there was a compromise at work in the 1530s, it was a middle way between several different sorts of inspiration; biblicism, anticlericalism, humanist reform and traditional Catholicism were all represented, as was an evangelicalism which fed into later Protestant identity, but which was in the 1530s more free-floating.

Some of the evangelicals, or early Protestants, around Henry were excited by the royal supremacy, the English Bible, the Ten Articles and the dissolution of the monasteries, but that is because they misunderstood what Henry meant by these policies. Despite some resemblances between the Henrician Reformation and the Protestant Reformation on the Continent, Henry's Reformation retained a basis in traditional Catholicism, and its reforming elements could not be categorised as either Catholic or Protestant in the sense these terms later acquired. Henry's reform in the 1530s and 1540s combined a deep traditional loyalty to the Mass with a clear commitment to evangelical advance. The way in which he purged holy days and altered the dedications of churches and cathedrals is a good case in point. The intercession of saints and the importance of patronal saints remained, but Henry focused on biblical saints, and God himself was the focus of most of the new dedications, involving one or all of the persons of the Trinity.[103] Traditional religion was to be brought into line with the inspiration of scripture. Persecution also gave a significant insight into Henry's religious ideas. His righteous indignation in the 1530s was focused on those who denied his supremacy and had the folly to side with the papacy, but it was also aimed at those who used the religious changes he had so carefully orchestrated as a justification for heresy.

The trial of John Lambert in 1538 for denying Christ's presence in the sacrament was used as a piece of religio-political theatre: the king, presiding as Supreme Head over the heresy tribunal, was clothed in pure white. Cromwell, ever adept at rendering Henry's understanding of himself into words, wrote to Wyatt and gave an account of the trial, which took place in the hall at Whitehall:

> It was a wonder to see how princely, with how excellent gravity and inestimable majesty his Highness exercised there the very office of a supreme head of his Church of England, how benignly his Grace assayed to convert the miserable man, how strong and manifest reasons his Highness alleged against him.

Cromwell thought the other rulers of Europe would have thought him 'the mirror and light of all other kings and princes in Christendom'.[104] This was indeed what Henry intended them to think. Lambert died at the stake for denying the presence of Christ in the sacrament.

The king who emerged during the course of the 1530s is the Henry VIII whom everyone remembers. The athleticism, chivalry and magnanimity of the young ruler gave way to the dominating, bulky figure of the Holbein mural, to the jealous authority which brought about so many judicial murders, to the busy and suspicious mind which sought to recalibrate Christianity itself. The unrelenting determination to secure the succession became tinged with a fierce desperation which hastened the death of three queens within the space of two years, finally securing the prize of Prince Edward's birth in October 1537. The fear and fury aroused by opposition left many dead at the king's behest. The destruction of the 1,000-year-old English monastic tradition saw an integral part of English society uprooted and communities shattered. The mature Henry VIII was at once imposing, frightening, and – to more thoughtful minds – not wholly convincing. His claims to imperial authority were at the same time astounding and rather vague; the religious rhetoric with which he justified his laws and proclamations remained questionable, in both its logic and its sincerity. To Henry's frustration, he discovered that he might be able to coerce his subjects, but he could not necessarily convince them. He had not been able to make them accept Anne Boleyn, and in a quietly insidious way, popular disaffection had played its part in her downfall. He had not been able to make them understand his religious vision; even his closest advisors persisted in misreading his intentions. He had discovered, however, what could be achieved by determined persecution of those who opposed him. He had become more majestic, less plausible, but undoubtedly a more terrifying proposition as king.

6

THE CLOSING YEARS,
1539–1547

I assure you that this lack of charity amongst yourselves will be the hinderance and assuaging of the fervent love between us ... except this wound be salved and clearly made whole.[1]

The 1540s are often characterised in terms of Henry VIII's physical decline and growing despotism: a bloated, suppurating monster of a man presiding vengefully over a wary court. This portrayal is in large part founded on the waywardness of his personal life; his daughters tolerated but still bastardised, his fourth wife dismissed after a fiasco of a marriage, his youngest wife executed after just nineteen months of wedlock, his last wife forced to stay silent as her friend, Anne Askew, was burned at the stake. Yet such wilfulness is also depicted as spilling over into the political sphere, with the king becoming more and more unpredictable and terrifying, vacillating between burning Protestants and hanging Catholics, favouring his councillors one minute and threatening or imprisoning them the next. The impression given is of a country ruled by tyranny, Henry's subjects rigid with tension, his courtiers hinting covertly at their dismay but never able to speak outright, his ministers continually afraid for their lives.

This dark but beguiling picture has many points of truth, but it is a very partial account of a much more complex narrative. It paints far too stark a picture of years which saw an efficient government, a stable society and a still impressive and competent king. It is true that the king's health was deteriorating, but since initially this just meant that he hunted closer to home, it is clear that he was far from incapacitated, and it has to be remembered that the Tudors suffered constant ailments as a part of everyday life, in a way which has only recently become unusual to those in more developed countries. The marriage to Katherine Howard did indeed prove a disaster, but almost entirely as a result of the young queen's folly, and Henry's last marriage to Katherine Parr was a notable success, which helped to foster an unprecedented amount of tranquillity and affection between him and his three children.

Religious policy in these years, which has often mistakenly been seen as a Catholic reaction, in fact continued to pursue moderate reform, and those who were persecuted were the extremists on either wing, leaving a stable body of more moderate believers within the Henrician church. Meanwhile, Henry faced the last major international conflict of his reign, with war in Scotland from 1542 onwards, and the last major encounter with France in 1544. Under the threat of invasion, Henry responded with such vigour that new coastal defences transformed the south coast of England and he himself led an army once more across the Channel. Thirty years on from his first expedition into France, the king was as determined as ever to display his military prowess, and the army he took to the Continent was an impressive force. His hopes for the future, however, rested on one small jealously guarded child, whose slightest ailment could throw the king into a fever of apprehension, and whose uncertain future lent a ruthless quality to his father's rule in these last years. Meanwhile, his nation seemed torn apart by religious dissension, and the 'lack of charity' bewailed in Henry's 1545 speech to parliament threatened to destabilise the country and with it his son's inheritance. It is important not to demonise Henry without understanding the political basis for many of his actions. Much of the suspicion and savagery of his political dealings must be seen as his anxious attempts to make the realm safe for the future King Edward VI, and at the last, a reflection of his agony that he seemed set to die and leave his kingdom to a child of 9.

THE CLEVES MARRIAGE

Henry mourned Jane Seymour with some sincerity, it would appear, but discussions concerning his new wife began almost immediately. It has been suggested, however, that Henry was best at falling in love on the rebound, and since in 1537 this could not apply, it was over two years before substantial progress was made towards finding him another wife.[2] Henry has a reputation for moving only too rapidly between wives, so it is salutary to realise that his contemporaries were deeply worried by his failure to replace Jane Seymour; for them, it seemed imperative that a king replace his wives with rapidity, in order to maximise his chances of producing the offspring on whom everyone's security rested. The Privy Council had advised him to consider marrying again within days of Queen Jane's death, yet negotiations moved only slowly towards a possible conclusion.[3]

In a conversation which took place in 1539, one former courtier opined to another, that 'methink it a great pity that the king is so long without a queen: his Grace might yet have many fair children.'[4] Many different candidates were considered, and five of them were considered seriously enough for Holbein to produce a portrait of them. The different women who were suggested as potential brides are often viewed as being the policy choices of different factions, with conservatives backing Catholic candidates, and evangelicals emphasising the charms of those from reformed states. The evidence suggests that Henry was first and foremost interested in their personal charms, however, and additionally tempted by the possibilities for foreign alliances which marriage might offer, with religion merely a partial contribution to the possible attractions of any such alliance. Certainly Henry considered several Catholic brides, but there was no hint that this might involve compromising the royal supremacy. He was more interested in their physical merits and intellectual attainments. Was their breath sweet? Were they musical? Was their bosom flat, or well-formed? These were the questions Henry asked of his ambassadors.

The possible candidates ranged from Mary of Guise, who eventually married James V of Scotland, to Christina, the widowed duchess of Milan, but generally speaking they indicated Henry wavering between a Habsburg and a Guise alliance. Indeed, the fact that he several times proposed marrying not just himself, but also all three of his children, to a nest of candidates from a particular background, shows the use to which he was trying to put these marriages. This was a technique Henry's father had used with some success. There were difficulties in the way, however. Both of Henry's daughters were technically still bastards, and showed no signs of being reinstated. Henry also expected any marriage alliance to be accompanied by an anti-papal stance; in the case of the Duchess of Milan, who was Charles V's niece, he demanded that Charles refuse to attend the forthcoming General Council called by the Pope, which was a highly unrealistic demand to make of someone who was struggling to crush the Lutheran cause within the Empire. There was also Henry's own reputation, which was beginning to count against him; the Duchess of Milan was Katherine of Aragon's great-niece, and reportedly believed that her great-aunt had been assassinated, while the fates of Anne Boleyn and Jane Seymour also raised her fears, for different but related reasons.[5] Henry had rather ostentatiously failed to protect and cherish his wives so far.

The choice finally fell upon Anne, daughter of the Duke of Cleves.[6] This is often mistakenly seen as an unequivocally pro-Protestant alliance, but in fact the Duchy of Cleves mirrored England quite closely, being committed to an Erastian and Erasmian blend of reform which stopped short of actual Protestantism. Anne's father had brought in a reforming Church Ordinance in 1532–3, which without breaking with Rome nonetheless emphasised the importance of preaching based on Scripture and the early fathers.[7] Anne's sister Sybille was married to the Elector of Saxony, so the marriage did bring a connection to the German Protestants. Yet this choice was not meant as a statement of religious alliance; viewed in diplomatic terms, it was rather one of the few which remained a possibility after the alarming development of June 1538, when Charles V and Francis I met at Nice and signed a ten-year truce. Since England was left out in the cold, the Cleves marriage was an attempt to salvage some kind of alliance from a suddenly inhospitable looking Europe. An alliance was needed, not only because Henry had been too long without a wife, but also because the truce of 1538 seemed to presage some kind of combined action against England. The Pope was preparing to implement Henry's excommunication, and at the end of 1538 sent Cardinal Pole on an embassy to rally Catholic support in Europe for an attack on England. When Henry despatched his envoy to Cleves in January 1539, his instructions show that he was ignorant of the duke's religious persuasion at that point, telling the envoy to enquire whether they were 'still of the old popish fashion', and if so, 'whether they will be inclinable to alter their opinions'.[8] England's chief need was for allies, and this was not the time to be too demanding about religion.

1539 began with an invasion scare. Fortifications were hastily constructed on the south coast, and as Hall recorded, 'his Majesty in his own person, without any delay took very laborious and painful journeys towards the sea coasts' to supervise proceedings. Ships were prepared for defence at sea, and troops were mustered for defence on land. In May the king reviewed the troops who had mustered from London. Hall's description again underlines the point that any show of power in Henry's England was accompanied by a gorgeous display. He wrote that:

> When it was known that the king would see the Muster, Lord how glad the people were to prepare, and what desire they had to do their Prince service, it would have made any faithfull subjects heart to have rejoiced. Then every man being of any substance provided himself a coat of white silk, and garnished their basinets [helmets] with turves like caps of silk, set with ouches [embedded gems], furnished with chains of gold and feathers: other gilted their harness, their halberds and poleaxes. Some, and especial certain goldsmiths had their breast plates yea and their whole harness of silver bullion.

He describes all the fields from Whitechapel to Mile End, and from Bethnal Green to Stepney, 'all covered with harness, men and weapons, and in especial the battle of pikes seemed to be a great forest'.[9] Henry sat in the gatehouse of Whitehall Palace to watch the procession, which lasted most of the day.

Preparations for defence against the enemy abroad were accompanied by vengeance upon the enemy at home. Cardinal Pole, who was rallying Catholic support for an invasion from the continent, had long been an irritant to Henry. As a cousin of the king, he had had a privileged upbringing, being educated at Magdalen College Oxford from the age of about 12, and then receiving the best available humanist education on the continent in Padua and elsewhere. He had initially helped the king in the campaign for an annulment, canvassing views from the university of Paris, but had gone the way of More and others whom the king had assumed would follow his lead but who had declared for the papacy.[10] His treatise *De unitate*, which was originally a letter to Henry arguing for the unity of the church and criticising the royal supremacy, was famous across Europe, and brought Pole to increased prominence. He was made a cardinal in 1536, and became an important figure in the field of Catholic reform. His activities had terrible consequences for his family in England, however, as Henry uncovered – or invented – the so-called 'Courtenay conspiracy'. The supposed treason of Pole's brother, mother and other associates was based on scraps of evidence, remembered conversations, perhaps above all on their communication with their brother abroad. Clearly Pole's family had deplored Henry's religious policies and his repudiation of Katherine of Aragon; more dangerously, they had speculated about what might happen if Henry died.[11] Pole's brother Lord Henry Montagu, and his cousin Henry Courtenay, Marquess of Exeter, were executed, along with Sir Edward Neville and a clutch of associates. Pole's grandfather was George, Duke of Clarence, brother to Edward IV; Courtenay's grandfather was Edward IV himself. Henry would not have forgotten these Yorkist ancestors.

Pole's mother the Countess of Salisbury was kept in the Tower for some time, despite being nearly 70 years old. As a former friend of Katherine of Aragon, and Lady Mary's old governess, her loyalties were always going to be questionable, and it did not help that she had Yorkist blood. There was a measure of justice in Henry's administration, however; these facts alone could not kill her. It was another example of visual treason which provided the evidence for her attainder: a coat of armour was discovered in her possession, decorated with the royal coat of arms, pansies signifying the Poles, and marigolds signifying the Lady Mary.[12] This was taken to mean that the countess was plotting a marriage between her son and Mary which might resurrect the old religion. There may have been some truth in this; certainly, when Mary came to the throne there was a strong body of opinion favouring her marriage to Edward Courtenay, the Marquess of Exeter's son, and Edward IV's great-grandson, who had been imprisoned along with his father as a boy of 12, and who was sufficient of a threat to the succession to be kept in the Tower throughout Edward VI's reign. The elderly countess was kept in the Tower until 1541, when she too was executed, just as Henry VII had executed her brother, the Earl of Warwick, over forty years earlier. She reportedly denied that she was a traitor, and so refused to lay her head on the block, and so was hacked to death by the executioner. Henry's remorseless pursuit of security had claimed yet another victim.

The invasion scare of 1539 died down within weeks, when it became clear that Charles V had other concerns, particularly the suppression of Lutheranism, which left him little time for an invasion of England. The episode had proved the futility, however, of Henry pursuing a marriage alliance with either the Habsburgs or the French as a guarantee of amity with either. The Cleves marriage proposal thus came to the fore, much encouraged by lavish (and inaccurate) praise of Anne's appearance. Diplomacy aside, enquiries as to Anne's 'beauty and qualities ... her shape, stature and complexion' had proved favourable.[13] The supposedly too-flattering portrait of her by Holbein seems in fact to have been completed when the alliance was already agreed. The treaty was signed in October, and Anne landed in England at the end of December. The king hastened to meet her, and came upon her at Rochester, where he reverted to the chivalrous patterns of his youth, and came upon her in disguise, dressed identically to five of his retinue, and bearing a gift which he said came from the king, before attempting to woo her. Anne was inexperienced in courtly behaviour, however, and ignorant of this kind of elaborate charade, she paid no attention to the giver beyond thanking him, whereupon she turned again to watching the bull-baiting which had been laid on outside her window by way of entertainment. This kind of courtly pretence had perhaps worked rather better when the king was young and handsome. Henry was forced to withdraw and change his garments, before returning to meet her formally.

This was an embarrassing beginning to an embarrassing relationship. From the first, Henry was repulsed by Anne's appearance, appalled that he had tied himself to a woman he found deeply unattractive, and angry and frustrated that there was no way he could find to withdraw from the impending marriage. They were married on 6 January 1540, two days later than planned, as Henry explored every possibility of escaping from the match. His Council failed to find anything; the often fruitful idea of a previous relationship was this time found to be no use. Anne had achieved little in her life so far beyond being a faithful daughter and learning how to embroider; no pre-contract could be discovered to justify Henry withdrawing at this late stage. He was committed. But he was far from happy about it, and complained with some bitterness to Cromwell, demanding (according to Cromwell's later recollections), 'Is there none other remedy but that I must needs, against my will, put my neck in the yoke?'[14] No remedy was found, and the king acknowledged the political pressures he was facing:

If it were not that she is come so far into England, and for fear of making a ruffle in the world and driving her brother into th'Emperor and the French king's hands, now being together, I would never have her; but now it is too far gone, wherefore I am sorry.[15]

If Henry was being forced into this marriage, it was not by any pressures brought to bear by Cromwell; his own reading of the political situation compelled him to proceed. It seems to have been genuinely a case of 'lie back and think of England'. On the morning of the wedding he is reported to have said, 'If it were not to satisfy the world and my realm, I would not do that I must do this day for none earthly thing.'[16]

The marriage was performed by Cranmer in the queen's closet at Greenwich; as ever, Henry preferred a private ceremony. Anne is described by Hall, 'apparelled in a gown of rich cloth of gold set full of large flowers of great and Orient Pearl ... her hair hanging down, which was fair, yellow and long'. The circlet of gold and gems she wore was also adorned with sprigs of rosemary. After the wedding, which was at 8 o'clock in the morning, the king and queen went hand in hand to the king's closet, or private chapel, to hear Mass, and then dined together; later that day after she had changed her clothes they went to evensong together before having supper, followed by banquets and masques.

Hall records that on the following Sunday, at the celebratory jousts, her costume 'so set forth her beauty and good visage, that every creature rejoiced to behold her'.[17] Every creature, it appears, apart from her new husband. Anne's purpose was to produce children, and had that seemed likely, no doubt the king could have continued his heroic self-sacrifice. But the match had gone from bad to worse, because Henry had found himself unable to consummate the marriage. Anne without her clothes was even more repulsive to him than Anne dressed, and he had been unable to maintain an erection and complete his duty to his realm and dynasty.

The delicate question of the king's sexual prowess had been approached once before during the trial of Anne Boleyn. Evidence then seemed to suggest that the king's libido was subject to a degree of sensitivity, or at least was sporadically daunted, probably by the unhealthiness of his lifestyle. The capacity which – if the gossip was true – had sometimes eluded him even with Anne Boleyn was absent altogether when it came to the second Queen Anne. According to Burnet, he gave a graphic account of the matter to Cromwell the next day. 'Surely, as ye know, I liked her before not well, but now I like her much worse. For I have felt her belly and her breasts, and thereby, as I can judge, she should be no maid.' This encounter with her flesh had left him so appalled 'that I had neither will nor courage to proceed any further in other matters'. In short, the king had 'left her as good a maid as I found her'.[18] In other words, she was still a virgin, and therefore a serious political problem.

This was a catastrophe; for Henry, for Anne, and for Cromwell, who above all others had brought about the match at Henry's request. It was also the spur to some grave consultations with the royal doctors, which have a humorous flavour to the modern reader, but must at the time have been conducted with extreme anxiety on all sides. Henry was advised not to try to force himself, but even with a more relaxed approach success still eluded him. He pointed out that he was not otherwise incapable; he had had '*duas pollutiones nocturnas in somno*', which was a solemn way of describing two recent wet dreams. But he found Anne an impossible proposition. It is hard to know, meanwhile, what was going on in her head. Since the king spent at least every second night in her apartments, her ladies were hopeful that she might soon be pregnant. She assured them that she was not. There then followed an ambiguous exchange with Lady Rochford, who must have had her suspicions, since as Anne Boleyn's sister-in-law she had been the one responsible for reporting that the king's sexual prowess had been a topic of discussion between Anne and her brother Lord Rochford. Lady Rochford said to the queen, 'I think your Grace is a maid still indeed.' The queen replied 'How can I be a maid and sleep every night with the King?' Lady Rochford responded, 'There must be more than that.' Anne explained that the king kissed her every night, and again every morning. Another of her ladies exclaimed, 'Madam, there must be more than this, or it will be long ere we have a Duke of York.' So, at least, the story has come down to us.[19] Anne is sometimes believed to have been excessively naive, but this seems too unlikely, especially in one whose assigned task was the procreation of royal children. It seems more likely that she was aware of Lady Rochford's meaning and was parrying it with the intention to confuse.

It was loyal of Anne to try to protect Henry's reputation, but their sexual difficulties made the marriage a lost cause. Cromwell seems to have made an attempt to encourage the queen's ladies 'to counsel their mistress to use all pleasantness' towards her husband.[20] The idea of Cromwell teaching Anne of Cleves the arts of seduction at one remove would again be funny, if it were not so sad.

The situation remained unresolved for several uncomfortable months. It was resolved by the method Henry had found so efficient in the past. He fell in love again, and spurred on by his amorous excitement about Katherine Howard, he found he had the courage and the ruthlessness to end his existing marriage. Anne was told to leave court, and moved to Richmond in June, where two weeks later she was told that the king wished to end the marriage. Within three days, Convocation had pronounced on the issue, and declared the marriage invalid. Henry's inability to consummate the match was taken as evidence of his lack of consent to the match. The always useful idea of a pre-contract (i.e. that a previous engagement had rendered her agreement to the marriage invalid) to the son of the Duke of Lorraine was again raised, and embroidered a little. Anne was at first upset, and cried sufficient to move the heart of the king's envoys. Clearly, and rather pathetically, she had enjoyed being Henry's wife. Despite the king's fears, however, after a little time she proved remarkably tractable and meekly accepted her fate. In one thing only she proved true to the description which had first attracted Henry; she proved to be gentle and biddable.

It was in Henry's character to be generous with those who submitted to his will. His response showed how obedience called forth his magnanimity, and also showed his tendency to equate his own will with that of God. He wrote:

> We take your wise and honourable proceedings therein in most thankful part, as it is done in respect of God and his truth, and, continuing your conformity, you shall find us a perfect friend, content to repute you as our dearest sister.

The letter then proceeded briskly to details of the financial settlement: he promised her the palaces of Richmond and Bletchingley, and a substantial annual income. She accepted dutifully, and wrote to her brother to tell him she would not be coming home. Indeed, Anne's anxieties seem to have been largely about what her family might think: when she promised her acquiescence, she vowed she would not change her mind 'neither for mother, brother nor none other person living'.[21] She also promised to send Henry all letters received from her mother or brother, and in her letter to her brother warned him that Henry's 'friendship for him will not be impaired for this matter unless the fault should be in himself'.[22] Yet when she returned her wedding ring to Henry, it was

'desiring that it might be broken in pieces as a thing which she knew of
no force nor value'.[23] Perhaps the bitterness of that one comment betrays
the disappointment of a woman who had not shared any of the king's
disillusion, who had been wholehearted in her commitment to their
marriage. Unique among Henry's wives, however, Anne went on to
enjoy a peaceful and prosperous existence as a respected member of the
royal family, at a safe distance from the formidable mother and brother
back in Cleves. She was also to die a quiet death.

THE FALL OF CROMWELL

Anne of Cleves may have departed peaceably from court, but her departure was accompanied by some savage political manoeuvrings. The
evangelicals had held out hopes of this marriage to the Elector of
Saxony's sister-in-law, even if Henry himself had shown no particular
signs of moving closer to the German Protestants. The king's heart was
now taken up with Katherine Howard, however, who had no evangelical potential whatsoever, and indeed not much inclination towards
piety of any sort beyond that dictated by convention. Henry, meanwhile, was still wary of the extremism which so many of his subjects
seemed, unaccountably to him, to be embracing. In particular, he
retained his particular loathing of 'sacramentarianism', the heresy of
denying Christ's presence in the bread and wine consecrated at Mass.
His performance at Lambert's trial as the guarantor of pure doctrine
was no isolated affair; this heresy more than any other always had the
ability to stir Henry to anger. Many of the evangelicals of the time also
still believed in the Real Presence, and saw denial of the doctrine as
erroneous: this gives some idea of how extreme such a belief was. The
king's unequivocal stance on this doctrinal point made it a useful
weapon for those who sought the downfall of their enemies, just as
Henry found it a useful way of delineating acceptable reformist interests from a dangerous inclination towards heresy. In both respects it
was to contribute to the downfall of Thomas Cromwell.

After the fiasco of the Cleves marriage, Cromwell's stature as the king's
most faithful and efficient servant had been called into question. We know
the Cleves marriage had some part to play in his downfall, if only because
of the anxious recollections of the matter which took place once Cromwell

was in prison, and seeking to restore his shattered reputation. His failure in the affair had left Cromwell vulnerable as never before, because the king's faith in him had been profoundly shaken. His opponents at court saw their opportunity, and told the king that he was guilty of heresy. On 10 June, as he sat at the Council table, the captain of the guard came to arrest him. His enemies watched it happen; Thomas Howard, Duke of Norfolk, and Thomas Wriothesley, Earl of Southampton, helped remove his badges of office before he was taken away. This is often portrayed as a victory for the conservatives, and overwhelming testimony to the power of faction at Henry's court. Yet there is also a contrary view which would see Cromwell's fall as the calculating act of a tyrant, with Henry seeking to distance himself from religious radicalism in the most dramatic fashion.[24]

The fall of Cromwell continues to evade any easy explanation. It is important not to ascribe too much influence to faction, however. Cromwell's fall did not lead to any major policy changes; diplomacy abroad continued as before, and domestic business proceeded as ever, with the king still deeply involved. Nor can it have been a straightforward consequence of the Cleves marriage, for Cromwell was still enjoying the king's confidence in April, and had been elevated to the peerage as Earl of Essex on 18 April. Undoubtedly factional rivalries played a part, but the conservatives were not able to topple a minister any more than Cromwell had been able to exercise independent authority. Factions and individuals were subject always to the king's control, and were only able to exert an influence where the king was already disposed to take a certain path. The conclusion must be that Cromwell fell because Henry chose to believe that he was guilty as charged. There were a raft of smaller accusations, but the main crime of which he was accused was that of heresy.

Rather than dwell on the composition of the different factions, therefore, we might look more closely at the charges. Cromwell was not just accused of being a sacramentarian, but of spreading heretical literature, licensing heretics to preach, releasing them from prison and protecting them from their accusers. He was alleged to have said that Robert Barnes spoke the truth, and to have been in correspondence with Lutherans. These letters, shown to the king, were apparently what had unleashed Henry's wrath, and made him determined to destroy this viper in his bosom.[25] And although these charges were given enthusiastic backing, even amplification, by Cromwell's opponents, they had not been able to invent them. Rather it was a case of emphasising Cromwell's evangelical inclinations to the point where Henry decided that Cromwell had not been honest with him, and that he was too great a liability to keep on the Council. Moreover, Henry often had great difficulty appreciating that those close to him had opinions which differed from those of their lord and master. The shock of discovering that Cromwell had ideas divergent from his own would have contributed to the strength of the king's anger; Henry hated all surprises which he had not instigated.

Cromwell was not the only one to die in July of 1540. In an extraordinary piece of political theatre, the king commanded the burning of three radicals at the same time as the execution for treason of three papalists. Robert Barnes, Thomas Garrett and William Jerome died at the stake; Richard Featherstone, Edward Powell and Thomas Abel were hung, drawn and quartered. Barnes, Garrett and Jerome had all preached in London, upholding justification by faith alone, and all three had made obviously insincere recantations under pressure.[26] Featherstone, Powell and Abel had been in prison for some time, which suggests that their execution was carefully staged for a reason, to demonstrate the true nature of Henry's religion, which even-handedly opposed both papalism and reformed radicalism.

That same reason probably lay behind Cromwell's fall from grace. It has been demonstrated that the fall of Cromwell can only be understood within the context of developments in London at this time, events which gave a new edge to Henry's fears of religious radicalism and also sedition.[27] We need to remember that ever since the Pilgrimage of Grace, Henry equated religious error with the potential for rebellion. Loyalty to the Pope or loyalty to Luther: both he regarded as a direct challenge to his authority. Barnes, Garrett and Jerome were not sacramentaries; in fact Barnes, ironically, had been one of those who instigated proceedings against Lambert in 1538. But they had a large popular following, and they readily preached in reproach of the king and in impassioned condemnation of the social sufferings which he might alleviate if he so wished.[28]

In 1540, then, Henry felt threatened as much by political subversion as by religious radicalism. Since the royal supremacy, of course, these two offences had all but merged into one. To dishonour or disbelieve the king's interpretation of the true faith was at the same time to question or undermine his authority. The Act of Six Articles, or 'Act abolishing diversity in opinions', had been an attempt to rein in one particular sort of religious radicalism. The dismay with which it was greeted by some must have compounded Henry's fears. The Act had sought 'the conservation of the ... Church and Congregation in a true, sincere and uniform doctrine of Christ's religion', and had moreover emphasised:

> as well the great and quiet assurance, prosperous increase, and other innumerable commodities, which have ever ensued, come and followed, of concord, agreement, and unity in opinions, as also the manifold perils, dangers, and inconveniences which have heretofore, in many places and regions, grown, sprung and arisen, of the diversities of minds and opinions.[29]

Henry could not have failed to notice that this Act had not been greeted with enthusiasm; two of his own bishops had resigned in protest. Hugh Latimer left Worcester and Nicholas Shaxton departed from Salisbury, and both were imprisoned. It would seem that Henry, despite being God's Vicar on earth – in England, at least – still did not have the power to 'abolish diversity'. One of the reasons for the deaths of 1540 therefore seems to have been Henry's sense of impotence in the face of evangelical advance. He could not control these reckless proselytisers; Cromwell could not control them either.[30] Priests were marrying, the Lenten fast was being broken.[31] This was precisely the kind of reformation Henry had always deplored: populist, uninhibited, outspoken.

This sense of a situation spinning out of control would have been compounded by the farcical recantations of Barnes, Garrett and Jerome in Easter Week 1540. Henry had expressly requested that a report on these be submitted to him.[32] All three made the official statements required of them, but managed also to include some statement of their true, unrepented, reformed beliefs. It was reported 'howe gayly they had all handled the matter, both to satisfie the recantation and also in the same sermon to utter out the truth'.[33] If there was one thing Henry really could not stand, it was being mocked. This light-hearted and dismissive response to his authority, given his exalted notion of his own divinely appointed role as king, must have appeared as hubris of the most offensive sort. It is unsurprising that Henry should have lashed out with such ferocity. He needed a highly visible and frightening act of punishment which would restore his subjects to a proper state of fear and respect.

Cromwell's fall from favour was an indication of his vulnerability once he had failed his monarch; it was also an indication of Henry's own vulnerability. The savagery of his vengeance was a sign of his alarm at the religious trends within his realm which time and time again he sought to control, but without success. It was a demonstration, not of the power of faction, but of both the king's power, and the limitations on that power. The religious atmosphere in 1540 was highly acrimonious, and Henry was deeply disturbed by his apparent inability to either quash residual papalism or restrain radical reformists. Cromwell was convicted by act of attainder; so too were Barnes, Garrett and Jerome; all of them made it clear that they were not entirely sure what they had done to deserve death. This lack of a trial, and this lack of clarity, indicate Henry's levels of anxiety, and show that these were primarily political deaths.

Cromwell's own religious beliefs evade easy definition, but it seems clear that evangelical leanings were ascribed to him by his contemporaries, and that he was at least perceived as being sympathetic to further reform, which is what sealed his fate. His diligence in implementing so much reformist legislation suggests that he was probably genuinely committed to the cause of reform, with a level of commitment which outstripped the king's own. When Cromwell was chiefly the architect and enforcer of the Royal Supremacy, this did not matter; once he was the named target of the Pilgrimage of Grace, it perhaps gave Henry pause for thought, but nothing more. But by 1540, with the king's fears mounting about the political threat posed by religious radicalism, Cromwell's evangelical commitment was become a serious liability. It should be remembered that William Jerome, one of the three burned two days after Cromwell's execution, was also the vicar of Cromwell's own parish of Stepney.[34] Cromwell was known to be the patron of Robert Barnes, even if he tried to distance himself from the reformer once he saw the dangers of this. It was Cromwell who had advanced some of the most outspoken preachers of the 1530s, even if his prime concern had been their capacity to preach the Royal Supremacy. Unfortunately for him, few besides Henry had the capacity to separate so completely the abuse of the papacy from the endorsement of Protestant doctrine. Nor does Cromwell seem to have been too concerned when anti-papal rhetoric spilled over into the preaching of further reformation. And when radical preachers came under fire from their more conservative bishops it was to Cromwell that they appealed.[35] In Oxford, the preacher Robert Wisdom at All Hallows gained Cromwell's protection against the wrath of

Bishop Longland; Wisdom was later prosecuted under the Act of Six Articles and only escaped arrest with Anne Askew by fleeing the country.[36] It may have been an exaggeration to call Cromwell a sacramentarian, but his identification with the reformist cause was an established part of his reputation.

It was for this that Cromwell died, not for any lack of loyalty to the king. As to this, a fit epitaph was supplied by Archbishop Cranmer, who wrote in amazement to the king, confessing himself astounded by Cromwell's treachery. No doubt he was trying to place the best possible complexion on the matter, since he had been associated with Cromwell in so many things, but it was also a brave gesture, to speak out for his friend in such circumstances.[37] His words also tell us something about the relationship between royal master and talented servant:

> he that was such a servant, in my judgement, in wisdom, diligence, faithful-ness and experience, as no prince in this realm ever had. ... I chiefly loved him for the love which I thought I saw him bear towards your grace, singularly above all other.[38]

In the event, it seems probable that Cranmer was not wrong, that Cromwell had loved his master, and sought to serve him. He had not perfectly understood him, however, and he had not been able to survive capricious fate when it came to the mysteries of the royal libido. Like Cranmer, his own evangelical leanings had outstepped those of his royal master; unlike Cranmer, he had proved dispensable. In subsequent edi-tions of the Great Bible, there would be a blank space where formerly Cromwell's coat of arms had stood. 'Those who live by the sword, shall die by the sword', said the Gospel of St. Matthew, which Cromwell had been so instrumental in rendering into English.[39] Some contemporaries noted unsympathetically that there was justice of a sort in Cromwell falling victim to the same kind of legal savagery which he had inflicted upon so many others at the king's behest.

KATHERINE HOWARD

The many policy initiatives of the 1530s had had mixed results, rather than the imperial and dynastic glory that Henry had intended. The break with Rome had met with unexpectedly resilient opposition, three marriages had ended in disaster, grief and embarrassment respectively, and the programme of religious reform had caused at best confusion, at worst rebellion. In particular, in his search for Catholic reform, Henry seemed to have unleashed Protestant heresy. His wrath at this unexpected development had swept away the chief architect of those policy initiatives, and Cromwell met his death in 1540.

Whenever Henry felt betrayed, he turned to a new beloved object to set matters right. So he had turned from Katherine of Aragon's obstinacy to Anne Boleyn's liveliness, from Anne Boleyn's betrayal to Jane Seymour's quiet and obedient affection; so too he had rejected Wolsey and turned to the Boleyns, and his army of scholars. It was essential to Henry's well-being to have men and women about him whom he could trust, and from whom he demanded unwavering loyalty, but his demands were high. Thomas Cranmer was one of the few who managed to serve Henry and keep the king's affection to the end, but he only managed it by putting aside some of his deeply held evangelical principles, as well as his wife. But Cromwell failed the king, and the swiftness of his fall mirrored the depth of the king's indignation: it was only in June of 1540 that his dishonesty with the king was revealed, and on 28 July he was executed. That same day, as if seeking solace for his latest disappointment, Henry married Katherine Howard.

If Henry was feeling disgusted and let down by Cromwell, he could at least feel sure that Katherine was no sacramentarian. His new wife was only 19 to Henry's 49, attractive, plump, vivacious, and not very interested in theology. Where his other wives had had quite notable scholarly and devotional interests, the only books associated with Katherine Howard are the pretty kind that could be worn attached to a girdle.[40] As a Howard, however, Katherine was from a family which was fairly reliably conservative in its religious loyalties, and had been raised since the age of about 10 in the household of the Dowager Duchess of Norfolk. If this was taken as a sign of her religious dependability, it seems ironic that what she mostly seems to have acquired in that household is a taste for amorous escapades. She was both sexually experienced and, it would seem, adventurous. After the fiasco of the Cleves marriage, perhaps Henry welcomed such overt attractiveness, and perhaps the fact of her being 30 years younger than him made her seem unthreatening. Certainly it was reported that he was taken with her from the time she first arrived at Court in 1539 to wait on Anne of Cleves. By the spring of 1540 he was giving her expensive presents, and her Norfolk relatives and Bishop Gardiner were hosting parties at their various residences in London, no doubt delighted that the new queen-in-waiting was likely to prove a distraction from any further evangelical advance.

Once the divorce from Anne of Cleves was through, on 10 July, Henry's Council thought it appropriate to implore the king to marry again, to secure 'some more store of fruit and succession'.[41] This was more than trying to please the king by urging him to do what he obviously wanted to do; another prince would make the succession a lot more assured. If Prince Edward were to die as Prince Arthur had, then the future looked dark. Less than three weeks later, the marriage took place, quietly, as suited Henry's tastes. The jewels with which he adorned his new queen were fabulous, and the famous Holbein miniature shows her wearing them. 'The New Queen has completely acquired the King's Grace', wrote the French ambassador, 'and the other is no more spoken of than if she were dead.'[42]

It was a long, hot summer, and the king and his new queen went on a long hunting tour, with their minds fixed on little but enjoyment. No doubt having a young, pretty, energetic wife helped compensate Henry for the fact that his own youth and beauty was all but extinct. The dimensions of his armour provide a graphic illustration of this. In 1514, his armour shows that he was 6 feet 3 inches tall, with a waist of 35 inches and a chest measurement of 42 inches. By the time of his marriage to Katherine Howard, his waist was 54 inches and his chest 58 inches.[43] This increasing obesity was accompanied by bouts of increasingly severe illness. In the spring of 1541, he lay ill at Hampton Court, having cancelled a proposed tour of the fortifications on the south coast. Illness made Henry angry and depressed by turns. The new queen was faced with quite a challenge.

Katherine is usually characterised as at best foolish, at worst completely immoral. She had redeeming features, however. She made efforts to establish harmonious relationships with all three of the king's children, even with Princess Mary, who was rather awkwardly about four years older than her new stepmother. She also received Anne of Cleves at court, and both women managed to overcome the embarrassment of a former queen doing humble obeisance to the girl who was her former lady-in-waiting. Henry, Katherine and Anne even sat down to supper together, with every sign of amiability. These were small but important achievements, given the potential for bitterness created by Henry's chequered family history. She also marked her formal entrance into London, in March 1541, by a plea for mercy for two prisoners in the Tower. One was the conservative Sir John Wallop, the other Sir Thomas Wyatt, the poet and courtier who had loved Anne Boleyn. Wyatt was pardoned on condition that he returned to his abandoned wife and be faithful to her.[44] If Henry was disposed to feel romantic about marital fidelity, he was soon to be cruelly disappointed. The evidence suggests, however, that Queen Katherine was warm-hearted, and that she tried where possible to soften antagonisms and reconcile conflict.

In the summer of 1541, Henry and Katherine went on a prolonged and unusual progress to the north of England, travelling as far as York. For a king who rarely left the south of England, this was a notable departure, an attempt to lessen some of the resentment left over from the Pilgrimage of Grace. The king behaved with great magnificence and benignly offered pardon and redress: if his temper was an indicator then it seems that he was enjoying married life. It is likely that Katherine found her husband physically unattractive, however, if not actively repulsive. He was bulky, unwieldy, by Tudor standards old, and there were ulcers on his legs which wept. She was used to flirting with gorgeous young men, and indeed continued to do so. By the time of the journey to York, she was doing more than just flirting.

Thomas Culpepper, a gentleman of the privy chamber, and thus an integral part of Henry and Katherine's private lives, had become her lover. Their assignations were arranged and protected through the complicity of Jane, Lady Rochford, the widow of George Boleyn. Having seen her sister-in-law executed for adultery had clearly not taught Lady Rochford to be more cautious. Perhaps, knowing that Anne Boleyn had been innocent, she thought that Katherine might as well be guilty, since there was no obvious link between crime and punishment at Henry VIII's court. It is also possible that Katherine had a slightly more altruistic motivation. It was important for her, for Henry, and for the country at large that she bear a son. It is probable that Tudor women believed that conception required an orgasm, and since it is highly likely that Katherine derived little or no sexual pleasure from sleeping with her husband, she may have sought to conceive by other means. But it is also clear that she was genuinely attracted by Culpepper, who was known for his good looks. One later witness testified that she had known the queen was in love with him, just from the way she looked at him.

The prolonged royal progress to the north of England was intended to counteract the divisions and hurts left in the wake of the Pilgrimage of Grace. A priestly rebellion in the spring of 1541 had made the royal presence desirable, and Henry was also hoping for a summit meeting with James V of Scotland. In York, Henry and Katherine received the local nobility and gentry divided into two groups, one loyal, one repentant.[45] Hall records how the royal journey was punctuated by submissions, sweetened still further by the addition of cash payments:

> the Town of Stamford gave the king twenty pound, and Lincoln presented forty pound, and Boston fifty pound ... And when he entered into Yorkshire, he was met with two hundred gentlemen of the same Shire, in coats of Velvet, and four thousand tall yeomen, and serving men, well horsed: which on their knees made a submission, by the mouth of sir Robert Bowes, and gave to the king nine hundred pound.[46]

Presumably the size of the offering had some correlation to the level of resentment previously felt, and now concealed, if not dispelled. The meeting with the King of Scotland did not happen, but Henry returned to the south and to Hampton Court for the feasts of All Saints and All Souls with some sense of contentment.

The feast of All Saints is a triumphant celebration; at court it was a Day of Estate, and the celebrations in the Chapel Royal included Henry's thanksgiving for his new queen. The feast of All Souls the next day takes place in a dark and solemn atmosphere, often with the priests robed in vestments of black, and it was on this more sober occasion that Henry, coming to hear Mass in his private chapel, found a letter on his seat. It was from Cranmer, and it communicated the awful intelligence that Queen Katherine was known to be a loose woman. This was not news to several people about the Court, but it had taken Cranmer to break it to Henry; probably nobody else would dare.[47] The shock, disillusion and humiliation must have been painful indeed, when Henry had been rejoicing in having found so sweet a companion. There was plenty of evidence to show that Katherine had had affairs both before and after her marriage, including the queen's own confession, patiently extracted by Cranmer.[48] Once more, the king's married life had ended in betrayal and disaster. To their surprise and consternation, Henry cried as he told his Council what had happened.[49]

Katherine's lovers were executed in December, and Katherine herself went to the block in February 1542. Lady Rochford died at the same time, marking a slight but painful note of continuity with the death of Anne Boleyn six years before. Lady Rochford's father, the avid translator Lord Morley, made a translation from Boccaccio's *De Claris Mulieribus* as a New Year's Gift for Henry in 1543. Containing as it did the castigation of loose women, as well as the praise of virtuous ones, it might be read as a graceful apology by Lord Morley for his daughter's behaviour.[50] But one quiet addition to his account of the death of Polyxena suggests his lament for his daughter, 'devoured ... to satisfy for another woman's offence'.[51] It is a small but telling illustration of the world in which Henry lived, at once sophisticated and brutal, where communications with the king were of necessity outwardly obsequious, yet might inwardly contain a bitter reproach.

REFORMATION

The religious policy of the 1540s has frequently been characterised in terms of a 'Catholic reaction'. One interpretation is that Henry had been pushed (in differing degrees) by Anne Boleyn, Cranmer and Cromwell towards the 'Protestant' initiatives of 1536–8, the Ten Articles, English Bible, Dissolution, 'Bishops' Book', and two sets of Injunctions. This was helped, it is argued, by a foreign policy isolation which left him reaching out to the German princes as potential allies against the Empire and France. This interpretation would then suggest that there was a backlash after the 1538 trial of John Lambert, culminating in the Act of Six Articles in 1539, accompanied by the fall of Cromwell, and consolidated by the marriage to Katherine Howard, with a justification being supplied by the failure of the Cleves marriage and growing rapprochement with the Empire. This interpretation can be varied slightly if you take the view that Henry was the deciding force behind the policy changes, but the central notion of a Protestant advance and Catholic reaction remain the same, and is neatly compatible with the idea of a Court ruled by faction, with Cromwell and Cranmer leading one wing, Gardiner and the Duke of Norfolk heading the other.

Recent work has shown, however, that this neat interpretation does not fit very well with the evidence. For one thing, the timing does not work. Long after Lambert had died, the Cleves marriage had failed, and the Six Articles had been passed, Cromwell was still in favour, being elevated to the peerage as Earl of Essex in April 1540. Even after his fall, one of the most important advances yet for reform was the proclamation of May 1541 making parochial failure to acquire an English Bible an offence punished by a fine. For another thing, the foreign policy context does not work. It was in 1538 that Charles V and Francis I signed a ten-year truce at Nice; the following year Henry was both encouraging negotiations with the Lutherans and preparing the way for the Act of Six Articles. Most importantly, the sweeping religious characterisation of these years just does not work. As had been the case in the years since 1533, Henry brought about various reforms, many of them tied to his ideas about the importance of scripture, whilst restraining those who went too far down the path of evangelicalism, and remaining particularly opposed to any hint of 'sacramentarianism', the refusal to believe that Christ was bodily present in the sacrament of bread and wine.

In other words, the years 1536–8 were not as hopeful for the evangelical cause as are sometimes made out, and the years from 1539 were not such a disaster for them either.[52] Although the Act of Six Articles had been a blow to some reformers, causing the resignation of Latimer and Shaxton, and the despatch of Cranmer's wife and children to the continent, they were less a reversal of previous gains than a reminder of the reality of Henry's convictions and objectives.[53] Henry remained consistent on several key points: he upheld the Catholic doctrine of the mass, he deplored clerical marriage, he disliked the doctrine of justification by faith alone. His reforms were evangelical enough to raise the hopes of Cranmer and others, but he was not breaking any promises when he placed limitations on evangelical advance in 1539. And after the Act of Six Articles a measure of evangelical advance continued through the 1540s. Since the fine commanded by the proclamation of 1541 was rather greater than the cost of the book, most parishes did indeed purchase their copy of the English Bible. The campaign against images continued, and the purge of holydays too, with the medieval practice of boy bishops being abolished. The dedications of the new cathedrals showed a confirmation of the trend towards Christ, the Trinity or at most biblical saints, with non-biblical saints such as St Swithun or St Frideswide being removed as patrons.[54]

Henry's own commitment to an English Bible remained a central part of his religious vision, and one which could not be relinquished, given how much he owed to his reliance on Scripture. His discovery of the Bible had been a kind of revelation, even if it was more noted for its political consequences than its spiritual inspiration. The Bible had brought him freedom from Katherine of Aragon, had given him the royal supremacy, and his relationship with it remained important. His ideas on how that text should be used, however, shed yet more light on his religious preoccupations. The Injunctions of 1536 and 1538 had made provision of the English Bible in parish churches a central requirement, and had encouraged the reading of it at the same time. There was always the risk, however, that the consequence of uncontrolled Bible reading might be further diversity and conflict. Henry was genuinely distressed each time it became clear that his reformist intentions had been misunderstood, and that his subjects had actually advanced into heresy.

The 1543 Act for the Advancement of True Religion restricted public Bible reading to licensed clergy, and to the nobility and gentry in the restricted context of their own households. Merchants, noblewomen and gentlewomen could only read it privately to themselves.[55] Since this piece of legislation went hand in hand with the promulgation of the 'King's Book', it is possible that Henry had decided that his own publication was a more reliable guide to the Christian religion than the Bible itself. This was in line with a recurrent tendency to improve on God, and expound Christianity in his own words.[56] This was the man, after all, who had wanted to rewrite the Lord's Prayer, finding that 'lead us not into temptation' was badly worded: Cranmer had gently but firmly pointed out that it was not up to mortal men to enhance the wording of scripture.[57]

This change of direction when it came to Bible-reading was important, because it actually marks the only really pronounced turnaround in Henrician policy. Yet just as the initial enthusiasm for an English Bible cannot be taken as a sign of Protestant advance, so too the restrictions placed on its reading cannot be taken as a sign of Catholic reaction. Nor can we perceive this reversal as the result of Henry's vacillations; rather it reflects what he had always wanted his reformation to be – biblical but measured, devout but not fanatical, educated but not populist. Like many who endorsed vernacular scripture in the early years of reform, he was forced to draw back when he realised its unforeseen consequences. Reformers in the London churches were reading loudly from the Bible at the back of the churches to drown out mass being said at the altars.[58] This was not at all what the king had intended.

Henry's views on the Bible remained Erasmian, for not only had Erasmus held back from the doctrinal advances made by Luther, he had also remained circumspect about the wisdom of allowing too much religious debate into the public domain. He had envisaged religious reform as being a matter for popes and princes, scholars and churchmen, for enlightened and civilised individuals such as John Colet and Thomas More, not inflammatory preachers like Robert Barnes and polemical writers like William Turner or Thomas Becon. Henry wanted a courtly reformation, not a popular one.

The *Necessary Doctrine and Erudition for Any Christian Man*, otherwise known as the 'King's Book', was given this name for good reason, since it was the result of Henry's reaction to the 1537 'Bishops' Book', and was largely based on his personal corrections to the earlier volume. It served to confirm the Act of Six Articles, but more than that, it was a lengthy exposition of all the central points of Christian doctrine, as Henry understood them. It is reasonable to see this work as an account of the king's own beliefs, since his own role in its production is well-attested. It is not reasonable to see it as a restatement of Catholic orthodoxy, and part of a Catholic 'backlash' in the 1540s. It was the fullest statement yet, both of the king's beliefs, and of his understanding of his role as supreme head. It began with a declaration of intent, and optimism:

> Like as in the time of darkness and ignorance, finding our people seduced and drawn from the truth by hypocrisy and superstition, we by the help of God and his word have travailed to purge and cleanse our realm from the apparent enormities of the same; wherein, by opening of God's truth, with setting forth and publishing of the scriptures, our labours (thanks be to God) have not been void and frustrate.

It went on to explain how this initial success had been followed by the work of the devil, who 'hath attempted to return again ... into the house purged and cleansed'. In other words, Henry in no way repented of his earlier attempts to reform the faith, but was now tackling a separate set of problems:

> hypocrisy and superstition being excluded and put away, we find entered into some of our people's hearts an inclination to sinister understanding of scripture, presumption, arrogancy, carnal liberty and contention.[59]

The response, which was intended as a definitive account of the Christian faith, is far from reactionary in its language. There is an Augustinian note sounded by statements that

> we cannot do of ourselves, but have need always of the grace of God, as without whom we can neither continue in this life, nor without his special grace do any thing to his pleasure, whereby to attain the life to come.[60]

This insistence on the inadequacy of man and his utter dependence on God's grace, was a recurring emphasis in late medieval devotion and the writings of the humanists. Luther had taken it, and forged it into the even more austere doctrines of justification by faith alone and predestination. These doctrines insisted that man was completely devoid of any merit, and that his salvation was wholly dependent on the mercy of God. Henry was never persuaded that this was true, but his religion was reformed enough to embrace the preoccupation with man's unworthiness, and the magnitude of the divine gift of salvation. Henry always retained an equal insistence upon the importance of good works, and the need to obey the commandments. Reformation theology is often caricatured as being a conflict over whether faith or works were the route into heaven, but Henry insisted that both were equally necessary.

In other words, Henry accepted 'justification by faith', but never allowed 'justification by faith alone'. The first chapter of the 'King's Book' tackled this problematic subject, and gave its own definition of faith, that:

> faith ... is the perfect faith of a true Christian man, and containeth the obedience to the whole doctrine and religion of Christ. And thus is faith taken of St. Paul, and in other places of scripture, where it is said, that we be justified by faith. In which places men may not think that we be justified by faith, as it is a

several virtue separated from hope and charity, fear of God and repentance; but by it is meant faith neither only ne alone, but with the foresaid virtues coupled together, containing, as it is aforesaid, the obedience to the whole doctrine and religion of Christ.[61]

Henry, then, was rejecting the particular Lutheran or Zwinglian interpretation of faith, and the process of salvation. But this work of 1543, like all other official formulations of Henry's reign, was still imbued with the wider spirit of reformation. It aimed to transfigure and uplift, and inspire with a desire to reach:

the true reward of all godliness, God himself: the sight and fruition of whom is the end and reward of all our belief, and all our good works, and of all those things which were purchased for us by Christ. He shall be our satiety, our fulness, and desire; he shall be our life, our health, our glory, our honour, our peace, our everlasting rest and joy. He is the end of all our desires, whom we shall see continually, whom we shall love most fervently, whom we shall praise and magnify world without end.[62]

Considerable effort had gone into making this work at once reformed, biblical, balanced and Catholic. The desire to avoid radicalism did not mean that the importance of extirpating superstition had been forgotten. In one notable area, indeed, the 'King's Book' actually went further than the 'Bishops' Book' and other earlier statements of doctrine: although it allowed prayers for the dead, it was the most complete refutation yet of the doctrine of Purgatory which was so central to the beliefs and practices of traditional religon.[63] For the first time, the place and name of Purgatory were dispensed with, and it was made clear that prayers for the dead, although good and charitable and commanded by scripture and the fathers, could not be applied to anyone in particular, and should therefore be also intended 'for the universal congregation of Christian people, quick and dead'. This single-handedly rendered a large part of the religious activity of the pre-Reformation Church irrelevant. There was also an attack on the attendant abuses which had been advanced under the name of Purgatory:

Under colour of which have been advanced many fond and great abuses, to make men believe that through the bishop of Rome's pardons souls might clearly be delivered out of it, and released out of the bondage of sin; and that masses said at Scala coeli, and other prescribed places, phantasied by men, did there in those places more profit the souls than in another and also that a prescribed number of prayers sooner than other (though as devoutly said) should further their petition sooner, yea specially if they were said before one image more than another which they phantasied. All these, and such like abuses, be necessary utterly to be abolished and extinguished.[64]

It was with this trenchant attack, on Purgatory, indulgences and abused images, that the 'King's Book' concluded.

There was, then, no clear-cut reaction to an earlier more Protestant religious policy, but the continuation of Henry's own religious reform programme: biblical, anti-superstitious, slightly idiosyncratic, Catholic in its sacramental doctrine, evangelical in much of its rhetoric. It has been suggested that if we were to identify a 'Catholic reaction', the most likely contender is the year of 1543, with the King's Book, the Act for the Advancement of True Religion with its restrictions on Bible reading and the attack on the evangelical book trade.[65] Yet even in this year, Convocation ordered parish clergy to read a chapter of the bible a week to their congregations. In 1544 it became more difficult to use the Act of Six Articles to actually secure a conviction, and at the same time, the implementation of an English Litany and the publication of an English primer were important achievements for church reform.[66] In short, the whole idea of progress and backlash is out of step with the evidence for Henry's convictions and his way of proceeding. He sought to foster moderate reform, and when this was misinterpreted as a justification for more zealous evangelical pronouncements, he corrected the mistake firmly, at times brutally.

It has been argued that at the end of his life Henry was turning more and more towards the evangelical cause, and that had he lived, the future of England would have been as a Protestant country. The case for this rests on the provisions of Henry's will, the way he educated Prince Edward, the state of negotiations with the German Lutheran princes, the introduction of the English Litany and Primer in 1544 and the moves towards the dissolution of the chantries. Individually, or together, these still fail to make a convincing argument. As will be discussed below, Henry's will was not about establishing Protestantism, but about doing his best to make his son secure. Prince Edward's education had been entrusted to humanists, not to Protestants. Negotiations between England and the Lutherans continued sporadically, but so did negotiations with France and the Empire; this was part of a wider diplomatic game. And against the further reforms of Henry's final years we might put his continued adherence to the Act of Six Articles, and his refusal to surrender the Latin Mass, or to give way on the central question of justification by faith alone.

Nor was Henry's insistence on moderation in his religious policy achieved solely by a balance of elements, weighing up Catholic gestures and providing their counterpoise with a similar number of Protestant elements. It is important to realise that the key elements of Henry's policies at this point defied easy inclusion in either category. His use of the vernacular is a case in point. The English Litany of 1544 was a supplement to the Latin liturgy, not a replacement of part of it; what was being implemented was in fact a combination of homily, litany and prayers to be used during processions. These processions were not a standard part of religious worship, but instigated on special occasions, often as a response to some time of trial, or an epidemic of the plague, '*causa necessitatis vel tribulacionis*'.[67] It was not particularly radical to have supplementary religious material of this sort in English; sermons had long been in English, and prayers also. If some reformers thought this was a sign of more reforms to come, they were misrepresenting Henry's own intentions.[68] If the new litany showed anything, it was probably the level of Henry's concern regarding the international situation, and his desire to have his military campaign supported by the nation's prayers. The English primer of the same year is also a quintessentially Henrician publication, 'set foorth by the Kynges maiestie and his Clergie to be taught, learned and read: and none other to be used throughout all his dominions'. Henry's concern was with uniformity of religious practice; English prayers had been a well-established part of devotional life since the fifteenth century, so the king was chiefly hoping to bring in standard formulations, in English and Latin together, for the sake of a 'quiete and peaceable life'.

Henry's religious outlook was given one last, characteristic expression by his address to Parliament in January 1545. He came in person to prorogue the session, a task usually assigned to the chancellor, and to deliver an oration which was closer to a sermon than a royal address. In particular, he appealed for unity, for an end to religious discord, for an avoidance of extremism. He invoked scripture, although with a certain lack of precision, as he reminded them that 'St Paul saith to the Corinthians, in the thirteenth chapter, "Charity is gentle, charity is not envious, charity is not proud", and so forth'. What followed, however, was only too precise. The king attacked the absence of love and charity and how some were too rigid in their old ways, others too reckless in embracing the new:

> when the one calleth the other heretic, and anabaptist; and he calleth him again papist, hypocrite and pharisee. ... I see and hear daily, that you of the clergy preach one against another, teach one contrary to other, inveigh one against another, without charity or discretion. Some be too stiff in their 'mumpsimus'; others be too busy and curious in their new 'sumpsimus', and sow doubt and discord among simple folk, who look to the clergy for light and find only darkness.[69]

Not only the clergy were rebuked; he also reproached the lords temporal for inveighing against the clergy, instructing them:

> If you know surely that a bishop or preacher erreth, or teacheth perverse doctrine, come and declare it to some of our council, or to us, to whom is committed by God, the authority to reform and order such causes and behaviours; and be not judges yourselves of your own fantastical opinions and vain expositions, for in such high causes ye may lightly err.

This repetition of Henry's claims to authority over the Church, which had been made so many times, in so many different ways, suggests that he had found it easier to banish the Pope than to replace him. The implications of this speech are that his subjects were still failing to take him seriously as a spiritual leader. Finally, he gave a telling comment on the purpose of vernacular scripture:

> And although you be permitted to read holy Scripture, and to have the word of God in your mother tongue, you must understand that it is licensed you so to do, only to inform your own conscience, and to instruct your children and family; and not to dispute and make Scripture a railing and a taunting stock against priests and preachers, as many light persons do. I am very sorry to know and hear how unreverently that most precious jewel, the word of God,

is disputed, rhymed, sung, and jangled in every alehouse and tavern, contrary to the true meaning and doctrine of the same.[70]

Scripture was a jewel, and jewels were not worn by ordinary folk. This had always been the understanding which underlay Henry's Reformation.

KATHERINE PARR

The religious outlook of the king in these years is perhaps reflected in his choice of his last wife, with whom he liked to discuss theological matters. Henry did not marry again until 1543. It would seem that he had been genuinely enamoured of Katherine Howard, and truly devastated by her infidelity. Chapuys thought that he had shown 'greater sorrow and regret at her loss than at the faults, loss or divorce of his preceding wives'.[71] He had mourned Jane Seymour sincerely, but then at least he had the delight of Edward's birth to raise his spirits. It took him some months to come out of his sombre mood, and over a year before he found another wife, which delay might indicate the level of his misery. His new wife was Katherine Parr, whose father had been esquire of the body to Henry VII and who had fought in France with the young King Henry VIII in 1513. Katherine's mother had served Katherine of Aragon, and had brought up her children to be unusually civilised and educated, even in a time when noble and royal children were educated to such a high level. Katherine was fluent in French, Italian and Latin, she read Petrarch and translated Erasmus and possibly Savonarola.[72] By the time Katherine caught Henry's eye in 1543, she was twice widowed, and childless, and considering a third marriage to Sir Thomas Seymour, brother to Queen Jane. Henry, however, intervened, and made sure that Seymour spent the next few years in the Low Countries or at sea.

Katherine Parr is generally portrayed as a sedate widow who was a sound choice for an ageing, infirm king, having already nursed two elderly husbands in their closing years.[73] In fact she was an intelligent, attractive, animated woman of about 30, who loved music and dancing, and dressed expensively and with flair. She was also fresh from a dalliance with one of the most attractive and reckless men at court: it was

Thomas Seymour who was later to endanger Princess Elizabeth's reputation and lose his head for treason. Katherine had educated and independent ideas and she would prove a capable regent when the king was in France in 1544, and an enthusiastic patron of pious scholarship. She perhaps had the same point in her favour as her predecessor, that she was not associated with any particular religious faction. Her first husband had had evangelical leanings, her second was more conservative: she herself patronised moderate Erasmians such as Nicholas Udall, and she had served in the household of Princess Mary, with whom she remained on affectionate terms as stepmother. It seems likely that Henry approved her moderation; he was later to prove menacing when she seemed to be straying too far towards evangelicalism. He probably also approved of her dress-sense; an early gift to her was some expensive items of clothing.[74] She liked diamonds, and dressed herself and her household in crimson.[75] In short, she was a more exciting choice as queen than is usually appreciated.

As ever, when Henry had decided to marry, he wanted it to happen with as much speed as possible. In July 1543 Cranmer issued a special licence and two days later the wedding took place in the queen's closet, that is, her private chapel, at Hampton Court. Significantly, all three of the king's children were present, as well as his niece Lady Margaret Douglas: it seems that Henry's thoughts were often with his family in the last few years of his life, and one of Katherine's great achievements was keeping some sense of unity between her husband and his offspring. The marriage was conducted by Bishop Gardiner. The frequent identification of Katherine with the evangelical cause is over-played. Chapuys reported the marriage back to the future Philip II and said hopefully, 'May God be pleased that this marriage turn out well and that the king's favour and affection for the princess [Mary] continue to increase.'[76] Katherine was devout, but her steady kindness towards Mary shows she was no tool of faction.

The royal household after 1543 seems to have achieved a certain measure of stability as a result of Katherine's gentle initiative. She brought together Henry's three children, and with them a grouping of scholars and courtiers who reflected her husband's humanist interests. In fact this last Queen Katherine was not unlike Henry's first Queen Katherine, with the same sort of pious inclinations, literary interests and a pronounced enthusiasm for education.

Under her guidance, one particularly important work of translation was undertaken. An abiding problem of Henry's reformation was how to exalt the authority of scripture, and broaden the knowledge of the Bible in English, without encouraging his subjects into error. His authorisation of the English Bible, as we have seen, had not at all had the effect he intended. Under Katherine's auspices, a project was begun to translate the paraphrases of Erasmus on the New Testament. Princess Mary undertook to translate the paraphrase on St John's Gospel. Here was one possible answer to Henry's difficulties; a work which could be read in parallel with the Bible itself, to point his subjects towards a reformed yet Catholic understanding of the text, and prevent dangerous speculation and misunderstanding. The work was not completed until Edward VI's reign had begun, but when it was, it was placed in every English parish church alongside the Bible, surely the last significant act of the Henrician Reformation.

Katherine herself also ventured into print, which in itself made her an appropriate partner to this bookish king. She published a book of prayers in 1545, and *The Lamentation of a Sinner* after Henry's death. She also inspired Princess Elizabeth to translate Erasmus's work *Dialogus Fidei* and an Erasmian work by Marguerite of Navarre, *The Mirror of Glass of a Sinful Soul*. Henry's children were being educated to such a level that the translation of devotional works from Latin or French was considered as suitable an occupation as the embroidery with which Elizabeth decorated her endeavours. Elizabeth's New Year gift to her father in 1546 was Katherine's book of prayers from 1545 translated into Latin, French and Italian, embroidered with the king and queen's initials and white roses to evoke Elizabeth's grandmother, Elizabeth of York, for whom she had been named. Elizabeth's preface to this book, written in Latin, referred to her father as 'a god on earth'.[77] Clearly more than one of Henry's key convictions were being reflected in his daughter's education.

The last years of Henry's life saw no diminution, then, of the intellectual life which he had always liked to foster at court. It also saw a continued emphasis on royal magnificence, in part expressed in the building projects of the 1540s. Just as St James's Palace in London was prepared for the son Anne Boleyn never had, so Oatlands and Nonsuch were built as satellite palaces for Hampton Court. Oatlands was to house the queen and her household when the king was at Hampton Court;

work began there in 1537–8, when six loads of fruit trees were brought over from the dissolved abbey of Chertsey, and it was seemingly completed in 1544.[78]

Nonsuch Palace was meant for Prince Edward. Work was begun there shortly after Prince Edward was given his own household, on 22 April 1538, which was the thirtieth anniversary of Henry's accession; it was at least partly habitable by 1541. The stucco panels at Nonsuch were meant to provide an education in pictures for the young prince, with a host of historical and mythical figures, a solid example of the 'mirror for princes' tradition.[79] A host of Caesars paid tribute to Henry's own imperial status. Nonsuch, according to a Venetian traveller in 1562, far outshone both Hampton Court and Richmond (see Plate 7). One of the chief craftsmen employed was Nicholas Bellin of Modena who had worked on Fontainebleau for Francis I; he was to remain a permanent fixture in England, with an annuity, until his death in 1569, and in 1544 was living in the 'Tombe House' at Westminster where Henry's tomb was being prepared.[80] The mottoes inscribed on the palace walls were largely taken from translations by Erasmus. The palace was a visual display of the ideology underpinning Henry's mature kingship, and an indication of how much he treasured his son.

FOREIGN POLICY

In July of 1542 France and the Empire went to war once more, which raised possibilities of returning to an earlier pattern of alliances, and once more making war across the Channel. The idea was kept quiet as England and France continued to pursue negotiations over the possible marriage of the Lady Mary to a French prince; these talks were bound to prove fruitless, however, since Henry refused to reverse his decision about Mary's legitimacy. Meanwhile, Henry was also pursuing secret negotiations with Charles V regarding a possible joint attack on France. Yet it was while meditating war with France that Henry found himself almost accidentally at war with Scotland. He had been making menacing noises to James V for some time, and had been irate that James had failed to meet with him during his progress to the north in 1541. In September 1542 negotiations were proceeding, with Henry demanding a release of English prisoners and James's firm commitment to a meeting that winter. The Scottish replies seem to have been vague, but not hostile, yet the Duke of Norfolk responded to Henry's impatient letters by unleashing a raid over the border to drive home the seriousness of the English demands. This had the opposite effect to that intended, and James V raised an army to counterattack in November. It was defeated at the battle of Solway Moss, and three weeks later James was dead, leaving his throne to his daughter Mary, just 6 days old.

Henry had won a victory he had not even aimed at. He decided to take the infant queen under his protection and betrothe her to Prince Edward. Unfortunately for the king, however, he never really understood Scottish affairs, perhaps largely because he tended to underestimate the Scots, taking an exaggerated view of what his own money and influence could bring about. On this occasion, since he planned to do nothing less than take over Scottish government, acquire custody of the small queen and reform the Scottish Church, he might have expected that it would be necessary to send a considerable force north of the border. Instead he tried to proceed through diplomacy, threats and promises, which had the combined effect of alienating those whom he considered to be his allies, and driving them back into the arms of the French and the 'Auld Alliance'.

In December 1543 the Scottish parliament annulled all treaties with England and formally renewed the alliance with France. Henry felt betrayed, and sent a punitive force into Scotland to punish Scots perfidy, and to quell the Scottish threat whilst he was busy in France. Even his own commander, the Earl of Hertford, pointed out that he would do better to occupy and fortify certain key strongholds, if he was to maintain his presence in Scotland. He opined that people would 'aid the king's army if they saw he intended to have a foot within the realm, whereas fire and sword would put all to utter despair'. Henry told him he was wrong, and commanded that he sack Edinburgh.[81] This Hertford did, and then withdrew, leaving the Scots even less disposed than before to accept English overlordship.

Henry was always a great deal more interested in making war in France than in Scotland. Of the two great victories against the Scots during his reign, Flodden had been to the credit of Katherine of Aragon and the Earl of Surrey (subsequently made Duke of Norfolk), and Solway Moss had also been the next Duke of Norfolk's rather accidental achievement. It was to France that the king preferred to give his more personal attention. In 1544, he went to war there, for the third and last time in his reign. It was the last grand martial flourish of a reign which had always been intensely concerned with international politics and the chance of military glory; and as before, the realities of warfare failed to match the exuberance and arrogance of the king's rhetoric. Nonetheless, it was an impressive body of men that was mobilised for the campaign. Henry himself led a third of the army, largely drawn from his court, Council and household, in an echo of the medieval affinity, but the other two thirds were raised by the more modern method of commissions of array, commanded by the Duke of Norfolk and Lord John Russell respectively.[82]

Henry's health was far from good at this point in his reign, but the resilience of the man is shown by the way he fought back against constant pain and physical decay in his determination to lead his armies to France. Prolonged negotiations which preceded any actual military activity show that his allies and his councillors alike were rather alarmed at the prospect of Henry actually venturing into battle. Chapuys suggested to Charles V, apparently at the bidding of Henry's Privy Council, that if the emperor declined to lead his own troops then Henry might also be induced to do the same, thereby increasing the chances of military success as well as safeguarding the king's health. Charles was not enthusiastic.[83] Negotiations laboured on, however, to somehow find a way of dignifying the proposed attack by this Catholic emperor and his schismatic ally on the French who were in alliance with the Turks. The chivalric and religious values of the time were being badly stretched; it is notable that the Anglo-Imperial alliance only managed to get round the embarrassment of Henry's title of 'supreme head of the church' by listing his titles only as far as 'defender of the faith', and then adding a masterly and craven 'etc.', a formulation which was to have a distinguished future history.[84]

The alliance with Charles V had been signed in February 1543, although for over three months it was kept a secret to enhance Henry's chance of success in his Scottish negotiations. In the summer of 1543 English troops went to help with the defence of the Netherlands, and there was a naval encounters with the French, but the main attack was planned for June 1544. The proposed invasion was on a huge and ambitious scale; both England and the Empire would commit an army of 42,000 men, and they would head for Paris by different routes. In reality, however, Henry's interests did not extend much beyond Normandy.

Although he dispatched his army under the command of the dukes of Norfolk and Suffolk, his letters to Charles V show that he was not completely sure about the wisdom of aiming at Paris. Upon arrival, the English army waited for instructions for several weeks while the king tried to recover his health and make up his mind. Norfolk was then told to lay siege to Montreuil, and after Henry's arrival in Calais in July, Suffolk was sent to lay siege to Boulogne. Henry argued that the capture of these two towns would facilitate the eventual advance upon Paris, but it was clear that he was far happier consolidating his foothold in Normandy.

It was also clear that the war effort was badly organised, and badly maintained. Continual complaints came from his commanders about the lack of everything necessary, from beer to artillery. From St Didier came the lament that:

> At our first coming hither we had flesh enough and scarcity of bread; and now we have bread and lack flesh; and by that time we are six miles further, I trust we shall have neither flesh nor bread.

Norfolk and his companions before the walls of Montreuil wrote hopefully to the King's Council 'if we might be furnished weekly of six or seven score tun [i.e. barrels] of beer from Bullen [Boulogne] we should make the best shift we could for other vittels.'[85] Meanwhile the queen, who made a point of reassuring Henry about the health of all his children when she wrote, assured Henry that she would send more ordinance, shot and '2000 shovels, spades and mattocks, if so many may possibly be gotten'.[86] This was a campaign involving much removal of mud. Henry still seems to have been capable of mustering some good humour, however, for his Council wrote telling Norfolk not to be dismayed by rumours of the Dauphin's approach, and:

> if the Dauphin do come indeed, whereof His Majestie requireth you to get certain [i.e. accurate] knowledge, to serve your turn, and to visit his godson, not doubting but the same will be brought ere he depart (if he do come) to acknowledge his duty to his Godfather.[87]

This last war saw some moderate success, for it led to the capture of Boulogne in September. Norfolk failed to take Montreuil, but he did at least manage to withdraw his troops without being defeated. However,

Charles V had decided that Henry had breached the terms of the alliance, and without consulting him, signed a peace treaty with the French. Henry tried to do likewise, but insisted that the French should ratify his capture of Boulogne and stay out of Scottish affairs, and this was to ask too much of them. Meanwhile, both England and the Empire continued to lay charges of deceit and disloyalty against the other. By the summer of 1545, the international situation looked unusually grave. England was at odds with the Empire, still at war with France, and doing badly with regard to Scotland, where the policy of repeated raids was achieving little, and indeed suffered a small but significant defeat in February 1545 at Ancrum. Its troops were still in Calais, diseased and disaffected. France was threatening invasion from Scotland and across the Channel, and the Lutherans, to whom Henry made another appeal at this time, were not interested.

In July 1545, therefore, England was seriously on the defensive. Henry deployed armies in Kent, Essex and the West Country to defend the south, and put Hertford in command of one force on the Scottish borders, whilst another force stood ready in Boulogne, and the fleet waited in the Channel. It was on 19 July, as the king dined aboard his flagship, that the French were sighted in the Solent. Two French landings, on the Isle of Wight and at Seaford, were aborted. On 9 August the fleet was ordered out of Portsmouth to do battle with the French, and on 10 August processions and prayers throughout the realm sought to mobilise the Almighty also. After some skirmishing, the French sailed home; like many military endeavours of this time, their efforts had been rather arbitrary, unsustained and ultimately ineffectual.

Nevertheless, hostilities had not ceased, and the ceaseless and complicated workings of diplomacy continued to exercise Henry, who paid careful attention to every twist and turn. One of the problems was that he was attempting to play the same sort of game that he had attempted in the first two decades of his reign, in a significantly altered context. Religious conflict, in particular, had complicated matters. The traditional alliances with Spain and the Netherlands, now united under the rule of Charles V, had been fundamentally weakened by the fact that Henry had broken with Rome and rejected Katherine of Aragon, whilst one of the major challenges faced by Charles was that posed by the Lutherans in the Empire, with whom Henry continued to negotiate. The old level of trust and cooperation in Anglo-Imperial relations could thus never be regained. England could not, therefore, hope to threaten France as it had in 1513 and 1523. Henry's attempts to enhance his authority at home had seriously compromised his effectiveness abroad.

The last major diplomatic objective of the reign was to recapture the Anglo-Imperial alliance, and Henry sent Bishop Gardiner, who had all the wisdom and experience he could hope for in an ambassador. Charles V was not sufficiently interested, however, and he continued to turn down offers of marriage between Henry's children and various Habsburgs, proposals of a meeting with Henry, and suggestions of a renewed attack on France. Charles was concentrating all his efforts on defeating the Lutherans. The best Gardiner could manage to extract from him was an Anglo-Imperial entente in January 1546. Meanwhile Paget and Tunstall were in France, where the German Lutherans were attempting to bring England and France together to help them against Charles V. Henry would not surrender Boulogne, however, and so the Lutherans went home disappointed, and Hertford was sent back to France to renew the war in the spring.

Yet when the spring came Henry had thought better of it. Possibly the huge cost of his involvements in both France and Scotland was beginning to daunt him. It was certainly taking its toll upon his subjects; it has been calculated that a prosperous taxpayer in the 1540s stood to lose two-fifths of his goods as a result of war taxation. In broader terms, the sale of crown lands to fund Henry's later wars effectively cancelled out the beneficial financial effects of the dissolution of the monasteries.[88] Perhaps too the king's own worsening health made him decide to be less ambitious, to safeguard what he already had rather than stretch himself still further. Peace negotiations began in April, and after many tense weeks, it was agreed that England would not make war on Scotland unless the Scots attacked, and that Boulogne would be returned to France at the end of eight years for the sum of 2 million crowns. Clearly Henry did not expect either of these articles to impede him; he meant to go on fighting in Scotland, and he meant to keep Boulogne. But it was enough to build a treaty on, which was celebrated in the usual lavish manner. Still, the garrison at Boulogne was reduced, but maintained, and when the French started building fortifications across the harbour, Henry gave covert instructions to have them destroyed.

By the end of Henry's life, international relations had acquired an even greater complexity than at the beginning of his reign, when they had been far from simple. The addition of religious conflict into an already volatile mix of vested interests, suspicions and ambitions meant there was no complete certainty behind any negotiated agreement, and very little sincerity either. To the end of his life, Henry remained active in diplomacy, constantly alive to the possibility of new alliances, constantly suspicious of the bigger players. France seemed to menace his possessions across the Channel, and threatened his objectives in Scotland; the Empire as it championed the Catholic cause always held possible menace for Henry on the grounds of his schism from the papacy. It cannot be said that Henry had a foreign policy as such. He sought security, and intermittently he sought gain and glory, but there was no clear path towards those ends in Europe of the 1540s.

THE LAST YEAR

The reign which had began with such high hopes was to end in a cloud of anxiety and vengeful aggression. The king's ability to compel his subjects to obedience was closely linked to his physical strength, and as his vigour waned, and his body began to rot, the political nation began to look towards the future, and to prepare for a new king. Since Prince Edward was still a child, the possibilities for political influence after Henry's death were broad and tempting, and that death seemed to be approaching.

The king's health had been causing concern since the summer of 1546. It is difficult to put this in proportion, since enormous care was taken with even the smallest royal ailments. Equally, a certain level of ill-health was a normal part of life in Tudor times, and the wealthy had such unhealthy diets that frequent digestive trouble was to be expected. It may even be that the king was so short of fresh fruit and vegetables he was suffering from scurvy.[89] He had also suffered with a sore leg since the late 1520s, with what was probably a varicose ulcer. The common story that the king suffered from syphilis seems unlikely, not least since none of his children demonstrated any signs of the disease, and there is no record of him ever undergoing the lengthy and painful treatment for this, which required six weeks of mercury treatment. It is more likely that he suffered from recurrent varicose ulcers, or possibly from a recurring bone infection resulting from a jousting injury.[90] Certainly he suffered from an ulcer in 1528 during a visit to Canterbury, when a local surgeon was called in and managed to cure him, Henry gave him an appointment in the royal household, such was his gratitude.

Then in 1536 came the fall during a joust which left Henry insensible for two hours, news of which possibly hastened Anne Boleyn's last miscarriage. This seems to have caused problems in his legs again, and from this time on he seems frequently to have suffered from ulcers on one or both legs which required sporadic draining. In 1538, when one of the ulcers closed up, it was reported that 'the humours which had no outlet were like to have stifled him so that he was some time without speaking, black in the face and in great danger.' It has been suggested that the king was suffering from thrombosis, and probably a blood clot which had travelled to the brain. If so, he was lucky to survive.

By 1546 it was clear to observers that Henry's state of health was worsening; the death of his favourite physician, William Butts, in the winter of 1545, probably also heightened his anxieties about his condition. The king's obesity had been giving concern for some years, although he was still able to hunt, once the awkward task of mounting his horse had been achieved. At Oatlands a special ramp was constructed to aid this. By the spring of 1546 he was having difficulty walking, however, even if he could still ride. A form of sedan chair, with in-built footstools, was constructed in which the king could be carried about his palaces.[91] He is reported as suffering from fevers, and from exhaustion. It has been suggested that he was suffering from Cushing's syndrome, a condition causing serious obesity, weakened bones, mood swings, headaches and fatigue.[92] Medical diagnosis at such a distance remains almost impossible, but Henry was definitely suffering from obesity, fatigue and a great deal of chronic pain. These in themselves might provide sufficient explanation for depression, irritability and frequent mood swings.

It is not necessary to seek a purely medical explanation for the temperamental difficulties which Henry was experiencing in the 1540s. We might just look at Henry's psalter, now kept in the British Library, which was written for him around 1540. Psalm 37, verse 25, reads 'I have been young and now am old', and in the margin, Henry wrote 'Dolus dictum' – 'a grievous saying'. If we remember the physical magnificence, the chivalric glory, the kingly magnificence, of his early years, the plight of this bloated, pain-ridden, disappointed old man seems painfully pathetic. We also need to remember the abiding anxiety which had been with him nearly all his life, namely whether he could secure the succession. In 1546 Prince Edward was only 9 years old. The last child to inherit the throne, Edward V, had been deposed and murdered by his uncle.

Henry must have been prey to a terrible desperation, longing to stay alive long enough to see his son grown to sufficient strength. The mood swings, the savage attacks upon his ministers and courtiers, the depression of his last months, are all understandable, given that the political security for which he had planned all his life looked set to evade him at the last. Every parent suffers agonies at the thought of dying and leaving their children still young and defenceless. How much worse it must have been for Henry, contemplating the likelihood that his precious son and heir might not survive the transition of power, that the dynasty his father had founded might be about to crumble, that his country might again be on the brink of the nightmare that was civil war.

It is in this context that we need to place the high-profile executions of Henry's last years. Perhaps the most shocking of these is the death, after torture, of Anne Askew. Anne was the daughter of a gentry family in Lincolnshire, married rather unwillingly to Thomas Kyme, and separated from him after her evangelical beliefs came between them. Bale said that 'in process of time by oft reading of the sacred Bible, she fell clearly from all old superstitions of papistry, to a perfect belief in Jesus Christ.'[93] She is known to have possessed a work by John Frith, himself executed for heresy in 1534 and when she came to London in 1544, possibly in search of a divorce, she became established in evangelical circles there. She was tried for transgressing against the Act of Six Articles in 1545, but released when the trial failed. A year later, however, a second investigation was conducted with much greater intensity, and Anne was interrogated by the Privy Council before being tried alongside the former Bishop of Salisbury, among others. Nicholas Shaxton, formerly Anne Boleyn's almoner, had resigned his bishopric in protest at the Act of Six Articles, and this heightened the significance of this trial. Once again, the nature of the Sacrament was at issue, but Anne's examination by a collection of the most conservative elements on the Council indicates that Henry was undergoing one of his sporadic anxieties about heresy.

Significantly, Anne was asked whether she had connections to five of the women who served the queen. Here we see an intermingling of different objectives. Henry had always been firm that sacramentarian heresy was to be wormed out and destroyed. The assiduity of his councillors in pursuing Anne Askew, however, was also a reflection of their anxiety about the influence of Queen Katherine. It seems likely that the queen's interest in religion had advanced no further than a mildly evangelical Erasmian kind of piety, but she was exceedingly devout, holding Bible readings with the women of her Privy Chamber, and more importantly, conversing with the king about religion. In the summer of 1546, however, one of these conversations annoyed the king, and he complained after her departure to Bishop Gardiner, who was conveniently in attendance. Henry is supposed to have said, 'A good hearing it is when women become such clerks and a thing much to my comfort to come in my old days to be taught by a woman!'. This suggests only irritation, but Gardiner's response was to offer to investigate the queen for possible heretical leanings.[94]

It is hard to know what to think about what happened next. Gardiner and the Council produced a list of articles against the queen which was signed by Henry. This list came, seemingly by accident, to be given to the queen, who must have wondered if she was to go the way of her predecessors; certainly she became ill and took to her bed. The king then despatched his doctor to her, a certain Dr Wendy, to whom he had confided his doubts about Katherine, whilst ostensibly binding him to secrecy. In fact, the doctor told Katherine everything, and she came to the king, declaring her total obedience to him and her submission to 'your majesty's wisdom, as my only anchor, supreme head and governor here in earth, next under God, to lean unto'. She explained that she had only discussed religion with him to divert him during his illness, and he reportedly replied 'And is it even so, sweetheart, and tended your argument to no worse end? Then perfect friends we are now again as ever at any time heretofore.' The next day the king was walking with the queen and the gentlewomen of her privy chamber when Wriothesley arrived with his henchmen to take the queen, her sister and two of her ladies to the Tower. But the king called him 'Knave! Arrant knave, beast and fool!' and sent him away.

It is from Foxe that we hear this story, and Foxe was never entirely reliable. No doubt he hoped to paint the conservatives here in the worst possible light, and yet there is no obvious propaganda point achieved by this story, which suggests that it may in essentials be accurate. The similarity with Cranmer's near fall from power in 1543, or Gardiner's the following year, suggests that this was a technique the king had evolved for maintaining the balance of power, using the workings of faction to deliver a reminder of his displeasure to those whom he wanted to control, but not destroy. If Gardiner did indeed volunteer to prove the queen's heretical leanings in this way, perhaps the king was affronted by such a response to what were merely grumbling about his opinionated wife. By allowing the conservatives to proceed against Katherine, but making sure that she knew of the plot against her, Henry was delivering a timely warning to both his wife and his councillors, that they should not try to influence him, and that religious policy proceeded from his authority alone. It was not a pleasant way of doing it, but it was undeniably effective. If the king was wearied by the remorseless scheming of the different factions at court, it is perhaps unsurprising that he chose to use their own methods to deliver a blow to those who sought to pressurise him. Intelligent, manipulative, and with a pre-eminent regard for his own royal authority, this would be a characteristic strategy for the king to adopt. It is also worth noting that although several of the participants in this drama must have badly scared, nobody lost their lives apart from the true religious zealots who could not be brought to acknowledge the king's laws. Anne Askew died a martyr, but Queen Katherine lived, and retained the king's affections, although she was quietly excluded from any position of authority over the future King Edward VI.

Henry's vengeance could be harsh, but it was more often than not based on substance. It could, however, be strongly influenced by the king's own fears, and these must lie behind the last execution of his reign. The final victim of Henry's vengeful unhappiness and anxiety for his son was Henry Howard, Earl of Surrey. Both Surrey and his father, the Duke of Norfolk, were convicted for treason in January 1547, but Surrey was executed on 19 January, and his father, whose execution was set to follow on 30 January, escaped death. Henry's own death on the 28 January meant the execution was suspended.

The life and death of the Earl of Surrey remain complex subjects, for Surrey was a conundrum to his contemporaries, let alone his biographers. His fall was a dramatic one, for Surrey had been a privileged member of Henry's court, raised as the companion of the king's much beloved son the Duke of Richmond, invested with the Order of the Garter, cousin to two queens, and an important military commander. He was known for his arrogance, painfully conscious of his high birth, and angry and melancholic by turns at the proliferation in government of men of lowly birth. He was also a very great poet, writing poetry which hints at his loathing for the politics of Henry's reign, but tells us nothing directly.

The crime that led to Surrey's death was the use of the arms of Edward the Confessor, and the unusual nature of this transgression has led many to conclude that this was merely a pretext for judicial murder, that Henry was bent on bringing down the Howards, either for their aristocratic pretensions or for their religious conservatism, although in fact that conservatism is by no means proven. Instead we should look more closely at this heraldic misdemeanour, because to Henry the point of it was that he believed Surrey and his father aimed at the crown. Surrey certainly held the opinion that his father was the only fit person to serve as Protector to the young King Edward in the event of Henry VIII's death. Surrey died, and Norfolk very nearly did, because of the potential threat they posed to the balance of power in the next reign.

Henry was dying, and he was afraid. His disquiet was behind much of the menace of these closing months of the reign. Just as the wound was suppurating in his leg, so the wound of religious division was weakening his nation. The significance of the metaphor he used to parliament in 1545 was a highly personal one, when he warned them: 'I assure you that this lack of charity amongst yourselves will be the hindrance and assuaging of the fervent love between us... except this wound be salved and clearly made whole.' He had issued a threat to Lords and Commons then:

> Amend these crimes, I exhort you, and set forth God's word, both by true preaching and good example-giving; or else I, whom God hath appointed his vicar and high minister here, will see these divisions extinct, and these enormities corrected, according to my very duty; or else I am an unprofitable servant, and an untrue officer.[95]

This was a heartfelt threat, but one he would be hard pressed to fulfil completely. It may even be that Henry was afraid for himself. He had dismissed enough 'unprofitable servants' and 'untrue officers' in his time, perhaps, to fear God's judgement himself for having failed in this most important of all his tasks.

By December 1546, Henry seems to have known that he was about to die. The queen was sent to Greenwich for Christmas, but Henry remained at Whitehall, and on the evening of 26 December he summoned his close councillors to his bedchamber, and ordered them to bring a copy of his will, last made in 1544 before leaving for war. He made some changes to the list of executors, removing Gardiner and Gardiner's friend Thomas Thirlby, Bishop of Westminster. The new will was drafted by Paget, completed by 30 December, and given to Hertford for safe keeping.[96] In all, he had sixteen executors, to whom he entrusted the regency of the realm during Edward's minority. After Edward, the throne was to go to Mary, and after her Elizabeth, on condition that they were to marry only with the 'written and sealed consent' of a majority of what remained of Edward's Privy Council. The importance of consensus was reiterated by the king's instructions: 'None of them shall do anything appointed by this will alone but only with the written consent of the majority'.

The more personal aspects of the will also provide some insight into Henry's character and convictions. Its opening invocation was 'in the name of God and of the glorious and blessed virgin our Lady Saint Mary and of all the holy company of Heaven', which was traditional enough. Unlike his father's will, which had appealed to ten specific saints – Michael, John the Baptist, John the Evangelist, George, Anthony, Edward, Vincent, Anne, Mary Magdalen and Barbara – Henry had no extraneous saints. His description of himself as 'immediately under god the Supreme head of the church of England' did something to outweigh the more conventional humility of his acknowledgement that he was 'insufficient in any part to deserve or recompence' the great gifts and benefits he had received in life. There was also a final firm assertion of the importance of good works, as Henry confessed that although 'we be as all mankind as mortal and born in sin', still he hoped that those 'dying in stedfast and perfect faith' and having executed 'such good deeds and charitable works as scripture demandeth', might look 'to be saved and to attain eternal life of which number we verily trust by his grace to be one'.

To speed this end, he left land worth £600 to the Dean and Chapter of St. George's Chapel, Windsor, for daily masses and four annual obits (commemorative masses). The obits would include a sermon, and in addition, a weekly sermon was to be provided for the townsfolk of Windsor. Henry also sought to revive the almshouses for poor knights first provided by Edward III; his daughter Elizabeth would eventually fulfil this intention. In his last will and testament Henry managed to pursue the same moderately reformed but doctrinally Catholic path he had struggled so much to follow in his lifetime.

The significance of the arrangements for a Regency Council take us straight to the heart of the king's anxieties as he felt death approaching. Established practice when an underage king was due to inherit was to appoint a Protector, or Regent. This had been the arrangement for Edward V in 1483, and for Henry VI in 1422, and on both occasions the new king's uncle had taken the role. Not since Richard II had come to the throne in 1377 had the regency been exercised by a 'continual council', and even then the king's uncle, John of Gaunt, had played a major role. Prince Edward had as uncle Edward Seymour, Earl of Hertford, who was already Lord Treasurer and Lord Great Chamberlain, whom Henry had trusted with military command in both Scotland and France. There was also Queen Katherine, whom Henry had named as Regent in his will of 1544, made – as was customary – before he departed for war in France. Yet Henry was too apprehensive of the dangers to entrust authority to any single figure.

The sixteen men who were to preserve the spirit of the dead king in their protectorship of the new King Edward were carefully chosen. The omission of Gardiner is said to have prompted one of those present to ask if he had been left out by accident, only for the king to retort that Gardiner's 'troublesome nature' had led to his exclusion. Henry reportedly said, 'Marry, I myself could use him and rule him to all manner of purposes, as it seemed good to me – but so shall you never do.'[97] More than anything, therefore, Henry seemed concerned to preserve stability during the always unstable interlude that was a royal minority.

Whether Henry wanted to guarantee more than just security, whether he also wanted to dictate the future course of religious policy, is hotly debated. Of the sixteen men appointed, Archbishop Cranmer, the Earl of Hertford and Sir Anthony Denny were openly committed to the evangelical cause. They were also, however, men whom Henry trusted – his faithful archbishop, his brother-in-law, a gentleman of his privy chamber. Others were more conservative in their religious leanings: Sir Thomas Wriothesley, Lord Chancellor; Cuthbert Tunstall, Bishop of Durham; Sir Anthony Browne. The rest are harder to place, and their subsequent careers seem to suggest that they were willing to follow royal will before any private religious convictions.[98] Arguing purely from the composition of this regency council, it cannot be said that Henry was making a final commitment to the evangelical cause. If anything, he seems to have sought balance, moderation, and consensus, and above all else, appointed men with whom he had been working closely and whom he felt he could trust.

The argument that Henry's final months saw a swing of the pendulum towards the evangelicals rests on several pieces of evidence. One is the replacement of Thomas Heneage in the privy chamber with Sir William Herbert, in October 1546. Another is the execution of Surrey, and the conviction of his father the Duke of Norfolk, who might otherwise be expected to appear in the list of executors. The final piece of the jigsaw is the decision to omit Gardiner from the list also. Yet, as we have seen, the threat posed by Norfolk and Surrey was not the threat to evangelicalism, but the more alarming threat to the dynasty itself, which had necessitated their destruction. Nor is it clear that either Norfolk or his son were unequivocal supporters of any religious faction, although Norfolk had tended to side with the conservatives against Cranmer in the 1540s. The Howard family later became famous for its commitment to Catholicism, but the third duke had sided with the king against Katherine of Aragon, brutally suppressed the Pilgrimage of Grace, and was not particularly known for any religious loyalties, while Surrey, if anything, had evangelical leanings, whilst remaining ambiguous in his religious loyalties.[99] Heneage seems to have been a religious conservative, but Sir William Herbert has no greater claim to evangelical identity than being married to Katherine Parr's sister.[100] Finally, Gardiner's commitment to the conservative cause was clear, but no less clear than that of Cuthbert Tunstall whom the king included. It seems likely that the king's own justification was truthful; Gardiner was troublesome, and headstrong, and it was for these qualities that Henry excluded him from the Regency Council.

This debate also rests on the assumption that the workings of faction were decisive in determining the policy decisions of Henry's reign. This biography has remained consistently sceptical of such a view. Factions were an undeniable part of political life, but their influence relied on their ability to align themselves with the king's wishes and bring about the developments which he desired. Yet, in these last painful and anxious weeks of the king's life, it seems probable that faction acquired a significance it had not formerly held. Whilst they lived in fear of the king, the workings of factions were necessarily subdued, and Henry had proved himself more than able to manage their scheming, using it to further his own purposes. But once it became clear that the king was dying, his authority began to wither, and all hopes became focused on the reign to come. Symptomatic of this is the fact that Henry VIII never actually signed his own will. He was too ill, and instead the 'dry stamp' was used, which gave an impression of the king' s signature which could afterwards be inked in. This had been a routine part of official business for some time. It does raise the possibility, however, that the will was a forgery. The fact that the will was not included in the list of 'dry stamp' documents for December 1546, but added to the list for January 1547 has also been seen as suspicious, as has the 'unfulfilled gifts' clause, which ensured that promises of land Henry had made before his death could be honoured after he had died. This last clause was to make a number of men very wealthy, most notably Edward Seymour and his associates.

Conspiracy theories are always tempting, but this one remains improbable.[101] William Clerk, clerk of the Privy Seal, recorded that the king delivered his will into the hands of the Earl of Hertford in the presence of ten witnesses.[102] It would have been well-nigh impossible to tamper with it thereafter, and the fact of it being signed by dry stamp was not remarkable. Nor is it surprising that the 'unfulfilled gifts' clause was included, given that the extensive Howard lands would be available for reallocation, and more importantly, given that Henry wanted the dictates of his will to be obeyed. If the price of his executors' loyalty was their own enrichment, then that was what the king needed to ensure. As it is, Henry's authority would fail to reach beyond the grave. Edward Seymour, Earl of Hertford, would establish himself as Protector within three days of Henry's death. Since he was elected by Henry's executors, the move was not illegal, but it was not the most obvious fulfilment of the dead king's wishes. If Hertford had arranged to have the will forged, he might have found it simpler to include Henry's sanction for his Protectorship. As it was, there was no need to forge anything. Hertford's election as Protector suited nearly everyone. Henry VIII's authority was to be abruptly terminated by his death, once again underlining the point that monarchy in this century was first and foremost personal monarchy.

Henry VIII died on 28 January 1547. At the last, he asked for Cranmer, who arrived in the small hours of the morning. This was how the deathbed scene was described by John Foxe:

> Then the archbishop, exhorting him to put his trust in Christ, and to call upon his mercy, desired him, though he could not speak, yet to give some token with his eyes or with his hand, that he trusted in the Lord. Then the king, holding him with his hand, did wring his hand in his as hard as he could.[103]

Here, of course, Foxe is laying claim to Henry for the Protestant cause. The traditional Catholic death bed scene, where the dying fix their eyes upon a crucifix, receive the last rites, and are gently conveyed into the afterlife by solemn prayers, is replaced by the simple demonstration of faith. Yet the replacement of Catholic sacraments by the Protestant doctrine of 'justification by faith alone' was something Henry never allowed. It is characteristic of the man that his final act should be one so full of ambiguity. We will never know for sure what he meant to convey as he clutched Cranmer's hand for the last time. It may well be that the archbishop's presence was not chiefly important for the religious reassurance it brought, but for providing a faithful friend and servant to be with the king at the very end. There is a sad irony in the fact that this man who was responsible for the deaths of so many who had been close to him, who had executed wives, ministers, and courtiers, had always craved so much the company of those he could trust.

Whatever the ambiguities of Henry's last moments, his commemoration and burial followed time-honoured tradition. His entrails were buried in the Chapel Royal at Whitehall, and his body lay in state in the Privy Chamber for three days, where the Holbein mural reminded mourners of the magnificence and the presumption of this king in his heyday. As specified in his will, masses were said for his soul. In every church in the land, dirges and requiems were sung. On 3 February, the coffin was moved to the chapel for ten days of requiem masses. It was not until 14 February that the funeral procession set off for Windsor, staying overnight at Syon on the way, as Edward IV's funeral cortège had done. Indeed, everything about the funeral obsequies was entirely traditional, closely following the precedents set by other royal deaths.[104] The coffin was carried on a gilded chariot draped with cloth of gold and blue velvet; on top of it the funeral effigy was dressed in royal robes, with imperial crown, orb and sceptre. It was preceded by all the chaplains and musicians of the Chapel Royal, 250 paupers in mourning gowns carrying torches, and gentlemen and knights with standards and the banners of descent. More of the household followed behind, including Anthony

Browne, Master of the Horse, leading the king's horse. The religious symbolism of the banners was unaltered from previous royal funerals; there was no sign that this king had transformed the English Church. When the procession reached Windsor there were more masses, and Bishop Gardiner delivered the funeral sermon. The vault containing Jane Seymour's coffin was opened and Henry was laid to rest beside the only one of his six wives who had fulfilled his expectations.

7

THE LEGACY OF HENRY VIII

I come no more to make you laugh. Things now
That bear a weighty and a serious brow,
Sad, high, and working, full of state and woe –
Such noble scenes as draw the eye to flow
We now present. Those that can pity here
May, if they think it well, let fall a tear;
The subject will deserve it.[1]

Henry VIII had every intention of being remembered as a great and glorious monarch. His tomb at Windsor was intended to set the seal on this
reputation; it was initially envisaged as a great triumphal arch bearing a
statue of the king on horseback. The classicism of the arch, and the
equestrian statue, in the most ostentatious Renaissance tradition, was to
be supplemented with a wealth of Christian imagery, paying particular
attention to the apostles, evangelists and doctors of the Church, and to
St George. Within the tomb it was intended that two figures should lie,
and as a Jacobean commentator described it, 'not as death, but as persons
sleeping, because to show that famous Princes leaving behind them
great fame, their names never do die, and shall lie in royal Apparels after
the antique manner'.

In other words, at the heart of the monument it was intended to
depict Henry and his only satisfactory wife, Queen Jane, in a manner

reminiscent of the tomb of Henry VII and Elizabeth of York, lying side by side. Yet as if to indicate how far the son's achievement had risen above that of his father, this would be crowned with the triumphal arch and the huge equestrian statue, 'of the whole stature of a goodly man and large horse'. At the very top, twenty-eight feet above the ground, would be an image of God the Father holding the king's soul in his left hand. It would have been a truly appropriate testimony to Henry's own idea of himself as King – as he styled himself in his will, 'immediately under God' – confidently appropriating Christian and classical imagery, the funerary styles of the past and of Renaissance modernity, the whole set within the chivalric setting of St George's Chapel, Windsor.

But as the Jacobean account concluded: 'Sic transit gloria mundi, For whosoever this King's fame was thus intended, yet that great work never came to perfection.'[2] All three of Henry's surviving children, during their respective reigns, intimated a willingness to complete the monument, but they never managed it. Some portion of a tomb was erected, but it remained incomplete, only to be defaced, dismantled and sold during the Civil War to pay the local garrison. All that remains today are copies of the four brass candlesticks that were meant to be a part of it.[3] Henry's remains lie in a vault with those of Jane Seymour, Charles I, and a nameless child of Queen Anne, under a plain black marble slab.

The fate of Henry's tomb could be held to provide a neat allegory for his life and legacy. The original design for the monument dated back to 1521, when Henry's European reputation was at its highest point, and it bore testimony to his close association with the Medici Pope, Leo X, who had given him the title of *Fidei Defensor*. Leo seems to have commissioned the design for this tomb from Bandinelli, a favourite of the Medici, in full support of Henry's pretensions.[4] The design of the equestrian statue and triumphal arch in particular had strong imperial overtones. At this point in the reign Henry and the Pope looked like each other's greatest ally, and Henry, ably supported by Cardinal Wolsey, appeared the model of a Renaissance prince. But as Henry's reign unfolded, these harmonious arrangements fell apart. Leo's cousin, Giulio de Medici, became Pope Clement VII, the Pope who was unable to end Henry's marriage to Katherine of Aragon. Henry's imperial pretension swelled out of all proportion, alongside his rejection of papal authority, and made him supreme head of the Church of England. Any continuing loyalty to the Pope became the worst possible treason; Henry even made a brief attempt to render it heresy.[5] Cardinal Wolsey, perhaps Henry's ablest and most loyal servant, fell victim to Henry's vengeful attack upon the Church that had failed him, and the King appropriated all that Wolsey had owned or enjoyed as Archbishop of York. The episcopal palace became Henry's new and magnificent palace of Whitehall, and the splendid tomb that the cardinal had been planning for himself was also confiscated by the king, who was to go on to seize so much else that had belonged to the Church. It was this tomb which was partially constructed at Windsor, only to be dismantled nearly a century later. Meanwhile the base of this structure, a black marble sarcophagus and platform, was destined to be relocated in 1808 to St Paul's Cathedral, where it formed the tomb of Lord Nelson. Nelson died a popular hero, lauded and lamented, as Henry VIII no doubt wanted to be. But Henry, in his attempts to acquire still greater security, power and prestige, overreached himself, and his kingship was to be tainted with suspicion and failure for the rest of his life.

Henry failed to fulfil many of his most fundamental ambitions. He failed to achieve any appreciable victories or conquests in France; he failed to secure the succession, leaving a child to inherit, and a wealth of complications surrounding his daughters' illegitimacy; he failed to entrench his vision of a reformed yet Catholic Church; and he failed to win the enthusiastic endorsement of the royal supremacy which he sought from his subjects. In more personal terms, he failed to secure the loyal marriage which he had idealised, and felt himself betrayed by a succession of those closest to him. In particular, he was failed by the two wives he had most dearly loved, and by the two ministers he had most trusted. The turbulent years of the 'King's Great Matter' were a watershed for Henry, betrayed by Queen Katherine of Aragon and Queen Anne in turn. Katherine, who had always been so quiescent, angered and appalled the king by her resistance to his attempts to declare their marriage a sham. Anne, who had so beguiled and bewitched him and who was surely the great love of his life, despite all his efforts had failed to make him happy, to give him a son, to be devoted and supportive once they were married, rather than tempestuous, jealous and flirtatious. This succession of bitter, minor betrayals from the woman for whom he had done so much surely prepared the way for him to believe that she had also betrayed him in sordid, multiple and incestuous adultery. After the terrible events of 1536, Henry always found it easier to suspect treachery, and his suspicions were accurate often enough to compound his unease. It is fitting that Thomas Cranmer was with him at the end; the archbishop was the nearest thing Henry had to a friend who had not let him down.

Yet if Henry's life was a failure in personal terms, he still achieved an extraordinary amount as king, and his reputation and royal image are as lasting and impressive as the changes he wrought to England's religion and government. The Holbein image of Henry as colossus, magnificent and unassailable in his personal majesty, has grown rather than declined in its vibrancy with successive centuries. It remains immediately recognisable, equalled only by the image of his daughter Elizabeth I, and it is notable that these two monarchs continue to provide unparalleled inspiration for books, films and television series. If Elizabeth has been portrayed by Sarah Bernhardt, Bette Davis, Glenda Jackson, Cate Blanchett, Judi Dench and Quentin Crisp, her father has been played by Charles Laughton, Robert Shaw, Richard Burton, Charlton Heston, Ray Winstone, Jonathan Rhys-Meyers, Eric Bana and even Sid James.[6] Father and daughter also have a great deal to do with making Dr David Starkey so well known. The Tudors have an enduring place within English culture, however complex and contested their achievement was.

English fascination with the Tudors may have something to do with the fact that English identity was so profoundly shaped by sixteenth-century developments. It was Henry who gave a lasting foundation to that identity, as he separated England from the rest of Christendom, while giving strictly limited advancement to Protestant ideology. England's emerging nationhood, so closely linked to its religion, which was neither Catholic nor straightforwardly Protestant, remained distinct and distinctive in consequence of Henry's extraordinary reign. The fact that, half a millennium on, we are still writing histories of the Tudor Reformation in which historians have first to declare their own confessional loyalties, shows that the debate Henry began is far from over.[7] Whatever else Henry's Reformation may have been, it was confusing, at the time and since. The subsequent history of the English Church was no less confused, although at times much more emphatically Protestant. 'From this story of confusion and changing direction emerged a church that has never subsequently dared define its identity decisively as Protestant or Catholic and that has decided in the end that this is a virtue rather than a handicap.'[8] The debate over the religious changes of the sixteenth century is still vibrant, immediate, frequently antagonistic and often still highly personal.

Henry's most immediate legacy was the rule of his three children. It is important to note that, whatever Henry's later reputation, he was treated with great reverence by all three of them, despite his cruel treatment at different times of both his daughters. This was not so much family affection as political sense; his majestic authority, and the fear he had engendered in his subjects, made him a godsend as a piece of political·rhetoric to three reigns labouring under the disadvantage of age and gender. Edward had of course been cast as a miniature version of his father even before he became king; the Holbein portrait of him as a regal toddler, aged about three, is slightly sinister in its resemblance to Holbein's famous depiction of his father (see Plate 8). Both wear the same distinctive hat with a white feather which also appears in Henry's book of psalms from 1540. Like depictions of the Christ-child, the young Edward lifts his chubby hand as if to bless the viewer; like Henry on the frontispiece of the Great Bible (see Plate 5), the place of God has been usurped. Just as Henry replaced God the Father, here now Edward replaces God the Son. A Latin inscription exhorts the child, 'Little one, emulate your father and be the heir of his virtue; the world contains nothing greater.'

Portraits of the older Edward develop the same resemblance. The portraits from both 1546 and 1550 by William Scrots again show us Henry in miniature. There are the same colossus-like pose, the same broad shoulders, the same ornate garb and hat, the same background of classical stonework. As king, Edward displayed many of the same traits as his father: his ostentation, his love of jewellery, his enthusiasm for music, sport, military display and his stern enforcement of the royal supremacy all show him emulating his father.[9] In the Elizabethan picture attributed to Lucas de Heere, *The Allegory of the Tudor Dynasty* (see Plate 10), Edward kneels at his father's side, almost obscured by his big sister. Mary is entering on the left with Philip II, followed by Mars, the god of war. Elizabeth, who comes closest to the viewer, enters hand-in-hand with the goddess of peace, followed by plenty. This painting was meant as a tribute to Elizabeth, and yet it is dominated by the central figure of Henry VIII. The message is that his children's rule remained contingent upon the achievements of their father.

Another famous depiction of Henry and Edward together is given by the picture titled *Edward VI and the Pope* (see Plate 9). Here Edward VI sits enthroned, but still takes endorsement from the figure of his father beside him, who indicates his son and successor from his deathbed. In the foreground, the Pope is crushed uncomfortably beneath the Word of God, evil-looking monks hurriedly depart, and the Regency Council look on solemnly as acts of iconoclasm are perpetrated outside. This painting has also been read as an Elizabethan work, and an exhortation to Elizabeth to continue the more unambiguous work of the Edwardian Reformation.[10] Even if it is earlier, the point remains that Edward VI's kingship was viewed as dependent upon his father's sanction, and that the 'verbum dei' imagery used by Henry had become a recognisable part of sixteenth-century visual culture. In particular, the image of the Pope crushed beneath the feet of the godly prince was to prove a recurrent theme. It would appear too in Foxe's *Book of Martyrs*, with Henry apparently using the Pope as his footstool.

Henry's religious symbolism was to prove especially long-lasting and extremely valuable to his descendants. Henry had portrayed himself as King David, or King Solomon, and in turn his children adopted Old Testament models of their own. Edward was King Josiah, the child king who rediscovered holy scripture, restored the Temple and purged the land of pagan worship. The fact that when King Josiah died, the people returned to their old pagan ways, was not emphasised by Edward's supporters until the accession of Mary completed the resemblance. Yet Mary too was sufficiently steeped in her father's biblicism, and blessed with her mother's erudition, to inspire comparison with the Old Testament heroine Judith. Elizabeth also compared herself to Judith, or to Deborah, but developed too the imperial line of rhetoric by appearing as the Emperor Constantine. In the first edition of Foxe's *Book of Martyrs* in 1563, the preface compared Elizabeth's reign to the rule of Constantine, which ended the persecution of Christians just as she had brought relief from the Marian persecutions to those of the true faith.[11] The ornate title-letter shows Elizabeth enthroned, very much in the style of Henry on the title page of the Great Bible. The Pope appears here too, not just crushed beneath her feet, but squeezed into the bottom part of the letter, clutching his keys, still wearing his papal tiara.

It was from the historical understanding evolved during Elizabeth's reign that Henry's reputation was given two particularly distinctive formulations. William Shakespeare's *Henry VIII* was to perpetuate not just the memory of the king, but his physical appearance. Samuel Pepys, in the late seventeenth century, noted that the actor who played Henry was dressed 'as we see him painted', which suggests that the Holbein image was central to that memory, a fact also confirmed by an engraving of 1709.[12] The performance history of the play shows that it has been all but impossible to separate the character of Henry VIII from this image; other Shakespeare plays are cast in modern dress, but the character of Henry VIII over the centuries has been dressed such that the king's own contemporaries would still have recognised him instantly.[13] The play itself is partly cast in terms of flattery to Elizabeth, which in the atmosphere of 1612–13, when the play was first performed, was also meant as an endorsement of idealised hopes for Britain's Protestant future. The play ends tactfully with the baptism of the baby princess, thereby avoiding some of the more appalling developments of Henry's reign.[14] Even so, it is striking that this work, which sought to praise Elizabeth, and cast Anne Boleyn as a rather unconvincing innocent, still gave a deeply moving and sympathetic portrayal of Katherine of Aragon. In one tense exchange with Wolsey, when he desires to speak with her privately, the Queen replies:

> Speak it here.
> There's nothing I have done yet, o' my conscience,
> Deserves a corner. Would all other women
> Could speak this with as free a soul as I do.
> My lords, I care not – so much I am happy
> Above a number – if my actions
> Were tried by ev'ry tongue, ev'ry eye saw 'em,
> Envy and base opinion set against 'em,
> I know my life so even.[15]

Katherine's lack of any moral qualms serves to underline the dubious moral standing of nearly all the other characters in the play. As we have seen, there is a different kind of ambivalence in Foxe's *Book of Martyrs*, where Henry is at once impressive as the scourge of the Antichrist, and pitiable as the dupe of faction.

One other Elizabethan observer gave a far less equivocal account of the King. For William Harrison, trying to describe England in its entirety in 1587, the reign of Henry VIII was a glorious one. One particular achievement was held to be the King's building works. Those palaces before his reign might show a creditable example of ancient workmanship:

> but such as he erected after his own device (for he was nothing inferior in this trade to Hadrian the Emperor and Justinian the Lawgiver) do represent another manner of pattern, which, as they are supposed to excel all the rest that he found standing in this realm, so they are and shall be a perpetual precedent unto those that do come after to follow in their works and buildings of importance.[16]

Harrison's words are a useful reminder that the material legacy of Henry VIII is worth as much consideration as any ideological inheritance. Although his great palace at Whitehall no longer stands, and Nonsuch and Richmond survive only in pictures, the additions he made to the Tower of London, Windsor Castle, Hampton Court, St James's Palace, Greenwich Palace and Leeds Castle still exist, or can be traced among what stands today. The great London parks – St James's, Hyde Park, Regent's Park – were his creation. The huge string of defensive fortifications along the south coast, from Kent to Cornwall, still bear testimony to Henry's military activities: castles at Deal, Walmer, Southsea, Portchester, Calshot, Hurst, Yarmouth, Portland, Dartmouth, St Mawes and Pendennis, most of which were built from scratch at Henry's instigation. Henry also established England's armouries, buying in expertise from the continent to ensure the most modern techniques were at his disposal. He advanced the development of the navy and left his children a formidable fleet of ships compared with what he had inherited nearly forty years before.[17]

Henry's material achievements also include Trinity College, Cambridge, and Christ Church, Oxford, although in material terms he is remembered just as much for what he destroyed as what he built. The devastation he wrought by the dissolution of the monasteries is witnessed by the ruined abbeys which still stand: Fountains, Rievaulx, Jervaulx, Whitby, Glastonbury, Kirkstall, Byland and Beaulieu. The abbey buildings which were almost immediately converted to domestic use often survive to give us an idea of how these buildings were converted to lay ownership, of which Cleeve Abbey is probably the best example. Cathedrals in Peterborough, Oxford, Bristol, Chester and Gloucester owe their existence to Henry, who created them out of former monastic foundations. Existing monastic cathedrals in Canterbury, Carlisle, Winchester, Worcester, Norwich, Ely, Rochester and Durham were allowed to continue as secular cathedrals, often with more or less the same personnel.[18] On a smaller scale, pictures, books, tapestries and other artefacts still recall the magnificence of Henry's court. The secular music which survives from his reign, and the sacred music from the Chapel Royal are an equally important reminder of the world he knew.

Most lastingly, and divisively, of course, Henry changed England's religion. How should we understand this? It is on this, more than anything else, that Henry's reputation stands or falls. Yet to some the English Reformation was 'the most decisive revolution in English history', while to others it constituted no very great upheaval: 'parish congregations went to church: they prayed again to their God, learned again how to be good, and went off home once more', in 1590 much as they had in 1530.[19] In such territory it is hard to know what to think. The battle has raged over this for centuries, and over Henry's own part in the drama.

> He gave up the Catholic faith for no other reason in the world that that which came from his lust and wickedness. He rejected the authority of the Pope because he was not allowed to put away Katherine, when he was beaten and overcome as he was by the flesh. He destroyed the monasteries, partly because the monks, and especially the friars, resisted the divorce; partly because he hungered after the ecclesiastical lands, which he seized that he might have more abundant means to spend in feasting on women of unclean lives, and on the foolish buildings he raised.[20]

Such was the judgement of the Elizabeth Catholic Nicholas Sanders, who found it easiest to blame developments on the king's sexual passions. (It is notable that even in this condemnation, the king's building projects figure.) Henry might himself have appreciated the literary technique; he too made some moral capital out of condemning others' lusts. The dubious morality of his own marital affairs was veiled by a public and high-minded stance on sexual ethics which involved closing the Southwark brothels and making lurid allegations about the sexual proclivities of monks.[21] Yet even those who saw the Reformation as a step forward have wondered at the morality of proceedings. In his biography of 1902, Pollard, who was largely impressed by Henry's achievements, summed up the religious changes in ambivalent terms:

> He directed the storm of a revolution which was doomed to come, which was certain to break those who refused to bend, and which may be explained by natural causes, but cannot be judged by moral considerations. The storm cleared the air and dissipated many a pestilent vapour, but it left a trail of wreck and ruin over the land.[22]

In particular, the impact of Henry's religious policies on the society of the time was a source of debate and disagreement at the time, and ever since. Before the 1530s were ended, some of Henry's subjects were beginning to protest that the dissolution had brought no relief to the poor, no improved access to education, none of the benefits which the king had promised. There was a tacit acknowledgement of these criticisms in the king's speech to Parliament in 1545, when he said:

> if I, contrary to your expectation, should suffer the ministers of the church to decay; or learning, which is so great a jewel, to be minished; or poor and miserable people to be unrelieved; you might say that I, being put in so special a trust as I am in this case, were no trusty friend to you ... neither a lover of the public wealth, nor yet one that feared God. ... Doubt not, I pray you, but your expectation shall be served.[23]

But their expectations never were answered. Nearly three centuries later, this was Henry's chief crime in the eyes of William Cobbett, to whom it was 'not a *reformation*, but a *devastation* of England', a change 'engendered in beastly lust, brought forth in hypocrisy and perfidy, and cherished and fed by plunder, devastation, and by rivers of innocent English and Irish blood', its consequences:

> now before us in that misery, that beggary, that nakedness, that hunger, that everlasting wrangling and spite, which now stare us in the face and stun our ears at every turn, and which the 'Reformation' has given us in exchange for the ease and happiness and harmony and Christian charity, enjoyed so abundantly, and for so many ages, by our Catholic forefathers.[24]

A modern reworking of Cobbett's themes sees Henry as 'the Great Egotist', the ultimate modern individualist, whose 'private conscience' was the basis for an attack on the communitarian principles of medieval faith and society, preparing the way for the capitalism which has 'ruined the planet'.[25]

The easiest judgements of Henry VIII, and the ones that are most memorable, are the ones that straightforwardly condemn. The amount of debate this one man has generated, however, suggests that the truth is likely to be more complex than these judgements would allow. Much of the suffering of his reign remains deplorable, but then this was an age in which religious error was persecuted with the conviction that it was too dangerous to let alone. Modern fears of terrorism have created an equally remorseless rhetoric, with as many crude and appalling conse-quences. The religion that Henry sought to create, however, was not so easily defined. He took away the monasteries, but he left us the cathe-drals. He brought the English Bible into several thousand parish churches, where still the Latin mass was being sung as it had been for centuries before. He aimed at moderation, this most assertive and immoderate of men, and he envisaged a version of the Christian faith which was both biblical and traditional, reformed and conservative. His methods were at times haphazard, and he had only partial success, but as a proposition it was at least interesting, and potentially more inclusive than the more extreme alternatives being posited from either side. Some fragments of the foundations he laid are still visible today, and even more visible is the uncertainty he caused. If we continue to be intrigued by Henry and his actions, it must be in part because we are still not sure what to make of them.

As we embark upon the twenty-first century, there are no signs that the debate about Henry VIII is losing its impetus, or its fascination. We remain captivated by the central figures in the drama, beguiled by them as individuals and by what their lives reveal about the intricate workings of Tudor culture, politics and religion. For some, the attraction of his reign lies in the complex negotiation of power between different groups within society, reflecting our growing interest in the subtleties of power relationships, and a sense that crude dichotomies between ruler and ruled fail to reflect the codes of honour, the duty of protection, or the interdependence between patron and client which shaped the political process.[26] Even in the unbalanced relationship between king and rebellious subject, there were obligations placed upon the ruler as well as the ruled. It is surely this sense of the intricacy of human relationships which ensures that faction continues to be central to debates about Henry. For others, Henry remains a tyrant, as he appeared to some of his more intelligent, perceptive and tormented subjects.[27] Meanwhile a growing awareness of the cultural diversity of Henry's court and capital gives us increasing understanding of the life lived by this King and his subjects. Perhaps it is precisely the scope, the diversity and the conflict within Henry's life and reign which make them both so interesting. Ruthless tyrant or betrayed husband; Renaissance prince or pious reformer; warrior, peacemaker, musician, lover, scholar, sportsman; capable of the best and the worst as father, husband, master and monarch; Henry embraced the extremes of human potential, and between his forcefulness and his fallibility his appeal seems set to last.

NOTES

INTRODUCTION

1   Sir Thomas Smith, *De Republica Anglorum* (1565), ed. L. Alston (Cambridge, 1906), 62–3.

2   Walker, *Writing Under Tyranny*, 1.

3   *CWE*, iv, 263.

4   See S. Brigden, 'Henry Howard, Earl of Surrey and the "Conjured League"', *HJ* 37 (1994), 507–37; eadem, '"The shadow that you know": Sir Thomas Wyatt and Sir Francis Bryan at Court and in embassy', *HJ* 39 (1996), 1–31; Walker, *Writing Under Tyranny*, 256–66, 301–34, 400–7.

5   Roper, *Life of More*, 228.

6   P. Collinson, 'De Republica Anglorum: or, history with the politics put back', in idem. *Elizabethan Essays* (London and Rio Grande, 1994), 1–27.

7   A. F. Pollard, *Henry VIII* (revised edition, 1905), 440.

8   Ibid.

9   Scarisbrick, *Henry VIII*, 677.

10 Colvin, *King's Works; Inventory*.

11 D. Starkey, 'The legacy of Henry VIII' in idem. (ed), *Henry VIII: A European Court in England* (1991), 8.

12 This belief in a prophecy may have been ascribed to the image after the execution. See P. Marshall, 'Papist as heretic: the burning of John Forest, 1538', *HJ* 41 (1998), 356; S. Brigden, *London and the Reformation* (1989), 290.

13 The heraldic charge against Surrey was contrived and arguably almost absurd, but it was sufficient to convict him. See P. R. Moore, 'The heraldic charge against the Earl of Surrey, 1546-7', *EHR* 116 (2001), 557–83.

14 W. A. Sessions, *Henry Howard, Earl of Surrey* (Boston, 1986), 13–14. See also S. Brigden, 'Henry Howard, Earl of Surrey, and the "Conjured League"', *HJ* 37 (1994), 507–37.

15 Walker, *Writing Under Tyranny*, 385.

16 C. L. Kingsford (ed), *The First English Life of King Henry the Fifth* (Oxford, 1911), 18.

1 THE EDUCATION OF A CHRISTIAN PRINCE, 1491–1509

1   Erasmus, *The Education of a Christian Prince* (Cambridge, 1997), 23–4.

2   S. B. Chrimes, *Henry VII* (second edition, 1977), 66–7.

3   Thurley, *Royal Palaces*, 34–6.

4   See A. J. Pollard (ed.), *The Wars of the Roses* (1995); C. Carpenter, *The Wars of the Roses: Politics and the Constitution in England, c.1437–1509* (1997); J. L. Watts, *Henry VI and the Politics of Kingship* (1996).

5   R. L. Storey, *The End of the House of Lancaster* (1966); R. A. Griffiths, 'Local rivalries and national politics: the Percies, the Nevilles and the Duke of Exeter, 1452–55', *Speculum*, 43 (1968).

6   J. L. Watts, 'Ideas, principles and politics' in Pollard (ed.), *The Wars of the Roses*, 110–33; S. J. Gunn, *Early Tudor Government 1485–1558* (Basingstoke, 1995), 12–13.

7   *Henry VI Parts I, II* and *III*. Henry IV produced two; Richard II, Richard III and Henry VIII just one apiece.

8   Gunn, *Early Tudor Government*, 13.

9   Chrimes, *Henry VII*, c. 3.

10 Ibid., 308–9.

11 S. J. Gunn, 'Henry VII in context: problems and possibilities', *History*, 92 (2007), 301–17.

12 Polydore Vergil, *Anglica historia*, ed. D. Hay, CS, 3rd series, lxxiv (1950), 145–7.

13 Chrimes, *Henry VII*, 212–18, 309–13.

14 Ibid., 93.

15 G. W. Bernard, 'The continuing power of the Tudor nobility', in Bernard, *Power and Politics in Tudor England* (Aldershot, 2000), 20–50; Bernard (ed.), *The Tudor Nobility* (Manchester, 1992), 1–48.

16 This is illustrated by the way in which the works of Chaucer were deployed in the Henrician edition of 1532. See *The Workes of Geffray Chaucer newly printed/ with dyvers workes whiche were never in print before* (London, Thomas Godfray, 1532); and the discussion in Walker, *Writing Under Tyranny*, 73–8.

17 Hall, i, 597.

18 *Henry IV, Part II*, Act 3, Scene 1.

19 E. Rummel (ed.), *The Erasmus Reader* (Toronto, 1990), 86.

20 Ibid., 97.

21 Juan Luis Vives, *The Education of a Christian Woman: A Sixteenth-Century Manual*, trans. and ed. C. Fantazzi (Chicago, 2000), 66–9.

22 Ibid., 67.

23   S. Thurley, 'Nonsuch Palace', in *Country Life*, cxcix no.31, 11 August 2005.

24   X. Brooke, 'Henry VIII revealed: Holbein's portrait and its legacy', in X. Brooke and D. Crombie, *Henry VIII Revealed* (London, 2003), 50.; See also S. Foister, *Holbein and England* (New Haven and London, 2004), 23–5.

25   Walker, *Writing Under Tyranny*, 9.

26   Scarisbrick, *Henry VIII*, 43.

27   The translation was the work of Sir John Bourchier, Lord Berners. See Carley, *Books of Henry VIII*, 73–5.

28   Byrne, *Letters*, 4–5.

29   Walker, *Writing Under Tyranny*, 9.

30   A. Walsham, *Providence in Early Modern England* (Oxford, 1999), demonstrates how these beliefs were not merely the province of zealous Protestants, but an integral part of early modern popular culture.

31   Cited in S. Anglo, 'Image-making: the means and the limitations', in J. Guy (ed.), *The Tudor Monarchy* (London, 1997), 29.

32   Edmund Dudley, *The Tree of Commonwealth*, ed. D. M. Brodie (Cambridge, 1948), 21.

33   Ibid., 31.

34   Ibid., 28–9

35   Ibid., 30.

36   C. L. Kingsford (ed.), *The First English Life of King Henry the Fifth* (Oxford, 1911), 16.

37   Ibid., 5.

38   G. Richardson, *Renaissance Monarchy* (Arnold, 2002), 29–32.

39   Three works translated from Plutarch were dedicated to Henry in 1514; see L. Jardine, *The Education of a Christian Prince*, xviii–xix. See also Stephen Baron, *De regimine principum*, ed. P. J. Mroczkowski, American University Studies Series vol. 5 (New York, 1990).

40   Hall, i, 30.

41   Dudley, *Tree of Commonwealth*, 27.

42   More, *Utopia*, 42.

43   See Walker's discussion of both Sir Thomas Elyot and Sir Thomas Wyatt in *Writing Under Tyranny*, 212–15, 305–6.

44   Erasmus, *Education of a Christian Prince*, 5.

45   Ibid., 89.

46   D. Starkey, 'Representation through intimacy: a study in the symbolism of monarchy and Court office in early modern England', in Guy, *Tudor Monarchy*, 50–1.

47   *LP* i (ii), 1852, 1870.

48 *The Antient Kalendars and Inventories of the Treasury of His Majesty's Exchequer*, ed. F. Palgrave, vol. 3 (1836), 393–9.

49 C. J. Harrison (ed.), 'The petition of Edmund Dudley', *EHR*, lxxxvii (1972), 82–99.

50 Scarisbrick, *Henry VIII*, 21–2.

51 S. Gunn, 'The accession of Henry VIII', *HR*, 64 (1991), 278–88.

52 Quoted in translation in S. Thurley, 'Henry VIII: the Tudor dynasty and the Church', in S. Thurley and C. Lloyd, *Henry VIII: Images of a Tudor King* (1990), 29.

53 P. Lindley, 'Innovations, tradition and disruption in tomb-sculpture', in D. Gaimster and P. Stamper (eds), *The Age of Transition: The Archaeology of English Culture 1400–1600* (Oxford, 1997), 80.

54 N. H. Nicolas (ed.), *The Privy Purse Expences of King Henry the Eighth* (1827), 9, 10, 279.

55 Ibid., 6, 5.

56 Ibid., 282.

57 Ibid., 4.

58 J. A. F. Thomson, *The Transformation of Medieval England, 1370–1529* (Longman, 1983), 9.

59 O. Rackham, *The Illustrated History of the Countryside* (London, 2003), 214.

60 Ibid., 21.

61 Ibid., 83, 97.

62 C. Dyer, 'Peasants and farmers: rural settlement and landscapes in an age of transition', in Gaimster and Stamper, *Age of Transition*, 61–76.

63 J. Hatcher, *Plague, Population and the English Economy*, 1348–1530 London, (1977), 65.

64 K. Thomas, *Man and the Natural World: Changing Attitudes in England 1500–1800* (London, 1983), 17–18.

65 Ibid., 19.

66 P. Ackroyd, *London: The Biography* (London, 2001), 171; see also the illustration between pages 136 and 137.

67 Rackham, *Illustrated History of the Countryside*, 63-5.

68 S. Thurley, 'Whitehall Palace and Westminster 1400–1600: a royal seat in transition', in Gaimster and Stamper, *Age of Transition*, 99.

69 Thurley, *Royal Palaces*, 40-44.

70 Ackroyd, *London*, 540.

71 Hall, ii, 277.

72 *The myroure of oure ladye*, ed. J. H. Blunt (EETS extra series 19, 1873), 7. The Latin version of the work had been written early in the fifteenth century.

73 Walker, *Writing Under Tyranny*, 29–32.

74   C. Dyer, 'English diet in the later Middle Ages', in T. H. Aston, P. R. Coss, C. Dyer and J. Thirsk, *Social Relations and Ideas: Essays in Honour of R. H. Hilton* (Cambridge, 1983), 191–216.

75   *The Boke of Kervynge*, ed. F. J. Furnivall (EETS, 32, 1868), 263.

76   Thurley, *Royal Palaces*, 156.

77   *Inventory*, nos. 56–7, 13.

78   S. Mennell, *All Manners of Food: Eating and Taste in England and France from the Middle Ages to the Present* (Edinburgh, 1985), 86.

79   Cavendish, 26–7.

80   Ibid., 27–30.

81   *Privy Purse Expences*, 3.

82   *The Boke of Kervynge*, 282–3.

83   Andrew Boorde, *A Compendyous Regyment or a Dyetary of helth* (1557?), ed. F. J. Furnivall (EETS, 32, 1868), 246.

84   S. Thurley, *Lost Buildings of Britain* (2004), 11–12.

85   Thurley, *Royal Palaces*, 161.

86   *Inventory*, no. 9313

87   Thurley, *Royal Palaces*, 176–7.

88   *Privy Purse Expences*, 18, 23.

89   Ibid., 17, 15.

90   See F. Kisby, "When the king goeth a procession": chapel ceremonies and services, the ritual year, and religious reforms at the early Tudor court, 1485–1547', *JBS* 40 (2001), 44–75.

91   Fox, *Letters*, p. 52.

92   *LP* iii (i), 1233.

2 THE FOUNDATIONS OF KINGSHIP, 1509–1518

1   Lord Mountjoy to Erasmus in 1509. See F. M. Nichols (ed.), *The Epistles of Erasmus* (3 vols, London, 1901–19), I, 457.

2   Polydore Vergil, *Anglica Historia,* ed. D. Hay, CS lxxiv (1950), 151.

3   See J. G. Russell, *Peacemaking in the Renaissance* (1986), Appendix A, 'Richard Pace's oration', p. 238.

4   S. Gunn, 'The early Tudor tournament', in D. Starkey (ed.), *Henry VIII: A European Court in England* (London, 1991), 47.

5   Vergil, *Anglica Historia*, 151.

6   *LP* i (i), 84.

7   Isabella's paternal grandfather, Henry III of Castile, had married Katherine of Lancaster, John of Gaunt's daughter by his second wife, Constanza of Castile. Isabella's maternal grandfather, John of Portugal, had married Philippa of Lancaster, John of Gaunt's daughter by his first wife, Blanche of Lancaster.

8   Erasmus to Paolo Bombace, 26 July 1518, in Carley, *Books of Henry VIII*, 111.

9   Carley, op. cit., 111–13.

10 G. Mattingly, *Catherine of Aragon* (London, 1942), 17–18.

11 Juan Luis Vives, *The Education of a Christian Woman: A Sixteenth-century Manual*, ed. and trans. C. Fantazzi (Chicago, 2000), Prelude, 13.

12 Ibid., 45.

13 Hall, i, 143.

14 Hall, i, 118.

15 Hall, i, 4–5.

16 J. Loach, 'The function of ceremonial in the reign of Henry VIII', *P&P* 142 (1994), 66–8.

17 Hall, i, 5.

18 Ibid., 48–55.

19 *CSPV* iv, no. 694 (p.293).

20 H. Ellis (ed.), *Original Letters illustrative of British History*, 3rd series, i (London, 1824), 34–5.

21 Fox, *Letters*, 82–4.

22 P. Ayris, 'Preaching the Last Crusade: Thomas Cranmer and the "Devotion" money of 1543', *JEH* 49 (1998), 683–701.

23 Thomas Elyot, *The Boke Named the Governour* (1537), f.95 r–v.

24 Dudley, *Tree of Commonwealth*, 103–4.

25 A. Ogle, *The Tragedy of the Lollards' Tower* (1949), pp. 152–3; a translation from R. Keilwey, *Reports d'ascuns Cases* (1602).

26 *Inventory*, p.196

27 Ibid., p.310

28 S. Gunn, 'Chivalry and the politics of the Early Tudor Court', in S. Anglo (ed.), *Chivalry in the Renaissance* (Woodbridge, 1990), 110.

29 *The Antient Kalendars and Inventories of the Treasury of His Majesty's Exchequer*, ed. F. Palgrave, vol. 3 (1836), 393–9.

30 Gunn, 'Chivalry', 112.

31 Ibid., 114.

32 Hall, i, 14.

33 Hall, i, 151.

34 Hall, i, 28, 21.

35 Hall, i, 18.

36 Hall, i, 30.

37 Henry VI may have briefly made Fortescue chancellor in 1461; he certainly referred to him as such. Fortescue, xxiv, 4n.

38 Fortescue, 4.

39 Hall, i. 144

40 Hall, i, 19.

41 D. MacCulloch (ed.), *The Reign of Henry VIII*, editor's introduction, 5.

42 N. Samman, 'The progresses of Henry VIII, 1509–1529', in MacCulloch, *Reign of Henry VIII*, 60–1.

43 Hall, i, 147.

44 Hall, i, 14–15.

45 *LP* i, 5ii.

46 *CSPV* ii, 11.

47 Ibid.

48 A. A. Chibi, *Henry VIII's Bishops: Diplomats, Administrators, Scholars and Shepherds* (Oxford, 2003), 46.

49 LP i, 842

50 G. Richardson, *Renaissance Monarchy* (London, 2002) 64.

51 *CSPS*, ii, 72.

52 Vergil, *Anglica Historia*, 197.

53 *RSTC* 5579, printed by Richard Pynson.

54 D. Baldwin, *The Chapel Royal Ancient and Modern* (London, 1990), 41.

55 Ibid., 24–5, 41–5.

56 P. Gwyn, *The King's Cardinal* (London, 1990), 4.

57 Ibid., 14.

58 *LP* I (ii), 1864.

59 *LP* I (ii), 1844.

60 C. G. Cruickshank, *Army Royal: Henry VIII's Invasion of France 1513* (Oxford, 1969), 13, 29.

61 Hall, i, 128.

62 D. Grummitt, 'The court, war and noble power in England, c.1475–1558', in S. Gunn and A. Janse (eds), *The Court as a Stage: England and the Low Countries in the Later Middle Ages* (Woodbridge, 2006), 148.

63 J. Raymond, *Henry VIII's Military Revolution* (Basingstoke, 2007), 137–8.

64 Hall notes that the king 'settyng a side al affeccion, caused him to be hanged'; i, 41.

65 Starkey, *Henry VIII: A European Court in England*, 65, 68–9.

66 T. F. Mayer, 'On the road to 1534: the occupation of Tournai and Henry VIII's theory of sovereignty', in D. Hoak (ed.), *Tudor Political Culture* (Cambridge, 1995), although see also C. S. L. Davies, 'Tournai and the English crown, 1513–1519', *HJ* 41 (1998), 1–26.

67 Thurley, *Royal Palaces*, 40–44.

68 Thurley, 'Greenwich Palace', in Starkey, *Henry VIII: A European Court in England*, 22–3.

69 Cited in Carley, *Books of Henry VIII*, 27.

70 Cited and translated in L-E. Halkin, *Erasmus: A Critical Biography* (Oxford, 1993), 37.

71 J. Woolfson, 'John Claymond, Pliny the Elder and the early history of Corpus Christi College, Oxford', *EHR* cxii (1997).

72 J. McConica, *The History of the University of Oxford, vol. iii, The Collegiate University* (Oxford, 1986), 339, 340, 67.

73 *LP* i (i), 1046.

74 Carley, *Books of Henry VIII*, 53–6.

75 For full accounts of these men see *ODNB*.

76 Erasmus, *The Education of a Christian Prince*, ed. L. Jardine (Cambridge, 1997), xxi–xxii.

77 Cited in Carley, *Books of Henry VIII*, 13.

78 Byrne, *Letters*, 70.

79 A. Atlas, *Renaissance Music: Music in Western Europe, 1400–1600* (London and New York, 1998), 373–4.

80 Ibid., 531, 536, 528, 689.

81 *CSPV* ii, 1010 (p.434).

82 B.L. Additional MS 31922.

83 Cited in G. Reese, *Music in the Renaissance* (rev. edn, 1959), 769. It remains unclear what fremen songs were exactly.

84 L. L. Perkins, *Music in the Age of the Renaissance* (1999), 660.

85 Atlas, *Renaissance Music*, 271.

86 *LP* iii (i), 505.

87 Cavendish, 134.

88 G. Elton, 'King of hearts', in *Studies in Tudor and Stuart Politics and Government* (4 vols, Cambridge, 1974–92), i, 104.

89 Historians who emphasise the importance of faction in the shaping of policy included Eric Ives, in *Faction in Tudor England* (revised edition, 1987), and *The Life and Death of Anne Boleyn* (2004), and David Starkey in *The Reign of Henry VIII: Politics and Perspectives* (1985) and 'From feud to faction: English politics

c.1450–1550', in *History Today* (November 1982), 16–22. Recent authors who take an opposing view include Peter Gwyn in *The King's Cardinal* (1990) and George Bernard in *The King's Reformation: Henry VIII and the Remaking of the English Church* (2005) and *Power and Politics in Tudor England* (2000).

90 *Writings and Letters of Thomas Cranmer*, ed. J. E. Cox (PS, 1846), 40.

91 The proper title of the 'Book of Martyrs' was *Acts and Monuments*. The first edition appeared in 1563, with three more editions before his death in 1587, and many more afterwards. For its importance in shaping Protestant identity see L. Colley, *Britons: Forging the Nation 1707–1837* (1992), 25–8.

92 Foxe, *Acts and Monuments* v, 260.

93 E. Ives, 'Stress, faction and ideology in early-Tudor England', *HJ* 34 (1991), 197.

94 Bernard, *Power and Politics in Tudor England*, 7.

95 D. MacCulloch, 'Henry VIII and the reform of the Church', in MacCulloch, *Reign of Henry VIII*, 174.

96 Ibid., 176.

97 Gwyn, *The King's Cardinal*, 6–19.

98 Cavendish, 8–9.

99 Gwyn, *The King's Cardinal* remains the definitive biography. See also S. Gunn and P. Lindley, *Cardinal Wolsey: Church, State and Art* (Cambridge, 1991).

100 *ODNB*.

101 Gwyn, *The King's Cardinal*, 351.

102 Cavendish, 12.

103 Ibid, 14.

104 *LP* iii (i), 592, 568, 570, 599, 613, 622, 634.

105 *LP* iii (i), 427, 431.

106 Cavendish, 25, 24.

107 Ibid., 30.

108 *SP*, vol. i, part i, no.1.

109 Elton, *Constitution*, 119–20.

3 THE LURE OF EMPIRE, 1518–1527

1 Hall, i, 198.

2 J. G. Russell, *Peacemaking in the Renaissance* (London, 1986), 10–20.

3 More, *Utopia*, 109.

4 E. Rummel (ed.), *The Erasmus Reader* (Toronto, 1990), 300.

5   D. Baker-Smith, 'Inglorious glory: 1513 and the humanist attack on chivalry', in S. Anglo (ed.), *Chivalry in the Renaissance* (Woodbridge and Rochester, NY, 1990), 131–2, 138–41.

6   Byrne, *Letters*, 4.

7   Russell, *Peacemaking in the Renaissance*, Appendix A, 234–41.

8   Hall, i, 170.

9   Gwyn, *The King's Cardinal*, 58–9.

10 Hall, i, 177.

11 Scarisbrick, *Henry VIII*, 100.

12 D. Hoak, 'The iconography of the crown imperial', in Hoak (ed.), *Tudor Political Culture* (Cambridge, 1995), 57, 60, 63.

13 R. Koebner, 'The imperial crown of this realm: Henry VIII, Constantine the Great, and Polydore Vergil', *BIHR* 26 (1953), 29–52.

14 Hall, i, 75.

15 Ibid., 83.

16 *ODNB*.

17 Hall, i, 177.

18 D. Starkey, *Reign of Henry VIII: Personalities and Politics* (London, 1985), 69–80.

19 Scarisbrick, *Henry VIII*, 163.

20 G. Walker, 'Faction in the Privy Chamber?: the "Expulsion of the Minions", 1519', in G. Walker, *Persuasive Fictions: Faction, Faith and Political Culture in the Reign of Henry VIII* (Aldershot, 1996), 35–53.

21 Thurley, *Royal Palaces*, 44–5.

22 N. Samman, 'The progresses of Henry VIII, 1509–1529', in MacCulloch, *Reign of Henry VIII*, 61.

23 *LP* iii (i), 416, 514.

24 Hall, i, 189.

25 Hall, i, 190; for the account in its entirety, see 189–218.

26 Hall, i, 198

27 Erasmus, 'The complaint of peace', in *The Erasmus Reader*, 310, 313.

28 Scarisbrick, *Henry VIII*, 158–60.

29 *LP* iii, 1.

30 One son called Henry was born in 1516. He died before 1522 when a second son was born and again christened Henry.

31 Hall, i, 75.

32 Gwyn, *The King's Cardinal*, 165.

33 A. Chibi, *Henry VIII's Bishops: Diplomats, Administrators, Scholars and Shepherds* (Cambridge, 2003), 26–8.

34 Scarisbrick, *Henry VIII*, 114–15.

35 Russell, *Peacemaking in the Renaissance*, 100–1.

36 There was possibly some kind of sliding scale of payment for the laity; see Gwyn, *The King's Cardinal*, 402.

37 Hall, ii, 44.

38 Hall, ii, 40.

39 See D. Starkey (ed.), *Henry VIII: A European Court in England* (London, 1991), 54–93.

40 Hall, ii, 84–8.

41 See Starkey, *Henry VIII: A European Court*, 94–9.

42 *LP* i (ii), 3581.

43 Ives, *Life and Death*, 85.

44 Nicholas Sanders, *The Rise and Growth of the Anglican Schism*, ed. D. Lewis (Rockford, Illinois and Tunbridge Wells, 1988), 25–6.

45 Bernard, *Power and Politics in Tudor England* (Aldershot, 2000), 12–16.

46 Bernard, *King's Reformation*, 4–9.

47 Ibid., 8. For the draft of the dispensation, see N. Pocock, *Records of the Reformation* (Oxford, 2 vols., 1870), vol. i, no. xiv, pp. 22–7. Scarisbrick, in *Henry VIII*, 215f., thinks Henry may just have been being optimistic.

48 Ives, *Life and Death*, 86.

49 Sanders, *Rise and Growth of the Anglican Schism*, 25.

4 DYNASTY AND SUPREMACY, 1527–1534

1 'An act that the appeals in such cases as have been used to be pursued to the see of Rome shall not be from henceforth had nor used but within this realm', in Elton, *Constitution*, no.177, p. 344.

2 L. Cust, 'Notes on pictures in the Royal Collections – XXXIX. On the portraits of King Henry VIII', *Burlington Magazine*, vol. 31, no. 177 (Dec. 1917), 218; H. J. Dow, 'Two Italian portrait-busts of Henry VIII', *Art Bulletin*, vol. 42, no. 4 (Dec. 1960), pp. 291–4.

3 *CSPV* ii, 624 (p. 248); 1230 (p. 529).

4 *A Glasse of the Truthe* (1532), Sig. A2v–A3v.

5 Byrne, *Letters*, 63.

6 V. Murphy, 'The literature and propaganda of Henry VIII's first divorce', in MacCulloch, *The Reign of Henry VIII*.

7 Byrne, *Letters*, 63.

8 Ibid., 66–8.

9 Ibid., 66. Henry here conflates two biblical passages: 1 Corinthians 3, v. 11 and Matthew 16, v. 18.

10 Cited in E. Rummel, *The Humanist–Scholastic Debate in the Renaissance and Reformation* (Cambridge, Mass.,1995), 97–8.

11 The term is usually ascribed to Flavio Biondo, d. 1463.

12 Rummel, *Humanist–Scholastic Debate*, 101.

13 Marsilius of Padua, *The Defence of Peace* (1535), f. 6r, f. 2v. For a discussion of how Henry deployed Marsilius's work as a part of his own propaganda, see S. Lockwood, 'Marsilius of Padua and the case for the royal ecclesiastical supremacy', *TRHS* 6th series, 1 (1991), 89–119.

14 *A copy of the letters / wherin the most redouted and mighty prince our souerayne lorde ... made answere unto a certyne letter of Martyn Luther* (1527), Sig. A ii r–v.

15 E. Rummel (ed.), *The Erasmus Reader* (Toronto, 1990), 222, 232–3.

16 *LP* iv (ii), 2868, 2870.

17 Muller, *Letters*, 6.

18 Ibid., 11.

19 Ibid., 13, 17.

20 Scarisbrick, *Henry VIII*, c. 7.

21 Murphy, op.cit., 138–9.

22 Bernard, *King's Reformation*, 17.

23 Scarisbrick, *Henry VIII*, 208–9.

24 Ives, *Life and Death*, 84.

25 Scarisbrick, *Henry VIII*, 213–15.

26 Murphy, op.cit., 144–5; Gwyn, *The King's Cardinal*, 522.

27 Murphy, op.cit., 146.

28 Hall, ii, 143.

29 Ibid., 145.

30 Ibid., 146–7.

31 Ibid., 145.

32 Scarisbrick, *Henry VIII*, 291.

33 Ibid., 282.

34 Cavendish, 83–5.

35 Bernard, *King's Reformation*, 30–43.

36 William Tyndale, *The Obedience of a Christian Man*, ed. D. Daniell (London, 2000), 26.

37 Simon Fish, *A Supplicacyon for the Beggers*, ed. F. J. Furnivall (EETS extra series 13, 1871), 1–2.

38 S. E. Lehmberg, *The Reformation Parliament, 1529–1536* (Cambridge, 1970), 81–3.

39 Scarisbrick, *Henry VIII*, 334.

40 Ibid., 340.

41 Bernard, *King's Reformation*, 37.

42 *The determinations of the ... vniuersities* (1531), f. 153 v.

43 *Dialogus inter militem et clericum*, ed. A. J. Perry (EETS o.s. 167, 1895), 1.

44 Ibid., 2–3.

45 *Dialogus inter militem et clericum*, 8.

46 *Hereafter foloweth a dyaloge in Englisshe, bytwyxte a Doctour of Dyuynyte, and a student in the lawes of Englande* (1530).

47 *A glasse of the Truthe* (1532), Sig. F i r.

48 Ibid., Sig. F i v.

49 S. E. Lehmberg, *Reformation Parliament*, (Cambridge, 1970) 130–1.

50 Ibid., 132.

51 'An Act concerning restraint of payment of annates to the see of Rome', in Elton, *Constitution*, no. 176, p. 341.

52 *EHD*, no. 94.

53 Scarisbrick, *Henry VIII*, 392.

54 'An Act for the submission of the clergy to the King's Majesty', in Elton, *Constitution*, no.175, pp. 339–41.

55 E. Ives, *Anne Boleyn* (Oxford, 1986) 175.

56 Ibid., 179.

57 *CSPS* iv (i), 224 (p. 352).

58 Thurley, *Royal Palaces*, 50–1.

59 G. Mattingly, *Catherine of Aragon* (London, 1963), 232–3.

60 Hall, ii, 197.

61 Thurley, *Royal Palaces*, 55.

62 Hall, ii, 205.

63 *LP* vi, 89.

64 MacCulloch, *Cranmer*, 70–7.

65 Ives, *Life and Death*, 157.

66 Lehmberg, op.cit.,163–9.

67 'An Act that the appeals in such cases as have been used to be pursued to the see of Rome shall not be from henceforth had nor used but within this realm', in Elton, *Constitution*, no. 177.

5 THE GODLY PRINCE, 1533–1539

1   From the Act of Supremacy, 1534; Elton, *Constitution*, no. 180, p. 355.

2   See S. Doran (ed.), *Elizabeth: The Exhibition at the National Maritime Museum* (London, 2003), 14.

3   Scarisbrick, *Henry VIII*, 421–2, suggests that Henry stayed away from Elizabeth's baptism out of disappointment, but in fact it was not usual for the king and queen to attend the baptism of their child.

4   L. G. Wickham Legg, *English Coronation Records* (Westminster, 1901), 241. These are my italics.

5   Ibid., 240.

6   See S. Thurley, 'Henry VIII: the Tudor dynasty and the Church', in C. Lloyd and S. Thurley (eds), *Images of a Tudor King* (Oxford, 1990), 28–9.

7   Holbein had also visited in 1526–8 when he painted Thomas More and his family, several of the Boleyn faction, and completed his first royal commission, a triumphal arch in a painting at Greenwich which commemorated Thérouanne.

8   Holbein's cartoon for this mural is on display in the National Portrait Gallery. A copy of it was made for Charles II by Remigius van Leemput in 1667, and this is now in the Royal Collection. Holbein's half-portrait of Henry VIII depicts the same Henry as the Whitehall mural.

9   K. Van Mander, *The Lives of the Illustrious Netherlandish and German Painters*, tr. H. Miedema (Doornspijk, 1994), I, 146.

10 X. Brooke, 'Henry VIII revealed: Holbein's portrait and its legacy', in X. Brooke and D. Crombie (eds.), *Henry VIII Revealed* (London, 2003), 10–17.

11 Ibid., 9.

12 Thurley, *Royal Palaces*, 54–5.

13 *Inventory*, 16569, 16586, 16589.

14 *Inventory*, 16644, 16655, 16634, 16651, 16644.

15 *Inventory*, 16698, 16719, 16737, 16726, 16730.

16 Thurley, *Royal Palaces*, 51–6.

17 Colvin, *King's Works*, IV, 3f.

18 Act for the exoneration of exactions paid to the see of Rome, in Elton, *Constitution*, no.179, p. 351.

19 Lloyd, *Formularies*, 3.

20 Act of Supremacy, op.cit., p. 354.

21 *Two London Chronicles*, ed. C. L. Kingsford (Camden Miscellany xii, CS xviii, 1910), 8.

22 For a more detailed account of Elizabeth Barton see Bernard, *King's Reformation*, 87–101; E. Shagan, 'Print, orality and communications in the Maid of Kent affair', *JEH*, lii (2001).

23 J. Guy, *Thomas More* (London, 2000), Chapter 10.

24 P. Pouncey, 'Girolamo da Treviso in the service of Henry VIII', *Burlington Magazine* 95, no. 603 (June, 1953), 208–11.

25 G. Bernard, 'The piety of Henry VIII', in N. Scott Amos, H. van Nierop and A. Pettegree (eds), *The Education of a Christian Society* (Aldershot, 1999), 86. Bernard has translated the letter from the original Latin version.

26 P. Marshall and A. Ryrie, *The Beginnings of English Protestantism* (Cambridge, 2002), 5–8.

27 *Miscellaneous Writings and Letters of Thomas Cranmer*, ed. J. E. Cox (PS, Cambridge, 1846), 118.

28 Daniel 6; v. 26. 'God of Daniel' has been altered to 'the living God'.

29 1 Timothy 2; v. 1–2.

30 T. C. String, 'Henry VIII's illuminated "Great Bible", *Journal of the Warburg and Courtauld Institutes* 59 (1996), 320.

31 See MacCulloch, *Cranmer*, 161, and Bernard, *King's Reformation*, 282–4, for two largely opposing interpretations.

32 Lloyd, *Formularies*, 12–13.

33 MacCulloch, *Cranmer*, 165.

34 W. H. Frere and W. M. Kennedy, *Visitation Articles and Injunctions of the Period of the Reformation* (Alcuin Club Collections, xiv, 1910) 2–11.

35 Cited in G. Mattingly, *Catherine of Aragon* (London, 1963), 302.

36 Ibid., 308.

37 *LP* x, 141.

38 The suggestion that this foetus was deformed and that Henry took this as a sign of Anne's adultery, or even consequently believed Anne to be a witch has been suggested, but remains unfounded. See Ives, *Life and Death of Anne Boleyn*, 297–8.

39 *CSPS* 1536–8, 39–40, 59; *LP* x, 282, 351.

40 *LP* x, 808.

41 Ibid.

42 G. W. Bernard, 'The fall of Anne Boleyn', in *Power and Politics in Tudor England* (2000), 80–107.

43 G. Walker, 'Rethinking the fall of Anne Boleyn', *HJ* 45 (2002), 17; Ives, *Life and Death*, 334.

44 Walker, op.cit., 21.

45 Ives, *Life and Death*, 342–3.

46 Hall, ii, 268; Lisle *Letters*, iii, 698.

47 L. de Carles, 'De la royne d'Angleterre', in G. Ascoli, *La Grande-Bretagne devant L'Opinion Francaise* (Paris, 1927), lines 1002–12.

48 Although see G. W. Bernard, 'The fall of Anne Boleyn', and 'The fall of Anne Boleyn: a rejoinder', in *EHR* 106 (1991) and *EHR* 107 (1992).

49 'Lust' in this context means 'joy'. The Latin phrase is usually translated as 'around the throne it thunders', but could be interpreted as a reference to Jupiter, meaning 'around the throne he thunders'. This could imply that Henry VIII was a vengeful god, or that he was being visited with the vengeance of the gods. See Walker, *Writing Under Tyranny*, 290–1.

50 *LP* xi, 860.

51 Lisle *Letters*, iii, 306.

52 *LP* xi, 860.

53 Elton, *Constitution*, no. 186, 374.

54 Ibid., 377.

55 Bernard, *King's Reformation*, 152.

56 Most of the observant houses were given away to other orders; Canterbury may have remained.

57 Erasmus, *Praise of Folly*, 165.

58 A. G. Dickens and D. Carr (eds), *The Reformation in England to the Accession of Elizabeth I* (London, 1967), 94.

59 Ibid., 95.

60 J. C. Dickinson, *The Priory of Cartmel* (Milnthorpe, 1991), 33–4.

61 R. Rex and C. D. C. Armstrong, 'Henry VIII's ecclesiastical and collegiate foundations', *HR*, vol. 75 (2002), 395–8.

62 Bernard, *King's Reformation*, 295–6.

63 Ibid., 298.

64 R. W. Hoyle, *The Pilgrimage of Grace and the Politics of the 1530s* (Oxford, 2001), 456–7.

65 Ibid., 457–8.

66 Ibid., 455–6, 457–8.

67 Bernard, *King's Reformation*, 304–5, 319, 440–2.

68 Ibid., 334.

69 Ibid., 400.

70 Cited in Bernard, 374.

71 *LP* xii (i), 479.

72 J.C. Dickinson, *The Priory of Cartmel* (Durham, 1991) 34.

73 G. Moorhouse, *The Pilgrimage of Grace* (London, 2002), 276–7.

74 Bernard, *King's Reformation*, 433–4.

75 S. Lehmberg, *The Reformation of Cathedrals* (Princeton, 1988), 84–5.

76 *EHD*, no. 104. See also Lucy E. C. Wooding, *Rethinking Catholicism* (Oxford and New York, 2000), 65–6.

77 Dickens and Carr, *Reformation in England*, 103–4.

78 *LP* xiii (ii), 866.

79 R. Rex, 'The friars in the English Reformation', in Marshall and Ryrie, *Beginnings of English Protestantism*, 38–59.

80 J. Loach, *Edward VI* (New Haven and London, 1999), 7.

81 Hall, ii, 280.

82 Lloyd, *Formularies*, 23.

83 *Miscellaneous Writings and Letters of Thomas Cranmer*, ed. J. E. Cox (PS, Cambridge, 1846), 469.

84 Ibid., 84, 89, 95.

85 A new English Bible had appeared in 1537, known as Matthew's Bible, largely based on Tyndale's translation and notes.

86 W. H. Frere and W. M. Kennedy, *Visitation Articles and Injunctions of the Period of the Reformation* (Oxford, 1911), 36.

87 It was at this time usual practice for people to confess and receive the sacrament only once a year, in Lent and at Easter, respectively.

88 E. Duffy, *The Voices of Morebath* (New Haven and London, 2001), 25.

89 R. Hutton, 'The local impact of the Tudor Reformation', in P. Marshall (ed.), *The Impact of the English Reformation, 1500–1640* (London and New York, 1997), 144–5.

90 Elton, *Constitution*, no. 4, p.8.

91 Elton, *Constitution*, no.30, p.62.

92 Walker, *Writing Under Tyranny*, 150–61.

93 Ibid., 154.

94 Ibid., 181–3, 192, 198.

95 Ibid., 268.

96 See S. Brigden, *New Worlds, Lost Worlds* (New York, 2000), 154–62.

97 Act of Six Articles, in Elton, *Constitution*, no. 190, p. 390.

98 Ibid.

99 MacCulloch, 'Henry VIII and the reform of the Church', in MacCulloch, *Reign of Henry VIII*, 178.

100 Richard Rex is responsible for elucidating this important motivating factor behind so much of Henry's religious initiatives. See Rex, *Henry VIII and the English Reformation* (Basingstoke, 1993), 17, 29, 103, 173–5.

101 Foxe, v, 535.

102 See G. W. Bernard, 'The making of religious policy, 1533–1546: Henry VIII and the search for the middle way', *HJ*, 41 (1998).

103 Rex and Armstrong, op.cit., 401–4.

104 *LP* xiii, 924.

6 THE CLOSING YEARS, 1539–1547

1 Henry VIII's speech to Parliament in 1545; see Foxe, v, 534–6.

2 D. Starkey, *Six Wives: The queens of Henry VIII* (London, 2004), 611.

3 *LP* xii (ii), 1004.

4 T. Amyot, 'Transcript of an original manuscript, containing a memorial from George Constantyne to Thomas Lord Cromwell', *Archaeologia* 23 (1831), 56–78.

5 Scarisbrick, *Henry VIII*, 464–5.

6 Her father died during the course of the marriage negotiations, in February 1539, so by the time she came to England she was the sister of the new Duke of Cleves.

7 D. MacCulloch, 'Putting the English Reformation on the map', *TRHS* 15 (2005), 79.

8 *LP* xiv (i), 103.

9 Hall, ii, 287–9.

10 T. F. Mayer, 'A mission worse than death: Reginald Pole and the Parisian theologians', *EHR* 103 (1988), 870–91.

11 Bernard, *King's Reformation*, 4.

12 Ibid., 423.

13 *LP* xiv (i) 103: 2.

14 *LP* xv, 823.

15 *LP* xv, 822.

16 Burnet, IV, 427.

17 Hall, ii, 102–3.

18 Burnet, IV, 430.

19 J. Strype, *Ecclesiastical Memorials*, iii (2), 221–2.

20 *LP* xv, 776.

21 *LP* xv, 925.

22 *LP* xv, 898.

23 *LP* xv, 925.

24 For a factional interpretation see D. Starkey, *The Reign of Henry VIII: Personalities and politics* (London, 1985),123. For an opposing interpretation, see Bernard, *King's Reformation*, 569–79. MacCulloch, *Cranmer*, 268–71, gives a more nuanced account.

25 Scarisbrick, *Henry VIII*, 491.

26 S. Brigden, *London and the Reformation* (Oxford, 1989), 310–12.

27 S. Brigden, 'Popular disturbance and the fall of Thomas Cromwell and the reformers, 1539–1540', *HJ* 24 (1981), 257–78. Brigden accepts the emphasis on faction of Starkey, Ives and others, but her depiction of tensions in London at this time is open to a different interpretation.

28 Ibid., 268–72.

29 From the Act of Six Articles; Elton, *Constitution*, no.190, pp.389–90.

30 Brigden, 'Popular Disturbance ...', 259.

31 Brigden, *London and the Reformation*, 300–1.

32 Brigden, 'Popular Disturbance ...', 265 and n.

33 Ibid., 266.

34 Ibid., 262.

35 J. Block, 'Thomas Cromwell's patronage of preaching', *Sixteenth Century Journal* viii (1977), 45–7, 49.

36 Brigden, *London and the Reformation*, 348–51, 370.

37 MacCulloch, *Cranmer*, 270.

38 *Writings and Letters of Thomas Cranmer*, ed. J. E. Cox (PS, 1846), 40.

39 Matthew 26:52.

40 Carley, *Books of Henry VIII*, 134.

41 L. B. Smith, *A Tudor Tragedy. The Life and Times of Katherine Howard*, (1961) 121f.

42 *LP* xvi, 223.

43 R. Hutchinson, *The Last Days of Henry VIII* (London, 2005), 142.

44 Walker, *Writing Under Tyranny*, 345.

45 *LP* xvi, 1130.

46 Hall, ii, 313.

47 MacCulloch, *Cranmer*, 287.

48 Ibid., 288.

49 *LP* xvi, 1334.

50 Carley, *Books of Henry VIII*, 63–4.

51 J. Fox, *Jane Boleyn: the Infamous Lady Rochford* (London, 2008), 312–14.

52 A. Ryrie, *The Gospel and Henry VIII: Evangelicals in the Early English Reformation* (Cambridge, 2003), 39.

53 MacCulloch, *Cranmer*, 249.

54 Rex and Armstrong, 'Henry VIII's ecclesiastical and collegiate foundations', *HR* 75 (2002), 401–5.

55 Ryrie, *Gospel and Henry VIII*, 47.

56   Cranmer, *Letters*, 83–114; Ryrie, *Gospel and Henry VIII*, 47.

57   MacCulloch, 'Henry VIII and the reform of the Church', in MacCulloch, *Reign of Henry VIII*, 163.

58   Brigden, *London and the Reformation*, 301.

59   See Lloyd, *Formularies*, 215.

60   Ibid., 216.

61   Ibid., 223.

62   Ibid., 252.

63   Ryrie, *Gospel and Henry VIII*, 50–1.

64   Lloyd, *Formularies*, 376–7.

65   Ryrie, *Gospel and Henry VIII*, 44–8.

66   Ibid., 51–2.

67   R. Bowers, 'The vernacular litany of 1544 during the reign of Henry VIII', in S. J. Gunn and G. W. Bernard, *Authority and Consent* (Aldershot, 2002) 151–78.

68   Ryrie, *Gospel and Henry VIII*, 52.

69   See P. Marshall, 'Mumpsimus and sumpsimus: the intellectual origins of a Henrician bon mot', *JEH*, lii (2001), 512–20.

70   Foxe, v, 534–6.

71   *CSPS* vi (i), 211 (p.410).

72   There has been debate over her knowledge of Latin, but this now seems to have been resolved. See *ODNB*.

73   It is now thought that her first husband was Edward Borough, her contemporary, who has been confused with his father in some accounts of Katherine's life.

74   Hutchinson, *Last Days of Henry VIII*, 57.

75   *ODNB*.

76   *CSPS* vi, (ii), 183 (p. 436).

77   S. Doran (ed.), *Elizabeth: The Exhibition at the National Maritime Museum* (London, 2003), p. 15.

78   Colvin, *King's Works*, iv, 207–9.

79   S. Thurley, 'Nonsuch Palace', in *Country Life*, vol. cxcix no. 31, 11 August 2005.

80   Colvin, *King's Works*, iv, 194–5.

81   See *LP* xix (i), 319, 348.

82   D. Grummitt, 'The court, war and noble power in England, c.1475–1558', in S. Gunn and A. Janse (eds), *The Court as a Stage: England and the Low Countries in the Later Middle Ages* (Woodbridge, 2006), 151.

83   Scarisbrick, *Henry VIII*, 575–6.

84   Ibid., 568.

85   *State Papers*, x, 5–6, 10.

86 Ibid., 28.

87 Ibid., 11.

88 R. W. Hoyle, 'War and public finance', in MacCulloch, *Reign of Henry VIII*, 98, 96.

89 S. M. Kybett, 'Henry VIII: a malnourished king', *History Today*, 39 (September 1979), 19–25.

90 C. Brewer, *The Death of Kings* (London, 2000); see also R. Hutchinson, *Last Days of Henry VIII* (London, 2005), Chapter 5.

91 Ibid., 149.

92 Ibid., 207–9.

93 John Bale, *The Examinations of Anne Askew*, ed. E. V. Beilin (1996), 93.

94 Foxe, v, 553ff.

95 Foxe, v, 535.

96 *NA* E 23/4/1

97 Foxe, v, 691; Burnet, vol i, book iii, 255. Accounts vary as to whether it was Anthony Denny, gentleman of the privy chamber, or Anthony Browne, then master of the king's horse, who asked whether the King really intended to omit Gardiner.

98 J. Loach, *Edward VI* (New Haven, 1999), 18–25.

99 S. Brigden, 'Henry Howard, Earl of Surrey, and the "Conjured League"', *HJ* xxxvii (1994), 507–37.

100 *ODNB* finds no evidence for his evangelicalism, describing his convictions as primarily Erastian.

101 For the most important contributions to this debate, see R. A. Houlbrooke, 'Henry VIII's wills: a comment', *HJ* xxxvii (1994), 891–9; E. W. Ives, 'The Protectorate provisions of 1546–7', *HJ* xxxvii (1994), 901–14; Ives, 'Henry VIII's will: a forensic conundrum', *HJ* xxxv (1992), 779–804; H. Miller, 'Henry VIII's unwritten will: grants of lands and honours in 1547', in E. W. Ives, R. J. Knecht and J. J. Scarisbrick (eds), *Wealth and Power in Tudor England: Essays presented to S. T. Bindoff* (London, 1978), 87–106.

102 *LP* xxi (ii), 770.

103 Foxe, v, 689.

104 J. Loach, 'The function of ceremonial in the reign of Henry VIII', *P&P* 142 (1994), 56–66.

7 THE LEGACY OF HENRY VIII

1 Shakespeare, *Henry VIII*, Prologue.

2 For the 1623 description of the model for this tomb, from John Speed's *History of Britaine*, see M. Mitchell, 'Works of art from Rome for Henry VIII: a study of Anglo-Papal relations as reflected in papal gifts to the English king', *Journal of the Warburg and Courtauld Institutues* 34 (1971), Appendix II, pp. 201–3.

3 S. J. Gunn and P. G. Lindley, *Cardinal Wolsey: Church, State and Art* (Cambridge, 1991), 267.

4 Mitchell, 178–89.

5 See P. Marshall, 'Papist as heretic: the burning of John Forest, 1538', *HJ* 41 (1998), 351–74.

6 See the introduction to S. Doran and T. Freeman (eds), *The Myth of Elizabeth* (Basingstoke, 2003), 1–2.

7 See, for example, C. Haigh, *English Reformations: Religion, Politics and Society under the Tudors* (Oxford, 1993), vii–viii.

8 D. MacCulloch, 'The myth of the English Reformation', *JBS* 30 (1991), 19.

9 J. Loach, *Edward VI* (New Haven and London, 1999), 130–4, 135–9, 152–8.

10 M. Aston, *The King's Bedpost: Reformation and Iconography in a Tudor group Portrait* (Cambridge, 1993). Her interpretation is open to question: see Loach, *Edward VI*, 187.

11 F. Yates, 'Queen Elizabeth as Astraea', *Journal of the Warburg and Courtauld Institutes* 10 (1947), 41–2.

12 G. McMullan, Introduction to the Arden Shakespeare edition of *King Henry VIII* (2000), 19.

13 Ibid., 38–40.

14 It should be noted that Shakespeare wrote this play with Fletcher during the reign of James I and VI.

15 Shakespeare, *Henry VIII*, Act 3, Scene 1.

16 W. Harrison, *The Description of England*, ed. G. Edelen (Washington D.C. and New York, 1994), 225.

17 See G. Moorhouse, *Great Harry's Navy* (London, 2005).

18 D. Marcombe and C. S. Knighton (eds), *Close Encounters: English Cathedrals and Society since 1540* (Studies in Local and Regional History, no. 3; Nottingham, 1991).

19 E. Duffy, *Voices of Morebath: Reformation and Rebellion in an English Village* (New Haven and London, 2001), xiii; Haigh, *English Reformations*, 295.

20 Nicholas Sanders, *The Rise and Growth of the Anglican Schism*, ed. D. Lewis (Rockford, Ill. and Tunbridge Wells, 1988), 162.

21 M. Ingram, 'Reformation of manners in early modern England', in P. Griffiths, A. Fox and S. Hindle (eds), *The Experience of Authority in Early Modern England* (Basingstoke, 1996), 71–2.

22 A. F. Pollard, *Henry VIII* (1930), 438.

23 Foxe, v, 534.

24 William Cobbett, *A History of the Protestant Reformation in England and Ireland*, 19, 3.

25 C. Richmond, 'The English Reformation: report from a stationary train', in Bernard and Gunn, *Authority and Consent*, 99–100.

26 See Griffiths, Fox and Hindle, *Experiences of Authority in Early Modern England*; M. Braddick and J. Walter (eds), *Negotiating Power in Early Modern Society* (2001); T. Harris (ed.), *The Politics of the Excluded c.1500–1850* (Basingstoke and New York, 2001); E. Shagan, *Popular Politics and the English Reformation* (Cambridge, 2003); P. Williams, *The Tudor Regime* (Oxford, 1979), part iii.

27 G. W. Bernard, 'The tyranny of Henry VIII' in Bernard and Gunn, *Authority and Consent*, 113–29; Walker, *Writing Under Tyranny*.

SUGGESTIONS FOR
FURTHER READING

PRIMARY SOURCES

The study of Henry VIII's reign must still take as its starting point J. S. Brewer, J. Gairdner and R. H. Brodie (eds.), *Letters and Papers, Foreign and Domestic, of the Reign of Henry VIII* (21 volumes, 1862–1932). See also *State Papers ... King Henry VIII* (11 vols, 1830–52), and *Tudor Royal Proclamations*, ed. P. L. Hughes and J. F. Larkin (New Haven and London, vol. i, 1964). For the views of foreign envoys see G. A. Bergenroth, P. de Gayangos and M. A. S. Hume (eds.), *Calendar of State Papers, Spanish* (1862–1954) and R. Brown *et al*. (eds.), *Calendar of State Papers, Venetian* (1864–1947). For a collection of primary sources chiefly concerned with legislation and administration, see G. R. Elton, *The Tudor Constitution: Documents and Commentary* (Cambridge, 1960). For the King's own letters, see M. St. Clare Byrne (ed.), *The Letters of King Henry VIII: A Selection with a Few Other Documents* (London, 1936).

Contemporary (or near contemporary) accounts of the reign include Edward Hall's *Chronicle*, properly entitled *The Union of the two Noble and Illustre Famelies of Lancastre and Yorke*, ed. C. Whibley (2 vols., London and Edinburgh, 1904); see too George Cavendish's 'Life of Wolsey' and William Roper's 'Life of More' in *Two Early Tudor Lives*, ed. R. S. Sylvester and D. P. Harding (New Haven and London, 1962). Other accounts include the first volume of Charles Wriothesley, *A Chronicle of*

England During the Reigns of the Tudors, 1485–1559, ed. W. D. Hamilton (vol. i, CS, new series, ix, 1875); *Grey Friars Chronicle of London*, ed. J. G. Nichols (CS, liii, 1852); *The Anglica Historia of Polydore Vergil, 1485–1537*, ed. D. Hay (CS, 3rd series, lxxiv, 1950) and Raphael Holinshed, *Chronicles*, ed. H. Ellis (6 vols,1807–8). M. St Clare Byrne (ed.), *The Lisle Letters* (6 vols, Chicago and London, 1981) gives an insight into a Tudor family close to the centres of power.

For the turbulent religious developments of the period, see John Foxe, *Acts and Monuments*, ed. S. R. Cattley and G. Townsend (8 vols, 1837–41); *Narratives of the Days of the Reformation*, ed. J. G. Nichols (CS, lxviii, 1859); N. Pocock (ed.), *Records of the Reformation, the Divorce 1527–1533* (2 vols., Oxford, 1870). Official religious policy can be traced through *Formularies of Faith put forth by Authority during the Reign of Henry VIII*, ed. C. Lloyd (Oxford, 1825) and *Visitation Articles and Injunctions of the Period of the Reformation*, ed. W. H. Frere and W. M. Kennedy (3 vols, Alcuin Club Collections, xiv, xv, xvi, 1910). John Strype, *Ecclesiastical Memorials, Relating Chiefly to Religion, and the Reformation ... under King Henry VIII, King Edward VI, and Queen Mary I* (3 vols, Oxford, 1822) provides both analysis and a collection of useful primary sources. L. E. Whatmore, 'The sermon against the Holy Maid of Kent and her adherents, 1533', *EHR*, vol. lviii (1943), pp. 463–75 is a useful example of politicised anticlericalism. B. Collett, *Female Monastic Life in Tudor England: An Edition of Richard Fox's Translation of the Benedictine Rule for Women* (Aldershot, 2002) gives an idea of monastic culture, and T. Wright (ed.), *Letters Relating to the Suppression of Monasteries* (CS xxvi, 1843) illustrates its dissolution. Erasmus's *The Praise of Folly*, trans. B. Radice, ed. A. H. T. Levi (London, 1971) gives an idea of the humanist reform agenda, and E. Rummel, *The Erasmus Reader* (Toronto, 1990) is an accessible introduction to the rest of Erasmus's work. J. A. Muller (ed.), *Letters of Stephen Gardiner* (Cambridge, 1933), illustrates the concerns of one of Henry's chief ministers. *Tyndale's New Testament*, ed. D. Daniell (New Haven and London, 1995) is a modernised edition of the 1534 edition. Nicholas Sanders, *The Rise and Growth of the Anglican Schism*, trans. and ed. D. Lewis (Rockford, Illinois and Tunbridge Wells, 1988) gives a superbly partisan account of the Reformation by a leading Elizabethan Catholic.

For an introduction to contemporary political thought see Erasmus's *The Education of a Christian Prince*, ed. L. Jardine (Cambridge, 1977);

Edmund Dudley, *The Tree of Commonwealth*, ed. D. M. Brodie (Cambridge, 1948); C. L. Kingsford (ed.), *The First English Life of King Henry the Fifth* (Oxford, 1911); Thomas More, *The History of King Richard III*, ed. R. S. Sylvester (New Haven and London, 1963) and Thomas More, *Utopia*, ed. P. Turner (London, 1965). Juan Luis Vives, *The Education of a Christian Woman*, trans. and ed. C. Fantazzi (Chicago, 2000), gives an idea of the opportunities and limitations of the female political role in the work designed for Princess Mary's education.

The material culture of the reign is given absorbing expression in *The Inventory of King Henry VIII*, ed. D. Starkey, vol. i (Society of Antiquaries of London, 1998).

F. J. Furnivall, *Ballads from Manuscripts* (vol. i, London, 1868) gives an insight into popular culture. Works published during Henry's lifetime can be read courtesy of the invaluable *Early English Books On-line*, to which most major research libraries and universities subscribe. The equally invaluable *New Dictionary of National Biography* is also to be found online and most public libraries now subscribe to it, as well as educational institutions.

SECONDARY SOURCES

Biographies

J. J. Scarisbrick's biography, *Henry VIII* (London, 1968) remains an important work, particularly helpful in its detailed yet comprehensible account of the canon law surrounding the campaign for the annulment. E. Ives, *The Life and Death of Anne Boleyn* (Oxford, 2004) is an absorbing as well as scholarly account of an extraordinary woman. P. Gwyn, *The King's Cardinal: The Rise and Fall of Thomas Wolsey* (London, 1990) is a magisterial work, which firmly debunks the huge number of historical myths surrounding Wolsey, and demonstrates the weaknesses of the factional interpretation of Wolsey's role. D. MacCulloch, *Thomas Cranmer: A Life* (New Haven and London, 1996) is an award-winning biography of Henry's archbishop which manages to be both a detailed work of scholarship and a moving account of a great man. D. Starkey, *Six Wives: The Queens of Henry VIII* (London, 2003), is hugely entertaining. G. Mattingley, *Catherine of Aragon* (London, 1942) tells the tragic story well.

For Henry's children, J. Loach, *Edward VI* (New Haven and London, 1999) should be read in counterpoise to D. MacCulloch, *Tudor Church Militant: Edward VI and the Protestant Reformation* (1999). D. M. Loades, *Mary Tudor: A Life* (Oxford, 1989) is usefully augmented by the essays in E. Duffy and D. M. Loades (eds.), *The Church of Mary Tudor* (Aldershot, 2006). See also J. Richards, *Mary Tudor* (forthcoming, London, 2008). C. Haigh, *Elizabeth I* (2nd edn, London and New York, 1998) is meant for students, while D. Starkey, *Elizabeth: Apprenticeship* (London, 2000) is intended for a wider audience. For some of the other characters who shaped Henrician England, try D. Daniell, *William Tyndale: A Biography* (New Haven, 2001); J. Guy, *Thomas More* (London, 2000); A. Fox, *Thomas More: History and Providence* (Oxford, 1982); D. Fenlon, *Heresy and Obedience in Reformation Italy: Cardinal Pole and the Counter Reformation* (Cambridge, 1972). M. Dowling, *Fisher of Men: A Life of John Fisher, 1469–1535* (Basingstoke, 1999) can be augmented by R. Rex, *The Theology of John Fisher* (Cambridge, 1991), while G. Redworth, *In Defence of the Church Catholic: The Life of Stephen Gardiner* (Oxford, 1990) might be read together with D. MacCulloch, 'Two dons in politics: Thomas Cranmer and Stephen Gardiner, 1503–1533', *HJ* 37 (1994), 1–22.

Politics

Good introductions to sixteenth-century England include J. Guy, *Tudor England* (Oxford, 1988) and S. Brigden, *New Worlds, Lost Worlds* (London, 2000). Two collections of essays provide a good starting-point for the study of Henrician politics: D. MacCulloch (ed.), *The Reign of Henry VIII: Politics, Policy and Piety* (Macmillan, 1995) and G. W. Bernard, *Power and Politics in Tudor England* (Aldershot, 2000).

D. Starkey, *The Reign of Henry VIII: Personalities and Politics* (1985) gives a distinctive account of the reign with a strong emphasis on the importance of faction; this might be balanced by the essays in G. Walker, *Persuasive Fictions: Faction, Faith and Political Culture in the Reign of Henry VIII* (Aldershot, 1996). S. J. Gunn, *Early Tudor Government, 1485–1558* (Basingstoke, 1995) provides a slightly longer context, and a thematic treatment of the business of government. The essays in G. R. Elton, *Studies in Tudor and Stuart Politics and Government* (Cambridge, 4 vols, 1974–92), are still important, even though his interpretations have been challenged since. Other useful articles include S. J. Gunn, 'The accession of Henry

VIII', *HR* 64 (1991), 278–88 and three by S. Brigden, namely 'Popular disturbance and the fall of Thomas Cromwell and the reformers 1539–1540', *HJ* xxxiv (1981), also ' "The shadow that you know": Sir Thomas Wyatt and Sir Francis Bryan at court and in embassy', *HJ* xxxix (1996), 1–32, and 'Henry Howard, Earl of Surrey, and the "Conjured League"', *HJ* 37 (1994), 507–37. E. W. Ives, 'Faction at the court of Henry VIII: the fall of Anne Boleyn', *History* lvii (1972), 169–88 can be balanced against G. W. Bernard, 'The fall of Anne Boleyn', *EHR* cvi (1991), 584–610 (reprinted in his *Power and Politics in Tudor England, op. cit.*). D. Starkey, 'Intimacy and innovation: the rise of the privy chamber 1485–1547', in Starkey (ed.), *The English Court: From the Wars of the Roses to the Civil War* (1987) gives a good account of Starkey's important theories concerning the privy chamber, but see also his 'Representation through intimacy: a study in the symbolism of monarchy and court office in early modern England', in J. Guy (ed.), *The Tudor Monarchy* (1997). Elton's thesis on the 'Tudor revolution in government' is brought under scrutiny in C. Coleman and D. Starkey (eds.), *Revolution Reassessed: Revisions in the History of Tudor Government and Administration* (Oxford, 1986). On Parliament, see S. E. Lehmberg, *The Reformation Parliament 1529–1536* (Cambridge, 1970), and by the same author, *The Later Parliaments of Henry VIII 1536–1547* (Cambridge, 1977). On different aspects of noble politics see S. G. Ellis, *Tudor Frontiers and Noble Power: The Making of the British State* (Oxford, 1995), and G. W. Bernard (ed.), *The Tudor Nobility* (Manchester, 1992). On popular politics, see A. Fletcher and D. MacCulloch (eds.), *Tudor Rebellions* (4th edn, 1997), also R. Hoyle, *The Pilgrimage of Grace* (Oxford, 2001); M. E. James, 'Obedience and dissent in Henrician England: the Lincolnshire Rebellion 1536', *P&P* lxviii (1970), 3–78, and E. Shagan, *Popular Politics and the English Reformation* (Cambridge, 2002). Popular politics are also addressed in A. Wood, *Riot, Rebellion and Popular Politics in Early Modern England* (Basingstoke, 2002); P. Griffiths, A. Fox and S. Hindle (eds.), *The Experiences of Authority in Early Modern England* (Basingstoke,1996) and T. Harris (ed.), *The Politics of the Excluded c.1500–1850* (Basingstoke and New York, 2001).

Religion

The history of religion is not really divisible from the history of politics in Henry's reign. For works which explore the interface between the two, see G. W. Bernard, *The King's Reformation: Henry VIII and the Remaking of the English Church* (New Haven and London, 2005); key ideas are also expounded in his 'The making of religious policy, 1533–1546: Henry VIII and the search for the middle way', *HJ* 41 (1998). See also Bernard's essay, 'The piety of Henry VIII' in S. N. Amos and H. van Nierop (eds.), *The Education of a Christian Society: Humanism and the Reformation in Britain and the Netherlands* (1999), 62–88. R. Rex, *Henry VIII and the English Reformation* (Basingstoke, 1993) is also required reading, as is Rex's article, 'The crisis of obedience: God's Word and Henry's Reformation', *HJ* xxxix (1996), 863–94.

J. P. D Cooper, '*O Lorde save the kyng* : Tudor royal propaganda and the power of prayer', in Bernard and Gunn, *Authority and Consent*, also illustrates the overlap between religious obligation and political duty. See also J. K. McConica, *English Humanists and Reformation Politics under Henry VIII* (Oxford, 1965) and R. McEntegart, *Henry VIII, the League of Schmalkalden, and the English Reformation* (Woodbridge, 2002).

For the country at large, the best introduction to the religious history of this period is P. Marshall, *Reformation England 1480–1642* (2003), while C. Marsh, *Popular Religion in Sixteenth-Century England* (Basingstoke, 1998) gives an excellent introduction to popular religion. For a European context, and a distinctive understanding of religious belief and culture, see J. Bossy, *Christianity in the West, 1400–1700* (Oxford, 1985). A. G. Dickens, *The English Reformation* (2nd edn, 1989) is still a valuable work, and a starting point for the Reformation debate, contested in very different ways by E. Duffy, *The Stripping of the Altars* (New Haven and London, 1992), J. J. Scarisbrick, *The Reformation and the English People* (Oxford, 1984) and C. Haigh, *English Reformations: Religion, Politics and Society under the Tudors* (Oxford, 1993).G. Redworth, 'Whatever happened to the English Reformation?', *History Today* (October 1987) gives some reflections on the debate. More detailed studies of religious change in its many aspects may be found in the following: M. Bowker, 'The supremacy and the episcopate: the struggle for control', *HJ* xviii (1975), 227–43, also her 'The Henrician Reformation and the parish clergy', *BIHR* 1 (1977), 30–47, and by the same author, *The Henrician Reformation: The Diocese of Lincoln under John Longland 1521–1547* (Cambridge, 1981). P. Marshall's articles, 'The rood of Boxley, the blood of Hailes and the defence of the Henrician Church', *JEH* xlvi (1995), 689–96 and 'Papist as heretic: the burning of John Forest, 1538', *HJ* xli (1998), 351–74, provide vivid insights into case studies of Henrician religious policy. Marshall's *Religious Identities in Henry VIII's England* (Aldershot, 2006) is also a valuable collection. For the reformation of bishops and cathedrals see S. E. Lehmberg, *The Reformation of Cathedrals: Cathedrals in English Society, 1485–1603* (Princeton, 1988) and A. A. Chibi, *Henry VIII's Bishops: Diplomats, Administrators, Scholars and Shepherds* (Cambridge, 2003). For aspects of the popular reformation, see M. Aston, *England's Iconoclasts*, vol. i (Oxford, 1988) and S. Brigden, 'Youth and the English Reformation', *P&P* 95 (1982) 37–67. Brigden's article, 'Religion and social obligation in early modern London', *P&P* 103 (1984) 67–112 gives an important insight into the state of popular religion before Henry began to tear it apart, and her *London and the Reformation* (Oxford, 1989) gives a matchless account of the complexities of the Reformation in the capital. For the beginnings of Protestantism, see P. Marshall and A. Ryrie, *The Beginnings of English Protestantism* (Cambridge, 2002), and Ryrie's *The Gospel and Henry VIII: Evangelicals in the Early English Reformation* (Cambridge, 2003). For an understanding of monasticism, see J. G. Clark, 'Reformation and reaction at St Albans Abbey, 1530–1558', *EHR* cxv (2000), 297–328, and J. G. Clark (ed.), *The Religious Orders in Pre-Reformation England* (Woodbridge, 2002).

Culture

On court culture, begin with D. Starkey, *Henry VIII: A European Court in England* (1991) and S. Thurley and C. Lloyd (eds.), *Henry VIII: Images of a Tudor King* (Oxford, 1990). H. M. Colvin (ed.), *The History of the King's Works*, vol. iii. *1485–1660* (part 1), (London, 1975), vol. iv *1485–1660* (part 2), (London, 1982), gives an invaluable account of the King's building works, including military fortifications. F. Kisby, '"When the king goeth a procession": chapel ceremonies and services, the ritual year and religious reforms at the early Tudor court, 1485–1547', *JBS* xl (2001), 44–75, gives an important insight into court ceremonial, while artistic patronage is discussed in M. Mitchell, 'Works of art from Rome for Henry VIII: a study of Anglo-Papal relations as reflected in papal gifts to the English king', *Journal of the Warburg and Courtauld Institutes* 34 (1971), 178–203. S. Foister, *Holbein and England* (New Haven and London, 2004) is a superb account of Henry's favourite artist. Exhibition catalogues are a useful aid; the Victoria and Albert Museum's *Gothic: Art for England 1400–1547*, ed. R. Marks and P. Williamson (London, 2003) is one of the best. On literary culture see J. N. King, *Tudor Royal Iconography: Literature and Art in an Age of Religious Crisis* (Princeton, 1989); J. P. Carley, *The Libraries of Henry VIII* (London, 2000) and J. P. Carley, *The Books of Henry VIII and His Wives* (London, 2004); A. Fox and J. Guy, *Reassessing the Henrician Age: Humanism, Politics and Reform 1500–1550* (Oxford, 1986); G. Walker, *'Writing Under Tyranny': English Literature and the Henrician Reformation* (Oxford, 2005). On material culture and environment, see D. Gaimster and P. Stamper (eds.), *The Age of Transition: The Archaeology of English Culture 1400–1600* (Oxford, 1997); O. Rackham, *The Illustrated History of the Countryside* (2003); and K. Thomas, *Man and the Natural World: Changing Attitudes in England 1500–1800* (London, 1983).

INDEX

Renaissance World

John Jeffries Martin

With an interdisciplinary approach that encompasses the history of ideas, political history, cultural history and art history, this volume, in the successful *Routledge Worlds* series, offers a sweeping survey of Europe in the Renaissance, from the late thirteenth to early seventeenth centuries. It shows how the Renaissance laid key foundations for many aspects of the modern world.

Collating thirty-four essays from the field's leading scholars, John Jeffries Martin shows that this period of rapid and complex change resulted from a convergence of a new set of social, economic and technological forces alongside a cluster of interrelated practices including painting, sculpture, humanism and science, in which the elites engaged.

Unique in its balance of emphasis on elite and popular culture, on humanism and society, and on women as well as men, *Renaissance World* grapples with issues as diverse as Renaissance patronage and the development of the slave trade.

Beginning with a section on the antecedents of the Renaissance world, and ending with its lasting influence, this book is an invaluable read which students and scholars of history and the Renaissance will dip into again and again.

ISBN 13: 978-0-415-33259-0 (hbk)
ISBN 13: 978-0-415-45511-4 (pbk)

Available at all good bookshops
For ordering and further information please visit:
www.routledge.com

England under the Tudors
Third Edition

G. R. Elton

'The best full-length introductory history of the Tudor period ... Written with great verve, it will delight both the scholar and the general reader.' – *The Spectator*

'Students of history owe Elton major debts. He has shown that political history is still worth investigation, that it offers the possibility of exciting discovery and genuine debate. He has demonstrated that scholarly work can be presented in prose that is witty, muscular, clear and above everything, readable.' – *The Times Education Supplement*

First published in 1955 and never out of print, this wonderfully written text by one of the great historians of the twentieth century has guided generations of students through the turbulent history of Tudor England.

Now in its third edition, *England under the Tudors* charts a historical period that saw some monumental changes in religion, monarchy, government and the arts. Elton's classic and highly readable introduction to the Tudor period offers an essential source of information from the start of Henry VII's reign to the death of Elizabeth I.

ISBN: 978-0-415-06533-7 (pbk)

A Political History of Tudor and Stuart England: A Sourcebook

Victor Slater

A Political History of Tudor and Stuart England draws together a fascinating selection of sources to illuminate this turbulent era of English history. From the bloody overthrow of Richard III in 1485 to the creation of a worldwide imperial state under Queen Anne, these sources illustrate England's difficult transition from the medieval to the modern.

Covering a period characterised by conflict and division, this wide-ranging single-volume collection presents the accounts of Yorkists and Lancastrians, Protestants and Catholics, and Roundheads and Cavaliers side by side. *A Political History of Tudor and Stuart England* provides a crucial opportunity for students to examine the institutions and events that moulded English history in the early modern era at first-hand.

ISBN 13: 978-0-415-20744-7 (pbk)
ISBN 13: 978-0-415-20743-0 (hbk)
ISBN 13: 978-0-203-995402 (e-book)

Available at all good bookshops
For ordering and further information please visit:
www.routledge.com